Tails in

I0652598

the

Tropics

BarbarianSpy

WARNING: This book is for sale to **ADULT AUDIENCES ONLY**. Contains graphic gay male sex, reluctance, multiple partners, anal sex, nongraphic violence, gay romance and gay love all of which may be considered offensive by some readers.

All sexually active characters in this work are at least 18 years of age.

BarbarianSpy
Jindalee St
Toronto, NSW 2283
Australia

TAILS IN

the

Tropics

BY HABU

Table of Contents

INTRODUCTION

Steamy climates. Hot men. Sizzling man sex. This meaty fifty-story anthology takes you inside the world's tropical zone, roughly between the Tropic of Cancer and the Tropic of Capricorn, in a whirlwind introduction to some of the hottest and most exotic male-male action and varied tales of taking you could wish for. We have served up for us herein spicy platters of drama, amusement, pathos, domination, discovery, arousal, melting of reluctance, irony, and surprise: your porn stars gone wild, your jungle soldiers in search of adventure, your older men dominating young hunks, your sex-rocked yachts, your gay bordellos and male prostitutes on the prowl, your no-swim suit pools, your exotic sex nests, and your hot night life and full-throttled spirals into seduction and realization of dreams and hot-blooded passion. So, pull on your Speedos (or not) and head for the tropical beaches of the Caribbean, the Atlantic, the Indian Ocean, and the Pacific to see how many ways and in how many different hot and humid locales you can be aroused and satisfied.

CARIBBEAN

Elusive

I waited until we'd almost reached Miami's airport, but I couldn't leave it here. "What's wrong, Zack? You've been pouty for days. You know I need this break."

"Yes, I know. And I can't go, I know that. Once your scenes are in the can, my editing work begins," Zack responded. But he wasn't looking at me. It was as if he couldn't look at me. He just had withdrawn into his corner of the limo seat. I scooted across to his corner and wrapped one hand around his neck and drew his lips to mine. My other hand went to his basket, and I traced the length of him through his worn jeans.

He returned my kiss hungrily, as if there was no tomorrow, and then he abruptly closed it down and turned his head away, his face pointed to the palm trees lining the approach to the terminal beyond the smoked glass of the Lincoln's windows.

"Zack."

"Go. Go with the wind, Dane Dixon," he muttered. But it came out choked. I wasn't amused. The line was from one of my least-favorite movie gigs, although it had been a crowd pleaser. And neither he nor I were fond of that name. And I knew then that something was seriously wrong. He only used my movie name—made fun of my work like this—when he was mad, or moody, or sad.

"It's only for a week, Zack. I need this change. The schedule's just too hectic. Just a week and I'll be back."

"Yes, yes, of course you will be," he answered in a small, distant voice. "And I hope you find it, whatever *it* is."

I didn't want to leave it there, but we had arrived at the terminal, and the passenger door was open. I took Zack's hand, trying to draw him across the seat and out of the limo with me so we wouldn't leave it there. But he resisted, refusing to be drawn from his corner, and I could tell from the murmurs and exclamations from the curb that I had been seen and recognized.

And if there were cameras, I knew I couldn't draw Zack out of the car with me.

A hell of a place to leave it. And how did he know I wasn't planning on coming back to him?

* * * *

I recognized what the driver the studio had sent to pick me up at the Acapulco airport had in mind the moment I caught sight of him when the first-class passengers were escorted off the plane. He was looking for faces only until he recognized mine and then his eyes went straight to my basket. It was a typical reaction; everyone who knew my movies wanted to have some sort of assurance that it was true. Well, he was a good-looking, sturdy muscle man, so I decided he might just get the tumble he was hoping for.

"This way, Mr. Dixon," he said almost reverently. "If you'll pick your bags out, I'll retrieve them. The limo is just outside the door to baggage claim. They didn't tell me where to take you, though."

"The Acapulco Las Palmes," I answered as we walked along the corridor. He wasn't Mexican. More Jamaican, I thought. Really nice build; bulging shoulder muscles; filled out the well-pressed black chauffeur's uniform really nicely.

"Of course," he answered, and he flashed me an all-white-teeth-parting-puffy-chocolate-lips smile that lit up the terminal. The Las Palmes was, of course, the premier gay hotel on the beach. If he'd ever wondered how much I was acting in my movies, this gave him some assurances.

"Clubs?" I asked as we neared the baggage claim carousels. "Appropriate clubs? They said my driver would have some brochures."

"Yes, sir. That must be the bundle of brochures they put in the backseat of the limo before I took off. And I'm at your disposal full time, sir. Whenever you are ready to go back out this evening, just ring the front desk."

We had reached the baggage claim just as the bell for the arrival of the luggage sounded and the carousel began to gin up.

"Thanks, umm—"

"Jomo. They all call me Jomo, sir."

"Thanks, Jomo," I said and gave him my best impression of a grateful smile. I turned toward the carousel to identify my bags, but I felt a tug on my arm, and I turned back to see that familiar look in Jomo's face.

"And when I said I'm at your disposal, sir, I meant I'm at your *full* disposal."

"Umm, thanks. That's very nice to hear, Jomo," I said. And it was, in fact, very good to hear. "Oh, there. That's one of mine coming down the chute now."

* * * *

Jomo must have called ahead to the Las Palmes as we approached it, because the front staffers were at full attention when the limo pulled up to the front entrance. I hadn't really paid any attention, as my mind was engrossed in the brochures I had found on the car seat advertising the gay clubs in the city. I knew I wanted to let loose, to do the town without the bevy of handlers I had to endure in L.A. and Miami, but I couldn't quite decide where to start. I don't know why, but there always seemed to be something out there, something more than where I was at any given moment, that I was striving for.

But we were at the hotel now; I'd have to decide on the clubs to hit later. The door to the limo was opening and several grinning faces were staring in at me. None of them dwelled on my face, though. I could see all of the eyes snap to my crotch as

I unfolded myself and stepped out onto the pavement. Well, this was what I got paid for. And I made damn sure my tailor knew that too. So, I gave them an eyeful.

Dozens of hands vied to carry my luggage into the hotel. I did like faces, though. And a variety of builds, but always something solid and well-muscled about them. From long practice, I made an instantaneous decision in favor of a small-but well-built young Hispanic with an angelic face and striking dark eyes above well-cut cheek bones. He had hung back, a little shy, but I got the impression that this was a pose he had learned to project to make himself distinctive. Slight, with a boyish figure, but when I looked at him and motioned to my luggage, he showed that he was strong as an ox.

I left Jomo looking hopeful with assurances that I'd need his services later and that I'd be calling him around 10:00 p.m., probably after a bath and shower and some supper, and I followed the tight-assed room boy to the bank of elevators.

The elevator went all the way to the top floor, while the room boy looked up at me with those bedroom eyes of his.

In the room, he opened and tested and pointed out everything he could think of, floating around the room, giving me his full "look at me" performance. When he couldn't think of anything else to demonstrate, he went to the door and turned back to me.

"Anything else you need, sir? Anything, anything at all that you want?"

And he was talking to my basket.

I walked over to him, a fair amount of cash visible in my hand.

When he reached out to get it, he looked up into my eyes again with "that" look.

"Yes, perhaps just one more thing," I said.

He smiled. He had put his hand in the one I was holding the money in, but neither one of us broke our grip. Then, with his other hand, he pushed the door to the corridor closed behind him and sank to his knees in front of me.

He unzipped me, and I thought he was going to swoon at what he found. But that didn't prevent from trying to swallow it whole.

He was gurgling and whimpering as he was bent over the foot of the bed and I was crouched closely behind him and stroking deeper and deeper into his channel. I had offered him an out when he had gotten the true measure of me, but, although he stuttered in reply, he insisted he was game and that he wanted to take it all. He had spread his legs wide when I first entered him, and he had cried out at the thickness and deepness of the invasion, but, once sheathed, I pushed his thighs in with mine and reveled in his tightness.

I rarely got partners of his size, and it was exhilarating to control a man in a boy's body, to overpower him so totally and to see such small, pert cheeks and a rosebud of a hole swallow what I had to drive inside him.

Yes, quite enjoyable. Very nice. But then, far from completion, my mind began to wander. He was panting and groaning and writhing under me, without a doubt getting the fuck of his life. Crying out that he was undone, crying out for more, for conquering of never-before reached depths, so beside himself that he was forgetting his well-learned English and was gurgling off into beleaguered, sputtering Spanish punctuated with sharp cries of the overfilled and fully transported.

But my mind was now elsewhere altogether. This was no longer something special to me, the ravishment of a luscious honey pot of a young man. Just never . . . quite . . . enough. The brochures of the clubs were fanned out on the bed beside one of the room boy's fists bunching up and knotting a large clump of the spread to the rhythm of the fuck. Putting my dick on well-practiced autopilot, I reached over for the brochures and fanned them out further. My mind wandered off on which of the clubs to start with and where to go from there.

* * * *

The limo was idling at the curb not far from the door of the club named the Open House, my ultimate choice for starting out the evening. I was laying back in the deep cushions, my legs spread, my trousers unbuckled, unzipped, spread wide apart, and Jomo kneeling on the floor of the car between my knees, a trembling fist wrapped around the base of my cock and his lips

17

straining to cover the girth of me. His chest was so bulky that I was straining to hold my legs out wide enough to accommodate him there between them on the floor of the back of the limo. He seemed determined to deep throat me, although I could have told him how likely that was.

His mouth was soft and experienced, his tongue knowing just how to caress the underside of my cock to the best effect. We were both sighing, and I felt a moan rise up from the center of me and escape to accompany the gurgling sound Jomo was making as he managed two more inches of me down the back of this throat. I lay my head back, closed my eyes, and placed my hands on this curly haired head to let the rhythm he was setting up with his mouth on my cock flow through me.

Ah, this was so nice, so soothing. It was heaven. Well, almost. Almost. Maybe.

My eyes slitted open and turned to the lit-up entrance into the Open House. A young man caught my eye as he looked around furtively and then slid almost sidewise into the club's entrance just as it looked like he was just walking by it. Young, blond, well groomed. He left the impression of someone who had heard about the underbelly of Acapulco and had flown down from Duluth. Maybe after long agonizing and struggling with himself. Clean cut, lithe, rather willowy, and with a dancer's gait. Someone who always wanted to and only now had built up the courage. But only courage enough to try it far from home, certainly not in Duluth.

I laughed, and thinking that it was because of what he was doing, Jomo lifted his head off my cock and looked up and laughed with me. He took it as a sign of approval, and I certainly didn't disabuse him of that impression. I *did* approve; I *was* enjoying it. But, I just seemed to be drifting away from it; letting it take its course; it was receding into the background.

The blond youth was in the foreground now. I had laughed because I was casting him in a role, just like I was making a movie. Filling in blanks that may not be there. But not knowing for sure was what was getting my juices going.

Jomo was quite surprised when I cut our little session off, pushed him gently away, and began to fasten up my pants. But I cajoled him by murmuring that he had gotten me hot for

18

the visit to the club and that we could resume our private pleasure later—that I wanted to give him some time to think about my cock working its way into some orifice other than his mouth. Jomo both groaned and grinned at that thought and let me go easily enough.

I found the bar in the darkened Open House. The room was small and the dance floor was even smaller. I ordered a drink and leaned on the bar, looking around the room for the blond. I expected him either to be hiding in a corner, building up the courage to make a move, or so determined that he'd be out on the dance floor already, his legs spread and off the floor and naked local boys sandwiching him with their probing cocks.

But he was neither. He was at the end of the bar, sucking up to a middle-aged tourist, who had the deer-in-the-headlights look of a not-so-sure neophyte that I had projected onto my vision of the blond at the club door. The blond was braying like a donkey at a weak joke the sweating tourist had made, and I heard a sum of money mentioned that I thought the blond should consider insulting, but he didn't. That's when I put my half-finished drink down on the bar top and turned and headed for the door. Vision shattered.

* * * *

In the backseat of the limo again, parked, idling again, not far from the entrance of the Club Picante. The windows were steaming up so that they now were almost as opaque from the inside as the outside. The hot breath was being supplied by Jomo. I was still fully clothed except for the spreading of my pants waistband and the hooking of the rim of my Calvin Kleins below my ball sac. The object Jomo was interested in was standing thick, and long, and proud straight up from my groin, reaching for the ceiling of the car.

Jomo was naked, though, facing me. I had wanted to see the ebony muscles rippling as he exerted himself. I wanted to test whether I could span his thin waist with my hands, although I couldn't because of the hard slab of stomach muscle, as finely formed as a Roman soldier's breastplate, that descended to the first fringe of curly black pubic hair. And then I wanted to run

19

my hands up the hard side of his torso, feeling every rib until I reached his pits, and I wanted to see that I couldn't hope to span that bulging chest of his.

I worried his plumped-up nipples with my thumbs as he positioned himself over my pelvis, fisting my engorged cock in place with both hands, each encircling my phallus but not touching the other hand.

He worried his entrance with the bulb of my cock for some time, obviously worried at being able to take it in. But I knew it would go in. It was one of the miracles of nature. It always went in. It often looked like an impossible task with me, but it always went in.

He grunted and strained and encased me at last, managing a couple of inches of me. Using the leverage of his knees on the cushion beside my hips, he then labored at swallowing a couple of more inches into his channel, all along muttering about some sort of comparison of what he was taking, declaring that a horse just didn't do it justice but not knowing of any other animal in the kingdom as well hung.

I didn't even ask him if he wanted to continue. He was lost in lust and determination. He had told me that he had volunteered to be my driver just for this possibility.

More inches and I was beginning to get that old feeling of detachment again, of seeking more, something else. Of getting on with whatever was next. Listening for a director to yell "cut."

But Jomo was prime meat. I needed to try my best. I needed to feel fully satisfied, and there was nothing about Jomo's beautiful body, given so openly and freely for me, that should not be satisfying.

I took over the fuck. I told him sharply to lean his shoulders onto the top of the front seat and just to hold himself in place above me. He did so, and then, gathering up all of the strength in my hips that I could, I grabbed him with my hands at his waist and thrust my pelvis sharply and viciously up into his lower belly, driving hard and deep up inside him with the full length of my cock. Jomo cried out in pain and shock and almost collapsed.

"Hold, Jomo. Hold. Damn it. Hold there."

He was moaning and giving out little yip yip sounds, but I held, arched up against him, balls to balls and sword sheathed deep inside him, until I could feel his channel walls flex and begin to ripple. And then, mustering all of my strength, I started to pump up into him in long, gliding strokes, while he began to move with me. His head was revolving on his shoulders, and he was giving fully satisfied gurgling noises. I moved my hands back up to his nipples and twisted them hard as he bellowed and shot his load up my belly and unto the underside of my chin. I almost simultaneously creamed his insides as now he did collapse his massive body on top of mine.

It was only then that I realized that my thoughts had turned to whether or not this would be a take or whether we'd have to shoot the sequence again. My body had been fully with Jomo, but my mind had drifted again.

As Jomo lay against me, his bulging body gleaming with sweat in the light cast through the foggy windows from the nearby club entrance, my eyes caught a change in the light. Someone was entering the club, casting a shadow. Cocky strides. Leather jacket, arms cut off, straining across tanned tattooed arms and torso of the finest cut. Dark, self-assured. An obvious top. One that would be cruel and would take and then take again.

I wanted to fuck him. This was the "next"; this was what I'd come to Acapulco for. It just hit me in a flash

* * * *

I was at the bar watching him at the pool table. He was good. But I was better. He didn't know that. I waited for him to demolish one of the local boys, and then I put my drink down and walked over to him.

"You're pretty good," I said.

"You look pretty good too," he said, with a sneer. His eyes traveled down me then, and I saw him hesitate, flinch. No longer that sure of himself, as his gaze reached my crotch.

"I meant your pool, but that too," I said. And then I went on. "But I'm better. Want to see?"

That had gotten him. "Big talk," he said. "For what stakes? A mouth that big should be willing to back it up."

"Fucking rights. Strip pool," I shot back, not wanting to give him much time to mull it over. "Winner take all."

His eyes went big in disbelief, but we had an instantaneous, salivating crowd now. He couldn't back down. If he did, he couldn't come in this club again.

I purposely lost the first couple of breaks, and I also purposely chose to strip off the trousers and briefs first. I wanted him to see what I would be fucking him with. And after that, he was lost. He trembled so badly on his cue striking that it was an easy win.

Several guys had to hold his arms down on the pool table with two others holding his legs spread. He was on his back on the table surface, and I had the barkeep hold a mirror up and someone lifted his head up by the hair so he could get a clear shot of me entering and entering and entering him. And then pulling back, nearly all of the way out, and then thrusting home again, in, in, in.

He was making a lot of noise for a tough guy. And it was quite obvious he had been an exclusive top to this point. But he could take any two guys here simultaneously after I was finished with him.

I was so sure, so sure when I was out in the limo and watching him enter the club that this was what I was seeking. The next step. What would satiate. But I wasn't more than half way through the fuck when the room seemed to go hazy, and the cheers of the salivating watchers grew hollow and distant. I found myself searching for the title of the movie this had been; when I had filmed this scene.

It wasn't all dim, though. There seemed to be shaft of light descending over to one corner. It illuminated a fine-looking man, not young, but not too old. Obviously rich. Fine clothes, elegant hands and movement. Handsome, patrician features. Casually, calmly lighting up a cigarette. The match the source of the light that had caught my attention. He was watching, like the others. But he wasn't frenzied like the others. His eyes were assessing eyes. I'd gotten that look before too. How high did I value myself? What would it take to buy me?

He was smiling, obviously enjoying the scene, but somehow as detached from the immediate scene as I had become. The sensation of the two of us being the only ones in the room.

I was still deep thrusting when he stood, threw some money down on the table, and extracted a card from the open wallet before returning it to the inner pocket of his silk sports jacket. He walked over to me. Our eyes were locked from the moment I had first seen him. The card drifted down from his long, sensuous, well-manicured fingers and floated to the top of the pool table beside the leather guy's trembling belly.

"Come see me," he said in a rich baritone. "Whatever you want, I can afford."

* * * *

Early the next afternoon I was covering the elegant patrician on a chaise lounge on the terrace by the pool of his villa high on the cliffs overlooking Acapulco Bay.

He was good, very good. He gave great, languorous head, and he took all of me in one long, sweet slide, his channel walls making undulating love to my cock as it took its long journey inside him.

I was sighing and moaning as contentedly as he was as we fucked.

A flash in the sun caught my attention, and I looked out over the cliffs ringing the bay. The young man, the Calvadistas, the cliff diver, was forming a beautiful arc with his slim, bronzed body as he floated in the air toward the shallow water below. He had to time his dive precisely to catch a large incoming wave to survive the dive. A beautiful body. An awe-inspiring dive. Something I had never, never seen in the movies before.

My cock engorged further, and the elegant patrician cried out in ecstasy at the extra length and girth, and began to writhe in earnest under me, losing his oh-so-refined control and pounding his pelvis more insistently against my crotch. Wanting more, deeper, harder. They always had trouble taking all of me, but they always wanted more.

I looked up again, zoning out on the body underneath me, sucking me inside with all its worth. Centering on the special gift I had to give.

My eyes and mind drifted back to the other cliff. I watched the graceful, lithe, bronzed body climbing back up to the top of the cliff. And, in my mind, I was climbing with it. And when we reached the top, I would lay him out on the cold stone, and I would dive deep, deep inside him. And this would be what I wanted. What would satisfy.

Or so I told myself.

The Other Side of the Island

"There, is that better?" Peitr whispered into my ear.

"Uhh. Yes, yes. That feels great," I answered, and my words turned into a soft moan.

"Yes, I can feel it in your body. You are a lot looser now. You are moving with me more smoothly. Is it because of the release of guilt?"

"Yes," I whispered. "This helps erase the guilt. It's as if none of this is something I could do anything about now."

"I thought so," Peitr whispered, and he began to move his cock inside me, dragging the head of his crocked dick along my ass canal at seven inches of depth, making my hips join in his motion. My eyes went to the ceiling paddle fan above us, gauging the thrusts of Peitr's hips against the flap, flap sound and movement of the paddles. I tugged a bit on the two silk scarves lightly tying my wrists to the headboard above me, seeking assurance that I was at least psychologically imprisoned and could pretend that I couldn't do anything to defend myself. Peitr's strong, solid Dutchman's body was closely covering mine on the bed, nipples to nipples and belly to belly. His legs covered mine, and I had my heels wrapped around his ankles. His arms covered mine, and he held his hands around the silk knots at my wrists, giving yet more of a comforting feel that I had no control over this. Only his hips and my pelvis were in motion, as the flap, flap of the ceiling fan above the brass bed moved what air there was in this dim-lit cabana across our naked, sweating bodies. Beyond the closed louvered doors, the heat and the jungle of the Caribbean island assaulted the small hotel cabana, trying invade our sanctuary. Strange bird calls screamed their annoyance that they couldn't get at us in our secret hiding place.

What a difference two days had made. A long weekend, but Cindy had to go north, into snow country, on business, and, for me at least, the winter had gone on just too long in the mid-Atlantic states. I'd had enough of the snow for the year, so I headed for the Dutch Antilles, and more precisely for the remote resort island of Cayo Grande, in search of sun, sand, and adventure. I had found all three in abundance, and the latter beyond my wildest notions.

Peitr had been the local Dutch guide I'd hired for a day of deep-sea fishing. We drank all day and cavorted around in our skimpy Speedos on his boat. We downed beer by sunlight, shared a couple of bottles of wine over our shell fish during the sunset, polished off a bottle of scotch under the moonlight, and I had awakened this morning with my back cuddled into his chest, his arms wrapped around me, and his dick seven inches up my ass.

I hadn't wasted my anger. I hadn't been sober to have made such a decision; if it had hurt too much, I hadn't noticed; and I'd always wondered what being with another male would be like. Unfortunately, at this point, I still didn't know what it was like even though I'd done the deed, so I was quite willing to find out when both Peitr and his peter had awakened and he'd started pumping me again.

Peitr, who obviously had not been nearly as drunk the night before as I had, remarked on how tense I was this morning in contrast to the wild fucking we'd engaged in the night before. I had to take his word for the wild fucking part; I hadn't remembered a thing about that. It had been his suggestion then that I be put under a mild restraint, and I agreed, and it had worked a charm. I was enjoying this fuck, and I wasn't feeling guilty about it. What was done was done. I couldn't pretend either that I hadn't done it or that I hadn't gone over the edge of arousal in doing it.

After we both shot our loads, Peitr untied my hands, and we glided our hands around on each other's bodies, trying to cool down under the flapping ceiling fan. Peitr lifted his lips from one of my nipples, crooked his chin on my shoulder near an ear, and asked me, "Have you ever done it with a black man?"

"No," I responded. "I've never done it before with any man before you."

"We have some magnificent native black men on this island. Have you ever thought of doing it with a black man?"

"No. . . . Well, yes, actually, I thought about that in college a couple of times. But I grew out of that."

"And now? The thought of a huge black cock churning around inside you? Does that sound pleasant, like a Caribbean adventure you might like?"

"Yes." Well, I had to be honest.

"I have business at the resort all day tomorrow. Why don't you take my boat out? Did you see that big rock formation coming down to the sea when we were about half way around the island yesterday?"

"Y-e-s-s," I answered.

"Pull into the beach just beyond that rock formation from here. You will see such a big, magnificent black man there. You will recognize him when you see him. Tell him you are interested in a waiheilah. Give him a fifty-dollar bill and ask for a waiheilah. Can you repeat that? A waiheilah."

"A waiheilah," I repeated. "OK, yes, I'll give that a try. Now, let's shower and eat and hit the beach. If I don't come home with a tan, Cindy will be suspicious."

The next day, I packed a small gym bag with shorts and a T for when the sun got too hot, struggled into my Speedo, and went out in Peitr's boat as he suggested to motor to the other side of the island. I found the little cove on the other side of the rock formation that came down to the water and pulled Peitr's boat up to just beyond the tide line. I looked around and saw nothing. But then, when my eyes adjusted in the sunlight, I saw that there was a grass hut of a pretty good size beyond the fringe of palm trees, and on the sand side of those trees, but in their shadows, was a long dugout canoe. And in the canoe, his massive back and shoulders turned to me, crouched a black giant of a man.

I knew instantly that this was the man Peitr had told me to seek out. I walked up the sand toward him. Something told me that he knew I was there and was approaching him. As I got closer, I noticed something very strange. The black giant wasn't alone in the boat. I realized that someone must be laying on his belly in the boat under the black man, because I saw two forearms dangling over the sides of the boat in the bow on either side. And they were of a very fair-skinned man. As I got closer, I saw a mop of bright-red hair on a head that rested on one seat slat near the bow of the boat. Following on behind this were the freckled shoulders of a lithe, sinewy man, whose hips rested on another seat slat toward the stern of the boat. The black man was crouched behind and above this seat slat, and, as I drew neigh, I could see that the black man, who had one strong arm planted in the small of the redheaded man's back, was pumping the most huge, blackest cock I'd ever seen in and out of the redhead's ass.

I stood there and watched in shock and awe for the longest minute, feeling my own cock coming to life at what I was watching. The redhead turned his face to me, and I recognized the Scandinavian tourist who had returned from the sea on Peitr's fishing boat the day I engaged Peitr's services.

"Yes, may I help you?" the black man asked me, without interrupting his rhythm, in a polite voice with a Dutch accent that resonated across the cove even though he had spoken in a soft tone.

"Peitr sent me," I stuttered out. "He told me to give you this money and to ask for a waiheilah."

"OK," the black man grunted and gave me a broad smile with flashing white teeth. "Excuse me," he said to the redhead and pulled out of him and rose and stepped out of the dugout.

I drew in my breath. He was completely naked, except for a thin leather belt around his waist attached to a knife sheath that ran down his thigh and held close to his leg with another

28

thin leather strap around his thigh at the bottom of the sheath. He was magnificent, just as Peitr had said he'd be. He was nearly seven feet tall and had European features but was black as ebony. This happy combination no doubt resulted from many generations of mixed breeding on this small island. And everything on him was big and round and curvy and rock solid, something that a bodybuilder would have paid big bucks and invested most of his youth in at a serious stateside gym. The biggest part of all on him was his dong, which jutted straight and long and thick and dripping with precum out from his body in honor of what he had been engaging in when I had arrived, and his big heavy balls that swung freely between heavily muscled thighs.

"Come over here with me, please," he told me. And he led me to the edge of the sand beyond the bow of the boat and took, first one of my wrists, and then the other, and tied them to cuffs that were chained to two palm trees. My arms were now chained out and above my head between the trees, and I was turned, helpless now, facing the boat.

"I'll be back shortly," he said, "This gentleman has a bit more time left on his hour." Then the black giant returned to the dugout, crouched behind the Scandinavian, and thrust his blunderbuster back into the redhead's ass. The redhead screamed out in ecstasy and set his hips churning as the black giant plowed him with deep strokes that brought his cock all the way out to the surface only to be quickly buried to the hilt. The black man only stopped long enough to slowly revolve the redhead on his cock and onto his back and then to start pumping again. The redhead yelled in delight in whatever language he preferred and brutally stroked his own cock until he'd shot his load all over the black man's belly. Then he just laid back and enjoyed the rest of the long ride and threw his head back and yelled in sheer delight as the black man no doubt came inside him.

Leaving the redhead lolling there in the dugout, the black man rose out of the boat and walked over to me in fluid, catlike motions. He stood in front of me and drew a thick-bladed knife out of the sheath on his thigh. Adrenaline pumped through my veins. Was he going to cut me? Here, in front of the

29

Scandinavian, who now was avidly watching us. The redhead was now slouched, facing us, on the seat slat at the stern of the boat, with his back resting on the stern and one hand firmly wrapped around his dick.

But the black man wasn't cutting me. With two swift slashes, he cut the fabric of my Speedo at the hips, and the remnants of the bathing suit dropped to the ground. The Scandinavian smiled broadly and licked his lips. The black giant sheathed his knife, knelt in front of me, and began tonguing and kissing my cock, which had been fully engorged from the entertainment he had been putting on with the Scandinavian fellow. I writhed in front of him, my wrists pulling at my bonds, and the redhead pulling vigorously at his prick, while the black man deep throated my cock and rolled and pulled on my balls. His hand continued on past the root of my cock, under my balls, and a long, plump finger found my asshole. I gasped in surprise and pain as he entered me there. The pad of his finger found my prostate, and I shot off down his throat in a lurch and a spasm. The redhead was thoroughly enjoying the show.

The black man rose and moved around behind me. He noticed the redhead lounging in the dugout and spoke to him sharply in some language I didn't understand. The redhead spoke back to him in a wheedling voice. He fished around in a pile of clothes at the bottom of the boat and came out with a wad of money that he waved in the air. Another verbal exchange between the two, and the redhead threw the wad of money out on the sand between the bow of the boat and where I was hanging. He then settled back in the dugout and resumed slowly beating himself off and watching the show.

The black man was behind me now, his hands on my hips, his thumbs pulling my butt cheeks apart, and his tongue searching in my asshole. We were both grunting as he slobbered into my hole and got his fingers in there. He was pretty brutal about this at first, but he seemed to come to realize that I hadn't had much attention in that department and became more gentle and caressing in his touch. His tongue was driving me crazy, and I was softly moaning for him and swaying my hips. I slitted my eyes and watched the hazy horizon where the azure sky met the cobalt sea. I was being mesmerized by the shimmering sea, nearly drifting off into a pleasurable sleep.

But I was awakened out my reverie by the sense that the black man was trying to get me to lift my legs. But I didn't know where I was supposed to be lifting them to. I felt the heel of one foot slip into a close hold on the side of one of the palm trees I was lashed between, at just above the level of my waist. I looked down and saw that there was a wooden foot hold nailed into the tree at that point. I understood now, and raised my other leg up to the foot hold on the other palm tree. The black man, who was much taller than I was, now had his strong thighs below me, and I felt the head of his cock at my asshole.

I gulped and let out a hiss of pain as he entered me with the head of his cock. He was so much thicker than Peitr was. I felt that this bulbous head was going to split me apart. But Peitr had been right. Once I'd seen this big, black tool, I'd known I wanted it inside me. The black giant rotated the head around just inside my hole as I accommodated to it. I huffed and puffed until the head got beyond my sphincter muscle, and then I felt like it would be OK, that I could manage him. He wrapped a strong arm around my belly, and the hand of his other arm went to my nipples, which he squeezed and rolled. I laid my head back into the hollow of his chest at the shoulder and moaned.

"Is it going to be all right with you?" he asked in a polite tone, his rich baritone voice echoing around the cove. "The thickest is in now. I sense you are new at this. I can manage without taking the big part of me through there, if you like."

"Yes, yes, I'm all right now, I think." I whispered to him. "I don't want you to stop. I want this. That big, black dick. All of it. In me."

And then I felt his thigh muscles tense and he was sliding that big, black, glorious cock up into me to the hilt, my ass walls undulating in appreciation as he glided in. His arm tensed around my belly and his fingers dug into my nipples. I arched my neck back and screamed to the swaying tops of the palms. The redhead applauded, as the black giant skewered me to the end and then began pumping me, shallowly at first at the deepest level, and then with longer strokes that brought the rim of his cock head to my prostate before he dove again.

31

After a good fifteen minutes of this stroking, the black giant pulled out of me and came around to where he was facing me. He was grinning, obviously very pleased with me. He gathered up my legs, pulling my heels out of the holds on the sides of the palm tree, had me wrap my legs around the small of his back, and then got his hips under me and entered me again from below and pumped his cock up into me like a piston. I arched my back, forced my hips up, close, into his pelvis, and threw my head back and watched the palm branches swaying against the azure sky again. The black giant palmed my butt cheeks. His lips came down to my nipples, and he sucked and rolled and nipped those with his tongue and teeth.

I heard a little cry and looked to the dugout, where the redhead was spouting foamy white cum into the air. Nearly simultaneously, I shot off another load of my own up the black giant's abs, and he flooded my insides with a very frothy Caribbean welcome.

While I was motoring Peitr's boat back to the other side of the island, I was grinning at the thought that if Peitr was fishing for a good fat tip for the weekend, he had not been fishing in vain.

La Lectura

"He was an old man who fished alone in a skiff . . ."

The rich, resonating, calming baritone of the La Lectura began to weave Ernest Hemingway's *The Old Man and the Sea* for us for perhaps the hundredth time, as we Torcedores settled once more into the rhythm of preparing our bunches of tobacco leaves perfectly for the press. We could not have done our demanding work without La Lectura, the reader who sat on the dais on the cigar factory floor, reading to us, first from the daily press and then from classical works—and sometimes, to our great privilege, reciting poetry to us in perfect rhythm to the set movements of our leaf bundling.

In this way he was not only transporting us from the onerous work of bunching the leaves of a perfect Vegas Robaina cigar in the demanding style of the Entubado, rolling each of five varieties of tobacco leaves separately and covering them with the binder Capote leaf before sending the bunch to the press, but also in transporting us beyond the drabness of the factory.

Day in and day out, we gathered in the dusty outskirts of Minas de Matahambre in Cuba's Vuelta Abajo region, famous for its premium cigars, at this dimly lit, factory—more a cavernous open-ended shed than a building—to repeat again and

33

again, the perfect bunching of cigars that each would sell on the European market for more than one of us made in two week's time.

La Lectura was salvation for us—and more for me than any of the other workers here. Only he, Estaban, and I were of Spanish stock. All of the other workers here, peasants all, were Mulattos or Mestizos. I had worked among them for nearly two years in almost complete isolation, and not only because of our different statuses. I chose to live not in the village but in a small, crude shack at the seaside, more than an hour's walk from the factory. Isolation was my protection; I had my secret to bear. I lived in fear that the others would find me out and I'd lose even this existence and have to retreat even farther into the island's interior.

I rested for a moment from the work of the Torcedore, the cigar roller, to gaze at Estaban, La Lectura, the glorious alien presence in this room, delivering culture and transport from this world of care in his rich baritone voice.

Estaban paused in his reading, seemingly sensing someone was watching him. I lowered my face, not wanting him to know it was me. But I slanted my gaze and saw Estaban's eyes stop and link with those of Teotilo, the dark-skinned Mulatto, small and somewhat effeminate of stature and slow of wit runner, who took our bunched tobacco packets from our rolling tables to the cigar presses. Teotilo was barely as old as I was, but he had been working here for ten years or more, since he had been a boy of no more than nine or ten. He was a good-looking young man of pleasant humor, despite the drabness of his never-varied, subsistence life. But, like any of us who could not escape this life, his prime would be over before he reached twenty-five and then, overnight, he would become an old man. In his case, as small-boned and thin and slow-witted as he was, I could not see him living into his thirties. But, then, maybe being a little dense helped him endure this monotony.

He had stopped in the rhythm of his running from factory tables to press and was looking at Estaban in total awe and admiration. Estaban was from Havana, another world altogether from Minas de Matahambre, a paradise, albeit thin veneered, of culture and sophistication and beauty to country peasants who had never been outside their isolated provinces in the remote peninsulas of Cuba. And Estaban was a handsome, well-built man of pure, patrician Spanish stock. This was in addition to being educated and refined and to having that rich baritone voice that had brought him to the highly honored position of La Lectura for one of the best of Cuban cigar brands, the Vegas Robaina, in the heart of the island's tobacco region.

I saw the grin spread across Teotilo's face as he realized that La Lectura had singled him out for attention and a smile. The women rollers near me, Estelle, Maela, and Yelina, all as smitten as Teotilo with the handsome, mysterious, velvet-voiced La Lectura, sighed at the realization that Estaban's smile was not for them and returned to their leaf bunching.

Teotilo seemed almost to melt on the spot in the sunshine of Estaban's smile, and I almost melted with him. I was so, so lonely among these Mulatto and Mestizo peasants, and so, so bored with the monotonous repetition of the leaf bundling. If it wasn't for Estaban—a Spanish city-formed soul like me—and his rich baritone reading connecting us with and transporting me to the outside world, I could not endure this existence for much longer. I would have given anything if that smile had been for me. But I could not even think of it; it brought me too close to the raw edge of my secret, what had banished me here in the first place.

"Ssst. You are lagging behind, Ramon," hissed Ernesto, the shift foreman, one of those barely thirty-year-old countrymen who had already collapsed in on himself in ugliness and ill health, one foot in the grave, the other foot on this factory floor until the day he no longer could stand.

"Take care of that one," Ernesto continued in a hoarse whisper, nodding his head toward the dais. "He does not belong here and may not be here for long, not if the rumors of what sent him out of Havana are true. Best leave him to the half-wit, if the rumors are true."

And then, leaving me to ponder that and to reach for a leaf of the first variety of tobacco to be rolled and bunched into a perfect Vegas Robaina cigar, Ernesto took two steps along the edge of the factory table and cuffed the runner, Teotilo, roughly on the back of head.

"The presses are waiting, dim-wit," he hissed. "Stop gawking and pick up the rhythm."

With that, La Lectura broke his glance at Teotilo, lifted the book in his hand, and began reading in that rich baritone of his, rhythmically, providing the beat for the preordained, precise, movement-efficient steps of the leaf-bunching process.

". . . and he had gone eight-four days now without taking a fish."

Not too many days after that a hurricane brushed past the northwest peninsula of Cuba in the night, appearing without warning in our remote, almost-forgotten Vuelta Abajo region, stripping the trees of their leaves and smaller branches and churning up the gravel and mud in the already deeply pitted paths that hardly classified as roads. I had no means of communication even if the telephone service had withstood the winds. And not knowing how Minas de Matahambre and the cigar factory had fared in the night's storm, I had little option other than to pick my way through the fallen debris for two hours on what was normally a one-hour trek from my seaside shack to the town.

Most of the workers were gathered at the factory when I arrived. The town's electricity was out, and, more seriously, the only roads into the town were impassible. Ernesto informed us there would be no cigar rolling that day. The freshness of Vegas Robainas had to be guaranteed, and there was no guarantee when a shipment could be gotten out of the town and to Havana, so production was just being suspended until more was known on possible scheduling. Ernesto did say that if I wanted the day's pay, I, as the strongest of the workers present, could stay and move bales of tobacco onto pallets in case the stream running next to the factory flooded. I readily agreed to stay, not wanting to miss the pay, such as it was, and having already walked into the town. There was no question that La Lectura would be expected to do such work, and Ernesto dismissed Teotilo with a sniff as being too small to lift the heavy bales and not bright enough anyway to understand where they should go to escape the danger of rising water.

For Ernesto's part, he happily decamped to the café in the town's square with Estelle for a thimble of wine and an unexpected fuck in the café's back room while his wife assumed he was safely hard at work at the cigar factory.

Not long afterward I was moving bales of tobacco into the factory's store room when I heard noises from a dark corner of the shed, behind some tobacco bales. Instinctively, I sauntered over to see what was making the noise and just barely was able to hold myself in check before revealing my presence, just on the other side of a stack of bales from where the two were fucking.

They were both naked, Estaban's finely formed, light-skinned body more easily discernible in the dim light. Teotilo's smaller, squatter dark-skinned body was belly down on a tobacco bale. The balls of his feet were barely able to stretch to the floor and he was rising and falling on his toes to the rhythm of the thrusts of Estaban's cock between his butt cheeks. Estaban was covering the small Mulatto figure closely from behind, his chest pushing Teotilo's down on the fragrant broad, compacted tobacco leafs at the top of the bale, and his mouth very close to Teotilo's ear. Teotilo's smile at the taking was beatific.

The sound that I had heard and that had brought me to this corner of the shed was the rich baritone murmuring of La Lectura.

He was reciting love poetry to Teotilo as he fucked him. "If I can stop one heart from breaking, I shall not live in vain. If I . . . ," he was whispering in the young peasant's ear. Teotilo certainly didn't recognize the poetry of Emily Dickinson when he heard it, but I, city raised in the family of a prominent doctor, did. But Teotilo obviously didn't care. He was completely transported not only by the fuck but by the overwhelming presence of the cultured and strong-cocked La Lectura. He was being taken into a new world of passion and desire he never before had imagined possible and possibly never again would be able to attain. This was his moment, the sum total of any excitement he would be able to wrest from life was, quite possibly, wrapped up in this fully possessing fuck by a master of lovemaking in the back corner of a cigar factory shed in the remoteness of the Cuban countryside.

And I was transported as well. Standing there, in the shadows, voyeuristically sharing in Teotilo's taking, my hand stroking my own hardened cock through the thin cloth of my trousers, I ached for what Teotilo was receiving. The husky-toned love poetry; the strong, virile body of Estaban encasing mine; the movement of his manhood inside me.

They were kissing now, and Estaban was stroking in a strong, steady thrusting. Teotilo was sighing and moaning. I was moaning too, but I didn't really realize I was until Estaban's head turned toward me.

I have no idea whether I retreated farther into the shadows in time, but I sensed that Estaban's gaze had taken me in, possibly not realizing it was me, but surely knowing someone was there. But it didn't seem to matter. Teotilo grunted and groaned at some more intense change in Estaban's fucking, and La Lectura began discoursing again, this time from Shelley, in a stronger voice than before, a voice that clearly carried to me halfway back across the shed to where I had been working and where I, full of envy and jealousy and want, resumed moving bales.

"I bring fresh showers for thirsting flowers, From the seas and the streams; I bear light . . ." Not only love poetry, I realized, but poetry that transported the one he was making love to out of this dreary existence. I ached for the attention that Teotilo, the half-wit Mulatto, was receiving, probably not even half capable of fully appreciating the gift he was receiving.

It did not get back to my shack by the sea until late that evening. I had worked hard all day, trying to purge myself of what La Lectura had awakened in me. Those dangerous secrets, the weakness that had caused me to escape Havana and to seek the isolation and scourge of the hard but honest work in the remote cigar factory. The urges were nearly overwhelming. I wasn't even sure I could return to the factory. Ernesto had been more right than he imagined. La Lectura was a danger to me. I wasn't even sure that my hands could control their trembling in La Lectura's presence and under the influence of his stroking baritone voice enough to be able to go through the demanding movements of the leaf bunching.

I stripped down to my undershorts by the door to my shack and pumped the water up until it rose up the water pipe by the door. I pumped for some time, standing under the cold water sluicing down onto my tired, aching, but yearning body. I dried myself with the towel hanging there and entered the dark single room of my shanty.

The voice was low, rich, husky, mesmerizing. "Shall I compare thee to a summer's day? Thou art more lovely . . ." Shakespeare. I had been chilled by the cold water sluicing over my body, but I began to tremble in earnest now, my knees knocking together. My first instinct was to turn and flee, but my feet moved on their own command. They drew me closer to my cot, to the source of the poetry.

"Come to me," La Lectura murmured. "You want me, don't you? I could see it in your eyes."

"No." I whimpered. But I was still shuffling toward the bed.

"No? Could I have been wrong?"

"No." I said again. This time so much weaker. Resolve draining out of me.

"No, what?" The voice. I would melt for the voice alone. But so much more was on offer than the voice.

"No, you weren't wrong," I capitulated in a whisper.

He was on his back on the cot, naked. Beautiful. Fully aroused. Ready for me.

I stood, at his direction, a leg on either side of the cot, over his chest, as his soft mouth came up to my cock and swallowed me and transported me beyond this world. He had lubricant and while he played my cock with lips and teeth, his fingers opened my canal and prepared me for mounting.

I stood there, whimpering and remembering. Remembering what had sent me into the countryside. Being overwhelmed with the realization of how much I had missed this, how much I wanted it. How much more I wanted it from La Lectura.

When we were both ready, he capped his sword and pulled me down onto the center of him. I cried out as ever before at the initial entry, but the memories flooded in, and my walls luxuriated in the expanding of the throbbing invasion and closed lovingly around his prodigious tool. He was holding me by my hips with his hands, but the balls of my feet knew the rhythm, remembered what to do, how to leverage off the floor on either side of the cot, and I was rising and falling on his manly staff, drawing him ever farther into me.

"I knew it. I knew it would be like this," he murmured, his voice turning dreamy. "I have wanted you since the first moment. I have dreamed thee; I have sought thy essence, to assuage thy sadness. To see thee smile; to smile for me alone, to melt and meld to me and to be mine to the depths of thee."

Not any poetry I'd ever heard, but poetry to me. The words of love I'd longed to hear for a lifetime, that I'd never even heard in Havana.

He had lifted his head to me and he was kissing my nipples and my sternum. His lips went up my chest and into the pit of one of my arms and he was licking and snuffling me in there, inhaling my essence.

"So young, and beautiful and perfectly formed," he was whispering. "And so tight and deep and warm inside. I want to possess you—to the quick, moving as one."

He was stroking my cock with his fist, and I was sighing and moaning for him, lost in his attentions; awed that he was making love to me with his rich voice and his throbbing cock.

When I had come in a great spouting of pent-up cream, he turned me on my belly on the cot and covered me closely with his body and began a rhythmic stroking of his cock down into me between tightly encased butt cheeks. He was growing larger and my channel was more constricted than before. The full circle of my interior walls felt every vein and tremble of his moving cock. And loved it, remembering, remembering.

I was so fully focused on the waves and waves of pleasure rising up from the center of me that I have no idea when he'd begun reciting again in whispering lips at my ear lobe " . . . Kissing with golden face the meadows green; Gilding pale streams with heavenly alchemy . . ." Surely Shakespeare again.

I melted and drifted off into another, more beautiful world.

I awoke hours later, in his arms, his cock tumescent inside me, spent after multiple takings and flowings in the earlier hours. His breathing was regular, and I didn't realize he was awake.

"You'll come when I call?" I was amazed, flattered that he even phrased it as a question in that rich, possessing voice of his.

"Yes. Anytime, anywhere."

"Here. Now."

And I was being lifted onto my knees, and he astride my hips and was quickly rising inside me again, and a hand came around and across my belly, taking possession of my ball sac and the base of my cock. And I was moaning and sighing and being stroked in dulcet tones with snippets of Shakespeare's sonnets as La Lectura, my lover, restored purpose and pleasure to my life. I could sing for joy now as I rolled those perfect Vegas Robaina cigars just as long as La Lectura was there on the dais and in my bed to provide rhythm and poetry to my life.

Haitian Carvings

I decided that if I was going to add Haiti to my list of countries visited, disembarking for a day's frolic in the fenced and well-guarded Disneyesque cruise line pleasure enclave of Labadee was the way to go. I was trying to push my collection over the hundred-country list, and, thanks to Henry Goslan the Third's money and patronage, I was well on my way.

Henry was pushing seventy, but he still wanted a companion to help him get around, to take care of all of the little chores he couldn't be bothered with, and to keep him warm at night. He was an elegant old man—quite a looker when he was younger, I was sure—and was generous and not too demanding. But there were times when I craved younger flesh. In the city that wasn't a problem. Henry was somewhat sympathetic to my needs and didn't shorten my leash—too much. But we'd been on the seas for a week now, and I was getting a little antsy.

I suggested several times how nice it would be to get out in Labadee and enjoy the day in the full-amenities resort enclave there—but even the descriptions of how easy they made wheelchair conveyance there didn't move Henry.

"I think a light lunch, a massage and perhaps a little fuck, and then you can certainly explore Labadee if you wish—for an hour or two. I can take a little nap."

An hour, two hours at the most, I thought. Just that long on my own. But I was grateful for that much time.

I picked up the phone and ordered Henry's lunch, and then half fed it to him, as he had little appetite but needed to keep his strength up. Then, after room service had cleared the lunch trays away I undressed Henry and laid him down gently in the middle of the bed we shared. I opened the cabinet and paused, wondering what he'd like me to be today. The cowboy costume won the day, because it was about the easiest to put on and I wouldn't have to make many adjustments along the way. Just low-rider jeans, a red bandana, and a cowboy hat. No boots. They would be too clunky in the bed.

Henry sighed as I gently rubbed his back and arms and legs with the special oil he liked. As I stood beside the bed, he reached over and slowly unbuttoned the fly of my jeans, pulled my cock out, and leaned over and ran his tongue over it before closing his lips over the head and helping me be ready for him.

I climbed over him and straddled his hips, being careful not to put too much weight on him, and moved my dick up and down between his butt cheeks and across his rim while I gently ran my fingers through the oil on his back and shoulder blades and lubed up my dick and his ass well with the special oil.

When I gauged his sighing was at the pitch where he wanted it, I slowly worked my cock into his hole and fucked him in slow, shallow rhythm. When I felt him tense, I took a long stroke deep into him, pulled back slightly and then drove in all the way one, two, three times, and he gave a little snuffly cry and jerked, dribbling his cum on the sheet under him. And then he promptly went to sleep.

I stood and cleaned my dick, still hard and not satisfied, stuffed it back in my jeans, without bothering to take them off to put briefs on, grabbed a tight T-shirt and my sea pass, slipped on a pair of loafers without socks, stuffed my wallet in my jeans back pocket, and was out the cabin door and headed down the stairs for the gangway as quickly as I could. I wanted as much alone time as I could manage.

I was sitting in the Dragon bar looking out to the El Tortue island, where they'd filmed part of the *Pirates of the Caribbean* movies, when the young Turk who was one of the ones who cleaned our suite on the ship stopped and asked me if he could join me.

I said OK, even though I suspected where this was heading, and I knew it couldn't go anywhere.

"I'm on furlough today—well for a few hours," Selchek said. He turned those dark, dreamy eyes he had on me and the big, all-teeth smile. "You been to Labadee before?"

"No, you?"

"Yes. And although it looks like every square inch is taken with recreational stuff and all landscaped and neat, I know of a trail or two that leads to small, private beaches—turned away from the tourist beaches. No one to see. No one to know what is happening."

He had the fingers of one hand playing in the hair on one of my forearms and the other on my knee under the table. His eyes told me everything he was offering. He cleaned our suite on the ship. He changed our sheets. He knew Henry and I were sleeping together—and it was pretty obvious what happened when we did.

"It's tempting, Selchek, but just not possible."

What I had with Henry was too good a thing. He didn't mind me going off in New York for an hour or two now and then. But he made quite clear he didn't want to know specifically what I was doing—and most certainly who I was doing it with. It was just too volatile for me to get anything on with someone from the ship.

The Turk looked glum and was about to say something else.

"It's not you, Selchek. It's the man I'm with. I can't. That's just the way it is. Besides there are rules about anything going on between crew and passengers. We could both get kicked off the ship."

"Ah, that is regrettable," was all he said, and he stood and slowly walked away.

But he left me with a hard on.

I walked the beach until I had my body under control and then I walked over to the artisan's village, which was a string—a long string—of open-air shanty stalls, opening out onto a walking deck—all made to look primitive and haphazard,

45

but of course it wasn't. There was little variety in the goods being offered. One shop was more or less like the next. Textiles or wood carving. Painted metal art and art on canvas that would look original and colorful when you got it back to the States, but here looking like there was maybe a dozen designs, painted over and over and over again.

And vendors all around, pulling at the tourists off the ship, wheedling them to look at their wares. "Just a look, sir, madam, no obligation. Special price just for you."

I did want to buy something, to help get some money in the economy of a superpoor country that recently had been hit by a devastating earthquake. But it all looked just too touristy.

It all became a jumble, everything looking the same— until my eyes were arrested for some reason by carvings in a stall that looked different from the others. The vendor there caught my hesitation—as no doubt they all quickly learned to do—and was up from his hammock and out onto the deck in a flash. He was a tasty little morsel. Short but slim and great muscle tone in his arms. He was wearing the pink shirt and tan trousers that they all wore in this overly planned false paradise. But his shirt was open down to one button at his waist. His chest muscles bulged despite his size and gleamed nearly black as the sunlight filtering through the exotic trees struck him. I sort of wondered if he'd oiled himself up and was offering more than wooden souvenirs.

He tapered down into a tiny waist, but I could tell by the way that his thighs worried the legs of the tan trousers that he probably was a soccer player. He wore a gold necklace with some sort of religious pendant resting at his clavicle, nestled between the swells of his pectorals.

A handsome face. Dark brown, the almost European features of the Caribbean mulatto and dark, flashing eyes.

"Special carvings. Just for you sir. You not find anything like them anywhere else here."

I almost believed him. What had arrested my attention was that the carvings were slightly erotic. It was subtle. I probably only caught on to the suggestive themes because I had an eye for erotic art. Henry collected it—he had masses of it in his New York penthouse.

46

This wasn't quite what Henry collected—what I could see was hetero, although there were enlarged penis images discernible in the curves of the carvings—in ebony and mahogany mostly, although some stone carvings too.

I had been trailing my eyes along the shelves, and the vendor had followed the focus of my gaze, all the time pointing this and that out and yammering on in repeated phrases of "This very nice. None like it anywhere here. You like? You buy? I wrap it for you."

He caught the dulling in my eyes as I didn't see anything that would be appropriate for Henry's collection. I wanted to please Henry, and I knew he'd like a nice piece of erotic art—if it was appropriate to his collection.

"I have more. More not right to show here. Come, come, sir, through curtain here. I have more behind."

I followed him into another shanty room immediately behind the first. There indeed were more wood carvings here—and more erotic. But still male on female (or female kneeling before male). A cacophony of fucking and huge penises. Nice and erotic. But not quite right.

"Yes, very nice," I said. "But not for me, thanks." I turned and started to pull the curtain aside to leave, but the young man grinned wide at me and winked.

"I understand. More. The same but different. You look, you see. I have more you will like. Beyond curtain there. You take look. you like. Good prices. Best in Labadee. No one else has these."

He shuffled me toward the back of the room and through a curtain into yet another room. And jackpot. He'd figured out exactly what I might be interested in. Carvings of men on men, in a huge variety of fucking poses. And carved penises. Huge dildos, their bulbous heads painted in bright red, or green, or yellow, or white.

I reached over and picked up one of the dildos with a red cock bulb on it. I ran my hand up and down it. Smooth ebony.

The vendor was watching me like a hawk. "Very nice. You take. Special price. Just today. Just for you."

I walked slowly around the small shanty room, taking in all that was on offer. I saw what I thought Henry would like almost immediately, but I was careful to pick up one or two others—never letting go of the ebony dildo with the red-painted head and a pair of plump balls at the base. We haggled and I slowly zeroed in on the piece I wanted.

"Oh, very, very, nice. Only $120 U.S."

"Maybe $40, I said—if you throw in this too." I raised the dildo. He, of course, knew I'd never let go of it.

He grimaced. "Oh no, no. Far too little. You can't get this art anywhere here. Anywhere in the world."

"Oh, maybe $60 for the two. Maybe more, but I don't think this really works." I held up the dildo again.

The vendor stood there, looking hard at me. "$100. Best price." He was sporting a beleaguered expression that I didn't believe for a moment.

I put the dildo back from where I had picked it up—which seemed to distress the vendor greatly—and turned to leave, giving him a smile and a shrug.

"$90 U.S. for both and I show you that red-headed penis work," he said in a strangled voice.

I smiled, seeing that there was yet another curtain at the back of this shanty room.

I played his asshole with the greased dildo in the small room at the back. A narrow table was set against the back wall, and he was perched on this, facing me, his trousers off, his hips rolled up, and his hands wrapped around his widely spread and elevated legs.

I worked him expertly, and when he started to enjoy it, I stood back, unbuttoned my jeans and let my hardening cock free. I dug into my pocket and extracted a condom and held it up for him to see.

His eyes were wide and buggy and his lips were trembling, but he wasn't making a break for it.

"$40," he squeaked with a whimper.

"20," I countered with, as I rolled the condom on my cock.

"$30," he croaked in a hoarse voice.

But now I was already at his entrance. "$20," I sternly said as I plunged my cock inside him, and he settled into concentrating on taking me all in without further haggling.

I took him long and hard—and with exuberance. I hadn't had young, fresh ass in so long that I fucked with abandon. Henry would have no cause for complaint. He'd get his titillating Haitian carved art for his collection. But for now, I needed this release.

And the young vendor was enjoying himself too. After he'd gotten me off well enough that I threw in another $10, he gave me a second toy, a string of graduated mahogany balls he took out from underneath the counter as I was leaving, helping him hobble along now on slightly bowed legs.

Back on the board that evening, I costumed as the gladiator, I delighted Henry so much with my purchases that I was afraid he might stroke out on me. He enjoyed the erotic carving I'd bought him immensely. And he enjoyed the work I did with the red-bulbed dildo within his channel just as much. He quickly went off in sleepabye land after he'd dribbled his cum in the sheets a second time for the day—an exhausted but very happy man.

I was still feeling my oats and devil-may-care—not carrying now if I was caught playing with the cruise staff or not—so Selchek was immensely surprised and pleased when I found him wandering down the corridor and I swung my free gift of the graduated string of beads in front of his face and asked him if there were any really private areas up on a deck with a beach lounger this time of night—and which was the largest ball he thought he could accommodate.

We discovered he could take the biggest in the wake of playing hide the red-painted ebony cock head. And then my cock afterward for nearly an hour as the waves of the Atlantic rolled on by beneath us.

Dominican Showdown

Twilight had set over the remote Puntacana resort beach on the Dominican Republic's southern coast, where the boyish, baking body of the young American tourist, Danny, had been staked out on a beach lounge under a palm tree all day. He watched the berry-brown Dominican beach attendant, all hulky muscle and graceful movement tidy up the beach area for the night. This didn't take long; it wasn't an onerous task in the off season when very few occupied the small vacation bungalows dotted around at the top edges of the small semicircular, pristine white sand beach of the cove. While the beach attendant worked, he frequently let his eyes stray to the stretched out, provocatively posed, and perfectly proportioned body of the American, the last resort vacationer remaining on the beach.

Danny turned onto his belly on the lounge and looked up toward the nearest bungalow, where the lights had just gone on. He sighed as he felt the strong hands at the waistband of his Speedo, and the suit being slipped down over his slim legs. A warm, naked, hard-muscled body lowered on him, stretching out on top of him. He let his arms dangle over the sides of the chaise lounge, his knuckles dragging in the sand on either side of it as the man above him turned Danny's head to the side with a hand on his cheek and took his mouth in a kiss. The small American, his body dwarfed by the massive muscularity of the Dominican, moaned with the feel of the cock head dragging on the small of his back. Coaxed by the touch of a hand, he spread his thighs apart. The beach attendant's cock, already half hard, dropped into the crevice between Danny's thighs, the upper side of it rubbing, rubbing, rubbing across Danny's puckering hole as the young man started to pant in response to the dry fuck.

A beefy arm laced under his waist and coaxed him up on his knees, as the Dominican's weight shifted. He no longer was lying on Danny's back. He was somewhere below Danny on the lounge. Danny grunted and gasped and spread his thighs further as a hand encased his engorging cock and a wet tongue went to—and into—his hole. He raised his arms above his head and grasped the top of the lounge. His eyes turned toward the foliage beyond the top of the lounge, toward the terrace of the bungalow with the lights on inside. There was another light, the glow of a cigarette, and the silhouette in the advancing dark of a figure sitting on the terrace.

Danny tried to stifle his moans and groans as his cock was pulled through his legs and a mouth swallowed it and a tongue ran up and down the sides of the shaft. He gave a little cry as the lips closed tightly over his bulb and the tongue darted into his piss slit. A thumb was buried deep in his hole, slowly moving in and out, opening him up to the shafting that soon was to follow, seeking and finding his prostate with its pad.

"Oh, yes, yes, fuck yes. Fuck me, fuck me," Danny murmured, knees trembling and slowly rotating his hips with the attention being applied to his cock and prostate. He was trying to be quiet. The glowing cigarette was just yards away. But he involuntarily cried out as the beach attendant rose up over him, crouched over his buttocks, grasped his hips with strong hands, and slid his cock into a shimmering channel, open to him and begging for his touch.

The fuck was a long one. The beach attendant was young and virile and had great stamina—and no doubt had been thinking of this encounter since earlier in the afternoon when

52

the two had established the twilight assignation. After doggy fucking Danny for several minutes, he turned the young American on his back, slid in between his thighs, grabbed Danny's ankles and raised and wishboned Danny's legs. As the Dominican thrust his shaft back inside the moist, now-gaping hole, Danny arched his back and panted and moaned. Danny was fucked hard and fast to the Dominican's first ejaculation. After the beach attendant had come, he moved down the lounge, pulled the spent condom off his cock and dropped it to the sand at the side of the lounge. He then lowered his mouth on Danny's cock and palmed Danny's pecs, worrying the young man's nipples, until Danny too had come.

The beach attendant moved back up Danny's body and they kissed, both enjoying the taste of Danny's warm cum. They lay thus closely embraced and moving their bodies against each other in a desultory fashion until Danny could feel the beach attendant going hard again. Danny was doing so as well. The Dominican went up on his knees between Danny's spread thighs and Danny narrowed his eyes in pleasure at the beautifully molded, berry-brown torso of his "For now" lover. He moaned at seeing the thickness of the man's cock, the cock that had just been inside his channel, expertly working him. The beach attendant smiled down at him, Danny watched as the Dominican slowly rolled on another condom.

Exhibiting both his strength and his control over the small, lithe-bodied Danny, the Dominican grasped Danny by the waist and raised his body in the air, over his, while he moved to stretch out his own legs toward the top of the lounge. Slowly he lowered Danny's body, Danny's knees going to the outer sides of the beach attendant's thighs and his face coming down to the Dominican's, where their mouths met in another long, lingering, tongue-possessing kiss.

"Perfect body, so small and perfect," the Dominican muttered as they came out of the kiss. "Such an amazing hole, first very tight and then opening right up. I didn't think it could, but it opened right up for me. You have taken many men, haven't you? That turns me on. And you are so flexible and graceful. Are you a dancer?"

"More in the line of an actor, I think you'd say," Danny answered, and then, with heavy breathing, "And yes, I have taken many men. Of those, you are one of the best. You have fucked many men too, I'll wager."

"And women too. It's part of the resort service."

"Fuck me again," Danny whimpered. "Just keep on fucking me."

Danny grasped and positioned the Dominican's cock while his own pelvis was being lowered to the Dominican's, and he lowered his channel on the shaft. Demonstrating his full acceptance, Danny leaned back and grabbed his ankles in his fists and fucked himself on the hard shaft as the Dominican laid back on the lounge and, smiling, arms crossed behind his neck, his muscular chest puffed out and heaving, watched Danny gyrate his body and ride the cock. After a few minutes the Dominican reached down with both hands and worked Danny's cock.

This time Danny came first.

The Dominican raised his torso up, grasped Danny's sides under his armpits, thumbs stroking Danny's nipples, and Danny arched his torso back over the upper section of the lounge and let his arms dangle at his sides and his head arch back, completely relaxed in his torso and his legs, every ounce of his energy and focus going to his channel and that thick, hard cock reaching up inside him. Again, the beach attendant resumed fucking Danny's channel with slow, forward and back, movements of his hips. Danny willed his channel muscles to undulate over the cock, to squeeze it and release it, squeeze it and release it. And with a jerk and deep-throated phrases of passion in Spanish, the Dominican ejaculated.

Alone, laying on his belly, panting and cooling down, listening to the waves lapping up on the beach and the breeze whispering through the palm branches, Danny raised his head and looked up at the nearby beach bungalow. The lights inside had moved to a different room. But the figure was still sitting on the terrace, the smolder of the lit end of the cigarette moving back and forth.

Danny turned and stretched like a cat on the lounge; raised his knees up, with his feet flat on the surface of the lounge; spread his thighs; and moaned quietly as he stroked his cock. His head was hanging over the top of the lounge, and his eyes were staring toward the foliage above him, picking out and following the movement of the cigarette tip.

The cigarette arced out over the terrace of the bungalow, landing in a planter, and Danny held his breath as he discerned the movement of a darker, bulky shadow rising from the patio chair in the darkness enveloping the bungalow patio. But then he heard the closing of a door and all was silent from the terrace. Danny's hand dropped away from his cock. He sat up on the side of the lounge and gathered up his beach items, looking up the beach toward his own bungalow.

* * * *

Danny was already stretched out on his "claimed" lounge under the palm tree on the resort beach in mid morning when a couple came out of the bungalow closest to him and moved to side-by-side lounges farther along the beach but close enough that Danny could hear that they were speaking when they did so but not their specific words. He watched them over the top of his sunglasses and a paperback novel held near his face as they laid out their towels and other beach paraphernalia.

They were a couple that would arrest most anyone's attention, so it wasn't notable that Danny would be scrutinizing them closely. They were mismatched. She was somewhat of a mousey woman, probably in her early forties, who was losing the battle of weight and didn't seem to know it. She was trying to wear a bikini and not pulling the effort off very well. Dishwater blonde hair, skittish movements, facial expressions that changed moods frequently, and a whine that Danny could hear from where he sat. She wasn't bad looking, just tired looking, nervous and giving off an air of defeat. She was on the beach to swim and went to the water, up to her knees, but no farther, almost as soon as they had reached their lounge chairs.

The man, in contrast, clearly wasn't there to swim. He was bare-chested, but wearing baggy shorts, and Danny doubted he was planning on swimming with the Smith and Wesson M&P 9 mm and holster buckled at his waist. From his attitude, he was there to continuously scan the beach, his eyes stopping for a lingering moment to focus on Danny with each sweep.

He was a mismatch with the woman in nearly every way he could be. He probably was in his late twenties or early thirties, was movie star handsome, gave off an aura of confidence and capability—and all business—and quite evidently was a serious bodybuilder. Whereas his body was a temple, the woman's was a 7-Eleven convenience store.

It was very hard for Danny to see these two as a couple. He continued to watch them both as surreptitiously as he could, while the woman waded around aimlessly and rather listlessly in the surf, flinching at any sound other than the cawing birds, rustling palm leaves, and lapping waves, and the man finally settled in to a wary seated position on one of the lounges. He slowly relaxed a bit while keeping an eagle eye on the woman broken by occasional scans of the rest of the activity on the beach—of which there wasn't much—and began chain smoking cigarettes.

After a while his eyes were going to Danny almost as often as to the woman in the surf, and Danny was doing all he could in posing in his skimpy Speedo on his lounge to encourage the scrutiny. The man was a real hunk, and the glances Danny devoted to the gun on the man's hip sent him into flights of fancy on the other gun he was packing. The shorts were baggy and the leg holes drooped, so that Danny fancied that he almost . . . almost . . . could see far enough up the curve of the heavily muscled thighs to see the hint of a cock bulb.

Almost imperceptibly Danny turned to his side, facing the man and, as he pretended to read his paperback novel, drank in the man's bulging pecs and ripped six pack through his sunglass lenses while his free hand glided over his sweat-glistened body. It wasn't long before Danny was rewarded with seeing the man's hand drop to his crotch. He was studiously not directly looking at Danny, but Danny knew that the man was watching him as surreptitiously as Danny was watching the man.

It almost seemed like the man was poised to rise and come over to Danny's lounge when the woman came out of the surf, dried herself off with a towel, said something to the man, and they returned to their bungalow.

Danny rose from his lounge then as well and walked in a graceful half-strut across the sand toward his own cabin, being fully aware that the man had come out onto the terrace of the bungalow and was standing there, smoking a cigarette, and watching Danny walk away.

That afternoon and evening it was like the paths of the couple and Danny were continuously crossing. In the afternoon, Danny went into the small village outside the gates of the resort to view the handicraft stalls, and the couple was doing the same thing. When Danny went to the resort's beach bar for a drink afterward, the couple already was there. The two were perched on barstools, side-by-side, although leaving the impression they weren't together, she morose and he observant, not saying much of anything to each other. They certainly weren't honeymooners, as anyone watching them for any length of time could tell.

Back in the village for an early dinner, both the couple and Danny had selected the same restaurant. The woman's eyes were darting everywhere while she ate, but Danny and the man mostly stole glances at each other.

Shortly after dark, Danny was back on his lounge, riding the cock of the beefy Dominican bartender who had been serving them drinks that afternoon. The Dominican laid on his back stretched out on the lounge, the palms of his hands fanned out on Danny's pecs as, facing the bartender, Danny crouched on his haunches on the man's cock and leaned his torso back with his hand's gripping his ankles. He was slightly raised off the man's crotch to give the Dominican room to fuck up into his channel.

Danny was moaning and moving his hips to meet the Dominican's thrusts, but his gaze was directed toward the fringe of the beach, where a figure was sitting, in the dark, on the terrace of the couple's bungalow and smoking cigarettes.

When Danny arrived at one of the village restaurants for lunch the next day, the couple was already there. But the man leaned over and said something to the woman, after which he took money out of his wallet and they both left the restaurant even though their food was only half eaten. The Smith and Wesson was still strapped to his waist. It was there every time Danny saw the couple.

Danny's own meal was only half eaten as well when two local policemen entered the restaurant, walked up to his table and politely but firmly requested that Danny accompany them to the local police station. There he was taken to a small interrogation room furnished with a wobbly wooden table and three chairs, one on one side of the table and two on the other. A large mirror was set in one wall, where the single chair faced. Danny was asked to sit in the single chair.

After a wait of nearly an hour sitting there all by himself, two men entered the room—an older-looking policeman and the man from the resort. They sat in the chairs opposite Danny, and the man opened a pouch he'd brought with him and had laid on the table and took Danny's passport; hotel reservation printouts for here and the Cayman Islands, where he next was booked at a beach resort; and plane tickets out of the pouch and laid them on the table.

"You've been in my bungalow," Danny said. "Those were in a locked safe."

"Yes, Mr. Wilson," the body-builder hunk with the gun on his hip said. "The local police are cooperating with me. It doesn't take much in the Dominican Republic to obtain permission to search someone's home. You have been paying a bit too much attention to me and the woman I'm with—enough to have raised questions why that was so."

"It's a small resort and off season," Danny said. "I didn't know that there were restrictions on where I could go just because you and your wife would be there too."

"She's not my wife," the man shot back. But then it seemed from the expression on his face as if he had said something he shouldn't have, and he regathered his approach. The policeman sat stoically beside him, arms crossed, saying nothing, quite possibly understanding little other than that there must be some reason for him to be cooperating with this other tourist.

Danny thought of asking the man—or the policeman—by what authority he was questioning Danny's activities, but he thought better of it and just waited for the man's next move, watching his face with a mixture of amusement and lack of worry.

"We are here for our privacy. I am, you might say, the woman's bodyguard, and I have to be very careful who shows interest in us."

"You've been in my bungalow. You've gone through my things," Danny repeated, gesturing at his documents that the man had laid out on the table.

"Yes, sorry."

"Did you find anything that would make you suspicious that I wasn't just here on a vacation?" Danny asked.

"No, we didn't. But you have been watching the woman closely. Can you say why?"

"I wasn't watching the woman," Danny said, giving the bodyguard a level, direct stare. "I was watching you."

"Watching me?" the man said, nonplused and surprised at the comment. "Whatever for?"

"I suspect—I hope—for the same reason you have been sitting and smoking on the terrace of your bungalow the last two nights and watching me—and what I was doing."

The three sat and stared at each other for more than a minute. Only the policeman seemed not to understand what was being said—and his English probably was very limited anyway.

"Tell me that I'm wrong," Danny said. "Tell me you haven't been watching me—and listening—with special interest."

Another pause of staring and then the man leaned over and said something to the policeman in Spanish. The policeman nodded, rose from the table, and left the room. The bodyguard also got up from the table, walked over to the door to the corridor, and closed and locked it from the inside. This was his one and only intentional act in that first coupling.

They fucked with the man standing with his back against the wall beside the mirror. Danny did most of the work. The man had clearly wanted to fuck Danny, but he struggled with the propriety of doing so, especially right there in the police station, until Danny seduced him with entreaties of need and with clever initiation of groping, moaning, kissing, stroking, begging, heavy breathing, and cock sucking—all out of view of the mirrored window in one wall.

Danny forced a position that the man could not resist and did not have to take responsibility for. Danny had his fists locked behind the man's neck and was draped on the front of the bodyguard, who, shorts down around his ankles but Smith and Wesson still buckled on a belt at his waist, was palming and spreading Danny's butt cheeks to give his cock maximum penetration of Danny's channel. Danny's legs were bent with his feet flat against the wall and out wide at the level of the man's waist, giving him the aspect of a crab attached to the man's pelvis. He used his feet for leverage. Taking full charge, Danny pumped his channel on the man's long and thick cock. Danny provided the Golden Ticket condom, Danny provided the opportunity, Danny provided the sensual touch, and, in the clutch, Danny provided the pumping action on the cock.

Until he was completely lost to Danny, and the irresistible need for him, the man was given no opportunity to withdraw from the brink of the abyss. What he did that night was, at least in his mind, a compensation for his lack of control and dominance earlier, letting a small, boyish-looking man dominate a macho, hulking dude like him. It became a matter of pride to reassert dominance.

That night after the resort's pool boy fucked Danny on the lounge under the tree and had gone, Danny rose from the lounge and walked over to the terrace of the neighboring bungalow. The bodyguard, naked, was sitting in a patio chair and smoking a cigarette. As Danny approached, he flicked his cigarette into a planter and raised and spread his arms, pulling Danny into an embrace as, facing him, the young man straddled the arms of the patio chair and lowered his channel on the man's erect, already-sheathed cock.

After Danny had ridden the cock to his ejaculation, the man gathered him up in his arms and carried him into the bungalow, into one of the two bedrooms; laid Danny down on his back on the foot of the bed; spread the young man's thighs, slowly slid his cock into Danny's channel; and fucked him, at great length in ever-more-rapid strokes, to his own ejaculation. As soon as the man could regain a hard staff, Danny straddled his pelvis and rode his cock again.

At length, exhausted, Danny and the man lay side by side on the bed, their hands roaming each other's bodies and Danny giving the man a hand job until with a moan and a sigh, the bodyguard drifted off into sleep. When the bodyguard's breathing had become regularized and he was quietly snoring, Danny carefully and silently rose from the bed and padded out of the bungalow, leaving the door behind him unlatched and slightly open.

He stealthily moved back to the lounge he had claimed for himself and lifted it and swung it away from the base of the palm tree, careful to muffle the scraping noise in the sand. Once the lounge was turned, he went down on his hands and knees and dug into the sand. Extracting the oilskin pouch that had been hidden under the beach lounge since the day Danny had arrived—two days before the couple in the nearby bungalow did—Danny carefully unwrapped the Beretta 92FS it contained, checked it over, and then screwed on the silencer that also had been hidden in the pouch.

They had been right, he thought. The best avenue of approach and the disarming of defenses had been through the sexual proclivities of the bodyguard. He already could feel the sweet taste of success. There hadn't yet been a witness protection arrangement that he hadn't been able to circumvent.

He rose and, holding the Beretta at the ready at his side, quietly and carefully stole his way back inside the bungalow.

Baggy Shorts

I think of the year of management training in Port-a-Prince, Haiti, as my year of discovering my fetishes.

The company's other American on-location trainee, Jake, thought, I'm sure, that I was concentrating on his typically long-winded explanation of why the Miami office hadn't sent in their lists for distribution of the sack-laden pallets on the floor below to southeast coastal U.S. cities, but I wasn't. I was sitting there, rocking back and forward in my worn leather chair, with my back to the whole spread of Haiti's Port-a-Prince harbor from my desk on the hot and steamy mezzanine above the dusty warehouse's coffee bean sacking floor and looking right past Jake, over his shoulder. I was focused on what was happening down at the reception desk outside the sales superintendent's office.

That new eye candy receptionist of the milky white skin, Emilee, recently arrived from Marseilles, was having her effect on the burly black policeman who was supposed to be scrutinizing the arrival on the trucks of the sacks of coffee beans from the plantations—to keep our company from shipping sacks of drugs along with the beans. They had become quite chummy in the two weeks she'd worked here. Now he was perched on the counter across from her desk in his khaki uniform, baggy shorts and all.

He was quite a looker himself. The milk chocolate color of the octoroon, descendant of French planter and black slave of Haiti's colorful past. Strong European facial features, with carefully curled and blown hair and the physique of a serious body builder. He was sitting on the edge of the counter and pulling his legs up with his hands below his knees. It was almost obscene. When he pulled his legs up, you could follow the curve of his meaty thighs right up toward his crotch. And now he was pulling his legs apart. If I'd been closer, I know I could see right up to where it got really interesting. And he and Emilee were just chatting away. It just wasn't natural the way he was showing leg, and it certainly shouldn't be going on in an office. Why, Emilee might be getting a real eyeful.

Then it hit me. Of course she was getting an eyeful. That's exactly what the trolling policeman—and she—wanted to be happening. And I couldn't help it; I wanted to be getting an eyeful too. My balls began to ache, and I could feel myself getting hard. Jake just droned on with his half-assed criticisms of the Miami office, though, oblivious to what I was trying to cop a look at over his shoulder.

My fetishes, those brought to me by Jimbo Jacques, were intersecting again. Glistening black muscle, an even blacker cock, and baggy shorts. I probably would not have ever known this turned me on if I hadn't come to the Caribbean islands.

I'd been in a real state for weeks, ever since the day I'd gone to meet Jimbo Jacques, the heavily muscled sack stacker I had melted to from watching his dancing movements and the undulating muscles of his sweat-glistened torso on the coffee bean warehouse floor for what had become a short midday suck session in the alley behind the warehouse and found he'd returned to one of the plantations without so much as saying good-bye to me. I'd grown dependent on the boners the beefy jet-black floor worker had given me—and then had given relief to. The least thing now put me in heat, and especially that intersection of glistening black muscles, an even blacker cock, and baggy shorts.

Emilee was getting up from her desk, and she and the policeman were disappearing into the floor superintendent's now-deserted office. Jake droned on as my mind was racing, imaging the small, milky-white, thin, all curves and roundness Emilee and the black, bulky, all-hardness policeman on the top of the superintendent's desk. Her running her hands up inside the legs of his baggy shorts; finding what she was seeking—revealing a ruby-knobbed cock even blacker than the rest of his skin. Him hiking her skimpy skirt up, tearing at her panties. And then him lifting her and setting her small pink rosette on his thick, raised, jet-black spike and fucking her, sliding the small of her back on the dull surface of the desk—jet black sliding into milking white and back out again. I felt myself panting at the image. And it wasn't Emilee I was panting for; it was the octoroon policeman, his imagined jet-black cock, and his baggy shorts—that intriguing tunnel up to his treasure chest.

I had to get out of there. I had to get laid. I had to get fucked now.

Jake was in midsentence when I just stood up, strode out of the office, and headed for the stairs in the shadows at the back of the mezzanine. Jake wouldn't think this was unusual. He knew his sermonized complaints were lame; I often walked out on him in these circumstances.

When I hit the baking tiles of the cobble stones bordering Port-a-Prince's teeming harbor side, I found myself walking away from the harbor and turning into the shadows of one of the alleyways leading to the old town's red light district. One night when I'd convinced the meaty sack handler to come home with me and fuck me into the next morning, he'd said I'd have to take him to an all-man's club to get him in the mood, and he's the one who showed me Papa Joe's. This had been no-holds-barred bar, where the local Haitian warehouse and plantation workers gathered and let off tension. It wasn't the place a visiting American looking for some male-male action would normally go. But what I needed now was to let off some tension, and I couldn't get the images of either my deserting jet-black hulk, Jimbo Jacques, or the Rosa-melting octoroon policeman out of my mind.

65

I walked into the dimly lit bar in my pressed khaki trousers and starched white sports shirt, which, along with my whiteness, screamed of out-of-place Norte-americano in the realm of the Haitian local sexual underbelly. I focused on the bar and walked straight there and ordered a beer before turning around, perching on a bar stool, and surveying the room.

At the other end of the bar from me, a lithe young coffee-colored, citified Haitian, obviously not long enough in the warehouse muscle business to really beef up, had been pulled into a hulky jet-black, not long from the rice fields guy perched on a bar stool facing out to the room, the coffee-colored youth's butt pulled into the black guy's package. Baggy pants must have been the signature apparel of those frequenting this bar, because the coffee-colored youth, who I heard referred to as Philippe, had on citified duds of droopy silky basketball shorts, a muscle shirt, and high-top sneakers and the black-black guy had on cargo shorts that hung low on his waist and a white T-shirt and heavy boots. What caused me to look in that direction was the black guy, arm muscles rippling, was pulling the muscle shirt off the younger man. I watched his huge black hands slowly glide down the youth's long, lightly muscled torso. I expected the hands to go under the rim of the droopy silk shorts, but they went down over the thin material of the shorts rested a moment on the youth's thighs, just above the knees.

Then the black guy's hands went under the hem of the basketball shorts at both leg holes, and I watched the material of the shorts bunch up and rise as the hands came up the coffee-colored Philippe's thighs and met at his still-encased package. The youth got a dreamy look in his eyes and began to purr. He was stretching his torso up inside the black guy's reaching arms and he threw his own arms around the back of the black guy's thick neck. They turned their faces toward each other and were both moaning and groaning as they kissed deeply. I watched what was going on in those thin, silky shorts, mesmerized with the rustling and tenting of the material at the crotch. The black guy was stroking Philippe off with one hand and doing something with the ball sack with the other.

The younger worker began to writhe in the black guy's lap. One of the hands of the black guy—the one that had been working the balls—came out of the leg opening to the shorts and moved to hold the younger man tight to him with a palm on his heaving belly. The youth was writhing about and he was giving little panting chirping noises, lost in a controlling jerk off that was inevitably going to bring him to orgasm as he was held tightly into the body of the black guy. I licked my lips in anticipation of what the black guy was going to do as an encore once he'd jacked the young guy off.

I sensed that someone was watching me watch the couple at the end of the bar, and I let my eyes sweep away from the coffee-colored youth being taken. I saw a man eyeing me from across the smoky room. Everyone else around seemed to be well into hooking up—some in fact were already fucking away on the cushy couches at the fringes of the room and on the carpeted stage area in the center of the room. I remember registering surprise at that point because he looked like the hunkiest of the lot, and yet he was the only one alone and not in some phase of fuck at this moment. Other than me.

He was wearing only baggy shorts and workman's boots—and a red bandana around his neck. His massive chest and bulky arm muscles also made clear that he was into heavy lifting work. Fine, heavy-muscled calves and thighs. I'm sure he could see how deeply in heat I was just from the way I looked at him—and that I liked what I saw in him. Neither jet-black nor mulatto, he looked more Jamaican. A rich brown but with European features reflecting some mix of ancestry. He gave me a little satisfied, knowing, possessive sneer, and then as he held my eyes with his, he pushed his butt forward in the lounge chair he was in and opened his legs, and, oh my, I could see a bulbous, red cap hanging low, near to the bottom edge of the bunched up shorts and I could also see all the way up to a heavy, hairy ball sack. His cock was several shades blacker than he was and his pubes were jet black, curly, and kinky.

I melted and he had me with no more than that. This was exactly what I was shopping for. I found myself rising off the barstool and gliding toward him. He had himself unzipped by the time I got to him, and he pulled me roughly to him, my legs encasing his. He made quick work of the buttons on my white sports shirt with one hand and the zipper on my khaki trousers with the other and pulled me down into his lap. He pulled the tail of my shirt out of my trousers, making no other move to strip them from me. But when he brought me down into his lap, we could not have been more intimately linked, the half-naked warehouse worker and the managerial clothed Norte-americano.

He pulled my pelvis right into his and my engorging dick entered the opening of the fly to shorts and both of our penises were there together in the tented area between where his denim and my pressed cotton met at the zippers.

He got a beefy hand in there as well and was stroking our cocks together—mine pink, long, and slender and his a regular super-sized, jet-black sausage—while his thick lips went to worrying my nipples. I arched my torso back and gazed around the room, watching others in various forms of fuck, knowing that soon, very soon, that jet-black sausage of his was going to fully possess me. I sighed and trembled as he stroked us together and worked his lips and teeth on my nipples.

I looked down at the pink cylinder being stroked together with the jet-black sausage by the lighter black fist, and I lurched and jerked, and sighed and groaned and creamed myself up into his kinky black pubes. He laughed and rhythmically squeezed our cocks, draining all he could from me.

And then he was pulling my trousers down and off my legs and he had his wide, callused palms on the backs of my thighs, squeezing them and appreciating that I was well worked too. Then he moved his hands to my butt cheeks and was raising them and settling me on his ramrod. I whimpered and protested a bit, not being ready for what he had for me—but containing my reaction, not wanting to scare him off, because this was exactly what I wanted. He wasn't the least bit afraid or reluctant; he just laughed and insisted on having me then and there. I felt the pain of that bulbous mushroom cap at my hole, straining at me, and then a sharp forcing sensation and he was inside me and sliding up and up and up. He was caressing all sides of me inside and stretching me, and my walls were starting to undulate—to work his sausage as they had worked Jimbo Jacque's prodigious jet-black cock. He was grunting his satisfaction.

I could hear myself groaning for him as he plowed up me, and I whispered dirty words in Haitian-kissed French to him, words I had learned from my short-time lover, words that aroused him in ways he transmitted down his shaft and into my center. I lifted both legs around the sides of the lounge chair and grabbed his massive pecs with my hands, my thumbs pressing on his erect nipples, struggling to maintain leverage, as he bottomed in me. And, with strong hands on my butt cheeks, he was stroking me up and down on his black-black sausage. Up and down and around and up and down. At first labored. And I was melting, and panting, and groaning, and crying for what he was so deeply and fully doing inside me, my own rehardened cock rubbing up and down on his heavily muscled, hair-matted belly, preparing to cream once again for him.

I had found exactly what I had come into this bar looking for and what a peek up those baggy shorts of his had promised me. He lifted my pelvis high off of him, pulling his cock completely out of me and then slammed me down hard while sucking hard on a tit, and I howled to the ceiling and spouted up his belly.

It was like my howl was the bell summoning the others to the main event, because some of the other muscle-bound, hulky, various-shades-of black Haitian workers gathered around.

The sausage man hadn't come yet. And after I did for the that second time, he stood up from the chair and turned me so my knees were in the chair and my arms and neck hanging over the back of the chair and then he slammed hard into me again and began riding me quickly and deeply. He was running his callused hands along the curves of my thighs and yammering something throaty and full of mirth in Haitian French to the other delighted Haitian workers gathered around me.

I knew enough French to know that he was making boasts of putting it to all the uppity white Norte-americanos from above the Caribbean, and his compatriots were laughing in agreement to fucking the northern fuckers. But I didn't care and I laughed with them. I didn't care as long as he continued pounding my insides with that jet-black cock of his.

He pumped me for a few more minutes and then pulled out of me and came around to in front of me and I was being face fucked. Another of the Haitian workers, with a thinner, but longer cock, mounted me then and came quite quickly, filling me with his cum at the same time that the first one was creaming my throat.

And then I was taken by a succession of beefy workers, including both the black guy and the coffee-colored youth, Philippe, I had watched earlier, working inside me with increasing ease, helped by a frothy mixture of shared cum. Several of them shed their baggy shorts in my sight before moving behind me and boning me with much excited yammering in Haitian French. It wasn't long before I forgot Jake's problem and the octoroon policeman and Emilee—and even my departed warehouse worker, Jimbo Jacques, ejaculating again and again, almost as often as I was filled.

For months afterward all I had to do was see a Haitian worker in baggy shorts and I'd go straight to hard—and it wasn't long before I found that the octoroon policeman was versatile enough to do me on the warehouse superintendent's desk too when that office was deserted. I was delighted to find that his cock was as jet black as I had imagined. I would make him lean back against the edge of the desk, and I'd reach up into the leg opening and pull his cock down to my searching lips and suck him to the top edge of arousal, the hem of those baggy shorts caressing my cheeks. And then, when he had me flat on my back on the desk top and my legs spread for him, all I had to do was lift my head and watch that beautiful black hunk of meat stroking in and out of my ass to come with loud gasps and groans just as I could hear Emilee do when she disappeared with him behind the frosted glass of the superintendent's office door.

Jake remained clueless to the end. He was flabbergasted when I put in for a permanent assignment to the company's Haiti office when my internship had been completed.

Key Westing

It was snowing in Washington, D.C., and after battling skidding cars on the Beltway for an extra two hours trying to get into work, I suddenly decided that it was time for me to head someplace sunny. It was my lucky day after all, because when I hit the office, everyone was in an uproar about reports from Havana that Cuban dictator Fidel Castro once more was on his deathbed. Bad news for Fidel and great news for me. I was a Caribbean and Spanish language specialist and, within hours, I was flying off to our little unit on Key West, the last of a chain of U.S. islands dribbling down from Florida toward Cuba.

I was able to hold on to my "put-upon" stoic face in negotiations with my employers over the short-notice, unknown-duration assignment to negotiate four days of expenses-paid vacation time on top of the news media death watch on Castro no matter how long it lasted. Time away from snow-clogged Washington at the gay capital, warm, and sunny-beached Key West. How could I have been so lucky? And to add to that, when I called my significant other, Brian, he jumped at the chance to join me on the trip. So, I slogged back to our apartment, and we threw our skimpy Speedos into a suitcase, and we were off.

If I thought it was going to be a few hours during the day monitoring the Cuban media and then afternoons on the beach and nights in bed with Brian, making wild love, I was shortly to be disabused of that dream. No sooner had we checked into the gay-friendly Atlantic Shores Resorts, within steps of the naval air station that hosted the unit where I was to work, than I was off to work and Brian was off to the Duval Street bars. For two days I was chained to radio and television receivers for double shifts and returned to the hotel room only long enough to catch a few hours of sleep—alone, because Brian wasn't there either of those days. He obviously had found the Key West night life much to his liking.

The third morning I was hurrying out to work as Brian was just dragging in, all disheveled, but with a sloppy grin on his face. I knew that expression; he'd been fucked hard and well.

"Hi there, Estaban," he said with a weak wave of his hand as he headed for the bed I'd just vacated.

"How nice of you to put in an appearance, Brian," I said, all of the frost of the distant Washington in my voice.

"Ah, man," Brian said, as he settled into the bed. "You oughta get some time off and go bar hopping with me. This place is a candy store of male pussy and hot cocks."

"I can see that," I said, my voice dripping icicles. "Your eyeballs are swimming in semen. I do so hope you continue to enjoy your stay on my nickel as I work my ass off to earn that nickel."

"Geez, Estaban. It's not my fault they've tied you to the job. When Fidel has kicked off, we can party straight for days. I'm just checking out the best places to do that."

"Well, if you didn't check them out so enthusiastically, maybe you'd be home in bed waiting for me one of these nights and we could at least do what we were doing in Washington. I didn't come to Key West to stop having sex, you know."

But Brian didn't have any response to this. Not because he wasn't capable of snappy banter but because he was already snoring away in the bed.

That night when I dragged back to the room, the lights were off and I assumed that Brian once more was out all night at the bars. But when I opened the door and the light from the hallway dimly outlined the bed, I saw something stirring there. So, at least he was home. But he probably was in a drunken sleep and would be no good to me tonight. And I badly needed some stroking tonight.

But before I could get the door closed behind me and turn on the light, I saw a torso rise up in the bed—and it wasn't Brian's. It was some heavily muscled and tattooed dude, whose naked butt was undulating up and down against another naked body stretched out underneath him, belly to bed. I recognized Brian's cries and grunts and groans of passion. The guy on top turned his torso briefly toward me, checking out where the light from the open door was coming from, and I caught the gleam of eyebrow, ear, nipple, and navel piercings in the reflected light. He saw me, but he said nothing and just swiveled back around and pumped his cock down in long strokes between the ass cheeks encased between his knees. So, at least Brian was home, but he was a little busy now—being fucked by some leather man he'd picked up in a bar.

I shut the door and just sort of collapsed in a chair by the window, listening to Brian's panting and moaning and cries of ecstasy at the stroking he was receiving.

I was so exhausted from the monotonous Castro death watch, during which Cuban media wasn't broadcasting anything even half way of interest to the U.S. government, that I dozed off while sitting in the chair. The first things I became aware of were two hands gripping the sides of my head, and Brian's visitor leaning down into me and giving me a deep, probing kiss. I discovered that he had a tongue stud along with his other body jewelry, and he was searching the tender inner linings of my cheeks with that. He sat down on my thighs, his legs encasing mine. He unbuttoned and spread my shirt open, and I felt the cold metal of his nipple rings as his chest rubbed against mine. His engorged, moist cock was pushing into my belly, and I discovered he had jewelry there too, a heavy Prince Albert cock ring pierced his mushroom cap.

I had never fucked on the wild side before, and a little thrill of a chill went through my body at these new sensations of touch. Tired and half dopey as I was, I took a bulbous butt cheek in each of my hands and pulled the leather stud into me, inviting him to make love to me.

And make love to me he did. He swayed in my lap, rubbing his torso against mine. I heard the unzipping of my pants, and he pushed the rim of my briefs under my balls and docked our cocks together. Neither of our dicks was something to sneeze at, although his was thicker than mine.

Then his knees were up on the arms of the chair and he was rubbing his cock, with the heavily metal ring, against my nipples. He pulled my shirt up and off my back and threw it aside, and then he was slapping his dick on my chest and into my arm pits—and then on my cheeks and forcing it between my lips. His Prince Albert punished my tongue and the roof of my mouth as he forced himself farther into me. He was so big and insistent that I could hardly keep from gagging, but I managed to deep throat him, and he was moaning his approval.

I felt a soft mouth come down over my own cock, a familiar mouth, and I knew that Brian had brought his head in under the leather stud's butt and had joined the party.

I assumed I would get the leather guy off in this position and Brian would get me off, which was not an unpleasant prospect, but I was wrong in that. The leather guy pulled his hard cock out of my throat, stood up from the chair, and pulled Brian back up on his feet. He had Brian roll a condom on his cock and then the two of them pulled me up from the chair and carried me over to the bed and forced me down on my belly. Brian came at me from above me, pushing his knees and thighs under my chest, and taking my head in his hands and forcing his cock into my mouth.

The leather stud was below me, tonguing and kissing my butt and then working his fingers in with some KY. He picked up two pillows and stuffed them under my belly, which lifted my butt at an inviting angle, and then he was pushing that thick cock of his into me. I tried to cry out my pain at the invasion, but Brian held my mouth firmly over his cock. I felt the Prince Albert ring rubbing the walls of my ass canal through the thin sheath all the way inside me. I was panting and trembling when his cock bottomed out inside me. And then he started to ride me hard. Stroking in deep and withdrawing nearly to the rim and then plunging in again and again and again. I grabbed around Brian's hips with my hands and grasped the brass slats of the headboard and held on for dear life. My head arched up off Brian's cock and I howled to the ceiling, but Brian just pushed my mouth back down on his cock.

I soon accommodated the leather stud and started to pump my pelvis back into him with the rhythm of his stroking. Brian and the leather stud were both grunting and groaning from the exertion and they came fairly closely together, Brian in spoutings down my throat and the leather dude by pulling out of me, jerking the condom off and spilling out across my back. The leather guy moved his pelvis up the small of my back, rubbing his cock through his spilled semen, and he and Brian kissed deeply.

The leather guy then disappeared from the picture and Brian turned me over and straddled my hips inside his thighs and brought his asshole down onto my cock. He rode my cock bareback in a familiar favorite coupling position of ours until I came deep inside him with a tired little sigh. Leaving me inside him to go tumescent, he then stretched his body down on top of mine and we slept.

I awoke the next morning on my side with my butt nestled into his crotch and his cock slowly stroking in and out of me in a side split. There was no evidence of the leather stud, and for all I could have proved, that whole scenario was an exhaustion- and frustration-induced dream after I had dragged in from a double shift over at the naval station and fallen asleep in this bed.

Needless to say, I was late to work that morning, but satiated and a good mood for the first time since we had arrived in Key West. My good mood was to blossom, because a dapper-looking Fidel Castro went on Cuban national television that afternoon to claim he'd been out of the country on a secret meeting with the Nicaraguan president for the previous week, and Washington once more called off the Fidel death watch. I was free now to check out Brian's research of the gay clubs and bars of Key West and to find a nice sandy beach on which to dream of the snow drifts plaguing Washington.

"No, not what you're wearing. Wear these."

"God, I can't wear those, Brian. I'd be a walking advert for 'Just bend me over and fuck me,' if I wore those downtown this evening."

Brian just gave me a hard stare. And of course he was right. After three hard double-shift days of work, that was exactly what I was going down to Key West's Duval Street gay strip to do—to get fucked. I took the mesh bikini briefs, the fishnet muscle shirt, and the tight low-rise jeans from him and struggled out of my preppy clothes and into my "fuck me" clothes. Brian, of course, was already decked out in his silver chain-mail mesh pullover shirt over gauzy white cotton pants. We were both wearing thin leather-strip sandals, happy to let our toes breathe after weeks of snow boots in Washington, D.C. I thought feet were very sensual, and I liked to show mine off.

We started the evening at Saloon 1 on Petronia Street, which I thought was a bit too leather and rough for the beginning of the evening. But Brian was three days ahead of me in checking out the extensive local gay club scene, so I just followed his lead. The stud who had fucked us both the night before in our hotel room, who turned out to be named Flash, was there and was looking mighty fine. He wanted the three of us to go right back to our room for an encore, but the evening's adventure was just starting for me, and I said, "Thanks but no thanks—at least not this early in the evening."

"You've not gonna find anything finer than me," he growled.

"You were fine, yes," I said soothingly, because, who knew, maybe he would be the best bet for the night. "But we're looking for a little variety tonight."

"I won't be far away," he said as he started to blend in with the crowd.

"Very comforting to hear," I called after him.

Brian was the forward, friendly type, and I could tell that he was ultra horny this evening, so I wasn't surprised that he let any of the guys buzzing around us feel him up. I didn't want the evening to end so fast with a rough gang banging, though, so I managed to extract him from Saloon 1 and get him moving toward the next club on his list.

We were back on Duval Street, and Brian pulled me into the Bourbon Street Pub. There were soft-core porn movies flashing on screens within sight of every nook and cranny in the dimly lit main room, the music was loud enough that my ears throbbed to the heavy beat, and heavenly barely legal young men in thong bikinis were playing poles at intervals along the top of the long bar. Brian was immediately surrounded by virile studs who he obviously had met and been very friendly with in earlier visits to the establishment, and he was quickly busy doing a lap dance on the crotch of a beefy Jamaican dude in baggy shorts and nipple rings who was perched on a bar stool.

I moved on down the bar and bantered briefly with a succession of muscle men on the make, all of whom seemed interested in what I might be interested in. I was still shopping, however. And I was enjoying the scenery working the poles on the bar top as well. One lithe young flaming redhead with good muscle tone and even better flexibility on the pole caught my eye, and I sat on a stool right under him and drank him in for two beer's worth of time.

After a while, I felt two muscled arms coming around on either side of me and nice big hands clamp down on the edge of the bar, encasing me but not too close. A rich baritone of a voice spoke into my ear, cutting through the noise of the music.

"Like him?"

I assumed he was talking about the dancing youth on the bar in front of me.

"Uh huh," I answered—because I did, indeed, like him very much. I usually wasn't in to barely legal guys, but this one had such a nice smile and clean-cut appearance. There was an air of vulnerability about him that made me want to just hug him and kiss away any of his fears—and then give him a few new fears to think about.

"He's mine," the voice answered. "But I might be willing to share."

I looked around at the source of the voice then. He was a handsome devil. Appeared to be in his early forties, but he was in great shape. Like the Jamaican, he was only wearing baggy shorts, which I was beginning to realize was the uniform of choice in the Keys, but no nipple rings here. He looked like a sleek CEO of a corporation, all blond, tending now to gray, and smooth and well-conditioned hard bodied. And if he owned the guy undulating around the pole, I guess he could have been a CEO of a corporation.

The guy was talking to me, and I had to make him repeat what he was saying because of the noise in the room. "Let's the three of us go upstairs to the New Orleans House. I have a room there. Or maybe downstairs to watch the pile for a while. It's time for Jamie to come off the pole, anyway, and it's getting a little crowded and noisy for me up here."

"The pile?" I asked. "And, pray tell, what's the pile?"

"You sort of have to see it to understand it," he answered with a rich little laugh. "And you can't see it if you don't go downstairs to where it's at." And then he raised his face and voice to the youth on the pole. "Come on down, Jamie. Time's up, and there's someone here who wants to meet you."

While Jamie came off the bar and, flashing a shy smile at me, was included with me in the zone that the older guy was creating with his encasing arms, I looked around for Brian, not knowing if it was wise for us to be splitting up. I wondered if he'd be willing to go check out this pile thing. But he obviously hadn't been similarly worried about me, because both he and the Jamaican were gone. This ticked me off a bit and probably was why I just threw caution to the wind.

"Sure," I said. "Let's go see the pile."

With Jamie leading the way through the crowd and the CEO-type's hand on my elbow, we moved to the back of the room, through a doorway covered by a beaded curtain, and down a long flight of stairs. En route, my guide established that his name was Kurt and that he thought I was really hot. Both of those seemed to be good things to know.

We were going down a hallway, and the sounds I was hearing from the other side of the doors we were passing tipped me off quickly that we were in a meet and greet (and beyond) area of the facility. One loud string of profanity cut me to the quick. I couldn't resist stopping in my tracks outside the door that was producing this sound and looking into the large window

78

in the door. Neither Kurt nor Jamie seemed to mind the stop, and both of them took in the view as well. Kurt moved in close behind me, and, as we watched what was happening in the room, he got his hands under the hem of my fishnet muscle shirt, and they eventually moved up to cover my chest and rub and tweak my nipples.

"You like that?" he murmured. "We could do that."

I didn't respond.

The room on the other side of the door was completely white and it wasn't very big. There was only one piece of furniture in the room, a small blue padded cube bed of some sort in the shape of a rectangle, with wedge-like risers at either end. The platform was in the center of the room. A naked man was reclined on the platform, belly down, with both his head and his butt elevated at head and foot. His wrists were cuffed to the lower sides near the head of the rectangle and his ankles were cuffed to the lower sides at the foot of the rectangle. He was positioned parallel to the window, so that what we were looking at was his right side. The naked man was Brian, and he was yelling his head off. That's what had made me stop. I recognized Brian's voice.

I could easily understand why Brian was screaming, because the Jamaican, sans his baggy shorts now and his magnificent torso glistening with sweat, was hunched down at the butt end of the rectangle with a manrammer in his fist, an over-nine-inch long and over-two-inch thick flesh-colored cock replica on a five-inch straight handle, and he was ramming the cock end of it in and out of Brian's asshole. With each thrust, Brian's body was lurching against the restraints at his wrists and ankles, he was thrusting his head back, and he was screaming to the ceiling.

I tensed up, ready to storm the room and save my significant other, when Kurt tightened his grip on my chest and whispered in my ear in that soothing baritone voice of his, "Wait. Listen. Listen to what your friend is screaming."

And, sure enough, when I allowed myself to zone in on Brian's voice, he was screaming, "Yes, yes! Harder. Deeper!"

Just then, having thrust the manrammer in, the Jamaican started rotating it inside Brian's ass, and he lowered his head toward Brian's. Brian brought his lips up to the Jamaican's, and they went into a deep kiss. I could feel Kurt's lips on the hollow of my neck then, and I looked around to check out what Jamie was doing. His eyes were glued to the coupling inside the room, and one of his hands was inside the pouch of his bikini briefs and was cupping his cock. I felt like reaching out and touching him, but I was afraid that Kurt would take affront at that.

When I looked back at Brian and his Jamaican, the manrammer was gone and the Jamaican was hunched over Brian's hips and his own rammer, a bit shorter and not quite as thick as the dildo, was busy thrusting in and out of Brian's captive ass. Brian seemed to be enjoying this as much as he did the manramming.

I gave a little sigh, which Kurt took as a signal that we could move on down the hall, and we were off. We were approaching the end of the hall, and the room it opened into appeared to be pitch black, but I could see flashes of neon-like colors of several different hues. When we reached this room, we stood just inside the door while our eyes adjusted to the darkness. Slowly, I began to see that the room was large and square, but that there was a circular room set inside it. That room was divided from the larger room by metal-framed floor-to-ceiling glass panels. And there was a padded railing encircling this room at knee height.

What was most intriguing, though, were the flashing neon rods I could see weaving in and out in no apparent pattern inside the glass room. The rods would undulate back and forth and up and down and would disappear and then reappear. On this side of the glass at irregular intervals were positioned couples of naked men in some sort of similar configuration that I couldn't concentrate on until I had worked out what was happening inside the glass-walled room. Kurt guided me around the side the glass enclosure until he found a spot where the man couples were not too close to us on each side.

I gasped as my eyes adjusted enough so that I could see that the center of the glassed-in enclosure was a large platform and on this platform was a writhing pile of naked men, all with beautiful hard-muscled bodies. The neon green and blue and yellow and purple rods were composed of fluorescent dildos and neon-colored condoms sheathing hardened cocks being picked out in a bathing of black light, and they were undulating and disappearing because the writhing mass of men was engaged in a wild, but languid group fuck. So this was the pile.

I was panting from the exotic live performance going on before my eyes. I was all atremble and my own cock was coming very much alive. Kurt, who was closely covering me from behind again, felt me melting down even before I began to moan my arousal.

Jamie stood a little in front of me and to the side, and one of my hands involuntarily went out and stroked his naked butt cheek. He turned to me and lightly kissed me on the lips.

"Do you want him?" the rich baritone voice whispered in my ear.

"What?" I asked huskily. But of course I knew what he was asking.

"Do you want to fuck Jamie?" Kurt asked more explicitly. "Do you want to fuck him right here while we watch the pile? You can fuck him if I can fuck you. He is willing. That's what his kiss meant."

"I don't understand," I mumbled. "Yes, yes, of course, but how . . .?"

And then Kurt and Jamie showed me how. Only then did I see the cuffs attached to the metal frames between the windows at a level slightly above our heads and that there were fur-lined knee cups set wide apart on the tops of the padded rail running around the glass enclosure. Now that my eyes had adjusted even more to the darkness, I could clearly see what the couples of naked men scattered at the rails around the glass enclosure were doing. One of each pair was cuffed to the metal frames at the wrists and their legs were spread apart and kneeling in the knee cups on the railings. Their partner was fucking them from behind. And I could see now that some of them were sheathed in the neon condoms and some of them were stroking their partners with fluorescent dildos. The watchers of the pile were part of the total performance.

Kurt handed me a tube of lubricant after he had cuffed Jamie and flicked off his thong. Jamie mounted the knee cups and I knelt and pressed my face between his luscious, sweet butt cheeks and tongued and kissed him until he was moaning and sighing and writhing and trembling for me. Kurt came back with two condoms. He had stripped off his shorts, and I saw that he was horse hung.

"Green or blue?" he asked.

"Green" I think, I answered. I didn't give a rat's ass what color, but I didn't want to take any time to put thought into it either.

"OK, blue for me then," Kurt said. And it hit me then that I had made a deal for the use of Jamie. The image of Kurt's long, thick cock surfaced immediately, and I involuntarily moaned in anticipation.

Kurt stripped off my jeans, leaving my fishnet shirt on. Then condoms were sheathed and cocks and asses were lubed, and I was soon stroking up into Jamie's sweet, tight ass and playing with his smallish cock and his pert nipples while we both watched the pile rise and fall and change shape and the neon-clad cocks and fluorescent dildos dance and appear and disappear inside the glass enclosure and around its edges.

I was pumping in rhythm to the perceived rhythm of the pile and joining my sighs and moans with all of the other couplings surrounding the enclosure, when I felt my own butt cheeks being pushed outward and Kurt was working his cock inside me.

I must have really turned him on, because Kurt came almost simultaneously with my ejaculation inside Jamie.

We held there, me going tumescent inside Jamie and Kurt inside me for a good twenty minutes, watching the pile. I was fascinated by the pile, and the undulation, and the moanings and sighings I was hearing were arousing me again.

Kurt felt my arousal and once again that rich baritone voice was whispering in my ear. "Shall we join in?"

"Join in what?" I whispered back

"The pile." Kurt whispered. "I think the pile is calling for you."

And we did and it was incredible.

Concern returning from being split from Brian, I didn't accept the invitation to spend the night with Kurt and Jaime in the hotel on top of the Bourbon Street Pub.

* * * *

When I returned from putting myself back together after experiencing the pile, I found Brian sitting primly at the Bourbon Street Pub's bar, apparently no worse the wear from the poundings he'd gotten from the manrammer and the Jamaican's own rammer. He was playing kissy face with yet another shorts-only dude. I pushed the dude off Brian with a "this one's mine" comment and told my freewheeling significant other that was time to move on.

"Fine by me," Brian said. I noticed that he was a little slow standing up, though. The Jamaican must have made quite an impression on—or, rather, in—him.

"Where to next then?" I asked.

"Back to Saloon 1," Brian said without hesitation. "I want to hook up with Flash again."

"Oh, God, all right," I said. I wasn't in the mood to fight.

We found that Flash had stayed put at the leather bar, just as he said he would, waiting for us to return. And he'd gathered a couple of friends he said wanted to meet us. The three were a motley group. Flash and the mountain of a man he introduced as Duane might have come from the same biker club. Duane was a good six foot seven, big boned, meaty, most of which was muscle, bald guy with a droopy mustache and a pig tail right at the back of his head. When I first saw him in the dim light of the bar, I thought he was wearing one fancy shirt, but it turned out he wasn't wearing a shirt at all. He was covered in an intricate black, blue, and red tattoo design that looked almost Oriental. When I was introduced and he shook my hand, I found that his mitt was about twice the size of mine.

"It's true what they say," he said, not letting go of my hand immediately, "At least about me." He said this with something between a smile and a leer on his face.

I was about to ask him what he meant, when he took my hand and wrapped it around his gigantic middle finger and slid the finger back in forth in my fist a couple of times. I got the point with that that his finger size indicated the size of another appendage and bit off any further question I might have. Brian moved in, with great interest, to talk with Duane, as Flash turned and introduced me to his other sidekick.

"This is Paulo. Paulo, this is Estaban. You'll like Estaban, Paulo. You're both Brazilian firecrackers."

"Argentina. My family's from Argentina," I said, for no particular reason.

Paulo looked way out of place in this group, though. Dark and handsome and almost preppy looking. I would have taken him for a model straight out of an A&F ad. He was finely muscled, but in perfect proportion, and there was no clanking jewelry or tattoos to be seen on him. I moved closer to him, involuntarily indicating that I was making a choice among all of them. Flash got the point immediately.

"I wouldn't be too fast making friends with Paulo, if I were you," Flash said. "Looks can be deceiving. He likes toys."

I thought that one over as Paulo put a proprietary hand on my elbow and Duane perched on a bar stool and brought Brian's butt into this lap.

"So, have you boys been discovering the clubs of Key West?" Flash asked as he took a swig from his beer stein.

"Just one or two," I answered. Paulo was lightly running his fingers up and down my arm, sending chills along my spine.

"And what do you think of Key West?" Flash continued the conversation.

"I haven't really seen much of Key West, I'm afraid," I answered. "I've been working practically nonstop until this evening, and Brian's the one who has been doing the exploration and having most of the fun."

"You've had no fun at all?" Flash asked, putting on a mock pout. I knew he was referring to the good fucking he'd given me the previous night, and I was quick to keep the record clear.

"Well, yes, last night the Key West I was expecting started, but thus far tonight all we've experienced was a brief stop here and then a longer time over at the Bourbon Street Pub."

"The pub," Flash said. "And did you go downstairs?"

"Yes, I've been to the pile, if that's what you're asking." Flash smiled broadly and I heard Paulo, now behind me, with both of his hands running up and down my arms and his hot breath at my neck, take a sharp intake of breath.

"Ah, yes, the pile," Flash said. "And experienced it as well as watched it?"

"Yes."

He smiled. "What else did you want to see here in the keys?"

"Well, I understood there are some really good, special beaches here, but I've been here four days and haven't seen any sand yet," I responded.

"Road trip," Flash called out to the group at large. "We know where they have the best beach in the world just waiting for you, up on Bahia Honda Key, not more than twenty-some keys back toward the mainland. And it has a nude section where they don't hassle anybody for anything, and it's gay friendly. Everyone to the car."

And that's all it took to have us all bundled into an old Chrysler Sebring convertible, just like nearly every other car riding the few stretches of road in Key West, and heading north up toward the toe of the Florida mainland in the early morning hours.

Flash was driving, and I was in front with him and spending much of my time telling him to keep his hands off me and his eyes on the narrow ribbon of road that was doubly frightening because it dropped off to ocean on both sides. Brian, Duane, and Paulo were in the backseat. For the first several miles, Brian was sitting in the middle, but it wasn't long until he was sitting on Duane's cock and shimmying his asshole up and down that pole. From the moans and groans Brian was emitting, I could tell that Duane hadn't exaggerated the size of his cock, because Brian was pretty good at taking them big, and he seemed to think he was having trouble with this one.

Paulo had taken something out of a duffel bag he'd brought into the car with him. He soon was hunched over Brian, and Brian was yelling to the passing wind something about shocks and his dick, testicles, and nipples. I didn't even want to know what that was all about.

I listened to Brian whimpering and looked out on the most beautiful, pristine-white sand beach I could remember ever seeing as we drove onto the Bahia Honda Key, turned off the road and drove parallel to the beach to the very end of the road. We parked under a sign warning the prudish that this was designated as a nude-permissible section of the beach.

Flash popped the trunk and Duane and I helped him carry a collection of beach towels and other paraphernalia over the line of dunes and onto the sand. Paulo carried only his duffel bag, quite possessively, I might add, and Brian remained prone on the backseat of the car, his still-trembling legs draped up on the back of the front seats on one side and the convertible's tonneau cover on the other side.

"You OK, Brian?" I asked before I followed our three hosts up over the sand dune.

"Couldn't be better," Brian muttered. "God has that guy got one hell of a cock—and Paulo and his bag of tricks . . ."

"Yes, well, we're here now," I said. "You comin' onto the beach?"

"In a few minutes," was Brian's dreamy-voiced reply. "Just give me a few more moments."

When I came over the dunes, I saw that the other three guys had pretty much set up our stake on the beach, having covered a fairly large area with beach blankets. All three were stripping down, and I took in a deep breath when I saw Paulo's beautiful Latin body. But I almost swallowed my tongue when I saw Duane stripped. His tattooing covered almost every inch of his body except for that monster cock swinging back and forth between his legs. And the contrast made the cock seem impossibly longer and thicker than it conceivably could really be. Flash's body was nothing to sneeze at either, but I've already come in intimate contact with that and enjoyed the effect of his various body piercings.

I shuffled through the finely grained white sand to the corner of their blanketed space and stripped down. Paulo watched me intently the entire time, a sloppy grin on his face, and I must not have disappointed him, because as soon as I was naked, he pulled me down to the blanket, my body stretched along his, and he began making slow, languid love to me with his gliding and fondling hands and his lips. I kept thinking of how Flash had told me to be very wary of Paulo, but no one had made such gentle and complete love to me before.

For the longest time Paulo possessed my mouth with his and rubbed the full length of his luscious body against mine. When his lips moved down to my nipples, I was able to look around the beach. There weren't too many other men out on the beach, as we had arrived quite early in the morning—but not earlier than the hot sun, however. Flash was nowhere to be seen, and I surmised that he had gone back to the car either to coax Brian down to the beach or to join him in the back seat for a fuck session of his own.

Duane, however, was very prominent. He had already made friends with a small-statured willowy Filipino guy who I had sort of noticed stretched out provocatively on a fairly substantial lounger not too far down the beach from us. The image of him when I was coming onto the beach flashed into my mind; a small, delicate effeminate type, stretched out on his beach lounge in a poster girl pose.

Well, he wasn't that way now, and Duane had been very quick in making his acquaintance, because Duane was now standing, feet buried in the sand, and legs firmly locked at the foot of the lounge, pointed out to sea. And he was wearing the willowy Filipino like a bib. The tiny figure was upended and draped down Duane's chest. Duane had his face buried between the Filipino's pert little butt cheeks, the Filipino's legs were spread-eagled out to the sides in nearly split formation, and he had both of his hands wrapped around Duane's tool and he was trying his best to get Duane's huge, bulbous mushroom cap into his mouth.

I lay there, fascinated by that tableau of the five-foot delicate doll and the six-foot-seven tattooed hulk in such a strange and intimate pose, and I moaned at what I was seeing and for what Paulo was doing in the journey of his lips around my body. He was working my navel with his lips now, while one of his hands brushed across and tweaked my nipples and the other one lightly glided on my inner thighs, causing me to spread my legs wide for him.

Paulo was crouched on his knees between my spread legs, cupping my butt cheeks in his hands, and making love to my cock, balls, and asshole with his mouth when I looked over at the incongruous biker-Filipino tableau again. Duane was already fucking his tiny prey now. The Filipino was facing him, but he was still draped down Duane's body. They were attached at the pelvises with Duane's gigantic peg impossibly buried in the Filipino's diminutive slot. Duane was holding the Filipino to him with his huge hands clutching the other's waist. The Filipino's legs were just bent at the knees with his calves flopping against Duane's hips in rhythm with Duane's cock stroking, and his back was suspended down toward the ground along Duane's well-planted legs. He was gripping Duane's calves as best he could with his hands in a an attempt to stabilize himself.

I was feeling distressed for the Filipino, who was fairly screaming his head off at the stuffing he was receiving, until his head turned to me and I saw the "well-fucked" expression on his face and hooded eyes that already appeared to be swimming in semen.

Paulo had his knees moving under my butt cheeks now and his hands on my hips, pulling my pelvis up his thighs and toward a very nice hard seven-inch cock. I looked dreamily and lovingly at him, fully prepared to take him, wanting him inside me now. No one had ever prepared me as well as he had for a good fucking. I was so mellowed out and aching for him that I didn't notice Flash and Brian coming down onto the beach arm and arm and Paulo motioning them over and I most certainly didn't see him open and search around inside his precious duffel bag.

I snapped to attention, though when I saw what he extracted from the duffel. I started to object and wiggle off of his thighs, but at his signal, Flash was above me holding my arms down and Brian was in back of Paulo holding my ankles.

Paulo very carefully and slowly strapped on the five-inch cock extender he'd taken from the bag. I was trembling and my belly was heaving at the very sight of it. It had thin leather straps that wrapped around Paulo's thin waist, holding it in place, covering his cock. The apparatus itself was composed of a cock ring to be snapped around the root of his cock and then four narrow, but thick leather bands running up the four sides of his cock, which would allow the side of his cock to have some sensation of the friction inside my ass passage. These leather strips were lined with silicon bumps that my ass walls were already undulating in protest against. And then capping the business end of his cock was a five-inch silicon extension.

I lay moaning as I saw that the extension was a bulbous head, just like a monster cock would sport—except that the cap was studded with silicon bumps.

I protested loudly and in vain, as Paulo started to work this enhanced tool into my ass. I was involuntarily writhing against the three of them, but this just made the attention the artificial cock head was giving to the rim of my ass all the more brutal, so I just collapsed and panted heavily.

For several minutes Paulo only pushed in as far as my prostate and he had me spouting cream all over my belly, and this settled me even more. At eight inches in, I was enjoying the fuck enough that Flash and Brian could release my arms and ankles and go do as they please. I saw Flash rummaging around in Paulo's duffel, extract some sort of leather apparatus, and he and Brian moved down toward the water. At eleven inches in, I was arching my back and crying passionately to the clouds scuttling by overhead, lost in the fuck, no longer wanting Paulo to stop. And then he started to pump me and I screamed in ecstasy and started to buck with his rhythm. I felt Paulo fountain his load around the sides of the extension and into the center of me and then we both began a long deceleration, bringing our breath and heart beats back into a calmer rhythm. Paulo remained nearly twelve inches deep inside me, though, and I wanted him to stay there.

I looked out to sea and saw a speedboat flash along the beach and then return at a slower speed, throttling down. I imagined that we were giving whoever was in the boat a great performance. Not just Paulo and me, who couldn't really be seen at that well, but the others. I looked over at Duane and his prey, and I know saw that the Filipino was on his knees on the lounge, with his chest on the surface of the lounge and his butt in the air, pulled a little toward Duane, who was hunched over the

Filipino's butt, one foot on the ground and the other foot on the lounge, giving him leverage to pile drive that huge tool of his down, almost sideways into the Filipino's incredibly receptive asshole. The Filipino was whimpering and purring at the same time.

But the real spectacle for the boater was the coupling of Flash and Brian. They were down at the water's edge, the surf swishing over their feet and ankles. Flash had a plow belt firmly in the grip of his hands and wrapped around Brian's belly, and Brian was bent over toward the ocean, his ass open to Flash's vigorous stroking down into him with his hard cock. He was pulling all of the way out and slamming back in, and each time he pulled out, the Prince Albert cock ring through his glans flashed in the sun. I wondered whether that was how Flash got his name.

The boat had edged into the beach now, and a well-cut black dude was clamoring out and stumbling up the beach. He bypassed Brian and Flash and came right up to Paulo and me. He pulled off his Speedo and he was on his hands and elbows over my body in 69 position and was sucking my cock and offering his to me. Paulo started stroking me with his enhanced cock again.

We must have enticed Duane, though, because shortly thereafter, he lost interest in his Filipino, who just collapsed on the lounger and whimpered and trembled the rest of the time we were there. Duane moved over to us and brushed the boater aside and pushed Paulo out of and off me. He then picked me up like I was a rag doll. With some effort from him, and considerable screeching from me, he pushed my ass down on his cock with him standing and me being held to his chest, and then he walked into the water up to above our waists and slid me back and forth on his cock, fucking me there in the water.

Looking back on the beach, I saw that Paulo, still encased in his extender, had the boater up on his knees and was deep fucking him doggie style.

After that initial orgy on the beach, we were all pretty spent. The boater hobbled back down to his boat, all grins, and sped back out to sea, and the Filipino just lay all akimbo on his lounge and whimpered and purred. The rest of us rested and swam and ate from a picnic basket Flash had been good enough to bring along and did a little more fucking until midafternoon.

Flash then herded us back into the Sebring and turned its hood south toward Key West. It was evening when we rolled back onto the pleasure island. I had thought Flash would drop Brian and me off at our motel, but he continued on through the town and past Duval Street toward the Truman Annex. He pulled the car into a narrow driveway beside a gingerbreaded shotgun house and parked in front a one-car garage in the back. The house narrowed as it spread back on the lot and there was a small swimming pool nestled between this wing and the garage.

While Duane took Brian to the pool to show him what a freshwater fuck would be like, Paulo, who I no longer thought of as the clean-cut preppy type, showed me that the garage wasn't for the car. Before I knew it, he had me cuffed into a sling hanging from a center beam that made me writhe and arch my back and scream to the ceiling and cry out in ecstasy for him and Flash to give me more, more, and deeper, deeper and longer, longer. This was the Key West I had imagined and looked forward to.

Unfathomable

I had sat there at Joey's beachside bar for more than an hour, watching the young man playing in the surf. When I'd first arrived at the bar, both bored and out of sorts, I'd seen him on his surfboard, riding the waves and doing quite well at it. At length, however, I saw him tire of that and come up on the beach and bury the tip of the board into the wet sand, with a strong force that, in itself, would have arrested my attention.

He was probably not over twenty and had a natural sensuality that made me catch my breath. He was tall, but not overly so, and on the lithe side, but even there, it was not at the expense of natural body tone, hard muscle, and a perfect balance of symmetry and beauty. His hair was dark, as were his eyes when he came close enough for me to see them. The hair was long and silky, and I was to learn it came down to below his shoulders, although when I first saw him it was tied back in a ponytail. The sun had tanned him deeply—he might even have been of Hispanic ancestry. His legs were strongly muscled without being heavy, and much of his body was covered—but again not overly much—in tightly curled black hair. His chin had that five-o'clock shadowing that so many young men prefer these days, and the body hair was more prominent on his forearms and legs and undergirded his pectorals, with a line running down his sternum and pronounced six pack and into the waistband of his low-rise, almost thong, navy-blue swimsuit. His nipples were pronounced, the aureoles large, and peeked out of his curly chest hair enticingly. A silver ring in one nipple only heightened the sensuality and mystery of him.

It was easy for me to be smitten. I had sent Scott packing earlier that day. It wasn't just that he had become grasping and was taking for granted that I would give him anything he wanted just to be in my bed when I wanted him there. I had become bored with him. His only conversation was about some electronic toy or clothing item he wanted. And he'd become untrustworthy, hanging out with other men his age, whispering to them knowingly—I'm sure talking to them about me and what I did for him—what he did to me. And his eyes had been roving, like he was looking for his next sugar daddy rather than concentrating on the one he had.

He hadn't been pleased when I'd had Thomas pack his bags and put them by the front door in the foyer and laid just enough cash out on the top of a suitcase for him to fly back to New York. But I had no commitment to him. I was bored.

Unfortunately, I also was horny and I hadn't thought ahead too well. I wanted what Scott gave me. I just didn't want it to be Scott who gave it to me. Always before when I'd come down here to the beach, I'd had someone in tow. I hadn't had to go to bars alone or hadn't had to try to cruise. I was a little too old for cruising, I had to admit. And I hadn't had to do it for years. I always brought my young men down from New York— where they sought me out. Where they wanted to be close to me, to be seen with Peter Cordell, to appear perhaps in photos in the society pages, where they would be lurking behind me and whatever beautiful supermodel I had on my arm for public appearance sake.

When Scott was gone, I walked the streets of the resort town, thinking that I would enjoy doing so when I was free and when no young man was cajoling me to look in this shop or that and to buy him this or that. But I quickly found that I didn't want to be alone. I just didn't want to be constantly wheedled to give, give, give.

I'd found myself at the patio bar off the back of Joey's—really just a vine-covered trellis over a deck out on the sand behind a rather seedy beach bar—and watching the activity on the beach. There wasn't much of it.

But my eyes would have picked out the dark, young man even if the beach had been crowded. He moved like a dancer. Fluid motion. As he moved, I could see his burnt-gold skin stretching over hard muscle. This was accentuated when he stretched out as he drove the front edge of the surfboard into the sand. In what was almost a connected, extended motion, he'd stripped off the tight black Lycra leggings he'd been wearing to surf—and I almost became breathless at seeing him just in a skimpy swimming suit. What were surely heavy balls and a thick cock were pulling the front of the thong-type suit down to where I could see a good inch of curly black pubic hair. I found that the beer glass I was holding was trembling. I wanted to palm his belly and move my hand down under that waistband.

After he had planted the surfboard in the sand, he walked slowly up the beach toward where I sat. His eyes were cast off to the side of me, though, and his feet were carrying him on a veering path off toward my left. For the first time I looked along the beach at the verge between sand and vegetation and saw that there was a line of red- and white-striped cabanas, the door flaps of some closed and of others lifted on stakes to make a sort of entrance porch.

The young man was moving toward the first of these, his smiling eyes latched onto an older man sitting on a beach chair in the shade of the open and raised flap of the first cabana to my left. The man looked like he was in his late fifties. A banker perhaps. He too was deeply tanned. His hair was gray, including a thick patch on his chest. I wouldn't say he was heavy, but he had the look of a man who once had been well-toned but was beginning to be defeated by time. Distinguished looking, though, at least from the side angle I got. And his eyes were plastered on the movement of the young man as he approached.

And whose wouldn't be? I know mine were.

The two only had eyes for each other, though, and as the young man drew closer, I saw that he had a gorgeous, almost mischievous smile that melted hearts and launched propositions.

The young man stood there in front the older man for a brief moment, as they conversed. The older man had been reading a hardback book, which he turned over in his lap without closing it.

I watched, almost in shock, as the older man put a hand on one of the younger man's thighs and the younger man leaned forward and took the older man's lips with his, while one of his hands slipped underneath the book on the older man's lap. The older man responded, the two of them still lost in the kiss, by raising his hand from the other man's thigh and cupping his basket through the barely covering material.

They came out of the kiss and the older man rose and turned and walked into the cabana. The younger man looked around—I looked away just in time for him not to think that I had been watching—and then entered the cabana as well, pulling the flap closed.

I sat there, trembling, for several minutes, not realizing that I was holding my breath until I almost passed out from the lack of oxygen.

I couldn't help myself. I was drawn to the cabana like a moth to the light. Standing and looking around to see if anyone was watching me, I sauntered—or tried to make it appear like I was aimlessly sauntering—off the deck and onto the sand. I'd already paid for my drinks. I walked off to my left, down the beach and parallel to the water's edge until I'd passed four cabanas. When I reached the fourth one, I walked around to the rear of that cabana and started working my way back toward Joey's, all the time looking around as casually as I could muster to see if anyone was watching me. There was almost no one there. It was late in the season and a weekday. The resort coast was nearly deserted.

I had already seen that the cabanas were constructed like panel flaps, so that the material didn't bend around the corners and the panels of the tents would lay flat when the cabanas were taken down. The material was slit there and the corners were held together by a series of ties from ground to roof. Standing at one of the back corners of the cabana, I could easily part the panels between ties enough to spy what was going on inside.

I almost gasped as I saw the older man, chest down on a beach lounge, and up on his knees, his buttocks in the air, with the younger man, crouched athletically over his hips, hands clutching the older man's waist, and slow fucking the older man, using the leverage of his feet on the lounge next to the older man's thighs for control in the rhythm of the fuck. The young man's black, silky hair had been let loose and it did, indeed, cascade to below his shoulders. It shimmered in the rhythm of the fuck. The sounds and murmurings both made indicated that they were taken with each other and thoroughly comfortable in the fuck. They weren't hurrying; there was nothing furtive in their coupling. This wasn't a chance encounter, I knew.

They were displayed at an angle from me, their butts toward where I was positioned. The older man's buttocks were milky white, but there were almost indistinct tan marks on the younger man's undulating buttocks. I watched, mesmerized, at the beautiful butt cheeks of the younger man clinching and expanding as he fucked the older man. And I gasped again when I saw the younger man's cock withdraw a good half foot from the ass of the older man without losing purchase and then sliding in again. And again, and again, and again.

My hand went to my zipper. In time, the younger man moved the older one to his back and crouched between his thighs, lifting his legs up and out, and continued fucking him in long, steady strokes. The younger man lowered his face to the older one's periodically and they kissed like longtime lovers.

The older man was moaning and clearly was in seventh heaven. Who wouldn't be?

When I had come, I zipped myself back up and withdrew. I couldn't bear anymore. I wanted the young man to do me too.

I left the beach then and went cruising. I knew all of the bars to go to, but it was low season already and the pickings were slim. I regretted having thrown Scott out now rather than when we got back to New York. But that didn't matter much. I wouldn't have wanted Scott for the same reason that I didn't find anyone in the bars that night who I wanted. I wanted the young man on the beach.

I spent a restless night, dreaming of me and the young, burnt-gold man with the long, silky black hair. I got up in the morning, went to the gym, and ate a humongous breakfast at a pancake house on the main boulevard. I was fagged out when I got home and fell onto the bed and slept for two hours. At three, I got up from the bed, already knowing where I was going.

I was the only one that early in the day on the back deck at Joey's on the Beach. The beach was deserted and the flap was down on my angel's cabana. That's how I was thinking of him— my own dark angel. And mine. After one beer, which I nursed for a half an hour, I started thinking of leaving the bar. But just as I was about to rise from the bar table, the flap came up on the cabana, and the young man jogged out into the sunlight. He was wearing a black bikini swimsuit this afternoon, the sides of which were held together by large metal rings. He had a large, multicolored beach towel under his arm, which he dropped on the beach a few yards above the high-water mark, and he was holding a pair of sunglasses in one hand, which he leaned over and put down on the towel after he had spread it out.

I took my breath in and held as I watched the muscles stretch in his lithe body as he leaned over the towel. He only lingered there a minute, though, before he turned and ran into the surf. When the water was above his knees he dove into an incoming wave and I lost sight of him. I didn't let my breath out until I had.

He was out of sight now, swimming out into the water, although I fancied I could see his head and the curve of his churning arms from time to time out beyond where the surf was breaking.

I turned my attention to the cabana. The older man emerged, raised the flap on the poles and stood there, his eyes shielded by a hand, obviously searching for his lover out in the ocean.

I couldn't help myself. As he stood there, I compared him to myself. He was older than I was, and not in as good a shape—certainly heavier than I was—and, although he'd been well-muscled at some point in his life, there was a sag of skin under his upper arm as he held a hand over his eyes. There were other signs that he was losing his muscle tone, and his tanned

98

skin looked just that way—tanned to a leathery brown. I fancied from what I could see that he wasn't as handsome as I was. I know, from my observations of the previous day, that he wasn't as well-endowed as I was. He could be richer than I was, although most certainly not as accustomed to fame—in New York and internationally, at least. I didn't recognize him as anyone of importance. Of course, perhaps my dark angel wouldn't be as impressed by the nature of my fame as some others would. Still, there was the possibility that my dark angel was a dancer; he certainly moved like one.

What did this old man have that would make the dark angel choose him over me? Nothing, I optimistically told myself. So, it was mostly a matter of getting the young man's attention.

While I had been assessing the older man who now was sitting in the beach chair under the cabana flap and had opened his book, the younger man had returned from the ocean and now was lying on his belly on the towel.

I gasped and my hand involuntarily went to my crotch when I saw it—it was lying there beside him on the sand, next to the towel. The black bikini. He must be naked, taking the sun in totally, I now realized. I ached to go out onto the sand and see him this way. It didn't matter that I'd seen him naked and fucking the older man the previous day. There was something so much more sensual about seeing him naked on a towel on the beach—where anyone else passing by could see him too.

I kept my eyes riveted to him, fantasizing going out there and straddling his hips, holding his cock erect as I descended on it, and leaning over and taking that nipple with the ring in my mouth and teething him until he groaned and lifted my face to his in a long, lingering kiss. When he turned over, I had looked away momentarily, and I castigated myself for not remaining alert and on watch, as if just a brief glance of him would make my day.

And it obviously would, because there, while I was watching him, he stood in all of his glory, facing my direction, his glorious cock and balls hanging free in a patch of black, curly hair between his thighs, as he reached down and picked up the bikini and put it back on, reattaching the rings somehow at his hips. That's when I saw that he had a ring in his cock head too, and I felt my sphincter muscle clutch, already feeling it rub against my inner channel.

And then he was walking. Not toward the cabana, but toward Joey's. I tore my eyes away from him, looking down into my almost-empty beer glass, as he climbed the three wooden steps to the deck. As I was looking down, I could see his feet and I wanted to groan. The feet were slim, but long, the toes also slender and long. And there was a patch of black hair on the top of each one. I was feeling very hot.

I heard him ask for a drink and then say, sorry, that he didn't have money with him and that he'd have go to his nearby cabana and . . .

I built up the courage to intervene at that point. I think my voice sounded strained and squeaky. Nonetheless I couldn't let the opportunity pass me by so I stood and offered to buy his drink for him—"and I need another beer too, bartender"—so that he could quench his thirst before having to traipse over to the cabana and back.

"Yes, thank you . . . if I can join you for the drink."

Could he join me? I was doing all I could do not to hyperventilate.

"Have you been swimming in the ocean yet?" I asked. "Is it too late in the season to do that? The temperature too cold?" I felt like an idiot for not coming up with anything better to say than this. And then he proceeded to confirm my idiocy.

"Surely you know I've been swimming in the ocean, Mr. Cordell. You've watched me do it, haven't you? Yesterday as well as today."

I was shocked, but then I felt all sorts of posturing and foreplay was being brushed aside. He obviously was in the game. And I knew this game so well. He was approachable.

"You know who I am, do you?" I didn't have to sound surprised. I was. Not necessarily that he'd know who I was, given what he obviously was. But that he would be so straightforward in getting to the bottom line. It was almost refreshing.

"Yes, of course. You're the Peter Cordell who produces for the Metropolitan Opera, aren't you? I read the New York papers."

"Yes, you have me there. And you are?"

"Raul. You can just call me Raul."

Ah, yes, Hispanic. I very much liked the passion of a Latin lover. Scott was West coast, sun, beaches, muscle shirts, and all about himself.

"Ah, the newspapers."

"And we have a few mutual friends too."

"Oh?"

"Yes. For instance, I know one of the members of the Met's permanent dance troupe. Jason Deavers. You might remember him."

"Yes, of course." Certainly I remembered Jason. I opened my legs for him nightly for a month two years ago. Raul most certainly was direct. Well, I could be direct too.

"I would like to see you. Away from the beach," I said. I turned my face to him and looked directly in his eyes.

"I'm rather attached," he responded.

"Yes, I have seen that. But you may be interested in reassessing your situation."

"I rather doubt that," he answered. I looked away then. This obviously was going to be expensive. He wanted to haggle. But then he surprised me.

"Did you know that they give performances in the old opera house on Duval Street?" He asked. "The local troupe is quite good, I think. I have an extra ticket for a performance of Mozart's *Idomeneo* for tonight. It's a powerful work—Greeks and fated lovers and tragic promises and all. Very melodramatic, but not much performed anymore. If you wouldn't be too averse to a busman's holiday . . ."

"He certainly is resourceful," was my thought as I clothed myself in a tuxedo that evening, after having already been to the barbers and then having a long shower and primping and making myself the best I could be. He was going to great lengths with me. This then, I knew, was going to be very, very expensive. But I had seen him fucking the older man, and I was assured that he would be very, very worth it.

The ticket he left for me was for one of the private boxes high up above and at the corner of the stage. It was angled, so that no one from the audience could look into the

101

box, and only singers positioned well up into the height of the set could see much of anything in the shadows.

I was the only one in the box until shortly after the first interval. In the interval, I had craned my head out around the edge of the box and scanned the audience and seen that, yes, both Raul and the older man were seated in the orchestra section. Raul looked magnificent in his tuxedo. That must have cost the older man a fortune. And the older man was probably paying for all of these empty seats in this box as well—and perhaps didn't even like opera. Raul had his hooks into that man really good. He should be grateful that I intended to take Raul away from him.

After the lights went down following the interval, I felt more than heard that someone had entered the box. I turned my face and saw that it, indeed, was Raul.

There were practically no preliminaries. I heard the zipper of his tux trousers being lowered after he'd sat in the chair beside me and felt the hand on the back of my neck, coaxing my face down into his lap. And to the glorious live, opera music of Mozart, sung rather well for the provinces, I gave Raul the best blow job performance I could muster up— luxuriating in my tongue's play with his cock ring.

He stopped me short of making him come, though, and I watched in fascination as he took a condom packet and a tube of lubricant out of his jacket pocket. He leaned over and whispered in my ear, "Strip off your trousers and briefs, please, and sit on my cock. Oh, and you look quite handsome tonight."

I sat, skewered by his cock, holding myself slightly off his lap at his request, bearing my weight on the balls of my feet, while I watched and listened to a Mozart opera on stage and he rhythmically fucked up into my channel. I made a little yipping noise each time that cock ring dragged across my prostate. He had his hands snaked up under my shirt and worried my nipples while I stroked my cock to completion. At his suggestion I had my linen handkerchief draped over my lap to catch as much of the cum I spouted as possible—to keep both of our tuxes clean. At the point of my ejaculation, his mouth went to the hollow of my neck and he lightly teethed my throbbing artery as I sighed my release. Timing was everything, and I knew I would remember that moment forever—the ejaculation came at the height of a love duet on stage.

He left me just before the second interval, after standing close beside me in the shadows and holding my face to his crotch as I cleaned his cock with my mouth and then helped to readjust his tux. As he was leaving, I gave him my card and hissed that I had to see him again—that he could come to my beach home any time he could get away. The sooner the better.

It had been the best of all setups for Raul to be moving to a new sugar daddy. Not only was he a hunk to view and a stud in cock play, but he was brilliant in his choice of claiming me. I—a veteran of the New York Metropolitan Opera—had never had such an uplifting sexual experience as being fucked to a live staging of a Mozart opera. I was bowled over. I was dangerously close to being in love. I certainly was in deep want and lustful need.

It was three maddening days before he appeared at my door. He was driving a BMW sports car that, I thought, must have set his older daddy back nearly a hundred-thousand. I had gone to the beach every day, spending the entire morning and afternoon at Joey's. But neither Raul nor his sugar daddy appeared the first day, and a family took up residence in the cabana the following two days.

He was all smiles and not the least bit apologetic for leaving me hanging. "I had business meetings," was all he said.

Yeah, right. He had business meetings. He was out spending daddy's money. That's what he was doing.

"It doesn't matter," I said. "I want you again." I took him by the hand. I planned to lead him right back to my bedroom, but Raul's Latin temperament was clicking in. We stopped in the middle of the living room and rocked back and forth against each other's bodies, kissing and feeling and unbuttoning and unsnapping and stepping out of clothes. And then, naked, we were kissing and feeling again.

He had extracted a condom and lubricant before his trousers hit the floor, and he simply pushed me back into the center of one of my deep couches and knelt between my legs. He worked my cock briefly with his mouth and then rolled my hips up and was going after my entrance with his lips and then

103

lubricated fingers, as I groaned and stroked my cock and floated on the clouds of heaven.

He fucked me there, crouched between my thighs, my ankles resting on his shoulders, and his hands working my cock and nipples. Bringing me to the brink again and again and then holding and then renewing the plowing until I couldn't take it anymore and ejaculated in a cry of ecstasy. Virile young man that he was, though, he continued stroking and I was ready to come again before he did.

We held there for several minutes, as I felt him ebbing away from inside me.

"That was nice," he said. "I do like a bit of variety now and then. If you are coming down next year, we should arrange to do this again."

"Next year?" I exploded in surprise. "I want you in the next ten minutes again. I want you every night. I want you in my bed."

"Sorry, old chap. I have a live in." Raul was almost jovial, as if he wasn't angling for anything at all here.

"A live in? That old man I saw you with at the beach?"

"Well, yes, actually. Teddy's my permanent. He indulges me with a side blow from time to time. I have rather a fetish for interesting older men. But we've been together for three years now—and I plan for that to last forever."

"Who is he? A Rockefeller?" I asked, becoming frustrated and a bit angry now. Raul hadn't even pulled his dick out of me yet. But he'd gone flaccid, and although I was trying to arouse him again, it didn't look like we were going to manage that. "God, I want you again now," I growled, giving up all of my pride.

"Sorry, Teddy and I fucked before I came over here and he'll want it again when I return. He's insatiable."

"Again who is he? Think of him and think of me. What does he have that I don't?"

"My love, actually. I'm sorry. But it's a permanent thing with us I'm afraid."

"What is he paying you? I'll double it. Whatever it is."

He gave me a funny look then and pulled out of me and walked over to the center of the room and started separating his clothes from mine.

"You don't know who I am, do you?" he suddenly asked, turning and looking at me hard.

"You're Raul. That's all you told me."

"Ah, well. We'd mentioned New York papers. I rather thought you had seen my photo in the society pages at least as often as I've seen yours. I didn't think I'd need to give you my last name. I'm Raul Delaplane. Of the Argentine Delaplanes."

Delaplane. The Argentine Delaplanes. Richer than anyone not from the Persian Gulf. Oh, shit.

Then he gave me the funniest look. "Oh, you thought I was some sort of gigolo and Teddy was my sugar daddy, didn't you?" As he was pulling his briefs on, still looking like a luscious dark angel, he reared his head back and laughed. "It's rather the opposite, I'm afraid," he said through attempts to cease chortling. "Teddy's penniless other than what I give him. He was my tutor, and my first love. And, I hope, my last love."

After Raul had gone, I lay there, my legs still open, mourning the loss of his cock, and contemplating how unfathomable this scenario of Raul and his old lover was. What was this fickle thing called love? I wondered. And would I ever find it for myself?

The Bonus

"Welcome to Key West, Mr. Jabril. You were quick getting out of the airport. Tuesdays are good days for traveling here."

Scotty was standing there on the curb outside the baggage claim area at the Key West air terminal much like last time and the time before that. He was leaning up against a red Jaguar XK-8 convertible and looking oh so preppy: spiky frosted hair, blue blazer over pink Polo shirt, white Ferrari Chino trousers, and brown loafers, polished up to a mirror shine. His smile was open and mischievous.

"Ah, you remembered me." It wasn't so much a pleased expression as it was a "You damn well better have remembered what I looked like" expression.

In contrast to Scotty's preppy blondness, Jabril was olive-skinned and dark haired. And muscular in contrast to Scotty's graceful litheness.

"Want to take a ride?"

Jabril didn't answer, and, indeed, Scotty didn't need an answer. He was here to pick Jabril up from the airport and deliver this luxury convertible. Of course he wanted a ride. It was just what Scotty said every time he picked someone up at the airport.

Jabril folded himself into the passenger seat, while Scotty folded his suit bag and computer case in the car's tiny trunk, came around to the driver's side, and slid in.

Most travelers flying into Key West rented a Mustang convertible. That was the standard rental of the Florida key. It had once been Chrysler Sebring convertibles, but tastes had changed in the past decade. And it was precisely because every other temporary driver on Key West seemed to be driving a Mustang convertible that Jabril had chosen a Jaguar. He had to pay a lot more at the Exotic Car Express than at Hertz, but it was worth the distinction from other travelers and it had its perks. He looked over at Scotty, his hair ruffling in the wind, his aviator sunglasses setting off his young, handsome face.

Scotty was just one of the perks. Scotty drove the Jag east around Roosevelt Boulevard, which semicircled the eastern edge of the key, turned west on Flagler and then north on Kennedy toward the eastern harbor and the baseball stadium. Just short of the baseball stadium he turned into the small, one-story building with the sign, "Exotic Car Express" over the plate-glass window and showing a Mercedes convertible on the showroom floor and drove back around behind the three-bay service wing off the showroom. He pulled in close to the building, turned the engine off, and lifted a set of keys to dangle between him and Jabril.

"The keys to the house are here too. Same place as last time."

As he held the keys out, Jabril held a fat envelope out and the two exchanged their treasures.

"Count it," Jabril said.

"I'm sure it's there. $1,500, right?"

"Right. I'll be back by 11:00 in the morning on Thursday. I have a flight at 12:30. You'll drive me to the airport." It wasn't a request.

"Yeah, sure," Scotty said as he opened the driver's door.

"Aren't you forgetting something?"

"Yeah, right." Scotty got out of the car, but only long enough to take off his blazer and lay it down on the fender of the Jag. While he did so, Jabril moved the passenger seat back as far as it would go and reclined it. Scotty got back in the driver's

108

seat; titled the steering wheel up as high as it would go; and, swiveling toward Jabril, unzipped Jabril's trousers and fished out his plump cock.

Jabril kicked off his right shoe and propped his foot up to where the windshield met the edge of the car door. Using his hands, he guided Scotty's head down into his lap and groaned a deep groan as Scotty's lips opened over the bulb of his cock and slid down the sides of his engorging shaft.

After a few minutes, in a voice thick with satisfaction, Jabril whispered, "Suck my balls too. It was a tiring flight."

* * * *

Jabril had donned stark-white Jocko David shorts with a Jocko mesh muscle shirt on top and white Crocs loafers to drive from the house on Virginia Street he'd been given the keys to just the few short blocks to the Bourbon Street Pub on Duval. He parked right out in front of the club by the fire hydrant and revved the engine before turning the car off, knowing that the men gathering around the entrance to the club would take notice of what he was driving and then, when he got out of the Jag, what he was wearing. And how good he looked in it.

He knew he looked good. He'd spent quite some time picking these clothes out and hiding them away for this occasion. His dusky skin, swarthy good looks, and well-cut body were set off perfectly in these clothes.

He was propositioned twice on his way into the club, but he brushed them both away with a smile. These guys looked like they wanted the same thing he did.

He bellied up to the bar, ordered a beer, and swiveled around to take in the scene while he waited for the drink to arrive. Even though it was a weekday night, the crowd was pretty good—and very good looking. Men were at the tables, making out and making deals. Men were on the dance floor, rocking against each other and fondling whatever they could grasp. And there was a cute young trick playing the pole at the other end of the bar.

Guys were brushing past Jabril and giving him the eye. He was giving a disinterested look back at most, but some of the smaller, cuter guys were getting smiles and meaningful looks back. The guys with piercings—not everywhere, but on the eyebrows and promising nipple rings as discerned under tight Ts—got special scrutiny. It didn't take long for the guys swirling around Jabril to catch the signals of what he was interested in.

When the drink arrived, Jabril pulled a twenty off a fat roll fished from the pocket of his shorts and put it down on the bar in full view of anyone looking and, when the barman picked up, Jabril signaled he was to keep the change.

In short order, a slim, blond guy with a small ring in an eyebrow and a ball piercing in his tongue slid onto the barstool beside Jabril. He appeared something on the younger side of twenty and had a pretty face and wavy blond hair. He had blue eyes and a sensual smile, with thick lips.

"Hi," he said to Jabril and flashed him a studied shy smile.

"Hi," Jabril answered back, giving the young man's eyes his undivided attention.

"The beer good?" the blond asked.

"Good enough," Jabril answered, although he hadn't had time to take a swig yet. And he knew full well that the young man knew that—he had appeared as the twenty was taken up by the barman. "You don't have a drink. You want one?"

"Yeah, sure, thanks. I'll take what you have."

Jabril didn't call the barman over, but he took the roll of bills from his table, flipped five twenties off the roll and laid them down, fanned out on the counter between him and the young man.

"Wow, I don't think the beer here is that expensive," the young man said. But the smile on his face showed that he wasn't being that naïve. "You got an oil well in your pocket or something? You one of those Arab sheiks?"

"It's not for the beer, of course," Jabril answered, just smiling and dipping his head at the young man's inferences.

The young man smiled. "My name is Trax," he said, as he laid a hand with long, slender fingers on Jabril's thigh. "They'll have a pile going soon downstairs," he said. "You want to start down there? They have cubicles too."

"I like my privacy. And I have an idea where I'd like to go. You want a ride in a Jag?"

The young man looked dubious, but by the way he licked his lips when the Jag had been mentioned, Jabril figured he'd heard about the nice one sitting outside.

Jabril took the wad of cash out and reeled off another hundred and laid it on top of what was already there.

Trax lost any squeamishness he'd had about going away from the club with Jabril then. He flashed Jabril a big smile and said, "Sure, I'd love a ride in a red Jag convertible."

So, Jabril thought, he'd seen it. He knew it was red and a convertible.

"Steve," Trax called out to the barman, who walked over. "Here, can you hold this for me? I'll be back in a while. I'm going for a ride with this gentleman." He handed over the cash and the barman took it as if this happened every day. And Jabril decided that it probably did. That Trax had put Jabril and him together in the eyes of the barman also wasn't lost on Jabril. It was insurance that Trax would be returned in one piece. The kid had looked young—and vulnerable—which, along with the piercings and his size and erogenous look had been what had attracted Jabril. But it was OK if he was a professional. For this money, he'd give Jabril a good time.

The money passed, Trax looked at Jabril and gave him a mischievous smile. He reached over and took Jabril's beer glass and downed a good third of it. He wiped his mouth with the back of his hand—which, in itself, made Jabril's cock twitch, and said, "You didn't tell me your name."

"The Jag is outside," Jabril said as he stood up from the barstool, not answering the question.

They fucked on a beach by a breakwater in the shadows of the walls of an old Civil War fortress, Fort Zachary Taylor, on the southern tip of the key. Trax was impressed that Jabril knew the best beaches to go to for a gay coupling, and Jabril had his assessment of Trax confirmed when his name was whispered in greeting from a couple of nooks and crannies in the breakwater as they found their own spot and Jabril spread out the blanket he'd found in the trunk of the Jag.

They weren't alone on the beach, but they weren't doing anything that everyone else wasn't doing, and the backdrop of sighs and moans and grunts and groans only added to Jabril's arousal.

Once naked, Trax had let Jabril initially take the lead. The young man laid back on the blanket and Jabril straddled his chest with his knees and fed his cock into Trax's experienced, but still soft mouth and enjoyed the play of Trax's tongue ball in the underside of his cock.

Once Jabril was hard and panting, though, Trax turned him onto his back and was the one straddling Jabril's hips, lowering his channel on Jabril's shaft, and riding him to a first, swift ejaculation. Trax had a control of his channel muscles, which assured Jabril that he knew exactly how to please a man and made a good living from it. For two hundred dollars, Trax realized that the one coupling would not be enough, and after Jabril had come, he pulled the swarthy man's torso up to his, and they sat there, facing each other, rocking back and forth, and kissing and fondling each other until Jabril had regained his stamina.

Then it was Trax laying on his back, legs raised and spread, while, his thighs shoved under Trax's buttocks, Jabril took over the stroking. His lips were lowered to the rings in both of Trax's nipples, and the young blond, as he no doubt was trained to do, was moaning and sighing how good a fuck Jabril was giving him.

Afterward—and following a period of holding each other and cooing like they were a pair of schoolboys discovering sex for the first time—they gathered up the blanket and their clothes and stumbled, arm in arm, toward the parking lot.

Trax stopped, though, as they heard short, sharp cries of passion from a pocket of sand surrounded by rock farther up on the beach. When he stopped, Jabril did too. "That would be Jewel. A tranny. Ever done a tranny?"

"No, never," Jabril said with hesitancy.

"She's fun. And she can make you come just with her sex moans. Fifty for her and another fifty for me, and you can do her."

"Here, now?"

"Yeah, why not?"

"You saw me lock my roll up in the car."

"We'll trust you for it. Come on. It will be fun."

Not getting an objection, Trax pulled Jabril over toward where the sounds had been coming from. They had subsided now, though, into just murmurings. When they came into the secluded circle, what they saw was the figure of a slim, black transvestite, with her skirt hiked up and white vinyl booted legs spread wide. They got a shot of both her asshole and her dick, so there was no question what she was. But other than that, she was a beautiful woman, with big tits jutting out from where her top had been pushed up to her neck.

Crouching next to her was a big bruiser of a truck driver type, his flannel shirt open and flapping around a heavily muscled chest and his lower extremities bare. His cock was nothing special other than the heavy ring in the bulb. This alone, though, struggled for Jabril's attention with the luscious tranny flashing her goods at him. Jabril had so wanted a cock ring himself. But, of course, he couldn't have one.

"Interested in seconds, Jewel? He'll give you fifty. And," Trax continued, turning to the bruiser, "you can do me for fifty too."

"Thirty," the truck driver growled.

"Forty," Trax countered.

But by then Jewel had opened her arms to Jabril and whispered, "Come to Momma" in a sultry voice and Jabril was sinking between her spread legs. One of her hands guided his face to her coin-sized aureoles, which he immediately went to sucking. Her other hand was guiding his cock inside her ass. Her channel muscles were even better trained than Trax's had been, and when she moved the palms of her hands to Jabril's butt cheeks, she began controlling a fuck that was sending Jabril up to paradise.

He turned his head to see that Trax was on his back and the truck driver was between his thighs and holding his legs up and spread with fists gripping the young man's ankles. Jabril's eyes went to the cock crowned with the heavy ring entering and pulling out of Trax's ass. All the way in and then all of the way out.

Jewel fucked him for forever, and sometime during the coupling, Jabril felt another set of hands on his buttocks and a tongue in his ass. This had never happened to him. This was an utterly fantastic feeling.

But then there was a new feeling at his entrance. Not a wet tongue. Something cold and metallic.

Jabril cried out and tried to pull away, but Jewel, with a surprising strong grip, laughed and pulled him closer into her smothering embrace.

"It's OK, honey. You'll like it. Just relax and go with it. Feel that cock ring?"

Jabril certainly did feel the truck driver's cock ring. And the cock that went with it. He thrashed and screamed, but it was no use. His cries turned into moans and grunts and then into sighs and whimpering; his thrashing moved to writhing—both of which only helped the truck driver to drive farther inside him—and eventually led to his body—the pain obliterated by the pleasure—joining with the rhythm of the fuck.

He knew he shouldn't be enjoying this. But Jewel's big tits and the way she could grip his cock and pull him inside her and her muscles undulating over his shaft—and that thick cock ring inside him and being filled and pumped, the ring punishing his prostate—were doing the trick. Making him moan and leak and twitch—he was going . . . over the . . . moon.

Later, when he was lying in a hot-water bath in the two-bedroom bungalow on Virginia Street, soaking his sore, swollen ass, and sipping wine, Jabril reasoned with himself that he had come for the adventure—that he'd wanted to experience the heights of arousal and sexual pleasure—and that, even though unplanned and something he'd never want to do again, he'd certainly climbed the heights this evening.

He fondled his cock, pressing his thumb into the slit of the bulb, wishing that he could get a cock ring too.

It had been all new and it had taken him to one height. But it hadn't really been what he had been looking forward to the most. Trax had seemed young and innocence, but he had turned out to be a professional. The Bourbon Street Pub obviously hadn't been the right place. There was just tomorrow now. He'd have to try again.

114

* * * *

Jabril walked down to the grill at the edge of the South Street beach for breakfast. He was in shorts and a sports shirt open to his chest. But he wasn't cruising; he just was after some breakfast and thinking that a walk would help ease the pain in his ass. And it was hot and sultry out. Much hotter than where he'd come from.

Six hunks were out on the beach in skimpy bathing suits, playing volleyball. One of them must have recognized Jabril, because he went around to the others and whispered something, and they all kept glancing over at him while Jabril ate his eggs and bacon and they continued their game.

Now that he thought of it, the guy who had started the whispering looked vaguely familiar. He probably was from the bar the previous evening or maybe even some earlier trip here, but Jabril couldn't remember much more than a hazy sense of knowing what he had inside that Speedo that was painted on him. So, probably an earlier trip. Jabril felt flattered that maybe the guy remembered him.

Their game apparently concluded, three of the guys came over and asked if they could sit with him. He was just finishing up his coffee, but he was polite and assented.

They were just talking about life around Key West and asking general questions of him in the context of their banter. But when their discussion got into the huge gay community on the key and then, more pointedly, when they mentioned the Middle East situation and asked him whether he thought that hurt the flow of oil from there more than it had, Jabril politely started to extract himself from the conversation and left them there. They didn't seem to mind. They were hunks, but this was his last day here. This wasn't what he was after.

Jabril had had such an exhausting night that his breakfast had come at 1:00 p.m. And still he felt hung over. So, the day half spent, he decided he needed a nap. He went back to the Virginia Street bungalow, swam laps in the pool that took up much of the lot that the house didn't cover, and then napped until late afternoon. When he got up, he padded to the

115

refrigerator and took two steaks out of the freezer to start thawing. Step one of his plan complete, he went into the bedroom and picked out the most nonthreatening clothes he had to wear. In the end, he picked what he'd planned to wear back on the airplane—khaki pants and a checked sports shirt. Nothing flashy; quite conservative.

Then he got in the Jag and drove down Duval toward Mallory Square. He parked there and started walking his way back, looking for a coffee shop. He followed along behind families with small kids, thinking they'd hone in on someplace that wasn't gay. He found what he was looking for on Fleming, just off Duval. An Island Joe's coffee shop and café. He went into the café, ordered a coffee and a sandwich, and sat near the back, where he could watch all of the tables.

His attention was drawn to a young, sandy-haired guy with glasses sitting at a table near the window, hunched over a computer. It seemed like his attention was focused on the computer, but as Jabril watched, he saw the young guy looking at other guys as they passed. He looked very nervous. But when other guys looked down at him—and especially if they smiled—the young guy would dip his head back into the computer.

He was good looking enough. A good build. But the glasses detracted. He was wearing baggy shorts and a T-shirt from some university. All Jabril could make out was "Florida."

The longer Jabril watched, the more he thought the guy wanted a hookup but had no idea how to go about it. If that was so, this was the guy Jabril had been looking for.

He'd finished his sandwich but still had half of his third cup of coffee. It was good coffee, but Jabril decided to invest it in his cause. He stood and moved toward the front of the shop, brushing by the young man in passing, and "accidentally" splashing his coffee on the guy's university T-shirt.

"Oh, god, I'm sorry," he said, as he started dabbing at the young guys chest with a napkin. The guy was firm under there.

"Uh, it's OK."

"No, it's not. I'm really sorry. I'll have to get that cleaned for you."

Without asking for permission, Jabril plopped down in the seat next to the young man. By the time they'd sparred on what Jabril wanted to do to apologize and what the young man didn't want to bother with, they had established that the young man's name was Gill and that he was a student in chemistry at the University of North Florida in Jacksonville—and a member of the university's baseball team. He was on a semester-at-sea course and his ship was docked at Mallory Square for the week.

"I'm in here hoping they put the Dolphins-Redskins preseason game on that TV up there. We don't get reception on the ship."

"That itty-bitty screen up there? You'll hardly be able to see it even if they have the game on. And you are going to watch it alone?"

"I don't mix much. Sort of shy. And I'm not from around here."

Perfect, Jabril thought.

"Nobody should watch the games alone. Which team are you a fan of?"

"The Dolphins, of course. They're a Florida team."

"Me too. I'm just going home to watch it myself. Some guys were coming over, but they all bugged out. And no one should have to watch a pro football game alone. Where's the fun in that?"

"I don't know."

"Say. Maybe you'd like to come watch it with me."

"Uh, I don't know. It's about dinner time and . . ."

"I was going to serve steaks. They're already thawing, and now I have too many. And we could get that T-shirt clean for you. I dirtied it; I should get it cleaned for you."

"I don't know . . ."

"I live nearby. Nobody should have to watch a pro football game alone."

"Well, I guess . . ."

* * * *

As Jabril hoped, the young Gill couldn't hold his beer all that well, and in the third quarter of the game, he already was woozy and nodding off. He was shirtless because his was in the dryer—and as a gesture of camaraderie Jabril had taken his shirt off too.

Gill had been impressed at the widescreen TV in the Virginia Street house pointed directly at a futon sofa. He'd also been impressed with Jabril's Jag convertible and with the jazzy bungalow on Virginia Street and even more at the pool that ran the length of the bungalow and took up much of the small lot the house was on.

He asked Jabril if he was some sort of Mideast sheik and if this was where he lived. And Jabril just smiled and said this was one of his homes away from home.

When they'd popped Gill's T in the washer, Jabril laughed and said he'd go skins then too. They sat on the patio with the lights on in the pool and ate their steaks and drank beer, waiting for the game to start.

Jabril became increasingly friendly and as Gill got increasingly blotto from the beer, he became increasingly yielding and his guard lowered and he began, slowly and in subtle ways, to reveal that he, indeed, had known before his ship docked that Key West was one of the gay capitals of the world, that he had heard that the gay activity was free and easy here, and that, yes, he'd always been curious, although he most certainly had never done anything about it. But his being in Key West had made him tingly and he had come off the ship and out into the town on his own just because it was arousing to think of possibilities and what fantasies he could pick up.

"So, you went to the coffee house thinking you might hook up," Jabril said. It wasn't really a question.

And Gill didn't provide an answer, although he blushed at having it openly said like that.

He was jolted into consciousness in the fourth quarter of the game to find that the back of the futon sofa had been lowered, that both of them were naked and stretched out beside each other, that Jabril's hand was encasing his cock, that his other arm was embracing Gill to him, and that he was kissing Gill's neck. What really brought Gill awake not long afterward— well, half awake—though, was that Jabril was working his cock into Gill's passage.

Gill drunkenly struggled, writhing in Jabril's embrace, and objecting in thick-worded babbling that made little sense.

Deep inside him and holding, Jabril shushed the young man, embracing him close, saying that he had told Jabril that this was what he wanted, that Gill knew this was what he wanted, and that Jabril was in the saddle now already. If he'd been a virgin before, he wasn't one now, so that bridge was crossed. That Gill should just lay back and enjoy what he knew he wanted.

Gill quieted down, but he sobbed and moaned and buried his face in Jabril's shoulder when he ejaculated under the attention of Jabril's pumping hand.

Jabril, taking Gill in slow strokes this first time, too had ejaculated into the bulb of his condom in the waning moments of the game, and they just lay there in each other's embrace, Gill softly crying and still trembling as the Redskins trounced the Dolphins.

Jabril reached over for the remote and clicked off the commentary, knowing Gill wouldn't want to be reminded of defeat. And they lay there, neither speaking, both trying to regularize their breath.

"I asked for it?" Gill weakly said in a whisper, at length.

"Yes. I guess the beer loosened your tongue. You told me that you'd come to the coffee house looking for a hookup, and when I appeared, that you hoped it would be me."

"I did?" Gill seemed to be confused, not being able to remember saying what he, of course, never said. But also unable to call it a lie. It had been obvious to Jabril that this was what Gill really wanted.

And this is what Jabril had come to Key West to do—to pop some young guy's cherry.

"I've got to go," Gill whispered.

"You'll want to shower. The pool looks inviting, though. Let's take a swim first."

"I've got to go," Gill repeated.

"You told me you wanted to swim. You told me you wanted me to fuck you in the pool. This is what you came to Key West for."

"I don't . . . I just don't . . ."

119

"Did you come off the ship to be fucked or not? Did you take this cruise because you knew it would stop in Key West and this would be your chance, or not?"

"Well..."

"You have nothing to protect anymore. I've fucked you. You've been fucked by a man. You're here, now. Who knows when you'll build up the courage to do this again. Enjoy tonight."

They went into the pool naked. Gill moved lethargically through the water, still dizzy from the beer buzz and the shock of what he had done—what he'd allowed this rich Arab to do to him, what he'd had to admit that he wanted.

Jabril moved to him in the water and embraced him and turned Gill's body to his. He wrapped one hand around his neck and brought his mouth in for a long, deep kiss. The other hand encased their cocks together and began to stroke. Gill trembled and shuddered and moaned as Jabril's tongue invaded his mouth cavity and took his breath away.

"I'm going to fuck you again now," Jabil whispered.

"Yes," Gill answered.

The second time Jabril fucked Gill was on the patio at the edge of the shallow end of the pool. Gill was on his back on a towel, his legs raised and spread over the water of the pool, gripped in Jabril's hands, as Jabril stood in the water and slow-fucked Gill's channel at the lip of the pool.

Gill sobbed again through the fuck.

"Remember, I've never before ... before today ... please be gentle."

Jabil slammed his dick home and started fucking hard. "You want it hard, I know you do."

Gill just sobbed and took it.

"Are you OK?" Jabril asked at the front door where they were both standing, neither really knowing what to say. Gill seemed sad and confused still—and embarrassed. Jabril was doing what he could to mask his elation.

"I've got to go," Gill whispered. "There's a curfew on the ship. I've got to get back."

"Do you want me to drive you?" Before the sentence was completed, however, Gill had faded into the darkness of Virginia Street, headed for the night lights of Duval.

Jabril showered and slipped, naked, between silken sheets, pleased with himself that the trip had gone so well. He'd have to get up early in the morning to get everything in the house back in exactly the shape he'd found it. When he returned the keys to the bungalow to Scotty, Scotty would want assurances that the owners would have no idea anyone had been there when they returned from their trip to the Redskins-Dolphins game in Washington, D.C.

He masturbated himself to sleep, reliving the moment when his cock had breached the young man's sphincter and Jabril had claimed his innocence. The young guy's virginity. What was his name? Jabril really wanted to remember the names of his conquests. He'd probably remember in the morning.

At 10:00 in the morning, while Jabril was finishing up with his housecleaning, there was a knock at the door.

He almost didn't answer it; there wasn't supposed to be anyone here. But he could see through the side window by the door that it was the young guy from last night—Gill. He remembered now. That was his name.

"Ummm. Hi. I just came by . . . I wondered . . . oh, god, I want . . ."

Jabril moved out onto the front porch and brought the door close to shut behind. "Uh, this isn't a good time, Gill. I've . . . I've got my stockbroker with me. But come back at 2:00. I'll have something for you then. I'll do you fine then. That's what you've come back for, isn't it?"

Gill hung his head and studied the toes in his sandals, unable to speak. Too embarrassed to say it. "Uh, OK. 2:00, then. I'll be back."

Jabril leaned over, cupped Gill's chin with his hand, and brought their lips together in a kiss.

Gill looked guiltily up and down the street when they parted, but he was smiling and there were tears in his eyes.

"Good-bye, Gill . . . for now."

* * * *

121

The flight into Baltimore-Washington's Thurgood Marshall International airport was an hour late arriving, but Angelo lived just a few minutes away, in Colombia, Maryland, so he had plenty of time to retrieve his Ford pickup in the distant shuttle lot and get home before Cindy was home from work and the kids were back from school.

He arrived in time to unpack and to hide his Jocko wear and the Speedo bathing suits in the bottom of the duffel bag with his tennis gear before he heard the lilting voice of his wife from the entrance hall.

"Hello! Is Mr. Gianinni on the premises? Mrs. Gianinni is home. Your truck is here; you can't be far behind."

"Hi, babe. Missed you. Have you missed me?" Angelo said as he walked slowly down the stairs and took his wife in his arms. He gave her a deep kiss and fumbled with the material covering her breasts.

"Down, boy, I hear the school bus. The urchins will be invading any moment now. Of course I missed you."

Later, when the kids had gotten the presents Angelo had brought them and had been bundled off to begin their homework, Cindy put a cup of steaming coffee down on the kitchen island counter, and Angelo perched on a bar stool.

"Everything go OK in Atlanta? The weather good? You got what you needed done?"

"Yep, everything good," Angelo said. "It rained Tuesday night, but I'd made it to the hotel by then." Angelo had quite carefully checked the weather in Atlanta every day he was gone. This was a standard Cindy question. She always asked it—just to have something to ask him about his business trips. It wasn't like she'd ever check. Angelo was so dull and predictable.

"Business was good too. I got everything done I went there to do." Angelo lifted his coffee cup to hide the sly little smile that that statement had brought to his lips. "But I'll have to go back in a couple of months. There always is more to do."

"They work you too hard at the office," Cindy said.

"It's a job. There are so many without jobs now. I have to keep plugging away at this one."

"Yes, I know. But you never get out to blow off steam anymore. When was the last time you played tennis?"

Angelo's heart skipped a beat at the mention of tennis and his thoughts went to whether that duffel bag was a good place for his stash. But, yes, of course it was. That didn't have anything to do with Cindy's mention of tennis.

"I have a good life. We have a good life, Cindy," he said as he reached over and took her hand in his.

"Yes the salary's good. But they really should give you bonuses—you deserve a good bonus for all these trips you take."

"I don't really see the possibility of that," Angelo said. But this wasn't the thought that came to mind. What he was thinking was how grateful he was that his boss gave bonuses—good ones. His most recent one, the one that took him to Key West, was for $5,000. But the best part was that his boss hated the IRS so much that he gave the bonuses under the table and admonished his employees not to let their spouses talk about them, which meant, of course, that none of them even told their spouses about the bonuses—so no one but he and his employees knew about them.

PACIFIC

Brazilian Soccer Team Balling

Pete and I had just finished playing a couple of sets of tennis at our Miami club and had sat down at a big courtside table for a beer before showering and leaving. Suddenly, five Latin hunks—all bulging muscles and steamy looks—descended on the court. We'd been told that members of a visiting Brazilian soccer team had signed up for the court after us, and I reasoned that these must be that lot. I could clearly see that they were all beautiful, with tanned hunky bodies and flashing pearly white teeth, as two of the Latin studs took to the court while the other three, after asking politely for permission in charming broken English, took the empty seats at the table Pete and I were sitting at. The three at the table introduced themselves as Filipe, Thieago, and Rafael. They told us the two on the court were the team offensive stars, Gustavo and Raimundo.

I quickly assessed all five and found them all to my liking—no, to my loving. I could already feel my cock stir. Gustavo was the only blond among the lot, and I wondered if he had some German blood in him. Whatever the case, he was just as heavily muscled and hunky as the rest of the team.

Pete got a little peeved when he said he thought it was time for the two of us to hit the showers and I said I wanted to stay around and watch the Brazilians hit the ball for a while. Neither of the two on the court were all that good at tennis, but they were mighty fine-looking athletes and moved with the grace of dancers. I knew that most of Pete's peeve was because I was warming fast to these Brazilians and I had promised him that he could fuck me after our tennis session. He saw the opportunity fading fast, and, in this, he was quite correct. Pete was a honey, but I literally melted at the thought of these five Brazilian hunks surrounding me.

After he saw he was in a losing battle with the Brazilians, at least for today, Pete stood and leaned down before he left and gave me a possessive kiss on the lips, no doubt in a last-ditch effort to mark his territory. I could tell by the hissing of released breath all around us at the table, however, that his gesture had had the opposite effect. It had sent a strong signal to the Brazilians that I could be approached by any of them who might be interested—and they all started showing their interest as soon as Pete was gone.

Thieago and Filipe, who were sitting on either side of me, moved in closer, while Rafael, who wasn't in reach of me, sent me steamy looks and tried out his limited English in chatting me up. Between trying to watch the somewhat fumbling tennis match and responding to Rafael, I didn't notice for a bit that Filipe was running his fingers lightly along the hair of my forearm and Thieago had a hand gently placed high up on my thigh.

Rafael called out something in Portuguese to Gustavo and Raimundo on the tennis court, and all five Brazilians had a good laugh. For the few moments I was there after that, I noticed that Gustavo and Raimundo were investing more attention into looking over at the table now than they were in wherever the tennis ball was going on.

Filipe had tightened his grip on my forearm and the fingers of his other hand were buried in the hair at the back of my head. Just as he brought my face to his and engaged me in a searching kiss, I felt Thieago's palm cup my basket. He said something like "Yiy, yiy, yiy," and then a run of Portuguese, and all five of the Brazilians were laughing again. Their laughs seemed more guttural now than before, however.

I disengaged from Filipe's kiss and noticed as I turned to ask Rafael what had been said that Gustavo and Raimundo were no longer hitting the ball back and forth. Now they were plastered to the wire fence just beyond our table, smiling big and licking their lips.

"Oh, Thieago was just saying that it was really hot out here and he really needed to take a shower," Rafael answered me with a big grin. "And we all agreed with him. But we are new here. We don't know where the showers are. Perhaps you could show us?"

The expression on Rafael's face left no doubt why they all wanted to find the showers, and they had turned me on to the point where I was more than ready to take on a whole Brazilian soccer team.

We left Gustavo and Raimundo blowing kisses at us and muttering what had to be very suggestive encouragements as the other three Brazilians hustled me into the men's dressing room, not seemingly at any loss on where it was located.

In the showers, I found all three equally arousing, attentive, and delightful. Filipe and Rafael were nicely hung, but Thieago had a veritable monster cock on him. All got hard quite quickly, with Thieago mainly watching, as Rafael sucked my cock under streams of water and Filipe worked my ass, first with his tongue and then with his fingers, and finally with what seemed to be his whole fist. I was well used, so only Thieago's cock gave me pause for any form of trepidation. While Filipe and Rafael were working me over, Thieago stood a bit off, but well in my vision, and entertained me with showing that he could make his cock get longer and longer and thicker and thicker.

When I had shot off, Filipe pushed my torso down with a strong hand, rubbed his cock up through my crack for a minute or so, and entered me forcefully from behind and started stroking me deep, while Rafael pushed his dick into my mouth and face fucked me in rhythm with Filipe's pumping. I thought this was mighty fine, taking it from both ends from two magnificent Brazilian studs. Filipe must have been overwhelmed at this opportunity, because he came quickly and removed his dick and went back to fingering my ass, now well-lubed with his cum.

When Filipe had a good bit of his hand up my ass, he called out in Portuguese, and I heard a reply that sounded like surprise and delight from the dressing room. Apparently, Gustavo and Raimundo had decided to change their game from tennis to some kind of other balling. As I worked hard to swallow the semen Rafael was now sending spouting down my throat, the five had a short discussion and I found myself lifted by Filipe and Rafael and delivered to the dressing room.

There I found Gustavo and Raimundo, buck naked, facing each other, in close, and straddling a wooden changing bench. Raimundo had his fist around two encased dicks, which were already hard. They were both long, Gustavo's a little longer than Raimundo's, but both were a little thin.

Filipe and Rafael, one on each side of me, lifted me by a thigh and arm each, with Thieago cupping my butt cheeks, and literally carried me over to the bench. These Brazilians were pretty good at their teamwork.

I started objecting loudly and giving a nervous scream or two as I realized what was going to happen to me. And then Filipe and Rafael inserted me between the facing Gustavo and Raimundo, and lowered my ass onto their now bundled, upward thrusting cocks. I nearly fainted as the two ramrods were forced up inside me. Laughter, moans, groans and Portuguese chatter abounded as Filipe and Rafael raised and lowered my pelvis on double throbbing cocks. Gustavo, who I was facing, had his fingers working my pecs hard, while Raimundo, behind me, had his hands wrapped around my waist and was helping to control the rhythm of the double fucking. I had my head thrust back on Raimundo's chest and was yelling in loud tones of protested pain and, yes, I admit it, pleasure at having taken two cocks working me in unison. More of that superb Brazilian teamwork.

So as not to raise alarm throughout the club premises, Thieago came up on the bench between Gustavo and me, hunched down a bit, grabbed the back of my head in his hands, and forced my mouth onto his gigantic cock. I did what I could to envelop his cock, but he was so long and thick that I could get less than half of it in my mouth. Some semblance of calm eventually came to the scene, which now was dominated by grunting, groaning, moaning, and sighing times six. Gustavo took my cock in his hand and treated it like the joy stick on his favorite sports car and was rewarded with three spurts of cum that were almost simultaneously coordinated with Gustavo's and Raimundo's ejaculations.

So, I had said I would take on the whole Brazilian soccer team, and this was what that was like. I must admit that it was more than a bit all right with me—certainly better than whatever Pete had planned for me this afternoon.

When most of us with cocks in play—Thieago still holding his shootoff—had come with great shouts of abandon and release, the various hands and cocks that were handling me disappeared. I collapsed, belly down, on the bench, and I heard happy chattering decreasing in volume as the Brazilian soccer team hit the showers, another stunning victory under its collective belts. Well, most of the team that is. When I was able to lift my weary head and chest from the surface of the bench, I saw that the giant Thieago was still there, giving me the eye, waving that monster cock at me.

With a big grin, he turned me on the back of the bench, spread my legs with strong arms and worked that huge cock inside my now-gaping asshole. With just one cock, he was stretching me more than Gustavo's and Raimundo's two cocks had been able to manage. I stretched my arms down and back and held tightly onto the legs of the bench as Thieago rode me hard, long, and deep—and to our great mutual satisfaction. I had no questions as to who the captain of this soccer squad was.

Creamy Thighs

Tight, hard, and hairless bodies with creamy thighs, resilient flesh on muscles of steel—and flexibility; flexibility is a must. I, Ricardo Humberto of Rio De Janeiro's DeAnima Ballet Contemporaneo, insist on that—and obedience and total subservience as well. And I possess them all. I fuck them all, women and men alike. I fuck them all regularly, without showing favor. That's the only way to keep order. And they stand in line, audition for the privilege of being possessed by me, regularly fucked by me.

Six men flying across the stage, dancing in the audition set to show me what they can do. Three I already possess; they are members of my premier troupe. Three others are auditioning for one opening.

One obviously has done his research well, knows what it will take to win the position. He has long, silver-blond hair, pulled back in a ponytail, but thus far he seems to fulfill the other requirements. It will be tough, though. There are two more days of auditions.

He flies through the air, legs higher and stretched out farther than the other two who are auditioning. And he knows he is auditioning for me by the way he is playing to me. And I highly suspect he knows all that is entailed in being in my premier troupe.

The first set is so invigorating that most take off their leotard tops for the second pass. The silver blond takes off his leotard bottoms as well. He's dancing in tiny briefs. He is lithe and has a long line and a natural effortless flow. He wants to show me his legs. He also has a well-developed chest and biceps—and a nicely projecting basket, the long line of the cock easily seen. This undoubtedly would be reflected favorably at the box office among the women patrons, and among some of the major male benefactors as well. This thought makes me smile. The silver blond catches my eye and shares in my smile.

They go through their set paces. All are flexible but none more so than the silver blond. He leaps right in front of me, turning his legs as he does so, so that I see the creamy thighs. He has done his research. He knows about me and creamy thighs.

The audition ends and I send all away—all that is except the silver blond. We stand there facing each other on the lit stage as all the others sort through their gear and depart through the stage door.

Then, in the silence, the silver blond slips off his briefs and pulls his hair out of the pony tail, letting it flow around his face and down to his shoulders. He stands there, legs slightly spread, arms out from his body at a forty-five-degree angle, palms turned toward me, a shy smile on his face, and a long slender cock dangling between his legs—standing there, in supplication, awaiting my bidding. Waiting for me to possess him.

He is hairless other than that silver blond hair cascading around his head—and hard as steel.

I slowly strip off my leotard, and he comes to me in light, dancing steps and raises his right leg, almost parallel to his body and leans it gently against my shoulder, exhibiting premier flexibility. His left hand takes both of our cocks together; his long slender one and mine, heavy, long, and thick, and holds them together as they both rise. I feel my chest swelling and rising and falling in quickened pace, while there is no trace of excitement or concern in his—total control.

I run one hand over his chest and torso; hairless, no sign of stubble at all; resilient skin covering hard-as-steel muscle. I run the other hand over the leg he has raised to me. Hairless, silky, creamy; I kiss and tongue the creamy calf and thigh while my other hand follows the line of his sternum down his tight abs, over his flat belly, and down around where he is holding our cocks together and to his balls. Not a hair or a trace of a hair to be felt—all warm, pliant flesh, covering muscles of steel.

He releases our cocks and pushes at my belly with the palm of his hand. I sit down on a mat, my legs stretched in front of me and a little open. He sits his pert little butt between my calves and lifts his legs up and out in front of my torso, pointing his toes to make his leg muscles tighten, and does little twirls in place with his legs.

I take each leg in turn and kiss and tongue them, from his heels down his calves and along his creamy inner thighs to where creamy thighs meet tender, hairless groin. He is sighing and moaning for me to sell me on the idea that he is thoroughly enjoying my fetish.

My lips travel back up his inner thighs, alternating legs, and, as they near the inner hollows behind his knees; he bends all the way forward at the waist and swallows my cock nearly whole. It takes superb flexibility for him to do this without lowering his legs from the attention I'm giving them. He's still auditioning.

When he has pumped me up with his lips, he digs his elbows into the mat and crawls his buttocks up my thighs until our cocks cross swords. With one hand, he positions the bulbous head of my horse-hung cock at his asshole and then resumes crawling his butt into me, letting his ass channel muscles grab my cock and pull it inside him.

He is panting and groaning and telling me what a nice, huge cock I have and how I hurt him and please him simultaneously, working hard on this private audition. I like being ingested by his ass just fine, but I'm still marveling at his creamy thighs.

At length, however, I do stand, maintaining my purchase deep inside him. He has one creamy leg running up my torso, and he wraps the other one artfully around my buttocks. He

135

arches his back toward the floor, playing the dying swan for me. I work on reviving the swan by putting a strong arm under his buttocks and using is as a lever to raise and lower him, while I pump him deep with my heavy, long, and thick cock. Some of his moans and pants begin to sound genuine.

In another demonstration of ultimate flexibility, he lets his legs down and does a slow spin and twist that moves me from facing him to being behind him with my cock still deeply embedded. His feet are on the mat now, and I'm behind him, my hands on his hips and fucking him with long strokes. I come deep inside him, and, to his surprise, I show him my own flexibility by putting my feet inside both of his and taking us down to the floor in a slow full split. I pull his back over onto my chest and reach around and slowly stroke his cock to eruption. He is mine now.

I can call off the auditions for the next two days. The male dancer opening has been filled.

Wait for Carnival

Ned Harrington had patiently waited for his young protégé. Ned had known for years that he wanted Devin; he'd known for more than a month he could have him. But everything had to be right, just right.

Ned and Devin's father, John Treadwell, had been long-time lovers. The Harringtons and Treadwells were among the first families of Charleston, South Carolina. Ned and Devin had gone to private school together; Ned had been John's best man. And the night before John took Helene to the matrimonial bed, Ned took John in the backseat of a Cadillac convertible. They initially had tried to stay away from each other after John Treadwell had wed, but their resolve was weak, and within a couple of years they had begun surreptitiously meeting for sex.

When Devin was six, John's wife, Helene, died in an airplane crash on her way to her usual summer retreat in Paris; John followed along behind her five years later in what would have been a suspicious hunting accident covering a suicide if Charleston society hadn't closed ranks around its own. John's death left Devin Treadwell an orphan. It also revealed that the Treadwells had been living well beyond their means for decades. Ned Harrington swept in and covered the family's debt and bundled Devin off to the same private school he and Devin's father had attended.

John wasn't nearly as successful in life as Ned was, and Ned had carried the Treadwells for years financially. He didn't give John and Helene money directly, but he made sure that business came their way and that the Treadwells could hold up their head at the forefront of old-line Charleston families.

Ned mourned the passing of John, but in Devin he had the spitting image of John. Patrician Greek god looks, a ready smile, natural athletic ability, curly light-brown hair, and an innate interest in men. And a "generation later" John to boot. Ned would not have disagreed with anyone who said bisexual preferences were inherited. The Harrington and Treadwell men loved their woman, but a good many of them loved their men as well. And the Harringtons and Treadwells had been linked in this way for generations. Ned had been initiated into male-male sex by his own father in the family's hunting lodge in the Great Smokey mountains and before that evening was over he had been taken as the lover of John's father as well in a threesome. It was almost inevitable he himself one day would seduce John.

Charleston society was one that was not as unique as the local patricians liked to suppose. It was all prim and proper and almost antiseptic on the surface, but underneath it was teeming with sexuality and a wild bent toward hedonism. In truth this was the same with many an isolated, highly stratified cast system, though.

Devin, the orphan Ned had taken on to raise as his own, worshipped Ned, and Ned figured it was only a matter of time till he could relive his love affair with John Harrington through his mirror-image son. But Ned wanted to do it right, and he wanted to do it away from the searching eyes and wagging mouths of the insular old-family culture of Charleston. And he wanted the taking to be special. Once he'd made love to Devin, he wanted to have Devin with him forever, taking the "spitting image" place of his true love, John.

All of Ned Harrington's carefully and well-laid plans for Devin almost were blown to the winds, however. Shortly after Devin's eighteenth birthday, the two of them had gone up to the Harrington family's hunting lodge in the Great Smokies. After a day of hunting deer, weary and tired but with Devin exhilarated about the stag he had bagged, the two drank a bit too much. Ned had always assumed that he would have to prepare Devin for him and methodically seduce him when it came time to take him.

Thus, he was taken by surprise when Devin put the moves on him, begging Ned to make love to him. Ned had showered and was sitting in the lounge of the lodge just in his sleeping shorts and a light robe. Devin appeared naked; told Ned he had wanted to be taken by him for years, stating that he now was of an age to make this decision for himself; and sank between Ned's thighs and buried his face in Ned's crotch.

This put Ned into such a sense of shock that he failed to react immediately. And within minutes, he was too weak and defenseless to the unexpected onslaught to resist Devin pushing the waistband of his sleeping shorts below his balls and taking his cock in his mouth. Devin's sucking technique was wholly unpracticed, but Ned was so taken with him—and had been for so long—that this hardly mattered in his arousal and the quickening of his cock. He lay back in his chair and moaned deeply as Devin sucked him hard.

Periodically Devin pulled his mouth off Ned's cock long enough to beg his mentor to make love to him.

Ned came back to his senses Just as Devin was taking charge and was coming down into Ned's lap and holding the older man's cock in position to penetrate his ass. He rose and pushed Devin off him and backhanded the young man across the cheek, sending him onto his ass on a bear rug in front of a roaring fire in a deep stone fireplace. Standing over the young man, looking so wounded and so vulnerable and yet so desirable and still desiring of what Ned could give him, Ned had to steel himself with all of his might. This was the same bear rug and an identical roaring fire where his father had pushed a cushion under his belly and fucked him for the first time and then invaded his mouth with his cock while John's father turned him, Ned's butt cheeks raised on the cushion, and came in between his spread thighs and fucked him as well. Then, spent and whimpering but filled with arousal, Ned had sat on the floor, his back against the warm stones of the fireplace, and watched

John's father put on a show of just how intensely and masterly he could fuck Ned's father. Ned had been taken into Mr. Treadwell's bed that night and shown just how filling and satisfying man sex could be.

"Have you done this before? With other men? Have you been fucking other men?" Ned roared at Devin in indignation. All of his plans, all of his careful work, and someone else had slipped in and taken this little bastard. The ultimate betrayal. A betrayal of all the John and he had been to each other.

Ned wasn't reasoning well; he was acting as if supposition were reality—and he was holding Devin up to standards he'd never enunciated to Devin. If Devin had been sexually active with men already, this was something he had done naturally. He had made no pledge of constancy to Ned; Ned had never asked him to do this, never demanded it of him. Now he was looking up at the man he worshipped with dismay, confusion, and deep embarrassment.

"No . . . no . . . never . . . never with anyone else. I've always wanted it to be you. I knew you went with men . . . I've always wanted that for me. Not just any man. You . . . never before. I wanted you to be the first."

Ned believed him, relief rushing in, the program salvaged. The awkward way Devin had sucked him was evidence he was telling the truth. And the young man looked so startled and contrite and openly shocked.

"I'm sorry, son. I never expected that you'd make the first move. I've always wanted you too. But it has to be special the first time. I'll think of some way to make it special. Something we'll always remember. And we'll always be together."

Ned had sunk to the bear rug and had taken a now trembling and sobbing Devin into his arms. They both immediately slipped into renewed arousal, and Ned took Devin's lips with his and they kissed passionately and deeply. Instinctively they each moved to take the cock of the other in their hands, and Ned permitted this much intimacy, a mutual masturbation to a shared climax with soft moaning and sighing. But no further than this. Beyond this, although the two came together regularly over the next couple of weeks, Ned would not permit the lovemaking to go farther for now. In fact, he wouldn't again, in those months building up to the full taking, let Devin touch his cock. Instead, he would take Devin in his arms and stretch out behind him and hold Devin tight, one hand playing his nipples and the other stroking Devin's cock relentlessly until the young man had ejaculated for him.

"I'll think of something special," he murmured as they lay entwined before the dying fire that first night.

"Please do it soon," Devin whimpered. "I don't know how long I can hold out." And then he gasped and began to groan and grind his pelvis against Ned's flank, as Ned took his cock in his fist again and masturbated him in vigorous and relentless strokes to a second ejaculation.

* * * *

Ned Harrington was perplexed about how he could make the taking of Devin special until one day, when he was walking down Charleston's Queen Street, he stopped at a corner for a light change and turned and looked in the window of a travel agency.

They were advertising special rates on travel to Carnival in Rio de Janeiro. Just the thing, Ned thought, and when Devin next lay stretched out in the arms of Ned and being stroked to completion—and begging, in vain, for Ned to move their lovemaking to a whole new level—Ned told him where they would be this time next week—fucking in a suite at the Mar Ipanema hotel in Rio and enjoying the sounds from outside of the annual Samba parade making its way to the Sambadrome.

Ned Harrington was a world traveler and thus he completely misjudged how overwhelmed Devin, who had never been abroad, would be by the sights and sounds and sensations of Carnival in Rio. Ned's idea was to have Devin completely devoted to and in thrall to him and only him in this foreign environment. But from the very beginning—starting in the airport itself, where a group of young, hunky Brazilian men honed in on Ned and Devin and swept them up in the gaiety of Carnival—Devin started to spin away from Ned. The Brazilian men were preparing a float for the gay procession in the Samba

Parade, and they declared that Devin would be perfect at the top of the float—and that, yes, of course, there would be a place for Ned as well.

From there the whole trip careened out of Ned's control. The Brazilians dashed all over town, Devin in tow, gathering materials for their float and costumes for Devin and Ned. The theme of the float was the Arabian nights, and both Devin and Ned were to be outfitted in diaphanous harem pants and turbans and nothing else but greased up torsos to accentuate their musculature. And the float needed to be prepared as well.

For two nights, Ned made careful preparations in the Mar Ipanema suite for a ritualistic deflowering of his young protégé. Devin was always working on the float with the boisterous Brazilian hunks, though. The preparations for Carnival had put Devin in high heat, so it wasn't a question of not wanting to lose his virginity to Ned—and, in fact, every time Ned appeared to check on Devin and on the progress of the preparation of the float, Devin begged Ned to take him off in a corner of the warehouse and relieve his virginity forthwith. But Ned was a stubborn man, and he had it in his head to do this in luxury and in a way that would always be memorable to them both.

At last he gave up and decided that it would have to wait for the concluding night of Carnival, when the parade was completed.

The day of the parade arrived, and all was in readiness. Ned was on the first level of the float, arm in arm with two of the Brazilian studs, while Devin was at the very center, top of the float, surrounded by several nearly naked Brazilian men. All were laughing and gay, and the Brazilians were passing around bottles of Cachaca, the local strong sugarcane rum, as the float started out in the Samba Parade, headed for the Sambadrome.

But the float never made it to that destination. The drunker the revelers on the float became and the more intense the gaiety along the parade route was, the hornier the Brazilian men got.

Ned was horny too. He looked up at the greased up, youthfully beautiful, nearly naked Devin at the top center of the float and he ached for him. He could hardly wait to get Devin alone in the hotel suite.

Sensing the heat rising off the handsome American, the two Brazilians at his side went into heat themselves. The float began to waver, the driver now being heavily under the influence of the Cachaca. The first Ned sensed something was unusual was as the float was staggering off the parade route and into a secluded park area to the west of the Sambadrome. And then he realized that his harem pants had been lowered and that one of the hunky Brazilians was beginning to suck his cock.

Ned recoiled and started to move out of the grasp of the young Brazilian making love to his cock, but this only pushed him into the encircling arms around his waist of the other strong and large-built Brazilian who was kneeling behind him and had inserted his tongue in the crease between Ned's ass cheeks.

Ned looked up wildly at the top center of the float—just in time to see Devin's ass channel being breached by the chubby cock of one of four Brazilians near him. One of the Brazilians was crouched behind Devin and holding him up in the air, while two at each side of Devin were hold his thighs wide and the four Brazilian was hunched between Devin's thighs and slowly feeding his cock inside the young American.

Devin was having a ball. Laughing and swigging from a bottle of Cachaca and egging the Brazilians on. Wanting to be fucked. Having been put off by Ned too long in the losing of his virginity.

Over the next hour, Devin's ass entertained the vigorous cocks of four virile Brazilian studs, all five lost in the hilarity and freedom of the Carnival Rio, while Ned, looking helplessly on at the ruination of all his careful planning, was being fucked from behind by his own two Brazilian companions, in succession. Ned finally broke away and waved for Devin to try to do the same, but Devin just waved a friendly smile at his benefactor and smiled broadly as several Brazilian men who had been at the lower edges of the float now start mounting the tiers for their own turn with the highly receptive and achingly handsome young American man.

Ned waited for two days for Devin to return to him. But at the end of that time, he decided he was waiting in vain—and the interest he had had in Devin had waned anyway when Devin was no longer pure and just beyond his reach. Ned left Rio never to see Devin again, although he continued sending checks regularly. He had simply waited too long.

Hurricane

The Colombian thug Arillano Galindo was rubbing his head dry with one towel, with another one wrapped around his waist, as he stepped from the bathroom into his sea view room at Cartagena's resort Caribe Hotel, when he was caught up short. Standing inside the closed door to the corridor was the waiter he had just been flirting with down at the hotel pool. He'd actually been assessing the young man as possibly part of the package he planned to deliver to the docks of New Orleans in two weeks' time—fresh ass for the male bordellos across the southern states of America. The young man was standing there, in a vest over his naked chest and short shorts—the uniform of the pool service—and holding a tray with a champagne bottle, a single glass, and a fruit plate on it. He was a Mestizo, highly valued in the trade, small of stature, almost boyish, dusky complexion but with blond-tipped hair and blue eyes. And he had the smile of a knowing flirt. Galindo probably wouldn't even have to whip him into shape if he took him to New Orleans.

"Compliments of the hotel management," the young waiter said with a smile. He moved to his right and put the tray down on the side of the dresser and then came back to the door, smiled, and said, "Anything else I can do for you, sir? Anything at all?"

Manuel was flat on his back on the carpeted floor, turning his head back and forth, crying out at the invasion, and digging his fists into the carpet pile. He was mouthing off like this was his first time, but Galindo wasn't buying that and he was feeding the young man's ass fast and deep—and Manuel was taking him in, stretching to accommodate him without apparent trouble. Manuel's butt was raised on three pillows from the bed; one of his legs rose up Galindo's chest, and Galindo held the other one out to the side with a fist wrapped around his ankle. Galindo was on his knees between Manuel's legs and raising and lowering his body in rhythm as his cock moved in and out, in and out inside Manuel's tight hole—at an ever faster, deeper pace.

Manuel groaned and moaned and slowly pulled on his own cock, as Galindo muttered what a nice, sweet, tight ass he had, murmuring that he should see the world, that his talents should be shared—and thinking to himself that, yes, this young, boyishly handsome waiter would command top dollar in the male bordellos of New Orleans. Maybe, he was thinking, he should consider pimping some of these guys himself and letting them keep more of the take. Galindo's share of the market at this point was not-fully-willing, expendable asses. It was almost a shame to throw someone as good at bottoming as Manuel was into that short-term pool. Almost. Manuel would return top dollar anyway—almost as much as if he was a virgin.

Galindo was even more pleased a half an hour later, when he had Manuel's belly up against the wall of the shower, under a cascade of water, and the little Mestizo was able to go with a power fuck. Galindo had to be careful with the small ones, like Manuel. He was built like a heavyweight prize fighter, with the brutalized face to match, and he sometimes lost control at the height of a fuck. He could get rough, and he could crush the smaller ones under him in the heat of lust. But doing it like this was OK. Holding Manuel by his waist and raising him up and down on his cock, and Manuel making all of the sounds of full-satisfaction taking that the marks like to hear. He didn't just lay there and take it; he moved his hips and touched his taker with his hands, and murmured his love for the cock and what it was doing to him.

Afterward, as they were stretched out on the bed and Galindo was enjoying Manuel's lips with his and the little berry-brown body, lithe and boy-like, with his gliding hands, Galindo whispered to him, "Are you free for the weekend? I have a very private island. I can make it worth your while."

"Yes, I think I would like that—if, of course, your pocketbook is of the same generous size as other parts of you."

"Well, I could be very, very generous. If you can show me that you can suck cock as well as you ride it."

Manuel then showed him that he, indeed, could suck cock very, very well.

* * * *

The speedboat was skimming across the water, the beach resort coastline of Cartagena receding behind them and an islet dead ahead. The waves were choppy and white capped, and the two men were breaking off from what they had been doing to look up at the sky. Arillano Galindo was sitting in the seat behind the wheel, his bathing trunks around his ankles and Manuel sitting on his cock, his hands trapping Galindo's wrists, as the older man steered the boat, and his ass rising and falling in Galindo's lap.

"I don't like the looks of the sky," Galindo muttered. "We'll make the island, but not with much time to crank up the boat in the boathouse. If we lose the boat, we're stranded for a couple of days."

"Stranded," Manuel exclaimed. "How big is this island we're going to anyway?" Manuel wasn't at all worried about the black clouds scuttling across the sky or the sudden picking up of the breeze and drop in temperature, or the whitecaps on the waves. This had been one of the riskier aspects of all this. The timing had been very touchy, and the primary plan required the hurricane that had been building off the coast of Cuba to be making an appearance here either later today or tomorrow. It now looked like tonight was going to be the night.

"It's small. Only has one house on it," Galindo said. "I own the whole island. I'll have you all to myself." He took one hand off the wheel and pulled Manuel in close in his lap and gave him a deep kiss in the hollow of his neck.

"If your island is small, it's the only thing about you that's small," Manuel whispered, and he wiggled his butt and was rewarded with a groan from Galindo as his cock touched all sides of Manual's undulating channel walls.

And once again the international trafficker in illegal flesh, Arillano Galindo, blessed his good fortune at having added Manuel to his collection at the last moment for delivery to the New Orleans auction house. Of course Manuel didn't know yet that he was going to be sold into the underworld of male brothels. And as long as Manuel was giving him a good time, Galindo wasn't going to tell the nice little piece of ass what was what. He'd have Manuel on the ship and sailing across the Caribbean before he had any idea what was in store for him.

"There, there. Up ahead. Do you see it? Isle de Turto. And it's all mine."

"Where? Oh, that? It *is* small," Manuel said. He was doing his best acting to convey the impression that he'd never seen the island before—although he had. He knew practically every inch of the island and the house on it now.

"Shall we take a spin around it and see it from all sides?" Galindo offered. "It would only take a couple of minutes. The storm should hold off that long."

"No, I don't think so. I think I want to see your bedroom first." It was the best Manuel could do on the fly. A trip to the other side of the island might have proved embarrassing to the fishing boat he knew was anchored just off the island over there. But the remark worked. Galindo revved up the engine and headed straight for the dock and boathouse.

Manuel thought the house was the perfect setup, and while Galindo was cranking the speedboat up out of the water in the boathouse, Manuel went on ahead, saying he wanted to look around the island a bit. He found the package he was looking for hidden behind a concrete vase at the edge of the stone terrace behind the house. He had its precious contents stashed away in his backpack well before Galindo came up the steps from the boathouse.

And as Manuel had requested, he was shown Galindo's bedroom first, and the wrist restraints in the headboard, and Galindo's ready cock, and the passage to paradise.

* * * *

Manuel woke in the middle of the night, encased in Galindo's arms, and in an instant he was fully awake to wariness at the sounds he was hearing—the whistling of the wind, raindrops smattering against the window shutters, and the beating of a loose shutter on a window frame. "Showtime" was the word running through his brain and he nudged Galindo—enough for the thug to wake up but not enough for him to think Manuel had purposely awakened him.

"The hurricane is here," Galindo murmured, half awake. But he became alert to the sounds of the storm quickly and sat up in bed. "It is time for me to show you the storm cellar."

The two rolled off the bed at opposite sides and reached for their clothes.

"Hurry, this way," Galindo muttered. Already the wind was howling rather than whistling.

"Just a second," Manuel answered. "I want my backpack."

They barely had made it into the store cellar under the house when the generator gave out and they heard sounds of the tin roofing giving way.

They were on a mattress on the floor, and Manuel clung to Galindo in fear of the night and the storm, and Galindo embraced him and comforted him. Manuel let his little hands roam around on Galindo's body, and they soon drifted into a slow fuck. As Galindo was at the point of ejaculation, the world caved in on him. Something hit him on the head, which stunned him, and something stabbed him in the thigh, which blacked him out.

Manuel dropped the length of wood he'd used to stun Galindo, put the syringe he'd used to put Galindo out for several hours back into his backpack, extracted a flashlight from his backpack, and went to the cellar door and let in the much-bedraggled team of U.S. intelligence technical experts.

The hurricane was passing by, but it didn't give them any help in their difficult task. Still, they were miracle workers and they had trained for this. They had brought all of the supplies they needed, and the team had every move planned down to the second. The first thing they did was turn the generator back on that they'd cut off themselves.

While they worked, Manuel, with pleasure, bloodied up the Colombian flesh-peddling thug's head more than he originally had and then bandaged it with his torn undershirt.

As the team was pulling out, layering a mass of splintered timbering in their wake, the last of them, the team leader, whispered to Manuel, "You sure you know what we need? We need to know where it is and where it's going."

Manuel nodded. His thoughts had been concentrated on that for days. They were simple questions, but the answers were worth all of the effort they were putting in to get them.

By the time Galindo came to, but woozily so from his head wound—although more so from the drugs Manuel had shot into his thigh once more—the cellar had been transformed into a collapsed building trapping the two of them in a small, but manageable air pocket, with no access to an exit. The timbers were stacked precariously to leave the impression that if someone started trying to move any of them, the whole lot would come down on his head.

"Where, what?" Galindo moaned as he came closer to the surface of consciousness.

"The hurricane collapsed the house on us," Manuel said. "You got hit in the head by a falling timber. We're alive, but we're trapped. I don't think it would be a good idea to try to move any of this debris."

"Alive but trapped," Galindo muttered and drifted off again.

He woke again in an hour, as the drug Manuel had shot into him was wearing off. There was enough still in him to make him confused, however, and Manuel was prepared to keep him in that state as long as he could.

"Where? Oh, yes, trapped in the cellar," he muttered. "How long?"

150

"You've been out for a day—through a night," Manuel said.

"Water. Thirsty," Galindo whispered.

"We don't have any," Manuel said. He put a sob into his voice, made himself sound like he was sinking in despair. "We're trapped . . . on an uninhabited island, under a collapsed house. Can't get out. We're going to die in here."

"No. We're not," Galindo muttered. "A night you say? We can hold out. Ship. Ship will be here tomorrow."

"A ship?" Manuel asked. "What ship?"

"They know I should be here; they'll see the house collapsed and will get us out. They can't sell the cargo without me. All those people will be useless to them. I'm the only one with the contacts in New Orleans and the way to get illegals in."

"People? Cargo? What ship? Where is it coming from? Where is it going?"

Galindo started to drift off again, and Manuel patted him on the cheek, a bit hard, actually. "Please, daddy, stay awake. I'm scared. What ship? I don't understand."

Galindo took Manuel in his arms and started to rock him back and forth. "Shush now, don't worry. It will be here tomorrow. Picking up cargo down the Nicaragua, Costa Rica, Panama coast. Sex flesh from all through the region. Love that in the south. Nice brown Hispanic ass—some fresh. New Orleans. Have it all set up."

"You're just trying to keep me from giving up, daddy. We've been here so long. I'm thirsty and hungry. We're going to die here. What ship, daddy? What ship."

"Shhh, shh, the *Grego II*. Wouldn't go by without finding me. Wouldn't do them any good in New Orleans."

"Oh, daddy," Manuel wailed—as he jabbed Galindo's thigh with the needle again and Galindo drifted off to lala land.

Manuel extricated himself from Galindo's embrace, reached into his backpack. took out a mobile phone, and punched in a number. "It's the *Grego II*, coming from Panama and headed to New Orleans for a sex slave trade auction. He expects it here on Tuesday. Now get me the hell out of here."

It had all happened in an eight-hour period from hurricane damage set up, to Manuel getting the information they needed from Galindo, to breaking the staged set in the cellar of a perfectly sturdy house and bundling Galindo onto the fishing boat on the other side of the island. They called in other teams to intercept the *Grego II* before it left Panamanian waters, the Panamanians being much more cooperative in these matters than the Colombians were.

As Manuel climbed aboard the fishing boat, he looked up at the sky, at the black cloud scuttling away from them up toward the Nicaraguan coast. He said a little thanks to Mother Nature for cooperating. Plan B for this operation would have been much, much more complicated and risky.

Tuesday at Three

All of his friends told Peter Townsend that he was crazy to buy the apartment in Cartagena, Colombia, in the luxury medium-rise building overlooking the ancient harbor, now yacht basin, as his retreat. But it was so convenient for him to sail his boat right up to the building's dock and whisk himself up to his retreat, with its heavy security, and Cartagena catered to some of the special interests he didn't want to own up to back in Chicago. When they said, "But Colombia, with all the drug warfare and the kidnappings of executives?" he'd just laugh and think to himself, "Hiding in plain sight."

He certainly didn't want to tell them that he made far more money from the drug running between Cartagena and Naples, Florida, on his yacht each year than his position as CEO of the major pharmaceuticals manufacturing corporation had made him in the last twenty years. What was a little balancing of Colombian drug cartels in the face of an early retirement without a financial care in the world—and with some added benefits in the meantime?

The sun was high over the harbor, beating down on the bulletproof glass covering his terrace as he swam lap after lap in the pool that took up most of the terrace he'd had covered and that jutted out toward the old castle walls guarding—not always successfully—the approach into the harbor for centuries. He was reviewing the distribution plans for this week's take across the States via his network of Florida bush pilots. He had to review the particulars every day; he had to keep it all in his memory; nothing was consigned to paper or computer file. He was careful and discrete in all of the activities he wanted to hide from his other world back in Chicago.

After he finished his laps and rested on the chaise lounge on the small square of terrazzo between the edge of the pool and the sliding glass doors into his living room, he planned to go to the closet in his guest room and cut the stash he'd just acquired into marketing share portions and pack it into sample drug kits he carried around with him on corporation business. Hiding in plain sight was a favorite ploy of his. No one had ever supposed that selected packets of dietary fiber powder his company was peddling to the world actually held heroin.

Laps and delivery network review finished, Townsend rose out of the pool and padded over to the lounge. He was in great shape for his forty-five years. His muscles were toned, his face was as square-jawed and handsome as his plastic surgeon could sculpt, and he'd managed to keep his own hair, although he'd stopped dying the hair at his temples when he was told that gray there looked distinguished on him. He was barrel chested and thickish in the waist, but he was just a solidly built man, with excellent musculature, a Neptune or Zeus rather than an Apollo or David.

Townsend lay back on the lounge and closed his eyes briefly. But after a few moments, he sighed and reached for the sex magazine on the table next to the lounge. He was keyed up and wanted to let off a little steam. He flipped the magazine over and started to peruse the photos. As he turned the pages, his hand slowly glided down his torso and under the waist band of his Speedo. As he became more engrossed in the photographs, he pushed the Speedo down and off his legs and started up a slow but steady rhythm of stroking his engorged cock.

He was lost, safe in his world of security, in his fifth-floor apartment, with the bars over the windows, solid bulletproof canopy covering the terrace, the latest in security alarm systems, and his small armory of personal protection assault rifles, most of them back in the closet of the guest bedroom with the drug stash.

He'd have every reason to feel very safe if the security alarm system had actually been armed that afternoon and if all of the double locks on the service door into the laundry room from the service elevator shaft had been bolted—if. But they weren't, just as the times that lax security at the Castillo de San Felipe de Barajas at the harbor entrance had nullified the protection of Cartagena at the wrong time when it was sacked by pirate navies more than a century earlier.

It took the two men practically no time at all to pick the locks of the service door and to steal silently into the apartment's laundry room on moccasined feet. They were dressed all in black, from nylon trousers, to Ts, to the silk hoods they pulled down over their heads before they carefully moved across the kitchen and dining room and into the living room, and positioned themselves behind the draperies on either side of the open sliding glass door out onto the terrace.

When they spied Townsend masturbating on the lounge by the pool, they smiled at each other and began to strip down to only the hoods covering their heads and knives in sheaths strapped to their thighs. The taller of the two, the dark Colombian, was also the younger of the two, strongly built, an obvious devotee of the gym. The cock he began to stroke while watching Townsend was long and thin. The shorter one, the darker Colombian, was of stouter, more solid build, probably the more heavily muscled of the two. His cock was barely noticeable when he first freed it, but it was impressively thick and was lengthening out nicely as he enjoyed the view of Townsend masturbating in supposed solitary splendor.

At a signal from the darker Colombian, the two moved silently out on the terrace, keeping to the late afternoon shadows for as long as possible.

Almost before Townsend knew they were there, the taller, younger one was straddling his chest and pushing his arms above his head. Townsend began to struggle, but then he felt the cold steel of a knife at the base of his ball sac. He saw that someone else was down there, but he couldn't make him out around the looming torso of the dark man straddling his chest.

In any event, Townsend's immediate attention was focused on that long thin cock slapping him in the face.

"Suck his cock and do it nicely or you lose your balls," a gruff voice rose from behind the young man hovering over his chest. "You can feel the knife, can't you?"

Townsend certainly could feel what thus far was the flat side of a hunting knife up under his balls. He also felt a large hand gripping his upper thigh.

The head of the younger man's cock was pressing at his lips, and, with the knife at his balls, there was little else to do but open his mouth to several minutes of sucking and gagging on a cock exploring his inner cheeks and the back of his throat.

He felt the knife being withdrawn, and he could see out of the corner of his eye a beefy arm swing over to the table. His bottle of lotion was taken up.

He felt cold cream being roughly fingered into his ass entrance, and Townsend began to squirm. But he stopped again as he felt the steel move up under his balls. Thick, moistened fingers were probing his ass, loosening him and widening him, searching deep inside him and pumping him slowly. He groaned and moaned in arousal despite his predicament.

The dark one pulled his dick out of Townsend's mouth and turned to say something to the darker one, who went back into the living room. He came back with a handful of condom packets. Still standing over Townsend's chest, the dark one made Townsend open a packet and roll the condom on his dick, while the darker one apparently was crowning himself. Townsend certainly couldn't feel a knife at his balls in that moment.

With a surge of strength that took the two by surprise, Townsend pushed up, rolled off the lounge, and lurched through the open glass doors into the living room.

Townsend stumbled toward the back of the apartment, toward the guestroom. The two caught up with him there. Leaning in the guestroom doorway, his back to the frame, the tall, dark one wrapped his arms around Townsend's belly and pulled the older man to his chest. The stouter, darker one faced Townsend and pulled his legs off the floor with strong hands under his hips.

Townsend moaned and threw his head back against the shoulder of the younger Colombian, as the dark one lifted his hips and forced his hole down on the younger one's upward-curved, engorged cock. Townsend writhed and struggled as he was being set down on the long, throbbing cock, but his efforts only served to ensure he was skewered to the deep.

He really cried out and began to grunt and groan as the darker one spread his legs with his own beefy thighs and crouched under his pelvis and started to enter his hole with a thick cock running up alongside the younger Colombian's thinner cock. The darker Colombian kept a firm grip on Townsend's thighs as the two double fucked the American executive, while the younger Colombian reached down between Townsend's and the other Colombian's bellies and fisted Townsend's cock and began stroking it in rhythm with the counterpistoning of the two cocks inside Townsend.

All three, otherwise silent with intense strain, were huffing and puffing and moaning and groaning at the exertion of the taking. Townsend came first, and the two Colombians came a short time later.

The American executive collapsed in a fully taken heap between the two hooded men as they pulled out of his channel and released their hold on him.

After a brief pause of regaining their breath, the two took him up again as if by prearranged agreement of a plan, the stouter man carrying his legs and leading and the younger man holding him by the armpits. The two hooded Colombians carried Townsend through the living room and into a narrow, terrazzo-floored room forming an L on the terrace with the living room. This room, probably originally part of the terrace, had a full glass wall looking out on the terrace and the side of the swimming pool and was furnished with expensive workout equipment, a tribute to Townsend's good shape.

Moving Townsend over to a massage table, they pushed him down on the edge of the table's end, his feet on the floor and his chest on the surface of the table. The younger of the two held a totally exhausted and sore Townsend down on the table with one fist in the small of his back and the other hand gripping the back of his neck, while the darker Colombian roamed around the room and found lengths of nylon roping.

Minutes later, Townsend's legs were spread and tied to legs of the table at his ankles and hips, and his wrists were tied to where the middle legs of the massage table frame met the top of the table.

Leaving Townsend there to moan and contemplate his possible fate, the two Colombians retreated to the kitchen and raided the refrigerator for beer and whatever they could find to eat to replenish the rough work they'd done—and to prepare for the rough work still ahead of them.

After they'd eaten and taken a piss and drank off another beer, they reentered the exercise room. They stood in full view of Townsend, and he trembled as they both rolled on condoms once more.

The younger one with the long, thin cock fucked him first. He just walked up behind Townsend and between his legs and thrust his cock deep inside Townsend's now-gaping hole and stroked hard and deep and fast. He reached up and buried a fist in Townsend's hair and arched the American's back toward him as far as the stretched arms and tied wrist would permit. He used his other hand to slap Townsend on the butt cheeks and flanks while he fucked him in a virile, relentless, long- fast-stroked taking.

Townsend cried out at the taking, and the young Colombian seemed to enjoy that and responded to every moan with a harder thrust, which produced a louder groan.

When the younger Colombian finished with Townsend, he slapped him hard on the rump and untied the American's bonds.

Townsend started to straighten up, but there was no time. The two Colombians were forcing him up on the massage table on his knees, and his chest and cheek were being forced down on the surface of the table. The stouter, darker Colombian was hopping up on the table, crouching over Townsend, his thighs encasing the American's hips, and he was working his thick cock inside Townsend and fucking him doggy style. The Colombian had his arms encircling Townsend's chest, covering him close, and he was gnawing on Townsend's ear as he fucked him.

This one was a whole new trial for Townsend. The second Colombian's dick was stubbier, but it was very, very thick, and he had a rotating motion he set it too that made Townsend feel all the more stuffed. After several minutes in this position, the Colombian went down on his knees behind Townsend and pulled the American up and back onto his chest and lap. He was able to gain greater depth this way.

Townsend was utterly exhausted, wondering what came next. As he felt the darker Colombian reaching his climax, Townsend looked over and saw the younger one pulled on another condom. Townsend shuddered in recognition of what came next.

In short order Townsend was turned on his back on the massage table, his legs spread up and out, and the younger Colombian stroking hard and deep inside him again for the last fucking.

After younger, fast-rising Colombian was done, Townsend was dragged between the two still-hooded men down the hallway and toward the back of the apartment. Inside the guestroom door, they pushed him to the floor and stood over him, fingering the handles of the knives strapped to their thighs and looking intently at him, ready for what came next.

Townsend looked up at them and spoke, in a hoarse whisper for the first time since the two had invaded his apartment.

"Next Tuesday, same time? Three?"

"Could we make it five?" the stouter of the two Colombians asked. "I'm getting my truck detailed that day."

"Sure, five is fine," Townsend said in a hoarse whisper. "You'll find envelopes with your fee in it on the credenza in the front foyer. Please leave by the service entrance."

El Presidente

"Mr. Winterberry wants to see you in the back cabin, Paulo."

Paulo Pulido unbuckled his seatbelt and gave a sigh. He was pretty sure he knew what came next. At least, though, perhaps the head of the Agency's special unit, informally known as the candy store, might shed some light on where they were going and why. At the moment they were approaching altitude after a straight-up lift off from Miami in a Challenger 604 corporate jet. And all Paulo could see out of the windows as he worked his way back to the rear compartment with its four plush seats, two on each side of the aisle, currently facing each other, were clouds and ocean.

As he entered the cabin, he saw that Sam Winterberry was alone and occupying the seat with its back to him on the right side of the cabin. From Paulo's approach, Winterberry was only seen as a head of well-groomed dark hair with graying at the temples.

"Have a seat here facing me, Paulo. I want to take a look at you. We haven't seen each other for several months."

Paulo moved past the seat Winterberry fully occupied, his bulk being more in bone and muscle mass, and turned and sat in the seat opposite. He let out a puff of air that was more a confirmation than surprise when he saw that Winterberry had his cock out of the fly of his suit trousers and was pumping it up.

"Do you know that this corporate jet flies at an average altitude of 45,000 feet and that this is approximately the level at which we're now flying?" Winterberry asked in a pleasant voice. He made no comment or gesture that indicated Paulo should be surprised that he was masturbating. And, indeed, there was no reason to expect Paulo to be surprised. Paulo was one of Winterberry's special agents, an agent employed for his sexual charms and ability to use those charms to collect intelligence. And Winterberry was his handler—in more than one sense.

"No, no, Sam, I didn't know that. Now that we're up at that altitude are you going to brief me on the operation you've called me in on?"

"In a bit, Paulo. Do you know how many miles 45,000 feet equates to?"

"No, I don't, Sam. How many?"

"Something over eight miles. Have you ever heard of the Eight Mile High Club, Paulo?"

There was a pause, and Paulo gave a sardonic low laugh. Sam was going to play it like some sort of sophisticated joke, he thought.

"Yes. It's just a term for those who have had sex on an airplane, preferably at cruising altitude."

"Very good, you got it in one." Winterberry's breathing was a bit heavy. He nearly had his cock worked up to full hard. "And are you a member of that club?"

"No."

"A more accurate answer, Paulo, would have been 'Not until now.' Strip off, completely, please, and come sit on my cock. Believe me, this is relevant to your mission. Make convincing love to me, please. Your continued employment with the Agency may depend on it."

For the next twenty minutes, Paulo fucked himself on Sam Winterberry's cock while sitting astride him, both facing him and facing away from him. Paulo was as much a slave to sex as he was to a very-well-paying job in intelligence. And Sam Winterberry was a master of fucking techniques. So, as much as

Paulo felt used, it didn't take him long to be lost in what the spy master was doing to him. Paulo was about to come, having shuddered at the angles and differing paces Winterberry was using to cock him, when Winterberry raised Paulo's channel off of his cock altogether and held him suspended there, above his lap. Paulo hated this part; the part where Winterberry usually made him beg for the fuck. And he always did beg for it.

"Sam, Sam, please," Paulo murmured.

"Tell me you want it," Winterberry muttered.

"Please, Sam. You know I want it."

With a guttural laugh, Winterberry slammed Paulo down on his cock again and finished him quickly. But Winterberry wasn't finished; he fucked on, and Paulo was vindicated in knowing, from Winterberry's groans and moans, that he wanted to be finished too. Paulo did a good enough job that, in his loss in the fuck, Winterberry had raised up and set Paulo back into the facing seat and was fucking hard down into his channel with Paulo's legs waving in the air at the fountaining of Winterberry's cum into the head of the condom buried deep in the younger, lithe man.

Twenty minutes after that, they were both cleaned and clothed and sitting opposite each other in the rear cabin of the Challenger 604 once more.

"I wanted to be sure you were the right choice, Paulo. That you still could deliver in positions like this. You did well, so we can proceed. You must know that I wasn't sure. I have a backup on the plane. If I hadn't been sure of you, I might have gone with Manuel."

"The assignment?" Paulo asked. He wasn't about to salivate all over Sam Winterberry about having had to prove himself worthy.

"We'll be landing at the Simon Bolivar airport in a couple of hours, Paulo. El Presidente, Eduardo Labarca, has become a bit too big for his britches and critical of U.S. society and policies. We are to bring him down a few notches."

"And so he's the target?"

"Our real target is his wife, Suzanne. Labarca is only president because of the support of his wife's brother, Jorge Facendo, commander of the armed forces. Labarca is a figurehead, but his anti-U.S. rantings have brought attention and business away from the United States to his country, so Facendo and friends seem delighted. We want to use the emotions of Suzanne Labarca to drive enough of a wedge in this happy family for them to squabble between themselves and forget us—but we don't want to upset the apple cart completely. Labarca isn't the most unsatisfactory choice the forces of Facendo could be backing."

"I don't do women," Paulo answered.

"No, that's not the plan. We want you to do Labarca. He's spending much of his time with his mistress at the presidential retreat near the Macuto seaside resort. We have arranged for you to be his chauffeur for those trysts, and we have outfitted the limousine with pinpoint video cameras and bugs. We expect you to seduce him and give us good video and audio during the drives back and forth to his mistress."

"I don't understand. If he has a mistress, why do you need me? Just put the cameras in their love nest. And what miracle do you wish me to perform with a man who has both a wife and a mistress already?"

"Labarca has the mistress—and the wife, for that matter—because that's what's expected in society down there. We know from his earlier history that not only does he prefer men but also that, before it was inconvenient, he went wild over your type. Photographs and videos of Labarca with a mistress shown to the wife and her military power brother would get nothing more than a smile; the same photographs and videos of Labarca fucking you will be incendiary in his social circles and should set his wife to clawing—not enough to get him ousted, because she also wants the position, but enough to disrupt his yammering at the United States. That Suzanne Labarca is a real tiger."

"That's it?" Paulo asked.

"Yes, that's it. Not a nuclear bomb; just a little attitude adjustment south of the border. We can be in and out as soon as you have gotten Labarca to be in and out inside that limousine. And speaking of in and out, we are finished here and you may return to the main cabin. Oh, and will you ask for Manuel up there and send him back here, please."

164

Manuel was a younger version of Paulo, a Mestizo, with an engaging dusky complexion contrasted with blond-tipped hair and blue eyes and with a more hopeful, innocent look about him than Paulo could manage after his time on the job. Manuel also was a noise maker. Paulo sat in the main cabin, listening to the sounds of Manuel's reaction to the testing Sam Winterberry was giving him in the rear cabin and, like the other agents on the plane, pretending not to hear anything. The long, drawn-out moanings Manuel subsided into, though, grated on Paulo's nerves. As much of a bastard as he thought Winterberry was and as much as Paulo would like to be able to resist being taken by the spy master, he had to admit that the man gave a superior cocking, and Paulo's ass twitched in regret that the moans were coming from Manuel and not from he himself.

* * * *

The first things Paulo noticed about El Presidente, Eduardo Labarca, were his arrogance and his complete self-absorption. He was not a handsome man, but he spent a lot of time on the sculpting of his body in the gym, and he spent a considerable portion of the country's treasury on his clothing and musky scents and haircuts and manicures. He carried himself like a president of a tin horn country as well. He wore a military uniform he hadn't earned covered with gold braid and medals that he couldn't even identify.

But Paulo determined immediately that he could be manipulated if the circumstances were right.

Paulo thought the wife and brother-in-law, on the other hand, were hard as steel and cold as icebergs. They were scary. The brother-in-law, in particular, was a towering, big-boned and –muscled hulk, who looked like he not only could, but would, with great pleasure, break a man in two on whim.

Paulo didn't envy El Presidente's position when those photographs and videos were presented to the scary duo, and he hoped that he himself would be well away before then. But he didn't think that getting the photographs would be difficult. He saw that Labarca was interested in him from the first time El

Presidente descended the steps of the presidential palace and entered the Bentley.

Paulo was grateful, though, that Labarca always was driven to his mistress's place in Macuto incognito and without guards. Paulo was his chauffeur for this trip purpose only and the Bentley was not the presidential limousine.

Labarca's sexual attraction to Paulo was registered almost immediately—whenever Paulo looked in the rear-view mirror, he saw Labarca licking his lips and looking back with slitted eyes—but Paulo had to use dynamite to move to the bottom line.

Paulo had been expertly fitted out with a chauffeur's uniform that was form fitting and left little to the imagination, and Paulo always was suggestively posed on a fender when Labarca approached the car—legs spread and hands near the crotch—and spoke to him in a submissive, sultry voice. And he touched Labarca when he was handing him into the plush, commodious backseat of the car. But, beyond the looks and the slowdown while looking as he approached the Bentley, Labarca wasn't making a move.

So, Paulo created his own move. On a rural stretch of a scenic back road drive between the presidential palace and Macuto one day, one of the tires on the Bentley went. Paulo had fiddled with the tire to make sure enough air seeped out of it for it to blow at approximately the point he preferred, and the tire cooperated.

"Conveniently," neither of the men had cell phones that day. Paulo had purposely left his behind, and he'd gotten Winterberry to arrange for a planted agent in the presidential palace to let the battery run down on the cell phone kept in the president's briefcase.

"I can fix the tire, sir, or I could walk for help. That would leave you alone out here, though."

"You can fix the tire?" Labarca said.

"I can change it out, sir. But it would be dirty work. If you didn't mind, I could do it if I put my uniform to the side. Oh, and could you hold the car keys for me?"

This idea suited Labarca just fine, and when he looked down at the keys Paulo had handed him, he smiled. The tag of the chain they were on had two male symbols interlocked. Labarca knew what that meant.

Paulo stripped down to just his briefs and boots, and Labarca stood there, panting, as Paulo showed off his muscles and grace to the best advantage as he worked. He had the tire changed just as soon as he knew Labarca was hooked.

Paulo tossed the spent tire into the trunk and came around the side of the Bentley and stood there, while the two eyed each other.

"Do you really want me to put my uniform back on, sir?" Paulo asked with a smile. "Or would you prefer we do something about that bulge in your pants."

"I . . . I want to fuck you," Labarca said in a strangled voice.

"I am at your service, President," Paulo said with a sultry smile, as he slowly pulled his briefs down his legs.

They fucked in the backseat of the limousine, Paulo lapped and rising and falling on Labarca's throbbing cock—and Paulo trying not to laugh at the memory of his testing by Winterberry in the same positions. He understood now that his coupling with Winterberry in the plane really had been a test connected with the operation—the mechanics of fucking in the backseat of a car. The musky scent Labarca used signaled to Paulo correctly, and he lifted his arms, one at a time, over El Presidente's face as they fucked and Labarca went wild at sniffing and tonguing the sweat in Paulo's pits.

At Winterberry's instruction, Paulo repeated the photo-session fuckings in the Bentley three times more in the next month—and Labarca loosened up to the encounters progressively more each time. He now sat in the front seat when Paulo drove him away from the presidential palace and played with Paulo's cock and nipples while they drove. When they reached a rural spot, Labarca pulled Paulo over on his lap and fucked him there. The third time Paulo wore briefs that hadn't been washed in a couple of days and that he had masturbated into, and Labarca went ape over those, putting his face into Paulo's lap as he drove and sniffing and sucking on Paulo's cock. The president kept the briefs.

Even the mistress seemed to be pleased. When Paulo picked Labarca up in Macuto now, the mistress came to the door with El Presidente and was all over him. Obviously Labarca's escapades in the Bentley translated well to his performance with the mistress.

Paulo avoided consummation—at least Labarca's—on the return trips to the palace in the capital, and by the third trip home, the dragon-slaying Suzanne was also meeting Labarca at the door with a smile.

For a brief time of less than a month, everyone seemed to be getting happier and happier. But the operational plan was to lower the boom.

* * * *

Even the best of intelligence operation plans have their flaws, and it sometime seems that the simpler the plan, the bigger the snafu.

In the case of this plan, when the boom was lowered, no one bothered to tell Paulo.

"You delivered the photos and videos this morning?" said Agent A.

"Yes, at 9:00 a.m., just as you directed," Agent B answered, turning to Winterberry and addressing the answer to him.

"I said tomorrow, idiot, not today. Somebody get Paulo on his cell phone," Winterberry barked.

"He never took it back after that time he didn't want to have it," answered Agent A.

"Oh, fuck," Winterberry growled. "Somebody get our asset in the palace on the phone and have him tell Pulido to clear out of there pronto."

But before anyone could do that, Paulo had been dispatched from the garages with the Bentley to the side entrance to the palace.

When Paulo stood by the rear door and opened it at the first flurry of activity inside the side door to the palace, out stepped El Presidente's brother-in-law, Gen. Jorge Facendo. And he looked like he was about to kill something.

168

Paulo trembled as he held the door for the general, having no idea why there was a change in routine, fearing the worst—that the operation had been uncovered.

"Where to?" he asked, trying to keep his voice calm, when he was behind the wheel.

"Toward the coast," growled the general. "I'll give you directions as we get closer."

The general directed Paulo off the main road when they got near the coast, over a rough track where no Bentley sedan should be expected to travel, and into a grove of trees at the top of a cliff from where the thundering surf could be heard even through the closed car windows with the air conditioning going.

Paulo had a premonition that this was probably one of the general's personal killing zones, and the jig most definitely was up for him.

"Get out of the car and strip and climb into the back," the general barked, and he had a gun to back up his demand.

The general totally and cruelly fucked Paulo for more than an hour in the back of the Bentley, rocking the heavy car back and forth on its springs, exercising the Bentley in ways it never had been exercised before.

The general also exercised Paulo well and made full use of the young man's flexibility. He took him with knees under Paulo's butt as Paulo laid across the backseat, with feet scrabbling for purchase on window frames and the roof of the car, and the general's hands on Paulo's throat. And he took Paulo bent over the short-backed center section of the front seat, with Facendo's back pressed to the ceiling and his cock pistoning hard and deep inside Paulo's channel and the general's chocking arm around Paulo's neck. And he took Paulo with Paulo's knees on the floor and his chest and cheek pressed into the back of the rear seat, the general's fists grabbing Paulo's hips and his cock pounding Paulo's canal from behind. And when Paulo was exhausted, the general sat back in the seat, with Paulo facing him and lapped and the general slowly pumping Paulo up and down on his miraculously fast-rejuvenating cock by wrapping his fists around the young spy's waist and lifting him up and down on his cock and Paulo flopping around like a rag doll. And then he made Paulo suck him off.

When they were finished, Paulo had come three times and the general four, and the floor of the backseat was littered with used condoms.

"Now you will drive me back to the palace," the general said, still waving his gun. "There you will be put under guard. But tomorrow I want you to pick me up at the same time and drive me back here. We bring guards. And today was just a taste. Tomorrow I fuck you so good; you won't be able to walk for a week—if we bring you back at all. And when I'm done, I'll give you to the guards. Then we'll find out who you work for and why."

* * * *

Three intersecting elements were on Paulo Pulido's side. Sam Winterberry saw that Paulo still had usefulness to the Agency's candy store program, the Americans had an asset embedded in the presidential palace, and when Paulo drove him back to the presidential palace, General Facendo was immediately embroiled in an ongoing slugfest between El Presidente and his wife and then he and his sister and his brother-in-law over what the general was doing out on the road with the chauffeur in the damaging photos and he forgot to place a guard on Paulo soon enough.

Paulo was whisked away from the presidential compound, the operation marked as a glowing success—not only accomplishing its original mission but collecting incriminating videos on General Facendo as well. And the Challenger 604 corporate jet, with Paulo in the forward cabin, was lifting off from Simon Bolivar airport before the radiator of the Bentley had cooled down, let alone the libidos of the president and general he'd left behind.

Once again, the jet zoomed right up to 45,000 feet and leveled off, and Paulo was only a third finished with the flute of champagne the cute little cabin steward had handed him before one of the other agents came out of the rear cabin and walked over to Paulo's seat.

"Mr. Winterberry would like you to join him in the rear cabin," he said. He could hardly keep the smirk off his face.

Paulo rose and sighed and started toward the rear cabin, knowing that another meeting of the Eight Mile High Club was about to convene. "He probably will even tell me it's my reward for an assignment well done," Paulo thought.

ATLANTIC

Bermuda Triangle

"A candidate for the Bermuda Triangle, might you say?" Dean said to Penn across the cocktail table. They were sitting at a window of the Splendor Lounge on the Champion of the Sea mega tourist ship on the first full night of its sail from Baltimore to Bermuda.

The two, both members of the ship's dance troupe were looking over a thirtiesh blond, well-formed, and obviously well-heeled hunk standing at the bar next to the bar stool-perching, equally matched blonde beauty in the minimal-coverage gold spangled top and miniskirt.

"Gotten particulars?" Penn asked Dean.

"Yeah," Dean said. "I've checked. They have one of the senior suites, and he's Samuel Heck of the Heck department store tribe."

Penn whistled. "So, a big fish."

"Yep," Dean said. "And I checked, because, maybe you didn't notice, but he had his eyes glued on the Viceroy Stage last night when we were dancing the muscle shirt number and his hand was in his lap working himself inside his slacks—only during the men's numbers, never during the women's. He's a closet brother if I've ever seen one, and I'm willing to bet his wife there 'don't know shit about that, honey.'"

"So, the Bermuda Triangle ploy, yes, I'd agree," Penn said. "The only question now is who's to make the move? You or me?"

"I'm best with a camera and you've been best with his type," Dean said. "So, you play lover and I'll do the clicking. Let's get over there beside them and start laying bait. If they open to us, I'll chat up the wife, and you can cut good ole Sam from the herd."

"Right, moving now," Penn said. "I don't think they've noticed us, so let's go out through the conference center and come in again through the front of the lounge and saddle up to the bar with them."

The ploy worked a charm. Penn and Dean bellied up the bar next to the Hecks and started talking about practice schedules, and it clicked with the Hecks that the two, young, very nice-looking guys at the bar with them were among the entertainers the evening before.

Happily, Susan Heck had taken modern dance—she certainly had the legs for it—so Dean slathered her up, using all of the butter he could churn out, while Penn had a more quiet, much more intense and pointed conversation with the mark. When Dean saw Sam Heck's hand go in guarded fashion to Penn's knee, he knew it was time to offer Susan a special five-hour beauty work over at the ship's spa on the ship's first day docked at King's Wharf in Bermuda.

Susan was ecstatic at the opportunity and left straightaway from the bar with Dean to check out the spa facilities and schedule her free appointment.

An hour later, when Dean returned to the cabin he shared with Penn, he found Penn waiting for him, all smiles.

"Is he hooked?" Dean asked.

"You betcha. We went almost directly to that men's room on deck four almost no one uses, and I gave him a blow job in one of the stalls. He's hot, hot for me and wants to go farther."

"So, which location are we going to use?" Dean asked. "No problem when. As I think you caught, dear little Susie is going to be stuck in the spa for most of the first day we have on Bermuda."

"I think that isolated grotto at the south end of Horseshoe Bay will do just fine," Penn answered. "The light's good there."

Penn rented a moped on the morning the ship arrived in Bermuda, assuring Sam Heck he was an expert in puttering about and also that he knew a really nice, isolated spot where they could have a nice swim and snorkel—something to be able to tell Susie that Sam was doing for a couple of hours that morning on his own—and all the privacy they needed.

Penn was pleased to see that Sam Heck was virtually salivating over the prospect of what they'd really be doing. When they got on the moped, Penn driving and Sam nudged in behind him, Penn could feel the rising need in Sam's loins and felt the sexual heat rising off him. As they puttered along at Bermuda's thirty-mile-an-hour speed limit through narrow roads, Sam had his hands on Penn's basket, working his cock hard through the material of his shorts and Speedo, in anxious anticipation. When Penn stopped at crossings, Sam kissed him in the hollow of his neck and ran his hands up under Penn's T-shirt and tweaked his nipples. Penn had no doubts at all that Sam was hooked and would give a highly photogenic performance as soon as he was given the chance.

Penn insisted they swim first, although all Sam could think about or talk about was fucking Penn. They wound up at a grotto-like small beach, enclosed on three sides by limestone rock formations, one of many such small, secluded spots along the Horseshoe Bay but one that was particularly hidden and almost never used to Penn's knowledge. They had arrived very early anyway, and there wouldn't be much of anyone on the beach at all until the afternoon.

Penn was afraid early on that he would lose control and the Bermuda Triangle ploy would go bust. They had swum out a bit, not far, because the water got deep quickly at that beach, and Sam had swum directly over to Penn and was holding him closely from behind, with one arm around Penn's chest and the hand of the other arm digging for his ass.

"Wanna fuck. Now," Sam was muttering. He had Penn, his legs spread and floating out in front of him toward the beach, lapped as Sam stood in four feet of surf, palming Penn's belly with one hand and fisting his cock with a hand running under the waistband of his Speedo with the other. Penn was enjoying this and didn't start to try to struggle out of the hold until the hand moved around his flank and into his crease. Penn jerked and gasped as an index finger breached the rim of his hole.

"No, not here, let's go back up to the beach," Penn cried out over the pounding surf. He was trembling and getting aroused more than he had anticipated. This Sam was a hunk—maybe even sexier than Dean was. Penn looked forward to the fuck, and Sam's fingers inside his hole were driving Penn crazy. He had been quick to offer to take this role with Sam because he had been drawn to him in the first place. He wanted the fuck.

He did manage to break away and head back into the isolated grotto, where they had stretched two large beach towels out on the fine-grained pink sand that Bermuda was famous for.

Sam had scrambled up behind Penn and tackled him at the edge of the towels, and the two wrestled playfully, working up their arousal to greater heights. Sam pushed Penn down flat on his stomach, saddled his pelvis on top of Penn's hips, and, holding Penn's arms down with his hands, began to mount the lithe dancer.

"No, no," Penn cried out. "I want to watch it stroke inside me. Here you on your knees, sitting back on your haunches, and me stretched out in front of you, with my ass cheeks on your thighs. Here in the sun, not in the shade. Yes!. Ahhhh . . . yes, Yess! Oh god, you are so big. Oh, god. Oh shit. Fuck me. Yesss. Fuck me!"

In a frenzy, Sam complied. Holding the more lithe Penn, with those firm and highly flexible dancer's legs, Sam pulled his lover for the day back and forth on his cock. Penn stopped the first fucking by ejaculating straight up into the air in an arc that could clearly be seen from the tops of the surrounding limestone formations. Then he pushed Sam onto his back, sucked his cock almost to ejaculation, and then fisted the hunk off so that he also spouted high into the air. After Sam had recovered and gotten hard again with the help of Penn's mouth, he doggy fucked Penn out in the sunlit center of the grotto until Penn spilled his seed. And as a finale and hour and a half after they had started, the flexible Penn rolled up onto his shoulders, his ass presented to Sam up in the air for a straight-down pile-driving fuck.

All of which looked quite convincing on camera, as Dean perched surreptitiously at the top of the limestone rock formation encasing the grotto and got pictures that left nothing to the imagination on what was being done in the grotto below and exactly who was doing it. This was one of Penn and Dean's favorite blackmail ploys that they had been working for two years on these entertainment troupe cruise liner runs from Baltimore to Bermuda. They certainly couldn't pay their rent on what the cruise line paid them; they lived quite well on entrapping and then promising not to tell on a series of well-heeled married cruisers. The three-way fuck—what they called their Bermuda Triangle ploy. The mark fucking one of them and then both of them fucking the mark.

Two nights later, while Susan was enjoying a follow-up free hair styling at the ship's beauty parlor and the cruise ship was on the return trip to Baltimore from Bermuda, Penn and Dean closed the trap on Sam Heck in his cabin.

Dean did the pitch. Penn was a little reticent about it. He'd really enjoyed the fuck and might have just forgotten about the blackmail part if Dean wasn't so insistent that they close it out. "So you see from these pictures, Mr. Heck, that it might be wiser if you . . ."

"Why the fuck would I care?" Sam said. "Frame them for all I care. Send them to the Baltimore *Sun*. It will only get you thrown in the slammer."

"I know you must be in shock, Mr. Heck, but I don't think you understand the gravity of the situation. If Mrs. Heck were to . . ."

"Mrs. Heck? My mother's dead. Why should she care?"

"No, no. He means Susan," Penn interjected. Sam glowered at him and Penn shrank away in embarrassment.

"Susan? SUSAN?" Sam grunted out. And then he laughed. "Susan Heck is my sister, dimwits. I don't have a wife. Everyone knows I'm gay. And very good at it, right, Penn?"

"Oh . . . yes, yes you are," Penn said, floored.

"Oh, shit," Dean said, in shock. He was faster at assessing adding to a total than Penn was.

"And so," Sam said, with a big grin. "Maybe I'll just keep these photos . . ." and with that, he turned and popped the photos into the room's wall safe and clicked the door shut . . . "and then it's you two who are fucked."

Penn and Dean looked at him with panicked expressions.

"But maybe if you were really fucked, both of you, hard, then we could just forget this happened."

Dean yelped, as Sam lifted him off the sofa with a strong arm wrapped around his waist and slammed him on the bed and started reaching below his belt in the back, down through his crack, digging for his ass.

Sam had finished with a panting and moaning Dean and was mounting Penn from the raised rear position when Susan Heck returned from her hair appointment.

Susan surveyed the carnage on the bed and gave a little sigh and pulled up a chair so she could watch Penn get fucked at close range. She loved to watch men fuck. She did ask Sam what they were doing, and Sam answered that they were playing Bermuda Triangle, a three-way, with him king of the top. They both laughed at that. Later Sam would give her a bonus thrill by opening the safe when they were alone and letting her examine Dean's glossy photo shots from the Horseshoe Beach grotto.

Gaycruise Daddy

"It's a great way to throw your money away; that's what it is."

"Well, let's see, Pete. How much have you spent on the site's hookup service, and how many guys have you actually hooked up with?"

"I've had some real hot conversations and cybersex with some of them," Pete sniffed.

"Purely in cyberspace, right? At, what, a dollar a word?" John answered, with a snort. "And I'll bet the photos they showed weren't any more of them than yours are of you."

"But three K at a single throw?" Pete retorted. "Just to go out in the ocean and back and watch young men fuck? And there won't be any hiding behind a fake photo for you, either. You'll have to be in a Speedo, or you'll stick out like a beached whale."

"The boat's going to Bermuda. We'll get off in Bermuda. I've never been to Bermuda. And, besides, I've got a good enough body," John answered indignantly.

Pete wheeled his office chair from beside John, where both had been staring into John's computer screen, and made a big deal of pushing his glasses down on his nose and giving John a sarcastic stare. That tableau held for about ten seconds.

"Well, I do for a man my age. Certainly better than yours."

"OK, I'll grant you both of those."

"And I bet I'm hanging lower and thicker than most of the young guys who will be on the cruise too."

"I'll grant you that too. But there's no chance any of the guys on the boat are even going to get an opportunity to see your—"

At that point Pete broke off because he saw one of the cashiers, Julie, standing in the door to the grocery store manager's office and looking pained. John noticed the change in Pete's demeanor, and his face swiveled toward the doorway.

"Yes, Julie, what is it?" John's fingers went instinctively to his keyword and toggled the screen from the homepage of the Gaycruiser gay male dating site to the chart of last month's inventory statistics at his Baltimore branch of Kroger's.

"A display got knocked over at the end of aisle three and there's pickle juice running on the floor and it doesn't look like Eddie's gonna get it cleaned up any too fast. He's already slid and fallen in it twice."

John took a deep breath and let it out in a sigh. "Thanks, Julie. Pete, could you—?"

"Hey, don't look at me, I'm management," Pete interjected. But he was already struggling to his feet.

"Yeah, but you're lower management and I'm upper management."

"Middle management," Pete muttered as he followed Julie's retreating figure through the floor and down the corridor to the main store floor.

What John was muttering at the same time as Pete walked away was, "Bermuda's gotta be better than this—and watching young guys fuck on a cruise ship will be a whole lot better than on a computer screen anyway."

* * * *

John was riddled with mixed emotions—nerves, arousal, a bit of dismay—as he stood in line waiting to register with the clipboard-laden, Speedo-clad tour director at the bottom of the

182

gangplank up to the sleek, small *Poseidon's Spear*, the cruise ship that was to take him two days out and two days back to Bermuda from Baltimore at the top of the Chesapeake Bay.

It was true, as he had actually hoped, that he was the only fifty-something man standing around waiting to get on the ship. The up side, though, was that the other men there were almost universally young hunks he would love to sink his dick into.

The cruise was one of the ones offered by the Gaycruiser Web site on a quarterly basis that augmented their on-line dating service. The fees were stiff, but the Web site no doubt thought that charging sixty men cruising for hookups on their site for the added hookup chance of four days out on the ocean on a sleek yacht where clothing was optional and fucking like bunnies was actually encouraged helped their paid membership statistics. Especially as extra money could be made from selling videos of the cruises on sex sites.

The cruise was going to be extra expensive for John. He had something of a plan—and there wasn't much of anything else in his life to spend money on. So, he'd reserved, and paid a high premium for, one of the suites on the ship. And before arriving, he spent weeks in the gym. His muscle tone was fine—for his age—but he had needed to get a little less thickish around the middle, and he'd at least partially succeeded at that. As he approached the cruise ship from the stern, he'd done a mental comparison of his torso with that of the Poseidon depicted on the fantail, and he didn't think he came off that badly. A man in his fifties had to be expected not to have a willowy figure. He'd had his gray hair styled and highlighted in a shimmery silver that caught the light and the loose hairs plucked from all of the unattractive places so that what was left on his chest was a pleasing—at least to him—patch that trailed intriguingly down his belly to his pubes, which he'd also had trimmed and shaped. He'd left curled tuffs in his arm pits, enough so that they wouldn't give the impression they'd been purposely shaved. And he'd spent enough time in a tanning both for a sort of all-over tan so that he wouldn't look like the office worker that he was when he got to the ship's pool.

And he'd bought some spiffier, expensive-looking clothes at the Tanger Outlet near the Chesapeake Bay Bridge. He'd been lucky to find a Speedo with a bull's eye design on it, sort of down and to the left on his basket, circling where his bulb rested, that would help emphasize his best feature—his thick, eight-inch cock.

When he got up to the tour director, a well-built hunk with blond-highlighted curly hair with a chiseled face and a practiced smile, he opened up his gambit.

"Ah, and you are?" the young man asked dubiously, looking down at his clipboard after a quick look up and down John and a slight sniff of his nose.

"Jonathan Pender. From Baltimore. Although, I'm not sure what home base was given you when the reservation was made. It could have been the Hamptons or Aspen too, I suppose."

The cruise director's slight supercilious smile had already started to turn more respectful as he found John's name on his clipboard, but, hearing what John said, he looked up with a far more welcoming—and interested—look on his face. John was also pleased to note that the men immediately behind him in line had stopped whispering to each other and were more attentive now too. At least they had stopped snickering.

"Yes, well it does say Baltimore, and I see that you are booked into the Neptune suite." This latter discovery had been the reason the tour director's attitude had already changed. "May I be the first to give you a hearty welcome aboard. My name is Tony and don't hesitate to ask if there's anything—absolutely anything—I can do to make riding . . . riding the waves a greater pleasure for you."

The young man fluttered his eyelashes and held out his hand for a handshake that held for several seconds longer than fully necessary and felt, John thought at the time, a little strange, because the young man had folded a finger inside the traditional grip and rubbed it across John's palm.

For a moment John wondered if this was some sort of signaling in the world of men who liked men—and he supposed that he should have spent more time researching on the Internet.

"It notes this is your first cruise with us, but I certainly hope it won't be your last."

"Yes, well," John answered, with a sigh. "The Hamptons usually are the best place at this time of year. But with the house refurbishing . . . well, I thought I'd try something a bit different."

"We can certainly offer you something different here, sir," Tony answered in a coquettish voice. "If you don't mind, I'll seat you at the captain's table for dinner tonight."

"That would be fine," John answered in a tone he hoped would convey that it was no more than what he would have expected anyway.

On his way up the gangplank, John was congratulating himself. He thought that was an auspicious beginning. And he hadn't even lied about anything. There always could have been a mix-up in listing his home in the reservation, the Hamptons no doubt *were* delightful at this time of year, and surely *some* house there was being renovated.

He gave a little chuckle, looking forward to pleasures to come, if he was lucky and clever. As he entered the ship, the first thing that caught his eye was an etching of Poseidon rising from the sea, with his trident a thick column rising between two meaty balls and ending in three hard-phallus points. He chuckled at this too.

He didn't do much chuckling that afternoon as the ship was steaming south down the center of the Chesapeake Bay and then turning southwest out to sea. As he had expected, all life gathered around the pool on the top deck in the center of the ship and most of the cruisers were starting their festivities early with drinking, cavorting in the pool, and sucking and fucking on the lounges. There were very few inhibitions to be seen and many an arousing distraction to watch. The young men were almost uniformly gorgeous, and the rewards for a voyeur were high.

As much as John liked watching, it was obvious that the young men weren't flocking to him. He had donned the bull's-eye Speedo and taken a prominently displayed deck lounge and laid a towel over his less-pleasing bits, but no one—with the occasional exception of someone doing a double take when seeing the line of his curled-around cock inside the Speedo—was paying much attention to him.

This changed a bit at dinner. He had to admit to himself when he looked in the mirror that he looked quite distinguished in his rented tuxedo. There was something about a tuxedo that brought out the best in a gray-haired, mature man, and John said a little prayer of thanks to the hair stylist he'd gone to rather than his regular barber earlier in the week.

The captain might not even have known that John was at the table that evening. The cruise director obviously was under strict orders to seat the most meltingly beautiful submissive young man on the cruise beside the captain on the first night, and they had not even made it to desert before they all had to rise when the captain did so as he escorted his entertainment for the evening from the table and to his cabin.

The cruise director obviously had similar plans for John. John had been conveniently seated next to Tony, and during their dinner conversation, Tony pumped John for background information, and John ran the thin line between being from a famous family of retailers and being the manager of a Kroger grocery store branch. John must have done it successfully and Tony must have heard what he wanted to hear, as, while those left at the table were being served coffee, Tony laid his hand in John's lap under the table—and, John was pleased to hear, gave a little gasp—and asked John if he could come to the Neptune suite later in the evening.

It was at this point that John knew that his scheme and the money he had invested in this cruise were going to pan out. When the cruise had come up on offer and while Pete and he discussed what young men seemed to be looking for when they played the hookup game on the Gaycruiser Web site, John reasoned that there were three reasons a young man would fuck a stranger. One, the stranger was a young hunk. This left John out, he readily acknowledged. But there were two other, more hopeful reasons. One was that they were looking for a good fucking and the last—the biggest reason by far, John thought after researching the traffic on the dating site—was that they were looking for a sugar daddy who would take care of them in the manner in which they would like to be accustomed.

Of the three, John saw his greatest hope as being the good fuck, because he had been magnificently endowed and had had decades of practice before his opportunities began to thin out as he aged, dwindling to nothing but memories soon after he pushed by fifty. Unfortunately, as John grew older, fewer and fewer young men who he fancied had stuck with him long enough to enjoy what he could give them down deep. And then John thought about the sugar daddy angle. He reasoned that if he got into it before others discovered the opportunities it accorded, he just might be able to play the sugar daddy card long enough to get his dick inside a couple of these studs and subdue them to begging for him. At that point, John thought, the good fucking might become as important to them as the sugar daddy aspect.

And, eureka, before *Poseidon's Spear* cleared Hampton Roads and was sailing out into the Atlantic, John's research assured him that he was the only one on this cruise who looked and acted the part of a sugar daddy—apart from the forties-something captain, who had his own entirely different avenue for dipping his wick as he pleased.

John left nothing to chance that evening. When he answered the knock on the cabin door and determined by looking through the keyhole that it was Tony, as expected, John had the lights out, music with a jungle beat going softly and subliminally in the background, and all he was wearing was a silver silk robe, open in a swath at the front that followed the line of his sculpted chest hair down to his sucked-in belly and then on down to where his proudly displayed penis and balls reached for the floor. The only light was what was coming from the corridor with the door open and a filtering of moonlight through the gauze draperies at the balcony door.

When the cabin door was closed and Tony was kneeling between John's knees as the grocery store manager sat on the edge of the bed, there was little light, and all Tony could concentrate on with astonishment and lust was John's engorging dick and the glorious difficulty—for both of them—with which he was soldiering to get it all in his mouth.

And the night had grown even darker when John laid back, stretched full length, on the bed and let Tony ride a cock that he had to work hard, with great groans and grunts and cries of passion, to accommodate. John showed him too, now that the atmospherics had been equalized and the rhythm of the beat of the music in the background was becoming more intense, that John's hands were not too old to massage Tony's cock in quite pleasant ways while he rode John's master phallus. This was something that many years of experience enhanced. A man of John's age and experience knew how to please another man—at least in the dark and with a thick, eight-inch cock. And a man of John's opportunities was far more attentive than a younger man would be to his partner's needs.

After working Tony's cock up, John moved his hands to the young cruise director's waist and tilted him slightly toward John's chest. At the same time John raised his knees between Tony's thighs, spreading Tony's thighs, and rolled his own pelvis forward. The head of his cock moved down to the pleasure spot inside Tony's channel that a seasoned expert like John knew was there. Tony cried out in never-before-felt pleasure as John's cock head rubbed across Tony's prostate once, twice, three times and then, as Tony gasped, plunged deep inside him, only to drag slowly back up his channel walls. Tony fisted his own cock and beat it to the increased intensity of the specially selected jungle music in the background. Rub, rub, rub, plunge, drag; rub, rub, rub, plunge, drag. And Tony soared over the moon and came in profusions of cum such as he'd never experienced before with a younger man. And then when Tony thought it was over, rub, rub, rub, plunge, drag. John had had years to perfect being able to hold off and to prolong.

Hearing Tony's moans was all John needed to know that a man with real experience was good to have on a fuck cruise.

When he left the cabin slightly before dawn, Tony seemed quite pleased with the two hundred-dollar notes John pressed into his hand after patting the sweet, tight buttocks he had had the pleasure of splitting a second time after Tony had recovered from his first hour-long ride on John's cock.

The young cruise director must have spoken of the highlights of the experience the next morning, as John hoped he would, because when he came out to the pool and settled on a prominently placed lounge, he wasn't alone for long. Several

188

young men gathered around him, asking about life in the Hamptons and Aspen and seeking advice on stocks and bonds and then, standing and posing for John and asking whether this or that muscle needed more definition or whether their tan lines showed too prominently. John laughed when one asked if he could dispel the rumors and see John's most important muscle, but John didn't give out easily. He teased them along while taking the opportunities as they came to cop a good feel here and there.

And they were ever so grateful when John was willing to rub the suntan lotion on them, particularly the young man wearing nothing who thought perhaps his cock might also burn if it was left uncovered and who lay there on John's lounge chair, John sitting at his waist, and smiled and arched his back and slitted his eyes and moaned as John expertly, forefinger pressing into piss slit, brought up the young man's own white fluid to spread on top of the tanning lotion on his cock.

When the saucy young drinks waiter brought back John's Tequila Sunrise, he asked the older man if there was anything else he needed in such a nice way and with his fingers tracing John's cock through the bull's-eye Speedo that John, at last, let him bring his phallus out into the air—which was especially good for John, as now all eyes were on that and he could stop sucking in his stomach and stretching to tighten up his pec muscles. As the young man lowered his mouth over the bulb of John's cock and started flicking John's piss slit with his tongue, John sighed in satisfaction and reached for the proffered cock of a deliciously divine chocolate young man sitting close to him on the neighboring deck lounge.

"I would very much like to take this lovely cock elsewhere," the waiter murmured to John after John had come and he was still slowly stroking John's cock. "May I come to your room tonight, Mr. Pender?"

"Alas, Emilio," John said, trying to feign a face of deep regret but saying the words with the greatest of pleasure, "I have three engagements already this evening. And there are limits to what I can do. I do have an opening or two on the return trip from Bermuda, though."

John knew he was on top of the world, though, when, as he was departing the pool area—and right out there at midday, under the sun, rather than in a dark cabin—the delicious young man the captain had no doubt fucked the previous night came up and begged to ride John's cock—right there and then. John picked the sweet young thing up and settled his butt down on the flight of stairs going up to the bridge—where he could see the captain watching them. The young man licked his lips and spread his legs and hooked his heels over the railing at each side, as other young men gathered around, their eyes locked on the weapon John was wielding between his legs. All sighed—not just the beautiful young man—as John slowly fed his cock inside him and changed the angle so that his bulb was planted on the young man's prostate. Rub, rub rub, plunge, drag; rub, rub, rub, plunge, drag. The young man cried out in ecstasy and writhed under John's masterful attentions, and all of the other young men around murmured and fisted their own cocks.

John went on forever—rub, rub, rub, plunge, drag—and the gorgeous young man whimpered and weakened and started to babble and his legs went to rubber and other young men had to lean in to hold them up and out as they gazed down at the root of the thick cock moving in and out of the puckered hole—shallow, shallow, shallow, deep, draaaagg back to the sound of a weak moan. The young man came but John didn't stop. He was tired, but this was lesson time, his time to make his point. Rub, rub, rub, plunge, drag. Rub, rub, rub, plunge, back, plunge, back, plungebackplunge, and the young man cried out as he came again with John. Moans all around as one by one, all the other young men came too.

After that, there was no question that whenever John could get it up during the cruise, he would have a fresh conquest moaning for what he could give them. No one on the cruise cared after that that he had gray hair and a thickish waist and age spots and a few wrinkles and sagged a bit here and there and couldn't play pool volleyball or drink the younger guys under the table. What mattered was what he could do between their legs on top of the table. No one even subtly quizzed him on how much he was worth in dollars anymore. He had a monster, talented cock, and he could give a guy the master fuck of his life.

It was so heartening, John thought, that the youth of the day could see what was important in life once they'd tasted it.

* * * *

"You look worn out," Pete said.

"I feel that way too." John fought hard to keep the smile out of his voice. He sighed heavily, for effect.

"Found you were too old for a cruise like that, didn't you?"

"It about did me in, yes."

"Didn't I tell you it would be a waste of money?"

"You sure did," John said as he turned away from Pete and toward his computer screen. He couldn't hold back the grin any longer. Of course, on a basis of pure cost-efficiency analysis, it probably was pretty pricey. He figured he'd wound up spending $4,400 in all. He tried to compute it in his head. Was it twenty-eight or twenty-nine lays? Uh, no, he wasn't counting those three times on the beach on Bermuda. And not the blow jobs either. Must have been over a hundred dollars an ejaculation. But then the food was good and plentiful and fully covered too. And the drinks. Maybe he should have drunk more booze—but where would he have found the time? He had an apartment here, so he really couldn't discount on the use of the suite.

"You look like you haven't slept in a week."

"Nope. Didn't get much sleep out there on the ocean."

"Just a ridin' those waves, right?"

"Yep, just riding away. Riding, riding, riding." Expensive rides, yes. But they came with the feel of young flesh, and the sound of another man's moans and begging for him. The feeling of being young again himself, wanted—by young hunks, ones he could feel in real life. Pete's way of using the Gaycruiser Web site services meant he rode alone.

"Well, I told you so."

"Yep, you sure did." John tilted the computer screen away from Pete's adjacent desk. This was his good thing. He didn't want Pete getting ideas and horning in. And most of all right now he didn't want Pete seeing that he was signing up for the fall cruise to the Bahamas on the *Poseidon's Spear*. It wouldn't be as expensive next time. Gaycruiser was offering him a professional discount.

And look, his profile on the Web site was lighting up like a Christmas tree. Requests for hookups—right here in Baltimore. So, maybe the cruise was going to be cost-effective after all.

Trawler Initiation

On a shrimp boat trawler well out to sea, you and a big muscle-bound bruiser of questionable intellect are telling me while we are taking a coffee break in the trawler I'd signed on for my sophomore summer in college that the senior crew all have privileges with the new guy. Just an initiation—like crossing the equator for the first time. But more fun.

What privileges and fun for who? I think, fear rising from my gut.

I'd been avoiding the bruiser because I didn't like the way he looked at me. But you've been nothing but friendly to me and have shown interest in who I was, why I was spending the summer working on a trawler, how old I was, did I screw all of the coeds—stuff like that. This, though. This, here and now, doesn't seem friendly—or maybe it seems too friendly. It has got me off balance.

You say you know I take cock because I'd been with the captain in his cabin the previous night and the bruiser heard how well I liked the captain's cocking. He says the captain was crowing this morning, saying he'd won the crew poll on who would be first.

Would it make any difference if I told you that the captain had gotten me drunk, and that I'd never done it before,

193

and that, other than the soreness, I wouldn't be half aware that I had done it last night? Somehow I don't think you'd care—or that the bruiser would care either. And the captain said he wouldn't tell anyone if I came to his cabin again tonight. And he said it in such a way for me to understand that it wasn't really a request—out here on the open water, where it's just those of us on this trawler.

Flustered, I say I don't know what to say. What I'm thinking is how the bruiser heard. The captain's cabin isn't anywhere near the quarters for the rest of the crew. But what I say is that I'm not easy like that, and will think about it.

I'm trying to remain calm—cool. Trying to cool man my way out of the cabin. But if they'd seen me riding the captain's cock that second time last night they'd have a right to think I sniffed after it anywhere I could get it. I'd just been letting loose. And he'd gotten me drunk. Three months on the sea completely free from the constraints of land and college. And the captain was a stud and a half and he wore practically nothing, just a Speedo—just like all of us when we are out to sea. It was just a fling. Just a summer madness to mark the end of the school term. And he got me drunk. I'd thought about it, yes, and I'd fantasized about it when I was thinking of signing onto the trawler, because I'd heard what could happen on these isolated vessels out on the open water. But I'd never done it before last night.

"Think fast," you say and turn to the bruiser and say, "What do you think, Big Jim? Right here on the table?"

The bruiser giggles, stands, and pops the biggest cock I've ever seen out of his Speedo. I'd been eyeing his basket for days, wondering who would be up to taking it that big. That was part of why I'd been staying away from him. In shock, I stand. You reach out and grip my forearm, but I brush your hand away and lurch for the hatch out to the deck.

I hear you both laugh as you start in pursuit. I make it only about thirty feet, in the bow and below the bridge. The bruiser pounces on me and brings me down on a coil of roping. I land on top of him, and he snakes heavily muscled arms around mine, pinning me to his chest. You lean down and pull my Speedo off my legs. The bruiser's legs then lace in between

194

mine, and he lifts and spreads his legs, so that mine spread and lift as well. I feel his thick, hard cock in the small of my back, snaking almost all the way up to my shoulder blades, it seems. I start to hyperventilate, but I know that won't help, so I start taking breaths in large gulps.

You are standing, looking down at me, and smiling. You push your Speedo to below your balls, showing that you're hard for me too. You go down on your knees between my legs, and I cry out as you slowly work your way into my ass.

I struggle, but it's useless, the bruiser is too strong for me. And the struggling only helps you move deeper inside me. I whimper as you stroke and stroke and stroke. I'm determined not to cry, though, to take it and then get as far away from here as possible. But what is far away on a trawler on the open seas?

Seeing that the captain has come out onto the deck of the bridge above us, I call out to him. He smiles and waves, takes a swig from his coffee cup, and turns and calls to the mate to join him. I see that he's pushed his Speedo down and is stroking his cock. No relief there. The black guy, Horace, who provides a lot of the muscle on moving cargo, has come up from the stern, hearing that something's going on. He's wearing a big grin and comes and stands beside us. He's got his cock in his hand.

"Relax kid," you say. "It's just the new guy initiation. When everyone's had a piece, we'll let you choose your two favorites for the rest of the voyage. Maybe they'll both enjoy you at once." You, the black guy, and the bruiser laugh.

I feel you jerk and come and then you are out of me and helping the bruiser free his cock from between his groin and my back. You are helping the bruiser find my hole with his staff. And when he has and I feel like I'm being split asunder, I start screaming anew. The mate is next to the captain on the bridge deck now. They are embracing and kissing and have taken possession of each other's cocks.

I can't stop complaining loudly from having the largest cock in the world pumping inside me. This isn't anything like the captain's. It isn't anything like I had from either the captain or you.

"Scream all you want, kid," the bruiser says in my ear in a hoarse voice. "There's empty ocean in every direction you can see from here, and we'll be out here for three months. And," he giggles, "a screamer makes me horny. And when I'm horny, I can go all day."

I believe him. I moan, starting to calm down, because the pain is turning into pleasure and I'm taking the biggest cock in the world. I'm taking the biggest dick in the world. I can't believe I'm managing the biggest dick in the universe. I'm wondering if it can get deeper from a different position. I shudder. I don't want to know that. But . . . but, of course I do want to know that. I'm taking the biggest dick in the world.

"Sweet ass," bruiser whispers. "And you like it. I can tell you like it. You wanna bunk with me tonight? I'll show you tricks you never knew. Maybe Horace can join us. You'll like that, kid. I can tell."

I'm thinking of the captain. I've got to go there tonight. But will he keep me all night? And, if not, will the bruiser be waiting for me? Can I take it? Maybe I'll need to be drunk tonight. Three months. Oh, fuck.

God he can fuck. God he can fuck.

I look up to see the captain and mate coming down the stairway, cocks in hand, smiling. I can barely hear what the captain is saying. "Great lay. Tight ass. Had him three times last night. I can tell you what he likes."

Azores Assignation

Edgar steadied himself against the bulkhead as the wake of a passing yacht sent his own ship to wallowing and scraping against the dock. He was hunched over the sink in the closely confined space, space being at a premium even in a Latitude 44 such as he'd sailed from Marseilles to the harbor town of Horta on Azores' Faial Island. He believed that he could find exactly what he wanted here, and he'd been preparing himself for the greater part of the morning to make the most of himself.

He was pleased enough with his form, fancying himself as looking a decade younger at least than his well-pampered fifty-two. He sighed at that thought, though, a decade younger not really making the difference he sought. It got no easier the older he got, although he found that a thick wallet helped considerably. He was leaning into the small mirror over the basin in the eternal search for gray hairs and plucking at the most noticeable ones; he was years beyond eradicating them all, and in Marseilles Tony had said his graying temples were distinguished, so maybe he should just make do with that thought. The wallowing of the ship certainly wasn't helping him in his quest, and at least he still had a full head of hair. There were men far younger than he was who couldn't say that.

He stood back as far as he could and peered into the mirror. Yes, everything seemed to be in as good an order as he could expect. He was really quite presentable. The thought of what he was about to do was arousing, and he felt the knob of his cock rub against the cotton of his stark-white cotton trousers. He had thought long and hard whether to wear anything under the trousers and was glad that he'd decided against it. He liked the feel of his cock being free and just below one thin layer of cloth.

Just one more thing: the hanky. He'd been intrigued to hear that they still followed the hanky code in the Azores. He was sorry that the code had gone out of style in Europe. The preliminaries could be a little difficult these days. It had always been so easy to tell when the hanky code was in vogue there. He reached over to his kit bag and pulled out the orange one. Yes, this was going to be an "anything, anytime, anywhere" day for him. At his age there was so little time and fewer and fewer opportunities. He no longer could be picky and spend time deciding exactly what he was interested in at the moment with any hope of finding a hookup. So, it was anything, anytime, anywhere for him—and he'd probably have to pay for it to boot.

While contemplating this, he dug into his kit and pulled out a tube of lubricant. Pulling down the rump of his slacks with one hand, he worked a glob of the lubricant into his hole with the other. He'd enjoy the squishy feeling of the lube inside his channel as he walked, and an anything, anywhere, anytime assignation could easily be one short on opportunity to prepare well enough. Pulling the slacks back over his plump rump, he dropped the tube in his pocket and opened the cabinet under the basin and selected three packets of ribbed condoms and pocketed those as well.

Edgar carefully folded the orange hanky and inserted it in his right shirt pocket, letting several inches of the hanky show. He'd selected a stark-white sports shirt to top his white cotton slacks precisely so that the bright orange hanky in his right shirt pocket could not be missed. Then, taking one last appraising look at himself in the mirror and convincing himself, by squinting, that he was seeing what he wanted to see, he turned, walked out on the deck of the tug-like yacht and across the teak deck and jumped up to the pier. Looking up at the tiers of buildings of the town of Horta rising up from the busy yacht basin, he smiled at the prospect of what lay ahead and set out for Peter's Café Sport.

At the café, Edgar selected a table back out of the sun, under the awning, near the side wall, and sat down, facing the yacht basin. There were few other patrons about at this time of the morning, which Edgar had been told was the best time for what he wanted. He ordered two Magna beers, which assured that the waiter wouldn't be back to fawn over him anytime soon. As he was nursing the first beer, he focused on exactly what he thought he was looking for.

The young man was perhaps in his mid twenties, dark-skinned, possibly Moroccan, but with handsome, chiseled features that hinted of French ancestry as well. Jet-black hair, close cropped, thick and curly. A three-day growth of beard that obviously was kept at that length because it suited the face well, although the impression was left that his hair grew quickly. Edgar contemplated how a hairy chest usually went with that— and was glad for that. Tall, well-muscled, but still looking very trim. The young hunk moved gracefully, like a dancer or an athlete as he picked out a table in the sun, on the same side of the café as Edgar, but choosing to sit facing the café rather than the yacht basin, so that he and Edgar were facing each other. He was sitting on the side of the table away from the other café patrons, as was Edgar. From the chest down only within the view of Edgar. He was wearing white, silky, draw-string shorts with a buttoned fly, and, similar to Edgar, a stark-white cotton sport shirt. Edgar sucked in his breath as he looked down at the young man's feet. He was wearing open-toed sandals. The feet were big and long, the toes long and plump.

And it was the sport shirt that caught Edgar's full attention. It was sleeveless, showing off the young man's well-developed biceps, and had button-down flaps on its shirt pockets. And attached to the right pocket was an unmistakable signaling device. Edgar's hands started to tremble and he had to set his Magna bottle on the table top. The young man had a black, rubbery cock ring, one of those ones with five knobs around the periphery, suspended from his right pocket. A giver.

Exactly what Edgar was looking for. Edgar felt his knees go weak. The cock ring must be at least two inches across. His eyes went back to those long plump toes. Edgar could feel his cock stirring.

A waiter was at the young man's table, and Edgar heard him order a bottle of Cergal beer, but when the waiter was almost back at the bar near the door into the café's interior, the young man rose and took two steps toward him and changed his order to a bottle of Magna. He had turned away from Edgar, Edgar gasped audibly when he saw a mustard yellow hanky peeking out of the left back pocket of the young man's shorts. It was a color Edgar knew well; it declared over eight inches of available service.

Edgar's hand went to his lap. His cock was hard, and he rubbed across it through the material of his slacks. Thank god the Azores were still on the hanky code system. Less than a half hour and Edgar had found exactly what he wanted. It was almost too good to be true. Then Edgar chuckled. Reality was what you made of it, of course.

He looked up to discover that the young man was looking at him and was smiling. The young man slowly lifted his bottle of Magna almost to his lips. Edgar watched in fascination as the young man opened his lips and pushed his tongue out into the opening of the bottle and pushed it back and forth into the neck of the bottle. Then he extracted his tongue and turned the opening of the bottle until it faced Edgar. All of the time the young man was staring at Edgar with a little smile of challenge in his eyes. Edgar picked up his own beer bottle in a trembling hand and slowly closed his lips over and down the sides of the neck of the bottle, slowly pulled it away and then took it in again.

The young man pointed down in his lap, and Edgar looked down to find that the young man had unbuttoned his fly and the side of a thick, brown cock was showing below a thatch of curly black hair. Edgar fumbled around in a pocket, nearly overcome with arousal, and pulled out his wallet and set it down on the table and laid one of the condom packets on top of it.

The signaling was complete. The contract made.

The young man stood and slowly walked away from the café, up the cobble-stoned street rising beside the café and up into the town of Horta, away from the piers. Edgar stood, still trembling and followed the young man at a distance of some twenty feet. The young man sharply turned to the right behind the back of the café and Edgar followed him back along a narrow path with the back wall of the café at one side and lush semitropical foliage pushing out into the walkway behind a short retaining wall on the other side. Far enough down the pathway that he could not be seen from the street, the young man sat down on the retaining wall. He was pulling off a sandal when Edgar reached him.

"Here suck these," the young man demanded in a rich, deep voice, in English kissed by a French accent, as Edgar sank to his knees on the pathway and took the long plump toes into his mouth and sucked on them. The young man had released his cock and was slowly pumping himself up.

"Now suck this."

Edgar sighed with pleasure as he turned his attention to the thick, brown cock.

"All of it. Take it all," the young man growled, as he palmed the back of Edgar's head and held his face close into his crotch. Edgar had all of the cock throated, but he began to gag as the cock lengthened and thickened inside him. He fought the gag reflex, though, because he was loving this, a vigorous young cock to suck on.

But then the young man was pulling out of him and standing and buttoning his fly.

"Come with me," he said. "I have a room nearby. I fuck you hard, yes? You pay me, yes?"

"Yes, yes, and yes," Edgar gasped out as he struggled back to his feet. Ninth heaven. Well worth the sail out to the islands.

In the small hotel room, less than a block from the café, the young man had only one question. "You know what the orange cloth means, yes?"

"Yes," Edgar said. "Anything, anytime, anywhere." But he was a little fearful when he said it because he could see what the young man had laid out on the nightstand next to the single bed—leather restraints, a ball gag, and a big, thick black rubber dildo.

In short order, Edgar was on his back, naked, on the bed; his wrists tied to the brass railing of the headboard over his head; the orange hanky stuffed in his mouth, held inside by the ball gag; two pillows under the small of his back, pushing his pelvis up off the bed, and a magnificently naked young man standing between his spread thighs and working the dildo inside his channel. The dildo was big and thick, but it wasn't as big as the nine incher pushing out of the black thicket of hair below the young man's belly.

Edgar was writhing and moving his pelvis off the leverage of his heels dug into the surface of the bed in countermotion to the invading, twisting dildo. The veins on his neck were bulging out as were his eyes, and he was screaming in muffled tones through the gag. Being taken hard. Loving every stroke of it.

When he was well open, the young man fiddled around in the pocket of Edgar's trousers and came up with one of the ribbed condoms, which he rolled onto his cock, barely being able to get it over what he was packing. He then pulled the dildo out, and almost teasingly, screwed it in one more time, to the bottom, to a depth and with the effect of lifting Edgar's pelvis off the pillows with a loud, muffled groan, pulled it out quickly, thrust it in again hard, and then pulled it out and exchanged it for a longer, thicker, throbbing, flexible brown cock. Pumping, pumping, pumping, while Edgar writhed and luxuriated under him.

Edgar achieved an ejaculation that far surpassed, both in force and in volume, any he had accomplished in his four month of cruising around the Mediterranean. He collapsed with a satisfied, exhausted sigh as the young man was still stroking deep inside him.

The young man smiled a sneery smile and said. "You want me to come too?"

Edgar wagged his head yes. He so wanted to tell the young man that he wanted him to strip the condom off and to fill him with his semen, deep inside him. But he was gagged and couldn't do that. A minor disappointment. But he wouldn't think about it, wouldn't let that mar the glorious fucking he was getting.

The young man was fumbling around in the pockets of Edgar's trousers again and came out with Edgar's wallet. Holding it up in front of Edgar's eyes, he said, in that deep, mesmerizing voice of his, "If you have enough for me in this wallet, I come. If not, I don't." He put his hand in the wallet and brought out the banknotes and fanned them out. "You are in luck. You have enough for bareback even. You want that?"

Edgar wagged his head yes vigorously, and watched in fascination as the young man withdrew from him and rolled off the ribbed condom.

The young man fucked him hard, fast, and deep then for several minutes, while Edgar arched up into him, spreading his thighs as widely as he could to get the full effect of the skin stroking on his channels walls. The young man ripped off the ball gag just before he ejaculated, and they cried out in unison at the prolonged bathing of Edgar's insides.

Edgar's blood was chilled while the young man was freeing him, when he said, "You came by yacht, did you not? I saw you walking up the pier. You have a nice yacht, yes? You have a lot of nice things on this yacht of yours, yes?"

"Umm . . . I don't . . ." Edgar murmured.

"We go to your yacht now, yes?" the young man asked, turning on that slightly sneery smile, which entirely changed the demeanor of his handsome face.

"No, no . . . I don't think . . ."

"We go to your yacht now yes." And it was no longer a question. The young man waved the saliva-slickened orange cloth in front of Edgar's face. "You signaled anything, anytime, anywhere. We go to your yacht now." He was holding Edgar close in to him and he took Edgar's mouth in his and kissed him brutally in a maneuver that ended in biting Edgar's lip and causing him to yip and gasp. The unexpected pain gave Edgar's dick a jolt. As brutal as the kiss was, it was also deeply sensual. Everything about this young man and everything he did to Edgar was arousing to Edgar.

The young man held Edgar's elbow to the threshold of pain as they stumbled down the cobble-stoned street and onto the pier. Edgar led him directly to his yacht, and when they were aboard, the young man pushed Edgar through the lounge and into the stateroom, pulling at Edgar's clothes and his own as they moved through the cabins. They were both naked again by the time they reached Edgar's berth. The young man pushed Edgar down hard on his belly on the berth and barked out, "up on your knees, chest down, and legs spread wide. Now!"

Edgar had barely gotten into the demanded position before the young man was saddled over his hips and was thrusting inside him again, bottoming quickly. He was holding Edgar up with a palm on his belly and was squeezing Edgar's balls and pulling on his cock with the other. His fucking was frenzied now, the sliding of the cock now completely unhindered, aided by the mix of lubrication and previous come inside Edgar's channel. Both were vocal now, the young hunk's deep bass drowning out Edgar's higher-pitched moans and groans and cries at the total magnificent fucking he was getting.

Edgar shot his load for a second time under the attention of the young man's strong fist—once more a large glob of cum in three strong spoutings. And then Edgar's knees gave out, and he sank stretched out full on the bed, with the young man coming down with him, his cock still deeply embedded, riding him hard for ten minutes more to his own ejaculation.

When he had come, the young man went into a slow collapse beside Edgar on the bed, both now stretched out full length on their sides, panting heavily, the slick sweat on the young man's curly-haired chest slicking up Edgar's trembling back.

Still churning languidly in a side-split, the young man brought his lips to Edgar's ear.

"Was that what you wanted, Ed? Did that do it?"

"Yes, Tony, that certainly did it. Did you see how strongly I came? This was just what I needed."

"Yes, I found it nice too, my love," Tony whispered. "But we could have had this fantasy back in Marseilles, you know. We didn't have to come all of the way to the Azores for this."

"Yes, but it pleases me, and I can afford it. Oh, god, to be as young virile again. I feel you rising again. I'm not sure I can . . ."

"Yes, you can . . . and you will," Tony growled in that low voice of his, already beginning to take control again.

To Die in Madeira

I closed my lips over Sir Guy's cock and pushed his foreskin down with them, my tongue going to opening and flicking down into his piss slit as my mouth slowly took more and more of him inside the moist warmth of my mouth cavity. He sighed contentedly and ran his fingers through my hair. He reached up and pulled my cock down to his lips and started returning the compliment.

We were half way through his massage, and I was on my knees and elbows straddled above him on the massage table in the sixty-nine position, careful not to burden his frail, tortured body with the weight of my hard-muscled 190 pounds. He was moaning softly and making feeble attempts to slowly pump his engorging cock up into the warmth of my mouth. I moved my forearms so that I could palm the flaps of his withered buttocks in my hands and both cushion his brittle skin from rubbing against the vinyl of the massage table top and help strengthen his attempts to pump up into me. I was careful not to thrust with my own cock, letting him do whatever he could with it with his teeth and lips. This wasn't for me; it was for him. I was just here to serve.

We continued in this position until he gave a little jerk and semen dribbled out of his cock at the back of my throat as he gave a little sigh and then settled down.

He thanked me in a faraway voice from some fantasy land or poignant remembrance of his past as I climbed back off the table and carefully turned him on his belly and resumed the regular part of the massage on his backside, ever so gently working what was left of his muscles and exercising his creaking joints.

"The ass, work the ass," he murmured. "And don't neglect the inside, please. Fuck me, please."

"Are you sure, Sir Guy?" I asked. "I fear I'm too big and heavy for you. I don't want to hurt you."

"You always say that," Sir Guy responded. "And you're always wrong. You're never too big for me. You're big, of course. But just right. Indulge me, please." And then he laughed. "I think my ass canal is the last youthful part of me. Still flexible after all these years. Still able to take the big boys."

"I don't know, Sir Guy. I don't know if it's wise." But I had already placed the pillow under his hips, raising his withered flanks, and I was gently massaging his buttocks in circles, ever widening circles that increasingly opened his crease, revealing a puckered hole. I let a thumb strum across the hole and leaned down and blew on it, and Sir Guy gave a little gasp and then a long sigh.

"What's wise?" Sir Guy asked "You afraid I'll die on your table? That you'll fuck me to death?"

"Umm, Something like that, I guess," I replied. It had taken several months for my massage appointments with Sir Guy to reach this point. He was living in one of England's most exclusive rest homes, tucked away riverside at Henley-on-Thames. I had signed on as a physical therapist there. I really fancied myself as a writer, but I couldn't see enough money in that for years to come, and the middle-aged men who picked me up in the men's bars for my main source of income and who I had gotten into a routine of massaging as foreplay remarked so favorably on the massages I gave—even what went before the massaging of their cocks—that I took a course of study in massage to add some legitimate income to my upkeep.

I had taken to the old folks homes, as the clients were of the gentle sort. But Sir Guy—I had no idea if he was really a knight, only that everyone called him Sir Guy, and I knew he must be loaded to be living where he was—had recognized what I was immediately. And he had slowly cajoled me into helping him be what he was. But I remained skittish of giving him what he always wanted, as he was so fragile and seemed close to a wasting-away death from the moment I met him.

"I'm not afraid of death," Sir guy continued, as I continued massaging his buttocks in circles and running my thumbs over his opening hole as they passed by. I thumped the hole with the pad of a finger, and it blinked at me and puckered up. Sir Guy groaned a "Yes, like that," and I pressed a thumb into the opening, which yielded to me and clutched at the invading digit. "And there is a certain kind of death I welcome and that there's no use living without."

"Oh, what's that?" I asked. I extracted the thumb and thumped it against the hole again, rubbed it across the hole three, four times, and then pushed it back in. His rim grabbed my thumb and pulled it in to the knuckle, and he moved his ass in little circles and moaned deeply.

"*Le petite mort*," he murmured through his sighs.

"What was that?" I asked.

"*Le petite mort*, the little death. Did you not read John Rhy's *Wide Sargasso Sea*?" He asked in a little gaspy voice. Paraphrasing poets, he presented each ejaculation, each orgasm as the point of a little death. "A death to be welcomed, wouldn't you say, Keith? And did you not know that the word for 'orgasm' and 'death' is the same in Olde English? I prefer that form of death. And when I no longer can die in that way, I welcome the death of the other kind; the final death. And you are helping me in maintaining the edge of life in these little deaths, Keith. Never forget that. Never think you are bringing harm to me in our massage sessions."

"Yes, sir," I answered. For indeed there seemed nothing else I could answer. I had grown fond of Sir Guy—to the point of becoming detached when I was wedged between the spread thighs of those middle-aged men from the bars and listening to them grunting and groaning as I split them with my thick cock and wondering if Sir Guy would still be there for our next massage session, if he had survived the week. But so far he always had been there.

"Now the ultimate kiss, if you please, Keith, with plenty of tongue. I grow weary but I must finish. I must have my little death again and pull one from you as well."

I lowered my face to his crease and blew on his hole again, which puckered nicely for me again. I brushed his rim with my lips and he sighed and trembled for me. As I invaded him with my tongue, he gasped and cried out weakly in passion. His hole spread wide. He started to squirm and his knees scrabbled against the surface of the massage table, but I held him firm with my hands on his hips, not wanting him to rub his thin-skinned knees raw.

"Deeper, deeper," he cried out, and then "Ahh, yes, yes, yes," as I pushed my tongue far inside him and moved it about. I could feel him opening up more. I feared what came next, but he seemed to be opening enough to take me.

"Now, now," He cried out. "Fuck me."

We'd been here before. There was no talking him out of it. I mounted the table and then crouched down over him from behind on the balls of my feet, suspended my pelvis over his hips. He was scrabbling back at my dick with his long, thin, age-mottled fingers, managing only to grab onto my ball sack and squeezing, which brought forth a long, low moan of my own.

I placed the bulb of my cock at his hole and let his rim muscles pull that inside.

Weak as he was, he was able to arch his back and gasp his appreciation of being invaded. I fisted the root of my cock and moved the bulb around in circles just inside his hole, which opened even more. His fingernails were now scrabbling at my thighs, and he was yipping his little "yes, yes, yeses" and begging me to get on with the fuck.

I let my cock sinking in about four inches, and I started a shallow, slow pumping, which I hoped would satisfy him. But, as always, it didn't. He urged me on.

I got a hand under his belly and fisted his cock, putting a thumb over his piss slit, so I'd know when he came again. He'd never let me stop until he came again.

And then, as slowly and gently as I possibly could, I sank my thick seven-and-a-half inches inside him, being as careful as I could not to put any weight on his body. When I bottomed, he jerked, and I felt the wetness of his ejaculation burbling around my thumb.

"Now you," he murmured through a gasp and a groan, and he took my balls his fingers and squeezed and pulled on them, as I started a pumping action in as slow and controlled a manner as I could. Again, he insisted on long, deep strokes. I lost control, as I always did, however, much to his delight, and he cried out for me to ride him hard and deep, as I started doing just that, ejaculating strongly up into him in three spoutings just before my leg muscles gave out and I had to roll off of the table and onto the floor.

"Thank you," he murmured. "I live yet again."

I returned to gently messaging his muscles and working his joints, which had now become knotted again at the limited, but unusual exercise they had gotten during the fuck.

"It wouldn't bother me, of course, to die on this table with your cock churning inside me," Sir guy murmured as I worked his muscles. His eyes were closing, I could feel his thin body relaxing, and I knew he was close to the restful sleep that concluded all of our sessions and that, alone, justified what we had done.

"But where I would really like to die would be to die in Madeira. Ah, to die in Madeira," he whispered, nearly gone now. "Would you like to see Madeira, Keith? You know, that lovely island in the Atlantic off Portugal?" he asked in his last waking breath. He was asleep and didn't hear my "yes."

* * * *

I had assumed it was just the ruminations of an old and wasting-away man, but, much to my surprise, Sir Guy actually did own a villa high on a hill overlooking a yacht harbor in Madeira, just to the west of Funchal. And when he asked me if I would take him there and stay with him and massage and otherwise service him until the end came, I didn't think very long and hard before saying yes.

I'd grown weary of making a living of fucking middle-aged businessmen sneaking down from London, Sir Guy had offered me more than that and the sporadic physical therapy appointments combined, and I could do my writing in Madeira as well as anywhere else—perhaps better, as new experiences would be all around me. Who wanted to read about pounding between the thighs of middle-aged men in the rooms above a Reading gay bar anyway? In any event, I didn't think Sir Guy would be long for this world now, and I was fond of him and thought he deserved to go where he wanted to go to die. It wouldn't be much of a demand on my time.

It turned out to be a bit more demanding of my time and of my hard cock than I had thought it would be. The breezes wafting through Sir Guy's open-walled villa hovering above the Atlantic restored his stamina considerably. I did think in the first week or two that this was just one of those fake flame-ups of vitality that often happened just before someone died, but it went on for months rather than weeks.

We were isolated up in the villa, just Sir Guy and me, other than the servants, who were not often seen and who spoke little English even when I encountered them. They all seem to glance down and away toward the marble-tiled floors whenever we passed in the hall. They surely knew why I was there and what I was to Sir Guy, but they chose to act as if I wasn't present at all. I began to feel stifled and trapped, but Sir Guy, sensing that I had become tense, alleviated my fears by giving me a tidy enough sum to return to England on my own any time I wished and to reestablish myself.

I did find more time to write than I had in Reading, but Sir Guy's sexual demands on me increased. As frail as he was, he always wanted me to take him hard and deep at the finish. Each time we enacted that little death he increasingly sought. And he always managed to maneuver me so that I gave him what he wanted. We normally had two massage and suck and fuck sessions a day on the terrace overlooking the small yacht basin, and after the first couple of nights, he also insisted on taking me into his bed at night and wouldn't release me until I had side-split him deep until he had achieved that little rejuvenating ejaculation of his and had felt me cream his insides. Then he would sleep the sleep of the dead. But, miraculously, each morning he would be alive—feeble and thin and living the on-the-edge life of translucent skin and bruising wherever I had gripped him harder than I should in the depths of our passionate fucking—but very much alive.

And each morning over breakfast on the terrace, I would suggest that perhaps we should take a day of abstinence, that the rest would do him good, and each morning he would demur and point to the massage table and say, "That . . . that and your magnificent hard cock, of course . . . are what keep me alive. When you deny me that, I will surely shrivel and die."

It took no more than that to hold me there with him, as the weeks turned into months and approached three-quarters of a year. Surely, I thought, it can't go on longer than this. And then I'd always reproach myself. I didn't want Sir Guy to die—not really. He was a good conversationalist and had a sharp, quick wit. And he had been very good to me. My cock was for sale. If not him, it would be someone else—at least until I started to grow old as well and dry out and wither and blow away as it seemed Sir Guy would do on any given afternoon.

Still, I felt isolated and trapped, and after six months of waiting for what surely would happen before the next dawn—but that never did—I started to take long walks by myself. And in search of company, I started to walk down to the harbor village at the foot of the cliff. There was a small open-air café there on the harbor wall that I began to frequent. And I was not the only one frequenting it.

One such regular was another Englishman by the name of Reginald. He was perhaps five years older than I was, close to thirty surely. A fine figure of a man, his muscle tone enhanced, I'm sure, because he was a part-time fisherman. I understood that he also was an artist and had come here a few years earlier. He'd just appeared in the village, looking for work, and an old fisherman had taken him on. One of the café's patrons had whispered between his fingers to me of a probable relationship between the young Englishman and the old fisherman and had given as proof positive the fact that Reginald had inherited the old man's boat, preferred fishing spot, and two-room flat above the small sundries shop across the cobble-stoned alley from the café.

Some afternoons I could hear the Englishman humming and singing softly to himself in his rooms above my head. One of his rooms was all windows, and I could tell that he was using it as his artist's studio. And I could tell by his humming that he was in his element when he was painting. I knew exactly how that felt. That's how I felt about my writing as well.

After I had been coming to the café for a month or more, he took notice of me, and if I was there when he came in from his brief fishing excursion of that day, he would come sit at the café. In time, there was a day when the café tables were all occupied and he asked if he could sit at mine.

We talked briefly of England and were both surprised that we had come from essentially the same area. I was from Reading and he had come down from London to a cottage outside of Caversham Park to paint. And for extra money, he'd worked a stint as an orderly in the same expensive rest home in Henley-on-Thames where I had done my physical therapy.

Then one day, abruptly, while we were drinking glasses of amber ale, he said, "I suppose the locals have told you how I came to have that fishing boat out there and the flat above."

"Ummm, yes," I said, "There was something about an old fisherman who had befriended you and who you assisted."

"They put it that way, did they?" He had a little sort of grin on his face.

"Well, no, not exactly that way," I answered, a bit nonplused.

"I'm sure they told you that I fucked my way to my small inheritance. Isn't that the exact way they put it?" The grin held on his face but was a little tighter now.

"Well, ummm, yes, that's what they said. But, you know . . ."

"They have that right. Exactly right. I've been watching you, you know," he interjected. "Could it be that you fancy me too?"

I paused, wondering where to take this, deciding that honesty was the best route. I hadn't had any variety in my sex life for months, and as generous as Sir Guy was, he wasn't

214

exactly fully satisfying for a young, vigorous, highly sexed lad like me.

"Yes, I guess I could say that I fancy you," I answered.

* * * *

We fucked in the sun-drenched studio room looking down onto the canvas umbrella tops of the harborside café. I gasped when I entered the room. A single, narrow, cot-like bed occupied the center of the room, and facing that, in a great circle all around the bed, were oil paintings. All were of young, well-hung naked men. Some of single men in erotic poses. Others of couples or threesomes in various sexual positions. The paintings were very well done and very arousing, highly erotic.

We stripped and wrestled on the bed for some minutes, both tops, both fighting for control. But fishing was hard, muscle-building work, and Reginald eventually wore me down and got behind me, trapping my arms over my head in a strong arm lock, and working his knees between my thighs. When he had worked his hard cock four inches inside me, I gave up the fight and started working with him. I'd been fucked before, mostly when I was younger and was being introduced to the life by my father's best friend. But it had been a couple of years since I'd last been taken, and so it took Reginald some effort and considerable groaning and grunting on both of our parts for him to bottom inside me, and then to hold while my panting and heaving subsided. And then he ran a strong arm around under my belly and raised my buttocks to where he could rise to his knees and get firm leverage. That accomplished, he began stroke me hard and fast. His thumb came up over my chin, and I took it inside my mouth and sucked hard on it to keep myself from crying out at the mixed pain and pleasure of his throbbing plumbing deep in my channel.

He came quickly in a flood of semen inside me, giving me the impression that it had been some time since he'd had a man. I thought that this might be so—that he walked a thin edge in this small village, considering how he had come to be one of the village residents himself. I supposed that the villagers kept a close eye on all of their young men, even without having ever

215

said anything to each other about it. He must have been looking for someone such as me to come along for some time. All of his sexual energy must have been projected into these paintings of his. But now, for this moment, all of the sexual strength of him was concentrated on that hard cock working inside my ass canal.

After coming in several jerks, Reginald let me free of his tight hold and rolled me over onto my back, He sank down on the floor at the foot of the bed and pulled me down to him, his hands gripping my thighs. And I felt the warmth of his mouth come down over my cock, and he sucked me expertly to ejaculation, with his tongue fucking my piss slit as deeply as he could penetrate me there.

When I had released my seed, he came back up on his feet and pulled my body back up the bed, turning me on my side, and stretching down along my back, the two of us plastered close together on the narrow bed. He lifted my leg, and I groaned and grunted as he ran his cock back up inside me, the entry this time more of a glide, aided by the cream of his earlier coming inside me.

The urgency and lusting of our first fuck behind us now, Reginald took me again with more care and more deference, asking me what I liked and what I liked better. My cries of passion and the involuntary churning of my hips told him what I liked best. I arched my back and turned my face to him and we kissed, his tongue caressing the insides of my mouth and flicking back toward my tonsils, while he kneaded and pinched at my nipples.

Spent, at least momentarily, his dick softening but still inside me, he asked me what had brought me to Madeira. I told him of Sir Guy and my service to him and that I was only here until Sir Guy passed on.

Reginald suddenly laughed and raised up on an elbow and looked down into my face.

"Why that old fucker. He bamboozled you too?"

"Excuse me?" I answered. Studying his face, looking for clues of what he might be talking about.

"Sir Guy is why I'm here too. He brought me out here five years ago. He said he wanted to die in Madeira. He had sweet talked me to be fucking him in that old geezer's home of his in Henley. Said he wanted to die in Madeira and would I bring him here to do so? Made it sound like death was imminent. I'll bet the old fucker will survive us all."

I started to say something, but Reginald stopped tweaking my nipple and raised a finger to my mouth, silencing me. I sucked the finger and then another two into my mouth. I felt his cock stirring again, rising again inside me. I reached back and palmed one of his bulbous buttocks cheeks and held him close against me.

"Five years ago," and he laughed again. "Well, we got out here and he came to life again and wanted to be fucked hard three and four times a day. I did that for months, waiting for him to die. But all he'd talk about were these little deaths of his—*le petite mort* he called it—and how they brought him life. And then I started coming down here and found this guy who appeared to be in a lot better shape than Sir Guy was and who was satisfied with a weekly fuck. One day I just didn't climb the hill again and I heard that Sir Guy had flown back to England. So, he's still alive, is he? And still getting away with this trick of his. I guess now you'll leave him too."

Reginald was fully hard again now. He plopped his cock out of me, though, and stood up behind my butt beside the narrow bed. I didn't quite know what he was doing—at least until I looked out at his paintings and saw in one a couple in a position that Reginald was maneuvering me into. My left leg was stretched out flat on the bed, and Reginald grabbed under my hip with his left hand and lifted my pelvis, while his right hand pulled up my right leg and propped it up along his chest. Then he swung his right leg over through my spread legs and to the other side the bed, where he dug in his heel where the mattress met the box springs. As he was swinging, I was crying out and grunting, because this maneuver brought his hard, long cock to my entrance at a side angle, and he thrust inside me and started caressing my channel walls with his cock bulb in places and ways it had never been made love to before.

He was stroking me hard and fast, and I was letting him know that I loved what he was doing to me. But at the same time my mind was processing what he had said.

No, I didn't think I'd be abandoning Sir Guy any time soon. I was fond of him, and I didn't begrudge him his little subterfuge in his clutching at whatever life and loving that was left to him. No, as long as I could occasionally break away to be mastered like this by Reginald, I believed I would be happy and content on Madeira—and in Sir Guy's bed—for some time to come.

Patience in Cape Verde

Stefan almost had me that warm afternoon in the summer pavilion of the Eisler country house in the Vienna Woods. We had played two sets of tennis, stripped down to our shorts in the unusual August heat on the mountainside above Vienna, and I knew by the way he looked at me that he wanted me. And, truth be told, I think I wanted him as well. I'd always had those urgings, but I had never given in to them.

Stefan had been an exchange student at my southern U.S. university in my sophomore year. We had struck up a friendship, and I had come back with him to Austria during a hiatus in my studies at the end of that school term. I wanted to be a writer, and I knew that the broadening experience of a European interlude would help me in that. Taking up Stefan's offer to stay with his family had been ideal. They were quite wealthy, they came from a titled family, and they traveled all over the region and had been good enough to take me with them.

Their son, Stefan, had been quite a hit at my somewhat provincial university. He was so sophisticated and so worldly, and it didn't hurt that he was achingly handsome. Solid

Germanic stock. Blond and blue eyed, sturdy build and well-muscled. He was the star of our soccer team and had taken us to a conference championship for the first time in the school's history.

He perhaps was a little too urbane for the university community, though, and he had been invited not to return for our junior year. Our sleepy southern town was sexually repressed, and Stefan was sexual and sensual to the nth degree, and openly bisexual to boot. The rumor was that he'd fucked a good two-thirds of the soccer team, and that part of the reason for their success was that they were so besotted with Stefan to a man that they went into superhuman overdrive in their games so as not to let him down.

Stefan had propositioned me as well several times in that year, pursuing me relentlessly, trying to wear my resolve down, but I was too strong for him. I knew my inclinations were dangerously close to what he wanted, but I had come from the small southern town the university was located in and I planned to remain there to take over a business that had been in my family since before the Civil War. I couldn't afford to indulge what Stefan had to offer. I would marry a cheerleader coed from one of the other prominent families in town, live in a southern colonial mansion on a golf course at the edge of town, and raise my allotted three and a half children and one dog and two cats.

Still, Stefan was not the type to give up, and I was fully on guard for there having been an ulterior motive for his invitation to me to summer with his family. I hadn't been totally cold to him. He had been raised on his family's Italian estate, and he was naturally expressive with his hands. I had let him become friendly with his hands—and I had thoroughly enjoyed his occasional attentions in that vein—but I had not come anywhere close to succumbing to his expressed desires for something more between us. He quite well knew what my limitations were and why I had set them.

After the tennis game, Stefan and I had dove into the pool, in our tennis shorts, to cool off, and I'd left him there, swimming vigorous laps and retired to the summer pavilion down near the small lake and dozed off on a chaise lounge.

I awoke with Stefan's full lips on mine. This was farther than I'd ever let him go before, and he had caught me completely by surprise. I had in fact been dreaming of someone very like him, so I was slow to draw away—in fact, I was holding up my end of the kiss. He was leaning over me, droplets falling off his hard, heaving chest onto mine, and he'd run a hand under the waistband of my shorts and was fisting my cock.

"No, Stefan," I exclaimed. "Too far . . . I don't want . . ."

"Don't tell me you don't want it, Jackson," Stefan retorted in a low, guttural voice. "Your dick tells me that you want it." He began to stroke me, and my cock did, in fact, belie my interest. "Just let me jack you off. You're driving me crazy."

"Not what you want, Stefan. You can't have what you want. You don't want to just use your hand on me. You've been very clear in what you want. And I've been equally clear that it won't happen. That it can't happen. I've been . . ."

"Just a hand job," Stefan wheedled. "That's enough. No more than that."

His lips returned to mine, not wanting to hear me say no, and he continued to stroke me inside my shorts. I struggled against him, but not for long. I didn't answer him, but my body answered for me. It started to relax, and I emitted a little moan through his searching kiss. He pulled away from my lips and gave me a radiant smile of victory and moved his lips to one of my nipples as he unzipped my shorts and pulled my dick out.

I was panting and moaning as his lips moved down over my belly.

"No, no," I whimpered. "Just the hand . . . ohhhhhh." He'd swallowed my cock. And it felt so good. I'd stop him. In a minute or two.

But then I felt the pad of a finger at the rim of my channel, and that galvanized me into full defensive mode.

"No, Stefan. That's enough. That's way more than enough." I struggled out of his grip and launched myself from the chaise lounge. I stood there, trembling, as I zipped up my shorts.

"You want me; you know you do. I want to fuck you and you want that too," Stefan said in a hoarse voice belabored by heavy breathing.

"No, it's not going to happen, Stefan," I responded, making my voice as cold and as unemotional as possible. "I'll leave tomorrow, if necessary. But this isn't going any farther."

"You are a tease," Stefan spat back. "You can't be as strong willed as you pretend. You wanted me just now; there's no question of that."

He had more to say, but I didn't hear it; I had turned and was moving up toward the house.

Neither of us mentioned the incident again—and nothing was said about my leaving early—but Stefan was cool and on the edge of being dismissive of me henceforth. I'm sure that I was the first person, male or female, who had ever turned him down. He continued to be friendly to me in front of his family, but there was an iciness in the air that even they could not miss. I decided I'd need to try to make some other arrangements for my European sojourn at the earliest possibility. Stefan wouldn't be returning to my university, so it could end here. And with luck, the yearning that I had for what he was offering would die here forever as well.

Less than a week later, Stefan told me that he'd been invited to attend a night of the Wagnerian opera festival down in the Volksopera in Vienna and asked me if I'd like to accompany him.

I jumped at the chance, tickets to the Volksopera being very hard to come by.

The patron who had extended the offer to Stefan turned out to be an international financier by the name of Klaus Gehler, who had a very good permanent box at the theater.

Gehler, a distinguished-looking Austrian not much short of sixty in age, was an excellent conversationalist. He also was an extraordinarily handsome and well-kept man of military bearing and close-cropped steel-gray hair.

During the first interval of the opera, he turned to me and fixed mesmerizing pale-blue eyes on me and floored me in a rich, smooth baritone voice, "Our friend Stefan here says that you are looking for a broader experience of Europe, Mr. Taylor. Perhaps I have a proposition for you."

I was looking for a change? I hadn't said anything directly to Stefan about that at all; nor had he broached the subject with me. I felt the anger rising inside me, but I held it in. I obviously was in the presence of a highly unusual man. He exuded power and strength—and elegance and refinement. I felt I was way out of my league here. But if Stefan wanted to brush me off, I certainly wouldn't give him the satisfaction of stepping on my tongue in the presence of Gehler.

"Yes, I was looking into some travel options," I said. "I came to Europe for the summer break to gather experiences for my writing exercises. The Eislers have graciously shown me many of the major cities, but I would like to get a deeper feel for the countryside while I'm here."

"A writer?" Gehler said. "Yes, I do believe Stefan told me that as well. That would fit perfectly. I write too, but something entirely more dull, I'm afraid. In my business I have to keep up a constant and voluminous correspondence. And my secretary, Frans, has had to go off on a family medical emergency. So, I am bereft and just about to leave for my retreat. It would work out marvelously if you could take on the role of my temporary secretary. Just for a month or six weeks. I would promise not to overtax you—to let you gain considerable experience and have time to write up your own notes. How would that sound to you, Mr. Taylor?"

* * * *

I would perhaps not have been quite so enthusiastic at accepting Klaus Gehler's invitation for a temporary appointment if I had known that his retreat was on a remote island of the Cape Verde chain, off the coast of east Africa and well within the tropical zone. I already felt isolation creeping around me as we motored from Gehler's larger yacht in a launch to the small island of Brava, which was only accessible by launches.

It was just the two of us, Gehler and me, in the launch other than the silent Spaniard who had seemed to have been in charge of the crew of the larger yacht. He was dark to the point of swarthy, with jet-black curly hair in profusion on his chest, arms, and legs in addition to his head. He was perhaps something around thirty and what I would call sinewy. Not hulking, but tall and so muscle hard that the veins popped out on the surface of his arms and torso because they had no fat to travel through. He had large, strong, long-fingered hands. He was brown as a berry and moved in the rigging of the yacht with the grace and dexterity of a monkey. He must have been a brawler, because he had perpetual bruises and stripe marks on his torso and arms and legs. The other crew members seemed anxious to stay clear of him, although there was no question that they jumped when he said to jump.

My feeling of gathering isolation wasn't helped as we neared the coastline of the small island and I saw Gehler's red-tile-roofed native stone villa hovering over the top of a cliff. There seemed to be only a narrow pathway through lush semitropical foliage rising and cutting back here and there from the pier to the top of the cliff. Gehler had told me that he came here whenever he felt the need to be entirely cut off from the world, and the immediate impression I got of the locale supported this completely. There was no other sign of habitation as I scanned the island upon our approach.

"Leave the luggage, Jack," Gehler said when the launch had been lashed to the pier and we'd scrambled up on the dock. "Estaban will bring it up."

I felt that the vines, large-leafed plants, and trees were grabbing at me as we mounted the pathway, which I found strange, as the Cape Verdes were, I thought, semiarid. I remarked as much to Gehler.

"Ah, we have Miguel and his now-deceased father to thank for that. Miguel is my gardener. I originally had my retreat in Bermuda until it got entirely too crowded, and when I moved down to here, I brought Miguel and his father with me. They are Portuguese. The gardeners of Bermuda are Portuguese, you know. We also brought the Bermudan techniques for gathering runoff water, and Miguel and his father created this paradise of vegetation similar to what I enjoyed on Bermuda. Don't you find it intoxicating?"

I just murmured a response that could be taken either way, because my immediate reaction was that it was stifling and a bit intimidating, but upon further thought, I guessed that intoxicating was just as good a term for it.

We brushed by Miguel near the first terrace. He was fighting with a stand of bamboo that threatened to obstruct the view of the ocean from that terrace. He was stripped to the waist of quite skimpy shorts. He couldn't have been more than twenty-five, which came as a shock to me. To have helped established plantings of this maturity in an unforgiving environment, he must have come here to work when he was a child. He was dark skinned, although not as dark as Estaban was, probably mostly from the constant exposure to the sun, and he was rather small in stature, but heavy with muscle in keeping with the hard work he had to do, which must have redoubled since his father had died. I wondered if he was the only gardener now. The estate obviously was large. Of course the landscaping, apparently on purpose, was wild and unruly on the ocean side of the house. But I could see around the side of the house toward the landward side, where there was a more park-like setting short of what appeared to be high stone walls surrounding the grounds on all sides except for the seaside cliff front. The walls didn't help me with my feeling of confinement.

The villa was in a rectangle, the longer side toward the sea, and it was built around an interior courtyard, complete with stone flooring and a pond with a fountain and the ever-present overflow of big-leafed plants and exotic-colored flowers. Hibiscus, bougainvillea, lipstick plant, hydrangeas, and banana trees predominated. The lounge area took up the ground floor of the side facing the sea, with Gehler's study and a small office he assigned to me above. The opposite wing, opening out onto the more formal, lawned park area had an open loggia with arched doorways on the ground floor and two bedrooms, each with bath, above. A hallway stretched across this section facing the inner courtyard, and a balcony ran the full length of this wing on both sides. The short wing to the west had a kitchen and storerooms on the ground floor, with a large dining room above with a bank of arched windows cut in the stone walls on each side. At the west corner, where the lounge was located on the seaward wing and the kitchen on the west wing, was located a breakfast room and staircase on the first floor, and a servant's room on the second. There were staircases and servants rooms in the other three corner sections as well. There were two more bedrooms with connecting bath on the second floor of the east wing. I was not shown what was on the ground floor of that wing. The sturdy wooden door to that was shut tight and had a padlock on it, and all of the windows were heavily shuttered.

What appeared to be the only house servant, a small, yet nicely formed African with black curly hair and features that showed some mix with European stock, barefoot and wearing only an orange-red sarong skirt tucked at his waist, had met us at one of the French doors from the upper terrace into the lounge and had followed Gehler and me around as Klaus acclimated me to the house. Klaus told me the houseboy's name was Jolo, and he just lowered his eyes in supplication, without sound, when I was introduced to him. He appeared to be hardly more than a boy, although Klaus told me that he had had him for several years. In the kitchen, we found a hulking German of coarse features and heavy musculature, perhaps in his forties, who Gehler introduced as Gerhardt, the cook and general housekeeper. Gerhardt leered at me in a manner that made me quite uncomfortable, and I was pleased when we moved on, climbing the stairs to the principle bedroom wing facing the landward side park area.

Gehler said that I would have the second bedroom in this wing, right next to his. Both bedrooms had two pair of double French doors giving access to the common balcony on the landward side of the villa. Gehler told me that it would be wise to leave the French doors open at night to catch whatever breeze could be captured at this time of year. He said the thick stone walls helped keep the villa relatively cool, but that, of course, there was no such thing as central air conditioning on the remote Brava island.

Remote indeed. I felt the remoteness. And all there was in the way of servants to take care of this estate were the cook, the gardener, and Estaban, as the general handyman when Gehler was in residence. I was particularly struck that there was no evidence of any women in residence. It struck me then that Gehler's secretary was male—and even his temporary secretary—me—was a man.

Gehler left me to think my increasingly disturbing thoughts and to watch Jolo unpack my suitcases and occasionally give me a shy, appraising look. He really was a well-formed young man, although it still was difficult to think of him as a man.

The first evening went uneventfully. Estaban and Jolo served us in the dining room, with me at one end of a table capable of seating eighteen and Gehler at the other end. Gehler was in good form with his conversation, making every effort to put me at my ease and to give me a brief history of Cape Verde and of this small island of Brava. After dinner, we sat in the lounge and had coffee and cognac, and Gehler puffed on a cigar, and then he gave me a couple of hours of dictation of business letters that indicated that his business interest were far, wide, and highly lucrative—and involved some of the major leaders of European countries.

Then, declaring he was tired from the sea crossing to the Cape Verdes from where we had taken ship, at Marseilles, Gehler said that he was going to retire. There didn't seem to be any question that I was retiring too. Gehler had that sort of ingrained power and authority. He spoke and all of those around him served.

I didn't resent his presumption, because I was probably more exhausted than he was. He still looked fresh and vigorous. He exuded power and vitality and, I had to admit, a sensuality that I found alluring despite myself. He was an uncommonly handsome man, and extraordinarily fine of figure, especially for his stated age.

I showered, padded out of the bathroom, a towel tucked around my waist, opened the French doors as I was advised to do, and, dropping the towel at the side of the bed, sank onto the silk-sheet covered kingside bed, under mosquito netting, and fell into a deep sleep.

I don't know how long I'd been semiconscious and aware of the sounds wafting in through the French doors, but when I was fully conscious, I realized I was listening to the sound of full-throttle sexual taking from somewhere beyond the French doors. I was shocked to find that I had my hard cock in my fist and that I had come. I rose quickly, in embarrassment, closed both of the French doors and went to the bathroom and cleaned myself off and collapsed back in the bed, my sleep for the rest of the night fretful and filled with feelings of concern and guilt. For hours I devised ways of saying that I must leave the island immediately, but dawn arrived with no inkling of how I could politely do that without revealing what I had heard.

The next morning Gehler was chipper and moved energetically around his study, dictating to me and being more effusive and jovial than I had seen him in the short time we had traveled together from Vienna to the Cape Verdes. He was wearing a T-shirt and shorts, and I was impressed at how well defined his musculature was and how well he V'd down to a thin waist at his age. Even at leisure, he wore his clothes elegantly, like a model for an expensive men's store. I had no doubt that his clothes had come from such a store.

He made no mention of whatever had happened during the night—if I heard it from my open French doors, surely he did as well, as he was in the room adjacent to mine. And I made no mention of it as well.

The next two days went uneventfully, with him somehow getting me to talk about myself and my hopes and ambitions without him revealing much about himself at all. But he was a brilliant man, well conversant with the politics and economics of the world, obviously earning his position in the world of finance honestly. And all the while there was the sense about him of a commanding general, holding the lives of all of his soldiers in his hands. Certainly that was how the three servants responded to him.

The next incident in what I came to realize was my spiral down into degradation, occurred two nights later. I awoke in the night slightly gaseous and knowing that all I needed was a glass of milk, as this was what had always worked before when my stomach was slightly off—the cook was an excellent one, but the Portuguese-based food that was being served was slightly more spicy than I was used to.

I had already found and drunk the glass of the milk from the refrigerator in the kitchen when I heard the sounds—quite similar to those of the other night. The sounds of sex. I was drawn to the sounds, which seemed to be coming from the lounge just a short distance away in the wing facing the sea.

They were mere shadows, but it unmistakably was the form of two men, one large and one small, having sex on the carpet in the middle of the lounge floor. The smaller man was on his belly, stretched out on the floor; the large man was crouched over the smaller one, at the level of his pelvis. He was on one knee and the other leg was thrown across the smaller man's pelvis. One hand of the large man was holding down the thigh of the smaller man and the other hand was palmed between the smaller man's shoulder blades. The larger man was fucking down between the smaller man's buttocks at a side angle. The sounds I heard were the sounds from the smaller man of his taking. They were sounds of acceptance and enjoyment. I couldn't readily identify who was there—and I didn't want to suppose. I didn't want to know. Still, I felt the shock of discovery—of being an unwilling voyeur; of hearing and seeing what wasn't meant for me—and then the greater shock of realizing that I was finding this arousing sank in. I was fisting my cock, which was engorging, and I suddenly was aware that I was naked. I turned to leave, only to find that the cook, his stare a leer of lust and interest, was hunched in the shadows, at the door that must lead from his quarters into the kitchen, his eyes glued to me. I blushed in embarrassment, his presence galvanizing me, and I slipped out of a doorway into the center court and ran for the stairs in the far corner of the villa and then to my room. I closed the door firmly behind me and buried myself in the soft bedding. And, once again, I got very little sleep that night.

I wasn't so much disturbed by what was going on in the house—my mind had worked that out early on, especially when no women surfaced in attendance. But I was partly disturbed that I was exposed to it and that I felt so isolated and unable to leave the situation. And I was mostly disturbed because of its effect on me. It was arousing. I had worked so hard to sublimate all of my inclinations in that direction. And here my body was fighting with me for control, wanting to succumb to the temptations. The only saving grace was that I didn't seem to be a focal point of Klaus's attention.

I sat up in the bed, adrenaline rushing from having admitted it. I knew that Klaus Gehler was the center of this taking. I admitted for the first time that the sounds of sex the other night had been coming from his bedroom—must have been coming from his bedroom. And, despite the shadows, I knew that the man in control of the sexual encounter tonight was Klaus Gehler. I just didn't want to think of him that way— as a sexual predator. But, no, I had to admit that wasn't quite right either. I increasingly was thinking of him in sexual terms. And as being desirable.

I buried my head under pillows and tried to steady my breath. I very definitely was deeper into a situation that I found disturbing and threatening than I wanted to be. I told myself I must fight it hard.

The next afternoon, Gehler told me that we would take a couple of hours respite from the dictation—that he planned to take a nap and perhaps, after a lunch in the breakfast room, alone because he was more sleepy than hungry, I might like to explore the park on the landward side of the villa. He said he thought I had not had time to walk those gardens yet, and he was correct in this assumption.

The park was more intricately landscaped than I had assumed at first. There were several hidden gardens, set off by dense foliage along the sides and at the corners, just inside the outer walls.

Once again I heard them before I saw them, and I should have just turned and gone back into the villa. But I didn't. I was compelled to follow the sound. Gehler was sitting, naked, on a stone garden bench. Facing him, also naked, and suspended over his lap, was Miguel, the small, young Portuguese gardener. Gehler was holding Miguel's left leg up high under his armpit, giving me a clear view of his cock pumping up into the young man's ass. Miguel was transfixed. His eyes were closed, and he was fairly purring and moaning in pleasure as he moved his hips in rotation, providing much of the motion that moved Gehler's thick cock up and down and from side to side inside his ass. Gehler's body was magnificent. Powerful and well-muscled, his belly flat, barrel chested, with hard biceps and thighs.

The two were kissing deeply when I first caught sight of them, and then Miguel took his lips from Gehler's and moved them down to Gehler's left nipple. I gasped at first seeing that Gehler had a silver nipple ring in his right nipple. This was so incongruous with his elegant, distinguished persona that this, more than the sexual act they were performing, aroused me.

I gave a little cry, having no idea if they heard me—and if they did, it didn't interrupt the rhythm of the fuck one iota, and fled back to my room. And, I'm ashamed to say, I lay, writhing on my bed, masturbating myself to climax, thinking of that nipple ring.

If the man tried anything like that with me, I would leave immediately, I told myself. I would swim away from the island if I could find no gate in the stone wall on the land side. I would not be used the way that Gehler had used both Miguel and Jolo. Yes, I admitted to myself. I knew in my mind that the small figure Klaus had fucked in the lounge on the earlier night had been the house boy, Jolo.

Another week passed by, and, although I heard Jolo being taken in Gehler's room on occasion at night, Gehler had made no move to take me. I at first was relieved. Then as the week wore on, I wondered why. I was better looking, better formed than either Jolo or Miguel. I wondered why Gehler had made no move on me. What was wrong with me? It all seemed so peculiar, especially since, after working the incident in the garden over and over in my mind, I had come to the conclusion that Gehler had wanted me to see what I saw. He had suggested I take that stroll in the park; he had said he would be napping, which he obviously wasn't doing.

And in the nights, especially on those nights I could clearly hear Gehler having his way with Jolo—or maybe Miguel—in the room adjacent, I found I couldn't sleep—that I couldn't calm down enough to sleep until I had exhausted my mind and my body. I took to masturbating to the sounds of the sex in the room adjacent. I had always masturbated to release sexual tension, of course. I just had not experienced sexual tension every night before now. And when my mind was drifting off—and even in my sleep—I conjured up the spectacle of Gehler fucking Miguel in the garden. And, oddly, I focused on that silver nipple ring, suggesting deeper, darker aspects to Gehler. Thoughts in this direction were disturbing. But increasingly they were arousing and compelling as well.

I found that during the day, as I was taking dictation from Gehler, I would look up at him. And I would see him undressed, fucking Miguel in the garden or Jolo in his bed or on the floor right where I was sitting. And I would go hard. Toward the end of the week, I was thinking of Gehler fucking me in the place of Miguel or Jolo. I resisted the image as long as I could, but slowly and surely I gave in to my arousal. And all of this paralleled the transition from fear that Gehler would make a move on me to questioning and experiencing rising confusion and ire that he had not.

I was thus in a state of high anxiety and arousal on the night that I found Gehler taking the Spanish seaman, Estaban.

Once again it was something that awakened me in the middle of the night. The cries were loud and they signaled pain—but they also were steeped in passion. And I knew enough Spanish to know that whoever was screaming out was begging for more.

The sounds were coming from the center courtyard side of the bedroom wing this time. I took up my shorts and pulled them up my legs and over my hips and padded out on bare feet, to the balcony across the hall above the courtyard. Light was streaming into the courtyard, and I was surprised to see that it was coming from the now-unshuttered windows into the courtyard from what had been the closed room on the ground floor of the east wing.

I moved silently down the stairs in a corner opposite to this room and then glided stealthily through the heavy foliage in the courtyard until I was positioned where I could look into the forbidden room. I nearly fainted at would I saw.

The room was a veritable SM chamber of sex, outfitted with more sexual bondage and torture equipment than I ever knew existed.

The Spaniard, Estaban, was suspended from a beam in the ceiling by restraints that stretched him out and barely enabled him to touch the floor on the balls of his feet. He was naked, glistening with sweat, his cock hard and bent up from his body in an arc. He was swaying and writhing under the hard, but not too hard, lashing a naked Klaus Gehler was giving him on his legs and torso and buttocks with a multithonged leather whip.

Gehler's cock was hard as a rock too and was one of the longest and thickest ones I'd ever seen. And I felt my cock go immediately hard too at seeing that he had a thick Prince Albert ring pierced through the glans of his cock.

Estaban's chest and arms and thighs and butt cheeks were covered with thin, red welts. And he was crying out for Gehler to fuck him. And I hadn't been standing there in the shadows, trying not to let my shorts fall and stroke my cock, but not succeeding in the effort, when all of my defenses melted away. I shocked myself. I was totally confused and ashamed of myself when Gehler moved to behind Estaban and thrust his cock up inside Estaban's ass and lifted Estaban's thighs with his strong hands to give him deeper purchase and started pumping him hard. And I was confused and ashamed because I was wishing that it was me rather than Estaban who was being fucked by Gehler.

I turned eventually and fled back to the safety of my room again. And again, as I got to the corner staircase, I saw the bulky German cook, Gerhardt, standing in the shadow of the kitchen door and watching me. And he had a stubby but extraordinarily thick cock pulled out of his pajama bottoms and was stroking it.

Gehler carried on his by-day pretense for three more agonizing days. Letting me smolder in the imaging of him taking me, letting all of my defenses melt away into the desire to be writhing under him. In the daylight, he continued to be the distinguished, elegant, no-nonsense international financier of late middle age, seemingly focused on his business needs, me just any scribe, not better than any other. Only there to take his dictation and key his correspondence into the computer, print it up, and prepare it for dispatch the next time Estaban took the launch out.

I still felt trapped on the estate, and on the small island, accessible only by a motor launch controlled by Estaban, who was controlled by Klaus Gehler. But it wasn't the physical entrapment that was tearing me apart. It was the sexual need that Gehler had aroused in me. Something that went far beyond

233

Stefan's attempts to break down my defenses. My defenses were long gone now. I ached for Gehler. I fantasized my taking by Gehler, and this fantasizing increased by day until it was all consuming.

Thus, I had no defense, no hesitation, no internal struggle on the night that I heard Gehler softly call my name from beyond the French doors of my room. I rose from the bed, naked, and went to the French doors. He was leaning back on the balcony rail, also naked, hard, magnificently ready for me. He extended his arm toward the open doors into his room, and I slowly padded through the door and over to his massive bed and, trembling almost uncontrollably, lay down on the bed, stretched out, my back to the French doors.

I felt him come down on the bed behind me, stretched full length behind me, close. I could feel his throbbing cock pressing at my back. I felt the coolness of the lubricant and jerked and let out a little cry of pain and surprise as he worked that inside my channel with thick fingers. He was kissing me in the hollow of my neck, and the fingers of his other hand were running through the hair on my head. He palmed my head and turned it to his face and opened my lips with his.

His tongue became more insistent, more possessive, searching deeper in my mouth. I wanted to escape him, but he held me fast. And then I felt his bulb at my entrance and he was pushing in. I wanted to scream in pain and invasion, and I began to struggle against him, but he was too strong for me. He wouldn't give up possession of my mouth, and I was having trouble breathing. I writhed against him, arching my back. But now he had one hand under my chin, pulling my head back toward him, holding me in a locked embrace. His other hand was palming my belly, pulling my channel onto his cock.

The pain was intense, but so was the wanting and the pleasure and relief that it finally was happening. I could distinctly feel the silver cock ring rub against my channel walls as it dug inside me, and I was panting hard, even though he still had possession of my mouth and was making it difficult for me to breath. I never could imagine that a tongue could get that far into my mouth. Realizing that my writhing wasn't helping, I widened my stance as much as possible, willing my channel to

234

open to him. He was going to plow me regardless now. His long, thick cock continued to invade, to stretch me and move to new depths. Relentlessly.

I knew he was taking his time, waiting for me to adjust. Being as gentle as he could be. I'm sure he knew that this was my first time. I was so sure he would be sensitive to my needs.

But then his own lust and desire took over. He pulled his tongue out of my mouth, and turned me on my belly, without losing the several inches of purchase he'd gotten inside my canal. He pulled me up on my knees on the bed with that palm on my belly, crouched over my hips, and thrust hard inside me. I yowled and widened my thighs. He then fisted my hair and bowed my shoulders back toward his chest, and went into long, deep stroking into me, continuing doing so long after he had bottomed inside me, and long after my knees had gone out from under me and I had collapsed onto my belly. He was riding my hips hard and relentlessly. And I was making all of the sounds of full-throttled taking that I had heard coming from this room on my first night on the island.

I was whimpering and sobbing when he was done, and he just lifted me up and slung me over his shoulder and returned me to my bed to suffer throughout the rest of the night—and, incongruously, to long for his cock to be buried inside me again.

For three days and night, we maintained the pretense. During the day he was all business, but business with a friendly, fatherly smile. And he was attentive to my every need and solicitous of my opinions. He said nothing about the nights during the day, and neither did I. I said nothing because I was afraid he wouldn't be there inside me in the night if I spoke of it in the day. And each night he visited my bedroom and fucked me, in a different position, but always with an intensity that took my breath away and left me begging for more.

On the fourth night, he lashed my wrists to rings in the headboard of my bed. And when he was finished with me, I was visited, first by Estaban, who fucked me hard, and then by the cook, Gerhardt, who fucked me even harder—no one coming to my aid at my howls of being taken like this.

The next afternoon, Gerhardt bent me over the kitchen table and fucked me again. And in the twilight, Estaban chased me down the pathway, reaching the launch as I did, and pushed me down on my back at the bottom of the boat, roughly forced my thighs apart and sank his knees and his cock between them. By now I didn't care. I was wanton. I wanted the fuck, whether from Klaus or Gerhardt or Estaban, it didn't matter. I wanted a strong dick moving inside me for as long as possible. I had shed the days when I had to pretend not to care, not to want to be fucking with a stud of a man. I wrapped my hand around Estaban's cock, trembling at the feel of the veins popping out on it and helped guide it inside. And I purred and ran my hands along the new welts in his sinewy arms and into the curls of his chest hair while he kissed the insides of my channel with those ropy veins of his cock.

In the following days, I sought out first Jolo, in the laundry room, and then Miguel, in a flower bed, and I showed that I could fuck cries of passion out of a man too. Now, when Klaus or Estaban or Gerhardt left my bed at night, Jolo would creep into it and receive what I had so recently been given.

On the eighth night, Klaus introduced me to his room of toys on the ground floor of the east wing.

After he returned me to my bed, he came down behind me, entered me in a side split, kissed and tongued the thin, red welts on my shoulders, and gently stroked deep inside me. He put his lips close to my ear and said, "Stefan arrives tomorrow. He wants to know if you will let him fuck you now."

I murmured a "Yes, of course," and moaned at the feel of the silver cock ring rubbing against my channel walls deep inside me, never wanting it to leave me.

PACIFIC

Five-Day Liberty

"Man, how did you score five days of shore leave?" Navy E-2 Tex Collins muttered, faking a hurt.

"Aced the last three inspections and built up my days," E-1 Randy Harrison answered. He was standing at the mirror just a couple of steps from their upper-lower bunk on the destroyer, the USS *Deringer*, parked just outside of the inner harbor at Manama, Bahrain.

"You're gonna' miss me," Collins said, making his voice into a pout.

"Yeah, I know," Harrison answered. He came over and sat on the bottom bunk next to the legs of his bunkmate. Harrison was in the midst of decking himself out in his sparkling enlisted dress whites, having put on the tight trousers. The white undershirt and the pullover tunic and blue tie still were draped on the hanger hanging from the corner post of the bunk.

Harrison was young—not yet nineteen—and on his first naval cruise. He was straight off the farm, strong of arm and chest and narrow of waist. He worked himself hard and looked good. His sandy-colored hair and pretty-boy face had attracted plenty of attention on their other berthings on the *Deringer*'s Mideast cruise, and Randy was pretty sure he could score well here.

Collins, older and wiser, had only managed to pull down two evenings of shore leave, and he didn't want to waste them yet. The *Deringer* would be in port at Bahrain's capital city in the Persian Gulf for a week.

The day was hot, and Collins was stripped down to athletic shorts, but still his dark, hair-matted chest was beaded in sweat.

"I know what you're gonna miss most," Harrison said, and then he gave a low laugh and worked a hand up Collins's thigh under the hem of the athletic shorts and brought it to rest on Collins's cock, which answered the call.

"You bet," Collins muttered. "How are you gonna keep out of trouble in Manama for four nights?"

"I'm not, I hope," Harrison said. He was encasing Collins's cock with his hand and had his thumb on Collins's piss slit. Collins shuddered and gave him a dreamy look. "Some of the guys have been here before and gave me some spots to hit in Bahrain. They say it's the playground of Arabia, and I mean to see just how playful it is."

"You've come a long way, Randy." Collins said it in a low growl of a voice, his hips starting to roll, his well-muscled body tightening up. He raised a hand and ran it along the well-sculpted, smooth-skinned pecs of his young protégé.

"Thanks to you," Harrison whispered. He withdrew his hand from the leg hole of Collins's shorts, but only long enough to move it to the older man's waistband and to pull that down to below Collins's balls. The senior enlisted man's cock was at full staff, and Harrison began stroking it with his fist.

What Randy Harrison acknowledged was correct. He'd gotten and given head before he joined the Navy, but it had been Tex Collins who, on dark, lonely nights tossing on the high seas, had taught Randy that he wanted cock and how to take cock.

"You gonna come back here for the nights?" Collins whispered.

"Not if I get lucky," Harrison answered. Then he leaned over and took Collins's cock in his mouth and started to give him slow, languid head.

"Gonna miss you those four nights, son," Collins whispered. "Oh, yes, Goddd . . . just like that. Softest mouth on the ship."

* * * *

Even with the address and the directions, Randy had a hard time finding the club. It was tucked away in a walk-down staircase from a parking deck under one of the new skyscrapers that had been thrown up almost overnight, mostly by Sudanese construction workers, in the cash-rich Gulf island state. Although there were cars in the garage, many of them stretch limousines with smoked windows, there didn't seem to be too many, and there wasn't anyone around—or there didn't seem to be anyone around.

Randy did sense that he was being watched as he moved across the concrete-encased cavern, but he didn't mind. He was here to be seen. He was decked out in his sparkling navy whites, and he knew he looked good in them. He moved into a strut, heading for the back corner of the garage, where he saw the innocuous sign with the words "Club Emile" on it, above a staircase leading down into the darkness.

On the half level below the staircase, Randy found a guy lounging against the rail who straightened up as he approached and gave him the once over. Liking what he saw, he smiled and beckoned Randy to continue down the stairs.

At the bottom of the stairway was a red door with another bouncer standing in front of it. He smiled as well and opened the door for Randy.

Beyond the door, Randy was standing on a landing yet another level above the floor of a whole other world than the one he had left. The smoke-filled room below was teeming with men. There was a lighted center area with a four-sided bar as its axis. Four silver poles ran up at the corners of the bar to the ceiling two stories up, and nearly naked young men were dancing the poles. Randy could hardly see the floor itself for the number of men swirling around, dancing to the music here—and engaged in close conversations there.

Some of the men were in jeans and T-shirts, but probably more than half wore the traditional *galabiya*, the long, white tunic of the Arabic Peninsula. The staircase Randy stood on was flat against one wall. The other three sides of the room each supported a two-story gallery supported on Moorish arches. These galleries were deep and in the shadows. There were banquette booths with tables along the back walls of these galleries on both levels, and Randy saw that many of them were occupied by men as well.

The liquor and tobacco—and recreational drugs as well—were openly in evidence, which, in itself would be enough to elicit a raid by the authorities—if Bahrain wasn't the region's wink-wink playground, and if the Bahrain authorities weren't very much cognizant and heavily invested in tucked-away clubs like this. The decibel level, when the conversation babble and the music the pole dancers were swaying to were taken into account, probably could be heard across the gulf in Iran.

The *Deringer* had just reached port today, and most of the sailors were husbanding the little shore leave they had, so Randy was the first spiffy U.S. naval sailor to reach this club during this port call. Many of the heads snapped around to take his striking figure in as he stood at the top of the stairs getting his bearings, and there was little doubt that Randy would not have to be buying his own drinks this evening.

Randy descended the stairs and walked over to the bar. A path opened for him as other men turned to give him an assessing stare—many wondering what his preferences were and what their chances were of being able to fulfill them.

Randy found an empty stool, perched on it, and signaled to the barman. But the time the barman had reached him, there was a middle-aged Arab in a galabiya at his side offering to pay for his first drink in salute to the U.S. Navy, and Randy thanked him without enthusiasm or encouragement, but nonetheless took the free beer offered.

He watched the young men on the poles—two Arabs, an African, and what was probably a Russian, for a few minutes while he got his bearings. Then he turned and surveyed the crowd. He was looking for something in particular, although he didn't want it this early in the evening. This was the first few hours of the first night of his liberty. He wanted to just feel free of the confining ship for a few hours—and to revel in the looks he was getting. He was probably the youngest man in the club, and he knew he looked good. He knew that two-thirds of these men wanted to fuck him—and he knew that two-thirds of them would also be happy to have him fuck them.

Most of them were Arabs, though. Randy hadn't come here to hook up with an Arab. He knew that's mostly what he'd find here in Bahrain, but he hadn't picked the port call. He would have been happier to be cruising in Scandinavian waters. He wanted a big man. A big muscled man with a big dick—like Tex was. But he also wanted a rich guy. He didn't really want to go back to the ship on the nights. And he didn't want to sleep in a flea-bag hotel, either, although from his walk in from the docks, he wondered if there were any hotel rooms in this town that went for less than $500 a night. He wanted a good-looking, preferably older guy—in his thirties, maybe—who oozed of money. And a European or an American.

He realized that most of these guys were Arabs—but he set himself to look right through them in search of the face and figure and style of the guy he was looking forward to sharing a free bed with tonight. But later. Not right away.

It wasn't long before Randy saw him. An elegantly dressed, distinguished-looking European who was perhaps in his early forties—graying at the temples, but filling out his suit like his body was pampered and well worked. He was sitting at a table inside the center area by the north gallery. He was with two other men, both Arabs, one in a Western-cut suit and the other in a galabiya. But all of them looked rich. Obviously a business meeting set to end with young men in their beds.

Randy had noticed the man, because he had already noticed Randy first. He was carrying on a conversation with his colleagues, but his eyes were on Randy. And Randy could see from the way the man's eyes were slitted and the flare of his patrician nostrils that he was interested.

It was too soon, but if, in an hour or so, the man had made an overture, Randy thought he was possibly the one to take him home.

Randy turned back to the bar to find a thuggish muscle man in black suit and black skin standing beside his stool.

"The shaykh would like to invite you to his table," the man said in heavily accented English. Randy couldn't determine the origin of his accent. Randy was from the Midwest; he had no interest in, or understanding of, foreign accents.

"Oh, he would, would he? I'm sort of still just looking around thank . . ." Randy stopped, because the thug had moved the lapel of his black suit to show the handle of what was causing the bulge at his left armpit. Randy got the subtle message.

"The shaykh would like to invite you to his table," the man repeated in a monotone.

As Randy was led toward the gallery at the western wall, he saw that only one of the banquettes in the section they were approaching was occupied. The surrounding tables were empty, which was rather a surprise in a room this crowded. Randy got the message that not only did this shaykh guy have muscle, but he also had clout.

Unfortunately, the guy sitting at the banquette who appeared to be the shaykh not only was Arab, but he also was wearing a white galabiya. He wasn't alone. There was a young guy in jeans, his T-shirt off, the Arab's hands on his chest and belly, sitting with him as Randy and the black-suited black man approached, but the guy in the galabiya waved to one of his goons from the group gathered at otherwise empty tables nearby, and the guy took the young man by the arm and pulled him out of the scene, with a farewell murmur of "Hold him for later."

Randy stood in front of the table, giving the guy in the galabiya a look see. He was maybe in his early thirties. On the thin side, but he had dark good looks, and he was groomed well. He also had an air of assurance that indicated he always got what he wanted.

"Are you from the U.S. naval ship that came into port today?" The man spoke good English—probably English English. Randy didn't know his accents, but he'd watched a few episodes of Masterpiece Theater. He thought he could tell real English when he heard it.

244

"Yes," Randy answered. "The USS *Deringer*. Good-will call in Mideast ports."

"And your name is, young man?"

"Randy. You can call me Randy."

"Well, Randy, you are a very handsome young man. Would you like to sit with me for a few minutes and share a drink?"

"Well . . . sure, for a few minutes."

"I'm drinking Scotch. Would you like that—or should we have another beer brought over?"

"Scotch is fine," Randy said as he lowered himself into the banquette next to the Arab guy and behind the round table. He figured if someone was going to pay for a Scotch, that would be just fine with him.

The Arab turned his face to Randy and gave him a little smile. His face was all right with Randy, but Randy still wasn't looking for an Arab to score with.

"Do you know what sort of establishment this is, Randy? Do you know that this is a men's bar—what I gather they refer to in the States as a gay bar?"

"Yes. That's what I came for," Randy said. The Scotches arrived and Randy took perhaps a bit too big of a slug of his and coughed. It burned like hell. It was probably the most expensive Scotch they served here.

The Arab gave a little laugh and said. "You can take your time with that. We can have as many as you want."

"Well, I'm only sort of just looking around at this . . ."

"Do you like men, Randy? Is that why you've come to this club tonight?"

"Well, yeah," Randy answered. "I know what kind of bar this is."

"And do you go with men, Randy?"

"Yeah, sure. That's what I like."

"You look quite smart in that uniform, Randy. Would you let me feel you . . ." he paused to watch Randy's reaction, and having done so and seen nothing that dissuaded him, continued, "for, say, $25?"

"Uh . . I don't . . . well, OK, for $25. Here at the table. Where it isn't too obvious."

No one spoke for the next several minutes, as the young shaykh turned to Randy in the banquette and, first, ran his hand up under the hem of Randy's naval tunic and undershirt and felt his hard stomach and chest muscles and lingered momentarily at his nipples. Randy worked at keeping his breath steady. Then the hand undid his belt and unzipped his tight trousers and palmed his cock.

"Yes, very nice. As nice as it promised to be," the shaykh murmured as he withdrew his hand. "Robert, $25, please, for this young man."

One of the thugs stepped forward with a wallet and doled out $25 in U.S. currency and laid it on the table in front of Randy.

"Would you like to feel me, Randy?" the shaykh asked.

"Well . . . I don't . . ."

"For another $25?"

Randy didn't say no, so the shaykh took Randy's hand in one of his and lifted up the hem of his galabiya with the other hand. Randy was a little surprised to feel naked flesh when his hand was put on the Arab's thigh, and he didn't encounter any undergarments on his way to the cock and balls. The shaykh held Randy's hand on his cock with his own hand.

"Is it satisfactory? You see it already is hard. Would you suck me for $100?"

"Here? Now?"

"You do give blow jobs, don't you?"

"Well, sure. But here, now? I'm sorry, but the evening's just begun. Maybe later, if I'm still around. No offence. It's a very nice cock. But the evening's still young."

"A hand job then. $50 for a hand job—on top of the $50 you're already getting. That's $100 for a fast trick. Very quick, then I'll let you go do your cruising, if that's what you want to do. And the offer would still be open if you didn't find something else you wanted. $300. I'll pay $300 if you let me fuck you."

Randy didn't answer, but he half turned toward the Arab and he started stroking the man's cock underneath his galabiya. The shaykh took his own hand away and leaned his head back into the padding of the banquette. He sighed and then moaned and groaned as Randy brought his cock to and then over the edge of ejaculation.

As Randy took his hand away and wiped it on the edge of the tablecloth, the shaykh opened his eyes and sat up.

"Thank you. You have a very nice touch. And you are a beautiful young man. Robert, please. $75 more for our young American sailor. And, Randy, I like you very much. I'll pay you $500 if you let me fuck you."

"I . . . I . . . really just got here. I'm just looking around at this point. But maybe later. Yes, maybe later." Randy stood and scooped up the rest of the money and stuffed it in his pocket after he had zipped his fly and buckled his belt again. Then he took a tentative step away from the banquette, looking from one thug to the other to gauge whether they were going to let him go.

But the shaykh signaled them away, and they all stepped back. Randy walked out into the center area and to the bar, without looking back into the alcove where the young shaykh was sitting.

He perched on a stool and ordered a beer and, seeing a pole dancer he thought was really cute, he watched him for several minutes. When he thought of doing so, he looked around for the European-type guy he'd picked out before, but he was gone and the table was now occupied by three queen types in ratty T-shirts, jeans, and heavily applied makeup.

Disappointed, Randy turned his eye on the alcove where the shaykh had been, but he was gone too.

This was just one of five bars Randy had been told about, and he was getting bored with this one, so he downed his beer, which he didn't have to pay for thanks to another unsuccessfully hopeful patron, and climbed the stairs.

He'd barely made it to the top of the stairs into the underground garage, when the lights of a nearby limousine flickered on and its engine roared and two thugs grabbed him from either side. The back door of the limousine opened as they reached it and Randy was literally thrown into the vehicle and the thugs came in behind him. The door slammed shut, and the limousine burned rubber toward the garage's exit.

* * * *

Randy was slung across the wide backseat of the Limo with his back hitting the corner where the top of the backseat met the window. He had the sensation that a crowd was milling around in that backseat, although the two thugs who had tossed him in the door and followed him were pretty much the bulk of what there was. Randy did see, though, that they'd propelled him past the seated figure of the shaykh he'd so recently given a hand job to.

The shaykh sat calmly in the middle of the backseat while one thug handcuffed Randy's arms over his head to a grab handle near the back edge of the ceiling, and the other thug was unzipping his navy white trousers and tugging them and his bikini briefs off his legs. One of the thugs was the black-suited black guy with the pistol at his arm pit. The other was an Arab. The money dispenser, Robert, was sitting in a jump seat across the wide expanse of flooring toward the front of the limo. He was just sitting there and enjoying the view. The young guy who had been taken away when Randy was brought to see the shaykh was naked and in a fetal position on the floor of the limo and forward of where the shaykh sat. Whether he was asleep or unconscious, Randy couldn't tell. Robert had a foot resting on the guy's waist.

"You have annoyed me," the shaykh said in a low voice. "We waited for you for too long."

"I didn't know you were waiting," Randy shot back. "No need for this."

He was grunting, though, because the black-suited black guy was fingering his hole with lube—and none too delicately. The shaykh snapped his fingers and pulled his galabiya over his head. Hearing the snap, Robert produced a condom packet from his trousers' pocket, slit it open, extracted the condom, and handed it to the shaykh.

Randy had the presence of mind to wonder if Robert was also going to roll it on the shaykh's rather normal-sized cock too, but it seemed royalty was able to do that sort of thing for themselves.

"You don't have to do this this way," Randy said again. "$500 is fine. I'll take cock and give you a good time. These handcuffs aren't necessary."

"You made me wait," the shaykh said. "I don't like that. And the $500 is no longer on the table now. Now I own you—if I like you. Otherwise . . ."

Randy started to object, but now he had two thugs at him, one on each leg, as they wishboned his legs and tilted his pelvis up. The shaykh came up between his spread thighs with his knees buried in the cushy seat.

Randy let out a gasp and a yell as he was skewered fast and deep and the shaykh started to pump him in quick strokes.

"You make too much noise." It was the first time Randy had heard Robert speak. Randy turned his head to find a cock being waved in his face as Robert hunched over him.

"Here. Suck this and be quiet. And be good," Robert commanded.

Randy did as he was told, and he started to let his hips roll with the fucking the shaykh was giving him. This was what he'd come out this evening to get. And this was kind of neat and arousing. Four guys all to himself. Him sucking one, the royal one cocking him, the black-suited black guy stroking Randy's cock, and the Arab thug playing with his balls.

The limo had come to a stop before the shaykh had ejaculated and Robert had covered Randy's chin and the front of his navy white tunic with his cum.

The four guys sat up and adjusted themselves. The black-suited black guy helped the shaykh put his galabiya over his head, and Robert was already exiting the car.

Randy took the moment when no one was paying attention to him to look out of the windows and reconnoiter. They were dockside in Manama harbor. Much of his view was blocked by a mammoth white yacht taking up a good third of the harbor and docked beside the limo, but Randy could see beyond it out into the outer harbor, where the USS *Deringer* rocked in the waves. So near and yet a world away.

"You may have him now, if you like, Tego," the shaykh said, as his two thugs helped him out of the back of the limo. Another one, probably the limo driver, an Arab wearing a galabiya, was standing outside the limo, holding the door open. "And if there's anything left of him when you are done, bring him to the ship. He still owes me a blow job—and Mustafa might be amused by him as well."

Randy eyed the black-suited black guy as he stripped his clothes off, folded them neatly, and laid them on one of the jump seats. He handed his pistol to the driver, who took it and also dragged the body of the young guy on the floor out of the limo and closed the door of the vehicle with an ominous click, leaving Randy and the black thug inside. The thug was a muscle-bound mountain of a man. And he had a big black cock, now in arousal, that put what the shaykh had to shame.

Despite the tenuous situation, Randy melted at the sight of the hunk. This was every bit as good as he had come out for today. There were only a few guys on the ship who cocked him who came anywhere close to what this black thug had.

The thug reached up and released Randy from his handcuffs.

"The shaykh likes it this way, but I like it a little different," he growled. "You make it to the door and out, past me, and I'll let you live. You don't even try, and you're a dead man."

Randy tried. But he didn't make it anywhere close to the door. Randy put up a good fight, just as he knew the black thug wanted him to do, but he lost, just as was OK with Randy. The limo rocked wildly, as the thug picked Randy up and threw him, butt first, into the center of the backseat—and holding his arms out with fists gripping Randy's wrists—forced Randy's thighs apart with his knees and skewered the young sailor's pelvis to the back of the seat with his cock. And he thrust and thrust and thrust, as Randy yodeled to the plush ceiling of the car.

While he was being fucked in this position, Randy could see up to the glass partition between the driver's compartment and the back of the limo. He couldn't see the young guy, but the head and shoulders of the driver could be seen in profile and he appeared to be humping something stretched out on the front seat. Randy wouldn't have bet against it being the young guy from the bar.

Then the limo moved like a wave on the ocean, as the black thug threw Randy to the floor of the vehicle on his belly, held the young navy man's arms pinned to the floor with his fists, and his pelvis pinned to the floor with his cock, and went up on his toes and proved he could do 500 deep-thrust pushups over Randy's body and slam down to the root inside Randy's hole with each downward thrust.

Randy didn't want to reveal it, but he enjoyed every thrust.

Then the thug let Randy put his now-rumpled navy whites back on for the short stroll to the yacht.

"You are good," the thug said. "We'll do this again later, maybe."

"What if I had not pleased you—or the shaykh?" Randy asked.

"You would not be walking to the yacht then," the thug answered simply. "You'd be fish food like the guy in the front seat's gonna be. The shaykh didn't much enjoy him. The rest of us are though."

* * * *

The shaykh's yacht motored out of the harbor and within hailing distance of the USS *Deringer* on its way southeast down the Trucial coast of Saudi Arabia toward the postage stamp-sized emirate that the shaykh could call his own—and where his command was law. Randy didn't see his home ship, however, because he was busy in the shaykh's stateroom, the shaykh on his back in the center of his bed and Randy, his hands tied together at the wrists behind his back, crouched between the shaykh's legs and giving him the slow head that the shaykh had asked for in the Club Emile and not gotten. After that, Randy straddled the shaykh's hips and took a long ride on his cock.

Randy did his best to make the servicing more than good. He didn't much like the idea of becoming fish food.

The shaykh had had a boy of his own lounging in the stateroom when the club party had returned, and this lad was none too happy to see the shaykh return with competing entertainment. So, after this one session and to silence the screeching of the jealous catamite, Randy was locked in one of the other cabins, where, through the night, he was visited by, first, Robert, who fucked him in traditional style, and then by the Arab bodyguard, Mustafa, who belabored him cruelly with a riding crop and positions Randy had never even imagined before. Later the black Tego joined them, and Randy was double-teamed the night away.

It had been the night that Randy had dreamed of having, this first night of his five-night shore leave. He hadn't been required to spring for a room—the appointments of the yacht were luxurious beyond his wildest dreams—he'd been well-fed with both food and cock, and he'd been taken in expert and imaginative ways throughout the night.

There were only a few wrinkles. He wasn't his own man at the moment, wasn't even in the country he was supposed to be in anymore. And he was steaming toward a country where the shaykh's word was unfettered law. These were pretty difficult wrinkles, to be sure, but he had three more nights of shore leave to get them ironed out. Randy was the optimistic kind. And he'd led a pretty lucky life until now.

Besides it was nearly dawn and he was still busy. Tego was sitting on his chest and feeding him with his cock, and Mustafa was busy trying to get both his dick and a dildo into Randy's ass.

And Randy was having too good a time to think much about tomorrow.

* * * *

The harem chambers Randy were escorted to after only a couple of hours of sleep were straight out of an Arabian Nights' fairy tale and had an excellent view of the shaykh's yacht—and another one that arrived in the late afternoon—riding at anchor in the Persian Gulf, from a belvedere, a covered porch, the only disadvantage of which was the iron latticework designed to keep the harem in and lusty marauders out.

There were only three other guys in residence in the harem, two young Arabs who chattered to each other in Arabic incessantly, and a morose European, who wouldn't even look at

Randy, let alone talk to him. Randy had no idea whether he could either speak or understand English, and Randy certainly couldn't speak another language; he'd never seen a reason to try to before now. All three treated Randy like he was temporary, and it pleased Randy to think he was too. He only had three days and two nights left on his leave pass. It would be murder for him if he didn't make it back to the ship on time.

Randy figured there was a women's harem here too, and from what he'd heard about Arabs, it stood to reason that they'd see the importance of producing sons even if their pleasures went in another direction.

He decided he was right, because they could hear the cat fighting from where he was and when he went out into the belvedere, he found there was another one right next to theirs and he could actually get a glimpse of women flitting around in the chamber that led from the belvedere. There seemed to be more in there than in the men's harem.

Randy thought they were being quite neighborly here, because the guards of the male harem included Tego and Mustafa, and Randy didn't have to get anyone else up to speed on entertaining him. Tego and Mustafa weren't shy about asserting their access rights to Randy.

He thought it was really good that the weather was so warm here, because they hadn't let him keep his navy whites. He was virtually naked in just diaphanous harem pants that hid nothing, a skimpy embroidered vest, and thick gold bands on his upper arms, wrists, and ankles.

That evening they came for him. He was taken to a covered pavilion overlooking the water, where a small band was playing weird tunes softly in the background and near-naked boys were passing trays to the shaykh and an older guest—a gray-haired Arabic man, not unattractive of face, who was burly but not exactly fat.

"Dance for them," Tego leaned over and hissed in Randy's ear when they had arrived before where the two men were reclining in a pile of cushions.

"I don't dance," Randy whispered back.

"You will dance tonight, or you won't see the dawn," Tego hissed back.

Randy was in a quandary. Three days from now he had to be climbing back up into the USS *Deringer* from a tender—or he'd be in a heap of trouble.

So he danced for them. He figured all they wanted to see was him move his body and swing his cock, anyway—and he seemed to be right; the two men seemed to enjoy him a lot, and they talked animatedly between themselves. To Randy's ears, it sounded like they were haggling about something and that the older man was frustrated and getting a little worked up. By the time both Randy's vest and harem pants had been tossed aside, though, the older man was all smiles.

Tego only had time enough to let Randy know he'd been sold to the older man before Randy was being bundled out of the pavilion by a new set of thugs.

The old man's stateroom in his yacht was more utilitarian than the shaykh's was, and the bed was in a corner rather than in the center of the room. There was a mat on the floor in the center of the room and a mean-looking hook in the middle of the ceiling with chains hanging down from it. And Randy soon found out that there were slots in his wrist bands that hooked quite conveniently in the ends of the chains and that, when he was hung from the ceiling, his feet barely touched the floor.

The older Arab had an amazing number of different toys to use on Randy through the night, and his cock was thicker and longer than the shaykh's too, so Randy's second night was just another version of how he had planned to spend the nights of his shore leave—and once again he didn't have to worry about room and board.

Randy thought this second night was great. The older Arab had made him come three times, and the hanging part was interesting and arousing—it was something he'd be unlikely ever to experience on board the ship. So, it was all good—maybe not every night, but as a new experience, it was just fine.

Randy was a seasoned seaman by the time his first cruise reached the Middle East, so he had no trouble, using his powers of observation and the "feel" of the float of the yacht, to determine that they were motoring northwest, back up the Trucial coast toward Bahrain, where they had started from.

* * * *

Bahrain, that playground of the Arab world, had a special beach, called the Shaykh's Beach, where the well connected could swim just like they do on the Riviera. In most places in the Middle East, an Arab man or woman who wanted to go into the ocean was covered nearly from head to foot, for modesty purposes and to keep the local Muslim clerics from separating their heads from their bodies.

If you could get permission to use Shaykh's Beach, though—and it wasn't guarded by anything more than common sense and the desire not to lose one's head—the women could go topless just like they did in Nice—and anyone could go bottomless too, if that was your desire. You could do just about anything you wanted there, actually.

Midafternoon of Randy's third day of shore leave found him lying on a beach towel on Shaykh's Beach, a Speedo at his side, his thighs spread open, and the thugs of the older Arab man who had bought him selling his ass to passing interested men by the minute.

Randy had to admire the way his new owner made his investments work for him.

The arrangement worked pretty well for Randy too. He was learning all sorts of new positions. He'd have Tex experimenting all the way back across the Atlantic.

The trip to the beach worked out well for Randy. There were lots of toys at the beach, and some Arabs who could afford them but had no fucking idea how to operate them.

When the two thugs and the guy who had been working between Randy's thighs had their attention arrested by the collision of two parasailers high in the air and over the water just off the beach, Randy merely struggled up from the towel and walked through what was a pretty crowded day on the beach and up onto the road into Manama. At the edge of the road, he stopped to put the Speedo on that he'd brought with him. He looked back to where he'd been holding court on the beach, and he saw his guards racing around and looking for him, but the numbskulls didn't seem bright enough to figure he'd head straight for the road.

Randy didn't know if Arabs knew anything about thumbing a ride, but he gave it a shot. A van stopped for him, and he saw too late as he approached it that the two guys in the front seat looked entirely too interested in the expanse of body his Speedo didn't cover.

There proved to be two guys in the back too, and they rolled the side door open, pulled Randy into the back of the van, and the four randy Sudanese construction workers worked over Randy's body in succession as the van drove slowly back into Manama.

* * * *

The third night of Randy's "liberty," although he wasn't thinking that word fit too well just now, found Randy in a small room at the back of a club in Manama, flat on his back on the bed, which took up most of the space in the room, and opening his legs to men who paid to get at him. The Sudanese in the van had sold him once again. Randy was amused to think that he was flipping over more transactions on the same piece of goods than a dollar bill moving around in a McDonald's.

Randy didn't mind it all that much. Three nights in a row now, and he was fulfilling dreams and fantasies that he'd conjured up all the way across the Atlantic and around the Horn of Africa. And he'd yet to spend any money on room and board. Of course he no longer had either his navy whites or the money he'd come with—but he still remembered his ATM number, and all he had to do was get to a banking machine and he'd have plenty of money to draw on. He'd have to think about those navy whites, though. He could hardly return to ship in what little or nothing he'd had to wear during the first half of his leave.

The guys who fucked him—mostly Arabs, of course—all had different techniques and fetishes, and he found the experience kind of interesting. Variety was the spice of life, he kept telling himself.

He didn't think too much about how he was going to get from here to the ship at the end of his leave, but he decided not to worry about that. He'd already been taken out of the country

256

and returned the next day, all without him having to do anything or to even worry about it. So, he had faith it would work out.

And early in the night it began, miraculously, to start working out for him.

The first evidence of this was when he looked up and found that his next customer was the European-style guy he'd seen that first night in the Club Emile and had decided he'd maybe like to have ball him.

And here he was, willing to pay to do just that. And he'd paid for an hour and a half of Randy's time, because he said he'd remembered seeing Randy and wanting to have him, and he liked to fuck real slow.

And that's how they did it. Randy gave him slow head to start with, bringing him all the way to ejaculation. And then, while the European guy was reloading and getting into the mood again, he massaged Randy's body and tongued him, all the way down to Randy's asshole, where he worked inside Randy's entrance and stroked his cock until Randy had come as well.

Early in the foreplay, the European let Randy know they were in the back rooms of the Club Emile, and Randy laughed at the irony that not only was he back in Bahrain but also back at the club from which he'd first been kidnapped.

Forty-five minutes into the session, when the European had just started fucking him, yet another fortuitous occurrence walked into Randy's lucky life.

He heard a voice out in the corridor that he recognized. The cocksmen on the USS *Deringer* liked to cruise ports in a pack. Chuck, an E-2, was the most forward of that lot. He was the first to head for the back rooms of a club to get a fuck. Randy heard him in the hall and knew this meant that other guys he'd fucked with on the ship, including his own bunk and fuckmate, Tex Collins, were probably in the club.

"Do you have some place we can really fuck?" he whispered to the European. "Some place less depressing than this? You could fuck me tonight and tomorrow night too—for free, for nothing more than a roof over my head and some food and beer if you have some place and will take me there now."

"I have a flat, yes. Just me. And I'd be delighted. But I know how it works here. We can't just walk out. You are money to these people."

"If I'm right, we can walk out, yes," Randy said. "And we should be able to get at least to the club floor easily. They think you're in here for another half hour. They won't be looking for you—or both of us—to be walking out."

The backroom guards did see Randy and the European leaving when they got close to the beaded curtain separating the back rooms from the club floor, but the two were out on the floor well before the guards got to the beaded curtain.

And Randy was living under a lucky star, because five of his burly USS *Deringer* shipmates were at the bar, in a group, and had already established a "don't fuck with us" zone.

"Hey, Tex," Randy called from across the floor. "Look what I got."

"The Frenchie looks good on ya," Tex yelled back, "but what is it with the Arabic nightshirt on you?"

"Long story, and I doubt you'd believe it if I told you," Randy answered as he and the European he had in tow reached the perimeter the sailors had set at the bar. "And long story short," he continued as he turned and saw the backroom goons approaching, "See those thugs walkin' on us? Me and this guy here need to get out of the club and away from them. Need your help."

"Sure thing," Tex responded. He had the other sailors formed into a wedge, with Randy and his friend in the center, in no time, and they had no trouble getting out of the club and past all forms of security.

In the covered parking garage, standing beside the European's Mercedes, Tex said he and the guys had to go back in the club. "Chuck's in there, and if he likes what he sees in back, the rest of us are going to dip too. We only got this one more night of shore leave, and we're gonna make the most of it. You goin' back to the ship now?"

"Nope. I got a date," Randy answered and he gave Tex a wink. "One thing you can do for me, though."

"Sure thing," said Tex.

"What's your address, stud?" Randy turned and addressed the European lounging against his Mercedes' fender. "Can you write it down for my friend here? And, Tex, I need a new set of navy whites to return to the ship in—no, don't ask; if you're good to me on ship, I'll tell you about it—could you bring a set of mine to this guy's apartment?"

"Sure. In the morning?"

"Yeah, if you can't be away from the ship longer—but I'll be there tomorrow night too—if I don't fuck up the hospitality."

"Boy, you know how to get the most out of a five-day liberty pass, don't cha?" Tex said, and he laughed. "Nice stud you got there. He should give you a good ride. And it only took you four days to land him."

"Piece of cake," Randy answered. "You have no idea what a ride these four days have been."

Curse of the Tan Tan

"Oh, Philippe. OH, Philippe!" The dark, handsome young Moroccan had been murmuring Philip's name when the American adventurer had started rimming him but was now crying his name out insistently as Philip split his curvaceous butt cheeks with his hard, throbbing cock and thrust down, once, twice, three times. "Philippe!" the Moroccan exclaimed and writhed under him with each deep thrust.

He was very good. The Moroccan bottom was very, very good—nicely formed and well-muscled, but willowy and compliant and with a boyish charm that was almost beyond handsome. Deep bronze skin, black curly hair, and fluttery eyelashes. His big brown eyes had a well-practiced "being taken for the first time, noncompliantly" look to them that was tantalizing to Philip. The exclamations of his name in French were very arousing to the American as well—a very, very nice added touch.

And the American was accustomed to having the best. The two young hunks were spread out on the wide, pillow-strewn bed in an executive suite of the Marrakech Millennium Hotel. The two had met for drinks in the swankiest bar Marrakech could provide, had eaten in one of the best restaurants in all of northern Africa, and had then moved to

Philip's suite at one of the hotels in the world, where Philip had quickly stripped Harun down, pushed him down on the bed on his belly, strapped his wrists to the headboard with leather bounds, and began taking him hard and rough. This had been fine with Harun. Everything had been prearranged. The American was accustomed to the best of everything, and Harun had been engaged from the best male brothel in the city.

"Philippe, O-h-h, Philippe!" Harun moaned, as Philip straddled his hips from above, a knee beside one hip and his foot planted firmly beside the opposite hip, as he fucked down into the Moroccan sideways from above. Philip liked unusual positions. And he was a connoisseur of sex. He had fucked like this all over the world. But this Harun was proving to be one of the best and most arousing.

"Call me Philippe, again," Philip whispered in a low, lust-choked voice. "I love it when you speak French to me like that."

"Oh, Philippe, Philippe, *mon amour*. O-H-H!"

Nearly an hour later, Philip, now stretched on his back on the bed and the lithe, flexible Moroccan was stretched out, belly up, on top of him, moving ever so slowly and languidly on top of the golden-blond studiously-muscled American stud. Philip had his pelvis plastered to Harun's pert buttocks and his cock was still churning deep inside the talented call boy. Harun's hands were now bound together and his arms were flung back so that his wrists rested on the back of Philip's neck, stretching his boyish torso out full. He had his heels dug into the bed and his pelvis lifted a bit so that Philip could thrust up into him. He was still moaning and groaning as if Philip was splitting him asunder, and, indeed, Philip had a tool that had that effect on most men.

Both men climaxed and Harun lowered himself onto Philip to rest, with the American still deeply encased inside him. Philip had the palms of his hands firmly planted on the Moroccan's nipples and was nuzzling Harun's neck with his lips and teeth, nipping at the other young man's throat to the point of nearly drawing blood. This was slightly painful for Harun, but he was a professional and the American had paid a small fortune for his attentions. Harun suffered far worse at the pleasure of the local, more demanding and stingy clients on a weekly basis.

Harun whispered above the sucking noises at his neck. "But I do not know why you tell me of this, Philippe, *mon amour*. This is something it is not wise to be mentioning at all in Marrakech. The Dakar Rally and its integrity are taken very seriously here in Morocco."

"I have money," Philip said with almost a pout in his voice. "All I want is for someone to take me and the Beast on the rally route for this year so I have a feel for how the course is. This is my first year. Some of the drivers have been doing this for years; they already know all about the conditions."

"But this time of year," Harun said insistently. "This is the worst possible time to be out on the desert in a vehicle. The Sirocco. It is . . ."

"I know all about the winds that rush across northern Africa and into Spain and France at this time of year." Philip said with a snort. He wasn't used to being opposed like this. Philip's father could buy Morocco if he wanted to. All Philip wanted was someone to guide him on the off-road vehicle rally course in anticipation of this year's dash from Lisbon to Dakar, Senegal, across the Sahara and down the western coast of northern Africa. And he knew there were rules against driving the course beforehand. That's why it was important to do so now, when the threat of the Sirocco winds kept prying eyes out of the desert quadrant. Philip had spent millions on the technology that had gone into the Beast. He had to win the race. And to do that, he needed to have a leg up on the others on the course.

"I'm sorry, it just isn't possible," Harun said, punctuating the "isn't" to end the conversation. He didn't mind getting fucked by this spoiled American; in fact, he rather enjoyed it. But he was a city sophisticate. The Dakar Rally was nothing to him.

"I'm sure there's someone on the street willing to guide me," Philip said stubbornly. "I will pay very well."

"If you go out on the street looking for this someone, you are sure to either be arrested quickly or get in with someone who will take you out into the desert and slit your . . . pay well, you say? Just how well?" Harun had just realized how many dirhams the brothel had been paid for his services this evening—more than a month's usual salary in his share alone. And such a waste. The American was so handsome and well

263

built that if Harun had met him by chance in the bar, he would have come back with him for free. But the American would have had to kept silent during the fuck then. Harun could hardly bear his arrogance and self-possession. The American was throwing money around like he had no idea of its value. And as Harun had already noted to himself, the Dakar Rally was nothing to him. He didn't care about its integrity or its rules.

"I'll pay $100,000 U.S. to the man who guides me and the Beast through the course to Dakar," Philip responded in a blustery voice.

There was a period of silence while Harun contemplated and Philip slowly fucked and chewed on Harun's neck.

"I'll take you there," Harun said at length in a quiet voice. "For that money, I'll take you there myself But how did your vehicle get that name?"

Philip laughed, happy now that he was getting his way. But, then, he always got his way. Money always won out. He pushed Harun up and off of him, waggled his baseball bat of a cock with his fist, and turned Harun back onto his stomach. "I named it after this. I named it after my cock. The Beast. I plan on fucking the competition in this running of the race."

And then Philip demonstrated once again why his cock was called the Beast, as he reversed himself above Harun, stretched out on his belly, and, once more pelvis to buttocks, but now Philip's hard, beefy calves encasing the sides of Harun's chest and his hands wrapped around Harun's ankles, Philip began pumping the ass of Moroccan prostitute-turned-road companion and guide again from above and down, while Harun writhed and groaned in genuine ecstasy under him.

"Philippe, oh, oh, Philippe," Harun was crying out. "PHILIPPE!"

* * * *

Three days later, as they approached the southern Morocco town of Tan Tan, where the desert dunes met the Atlantic Ocean coastline, the Sirocco hit them in a swirl of dust that obliterated their whole world. They literally couldn't see more than two feet in front beyond the mud-caked windscreen of the Beast.

"Quick, pull in over there. Over there, where we saw the ruins of a large compound before the Sirocco descended," Harun yelled above the whining of the dust-laden wind.

"Time. We don't have the time," Philip yelled back. "We're two hours behind my calculations of a winning pace. We must press ahead."

"We can't possibly keep going," Harun screamed back. "The engine will quickly clog in this dust storm. The dust will get into everything." And in fact, both of the men were already covered with dust even though the Beast was locked down as tight as a ship.

"No worries," Philip retorted with bravado and a grin. "This is a multimillion dollar machine. This has been designed for any . . ." The grin slid right off Philip's face, as a painful clanking and wheezing sound wafted up from engine compartment of the Beast.

"Quick, as I said," Harun persisted. "The vehicle—and we as well—need to get under cover immediately. There, there. Drive in that direction. Now! Oh, God, what was that?"

Philip had turned the wheel and headed in the direction Harun had pointed, but just as they saw a crumbling mud-brick wall and an opening big enough for the Beast to fit through, there was a swirl of something black and enveloping across the windscreen and the sensation of a flash of white fangs. Something was out here with them. Or so it seemed. But it was over in a flash. And whatever it was, it was as much beleaguered by the sudden Sirocco as they were.

When they had gotten through the opening in the outer wall, they were in luck. This was some kind of fortress from ages past and there were still some building standing with roofs on and openings on the side away from the direction of the Sirocco wind for them to pull the Beast in under cover and then for they themselves to grab blankets and some provisions and retreat beyond doorways with doors they could close and escape through a series of rooms to a sufficiently sheltered space to hold back the Sirocco.

It was dark in the room they finally entered, but only because the Sirocco had blackened the sky. There were several rents in the crumbling wall, which, luckily was set away from the wind, that the room would be lighted well on a normal day. They had a battery lantern with them, though, so Philip wasn't worried about the dark—at least for now, for as long as the batteries held.

When Philip looked up from spreading the blankets and fussing with the provisions they had brought in, he saw that Harun was nervously pacing back and forth from end of the small room to the other. Harun obviously was worried about something.

"It's fine," Philip said. "I've read up on the Sirocco. At this time in the season, this should let up in a couple of hours. A few hours and we can be on our way again. And we're almost to Laayuoune. We can reprovision there."

"I only noticed from the signs on the walls in the rooms we passed through to get here where we are," Harun said. And there was something dread-based in Harun's voice that made a chill run down Philip's spine.

"What are you saying? Where are we?"

"This is an old French Foreign Legion post," Harun said. "We're actually on a cliff overlooking the sea. The legion was here because piracy was rampant here at one time. The trade route goes right through here, and the pirates would land just long enough to snatch their fill of goods and slaves and be off on the sea again. And then they often sailed into the arms of other pirates awaiting them just over the horizon. There are several burned hulls of ships washed up on the rocks below this cliff."

"Yes, so?" Philip asked.

"So, there are legends about this place," Harun said. "The post was well manned, but one season it suddenly became deserted."

"Deserted?" Philip snorted. "So where did all the legionnaires go?"

"That's just it," Harun responded, and there was fear in his voice. "The villagers in Tan Tan had been having trouble with wolves, or so they claimed—and if there ever were wolves

266

here, the pirates must have brought them, because this isn't a natural habitat for such creatures. But some of the villagers had been found dead, their throats torn open and their bodies ravaged. But then their local magic men, you call them witch doctors, had the villagers stay close to the village and the village lighted with great bonfires day and night, and the problem stopped, at least down there."

"Stopped," Philip asked with a superior tone of disbelief. "Just like that? For how long?"

"Well, forever," Harun said. "Because they are still doing it, still keeping their village well lit. The legend was that strong. Men have continued to disappear from the village from time to time, but while the slave boats were passing, that was ascribed to the pirates or to warriors from nearby villages. And now when it happens, they just assume the men have been blinded by the promise of the big city lights and have gone to seek their fortunes. But legend was reinforced by what happened here in this fortress."

"What happened here?" Philip asked. He was toying with Harun now, mocking him. The man claimed to be a city sophisticate, but you scratch an African and they will go native on you in a flash.

"No one knows. There were thirty men or more in the legion unit here, but one day, when none of the legionnaires had come into Tan Tan to drink and fuck for some time, a few of the villagers were brave enough to come up here—but they found the place deserted."

"No doubt they just found the drink and prostitutes more palatable up in Goulimine and then found it was too long a distance to go back and forth and just deserted en masse," Philip said with a laugh. But then he went on. "You say there was no accounting for what could have happened to them?"

"Well, there is the cliff and many skeletons have washed up on the rocks below. But it would be unthinkable that thirty strong men would all have fallen off the cliff to their deaths below in just one season. And where there are ancient hulks washing up on the rocks, there are sure to be skeletons as well."

"A version of the big city lights as opposed to the dreariness of the foreign legion life sounds the most plausible to

267

me," Philip said with a sniff. He was fiddling with the lantern now. The light had dimmed. They may be in the dark soon.

"Shush. Did you hear that?" Harun said with a tremulous voice.

"Hear what?" Philip asked absentmindedly. He had turned to bunching up blankets on the uneven dirt floor and testing to see how hard the ground was. He had unbuttoned his shirt and stripped it off.

"It sounded like some sort of animal—a howl of some sort."

"I didn't hear it. And there's something I want to do now. Something I've paid good money for and haven't had since Goulimine. And I have no intention of going into Tan Tan for it in this dust storm, either. So get your sweet little ass over here. I paid for your ass." Philip stood and unzipped his pants.

For the next three-quarters of an hour, Harun's mind was completely absorbed by something other than the disappearance of the legionnaires, as he spent much of the time rolled up onto his shoulders and his buttocks up in the air, while Philip crouched over him, his thighs pressing in on the Moroccan's hips and his cock jackhammering down into Harun's ass canal. The American was paying well, so Harun writhed and whined and moaned for him. It wasn't long though before the Moroccan's grunts and bleetings were genuine, though. The American was an expert in what he did as well.

When Philip had had his satisfaction, Harun took a towel and a canteen of water and slipped out of the room, saying he'd find some corner to relieve himself and get cleaned up a bit.

Philip busied himself with eating some the delicacies he'd packed and checking over the maps to familiarize himself with the next leg of their journey. The light from the lantern was growing dimmer and dimmer. Philip hoped the Sirocco would give up its grip on the land soon.

He had no idea how long he'd been amusing himself before he realized that it seemed a long time since Harun had left. After several more minutes, Even though the light was nearly gone, Philip had recharged his own batteries and felt like another fuck, so he went looking for Harun.

They were three rooms away. Philip was so surprised by what he saw that he stood there, dumbly for the longest time, trying to figure out what he was looking at.

It seemed to be a large square of black silk mounded over something in the middle of the room and undulating up and down, the cloth rippling out from the center to the sides.

He must have made some sort of guttural noise, because the cloth suddenly rose up higher and swirled as a monstrous figure turned toward him. It was both man and beast. It had to be at least seven feet tall. The black material, which proved to be a cape swirled away from the body of the man beast as he turned and snorted and eyed Philip with great interest. It was the shape of a man, but everything about it was exaggerated, the whole musculature—big and bulging and plump, a veritable champion of champions among body builders—right down to the most monstrous cock and bulbous, low-hanging balls Philip had ever seen. The beast was hairy, black curly hair covering him almost to the point of identifying as nonhuman. But, no, it was definitely a man. All man—and inch and more a man. And his face was malevolence itself. Not ugly—in fact, square-jawed handsome in a wild, rugged way. But the eyes were red, blood shot, and the flashing teeth were white and sharp, with pronounced fangs . . . and they were dripping in blood.

That's when Philip noticed that the beast wasn't alone. The cape had been covering not only the beast. Harun, but a pale and diminished Harun, was lying there under the beast's crouched body. Harun's legs were spread wide and the beast was kneeling there between Harun's thighs. The Moroccan prostitute was white as a sheet and wasn't moving. He, in fact, looked entirely drained of life. The beast had a huge hand under Harun's buttocks, holding his pelvis up, and it was obvious that the beast had been fucking Harun when Philip appeared. And Harun's head was lolled over to the side at an awkward angle and his blood-covered neck was arched and exposed. His eyes were open and glazed, but there was a wan smile on his face as if he had supremely enjoyed whatever had happened to him.

A moment of sniffing each other out, and then the beast gave Philip a languid, very-pleased-with-itself look and then almost nonchalantly pushed the head of its dick into Harun's yawning hole and slowly, ever so slowly, made every inch of its cock disappear. Philip was panting hard and giving little gasps as he saw that huge cock slowly disappear inside the hole he had so recently been splitting himself. The beast smiled, eyes intently and warily watching Philip as Philip's eyes were glued on that huge tool moving slowly, deliberately, in and out. A flow of semen, much too full a flow for a normal man, was seeping out of Harun's hole each time the mushroom cap appeared, only to descend again in the slick lubrication of the beast's own cum. Whenever the mushroom cap slurped out of the hole, Philip could see a steady stream of white cum dribbling down from the slit. There was no reaction from Harun. He was slumped over, collapsed into himself, gone.

Philip and the beast were suspended in some sort of standoff. The beast seemed content with his total taking of Harun as long as Philip stood there in rigid shock. Philip broke the silence and the form first by screaming and turning and running for the inner chamber. He'd brought a gun in. All he could think of was that he needed to reach that gun.

The beast was loping behind him and gaining ground. Philip could hear its snuffling and heavy panting quick on his heels, and he had barely reached the door into the inner chamber, when his ankle was gripped and his body came crashing to the ground. He continued as best he could, the adrenaline pumping and moving him forward, dragging himself toward the center of the room, toward the satchel where he'd put the gun. And the beast was crawling up his back, covering his body inch by inch, ripping at the clothes he loosely draped back on his body after fucking Harun with its nails and teeth, stripping him naked.

* * * *

Philip collapsed on the ground under the weight of the beast when he was just a few feet away from the satchel. He stretched out his hand and felt the leather of the satchel. But he saw a long, heavily muscled, hairy arm reach up and a strong fist closely around his wrist, and he was being pulled back. Fully covering Philip's back, the beast wrapped his arms around

270

Philip's chest and stomach and was pulling him up onto his knees, hugging Philip's shoulder blades into its hunky pecs, holding Philip close to its chest. A hand went down to Philip's belly and then on down and took a firm grip under Philip's exposed balls and pulled Philip's hips upward along its own heaving belly.

Philip screamed as he felt the size of the beast's gigantic mushroom cap at the entrance of his ass canal, and then he cried and moaned, "No, no, no," as the beast brought him slowly down and down and down onto the semen-slick monster tool, impaling his ass canal on an impossibly long and thick—and well-lubricated—cock.

The beast had Philip entirely under his control now. Philip's ass was skewered firmly on its cock and his arms held the American close to its chest. They were erect, on their knees, but the beast was able to slide Philip up and down on its torso at will. The beast was simply too big and strong for the pampered American. Philip, arms flailing until they became too heavy and just hung down his side, gasped and groaned and heaved and panted and cried out as he descended on the beast's throbbing manhood. But the beast was almost gentle now. He was pulling Philip onto him slowly, making an effort to let Philip stretch as best he could, and he was nuzzling Philip's neck with his mouth, giving him a long kiss there on the throbbing artery stretching down his neck, just under the surface of the skin. A kiss of lips and tongue and then teeth.

The teeth. The teeth. It felt like only pin pricks, but increasingly Philip felt the sucking sensation, the feeling of flowing. His blood, flowing out of him. Draining from him.

The beast was making a low humming sound, a soothing sound—almost a lullaby tune. Enjoying its feeding in every way. And, having bottomed out and given Philip's passage walls an opportunity to stretch to him, the beast began lifting and lowering Philip on that massive cock. the black silk cape was rippling around the two of them, caressing Philip's bare arms and shoulders. One of the beast's large hands encased one of Philip's pecs and a thumb and forefinger were applying and releasing pressure on a nipple to match the rhythm of the gentle fucking and sucking. the beast's other palm was on Philip's lower belly, holding the young American close to him, and long sensuous fingers stretched to either side of Philip's cock and applying rhythmic pressure to veins at the base of Philip's cock that caused him to harden and ejaculate quickly and then harden quickly again and ejaculate again.

For the first time in his life, Philip did not have control. He was being played and drained. Completely defenseless and becoming increasingly so.

Philip was losing interest in escaping. The fuck was glorious, and he was growing weaker and more disoriented, but, at the same time, rising in arousal. The beast was filling him, deep, with one long, flowing ejaculation. And Philip's own cock was being milked again and again with great expertise and satisfaction.

Philip's head lolled to one side. He was loving the feeling of the flowing of the blood from him to the beast; he felt like they were one, supreme, well-oiled fucking unit. He knew why Harun had the silly, satiated smile on his face. On and on the beast was fucking up into him, reaching new depths with each slow pump. And flowing. Not a single, jerky cum shot spouting, but a flowing of warming essences. Philip's blood was being exchanged with a flowing of numbing semen.

The young American was drifting off and he was doing so with only the mild regret that he might not be able to feel the full effect of the total, possessing fuck if he lost consciousness.

But then there was a howling screech, and a tearing sensation at both throat and ass as the beast lurched and jerked this way and then and pulled out of and away from Philip and went racing out of the room in an awkward, bent-over lope with a deafening scream. Philip just collapsed on the floor, too tired and drained to move. But his eyes flitted open . . . to find that the room was now bathed in light streaming in from the chinks in the crumbling walls.

Philip lay there for some time, maybe even hours. He had no idea how long he was there. He only knew that slowly, slowly his strength was coming back to him. He managed to drag himself to the center of the room and eat and drink from the provisions he'd brought in. And, eventually, he was able to stand and to walk. He gathered up the satchel, remembering to fumble around and extract the gun he'd placed there.

Then, holding the gun in front of him with trembling hand, he tentatively moved out of the room. He instinctively moved from one well-lit spot to the next, not even consciously knowing why, just knowing somehow that that was an important thing for him to do. He could see his vehicle, the Beast, under its cover when he emerged from the building. He didn't fully comprehend what it was at first, but he slowly fixated on the knowledge that the Beast was his salvation and that they had parked it here for its safety. That's how he thought of it—that "they" had left the Beast there. But he was all muddled now. Who were the "they"? Had he come here with someone or had he come alone? He couldn't quite be clear on that. There certainly was no one else about now. And what had happened? He knew he was incredibly weak and that his ass felt like raw hamburger and his inner thighs felt sticky, but he couldn't fully comprehend what had happened—or how long ago it had happened. Everything was still a hazy blur. Oh, why did he feel so weak?

Something about driving to Dakar, though. He looked at the maps he had with him, and, sure enough, a road was marked that ended in Dakar. Well, he'd just get in the Beast and start driving in that direction. Maybe somewhere down the road his ears would stop ringing and he'd remember more.

But he wasn't even sure he wanted to remember more.

Ethiopian Cabin Boy

To my surprise, when I was training for intelligence gathering, I discovered that my line of work wasn't as pristine sexually as I had tried to convince myself it was. I should already have been aware of this, as I had already gotten hints of my spy masters looking the other direction during my assignment to Bangkok when it pleased them to do so. And in my training, I learned that they could be pleased to do so if the intelligence needed was considered very important and when the options of "getting the goods" were restricted.

I was sent into the Middle East and stationed in Cyprus, which is now considered in relationship to the Middle East somewhat like Switzerland was considered to Europe in World War II—a safe haven where spies can meet on neutral ground and where it is considered ungentlemanly (although it does happen on occasion) for "wet" (meaning doing someone to death) operations to be conducted. And it wasn't long before I learned how far I might be expected to go to "get the goods" in my job. It was also where I quickly found a new answer to one of three questions that had perpetually come up in the world of "bottoms" in my Bangkok days: This question was "What was your longest?" One of the other questions, "What was your thickest?" would also be answered when I lived on Cyprus, but during a different tour a decade later. The remaining question, "What was the most satisfying?" had already been answered years earlier in Bangkok in the form of a black Army officer (who, with his ten by two dimensions, almost answered the other two questions as well).

The "longest" question was answered in the form of an Ethiopian cabin boy on the yacht of a Saudi businessman at anchor off the Larnaka waterfront. This promenade, very European in atmosphere, enjoyed a deep, flat beach separated from a long hotel and sidewalk café front of gaily decorated umbrellas and tables by a wide boulevard. The boulevard was anchored at one end by a yacht marina and at the other by the medieval harbor castle where Richard the Lionhearted married his shipwrecked Berengaria.

After our encounter, the Ethiopian had me singing a couple of octaves higher than normal and walking around tenderly—although the later part might have been caused by the escapades later that night. I can't attest to how long the Ethiopian's cock was, but both my eyes and my intestines are quite sure they've never seen or felt a longer one.

When he took me, we were in a lower-deck cabin of the yacht, where you couldn't stand up straight except in the middle of the room. A double berth went in under the bulkhead. The Saudi owner of the yacht and I had just agreed on some successful business of a nefarious government nature, and the Saudi had been very attentive to me and let me know he wanted to fuck me. I had met him at a couple of embassy cocktail parties earlier and apparently had made a very favorable impression on him. I could tell by the way he looked at me that he fancied me, but I didn't make the connection at the time when I was assigned to contact him. My spy masters wanted the deal to go well, and I had been told to do what it took to conclude the deal—and I subsequently came to assume that my masters knew exactly what the Saudi businessman was interested in getting in return for his vital information. So, when he so directly propositioned me and connected it with his willingness to provide what I had come for, I said I would sleep with him that night on the yacht. Clearly delighted, he responded that, in appreciation, he'd send me a gift before dinner.

An Ethiopian cabin boy—not a "boy," of course, but an adult young man—had been gliding around the yacht all day as it wallowed off the colorful Larnaka waterfront, doing this and that. He was incredibly tall and thin, really out of place on a yacht with cramped head room, even if it was large. When I opened the door of my cabin to him, he was carrying a tray with a bottle of champagne and one glass on it, but I knew right away that he was my gift, because he was nude. His pecker hung down almost to his knees, it seemed—and this thighs were unusually long in themselves. I had never really thought about whether the unusual height on some African tribesmen had a relationship to dimensions elsewhere, but just then my education in that department lengthened considerably.

There was no thought of me refusing this gift from the Saudi; he hadn't given me the promised information yet, and this was no time to rock the boat—other than the rocking the Ethiopian was about to do with his performance on my body, of course.

I was still in just my Speedo, so there wasn't much undressing required. The tray also had a bottle of KY and a couple of condom packets on it, and the Ethiopian just slid off my Speedo and knelt there and sucked me hard, while pulling his own meat to erection. I fell back onto the bed, which was low to the floor, while he lathered himself and my hole up and rolled on a condom. He wishboned my legs up and out and I dug my feet into the low bulkhead that stretched out over the berth. He then knelt between my legs and just fed and fed and fed and fed that long eleven- or twelve-incher up into me.

At first he moved my hand to my ass and had me cup my fingers there so that he was pushing his cock through my cupped fingers, giving him a hand job as well as him giving me an ass fuck, when he entered me. I gasped as he reached a depth inside me I'd rarely felt before even though he had to go three inches through my fingers before entering me. But he laughed hoarsely as I panted and moaned to accommodate him. And then he brushed my hand away and I arched my back and cried out my astonishment and passion as he just dug deeper and deeper inside me. It wasn't all that painful, because his cock was pretty thin, but he had to have gotten well up into my intestines and stretched them out where they'd never been touched by a foreign object before.

I looked up as he was doing this, and the Saudi was lounging in the doorway, watching me get royally fucked. The Ethiopian pumped me that way for a while and then turned me over on my belly and got that cock even farther up into me, taking it all out and then just slamming all the way back in repeatedly until he needed to come. And he withdrew then, ripped the condom off, and shot off all over the small of my back. I was digging my fists into the bedding as best I could to hold position while he jackhammered into me. I'd already come twice by then myself, once with the help of his mouth and then with the help of his hand.

The Saudi just stood there and watched with slitted eyes, and he kept his hand busy with his own cock. His "gift" to me was even more another gift to himself. He really wanted his entertainment worth for those precious secrets he held, and the long, long Ethiopian and I gave him quite a show.

That night the Saudi and his bulky bodyguard did me in a sandwich in an all-night fuck fest in the main cabin, which was not nearly as cramped as mine was. The Saudi's equipment was nothing to write home about and he came quickly, but the bodyguard had a really thick piece and was a fast reloader and had a vigorous, long-endurance pelvis action. Lots of nice muscle. He's probably the one who was responsible for my bowed legs and shuffling walk—and big smile—the next day.

They did me in turn. Then, as a finale, the Saudi really wanted to get his cock in there with the bodyguard's, but I wasn't having any of that, needed secrets or not. The bodyguard alone was much too thick.

I never did drink the champagne, and I can only surmise that the information I collected was worth my effort—at least my masters were well pleased when I returned, and they asked me no questions about my use of trade craft in getting the goods.

To Serve

"I'm sorry, what was that you just said, Mrs. Pettington?"

What a tiresome woman. I had just now been distracted from listening to her by the way she snapped her fingers at Kisula and then gave him a distasteful look when he refilled her coffee cup.

"I said, Mr. Woolston, that I hardly think we need worry about these rumblings from the tribal huts. England has held this protectorate in Tanzania since the war, and we will do so as long as the London cafés need their coffee."

"I do hope so, Mrs. Pettington, of course," I said. "But still, I do advise you—and Mr. Pettington—that you'd best make contingency plans on sharing out the holding of your coffee plantations so that production won't lag, if the Nyerere government is brought in as rumored. I don't think he will rush to nationalize as long as we have a transition schedule that will continue to keep production at a robust level. The new Tanzania will need this trade just as much as the old one did."

"The new Tanzania," Mrs. Pettington snorted. "No such thing."

And then she turned to Kisula, who was standing, ready to serve, in the doorway into the residence and gave him the evil eye. "You aren't listening, are you, boy?" she exclaimed sharply.

"No ma'am," Kisula replied. "I am here to serve. But if you prefer, madam, I can remove myself."

"Yes, do," Mrs. Pettington said sharply.

I sighed and looked out from the covered veranda, beyond the long lawn, toward the shimmering, blue Lake Victoria. Sitting here, with the lush frangipani and bougainvillea clambering over the porch posts and framing what was, to me at least, the most beautiful vista in the world, I could only sigh at what was—in contrast to what inevitably was to be.

The Mrs. Pettingtons of the world would never see it until too late. We would not make the seventies—hell, we wouldn't even likely make the mid sixties—with the World War II British colonial system that was trying to hold central-east Africa together for God and Queen.

The coffee trade must continue. The Pettingtons were one of a handful of British plantation owners in this region of Tanzania, in the robusta-growing flatlands of Mwanza on the southern edge of Lake Victoria, who produced much of the coffee beans being exported to Europe. If . . . no, not if, when the native Tanzanians took the reins of the government at the end of a British UN protectorate that had gone on longer than anyone could have imagined it would, there would be inevitable and massive changes in the economic and social structure here. The Pettingtons must realize that. Surely they couldn't be that dense. I had invited them to come into Mawaniza, to my residence, to discuss this. And only the hard-boiled wife had appeared. The husband no doubt was sticking his head in the sand, full of hope and a prayer, on this one.

The others were beginning to sell an increasing number of shares in their plantations to members of the Sukuma tribe. The Pettingtons were one of only a few families holding out. But they were the largest of the landholders. They also were the most racist of them all.

"Really, Clive," Mrs. Pettington was whispering in an insistent voice. "Do you just let him stand around and listen in to your conversations like that always?"

"Kisula is—"

"One of them. A Sukuma. I declare they are going to murder all of us in our beds one of these days. And he's a big bruising one. And so uppity."

I was confused about what she meant by uppity—but only for a minute. I remembered how surprised she was when she had arrived and asked Kisula a question, and he had answered in more cultured British tones than she could manage with her Cockney background. Her attitude toward him had gone considerably downhill from there. I so wanted to point out that Kisula was the son of a Sukuma chief and therefore of higher standing in his culture than she, a butcher's daughter, was in hers.

"You don't need a native houseman, Clive. You need a wife—and Indian servants. The only trustworthy servants here are the Indians."

"Perhaps we should talk about the harvest projections before you leave, Mrs. Pettington," I interjected. The sooner I got rid of this horrid busybody, the better, I thought. Her milquetoast husband was so much easier to deal with, but it was a mistake to try to reason with either of them. Trash. These people were trash. Mr. Pettington had been sent out here precisely because he had married Mrs. Pettington. Lord help them if they were forced out of their holdings and shipped back to London. No, not if . . . when.

"First, I really would like to have another cup of coffee, Clive, if you please. Where is that darkie anyway?"

"You insisted—" I started, supremely exasperated at this point, but Mrs. Pettington pressed on.

"My Indian houseman would have seen the cup empty long before now. Such sloven fools, these Sukuma natives."

I rose and reached for the coffee pot in the center of the table, but a strong, brown hand was there before me, and Kisula was pouring Mrs. Pettington another cup of coffee and whispering deferentially, "Yes, ma'am, thank you ma'am."

"You *were* listening in, weren't you?" Mrs. Pettington growled. Then she turned to me. "Clive, really . . ."

I had a splitting headache before I could dislodge Mrs. Pettington. I also had heard more than I'd ever want to know about the status of the available and suitable young women from Mawaniza all the way to Mount Kilimanjaro.

"You are a sturdy and handsome man, Mr. Woolston," she had said, "and quite well fixed and stable in your coffee exporting district manager position. I can bring you into contact with any number of suitable young women. You must come out to Green Gate Farm in the spring. We must get you settled. And I have several very good Indian servants in mind. I . . ."

Kisula had diplomatically withdrawn from the porch as the sun dipped lower and lower to the west of the lake and Mrs. Pettington showed little inclination to leave.

I did not offer her supper, however, and she eventually got the message and huffed off in the backseat of her vintage Bentley, being driven by one of her stiff-form Indian servants.

I entered the house, and Kisula was standing there, looking sympathetic. I could not face him after the ugly treatment Mrs. Pettington had given him. I didn't know what to say. And so, as usual, I retreated into my English-bred refusal to face reality.

"I have a headache and it's been a long day, Kisula," I said. "I think I shall retire early without supper."

"Yes, thank you, Master Clive," Kisula answered in that perfect King's English of his, learned at a local Sukuma school as insistent on the fundamentals as the best of our British schools in the protectorate were. "Do remember to open all of your windows tonight and to close up the mosquito netting. It will be a hot night, and you will be glad of the cross ventilation."

I went to my room and picked up a novel, a new Irving Stone best-seller, *The Agony and Ecstasy*, the title of which made me laugh at the irony it evoked. It represented my current existence perfectly.

I stripped down and pulled on my sleeping shorts, taking very much to heart that tonight would be a scorcher, and I padded around the room and opened floor-to-ceiling windows. I stood at the windows overlooking the lake for several minutes and savored the beauty of the approaching evening. A light rain had started to fall, which was a blessing. The night now wouldn't be quite as hot as anticipated. The sound of the raindrops on the tin roof were soothing, and it didn't take long for my headache to drift away—along with all memories of Mrs. Pettington's horrid visit.

Drawing, almost unwillingly away from the window, not knowing how many peaceful twilights like this I would be able to enjoy in Tanzania on the cusp of independence, I closed the inside shutters over the open window and then padded around to the other three walls, each with two windows, and shut those windows as well.

The rain would have forced the mosquitoes into hiding out in the garden wherever they hid during a rain, but I knew it would only be a matter of a half hour or so until the rain stopped and they would start seeking out their human prey. I climbed through the gossamer mosquito netting, my Irving Stone novel in hand, and pulled it to again and settled on the white linen bedspread, not bothering to turn it down to sleep on the sheets and I was ensconced in a world of cloudy white, floating, as, after only a few pages of reading, I slowly sank into a peaceful sleep, in a world where there were no cares, no injustice in the world—and no Mrs. Pettingtons.

Hours later, in the dark of the night, with the crickets in full chatter, the shutter on one of the windows facing the front veranda opened silently, so silently that I didn't hear it. Nor did I hear the pad of bare feet on the polished wooden floor, or feel the added wisp of breeze as the mosquito net was parted, briefly. I was in such deep sleep that I didn't feel the crisp crackle of the starched white linen coverlet or my book being carefully lifted off my chest and moved to the nightstand or the slight creaking of the mattress as 180 pounds of muscle lowered itself beside me.

I did awake—nearly—though, to the strong arms embracing me and the hot breath of my lover on the hollow of my neck and his lips closing on one of my nipples.

I sighed in recognition that Kisula had come to me in the night. I had not expected him to. I had expected him to be angry at the way I had let him be treated by Mrs. Pettington. I felt so ashamed and so helpless. I could not expect him to visit me— my lover, my master.

But he was kissing me, and he slid his hand below the waistband of my night shorts and he found me down there and was bring me to life.

I moaned and turned my face to him, and we kissed. I opened my lips to him, surrendering to his mastery, and his tongue entered my mouth, victoriously. But it was not a victory of the sword. It was a victory of peace, of yearning love.

When his kiss had finished, I was moaning at his possession of me. My hips were rising and falling with the stroking of his hand on my cock.

"I'm sorry, Kisula," I whispered. "She was such a cow. I should have—"

"Shh, shh, Master Clive," Kisula whispered in that cultured English of his. "You cannot control it. It is what it is. But now is now."

I reached down and put hands on his hips, and, knowing what I was offering, Kisula rose and knelt over me, his knees on either side of my waist and his hands reaching for the top of the headboard above my head, as I raised my face to his fully engorged cock, opened my mouth over the tip of it, and began to give him deep-throated suck.

He was big—long and thick—beyond that of any of the Europeans I had been with before. And he was hard bodied and meaty. Not an ounce of fat on him, but a heavily muscled ebony beauty, chocolate brown skin with black tattooing. Who would have known that the Sukuma produced such magnificent specimens of men?

Or that Kisula had come to me, was showing me the depths of ecstasy I never before had known. The agony of being here, in Tanzania, at a pivotal time like this, when time itself held its breath, not knowing, not wanting to even think, of the dangers around the corner. And the ecstasy of Kisula devoting himself to me, giving himself to my needs. Making love to me in the dark of the night while all of Tanzania held its breath— imbuing me with Africa when his hot, brown, throbbing cock took possession of the very center of me.

Kisula was moving down my body. Kissing his way down my chest and my belly and possessing my cock between his thick lips, as I groaned and moaned my love for him. My

284

surrender, willing him to do whatever he wanted with me. His lips were moving lower, tonguing at my channel opening, taking my hands by the wrist as I moved them down to stroke the tight black, thick curls on his nearly shaved head.

I was writhing under the attentions of his tongue, moving my hips to his invasion and begging him to give me relief, to take me now, wanting the fullness of him inside me, opening me up, stretching me, and moving inside me, throbbing cock gliding along undulating channel walls.

But tonight, he didn't listen. Tonight he continued to fuck me with his tongue, bring me to the brink, and then send me cascading over the edge in a cry of passion and release of my seed up my belly.

And then he was laughing lightly and rising over my chest and widening the stance of his knees, pushing my thighs farther apart and pushing his knees under my buttocks, and causing my pelvis to rise to him. And then, still holding my wrists in his strong grip, he was entering me and entering me and entering me. I cried out a primeval cry in the taking, the never-ending taking, as he sank deeper and deeper inside me, spreading my channel, pulsating in its welcoming rhythm to the throbbing of his possessing cock. As he slid ever farther inside me, dividing me, splitting me in two. I began to moan and to groan and to move my hips, fucking myself on his gigantic possessing ramrod, begging him to take me to paradise.

He laughed softly again and began to pump me. And to pump me and to pump me, as my spirit floated up from the bed and out onto the lawn and then over the lake. Forgetting all of my cares, all of my worries, living in the moment of the magnificent fuck. Becoming one with Kisula, becoming Sukuma, becoming Africa.

I panted and lurched in answer to his jerks and murmurs of joy as he ejaculated in three forceful flowings deep inside me.

Later, as the first birds of the morning presaged the start of another day on the banks of the shimmering blue Lake Victoria, I turned my face to Kisula, as I lay in his embrace, both of us on our sides and my buttocks spooned into his groin.

"Kisula, I can't go on like this. I'm so, so sorry."

"Hush, hush now, Master Clive," Kisula whispered. "It is what it is."

"Kisula, I wouldn't for a million years. . . . I love—"

"Shh, shh, Master Clive. You must not say it. This is Tanzania. You must not."

"But are you happy, Kisula?" I asked, somewhat idiotically, grasping for anything that would make me feel better—not so much the ugly European.

"My cock is happy," Kisula answered "That is enough. Can you feel my happy cock?"

And I could. Kisula was hard again; his cock had been encased between my thighs under my balls and he had been slowly moving it back and forth, causing me to breathe heavily and to start to moan.

"Yes, yes, I feel it Kisula. You are so huge. I cannot believe that I can—"

"Mr. Cock would like breakfast, Master Clive. Do you think Mr. Cock could have his breakfast before we rise and meet the day?" And there was that pleasant little laugh of his again.

"Oh, yes. Oh, god, yes," I murmured. And then I jerked and grunted as Kisula raised my leg for greater access, and Mr. Cock entered me and started to greet the day, as I groaned and moaned and melted to my African lover.

* * * *

It was the most important meeting of my year. The inspection trip by the country director of the coffee importing company, Sydney Thornton. The company had the protectorate divided into two production districts, but Thornton's district was much the larger, and he was the man in charge out here. My district, covering the area on the southern rim of Lake Victoria, produced the robusta blend of beans, But this was less than 15 percent of our coffee bean exports from Tanzania. Sydney Thornton, from his own coffee plantation at the base of Mount Meru, to the east, in the uplands that included Mount Kilimanjaro, supervised the bulk of the coffee bean production in the arabica beans.

Sydney Thornton was a large, rotund man, of slow, cane-assisted gait and heavy breathing at the least sign of exertion. He must have been sweating up a storm under his starched white suit, but he somehow soldiered on, without mussing a crease or showing discomfiture in any other aspect than his "might this be the last gasp?" belabored breathing.

I greeted him at the top of the stairs from the beaten-dirt driving court to the veranda and we sat at the same table where Mrs. Pettington has so recently tortured me into a splitting headache.

I barely knew Sydney Thornton. I had passed through Arusha, where he kept his offices, while en route here the previous fall, and he had been polite and correct, but he had not invited me out to his coffee plantation on the lower slopes of Mount Meru. He had told me he'd been here since the Germans held the country and called it Tanganyika, that his whole life had been devoted to raising and perfecting the coffee bean, and that he wouldn't recognize England if he were suddenly set down in it.

I felt sorry for him now. What did a man like him do when independence came and his land and livelihood—and mere presence—would no longer be his to decide?

But still, he sat there before me, not even acknowledging Kisula, as the beautiful Sukuma man stood differentially over him and offered him his choice of coffee and biscuits in that subservient murmur of his. At the moment Sydney Thornton seemed to me wholly, painfully England and all that arrogant subjugation of one peoples by another represented. The specter of the Mrs. Pettingtons of Britain's colonial world rose before my eyes and merged with this lump of a man, in his perfectly pressed, almost-intolerably hot white linen suit, stubbornly forcing the reality of Africa to bend to the old-world demand of the British Empire.

And I snapped.

"I'm sorry, Mr. Thornton. I cannot pretend any longer." And I turned to Kisula and said, "Come, Kisula, come sit here beside me. We will host Mr. Thornton together as we are. As equals. As full partners."

Kisula's eyes opened wide and I could see him start to tremble. The whole, false world order of the genteel British colonial system was crashing before our eyes, here, on my Veranda on the shore of Lake Victoria. And a burden was rising off my shoulders. It no longer mattered. My job for the British system no longer mattered to me. I would take my stand and live with my banishment.

"Master Clive . . . No. You should not—"

Kisula was beside himself with concern. This obviously was too much for him, too soon. But I did not care. The Africans were going to seize their lands and their dignity from the white man, the colonial empires, one way or the other. I could not wait. I owed it to Kisula not to wait.

I laid my hand on Kisula's arm and reached over with the other and gently took the coffee pot from him. And then I pulled him over to the chair next to mine at the table and gently pushed him down into the seat with my hand now on his shoulder.

Kisula sat as if in a trance. His face was frozen in shock. I put a coffee cup and saucer in front of him and slowly poured him a cup of coffee. All the time, I could not bring myself to look at Thornton.

I started to speak. "I'm sorry, Mr. Thornton, but it's time for the change. We must change ahead of a forced transition that will take the company out of our hands, whether we like it or not. Kisula is the son of a chief of the Sukuma. They will own and control all of the coffee plantations in this region soon— perhaps within a couple of years. It's time to wake up to reality. Kisula is my partner. We can't do better than to start including him and the Sukuma in our plans."

It was only when I had finished this speech, delivered rapidly, almost in one breath, for fear that if I had stopped, I could not complete it, that I looked up, first at Kisula and then at Sydney Thornton.

Kisula still sat, in shock. But he sat tall. All of the Sukuma sat tall. They were a proud people, with every right to be.

But when I looked at Thornton, what I saw was not at all what I expected to see. He was smiling. Not a broad smile, but a small, knowing smile.

"I'm . . . I'm sorry, I—" I started to say, the horror of what I had done beginning to dawn on me.

"Not at all. I quite agree," Sydney Thornton said. "I rather hoped we could start talking about how we maximized our position in the inevitable transition to independence in Tanzania. I welcome Mr. . . . um, Mr. Kisula to the discussions."

I sat there, paralyzed at the moment. He didn't fully understand. Should I leave it like this? No, I had come this far; it wasn't fair to Kisula to leave it like this.

"I don't think you completely understand what I'm trying to say, Mr. Thornton." I said, and then I raced ahead lest I never would say it. "Kisula is my partner, my full partner. My life's partner. No, Kisula is the master of my life. If you wish me to tender my—"

"Let's have none of that, young man," Thornton interrupted in an amused voice. I was taken aback by the hint of a twinkle in his eye. "Perhaps, Mr. Woolston . . . Clive. Perhaps when you come up to Mount Meru next, you and Kisula will be kind enough to come out to my plantation. There you can meet my Maasai wife. She too is my master, and our coffee plantations are already registered in her name. You see, Clive, there's a reason I have never gone back to England in all of these years. I too, just like you, am now married fully—and quite happily—to Tanzania."

Disintegration

It had taken me three weeks to get to the real reason I knew I had been sent to Rhodesia. But here I was, in the lobby of Salisbury's Meikles Hotel, waiting for Section Officer Gavin Coetzer to drive down from Morris Depot along The Avenues to take me out to Alister's farm. I pulled at the tops of my long socks, still being self-conscious about the art of wearing shorts as every-day attire, as the well-oiled routine of the fine old hotel swirled around me, just as it had for over a century, and just as it seemed to intend to do for another century.

But I knew better.

That ostensibly was why the Foreign Office in London had sent me out here. They couldn't figure the rebellious Ian Smith regime out. Was he really trying to save Britain's interests here, or was Rhodesia, as he suggested, descending into chaos because Smith was being isolated? A bit of truth in all, I had found, although there wasn't much question that Rhodesia was headed toward chaos in any event before we saw the dawn of the 1980s. The vibes for native African independence were just too strong. No economic reasoning was going to win out over the thrust for freedom and independence.

But the real reason I'd been sent was because of the influence of the Earl of Devon. Lord Clarence had already

291

decided where Rhodesia was going, and he didn't want his daughter sinking into that pit. It was my misfortunate to be on duty on the Africa desk and to have once been engaged to said daughter, now Pamela Cullingworth. This was a memory I could well have done without.

Although I wouldn't say that I would have been miserable with Pamela, we were both marrying for convenience, and she was a distracted lass and treated me like a donkey—to extremes, in fact, at the time. For her part, her father, who was a stuffy, self-important Earl even in those days, was trying to marry her off as quickly and as well as possible to avoid scandal. She'd become inconveniently pregnant—although she mercifully lost the baby—which simply wasn't done in her circles in those days. And, worse, the man in question was an Indian—an Indian from Bombay. I rather suspected she seduced the poor lad just to stick it to her father's world.

For my part, I was trying to stave off an even more sinister scandal. I had fallen into one of those too much love on top of too much hate situations at university. Alister Cullingworth was a senior boy at my university, two years ahead of me and also the son of an Earl. Alister was insufferable because he was the son of an Earl, just as Pamela could be unthinking and rebellious because she was the daughter of an Earl. But Alister was even more insufferable because he was the third, "left out," son of an Earl. His life at school had been one of trying to make up for this and forcing the rest of us into his entourage. And he had the most maddening—and mad—ways of exhibiting this. I had felt well shed of him at the end of Alister's next-to-last term.

But I was wrong.

"Ready to go, Sah?" the blond-headed, beefy, thoroughly Afrikaaner Gavin Coetzer said to me from the lower stoep, the Afrikaaner version of steps up to the veranda, of the Meikles entrance. The query was accompanied by me a sharp salute and professional click of his highly polished heels. And very nice heels they were too.

"Yes, of course, Gavin," I answered, "and do call me Brian. I'm not even all that officially here."

"Yes, Sah . . . Brian." And then Gavin gave me a grin that showed that he was quite willing to dispense with the niceties for this little jaunt of ours—a jaunt that had played on me like a toothache all of the way from London. I liked his smile immensely.

"I do hope you don't mind going out to the Cullingworth farm, Gavin. I know it takes you away from your police duties."

"Yes, it most certainly does," Gavin said with another grin, as we climbed into the dark-green Land Rover. I was teasing him, of course. I knew he'd be glad to get away from the regimental spit and polish of the British South African Police barracks for the three days I planned to stay in Beatrice.

Beatrice, a good fifty miles south of Salisbury on the road to Johannesburg and straddling the sometimes Umfuli River, was the nearest town to the Cullingworth farm that had some semblance of a hotel. I had no intention of being housed by Alister and Pamela, and I needed somewhere I could hole up for two nights while I attempted to cajole a disaffected daughter to do what she'd never do if she knew that was what her father wanted her to do. This, even though it was obvious to anyone with eyes and good sense to know that Rhodesia was on the edge of disintegration that could bode nothing but danger for a British expatriate landowner trying to eke out an existence there.

As we turned off the highway to Johannesburg and started to bounce across the hard dirt road into the Cullingworth homestead, I could sense the tension in Gavin despite his free-flowing, loose discussion. This was a dichotomy that had hit me repeatedly during my investigations in Salisbury and that would continue to assail me at every turn: the seeming informal, slow flow of life in unending pattern in a Rhodesia that was, at the same time, one match away from an explosion.

I could tell that there was some sort of match like this under Gavin's tail as he not so cleverly quizzed me on my relationship with Alister Cullingworth and his wife, Pamela, the deceptively delicate and high-strung beauty queen that Alister had overpowered; snatched from both the afternoon teas in British palaces and, not incidentally, me; and taken off to a rougher, cattle-raising life in the dusts of Africa. I remember being amazed for several years that Pamela Cullingworth had neither returned on her own to London nor succumbed in the African veld. But, with Pamela, one never knew. I still, after all these years, don't know if Alister snatched Pamela from me or if Pamela snatched Alister from me. I only know I had taken the brunt of the game—probably from both of them.

His last term at the university Alister had decided that I was his project for the year. He pursued me, alternating between torturing bastard and best friend until he had worn my defenses completely down. And then one dark, rainy afternoon, he had gotten me drunk and fucked me on the narrow bed in my tower chambers. I'm sure he saw that as some sort of fulfillment of a campaign of domination. But at the time, I saw it as a liberation, and for weeks I joyfully spread my legs for him upon demand. The euphoria was short lived, however, as rumors started to spread, as they do at Oxford, and they were easily accepted, as also happens at Oxford. Alister was above such a scandal, but my family was still very much on the make in London society, and I didn't have to be told that I needed to scotch the rumors.

Thus the convenient engagement to Lady Pamela. Her family was relieved that at least my family had money and was on the ascendance, and my family was delighted to be rubbing sex organs with the entrenched nobility.

And that, more than any other reason, I supposed, was why Alister had decided that he must possess Pamela—because I had her and because he no longer had me. I couldn't think of any kinder word for Alister's acquisitions than "possessed." At least that was my take at the time. In calmer times, I had to acknowledge that perhaps it was all just another one of Pamela's bird flipping statements to all that was noble Britain.

"So, you and Alister aren't all that good friends, then?" Gavin said after I made my views of Alister as well known as I felt was politic.

"Oh, no, Alister has always been an ass. And he was very much a bother at school."

"Quite." Gavin said, putting a succinct finish to his view of Alister as well. "And Lady Pamela?"

"Oh, we knew each other at one time. It's her I'm here to see, actually. At the behest of her family, but please don't say anything about that until I have. I can't say that I have much hope of success in what I have to tell her, however."

I had no intention of telling anyone here fully what Pamela—and Alister—and I had once had.

With that, Gavin's tension seemed to evaporate, and we became quite good friends while bumping down that road.

As we came upon Devon Cottage, which was what Alister had pointedly named his typically British colonial-designed rambling stuccoed bungalow with broad verandas all around to fight off the African sun, I sucked in my breath and marveled yet again at another reflection of the Rhodesian dichotomy. We were driving out of the dusty range, where the only color and animation was in the Hereford cattle of the Cullingworth holdings—even the leaves of eucalyptus trees were a dull brown from a thick coating of summer dust—to a riot of color in the full-blooming hibiscus hedges bordering the bungalow's verandas, rising to scarlet bougainvillea vines on the columns and the colorful flower garden, a swarm with the miraculous flitting of butterflies, placed strategically, if somewhat forlornly, between the vehicle circle and the crumbling stone veranda steps.

Alister was standing at the top of the veranda steps—and sneering, the pose in which I could most clearly remembered him.

"So, ugly as always, Kennelly, I see," he said, that mischievous, superior sparkle still in his eyes—the rigors of the African veld had not beaten that out of him. "And my favorite policeman, Gavin Coetzer."

He turned then and spoke back into the dark interior of the veranda. "Come greet our long-lost friend and our very good friend, Pamela. Come all the way from London and Salisbury, respectively, just to pay their respects to us." This was nowhere near kindly said.

The same old Alister Cullingworth. This was going to be three unpleasant days. Then I saw Pamela, as she slowly emerged from the shadows, her eyes looking down, not at me. Her countenance was shocking. She was still as beautiful as ever, but the rosy complexion she'd had in England had turned to a china-white pallor, incongruously so after these years of living under the African sun, and she was so thin and delicate-looking that I couldn't see how Alister had failed to break her in two with his sharp tongue ere now. She once dominated all men just with the uncertainty of what she might say—and the certainty that what she would say could cut a man to quick. There was no evidence of that now.

She muttered something in the way of a greeting, and Alister, who also was thinner than I remembered, but in the sunburnt, wiry muscled way of a hardscrabble farmer, placed his hand on Pamela's arm and guided her back into the shadows. He lifted his other hand toward us in a halfhearted invitation to join them on the veranda.

When I reached the top of the stoep, I realized that there was another, as yet unheard from, party hunched on the far side of the round, rough-wood table that was surrounded by six leather-seated African barrel chairs.

"Brian, this is Doctor Nicholls, our local witch doctor," Alister said in what seemed an almost grudging introduction. "Angus . . . hello, Angus. Want to put that glass down and greet our guests? Angus, this is my old school chum and current British spy, Brian Kennelly, out to drive London's last nail in our collective coffin here in Rhodesia. Gavin, I'm sure you know. Although perhaps not as well as you want to know. Or that our new friend Brian might want to know either."

Gavin, who I focused on at the corner of my vision, looked embarrassed at this comment. For myself, I had no idea what Alister meant, but I assumed at some point he would use those words to try to hurt and attempt to control me. In that brief, acidic introduction, I felt all sorts of innuendo flying around. But everyone else was ignoring whatever elephant was lurking in the shadows, so I did so as well.

I leaned over and shook Doctor Nicholls's sweaty palm, having a little difficulty disengaging from his surprisingly strong grip, and stepped back, as Alister and Gavin played a little game of musical chairs on who was going to sit on the near side of Pamela. She had sunk into the chair next to the doctor and seemed to keep withdrawing in upon herself even after she was seated. I instantaneously found myself wondering if she was on drugs. Her eyes seemed to be continents away, if not altogether dead. Not at all the mischievous and havoc-rending Pamela I'd once known.

While Gavin and Alister fought for the chair next to Pamela, with Alister finally taking the position, my attention was arrested by humming and clicking noises coming from the interior of the bungalow. The front door was just to the right of where I stood. The interior was dim, but I slowly focused on a handsome, well-built Shona youth of twenty or so, who, dressed incongruously in a colorful sarong-like skirt and a stiff white butler's jacket, was skating around the wood-parqueted floor of the house's main living room in his bare feet on rags. He was polishing the floor and had already brought it to a high sheen.

I was shaking my head at the new memories I was gathering of southern Africa as I plopped down in the seat between the doctor and Gavin. I had the impression that perhaps Gavin had a thing for Pamela and that Alister probably was fully aware of this and, like he once toyed with me, was both encouraging and fighting it. In a fair fight, the strapping blond Afrikaaner could take Alister, I knew. But I also knew that any fight Alister would be in would not be a fair fight.

"Shall we leave our visitors dry, Pamela?—no, not you, Angus; I've never seen you dry and you are hardly a visitor—or do you remember how to be a hostess?"

Pamela lifted her eyes for the first time since we had arrived, and I could see a brief flash of life in them. But then it evaporated and her head sank again. She was not rising to whatever bait Alister was laying before her. With a sneer and a grimace, Alister picked up a brass hand bell on the table and rang it with two quick flicks of his wrists.

The smiling white-jacketed Shona youth appeared in the doorway immediately.

"Tea and whiskey, Penny. Now . . . please," Alister spit out in a perfunctory and dismissive command to the house servant with just a hint of a belated, and seemingly begrudged, perfunctory politeness at the tail. I got the distinct impression that the "please" was only because of the unusual presence of guests. Then, turning his anything but genuine smile on those gathered, Alister lost all interest in the servant, who bustled around the table, quite efficiently filling our glasses and setting down a plate of digestive biscuits. Britannia forever, wherever the sun was setting over a yardarm, either seen or unseen.

The rest of the visit went generally the same way Rhodesia's future was headed. Innocuous and seemingly endless small talk in a languid discussion matching the afternoon heat beating down on the bravely forlorn flower garden, innuendo that touched on reality and then skirted quickly away, and an underlying tension that everyone wanted to play with but no one wanted to ignite—at least among the three of us who talked.

The conversation was carried by Alister, Gavin, and me, with me trying to work in the threat that these people were living under, Gavin being mostly unbelieving and unaccepting, and Alister being sarcastic about all that I was saying—and barely civil to either one of us. All the time Pamela sat there, hands in her lap, looking at her palms, and apparently pretending to be far, far away. You'd think she would have had something to say to or ask of me, her long-ago fiancé. But I couldn't now be sure she remembered me at all. She certainly wasn't indicating she did.

Doctor Nicholls, for his part, three sheets to the wind and looking crumpled in his bush shorts and the khaki shirt that almost met across his sunken chest and the start of a pot belly, was paying more attention to me than he was to the conversation. His eyes were slitted as if he was reliving some miraculous operation in years past, but his knees and thighs were rubbing against mine, and at some point he placed a hand on my thigh. But I simply took it and placed it back in his lap. I was used to his type. I'd been known as somewhat of a pretty boy at Oxford, and I had learned to fend off fellow students and tutors alike—until along came Alister, of course.

After an eternity of saying little and meaning much more, Alister abruptly cut into a friendly argument between Gavin and me on whether the British South African Police should be disbanded as a vestige of colonialism.

"I'm sure you're tired, Gavin. And you have to make sure our spy here gets that best bed in our luxurious little flea bag in Beatrice. So, run along now. I want to beat out of our dear, dear Brian the real reason he's come to the middle of nowhere. Surely not to gloat; you never really had it in you to gloat, did you, dear boy?"

I cleared my throat and then I dove right into the center of it. I hadn't wanted to come. I hadn't thought it would do the least bit good if I came—and I told Pamela's father as much. So, there was nothing to lose, really.

"I've come to talk to Pamela, actually. On the behest of the Earl. I—"

"Well, then, by all means you have at her. She's all yours—not that you can keep her, of course. You never could do that." And then, with a laugh, Alister had gotten up out of his chair and headed into the darkened interior of the bungalow with a bellowed, "Penny!"

And when he'd gotten to the door, Alister turned, gave Gavin that smile of his that couldn't really be taken as a smile, and said, "And, Gavin, take Angus with you. And see that he gets bathed. I think he'll quite enjoy that." A hearty laugh and then Alister had turned and disappeared into the maw of the bungalow. "Penny. Penny! Where the fuck are you?"

This was much too—and most probably beyond—the point, but Gavin was ready to leave anyway. One last questioning look at me and Gavin hoisted Doctor Nicholls up with greater care than I'm sure Alister would ever have expended on the old gentleman, folded him into the Land Rover, and rolled out slowly in a great cloud of dust.

"I want a drink, and I don't want it here," Pamela said as we watched the Land Rover drive off. And now, with Alister gone, I could feel some of the old steel in her in the strength of her voice and the set of her shoulders.

That was fine with me. I needed to talk to Pamela to see if she'd heard anything I was saying about Rhodesia's future— and especially of the futures of the white farmers in Rhodesia— and I thought what I'd have to say would be something I couldn't say around Alister, who had made clear in our earlier conversation that he didn't believe in the least that Rhodesia was disintegrating. I owed Lord Clarence at least the respect of being totally and brutally honest with his recalcitrant daughter.

"We could go into Beatrice," I said as we climbed into an old rusting VW sedan. "I understand there's a bar at the hotel that is as close to respectable for a European woman as you have here."

"A white man's bar," Pamela said in disgust. "No, I have something I want to show you."

We drove nearly all of the way back to Salisbury, but in the southern outskirts of the city, Pamela turned off toward the west. She handled the sedan with the expertise of a lorry driver.

"Been to Epworth during your spy mission here?" Pamela asked.

"No. And I'm not a spy, Pamela," I answered with a show of impatience. Alister had gotten to me on this subject, and now Pamela was being feisty about it too. They both always knew how to get to me, making me feel like the dope on the rope. "I'm here just to check on the atmosphere, just an independent check on the reports being sent in to London on the situation here."

"And you are not here to drag me home, to dear old England, at the behest of my father?" Pamela asked. "You needn't lie."

"Nor will I. Yes, part of my brief is straight from Lord Clarence. He wanted me to discern whether Rhodesia is reaching the breaking point for white residents. And if so, he wanted me to try to convince you to come home. For you, at least, to come back to England for a while, a visit if you won't stay longer, even if Alister won't come. Is that so hard for you to understand and accept?" I saw no reason to prevaricate about Lord Clarence's concern and his assignment to me. Pamela could take it or leave it.

"He hasn't spoken to me for five years," Pamela muttered under her breath.

"Nor have you spoken to him, I'll wager," I shot back. "But he's showing concern now. And now that I've seen you, I can understand your father's concern. Africa is eating you up."

"Ah," Pamela muttered under her breath. "Your disinterested concern for me is very touching." She then stopped the VW abruptly in a flurry of rock and dust beside a weather-beaten wooden shack at the edge of a Shona kraal. The walled village consisted of a large number of round African buildings with thatched roofs that I'd been told were called rondavels. These were set haphazardly inside a low stone wall.

"Welcome to Epworth," Pamela threw over her shoulder, as she opened the driver's door of the VW and rolled out. "Time to wet our whistles. And then what I had to show you." She was already inside the door to the shack before I'd gotten out of the sedan and followed her. This persona was quite shocking—not unfamiliar, just shocking that she could turn on the old Pamela so loudly after that weak church mouse performance back at her bungalow.

The interior was dim; the room seeming larger on the inside than on the outside. There were three tables, but everyone in the shack, all Shona men of advanced age, was gathered around the bar. They stopped talking when we entered, and they stared. But they were staring at me. I got the impression that Pamela was a regular, which was perhaps the most shock I'd had on that quite disturbing day.

Pamela gave them a sweeping, sharp stare, and they went back to their talking in click-clacking musical sounds and drinking, which they did as any man would.

One of them sauntered over with two dusty bottles of chibuli, what passed for beer among the Shona, and Pamela and I sat, in silence, and drank. After we'd drunk those, there was another round of beer, and then another, and still Pamela didn't speak. But I could tell she was building up to something. She had that little smile on her face that she'd had all those years ago when she was ready to perform her bird-flipping routine at the Ascot races or someplace equally staid.

Nearly an hour had gone by when she stood up straight unexpectedly and said, "Come along. I want to show you something."

I stumbled out of the shack into the blinding sunshine in her wake and followed her into the depths of the kraal on unsteady feet. After a while she stopped at the door of a rondavel and bellowed, "Ado, it is I, your adoring wife. Home again for a short visit."

Two figures appeared at the entrance to the rondavel. Two small children. Cream and sugar brown; features not entirely Shona.

301

I knew before we entered the rondavel. A young Shona man, tall and willowy, but with obvious strength in him, with wiry, sinewy muscles. A runner, an endurance runner. And a handsome and proud-standing representative of his race. He was wearing only a sarong-like, brightly colored length of cloth around his middle. He had been using a grinding stone to sharpen a long spear, which marked him as a tribe hunter, and he did a double take when he saw me with Pamela, but he showed no evidence of embarrassment or subservience.

He nodded to Pamela and then to me, and then he shooed the two children out of the rondavel. While he was doing this, Pamela took two leather-seated African barrel chairs and set them facing each other, about ten feet apart, and motioned me to sit on one of the chairs, which I did.

Then Pamela motioned the Shona warrior to sit in the chair, and she unknotted his loin cloth and pulled it off as he sat down. Pamela moved to behind the warrior, turned him facing me, and nuzzled her chin into the hollow of his neck. Then she unbuttoned her dress all the way down and pushed it off her shoulders. She wasn't wearing a bra. She pulled his head back between her breasts and he reached back with one hand and cupped one of her breasts. At a muttered command from her, he reached down and started stroking his cock with the other.

I was mesmerized by what I was watching. And I was watching him, not Pamela.

As his cock lengthened and thickened, Pamela ran her hands down onto his chest and toyed with his nipples. All the time she was watching me, maintaining eye contact, enjoying telling me something definitive.

When she had stripped off her panties, come around the chair, and sat in his lap, facing me—holding the root of his cock in position until it was logged inside her cunt and then descending on it—I finally found my voice.

"Pamela," I said in a strangled voice. "You don't have to do this. I understand." But that didn't stop anything. She was too absorbed in her "husband's" fucking. I could take no more and rose from the chair and pushed my way through the beaded curtain across the rondavel's door.

She spoke as I left the hut, "Oh, do you fully understand, Brian? When you return and report to my father, I want this image to be locked in your brain. I want you to tell him that I have no plans to return to English . . . that I have family roots here."

I didn't turn, or say, anything, though. I just went on out into the blinding light of the sun-baked kraal. The two half-breed urchins were standing next to the VW when I got there, and I gave them each a few coins, the least I could do for the disintegrating House of Devon.

I sat in the sedan, not knowing what to do, baking under the sun. Not even wanting to go back into the shed that passed as a bar. Knowing that all of the eyes in there would be laughing at me. After about a half hour, Pamela appeared at the rondavel door, still buttoning her dress, not the least bit interested in what anyone saw or thought.

She walked directly from there to where I sat. "You . . . may . . . leave, Brian . . . if you've seen enough. You can take the sedan and just leave it at the hotel. I have friends and family here who will take me home in the morning. But I think we are finished now, you and I. You may tell my father what you like. Of course, if you want to stay and see how fully a white woman can fuck her Shona man . . ."

But I had already slid over into the driver's seat and was meshing the gears in the VW, grinding it to life. When I got to the hotel in Beatrice, I wasn't surprised to see Doctor Nicholls slumped in a stool at one of the tables, but I was quite surprised to see Alister similarly slumped on a high stool at the bar. He was smoking and had a tumbler of what seemed to be hard liquor in front of him. He didn't look at me when I came in, but he took a long puff on a cigarette and then brutally crushed it out in a plastic ashtray on the bar top. He then rummaged around in his shirt pocket, extracted another cigarette from a crumbled packet, and lit it after several tries of firing up a match. I could see that his hands were trembling. And I wasn't the least interested in a question from him about where Pamela was. My mind had been in a mess all the way back from Epworth. Those two mixed-colored children. Two of them.

I started to turn to walk up the stairs to the rooms on the story above, but as I started across the room, Doctor Nicholls laid a hand on my sleeve and arrested my movement.

"Could you spare a moment for an old man, sir? I do want to apologize."

What could I do? I sat at the table beside the melancholy doctor.

"Can you forgive me for my behavior this afternoon?" he mumbled. His eyes were bloodshot and there were tears in them. "I don't know what came over me. I'd had too much to drink, of course. It's just so lonely out here, and I have . . . sometimes I have . . . these urges, you know."

"That's quite all right. Think nothing of it," I answered quietly, trying to put on my "understanding" face. Perhaps I was being too sophisticated London and not enough raw Rhodesia, though, because Nicholls took that as encouragement rather than a polite sendoff.

"It's that we don't get many fine looking visitors like you out here, Brian. Refined men. Men of brilliance and presence, if you know what I mean."

"Ummm, umm," I murmured, more focused on politely refusing the drink Nicholls was pushing toward me than in listening to what he was saying.

"I was thinking. Perhaps . . . Well, I was thinking. Perhaps you could come up to my rooms for a drink."

I was fully focused on Nicholls now.

"Umm, thanks for the offer, Doctor. Very flattering indeed, but I think not. I think I will go up and wash the dust of the road off me and take a nap."

"I have the best bathtub in the hotel in my suite of rooms," Nicholls babbled. "You could—"

"Again, thanks, but I'll manage." I looked over at the bar, half afraid Alister was drinking all of this in and setting himself up for one of his embarrassing moments, where it always seemed to be me who was embarrassed. But Alister was no longer at the bar, or anywhere else in the room that I could see. When I had been able to extricate myself from that clumsy proposition, I went straight to the bathroom at the end of the hall my room was on and soaked in the tub for a good twenty minutes, trying to wash away much more of what I'd learned of Rhodesia than just that it was covered in dust.

Padding back to my room with a towel wrapped around my midsection, I discovered where Alister had gone. He was in my bed, naked, smoking a cigarette, and still with half a tumbler of liquor to drink.

Perhaps if I hadn't had the double shock of seeing Pamela and her well-endowed Shona "husband" in coitus and then being propositioned by Doctor Nicholls, I would have had the resolve I needed to resist the situation. But this was remote Rhodesia in its death throes, and all of the frustration and inevitable sinking into oblivion that I had been experiencing for the past three weeks flowed over me.

We didn't speak, but, as I approached the bed, Alister rose and stood, nonchalantly and insolently, before me, ever so sure of himself. He was in full erection. I said nothing. Nothing had changed between Alister and me in all of these years. I simply dropped my towel and went onto the bed and spread my legs for him. He entered me with a force and brutality that hadn't changed a zot over the chasm of the years since he'd last fucked me. He was a demanding, rutting animal with a wild, crazed piston movement to his pelvis as he pounded, pounded, pounded all of the anger of his unfulfilled life into my ass channel.

I knew I should honor the sanctity of their marriage, or at least stay well clear of how badly I always was used by them both. But I had just come from a cruel show of just how much sanctity was in that institution. And, to be honest, I wanted this. I reveled in this. I wanted Alister to be rough and cruel with me. And he didn't disappoint. He was fucking me like he was trying to fuck Africa out of his system. As if there was no tomorrow. And perhaps there wasn't. At least for Africa. And for Alister and Pamela.

Alister fucked me into an exhausted sleep, and when I awoke, he was gone. I drifted down to the bar for a drink before a late dinner. I was all alone in the bar. The doctor had beaten a defeated retreat.

But, no, I wasn't alone. I heard sounds from behind the bar, beyond a beaded curtain that covered a doorway behind the bar. I was drawn to the sounds, seeking the barman so that I could have that drink.

They were in the shadows just beyond the beaded curtain, up against the wall. Alister, now the prey rather than the hunter, his back rubbing up and down the wall, his shirt front open to Gavin's hungry lips. Gavin standing, facing him, feet firmly on the floor, leveraging off the balls of his feet, his shorts down around his ankles and Alister's trousers in a puddle on the floor. Gavin, young, virile, in superb shape. A cock that put mine to shame. Alister's knees gathered up on Gavin's hips, and Gavin fucking up into him, pushing his sun-bronzed shoulder blades up and down the wall with deep thrusts. Alister's face was lolled over in my direction, and he was staring at me, but not seeing me. A vacant look in his eyes. Just another fuck. Just as my stolen moments with him had been. Just thrusting yet another one-finger salute to Africa and to what he knew Rhodesia and his existence here was descending to. Into chaos. But not a chaos of heat and passion. A chaos of numbness and emptiness. And of head-shaking indifference and insanity.

I retreated as quickly and quietly as I could and ate a morose and largely untasted meal in a scruffy dining room with faded brocade curtains and chipped chinaware celebrating the centennial of Queen Victoria. No other soul about me, other than the nearly invisible servants, to prevent my mind from racing about all that was being lost, all that made little sense, but just continued its swirl down into the vortex.

I spent a sleepless night, struggling with myself and with the situation. I couldn't just abandon what I had come to realize brought me to Africa. It hadn't really been London that sent me here—and certainly not Lord Clarence. All along my subconscious had known I'd come for some sort of resolution of a past with Alister and Pamela that I couldn't shake. I couldn't just abandon that realization now and return home meekly. They both seemed to be crying out for help. I believed, then at least, that they wanted me to save them. I was the link between them, the thin strand that held them together, if anything held them together any more. I told myself this, and I let it repeat itself in my mind until I believed it. They just didn't know how to tell me any other way than as they were acting out. My presence had pushed them both over the edge.

I owed them nothing. But I hadn't recovered from either one of them. I was convinced that I had to save them both to be able to save myself—and to put the past with both of them behind me.

Tomorrow. Tomorrow I'd drive back to the bungalow. I'd be strong. I'd convince both of them to pack immediately, and we'd be back in Salisbury and at the airport before they would withdraw into their cynical defenses. That's what they were begging me to do—in their own way. Pamela's father was right to have sent me. No one else could do this.

I was pulling quietly up to the bungalow not long after the break of the next day. The landscape was magnificent at this time of day. I could see how Africa could get its talons in a person. I could understand why Pamela had made the choice she had. But this wouldn't really be hurting Pamela—or Alister. This would be releasing them both. They were begging to leave the disintegrating Rhodesia behind and return to their roots in England—to stability and sanity. To what was expected of them, both children of nobility.

All was quiet at the bungalow. For some reason I had assumed that I'd hear Alister's booming voice, his acid tongue at work, if he had returned already. Or see Pamela sitting on the veranda, looking dazed and unattached to the role that had been assigned to her. I quietly mounted the stairs to the veranda. I stood, ready to knock at the door, but then I heard the moaning. My heart went dead and it was on leaden feet that I pushed the screen door open and crossed the highly polished parquet floor and looked into the bedroom beyond.

They were stretched out in the middle of the massive stinkwood four-poster bed, covered in the brightest of white muslin. They were both naked. Alister was lying on his back in the center of the bed, his knees wide, the heels of his feet planted on the bed, and rocking his pelvis up and down.

Penny, the young, muscular Shona house servant, was crouched between Alister's knees, his hips pushing in and out in rapid motion, the muscles of his bulbous butt cheeks contracting and releasing, fucking Alister hard and deep.

Alister was moaning and sighing as he'd never done for me or, last evening, for Gavin either. He was murmuring to the glistening brown servant in that click-clacky language of the Shona. Alister was writhing under his Shona lover, lost in languid, mutually passionate love as he had never been with me. He was crying out in a voice of passion that I had never heard before.

Gavin found me at the table in the hotel bar an hour later.

"About ready to return to Salisbury?" he asked. He was wearing that comfortable grin of his, no cares in the world, not having heard or absorbed anything I'd said on the bungalow veranda the previous afternoon.

"Yes," I answered and took a long drag on my bottle of Lion lager. "All ready." "Done everything here that needed to be done?" he asked.

"Yes."

"I hope you didn't mind the doctor much. He's a good doctor. Better than we could get out here otherwise. He just had to leave London. He's no harm really." "No, there was no bother," I answered.

"He's the one I worry about most," Gavin said. "When the end comes here, he's really the only one with nowhere to go but also no prospect of staying. The Shona don't really appreciate his activities among their young men."

I looked hard at Gavin. So, he had been listening yesterday after all. He didn't have to be convinced of Rhodesia's descent into chaos. And now that I looked at him, I could tell he'd be all right. He'd trained hard and well for the British South Africa Police. He'd have options.

"You?" I asked.

"I've been looking at brochures on Australia," Gavin answered. And then he smiled. "A big country, a lot of space. Not so many people. Not that far off of what I grew up to. Before recent years."

"But the Cullingworths?" I then said.

"Oh, Alister and Pamela? They'll do whatever they'll do. They are inevitably part of this land now."

"But how can they . . . stay together? They hate—"

"What makes you think they don't love each other?" Gavin asked. And when I looked into his eyes, I suddenly realized that he was a far wiser man than I was. That he knew all there was to know. "They are Africa. They will stay here, together, to—and beyond—the end. Together."

Perhaps it was I who had not understood, I realized.

"There is something I understand," Gavin said, turning his face to mine. "I understand what Pamela was to you—and what she did to you back in England. Beyond that I understand what Alister was to you . . . and what he did to you. What he did with you yesterday in your room. Yes, these walls are paper thin. I would like . . ."

He didn't complete that sentence, but I felt his hand on my thigh. Commanding and inviting. In turn, I gave him a look that no man of his proclivities could misunderstand, and I let him take my arm and climb with me up the hotel stairs to my room and then to fuck all thoughts of disintegration and of Pamela and Alister, of Africa and doomed Rhodesia, out of me. As he stroked down hard into me, I rubbed the heels of my feet along his knotted calves and ran my fingertips across the firm straining muscles of his back and stared out the window at the blue, cloudless African sky, looking for my plane to materialize from out of the sun. Ready to let go of the ghosts of my past and of Rhodesia and all it stood for.

I arched my back and cried out and panted hard, as, thrusting, thrusting, thrusting, the virile, young, primeval rutting Afrikaaner drummed the wild rawness and bald honesty of Africa deep inside me.

Congo Drums

The riverboat hit a log, or something, on the hull right at my head, and I woke with a start. The first sensation in the soft, wavering light of a single lantern hung by the doorway was the sound of the drums and low chanting from somewhere above. The driver and cook at it again. The sound was monotonous and comforting all at the same time. It also seemed to be richer than before, almost stereophonic, and the second sensation to reach my senses was the dull thumping against the cabin wall above my head, which was what was providing the stereophonic effect of the drums. The Millers were copulating again to the rhythm of the drums. Who would have known the old man had it in him to fuck so often and so long?

Heavy breathing, inside the cabin, reached me on a third level of sensation. I rolled over. Ethan was slouched, naked, in the chair, legs spread, a shock of salt-and-pepper hair hanging down over one eye, the other eye boring into me. He was slowly masturbating himself—also to the rhythm of the drums. He had a trim and scarred, but hard, body, well built even though he was pushing fifty. He'd had an active life and it showed.

A chill went down my spine. This was Africa. Raw, primeval, and sensual. Instantly feeling the mood and the need of the drums, I turned toward Ethan; stretched my body out, unwinding every bunched muscle like a jungle cat waking from a nap; arched my back; and moved my hand down to my own hardening cock. I lay there on the lower bunk and Ethan slouched in his chair, each of us silently and intently staring at the other, both working our cocks up, panting. Knowing we were going to fuck. Already fucking each other even though we weren't touching. The drums picked up their beat, as did the thumping on the wall above the bunk. In a separate dimension, the cry of a native woman from the deck overhead cut through the rhythmic sounds followed by the growl, in his distinctive South Afrikaaner dialect, of the guide, Bull. "Spread 'em wider, you native doxy, and stop your yowling. Stop acting like you've never been fucked before."

Bull had broken the spell in the cabin.

"Come. And bring a condom," Ethan commanded in a hoarse whisper. I knelt between his spread thighs and opened my mouth over the bulb of his cock, being rewarded with a long sigh and the feel of his long, sensuous fingers gliding through my hair, holding my head into his crotch.

Ethan enjoyed the exotic, picked up from his extensive world travels. He fucked me without leaving his slouched position in the chair, my body swanned out from his torso and over his thighs, my feet hooked on his shoulders, him grasping my wrists and, bowing my arms back, my torso arched out over his thighs. With his cock throbbing and making slow and shallow strokes deep inside me, he maintained the rhythm of the drums, slowing in the wake of the sharp cry of release by the native woman overhead and the sudden ceasing, with a jolt, of the cabin wall thumping. With a tightening of Ethan's body, a jerk, and the sound of a gasp and a sigh, I felt him fill the bulb of the condom, and he slowly lowered my chest on his thighs without extracting his cock from my channel. We both held there, panting heavily. I knew he'd fuck me again once he had regained his breath and the hardness of his cock.

That's why we went together so well. He could fuck forever and I wanted it that way. Had we brought enough condoms on this journey?

Stretched out on the bunk, me on my back on top of him, his cock inside me, Ethan slowly masturbated me to my own ejaculation and nibbled on my ear, whispering endearments to me. Then we both slept, sensitive to whatever scant breeze invaded the cracks in the hull of the Congo river steamer to cool the sweat on our bodies.

I woke up in the darkest of the night to silence other than Ethan's heavy breathing and his hissing through chattering teeth. The lantern had sputtered out, the boat was gently rocking from side to side, and, although there were sounds of low muttering in a foreign—to me—tongue coming from overhead, the drums and chanting had stopped.

Ethan and I were both bathed in sweat—his—as were the sheets. He was mumbling and shaking. I felt his forehead, which was burning even though his teeth were chattering. I scrambled out of the bunk and pulled the blanket down from the bunk above, which was supposed to be mine but which Ethan hadn't allowed me to occupy in the six days of our river journey. It had been nearly a year of absence since we'd met up on this safari, and he insisted on going to sleep with his cock inside me every night. This was fine with me.

I bundled him up in the blanket and, not knowing what else to do, went looking for Bull, even though I felt intimidated by the man.

Bull, bulky, but not fat, all muscle and power, seemingly took up all of the space in the cabin as he squatted and peered at Ethan's trembling body.

"Yep, malaria. For sure. Where's he been?"

"Everywhere," I answered. "He does TV documentaries from the ends of the earth. He's been doing a film on lingering insurgency in Angola."

"Yep. Probably got it there. Could have got it here too, but it wouldn't show up this bad in seven days if he got it here. We'll have to have him sent back to Kinshasa when we reach Lokutu Mombongo later this morning."

Bull was giving me an appraising look as he said that. I only then realized that I was naked.

* * * *

"The question, I suppose, is whether we press on or call this off for now." Although this was on everyone's mind, it was Sondra Miller who asked it. Of all the people here, she was the one most out of place—and well aware of that. A statuesque blonde who looked every lovely inch the runway model that she was, she would look good in any setting—but a lot better in most every one other than the upper Congo where we now were. Her voice sounded just slightly bored when she'd said it, but everyone was aware of the hope behind her words.

"Of course not. We've come this far," her husband, Charles, answered, an edge to his voice. "Ethan said he already had enough notes to begin the documentary as long as I was still in. Jim here can take notes for the rest of the journey. What say you, Sean?" he asked turning to me. "You are the editor on this and have talked with Ethan on his vision. Can we do the rest of the research without him? We'll have to come back to do more filming when the script is together anyway."

"Probably so," I answered, not looking at Sondra directly to see if she'd mar her pretty face with a scowl but looking, rather at Charles's young, black secretary, Jim Jackson, to see how closely he was watching Sondra. Very closely. A pity, I thought. With Ethan gone, Jim Jackson was looking very good to me. And I needed almost constant attention.

I wondered why Sondra had come on the safari at all. Probably didn't want to let Charles Miller's money out of her sight for very long. He was a good thirty years older than she was and definitely of the florid-faced, slightly pudgy aspect. He was the money behind this documentary film and Ethan had told me to treat the man right. Thus far I hadn't had many dealings with him, but he seemed the all right sort. He certainly didn't flaunt his wealth—not like his wife did. She was wearing diamonds even though we were sitting on the banks of the Congo at Lokutu Mombongo in a primitive tent camp. The guide had said that it was best to camp in tents in the open under mosquito-repellent lamps whenever we could, as the boat cabins would be harder to protect against the mosquito.

If Ethan was any evidence of this, Bull was right.

Ethan had been bundled off in a float plane by noon and the others had gone on to their daily excursion to the Lokutu Oil

Palm plantation. Sondra had shown more interest in this outing than in the ones of previous days, probably because the plantation owner was a Frenchman with a roving eye, a good physique, and randy banter. Sondra very much gave the impression that she needed to be bedded constantly. I didn't fault her; it was my sin as well.

"The safari is already paid for," Bull interjected. "We can take you back now, but there won't be a refund."

"We won't be going back," Charles Miller decreed. "I've already sunk too much money into this documentary to abandon it now."

"Good," Bull said, the palm of his hand going to the buttocks of the young Congolese woman laying the place settings at the camp table. "We leave on the boat at daybreak tomorrow. We'll reach where the Congo is at its widest, where you will see a vast field of hyacinths on the water and visit the Bafoto pygmies."

"Ethan told me about the hyacinths," Charles said, turning to his secretary, Jim. "Be sure and have your video camera for those, Jim. Ethan will want coverage of them. You'll have to do the photography now, if Sean doesn't want to do it."

Miller had turned to me. "Sorry," I answered. "I'm terrible at it. Ethan asked me to begin on the script."

"I suggest an early night," Bull said, as he stood up and put a hand on the small of the Congolese woman's back.

I chose to take in the twilight and sunset over the Congo River before turning into my solitary tent—the first time I would be sleeping alone on this trip. Ethan and I had met in Bangkok when we both were covering a coup there, me for the Associated Press as a journalist and editor and he as director of a documentary. We each retreated into a bar on Soi Cowboy off Sukhumvit, near the international enclave, to escape the teargas of a spontaneous clash between the police and university students. It proved to be a gay bar, and after several drinks, Ethan fucked me in a small room beyond the beaded curtain at the back of the bar. After the teargas cleared, he took me back to his hotel room and fucked me repeatedly there. He was nearly fifteen years older than I was, but I liked older men, and he was hard bodied and fully capable. We had met sporadically, as on this safari, and worked together and fucked periodically over the past seven years. If anything, he got better at it with age.

Now he had deserted me near the end of the earth, up the Congo. The sex the last seven days had been as good, if not better, than it ever had been and we were reaching a shared rhythm that raised possibilities of a more permanent living arrangement. But now he had malaria and was probably in a hospital in Kinshasa awaiting medical evacuation back to the States. I wasn't even sure how to contact him in the States. Charles would know, though. I'd have to ask him.

It was dark enough that night was stealing into the clearing between the tents and the central fire was dying down to embers. The driver and the cook were starting up the drums. The cook was an old man, but the driver was young and heavily muscled and quite handsome. He also moved with an assurance and with sensual grace. I had stolen glances at him with possibilities in mind the first seven days, even when I was being possessed fully by Ethan. I wondered if he . . .

I found my hand wandering down to my crotch, not even thinking if I was safe from observation. The clearing seemed deserted other than the low sound of the drums and of the soft chanting by the two Congolese men. As the darkness drifted in, though, the glow of the lights in the tents almost made their walls transparent, and the shadows from inside them caught my attention.

Bull's idea of turning in early was fucking the young Congolese woman in his tent. I could clearly see their silhouettes against the tent walls. He was standing up and taking her, with her bent over in front of him. I watched for nearly an hour as he turned her and she just flopped back, her arms dangling down to the floor and her head thrown back, while he clutched her buttocks and fucked on. I wondered if she was still conscious. And more than that, I wondered what it would be like to be in her place. There was similar activity in the Miller's tent, where the copulating couple was more reclined and he was stretched on top of her, his buttocks rising and falling, again to the rhythm of the drums.

I almost resented the others getting what I wasn't getting—and now wouldn't get until the safari was over.

Charles Miller walked into the light of the clearing from the direction of the boat. He had a bottle of scotch under his arm and was holding two glasses with his fingers. As I watched him approach, flabbergasted and letting my eyes dart to his tent and what was obviously happening therein, I couldn't help but gasp my surprise that it wasn't him in the tent. The woman there most certainly was Sondra. He calmly sat down beside me where we could both watch his tent and said, "Share a scotch with me and enjoy the show together? Sondra gives a good fuck."

While we were both on our second glass, with the fucking still going on in both tents, he turned to me, laid a hand on my thigh, and said, "I'll give you fifty dollars if you'll let me suck your cock. Ethan said you'd be good to me if I asked."

I didn't need the fifty dollars, but after the silhouette shows I'd been watching, I certainly needed the attention to my cock.

So that was what Ethan meant about treating the angel for his documentary well. I unzipped my shorts and he crouched between my spread thighs, fished my cock out, grasped it at the root, and closed his mouth over it. He gave expert head and welcomed the facial I gave him. I wasn't quite as melancholy at Ethan's absence anymore.

All melancholy was dissipated in the night when I felt a body stretch on top of mine as I lay on my belly on my cot in the tent I shared with no one. In the dimness of the glow of the pulsating mosquito repellent lanterns I could tell that the heavily muscled arms lying on either side of mine were black as ebony. Outside the tent, a drum beat softly started—and a low chant— but it was the sound of only one drummer, one chanter.

A whispered question in my ear, the accent more French than English, but very polite under the circumstances. "Please, may I. Will you receive me? I was told you would want me. I fuck good. You been watchin' me from beginning. I seen you . . . have wanted to fuck you."

"Yes," I whispered back, aching for the sex that was being denied me in Ethan's absence and thrilled at the feel of the size and insistence of his phallus at the small of my back. I turned my face to his and opened my mouth to him, and he pulled my tongue into his mouth and sucked on it as he moved his lithe, hard body on mine, showing me what French kissing was all about.

"Oh, shit. Fuck me," I whimpered when coming up momentarily for air, as, by instinct, I raised my buttocks to him and opened my legs, permitting his cock to move into the crack. He rubbed the upper side of the hard phallus on my hole, again and again, dry fucking me already as I gasped and writhed under him. He grasped my wrists and held my arms above my head. I recognized the signaling that he would fully possess me, and as we came out of the kiss, I took a deep breath and murmured, "Yes, yes, fuck me hard."

He laughed, a low guttural laugh, and, murmured, "It is good with you? You want me fuck you, yes?"

"Yes, yes, I want you to fuck me good," I answered with a gasp. "Don't ask for anything; just do it. All of it."

The weight of his body came off me and he was licking and kissing down my back. But that wasn't what had my attention. He already had a moistened finger exploring my asshole. He was on his knees between my spread thighs, and as I lifted my buttocks higher in the air, his mouth went to my ass and a hand grasped my cock through my thighs and he was stroking it.

"Please, please," I groaned. "Fuck me." I was clutching hard at the thin foam mattress and rubbing my cheek against the rough cotton sheet.

I groaned when his lips left my hole to be replaced by a thumb and his mouth swallowed my cock. I moaned and writhed under him, until he immobilized me more by moving a knee up next to my waist, holding my chest down with a fist between my shoulder blades and began roughly working my hole with three and four fingers.

"Please, please," I whimpered.

And then he was straddling my hips, crouched over my pelvis, and feeding his cock inside me. When he was deep inside, he encircled my chest with his arms and brought me up on my knees in front of him closely plastered against his chest. One strong, muscled arm extended up my chest and he held my head close into his shoulder with a grasp on my chin. He was stroking my cock with the other hand. Then he began to plow up into me in earnest in long, strong jabs, making little grunting noises, while I egged him on with continuous babbling that he probably didn't understand a word of. He was longer and thicker than Ethan was, and more vigorous in his stroking and longer lasting. I came long before he did, and then again when he flipped me over, wishboned my legs, and took me from the front, with me glorying in palming his hard, glistening, ebony-black chest and thrumming his quarter-sized aureoles with the pricks of blue tattooing circling them.

When Bull came to rouse me near dawn, I was flat on my belly on the cot, my arms hanging down, with my knuckles dragging on the earth of Africa, and burbling my appreciation for the night.

Bull gave me a quizzical look, and I was trying to think of something to tell him to explain how exhausted and fully satiated I was when he obviated that. "Was it OK with you?" he asked tentatively. "When we were putting Ethan Woodsmall on the plane, he was begging me to arrange for someone to take care of you. The driver has been—"

"Yes, that's fine. It was more than fine," I answered.

"Do you want him again? I can always cut it—"

"Yes, he's fine. Send him every night."

"Also, If you're interested, one of the boat men. The young one who wears the orange and red dhoti—"

"Yes," I murmured. "I know who you mean. Yes, him too."

"Separately or together?"

"Whatever."

I was hoping he was going to mention himself. But he didn't. He just smiled and whistled. Then with a, "Breakfast in ten, and then it's steaming on to Lisala," he was gone from the tent.

Groaning, I struggled out of my cot, my mind going to the Congolese young boat man who wore the orange and red dhoti, the scarf-like long skirt, leaving the chest bare, that men of his ethnic origin wore—tall and rangy, not a black man, but an Indian. But I'd gotten a peek at his cock. Very, very long. Long and think, like a snake.

I found how very long later that morning as we steamed up the Congo en route to the town of Lisala, where we were to have our afternoon outing and camp for the night and which the Congolese safari staff twittered excitedly about as the highlight of our trip. Such morning boat trips had become somewhat of a monotonous glide up the river, staring desultorily off into the jungle in continual search for a view of exotic plants and animals that we had seen hundreds of times before on lower stretches of the river.

The chief boat man was standing at the wheel, with one of his subordinates kneeling at the bow and watching the water for possible dangers to the boat's hull floating in the approaching stream. I didn't know where the other boatman was at the moment, the tall Indian with the orange and red dhoti. When we'd first boarded that morning, he'd been there near me, helping me aboard and then touching me and smiling, paying particular attention to me. And then as we were settling on the benches and the boat was pulling back into the midstream, coming back close to me, leaning down and whispering, "The guide, he said—"

"Yes, that will be fine. I wish it," I broke in, not wanting him to complete whatever he was going to say. It was a weakness of mine, wanting men's cocks—and as many and in as much variety as I could get them. I had gone exclusively with Ethan for the first seven days. After being plowed by the driver the previous night, I realized that if Ethan hadn't been taken away, I might by now be feeling the frustration of just his cock. It wasn't what I was used to, and, upon reflection, I realized I had been eyeing not just the driver, but the Indian boat man and Bull and even the secretary, Jim Jackson, for days before Ethan left us. They probably noticed that I had. I'm sure the driver and the Indian wouldn't have been as forward with their intentions if I hadn't been unconsciously signaling them.

"It is very long," he whispered. "Some men don't—"
"I've seen it. I want it."

The Indian smiled, touched me on the hip, and melted away.

Jim Jackson was at the stern, where the Congolese woman was washing out some clothes. Despite the language barrier between them, I expected to see them disappear below at any moment. The biggest wrinkle was that the young driver was there too, probably trying to cajole Jim to give him the same thing Jim was trying to get from the woman. Neither Bull nor Sondra Miller were in evidence on deck. I knew where Charles Miller was, though. He was sitting close beside me on a padded bench, set where we could watch the southern bank of the river glide by. He had an arm around my shoulder, and he had my cock out of my shorts and was slowly masturbating me. He was purring like a kitten and was kissing and licking the side of my neck.

"Would you like me to go below with you?" I asked. Ethan had told me that Miller was a necessary evil to getting this documentary in the can and I didn't have any other prospects for projects at the moment—and the driver had cocked me so well that I was feeling generous and not too picky.

"No, dear boy, thank you," Miller murmured. "This is quite nice as is. Just get nice and big and come for me, and I'll be satisfied."

That's when I realized that he couldn't get it up and that this was the next best thing. That's why he was so calm with his secretary, Jim, fucking his wife. Sondra probably hadn't agreed to come on the safari at all without a boy toy. I felt sorry for Miller, and when he pulled my head back and put his lips on mine, I gave him a kiss to remember. I also ejaculated for him, and although he dipped his face down to my lap to clean me up, I stood afterward and said I would go down to my cabin to clean up better.

Jim Jackson had the Congolese woman bent over a crate and was fucking her from behind when I reached the top of the stairs down into the cabin area. The driver was sitting on another crate and watching.

I heard them as I was coming down the steps into the lower corridor. The door to the Millers' cabin was slightly open and I looked in as I passed. Bull was naked and on his back on the double bed in the cabin, and Sondra, also naked, was straddling his pelvis and riding his cock. Before I moved on, I saw her dip her face down to his and him run his hand into her luxuriant cascade of blonde hair and take her lips in his. He brutally attacked her lips and, with a tug of her hair and a thrust of his hips, turned her in the bed and was mounting her to take over the driving. She threw her head back and laughed a hoarse, lusty laugh and then cried out as he thrust hard up into her.

I ached to be so lustfully and roughly handled.

Knowing now that Miller couldn't perform for Sondra, I felt much more forgiving of—and a kindred spirit with—her. I passed on to my own cabin door. The Indian, sans his dhoti, was waiting patiently for me in there. If one can say they were fucked gently, this would have been that fuck. I sat in the chair that Ethan had slouched in just a couple of nights previously, while the Indian gave me the most sensual blow job I think I've ever had. I tried to return the favor with him standing and me kneeling in front of him, but I doubt I succeeded all that well. He was just too long for me to come anywhere close to deep-throating him as he had done for me.

He then amazed me with his strength. He appeared so tall and thin that I could not imagine that he had the strength to lift me and stand, a bit crouched, in the center of the cabin, while I wrapped my arms around his neck and my legs around his waist and he entered and entered and entered me with that long, snake-like cock of his and rotated it around inside my channel and stroked it in long glides in and out until I was yodeling to the ceiling and no doubt announcing my very satisfactory taking to all aboard the boat.

Later he took me even more slowly and sensually, face on, atop the bunk, with me looking down the length of our torsos and watching how impossibly all of that was slowly sliding up inside me and, though going in rock hard, seemed to have the flexibility of a hose inside me, finding every nook and cranny of my channel and caressing it with the bulb of the cock.

The Millers, Jackson, and I all had to contain our mirth later in the day when we were shown what the Congolese considered the highlight of the safari, which was a tree commemorating the birthplace of their former leader, Mobutu Sese Seko, founder of Zaire. The members of the party, each giving looks to the other, properly praised the event, though, not wanting to be on the bad side of any of the Congolese this far up the remote river. Charles made a great to do of directing Jim to take multiple photographs of the site, but, in sotto voce assured him that they didn't need to be good photographs.

I felt a chill in the air that evening after we had finished our dinner at the campsite in Lisala. No one else claimed to feel it, though, so I put it out of my mind. Once again Bull suggested that we make an early night of it, as we were pressing on to what he called a "beautiful fishing village" at Laté. The rest of us interpreted that to mean that we had to stop somewhere for the night before going on to something we really wanted to see, so it might as well be at the collection of mean little huts at Laté. We had come for the excitement of the national animal preserves, and it was taking us considerable time to find them.

With a smile Bull told us that we would be crossing the equator in merely five days. We all suppressed groans. We wanted the experience of crossing the equator, but we weren't wild about the idea of having to wait for five days to get it done in what had become one monotonous day after another if you didn't take the good sex into account. I was willing to take the good sex into account.

No, not the good sex—the great sex.

At dark that night, Charles Miller appeared from the direction of the boat with another full bottle of scotch under his arm, causing me to wonder just how many bottles he had brought on the journey and if he was thinking of the need to ration them for the return trip. The driver and cook were on the drums again, and, again, Miller and I sat parallel to the Miller's tent so that, while he was slowly and expertly sucking me off, we could watch the show in his tent. Tonight it was a spectacular silhouette show, with Jim and Bull standing, facing each other, and Sondra suspended between them and taking cocks in both entrances.

I wondered how Miller could so calmly take this until, as if he could read my mind, he said, "I can no longer give Sondra what will keep her with me. And I enjoy watching those who can, servicing her."

I had to agree that that was simple enough. Thanks to their performance, I was quite randy when I went back to my tent. Thanks to the driver and the Indian boat man, my randiness was fully serviced. I had watched Sondra get double plowed one way. The driver and the Indian showed me there was more than one way to double plow.

I was quite content riding the driver's cock, facing his face, as he lay on his back on my cot. I lost my contentment and gained a half hour of "Holy Fuck!" when the Indian slid in behind me, encircled my chest with his arms, pitched me forward, and entered me with his snaking cock on top of the driver's thick one. They played me like a calliope and left me just a few hours before dawn, exhausted, sweating profusely, and with my tongue hanging out.

The sweat turned out not to be from the sex. By the time Bull entered my tent at dawn to rouse me, I was wrapped in a blanket alternating between chills and hot flushes, sweating like a pig, and chattering my teeth.

Bull pronounced the dreaded word: malaria.

As I was being bundled aboard the float plane, I heard the drums playing. It seemed to me that they were a bit more loose in rhythm and had a lighter beat than before the driver fucked me. I hoped I'd had a good influence on the driver's music. Bull was helping to tuck me in on the plane and was regretting that I hadn't been able to stick it out to cross the equator later in the week. My regret was that I had to leave before I had experienced Bull's cock—and Jim Jackson's, for that matter. The medic was looking really good to me, and I wondered what might be possible on the way back to Kinshasa. Would the plane fly high enough to qualify for the mile-high club? I wondered.

Snaked on Anjajavy Beach

I had both the advantages and curses of being a rock star. I could afford to go anywhere I wanted on the spur of the moment or as the mood hit me, but if a mood hit me that would land me in the tabloids, I'd better be prepared to go to the ends of the earth.

The mood had hit me to get the most exotic and total fuck that I could find by the most talented cocksman I could attract. I had been on a road tour for months and could have had any woman I'd wanted during that time. But revealing what I really wanted just wasn't the type of publicity the band—or its teenaged-girl-based fan club—could use. And that's why on this particular evening I found myself on Anjajavy Beach on the northern coast of the island of Madagascar in search of relief for this heat I'd been in for a total plowing for the last few months of what must have been the longest road show concert series any international band had ever done.

My voice was hoarse from all of the performances, and my ass was twitching for attention. Madagascar wasn't necessarily the end of the earth. But it was so open to accommodating what I needed without a whole lot of publicity that it seemed the right place to be.

I'd heard that Howard's Bar on the fringe of Anjajavy Beach was the place to hook up. So, long after the sun had gone down, I entered the garden bar dressed in my most fetching low-rise stonewashed jeans and a pair of loafers and showered body and shampooed hair and nothing else other than a friendly smile that had been plastered across numerous music, fashion, and gossip magazine covers.

The party was already in full swing. A couple of bars were set up under palm trees surrounding a meandering concrete terrace with a pool, many clumps of lush tropical vegetation that provided a good many discrete pocket garden areas, and a network of muted lighting that highlighted the central dance floor and provided good mood light to all of the other nooks and crannies about. There was a good crowd already partying—all hunky-looking men and all obviously either on the make or well into making or being made. A band of Indian musicians was doing a creditable job off to the side of many of the hit tunes of the day, including several that I had recorded to platinum myself.

I recognized some of the men there and was surprised to see most of them here; I didn't feel so isolated now in what I had to do to keep public face. But as long as they didn't do a double-take at seeing me, I wouldn't mess with their desire to hang out without being outed either. Still, with all of the talent in evidence, I was both surprised and a little gratified to note that all eyes at least stopped when they saw me and a good many lingered there—with some even bold enough to give me a come-hither look that I knew so well when I was on vacation from my public world.

I could feel my butt twitching. One of these hunks was going to top me tonight—sometime before I left Howard's Bar—and I wasn't going to let him go until he'd done me royally. I was going to work some unsuspecting guy to exhaustion tonight.

I sat at a bar stool watching the crowd and brushing off the braver of the swirl of cruisers who approached me with their tongues hanging out, whether attracted by recognized celebrity or my hours spent in the gym and grooming shops I knew not—

nor did I particularly care. Any brand of honey would do tonight as long as the bees had nice bods, big dicks, and a lot of stamina. I wanted something special—and I wanted it soon; I'd flown all the way from L.A. for this.

Within about ten minutes, I'd seen him. I was sure that I saw him before he saw me. He was at a table with three other capable-looking muscle men—and he was the hunkiest of the lot. I could hear their boisterous conversation well enough to tell that they were all Aussies. He had the size and physique of a footballer and the face of a movie star. All blond good looks with enough of a tan to make him look like a serious outdoor sportsman. He was wearing baggy cargo shorts and a godawful Hawaiian shirt unbuttoned and hanging loose to reveal a serious bodybuilder's torso. I decided that if he had a cock to match that, he could very well be in for a special treat tonight.

He must have felt someone watching him intensely, because he turned to me, made eye contact, and gave me a glorious smile.

I was about to go over and tell him he was the night's lucky winner when a swirl of bodies came between the two of us. His table was across an edge of the dance floor from where I was sitting, and the singer of the band that was playing had put on a hard sell for dancers to flood the floor. They had done so. And out of that new, distracting wave of dancers, my attention was torn away from the Aussie hunk and found a new, fascinating focus.

There, highlighted by a traveling strobe light that must have been guided by a real fan in the lighting booth, was a sight that took my breath away. The dancer was Sri Lankan. He had a rich chocolate-brown body that was well muscled but that also was as lithe and as flexible as anything I'd seen on a man. He had a healthy head of black hair and a face so chiseled and fine boned that it was hard to think it was natural. But it was his torso that mesmerized. He was undulating in perfect harmony with the music in a slow, sensual motion that stretched and highlighted every muscle. He was wearing a island-style sarong skirt that barely covered his hips, and considering the movement of his body, it was hard to understand how the sarong stayed in place. As beautiful as the movement of his torso to the music was, however, what was primarily arresting was his body tattoo.

He had a gorgeous, almost luminous, rendering of an intricately scaled snake, in reds, greens, and purples, coiled around his midsection and winding up and around his left shoulder. The head of the snake, which, when examined closely, evoked the beauty and features of the dancer himself, dipped down and looked out—straight at me; always focused on me—from his sternum at the center of his torso just below his pecs. And when I was able to pull my gaze from this as the dancer made the snake sway back and forth with the undulating of the music's rhythm, I followed the tail of the snake. It wound back around to the front of the Sri Lankan and came just to below his puckered navel and then disappeared down and beyond the dipping waistline of the sarong, toward the very center of the dancer.

The dancer had seen me. The dancer had chosen me. He moved to directly between me and my line of sight on the Aussie hunk and stood there, dancing only for me. Swaying to the music for me. Undulating his snake tattoo in a mesmerizing movement that held my attention entirely and aroused my already oozing juices. The Sri Lankan was dancing with his hands too, turning them in impossible positions to the rhythm of the music. They were beckoning to me, and the dancer was slowly retreating from me, but drawing me with him.

I had no idea I'd left the bar stool and was following the swaying snake until we were beyond the dance floor and entering one of the more private parts of the garden, still within sight of the swimming pool and well within hearing of the band music and softly lit, but somehow completely cut off from the swirling vortex of cruising men on the dance floor and at the bars. The achingly handsome Sri Lankan was still moving with the music, undulating his muscles and that fascinating snake. I was charmed. He drew me over to a velour-covered padded lounge chair, one of a large set scattered around the pool area, and I sank into that without being fully aware that I no longer was sitting at the bar.

The Sri Lankan swayed in front me to the music, drawing ever closer to me. The snake was holding my attention enthralled. I felt the long slender fingers at my waistband and the button being undone, and I heard the zipper being slowly worked down. And I felt my jeans being pulled off my legs, but I had eyes only for the undulating of the snake tattoo. It seemed alive. Sensual, not the least bit frightening.

The dancer leaned down and his handsome face crowded my vision. He was smiling and telling me how beautiful I was and asking me if he could fuck me. His long slender fingers were stroking my cock. And of course I told him he could fuck me. That's what I'd come here for. Exotic relief. And this was far beyond my wildest dreams.

He gave me a deep, possessing kiss on the lips, and his tongue darted inside my mouth. Here, there, everywhere. Exploring, slithering inside me.

He moved one of my hands to the knot at the waist of his sarong and whispered that I should untie it. All the time, he was swaying to the music, his muscles and that snake undulating in breathtaking motion. My hands were trembling and it took both of them to undo the knot. When I had finally managed to untie it, he stepped away from me as the silk of the sarong slithered down his legs and puddled on the concrete of the pool deck at his feet.

I gasped when I saw him naked. The tail of the snake wound down his groin and onto his penis and encircled it twice before ending just short of the cut glans head and on the top surface of his cock. His cock was long and curved up in tumescence. I had gasped mostly, though, because his bulbous dickhead had been rouged the same color as the snake head on his chest and two tiny green eyes had also been inked in. And, most maddeningly of all, he had a stud in his penis head and attached to that was five or six inches of thin red ribbon, slit most of the way from the tip. The forked tongue of the snake.

"Do you want to make love to it before I fuck you?" he whispered to me in a sing song voice.

Of course I did. He continued to undulate his tattooed torso in front of me to the rhythm of the music as I played his long, rouged cock with my mouth. He was humming to the music in half tones that harmonized with what the band was playing but that made the music into a more mysterious, sensuous sound. And somehow he managed to reach my cock with long sensual fingers and augment my arousal as I made love to the snake between his legs.

I heard rustling in the bushes and looked up to see that the Aussie who had first arrested my attention had followed us. He sat down on stonework surrounding an area of foliage in the shadows not far from us, and I heard the sound of a zipper, and he pulled out a cock even larger than I had hoped he had and fingered it as he intently watched with slitted eyes the Sri Lankan taking me.

Even before the Aussie arrived and settled himself, the Sri Lankan pulled away from me and, moving strong hands behind my knees on both sides, slid my body down the lounge chair so that my butt hung over the side, and spread my legs wide.

A light over the chair in a palm tree played down on us just right to focus down along a torso that was still swaying to the music. My eyes moved down from the undulating snake head on the torso to the approaching snake head at the end of his long, upward curved cock, and the light gave me a full view of him slithering inside me and giving my passage walls the combined thrill of dancing, swaying, a cock stud, and that swirling red-silk ribbon cock tongue.

He was striking inside me. Again and again. Biting every inch of my passage with the stud. Slithering that tongue inside, going ever deeper with each strike. I was lurching and moaning and groaning and begging him to fuck me forever just as he was doing. And the Sri Lankan was still swaying to the music and gliding his sensuous fingers over me and working my cock like the gear shift on a fine sports car.

I was turning my head this way and that way, glorying in the sensual fuck. I saw that the Aussie was highly aroused as well and was running his meaty hands over the deep curves and bulges of his muscles. His thick cock was standing out what seemed a full foot and he had his thumb on the head of it and was moving it in a slow, languid motion.

And now there were others there too. Not much different from one of my rock concerts—except that it was the Sri Lankan playing me to perfection rather than me taking the lead in entertaining the crowd. One of the small islanders had moved to the Aussie and, naked, was sitting, facing me, in the Aussie's lap. The Aussie was moving the smaller, bronzed islander up and down on his cock, controlled by strong hands around the smaller man's waist. The islander's head was lolling around on his shoulders, lost in the skewering by the larger man's prodigious cock. But the Aussie's eyes were on me. He, along with the Sri Lankan, was fucking me with his eyes. And I knew that later, when the Sri Lankan had done with me, I would be down in the shadows on the beach, being fucked by the Aussie in the same long masterful strokes with which he was taking the small islander.

The one light playing down between the torsos of the Sri Lankan and me, both swaying to the music of the fuck and slamming against each other, the snake between his legs slithering out and then slamming back into its hole. Repeatedly. Again and again. In rhythm to the music. The men gathered around were watching and fingering each other. One man was standing behind another, smaller one, and fucking him hard from behind. Lifting him with each thrust. Each thrust of his was timed with an appearance and holing of the snake between the Sri Lankan's legs.

I was getting exactly what I'd come for. I lay back and watched, along with the others, the rhythm of the Sri Lankan's fuck, knowing that I was the one getting the fullest enjoyment of it.

Laying and watching. No sense of time. Never wanting it to stop.

All the way out, the Sri Lankan pulling his hips back and then, with a hissing sound, striking hard, deep, swiftly, accurately to my center. Once, twice, five times. Both of us coming in a flood. I collapsed into the lounge chair, as the Sri Lankan slithered away into the dark. My eyes opened to the view of the massive Aussie standing in front of me, his cock heavy and hard. Reaching down with his muscular arms, he gathered me up and slung me over his shoulder and walked into the dense jungle, my head and arms dangling down his back.

Thrusting again and again in the dark. Not a snake this time. A battering ram. My cries of passion mixing with the jungle sounds of the night and the far-off sound of the band playing, the thrusting and heavy breathing continuing well past the end of the music. The music now being his grunts and my groans in a seemingly near-ending progression of thrusting and spouting, thrusting and spouting.

I woke the next morning lying in a bed of ferns against the smooth-wood trunk of a many-branched tree, my knees bent, legs spread, ass channel sore, and still purring.

SOUTH ASIA

Indian Magician

I now understand that my subconscious was miles ahead of my "surface" brain on knowing what I wanted. Male models apparently are as justly characterized as thick brained as female models are reputed to be. There was no blame to cast; I'd seen the Indian doctor (if he really was a doctor) work the young men on the gym floor and in the shower room. There was no reason my surface brain wouldn't know he was a sexual predator. In the end, I'm really glad it happened, though.

The Indian was a magician really—and I was the world's worst dummy. The first encounter happened without me having a clue about what had happened even when it was over. I was a few years older than those the Indian was targeting at the gym in New Delhi that I frequented when I was assigned to the U.S. embassy there—and he was a good twenty years older than I was. He touched me in the sauna, and my cock burbled out juice without warning and certainly without my really realizing we were having any form of sex. He had a mesmerizing voice, and I got horny without the usual arousal mechanisms—no warning really. He was doing this monologue about being circumcised or not in those doctor words of his, as if we were having an academic discussion or a medical consultation, and he had his long, thin fingers on my cock head before I really knew what he was doing. I was so surprised that I shot right off. I was greatly embarrassed, thinking I had probably misjudged his intent and now he'd think I was queer. I left the sauna in a highly confused state.

For his part, he probably just thought I was performing a hard-to-get mating dance. I hadn't clocked him when he got hold of my cock. I'd just sat there and stared dumbly.

I stewed about the encounter for a week, and although I didn't think I was attracted to South Asians, this one was quite handsome and distinguished and sensual looking. The next time we were in the sauna alone, I more or less set myself up for the pass, thinking he probably wouldn't even make one and I could put my confusion to rest. I stretched out on my back, towel loosely around my waist and stretching down to my knees. He came in and sat on the bench below me and in back of me. In somewhat of a trembling condition, I spread my thighs so that from where he was sitting, he could see up under my towel and check out the goods (if he wanted to). He obviously wanted to and liked what he saw.

An electric jolt went through me and I suddenly knew we were "doing something," when I felt his strong, long fingers on my foot and he was massaging it—the sole and the toes— and slowly pulling on toes in a sensual way. I went hard. He slowly worked his hand up my calf and knee and under the hem of the towel. That's when he started murmuring to me how nice my body was—and I was narcissistic enough to melt to his seduction. He'd seen me work out on the gym floor, he said, and he knew I was in TV commercials. I had worked in movies in the states and the Indian films loved to have Americans in their TV commercials. His hand slowly went up the inside of my thigh, and he was lightly stroking my cock. I shoot off almost immediately again. And, thick lunkhead that I was, I apologized for early ejaculation. This hadn't happened to me with women. Obviously the new experience with men was just that much more arousing.

Still holding my cock, he said he could teach me some techniques that would help with that problem—he was talking like a doctor and like it would be something I could use with the women I was with. I weakly said I didn't have a problem with women, but I was talking pretty weakly because my attention was riveted to what he was doing with his hand. He was palming my cock and stroking the piss hole with a thumb, rubbing my ejaculated cum around the head. He was still talking clinically enough that I was fooling myself a bit about what was going on. I said I'd think about it.

The next week, he overheard me being told that my regular masseur wouldn't be there that afternoon—I always worked out, showered, and then was rubbed down. The Indian then asked me while we were still out on the floor exercising whether I'd like to come back to his office, which was in his home, after we worked out and he'd give me the massage I was missing. I was all aflutter, still not positive where this was leading, when we got to his place. He did have a massage room with a padded table and all. And he massaged my back and legs and arms with oil—doing a better job than my regular masseur did. He told me to roll over on my back, and when I did so, I saw that he now was naked. He was tall and lithe, but very well muscled, and he had a thin but very long dong. It wasn't hard at all, so I rationalized that I was pretty safe.

He was massaging my front with oil and my cock was standing up straight—and I was very embarrassed, not being able to control it and still figuring there was an outside chance he wasn't trying to do me, that this was all a misunderstanding on my part. When he got to my pelvis, he slowly jerked me off, his hand slick with oil, murmuring that I was just to relax. I made some embarrassed comments about being sorry I'd gotten hard, and he could just try to ignore that, but he was soothing me with words to the effect that the Indian massage method included an "evacuation of the pent-up essences" and it was all very normal in the Indian context. But even then he was starting to teach me control. He'd pump me up and then hold off until I cooled. My cock and his hands were so oiled that there was little friction at all in what he was doing. At last he let me ejaculate and cleaned it up with a towel. He then massaged all of the muscles on my front side real well again and I got drowsy.

He came around to above my head and he was massaging my temples and really putting me to sleep. He put his hands on my upper sides and pulled me up on the table until my head dropped off the end of the table and he was still working my temples. Then I felt his cock at my lips and he was pushing in, suddenly very hard. I was shocked because he had hardened up almost instantaneously (something I later learned was in his bag of tricks). He didn't push far in, but I sort of spit it out and told him, rather frightened, that I'd never sucked a man before—that, in fact, I'd never had any form of sex with a man until now.

He went all impressed and joyful at the news that he had a virgin on his hands. While I had been wondering what was going on, he had just thought I was into a foreplay game. He asked me if I'd let him initiate me. He begged me to let him prepare me for future encounters. He entreated me that I'd never have anyone as gentle and skilled as him if I had any inkling I wanted to be with men. He flattered me by wondering how anyone who looked like me could have gotten this far without going bi. He showed me a picture of his wife (it really was his wife, I found out later) and assured me that many men took pleasure both ways. Something inside me told me I didn't want to deny myself any opportunities to full sensuality, and I gulped and asked him if he really would be gentle. (I didn't think to ask him why I wasn't going to be fucking him instead, if I was all that hot.) To prove he would be gentle and careful, his cock did go back into my mouth, but only a little ways, and rotated around. He said we wouldn't have to get much into that for now. (My guess is that he wanted to get his dick up my ass before I thought better of the situation.)

He sent me off with an enema bottle then, saying I'd be more comfortable if I was cleaned out—and he went off to take a ritualistic shower (he said). He didn't want me to take a shower, I guess, because he wanted to roll around in the oil I'd been basted in.

When I came back, he had me go up on my belly on the table—I was oiled up so well now I could have slid off the table. I assumed he'd suck me off to show me how that was done, but he obviously was going straight for the main event. A virgin is a virgin. An American male model virgin in the grasp is probably a trip to Nirvana for a randy gay Indian. He put a pretty bulky pillow under my belly to lift my pelvis up. He then got up on the

338

table, pushed my thighs wide, and got down behind me and tongued my asshole for a while. His tongue also went to the underside of my cock and around my balls and across my inner thighs in this process. All the time he was telling me how nice I was and assuring me that I was slowly opening and that I'd be well open before he mounted me.

He actually said that—that he would be mounting me. For some reason that sounded really sexy to me.

He was pretty good at his word on that. He patiently worked on me for an hour or more (during which I shot off a couple more times, with his encouragement and clucking that I had nothing to be embarrassed about—I could reload within twenty minutes in those days and shoot off five or six times a night when I was really aroused). Varieties of lubricant were applied, some of which was for deadening the area (and probably was illegal). After his tongue, he went to fingers. He had long, sensual ones, and he could easily reach my prostate and showed me how he could make me shoot off just by rubbing me there. Then well-oiled fingers probing deeper. Whatever he was using to deaden pain was only used on the rim and just a few inches inside, so he could be in a couple of inches before I even knew I was being skewered. He showed me a couple of smallish dildos of increasing size before he lubed them up and screwed them into my ass and around. Not much pain in any of this, and I was jacked up to the roof at the very idea of what was happening to me—the sheer risk and adventure of it— and the fact that I'd finally been brave enough to give it a try.

After more than an hour, I felt his cock at my back door, and he very slowly entered me—and entered me and entered me and entered me. That was one long cock. It felt like the uncoiling of a snake inside me. He had one of those "bent up" cocks too, so I could feel the head dragging along my ass canal walls as it plowed up me. There was some pain now, but I'm sure minimal pain for a first time. I'd been as gently prepared as I could wish for. He rode me, slowly pumping me deep, for a good thirty minutes, drawing out his pleasure with the virgin as much as he could, I suppose. He was braced on his knees behind me and either kept his hands hooked over my shoulders or palmed flat on my shoulder blades as his cock worked me. He was chattering away in his singsong voice, no doubt keeping me calm and mesmerized, and I could tell that the experience was quite arousing for him too, because he came quickly (for him—he was the master of self-control). His ejaculation felt like a warm oozing inside me, sort of a foreign tickling sensation.

He held there for a while, his cock buried to the hilt, massaging my muscles again and telling me what a lovely young man I was. I felt him go flaccid inside me, which left me with a strange feeling of loss. But he just kept massaging me, not letting me up. And I felt him start to engorge and fill up my ass canal again. I didn't feel sore inside, but the deadening was wearing off on the rim of my ass, and I felt a little chaffed there. It was obvious that he wasn't going to let the virgin get away with one screwing.

He pulled out of me and walked down the table on his knees, pulling me with him, until we were both standing on the floor at the edge of the table, and then he bent me over, my chest on the table, my legs wide, and he folded himself over me as well and slowly entered me a second time. This time I felt some pain at the entry and let him know he was hurting me. He shushed me like one would do a fussy baby and just kept plowing up me. He said he wanted briefly to let me feel another type of fucking and that he knew I'd enjoy it. He squeezed my thighs with his, which tightened my canal around his cock and then he took me in long strokes, nearly all the way out, and then all the way back in. He did me for about fifteen minutes this way, and I was very vocal with this one, arching my back up to him and writhing my hips around. This is where I first experienced pain mixed so heavily with pleasure that I both was yelling that he was hurting me and pleading with him to keep pumping me. He claimed to really like my reaction to that position—and chose to keep pumping me.

Then he turned me on his cock, while pushing on my back onto the massage table. He spread my legs, and, saying this was yet another style I might like, he gave me a mixed-routine fuck. He'd pump me from the front with fast shallow strokes for five minutes, then take the root of his cock in his hand and rotate it around inside me, hitting all the walls with that bent knob of his. Then back to the short, fast strokes. I did a good bit of grunting and moaning for him in this position—and wondering if it was going to ever stop—not at all sure I wanted it to. He went deep then for about three plunges and he had come again.

We showered together and that's when he went down in front of me in the cascading water and sucked me off. He did it quickly that afternoon. In later sessions he showed me he could drive me wild with his tongue and mouth work on my cock.

After drying off, he took me to his bed, and after lubing up my hole and his cock, he fucked me again in a side split—me on my left side, he on his left side behind and under me, his left arm under and around me, with his palm fanned out over my belly, his right hand holding my right leg up in the air, and his cock stroking up into me from behind and below. During this, he started showing me that men could exchange sensual kisses. After he was done with me in that position, I was exhausted and slept in his arms for over an hour, with his cock up my (now throbbing and sore) ass.

So, it took me a hell of a long time to get around to any "firsts," but then my real first was a doozy.

The Indian gave me ointments and lubricants to cut down on the "getting used to it" pain, and a collection of ever-larger butt plugs—that didn't stretch the rim too much, but that stretched the first three or four inches inside, so that big cocks could get in and not do too much damage.

Good thing I had this preparation and the first encounter/training I had with the sensitive Indian, because about six weeks after that, I was trapped in a massage room at the gym by a Swede with a thick good eight incher and was taken roughly and in no uncertain terms and little choice in the matter (of course, it was all my fault as I had purposely given him a good look at me and acted a little provocatively in the shower room to check out my effect on other men). With the preparation the Indian "doctor" was giving me, I actually enjoyed the Swede.

Mumbai Glitter

I was bent over on my belly on the conference table, high in the glass-windowed office building overlooking the harbor of India's busy financial center Mumbai, formerly Bombay, and the hunky blond attorney was riding me hard from behind. I still had on my tie; my shirt, unbuttoned; and my shoes and socks clipped to supporters wound just below my knees. But otherwise I was naked. He started a maddening rotation of his cock inside me, and I was giving little urping sounds. To let the others see the pain and ecstasy this master cocking brought to my facial expression, he pulled my head up by pulling on my tie, which he had spun around to my back to give him reins for his hot ride of my ass. All the time he was telling me what a hot performer I'd be in his nightclub act. My own boss, the Indian who headed up the Mumbai office of an international consortium, and the two Japanese businessmen were sitting there, mesmerized by the exhibition the blond and I were putting on, their hands in their laps, working their own meat. The blond released the tie and his hands went to holding my hips still as he stroked hard in and out of me. I could feel his gold cock ring kissing the sides of my inner canal as he pumped me.

The golden blond was telling me what a good fuck I was, that he wanted to have more of me. He was asking me how I was enjoying the ride, and I was panting and groaning my approval of his eight inches working hard inside me.

My boss rose from the table, engorged cock in hand, and came over and tweaked one of my nipples while he kissed the blond deeply. Then he told the blond that it was time for the Japanese businessmen to take over with me and that he wanted the blond's cock in his own ass now.

The blond withdrew from me, the Japanese businessmen already eagerly standing in line behind him, and a large cock was exchanged for a medium-sized one, which, however, was more active and inventive in its exploration of my ass; the other Japanese businessman knelt between me and the table and started playing my cock and balls like a flute with his sensitive mouth.

The blond had planted my boss on his back across the narrow conference table from me, and my boss and I engaged in deep kissing and exploration of each other's torsos with our hands, as the blond spread my boss's legs and plowed into his ass. I lifted my head up from my boss's as the blond brutally entered him, and I held my boss's head between my hands, both of us connecting on what was happening in our asses with a variety of expressions on our faces.

When the Japanese and their blond attorney were finished sealing our multimillion dollar deal, they left my boss and me there on the table, consoling and rejoicing in each other and at our success at and on the conference table.

In parting, the golden blond came back to me and gave me a kiss. He flipped a business card out and said that I should visit his nightclub in the Calaba gay district of the city for the experience of my life; that the card would give me a free pass and free drinks. And that he would throw in another wild, free fuck as well if I was interested.

Try as I might I couldn't get the blond out of my mind. I hadn't seen many northern Europeans since I'd arrived for my internship in the Mumbai office, and he was a pleasant change from the South Asians I'd been cavorting with since I got here. He had ridden me hard, but he hadn't finished me off. I developed an obsession that he finish me off, that I feel the explosion and bathing of that eight-inch ring-headed cock of his deep inside me.

* * * *

Three nights later, the blond's business card in hand, I was standing at the dimly lit walk-down wooden door under the iron porch above of a dark building in the heart of the Calaba district. Only the blinking sign announcing "Club Pan" beside the door assured me I was in the right place. At my ringing of the bell, the door opened just a crack, but enough for me to show the business card, with the scrawl of the blond across it. Then the door opened enough for me to slip through, but then it shut again with a solid, final sound. The vestibule was dark, black drapery on black walls, ceiling, and floor. The half man who admitted me was also dark—but not a South Asian, it didn't seem; he seemed to have more of a Mediterranean look about him.

I say half man, because he was togged out as a wood nymph, or a satyr, or whatever they call those horned men with the legs and feet of a goat. This one was slender as a reed, with black curly hair, a small goatee, little pointed horns above his temples, black eyebrows curled up at the ends, and an interesting array of black tattooing on his naked torso. The most prominent of these, as I could see when he turned to guide me beyond a beaded curtain into a large step-down, smoke-filled room, was a chain of interlocked heart shapes descending from this hair line at the back of his head down to where the goat's pelt started just above his crack at the bottom of the small of his back. His legs, as I already indicated, were pelted like a brown goat's, and his feet coverings were made out like cloven hooves. Most distinctly, though, was that his cock and balls hung free and there was a circular opening in the pelt at his rear where his asshole lurked.

The nymph swished his tail saucily as he guided me through the dim, smoky room to one of four long bars by the back walls on either side of what looked like a small diner theater, with three tiers of descending levels going down to a circular stage in the center. Everything was black. The bars were black, the carpets and walls and ceiling were black, and the couches set around on the descending tiers, more like the lounges in those Roman banquet movies, were also covered in black material. Even the stage was black; it was square but had a round, revolving platform set into it. And standing up from this platform was an eight- or nine-foot high, widely spread X-shaped apparatus, with the cross-over set so that the upper portion of the apparatus was larger than the bottom. This was made out of some sort of transparent Lucite-type material. Near the four corners of the stage were poles made out of the same transparent material that went up to the ceiling. The poles were some sort of hollow tube filled with a liquid in which glittery gold confetti floated.

The theater was dark, although I could hear the sound of moaning and activity that told me that something was happening down on those lounges on the descending tiers—and as my eyes adjusted to the dimness, I could see that there were pairings and small groups of men dotted here and there, becoming very well acquainted with each other. It must have been early, however, as the theater was only about a fourth full of these fully occupied patrons. Not all of them were Indians. There was a smattering of Westerners, and I might have recognized a couple of the Japanese men as those who had been at the meeting at our offices the other day.

The nymph whispered something to the bartender, yet another satyr, but a larger version than the young man who had admitted me to the club—indeed all of those serving the patrons were decked out in the same motif. The younger man pointed to the business card that I carried and then told me I could order anything I wanted—that the bartender was at my beck and call. That was very nice to hear, I thought, as I checked out the very presentable, broadly smiling bartender, not leaving out a peek over the bar at what he was packing between his legs. There was nothing there for him to be ashamed of.

As I sat back and drank my first drink and observed the atmosphere, I saw that activity had started down on the stage. The four poles now were occupied by male dancers—all young, dusky-skinned, lithe nymphs just like the door keeper.

Strobing white lights started to work the room, and I now was getting a sparkly feeling of glitter everywhere. That's when I noticed the decor of the room. Cylinders of glittery gold hung on wires above the stage area in thick profusion, and as the lights strobed, they bounced off the glittery gold sparkles and brought the arena to life. I noticed then that the lights were picking up glitterings on the tiers down to the stage as well—just here and there, but enough to make my eyes dart around the room, increasingly picking out very intimate embraces and activity going on at the lounges.

A few of the glittering cylinders were on the floor of the stage, and I assumed that they had fallen from the wires. But I felt a chill and a tinkling sensation going down my spine as I realized otherwise. From the third tier in front of me, my eye caught a naked figure rise from one of the lounges, and I caught the bounce of strobe light off gold glitter as he glided down to the stage and came up with one of the gold glittery cylinders and threw it down on the stage floor. Condoms. These were glittery gold condoms. Used condoms, merging the activity in the audience with the entertainment on the stage. The club's decoration was both evocative and functional. I watched in awe as the figure pulled another cylinder off a wire hanging down toward the stage and glided back up to the third tier, no doubt for another round of pleasure.

Four beefy satyrs had arrived on the stage now and were cuffing the pole dancers who had preceded them to the poles and, one muscled satyr to one lithe pole-dancing nymph, were beginning to perform a duet of love dance for the patrons. Each of the muscled satyrs was outfitted with a glittery gold condom.

The club was beginning to fill up now, and all of the patrons I saw coming in were handsome and well built. The club has developed a winning clientele. The performers on stage were turning me on. Already one of the beefy satyrs had filled his glittering condom and had thrown it to the floor and was pulling another one down from an overhead hanger and sliding it on his hard, curved up tool. He quickly was ready to resume his dance with the younger nymph, who was contorting his body around the pole, seeking a new and interesting position to be taken by his partner. All of this for the enjoyment of those in the audience, most of whom were so absorbed in filling out their own glittery tubes to give full attention to the floor show.

I felt my tool pushing against the fabric of my trousers, and I reached down to stroke myself, only to find that I'd been so absorbed in the atmosphere around me that I hadn't notice there already was a hand there. I turned to see a nice, square-jawed face with bedroom eyes. But I only caught a glimpse of the man who had taken interest in me when the bartender said something gruff to him and he was gone. I was a little annoyed, because I hadn't asked the bartender to run interference for me.

And I was about to say something to him, when the lights went brighter on the stage and the heart-stopping golden blond who had invited me here appeared. He was decked out in leather, but it was all of a glittery gold color, from the chain criss-crossing his chest, to the boots, and arm bands, and a riding crop with a billy club-like handle—but no other body attire except for the glittery gold condom trying its best to cover his eight inches of horse-hung meat.

He walked the four corners of the stage briefly, flicking bottoms here and there with his riding crop and inserting hands into this and that undulating position, and then he came in front of the revolving transparent X apparatus and spread his arms wide, muscles rippling in the strobe lights, and all action on the stage stopped in mid fuck.

"Do we have a volunteer this evening, gentlemen?" he asked the now-filled house in a booming voice.

The strobe lights revolved wildly around the theater and then all merged—on me.

Before I had time to react in any way, I was being bustled down to the stage by my babysitting bartender and a few of the other club satyrs and was finding that the transparent X apparatus had cuffs on it that, when I was trussed up, stretched my arms and legs out wide and securely in place.

I had become a focal point for the floor show. For the next half hour or more, as the satyrs returned to pole fucking the nymphs and the well-used glittery condoms from the audience and the corners of the stage continued to build up on the floor of the stage, the blond god teased and tormented me. He prodded and pinched and kissed and tongued me endlessly and

348

to distraction, as I revolved around the arena, cuffed to that transparent X. He flicked me with his riding crop and applied love slaps to my butt and hips and thighs and chest. He twisted and pulled at my nipples and balls until I screamed my awareness of the sensual cruelty in him. And then he fucked me with the greased butt end of his riding crop, stretching and preparing me for his even longer and thicker gold-glittered tool. All the time I was revolving, giving the club patrons a look at the glorious torment from all angles, writhing and bucking with and against the butt end of the riding crop, testing the rock-solid holding strength of the X apparatus.

The tiers running up from where I was being displayed were a teaming mass of undulating bodies and young, naked men descending to the stage and tossing their offerings of spent glittery gold condoms at my feet and then grabbing a replacement off the handing wires and remerging with the slithering pile of man flesh stretched around the room.

The golden god was behind me now, his hands on my shoulders, and his glitter gold cock slapping on my butt cheeks and working its way up and down across the puckered, moist rim of my asshole as he stroked up and down inside my butt crack. The bulging head of his dick came ever lower as he stroked up and down inside my crack, with each stroke now more centered at my hole, until with one long stroke he entered me deeply, strongly, and painfully. I lifted my head and howled to the ceiling and a cheer went up around the theater.

There was more of a hush now, much of the attention on the blond god and me rather than on each other, as two the satyrs left tormenting their nymphs and uncuffed my legs and held them higher and stretched out more as the blond relentlessly pumped my hole with long, deep thrusts, giving all in the audience a good view of my plowing as the stage revolved slowly around and around.

I was not shy in voicing being well fucked, and another cheer went up as my ejaculate shot out across the dozens of glittery-gold used condoms littering the stage below me.

The golden god also yelled his delight and joy when he had cum deep inside me, and he swiftly parted from me and jerked off his spent condom and tossed it out into a roaring audience. Then he strutted around the stage, flicking the poled nymphs playfully with his riding crop as, one after the other, the four muscled satyrs plowed me and added their glittery gold condoms to the offerings at my feet.

When they had done with me, my wrists were uncuffed. But then I was pushed to my knees, with my heaving chest forced into the V of the X apparatus, and my wrists were cuffed again at a lower position. The blond then presented his cock to me, me knelt on one side of the X and him standing at the other side, and I sucked him to life again as the stage continued its endless revolutions to show the entire audience the full effect.

When he was once more in engorged full-eight-inch fucking form, I was uncuffed and simply sank to the floor, exhausted. But once more the golden god's tool was adorned with glittering gold and he took me one last time on the floor at the base of the X apparatus. He fucked down into me deeply and strongly as I lay whimpering and moaning on my belly on a pile of used glittery gold condoms on the revolving stage— loving every golden stroke he took.

Raja Obsession

He had become obsessed with me. The holiday party was large and boisterous, and our eyes met across the room and he gave me a brilliant smile. His eyes were a liquid brown; his skin the color of nutmeg, his stature straight and tall and confident. He was in his element here; I was not.

A short time later, he sat down beside me with people swirling all around us and put his hand on my thigh and gave me that brilliant smile again. I tipped my glass to show I needed a refill and glided away from him, not wanting to make a scene. Not long after that, he trapped me in an alcove and kissed me on the lips and put a hand on my crotch. He managed to whisper "I want you; I want you now. I want to feel my cock inside you," before I broke away and put as much distance as I could between him and me. As soon as I could make my way to the door, I left, and walked back upstairs to my hotel room.

His obsession had disturbed me greatly. I'd been propositioned by men before, but never so blatantly or persistently.

When Geofrey had died, I had taken to travel to assuage my grief and reorder myself for a new life, whatever that had been. Geofrey had always wanted to do a Raja tour, a slow journey through the South Asian continent in pursuit of capturing the good life of the British Colonial period. It was what he had written about in his novels, but, strangely enough, he had never experienced the essence of the period that he had been praised for attaining in his writing. I had already traveled through India, stopping at all of the grand dame hotels of the British Raja, and on New Year's I had found myself in Kandy, the old cultural capital of Sri Lanka, at the venerable Citadel Hotel, perched on the edge of the Mahaweli River.

As I had traveled across the subcontinent, I had discovered that I was attracted by the South Asian men, and, the farther south I traveled, that I was aroused by them. It was thus that I had been disturbed by the forceful attentions the finely formed young Sri Lankan man, obviously of ancient royal stock of Kandy's past.

I showered, opened the widow onto the terrace to take advantage of the breeze wafting across the top of the city from the Mahaweli River before my room, and lay down on my bed, naked. I was drowsy, a little drunk, and disturbed. I couldn't get the man's handsome face and brilliant smile out of my mind. What could he have seen in me to have formed such an obsession? I wasn't that way; I didn't go around advertising myself.

The breeze from the terrace caressed my body, and I found myself gliding one hand around my torso and pinching at my nipples, while slowly stroking my cock with the other hand. Hardening my cock and relaxing myself in my own way as I drifted off to sleep, as I often did on these breezy nights in the city.

I heard a sigh and moan and my eyes popped open. He was standing there in the moonlight from the open terrace door. He was naked, and he was beautiful. And he was fully aroused; the obsessed man from the party. His eyes were captured by the sight of my hand stroking up and down on my cock.

He came down on the bed below me and wrapped a hand around my engorged cock and covered the end of it with his mouth. He rotated my cock in his mouth while his tongue slid over and around its helmet, and he sucked it with his tongue flicking the slit at the end of the helmet. Then he swallowed me down to the root and applied even pressure all up and down my cock. In shock, I let him do this to me. And when I recovered and put my hand down to his head to pull him away from me, he took my hands in his and slid them out to each side of the silken bedspread, while he started to pump my cock slowly with his mouth.

I don't know why, but neither one of us spoke. I had been so close to sleep that I couldn't be fully sure this wasn't just a dream, just an extension of my masturbating myself to sleep after having encountered a man who claimed to want me, to want his cock inside me. It was a sensation I'd hadn't had in months and that sent a chill of fear and anticipation through me.

He took my right hand in his and guided it to my cock. I felt powerless and just let him take the lead. He entwined his fingers in mine and then wrapped both hands around my cock, his hand guiding me in stroking myself. His eyes glittered as he watched me masturbating under his guidance. I sighed and arched my back, feeling so much more aroused than if I had been doing this solo. I—or, rather, we—brought my throbbing tool close to ejaculation, and when he let go of my hand, I was too near to climax to fight him for what he obviously wanted from me.

His mouth once more slid down over my cock. My hands went to entwine themselves in his beautiful jet-black hair, and his hands slid up my sides and buried themselves in my chest hair. He was rubbing and rolling my nipples when I shot off down his throat, in three strong and satisfying spasms.

He sucked me clean and then sent his lips and tongue on a journey up across my belly and my abs and onto my pecs and nipples and then into the hollow of my neck and, at last to my mouth. He enveloped me in his arms, there in the dark, the breeze caressing both of our bodies, and our dicks entwined between our bellies. Mine was soft but quickly reloading and his was hard as a rock and gigantic and pushing insistently up my belly, reaching for the cleft between my pecs.

I was struggling to get free, but he was too strong for me. We rolled in the bed, limbs and cocks entwined and dueling, until I was exhausted. He then turned me on my belly and kissed and tongued his way down from my shoulders to the small of my back. He pulled my butt cheeks apart with strong, wide hands, and his tongue and lips went to my tight, long-unused asshole. A hand snaked up between my thighs, and I rose my hips a bit while he rolled and gently squeezed and pulled on my balls. My cock was coming alive again, and he pulled that on through between my thighs and alternated kissing and tonguing my hole with kissing and tonguing the helmet on my cock.

His full attention went back to my asshole. His hands were kneading and rolling my butt cheeks, and I found I was grinding my cock into the bedspread, fucking the bedspread. His hands encased my pelvis, and he helped me with the grinding. Then he was only helping me with one strong hand, which had had run between my legs and fanned out over my lower belly, using his elbow to help hold my pelvis up from the surface of the bedspread to help me stroke the underside of my cock along the silken cloth.

He started inserting fingers into my moistened and loosened hole. He managed to insert two fingers to where my sphincter muscle picked them up and drew the index finger to my prostate gland. When he'd rubbed across that a couple of times, I came again, for a second time and collapsed onto my belly. His fingers had maintained hold, however, and he continued to finger fuck me for several minutes, the big palm of his other hand firmly planted in the small of my back, symbolically asserting his control, his possession of me.

I don't know why, but I just laid there, letting him have his way with me. He was dominating me in silence. Still neither of us had spoken.

He turned me on my left side, as he stretched his body up behind me. His left arm went under me and wrapped around and he cupped my right breast with his left hand. I raised my right arm over my head and my left hand lowered to languidly play with my recovering cock and my balls.

He rose up enough over me to give me a deep kiss and then he settled down below me, his pelvis nestled under my butt cheeks. His alarmingly long cock had pierced its way through my thighs and the head had come out under my balls. I managed to reach and fingered the helmet of his cock, working up precum and sliding it around on the sensitive knob, until he moaned and I could felt him quivering. He stroked my cock and cuddled my balls for a short while and then brought his fingers to mine on the head of his cock and helped me excite him there.

He sank his face into the hollow of my neck and found the throbbing carotid artery there and sucked and kissed at that, while he raised my right leg in the air and I felt the head of his cock at my asshole. I moved to escape him and lurched a bit as the helmet went in up to its rim. I cried out then, the first time that the silence had been broken. He buried his left hand into my chest, holding me firmly there, and his teeth pressed firmly into the hollow of my neck, as he forced his cock in a good five inches. I jerked and shuddered as the helmet of his cock dragged across my prostate.

I was panting from the feeling of being stuffed and from the initial pain. He held there as the pain slowly subsided and whispered endearments in my ear. "Ah, it will be fine; the pain will go away. You're so fine, such a beautiful body. I've been obsessed with you all evening. A nice tender, tight ass; I love the feeling of my cock up this sweet ass."

When he felt me relaxing a bit, he pushed in another couple of inches and then started pumping me in short strokes, never coming back more than a couple of inches. He lowered my right leg down and back, which made my canal all that much tighter, and he spread his right hand across my belly.

He must have stroked me like this for a good ten minutes, whispering encouragement and voicing how much he loved being in my body all the while.

It was like I'd been hypnotized. I just lay there enveloped in his embrace, letting him do what no man had ever done to me before.

I thought that it was long past when he should have come and left me, but his stamina was amazing, and I wasn't anywhere close to end of this ravishment. He had grown a couple of inches and now was at least seven and a half inches into me.

Before I knew it, he had pulled out of me, and I started to rise, thinking this was over, but he just laughed and slapped me on the butt, and rose from the end of the bed on his feet. He flipped me over on my belly and pulled my hips back to the end of the bed and entered my asshole with that big rod again. He had his hands on my hips and he just brought me back onto his skewer. He went in at least seven inches this time and then pushed to eight or more and deep stroked me. He stopped occasionally and rotated his cock around inside me, giving special attention to the walls of my canal.

After an eternity, he turned me again, this time onto my back and without losing purchase with his cock and he seemed to attain even more depth. He was churning around inside me nine inches or more deep, and I was holding him to me, seeking as much intimacy as I could get. His pelvis was riding up on my buttocks. We were belly to belly, heaving chest to heaving chest. His arms held me fast to the surface of the bed, his hands cupping my head, his mouth kissing me wherever it could reach. I held his chest close to me in my enveloping arms and had my legs tightly wrapped around the small of his back. My cock was being stroked between our bellies by the rocking and churning of his pelvis, and I came for the third time just before he shot his load deep inside me.

He slid both of us up onto the bed and collapsed on top of me, enveloping my body once more with his arms and searching from my mouth with his. When his mouth had dropped to the hollow of my neck, I looked over toward the terrace door and saw that dawn was near.

We slept, and when I awoke the day, was bright and full. And I was alone. I was murmuring Geofrey's name, but I was thinking of someone else entirely. Geofrey had never loved me as my obsessed Sri Lankan lover had. I was not sure—I would have to think on it—but my Raja journey may have come to an end.

I lay back down on my bed and started to languidly masturbate while my mind searched for clues on how my obsessive lover got to me—wondering now if I even could be quite sure that wishful thinking had been my lover in a drunken dream. I closed my eyes; arched my back; imagined a strong hand on mine, guiding the stroking of my throbbing cock; and gave a little cry of pleasure as release flowed up through me and fountained onto my belly and thighs.

Sweet Sanjay

I heard my name being called out from the midst of the teeming horde pressing in on the barriers after customs in New Delhi's Indira Gandhi international airport, and a head and arm waving a sign was bouncing up and down over the tumult. The sign the young man was carrying said "Clifford Jenkins" with "New York" written under it. That was me. But I wasn't being met by anyone that I knew of. The young man obviously thought I was, though, as he was pushing his way through the crowd, moving toward where I would have to join the crowd myself at the end of the separated-off corridor. He had his eyes on me and was waving just for me.

"Mr. Jenkins?" He held up a photograph that clearly showed that I was the man he was looking for. "I am Gupta," he said, as he came up to me. "I am your escort here in India."

"My escort?" I said, not comprehending.

"Yes, yes. I take you to Chennai to find Tamil translator. I speak Tamil and Gujarati and very, very good English. I guide you where you want to go down in Tamil Nadu. I guide you here in New Delhi too."

How did he know why I had come to India and what I was to do here? I stared at him blankly.

"Khurana. I am cousin to Khurana. Khurana, who works for you in New York. He tell me to meet you and to guide you and to take care of you."

Ah, Khurana Bhutra. One of the news agency's Indian translators in New York. One who was very good at what he did, but who also was irritating and demanding. It had been Khurana who had set off this notion that the international news agency I worked for needed another Indian translator in New York. We had taken on some government translation work in Hindi and Tamil, and Khurana had insisted we had to have another Tamil speaker to handle it.

"Come just this way. I have transportation. What is your hotel, please."

He had taken charge, and one part of me was very glad he had. I was overwhelmed by how many people were swarming around in the airport, jabbering in a mix of languages, some I didn't know, and many of these people—too many—looking emaciated and holding their hands out in supplication, their eyes big with hope, their hopes somehow focused on me.

Even as I let the young man, Gupta, lead me along through the crowd, him now rolling my suitcase so that there was no question I would follow along, I could see the hope in his eyes too. He somehow needed to establish favor with Khurana; he needed to do this service. How could I politely deny him? This ploy was just like Khurana, though. I could manage this on my own, but Khurana wanted me to be in the position to owe him as well. So I was being forced to need something from him. He was always doing this around the office—and then calling in on a chit I hadn't asked to possess and often didn't realize would have been seen as a favor from Khurana until he made a claim against it. It was maddening, but he did it expertly.

Gupta was as thin as many of those pressing about me, but he looked more strongly built than most, and he also was a handsome young man, neatly dressed in a white shirt and khakis and with clean tennis shoes, I noticed. I noticed they were clean, because so much of what others were wearing, especially their shoes, weren't clean, were in tatters. Even here, in the airport, the filth under foot was noticeable, as was the scruffiness and dinginess of everyone's shoes—those who were wearing shoes. Most were in some sort of thin sandals or were barefoot.

He had expressive brown eyes and a shock of unruly jet-black hair, and, surprisingly, since most around us were dusky skinned, his skin was alabaster white. Khurana was similarly pale and somewhat superciliously had told me it was how you could tell the purer descendants of the Mogul rulers from the masses. And, indeed, Gupta cut his way through the crowd as a prince would. The mass parted for him, and we shortly were on the curb at a cab stand.

I was sweating profusely already from the sweltering heat I had been slathered in from the very doors of the passenger jet and from the press of the crowd, starting in the arrival lines at passport control. I couldn't help myself. I was glad that the young man was here, even though he was holding my elbow possessively.

"What hotel?" he repeated.

"The Ashok," I answered.

"Ah, very, very good hotel. Khurana picked well."

I would have retorted but for the fact that Khurana, indeed, had suggested the accommodations. And later, as the cab approached the sprawling hotel, looking every inch like a raja's palace, I reluctantly had to thank Khurana under my breath for his choice.

I felt no disappointment all the way through the efficient check-in process. In contrast to the airport, all here was calm and long stretches of regal furnishings in cool fabrics and marble walls with few people in sight, or, rather, with everyone in sight looking attractive and well heeled, and at their leisure, not in a hurry to be anywhere. This contrast had already hit me as the cab that, as Gupta had said had been waiting for only us beyond the cab stand at the airport, drove through Old Delhi into New Delhi. The atmosphere turned from filth, heat, oppression, and teeming and seemingly hopeless and helpless masses, to, as we entered the new city, cool greenery, serenity, majestic buildings set in vast gardens, and the near absence of people on the streets. There were no sidewalks here; pedestrians obviously weren't welcome.

"Most Indians cannot enter New Delhi," Gupta answered to my question on this. "It is for the government and foreigners. As an Indian from the old city, you must work here or obtain a pass to visit."

I was disappointed in the answer—the thought that the people's government wasn't accessible by the people themselves, but the foreigner in me couldn't help but be pleased at the lack of pressing humanity and the frustration of the wants and needs of fawning South Asians closing in on me.

My room was large, appointed in cool silks, and wood paneled. The two windows looked out onto a vast green lawn. The bath was marble and also luxurious in its waste of space. The tub was sunken and square, enough for a couple, and I immediately had visions of honeymooners spending their entire hotel time together in the tub.

Gupta had left me at the reception desk, with the promise of meeting me again at 10:00 a.m. the next morning after I had breakfasted, saying he'd show me around New Delhi in the one day I'd scheduled to be here. After two nights here to acclimate myself, I would be heading south, to Tamil Nadu, and the city of Chennai, once called Madras, and the center of the Tamil-speaking population.

An assistant manager and a bellhop took me to my room. And then there to greet me in the room, head bowed in respect, was a young male room attendant, berry brown, demure, and quite handsome almost to the point of being pretty. He was dressed traditionally, in a white silky dhoti—the traditional skirt that Indian men wear that is a gathered length of material bound around their waists and nearly touching the floor—topped by a white silky vest tightly hugging his chest. His midriff was bare, and I was surprised to see a ruby-red gem stud in his belly button. He was wearing bangles around his wrists and ankles too that jangled a bit when he walked, and he was barefoot, with silver rings on a few of his toes.

I thought the assistant manager looked down his nose a bit at the young man as he was handing over the room key to me and the bellhop looked away until I pressed a generous tip in his hand, but then he thanked me politely and withdrew. The assistant manager treated me like visiting royalty, and I had trouble stopping him from fussing around to show me the room's amenities despite my early conveying of another generous tip to his palm.

I listened to the room boy jangle his bracelets as he unpacked my bag and stowed the clothes away in bureaus and armoires as if I was going to stay a month, while I wandered around the room, contemplating taking the shower he had hesitatingly suggested after my grueling travels—which I had to admit were pretty grueling. I stopped at a large bouquet of flowers and a bucket of ice cooling a bottle of wine and noticed there was a card in the flowers. "Welcome to India. Enjoy. Leonard," the card said.

Ah, that explained the hospitality, I thought. Leonard Wright—Sir Leonard now—was an old, very close, friend of mine from his BBC days and my early news agency days. We'd first met at the Henley Regatta when he'd been with BBC Monitoring in nearby Caversham Park and I'd been working for the U.S. government news agency. I'd later settled in New York with a private news agency and married my Jennifer, a stockbroker, who came with a powerful father as well as with a Fifth Avenue penthouse apartment that I loved and would be hard pressed to give up. Leonard had married even better. An Indian correspondent then in London, Manjula, a woman who had returned to India and to politics and had risen to near the top of the Congress Party. She was cabinet secretary of something or other now, although I never could remember which one. Her position was so important that Leonard too had been living here for the last decade.

I wondered how he knew I'd come to India. But then, through his wife, he probably knew everything that happened in India. Thinking back on my relationship with Leonard, I poured myself a glass of wine, saluted him silently, and took a sip. It was first-class wine, as I was sure it would be, knowing Leonard.

I heard the bath water running in the bathroom and I moved in that direction, stopping in the doorway in surprise and shock.

The room boy was drawing the bath. He also, though, had stripped off his dhoti and vest and was only clothed in the bangles, the navel stud, a silver nipple ring, and a shy smile.

I was about to say something when he held his hand out and I took another small card from him. "And above all else, enjoy this. He cost a fortune. Leonard," the card read.

I smiled, as the room boy started unbuttoning my shirt and raised up on his toes and kissed me shyly on the lips.

"You will have me?" he asked in a soft voice.

"Oh, yes, I most certainly will have you," I answered and took another sip of wine as he went down on his knees in front of me, unzipped my trousers, lowered my briefs, and took my cock in his mouth.

The memories of Leonard. We not only met at the Henley Regatta and both covered the event for our respective organizations, but we also got sloshed on ale together, conversed long enough together to know what each other wanted and that we wanted it from each other, and fucked and slept the sleep of exhaustion together. Leonard was interested in a particular sex technique, and I was interested in providing that same technique, so our coming together had been a miraculous event. He often said that I didn't look and act in public the sort of man who I was like that in bed; in turn, I told him that he looked just the sort of man who looked for that in another man. Neither of us took umbrage, delighted that we had fallen in with each other.

For eight years we conveniently met all over the world on assignments and tumbled into bed together as quickly and for as long as possible. Leonard was an old English school submissive bottom and I was a power top. We enjoyed each other immensely. But then he married for advancement first and I did so afterward—not in any sort of revenge, but in search of the luxuries of life. And, although we still coupled a few times after that, Manjula became a much-investigated politician in India and that was that between us.

It stood to reason that Leonard wouldn't meet with me here in India, on his own home ground—but also that he would make the gestures of welcome that he had.

I fucked the room boy in the double tub, laughing at the image I'd had when I first saw it of honeymooners who wouldn't leave it. After scrubbing me, he had climbed into the tub and, facing me, settled his channel, challengingly and evocatively tight given that he was a rent boy, on my cock and, leaning his body

362

back, had grasped his ankles. I bent my face down to his nipples and pulled at the ring with my teeth until he was giving little gasps and whimpers. I had established that he was an adult, but he had the slim, soft body of a boy. He told me that he was as many adult Indian men were, spare and small, but an adult nonetheless. I reveled in that and in Leonard, also small, knowing what I liked. I pulled his pelvis up from my buried cock, which could accommodate considerable upward pull without dislodging, with my palms grasping his small buttocks orbs, and my lips traveled down his sternum to his navel, where I grasped the ruby gem in my teeth, pulled it out, spit it out of the tub, and stuck my tongue in his navel. He was trembling and murmuring in some language I didn't understand and then gasped, as I lightly teethed the smooth, soft flesh around the navel.

He cried out and began to jerk and writhe as, grasping his waist now, I slammed him down hard on my cock. Lifted him and slammed him down; lifted him again and slammed him down again. Lifted him and slammed him down. Lifted him and . . . until, with another cry, the water between our bellies became cloudy white with his cum. He had lost his grasp of his ankles and now was grabbing at my sides, digging his fingernails into my flesh.

I enjoyed the heightened sensation the pain gave me—enjoying more the mixture of pain and passion in his eyes. His head was slanted to one side and he was eyeing me out of one eye, the other one being covered by a hank of his silky, black hair. The look was a mixture of wariness, awe, lust, and pain. With one hand I cupped the back of his head and brought his lips to mine in a brutal, possessive kiss. I encased his small cock and balls in the other hand and squeezed, causing him to gasp and whimper at the double assault.

Then, abruptly, I released him at both ends, gripped his waist in my hands again and renewed slamming him up and down on my cock until I too had ejaculated and he was just flopping around like a rag doll.

He had endured it all without throwing up any defenses. Leonard must have explained my need well in engaging him, although he still seemed to be surprised at the reality of it.

Leonard knew I wanted full control and mastering, full domination.

The room boy rubbed me dry with a towel, slowly and sensually, as if he hadn't been fully and forcefully taken in the tub. Then he suggested a massage. During the massage, and when I was completely relaxed, he started giving me a blow job. I put up with it until I was fully engorged and then I heaved myself off the massage table, grabbed him around the waist, and carried him, easily, over to the bed. I slammed his back down on the foot of the bed, his eyes wide in surprise and all of the breath knocked out of him, and slapped his legs apart. Grasping an ankle in one fist and raising and spreading that leg, and, after stuffing my cock inside his tight hole as he grunted and groaned, I grasped him by the throat with the other hand. He arched his back and babbled to me intelligibly as I fucked him hard and fast to a second ejaculation.

Afterward, after I'd taken a shower, I asked him how long he'd been engaged for.

"For the night, sahib," he answered with a sob. He was curled up in a fetal position on the bed. I had no idea how genuine his distress was, although during the fucking he'd tried to assert that I was thicker and longer than other men he'd lain under. I patted him on the buttocks and told him I would be going to the dining room for dinner, which would give him a chance to get something to eat too, and that I would be gone for an hour or more.

"Is this too much for you?" I then asked. I was being rougher than even was normal for me. I hadn't had male sex for months, because I hadn't traveled from New York for some time and I wouldn't go there in my home environment. But I couldn't help myself. This was what I liked, and I was keyed up from not having had it for months. I wasn't beating him, I just was hung and preferred to fuck hard. I wanted a tight hole—and the feeling of taxing it to the limit.

"No, sahib," he said with a sniffle. "It is hard but . . . but it is so . . . I don't know. The harder you are with me, the higher in the clouds I go, and the more I want."

"Then I expect you to be naked and on the bed when I get back."

"Yes, sahib."

He was good and I hadn't had a good, freestyle fuck in some time. I walked on eggs in New York with Jennifer. I wanted to make the most of this gift.

Sometime after 9:00 p.m. I shot another load. The room boy's torso was arched out from my belly, my hands gripping his sides half way between his waist and his armpits, his arms dangling down to the surface of the bed, my knees wedged under his buttocks, his knees bent and his feet flat on the bed behind me. His ankle bangles jangled quietly with each of the thrusts I made inside him for more than a half hour. I was tired, but he was exhausted. When I fired off, I stretched out beside him, and wrapping the fingers of one hand around his cock—it being too small to take a full fist—I slowly masturbated him to a moaning completion.

I was getting on in years, so I mounted him again only twice more in the night. He gave every impression that that was three more times than he had expected this gig to entail.

He served me breakfast in the room the next day, him redressed as when I'd first seen him and me in briefs and a silk hotel robe. He told me he was leaving then and one of the regular room attendants would be taking over the duties.

"The hotel room boy isn't—" he began to say, his head lowered demurely and looking shyly at me.

"I understand," I interjected. "And, please, come over here."

He walked over to me gingerly and with some apparent reluctance, probably expecting me to brutally attack him. But when he reached me, I placed a wad of rupee bills in his hand, probably far more than he made in a week of regular johns. Giving me another shy smile, he moved back to the door.

"And . . ." I realized I'd never asked him his name, so I pressed on without using a direct address. "You were very good. I know I am demanding, but you were very good. I will make sure I make that known to those who arranged for you."

"Thank you, sahib." He smiled a little smile. He seemed grateful. I didn't know if this made up for how forceful I'd been, but I hadn't been able to help it. It had been quite some time.

"I was going to ask if you managed to find your red gem, but I see that you have."

"Yes, sahib, I did. Thank you, sahib. And your staff, sahib, I have never . . . no man has ever taken me so cruelly but made me want more. I don't know . . ."

He didn't have a chance to finish that, as there was a soft knock at the door. He opened it and there stood Gupta. I felt a little flash of irritation, having understood that he would meet me down in the lobby at 10:00 and it was only 9:00. But there he was.

He stayed in the outer corridor briefly, exchanging a few remarks with the room boy, and then he came into the room.

"I thought rather than New Delhi that you might want to see the Taj Mahal and the Red Fort instead," he said, "since you only have one day in the city. Much of what you can see here would be from inside a car, and I have hired one to take us into the countryside."

"Thank you, Gupta," I said, fully aware that we already were on his schedule, not mine. I dressed there in the room in front of him, and he watched my every move.

It was an exhausting day, but, I had to admit, a good one. I would never have been able to arrange to see all that was covered on my own, and Gupta was an expert guide, filling my head with information but all of it interesting and enlightening, nothing frivolous or tiring.

That night I ate alone in the dining room and returned to the room somewhat regretting that Leonard hadn't booked two days with the nameless rent boy. I read until I couldn't keep my eyes open, and then lay, naked on the silk sheets, welcoming every wisp of breeze stirred up by the ceiling fan overhead.

Late in the night, not even having heard him enter the room, I woke up to a chest pushing my thighs open below me, one hand encircling my cock and another one cupping my balls, and a moist mouth descending on my cock.

Leonard, playful Leonard, I thought. You did go for the two nights.

But then I sensed as the body came up over me that it was somewhat more substantial than the rent boy's had been. And the hands grasping my wrists and forcing my arms over my head were much stronger than the rent boy had demonstrated in capability. My eyes shot open. I was looking into the face of Gupta.

I didn't fuck Gupta, although I struggled for control to do so. He fucked himself on my cock. Pinning me, with strength I could not have believed a man of his size and physique could have, he mounted my cock and vigorously pounded his channel on me, strongly resisting every attempt of mine to gain control and to regulate the fuck.

Exhausted from the day's excursions, I finally just relaxed, turned my head to the side, and didn't try to move my pelvis again until the throes of ejaculation approached and then I was strong enough, briefly, to counterpunch him for a few thrusts, to arch my torso and head back, and to cry out to the ceiling as I bathed his insides with my cum.

"Ah, I knew you would want me," he murmured.

Even as he stretched beside me, he held me in a strong embrace that would have taken much effort to escape from. A half hour later, he repeated the earlier, controlled fuck, and, although his embrace following that was more relaxed and he soon was snoring softly, I was so spent I made no effort to repel him. Mentally, though, although I didn't find his method of fucking arousing to the levels I went after, it wasn't like I didn't accept him. This just wasn't how I liked to fuck. And even then, I recognized the danger of Gupta, and by association, Khurana, knowing that I fucked men. How had he found out? The brief conversation outside the door to my hotel room with the rent boy?

He was gone in the morning, but I barely had time to shower and repack, when he was at the door saying we needed to get a quick breakfast at the hotel's buffet, as our plane would be leaving soon.

He did not mention the visitation in the night, and neither did I. But on the plane, with the two of us the only ones occupying the seats on one side at the window, he let his hand move to my crotch, possessively. I can't claim that what he then whispered in my ear didn't let him feel some effect with his hand covering my crotch. His wasn't my preferred sex partner, but it wasn't like he was raping me. I sought out release as much as the next guy, and what he was describing did heat me up.

* * * *

When we arrived at the hotel in Chennai, chosen for its proximity to the American consulate and because of its American brand name, Sheraton, I thought at first that a massive mistake had been made. The roads around it were nothing but mud and there was a cow in the lobby. I soon was to learn, though, that this was mainly the way it was in Tamil Nadu. I chalked that up to a plus for finding someone who qualified for the job I had and who wanted to get out of this area of the world.

On the whole, the people were shorter and smaller and browner than the Indians in the New Delhi area. Like many in the developing world, they tended to appear attractive when young but to age quickly when they reached their forties and, generally, to be completely spent by their fifties. On the way from the airport in an open-sided cab, Gupta pointed out several men to me who appeared to be in their mid-teens but who he said were in their late twenties. He apparently told me that as a warning of what to expect in looks from the translator prospects I would be interviewing and testing, but I'll admit that, already being heated up, I viewed them as potential sex partners. I liked to fuck smaller, young-looking men. I liked to overpower and fuck them hard. When away from New York and cruising for men to manhandle, I found I often gravitated to South and Southeast Asian men, as they generally were small—and tended to have tight channels.

I needed a hotel near the U.S. consulate on Gemini Street, which was also only a couple of blocks west of the Bay of Bengal and a long, narrow beach called Elliot's Beach, because the interviews and testing were to be conducted there. It wasn't public knowledge, but my news agency did work for U.S. intelligence. We were adding the Tamil translator because work we did for the Agency justified the added position. The intelligence section at the consulate was helping me by giving me interview space and by having already weeded the candidates down to twenty who not only had the skills but also could pass scrutiny on entering and working in the States. I was to be aghast when I arrived at the consulate and found out that there had been more than 200 applicants for the position, which lent credence to my thought that this was an area of the world that many wanted to get away from.

There was only one room booked for me at the Sheraton, and although the place seemed deserted the entire time I was there, the desk manager insisted that they had no more rooms available to accommodate Gupta. I had let Gupta go into the hotel ahead of me, not believing that it really was the hotel where I was booked and not wanting to lose the cab if we had to find another hotel. I've ever since thought he paid the desk staff to say they were booked up. Without consulting with me, Gupta told the desk manager it would be just fine for us to share the room. I said it would be only if it were just for the one night. Otherwise we'd go to another hotel. The desk staff sheepishly acknowledged that they could find a separate room for Gupta after the first one.

Gupta made the most of that one night. As everywhere I went in India, we had arrived hot and sticky and showers were in order as soon as we got to the room. I let Gupta shower first. When I emerged from the bathroom, with a towel around me, he was sitting on the edge of the bed, naked, and pulling on his meat. His cock was long for his size when it was erect, but it wasn't thick. His sex talk on the plane had already had me hyped, so when he urged me over to stand in front of him, I responded. He stripped my towel off; got both of my wrists in an iron grip behind my back with one of his strong hands; moved the other between my thighs, with the heel of that hand under my balls and pushing them up and an index finger at my asshole; and he sucked me hard with his mouth. When he was ready to fuck, so was I.

I had never fucked up against a wall quite like he fucked himself on me then. I was backed up against a wall and he hung, facing me, on my front with his fists locked behind my neck. I was supporting and separating his buttocks with the palms of my hands, but, probably looking like a crab, he had his feet plastered to the wall, wide, on either side of my hips, and was pushing and pulling his channel on my cock, fucking himself until we both ejaculated.

I never felt more under his control, almost a prisoner, as I did at supper time, when we went out looking for a restaurant. The town was almost as teeming with people—and needy-looking people—as Old Delhi had appeared. They were just smaller and blabbered more, with almost no English to be heard. They also smiled and laughed more and were more expressive with their hands. But I felt totally lost, completely reliant on Gupta for everything. I could have eaten in the hotel dining room, of course, but he didn't really give me that option. He just ran ahead of me, out of the hotel entrance, urging me to follow.

That night was more of his controlling sex. I was providing the cock for his channel, but he was controlling how the cocking was done and was providing most of the pumping action. He kept telling me that he was giving me the best fucking I'd ever had, and I was just too polite to tell him otherwise. His mind and mouth were always running way ahead of me, like he wasn't even listening to anything I said anyway. In that I could definitely see the family resemblance between him and his cousin, Khurana, in New York. The more frustrated I got with Gupta here the more frustrated I got with the Khurana I knew I'd have to return to—and to tell how helpful his cousin had been to me—and to wonder what his cousin was telling him about the sex I had with men.

All of the candidates were excellent. The consulate had done well in reducing them to the most likely. My interest gravitated toward one in particular, a young man named Sanjay. He was so handsome and beautifully formed and had such a winning, shy smile, though, that after the first round of interviews, I had to tax my brain on whether he really was that much better as a candidate or did I focus on him because of sexual interest. I certainly couldn't deny the sexual interest. And the way he looked at me under long eyelashes and with sultry eyes made me think he had a sexual interest in me too. He wore his straight, black hair in a ponytail, and I fantasized unbinding and running my hands through it as it cascaded to his shoulders. My attraction to him worried me.

It didn't help that he scored the best in the initial language tests I gave the twenty candidates.

They had all stayed for the entire work day, and at the end of that day, I called them together to let them know which ten I wished to have come back the next day for a second round of interviews and testing.

Sanjay was one of the ten, and the look of gratitude he gave me when I told him that he was ripped at my heart. There was no question he wanted to get out of Tamil Nadu, and the look he gave me made me think he'd do almost anything to do so. I had no trouble fantasizing what he could do for me, but I knew I had to separate the personal from the professional.

Alone in the testing room, I poured over the test results and the personal folders, trying to pick out the best of the best—but really, I knew, also trying to find some way of legitimately disqualifying Sanjay. He made me feel like I'd rarely felt before about a man. And the few I'd felt about in that way had endangered my cushy life in New York. I could not have that. Still, looking at his photograph in his folder was like being a moth drawn to a flame for me. He looked entirely too young. But a check and a cross-check with other information revealed him to be twenty-three. It was the ideal age for who we were looking for for the translator's position. To have gained the language and area-knowledge skills he exhibited by the age of twenty-three marked him as highly intelligence and quick to process and assess.

No way could I put him lower than the top three.

When I left the consulate, I didn't want to go back to the hotel just yet. Gupta was supposed to have moved to his own room by now. But even if he had, I wasn't anxious to move back into his controlling sphere. I could hear the ocean from the street in front of the consulate, so I picked my way through the muddy streets there and, shortly, found myself at the edge of the beach overlooking the Bay of Bengal. From here the sea looked vast and the beach looked almost pristine, even though it bordered a teeming city of nearly five million. That figure alone made me shudder—a city that few in the West even knew about located near the end of the earth and with five million inhabitants.

There were only a few people out on the beach, most of them just standing and looking out to sea. I fancied they all were seeking a private moment, turning toward a vast emptiness and away from a human anthill.

He was standing about half way between the upper edge of the sand and the waves lapping up on the beach. For some reason I recognized him even from the back—out of all of those five million people in Chennai—and even though he no longer wore the clothes he'd been interviewed in.

He was short and a rich brown, but unlike so many in the north, he wasn't thin and emaciated looking. He was beautifully formed even by Western standards. He was bare above and wearing a white dhoti flowing down to his ankles. The dhoti was being ruffled in the sea breeze, and occasionally opened enough to show a well-turned, if miniature, calf. His feet were in thin-soled sandals. His biceps and shoulders were well muscled, and there was a dip from his shoulder blades and broad shoulders down to a thin waist before his buttocks flared out in back. Not his hips, though, he didn't have the hips of a woman.

When I came up beside him, I saw that he had his arms folded across his well-muscled chest. A gold medallion on a thick gold chain hung from his neck, the medallion nestled in the cleavage of his chest. He had a sweet, enticing scent about him. Of cloves and cinnamon, and I ever after was to think of the sweetness of these smells when I thought of him.

"Hello," I said. "It's Sanjay, is it not?"

"Yes, hello, Mr. Jenkins," he answered in a soft voice. "Did you hear the sea calling?"

"Yes, exactly," I answered, a bit surprised because only now I realized that this was so. "Did you as well?"

"Yes, I often come out here to listen to the sea. Often I need to withdraw."

"Withdraw?"

"Yes, from Chennai, from the taboos of Indian society."

"I'm not sure I know what you mean," I answered, my heart beginning to beat faster, because I had a definite inkling that I did know what he meant.

He turned and gave me a sharp, knowing look, that went to the quick of me. Then he returned his gaze to the sea. "I have a feeling that you do know."

My heart was racing. Should I just pretend I hadn't heard him say that? His voice was low. Could he believe that a statement that stripped all pretense from me had gone unheard?

"You did well in the interview and the testing today," I said.

"I'm glad to hear that."

"Very well."

"My heart soars at the sound of that."

There was silence between us for nearly a minute, but it wasn't an uncomfortable silence. It was more of a building of the senses and of a sensuality in just being close to each other. I certainly felt it, but I felt the heat of it coming off his body too, even though the sea breeze was getting chilly. I moved a hand out from my body, toward him, and although I didn't see him noticing I'd made that gesture, he placed his hand in mine.

"If I asked you to come with me, now, would you do it?" It was not of my own will that I said that; it just came out of me.

"Yes."

"I'm not talking about for more testing for the position."

"I know you're not."

After double locking my hotel door to bar a visitation by Gupta, I began the evening- and night-long fuck of Sanjay on the bed in my hotel room with the small of his back on the foot of the bed, his legs running up to my shoulders on either side, his feet only reaching the hollow under my shoulder bones and with my palms on his pecs and puffed-up nipples. As with the two Indians I previously had fucked, it was hard going getting the thickness and length of me into his tight channel. But with Sanjay I took my time, and we were both panting and breathing heavily and groaning at the effort. But I was inside and fully buried, amazed that he had taken all of me. He was trembling and watching my eyes with his, big and brown under think, long, black lashes, looking like a deer in the headlights. But I could see trust and acceptance in them as well.

I leaned my face down to his and ran my hands behind his head, lifting his face to mine. My fingers broke the band he was using to gather his hair into a ponytail and then ran through his long, dark hair as it cascaded down to his back. Our lips met in a tender kiss, which turned into one of mutual hunger and need . . . and I began, slowly to pump inside him in long, slow strokes. His cock wasn't small for a man his size, and it continued to harden as I fucked him. But he didn't ejaculate. He clutched my arms with his hands and moaned deeply, but he remained tense, not relaxing into the fuck, almost as if he was just enduring it.

I slowed the pumping, trying not to hurt him any more than necessary. Being surprised he had accommodated my cock in his confining channel, and feeling him so small, I wanted to maintain control of myself and was giving him a gentle, loving fucking.

For once I wasn't thinking only of myself and my own pleasures; I was thinking of his enjoyment as well—and his endurance.

I changed the position, moving him onto his belly on the bed, and I stretched out on top of him, bearing most of my weight on my elbows and knees, but my cock buried, again, to the hilt in his channel and me trying to touch him in as many places as I could—my lips in the hollow of his neck, my toes rubbing his calves—as I slow-plowed and he moaned and groaned.

But, to my surprise and concern, I soon realized that his trembling came from his soft sobs.

"Am I hurting you?" I whispered. "Am I possessing you too much?"

"No, not that," he murmured. "I just was expected something more—something different from a man your size. I'm not porcelain. I won't break. I want to be worn out, taxed to the limit, fucked hard. Punished. You have such a big cock that I expected more. I thought that you would . . . could . . . when I am taken I want to be taken totally, no prisoners spared. I want to know that I have been . . . fucked."

I fucked him then as I had done the rent boy in the tub, my knees jammed up under his buttocks, his torso flopped back in front of me, arms dangling down to the bed surface, head arched back, a cry and big "Oh" on his mouth, and, hands gripping his waist, pulling him hard off and on my cock.

I rode him doggy style with him bent over the arm of an easy chair and me using his gold chain as reins. I fucked him standing up with him draped on the front of me, fists locked behind my neck, knees hooked on my thighs and, me, palming his buttocks, brutally jamming him on and off my cock—and then still standing, with his torso bowed over the bed, me grasping his wrists and holding his arms taut, and him locking his ankles behind my thighs and me thrusting, thrusting, thrusting.

After his third ejaculation and my second, we fell in a heap on the carpet, panting and heaving and grunting and groaning. He cupped my face in his hands and we kissed deeply, after which he said in a hoarse voice, "Yes, just like that. You are a horse and your fury, your cruel, total taking, arouse and satisfy me fully. Most Indian men copulate too delicately. This, this is what I've wanted, what I've dreamed of getting."

I fucked him, brutally up against the shower wall under the streaming water with his knees hooked on my hips, my lips and teeth working over his mouth and his nipples, and thrusting up deep inside him again and again and again.

And I mounted and fucked him hard three times in the night. After the last time, I ached to possess him as fully as I had the first time, to become one with him, our minds and bodies fused for all time. Between fuckings we lay close together with our arms entwined and our hearts beating together in unison as I drank in the clove and cinnamon sweetness of his scent.

I left him in the morning, on his back on the bed, his knees bent and legs spread, an arm thrown over his eyes, and moaning softly.

I scheduled him ninth out of ten interviews and tests that day to give him a chance to recover and be there on time. With a heavy sense of regret, though, I had already decided I would not hire him.

Sanjay aced the second interview and got all of the test questions right. I didn't tell him that, though. At the end of the day, I told that he had done well on the tests but not nearly well enough. He seemed more resigned than crushed when I told him this, and it occurred to me that in a city of five million with less than a third of that many jobs, interview rejection must be the assumption of all candidates. I mourned that that was so. But mostly I mourned that I could not give Sanjay the job.

I looked for signs that he had expected to get the job because he'd let me fuck him. But I saw none. If I'd seen that, I would have offered to pay him a large sum. Not having seen that, I felt I couldn't insult him with suggesting he was a whore.

"Does that mean . . . that we won't be together again?" he asked with sad eyes.

"Probably. I'll make my final selection tomorrow and the consulate will handle the processing from there. I'll fly back to New Delhi and then back to New York." I tried not to make it sound too hard, but I also tried to make it sound final—and inevitable.

"Oh. Did you not like me? Did I ask for too much?"

"I liked you fine. It was good. Very good. We just won't be on the same continent." And that indeed was the crux of the matter. I certainly did like him. I thought that I might even love Sanjay. I knew that his body brought me great joy, and I loved fucking him. But he could not be in New York. I could not trust myself with him in New York. I could not rock the boat with Jennifer that way. My cushy life was too important to me. I steeled my heart and wished him luck. I said I would put in a good word for him to the consulate for the possibility that they someday might need an excellent translator.

He left quietly, and if it was a sob I heard when he got to the door, I pretended that I didn't.

That night, after he had ridden my cock, Gupta quizzed me on how the candidate search was going—and pointedly asked me if I'd found anyone who spoke better English then he did. Nearly half of them did, but I diplomatically brushed on, concentrating on what else he had asked.

"It was hard deciding. I still have work to do on it tomorrow, but I think I will be ready to leave the morning after that. You can go ahead and look into flight schedules back to New Delhi for us. There is one, named Sanjay, who is beyond excellent."

"The well-muscled, dark brown one with the pretty face and ponytail?" Gupta asked.

"Yes," I answered, disconcerted because I had no idea when Gupta might have seen Sanjay. Did he, perhaps, see him leaving my room this morning after I had left?

But he didn't pursue the point. And he didn't try to maneuver me into another fuck. He dressed and left the room. I double-locked the door behind him, showered, and got my first full night's sleep since arriving in India.

I woke up full of remorse. I couldn't do this to Sanjay just because he was such a good and willing lay. It wasn't just to him. I had to include him in the last set of candidates. I breakfasted with Gupta in the Sheraton coffee shop and called the consulate and asked them to send someone to inform Sanjay he was still in the running and should appear at the consulate for another test if he was still interested in the job. I had his folder and read his address over the phone to the secretary at the consulate.

Between the second and third interview of the five I'd called back—six, counting Sanjay, Gupta appeared at the consulate and called me aside.

"I went to this Sanjay's home to make sure he got the word you would test him today," Gupta said. He was wearing a sad face and spoke slowly and haltingly.

"Yes, and?"

"I'm sorry, Mr. Clifford. Sanjay took his life last night."

"Took his life?" I heard him, but I rejected what he had said. It couldn't be. It was just too horrible.

"His family said he went down to the sea and just swam out into the water. They recovered his body this morning."

I sat down hard on a bench in the corridor, my ears buzzing. I felt like I was going to be sick.

"But I don't know why you need to continue the interviewing," Gupta said. "I think we both know I am the best man for the job. Khurana told me all about what was needed, and I have prepared myself. I have even let you make love to me. I think it's obvious the job should be mine. When I am in New York, you can make love to me as often as you want to."

377

I looked up at him dully, the horror of what had been happening to me sinking in. It all had been engineered by Khurana—to get his cousin the job. Just as upon hearing that Sanjay was beyond my touch now and realizing that I loved him and my heart had rent, hearing what Gupta had said—so crassly transitioning from telling me that Sanjay was dead to making a claim on the translator position—and saying that he had let me fuck him when he had controlled all of the fucking—I woke up and my heart snapped back together and hardened.

"You can't have the job, Gupta. Not only are you not as qualified as any of the five I'm interviewing today, but you cannot have the job precisely because we have fucked. I can't let you come back to New York with me as a man I'm fucking. I can't do any of that in New York. I am married. I have a reputation."

"But we *have* fucked, and I can say that all the way to New York if I must," Gupta said, his tone just as hard as mine.

"You want a job, I'll give you one. But here, in India," I said, realizing the truth of what he said about knowing already that I went with men and my mind already racing ahead to repair my folly. "We are opening an office in India. Khurana will come here as chief. And you can work in the office, but only as long as you keep your mouth shut—and your body in India."

We'd only talked at the corporate level of opening an office in India and no one had mentioned sending Khurana here, but I could make it so. I knew I could. Now I couldn't have Khurana in New York either.

"I think you should make your own way back to New Delhi," I said. "I will be traveling separately now."

I stood up and marched toward the entrance of the consulate, right by the receptionist, not seeming to hear her trying to tell me that the five remaining candidates were here now and ready to be interviewed again.

I walked to the beach and stood there, looking out to sea. And I wept. After I had no more tears, I opened my briefcase and fished out Sanjay's folder. It took effort to find flowers and to make my way on my own without help to the address Sanjay had given, but I did it not only because it was the right thing to do, but also as a token of atonement. Perhaps I personally hadn't caused Sanjay's death, but I had provided that last push over the edge for him, that last rejection, both sexually and as an opportunity to escape out into the larger, more forgiving and supportive world.

"Sanjay, he not here," the old crone said when she opened the door of a small shack in a sea of temporary hovels.

"Yes, I know. I am so sorry. I am a friend. I've come to—"

"He has gone to Mumbai, this morning. A man from New Delhi came and gave him money and Sanjay has gone to find job in Mumbai."

I swallowed my breath, almost choking. So that's how it was, what Gupta had been up to. I could have cursed him, but I was too elated in knowing that Sanjay hadn't died. "Mumbai? Where in Mumbai? How can I contact him there?"

But she was already closing the door on me. She had taken the flowers, though.

I had lost him once; I couldn't lose him again.

In the airport, after changing my ticket to Mumbai, I found a telephone and called Leonard's office in Delhi. My name was enough for me to be put directly through to him. It always had been. We had met periodically over the years, arranging our meetings by phone to our offices under the guise of being old, dear friends—which, of course, we were.

"Leonard. Yes, I'm fine. But I need something urgently. Even Indian citizens have to register when they move from city to city, don't they?"

"Yes, certainly, but it isn't really as draconian as you might—"

"I'm not judging that. Listen, can you, from your position, or from Manjula's, tap into that system and locate someone?"

"Yes, of course, for you, if that's what you—"

"Yes, good. I need a location for a Tamil Nadu citizen arriving in Mumbai today from Chennai." I gave him Sanjay's name and as much of the personal information from his folder that Leonard needed. "I'm headed for Mumbai myself and will give you a call from my hotel when I get there."

"No, nothing's wrong. I have selected him for a position and must get in touch with him as soon as possible."

My relationship with Leonard was such that I couldn't tell him that, although I *would* select Sanjay for the translator's job, his more significant position would be under me and that the touch I was looking forward to was that of my thick cock inside his tight channel.

I had no idea what I'd do about the life I led with Jennifer when Sanjay and I got back to New York. But I was reassessing my priorities as I chased the man I loved across India, and something would work out. I had to believe that it would. I pulled a handkerchief he had left behind in my hotel room out of my pocket and raised it to my face. I ingested the sweet smell of cloves and cinnamon, feeling Sanjay close beside me.

Satisfaction Ashram

As I stood outside the entrance to the old British colonial-style Windsor Hotel in Nuwara Eliya, Sri Lanka, in the shadow of Mount Pidurutagala, waiting for someone to take me up to the ashram, I couldn't believe how far—and how far back in time—I had moved from Teddy's cabin in the Catskills. From the moment Teddy's business partner, Mort Whitley, drove up to the cabin and told me how remorseful Teddy was over the fight we'd had and that he wanted to make it up to me by letting me go on that yoga retreat I'd wanted to do for some months, it had been one long, swift journey on progressively more primitive modes of transport.

I was surprised that Mort was being so helpful in acting the go-between like this. I'd always thought that he saw me as competition with Teddy—not in a sexual way, but for Teddy's attention. There was always an edge in the way he responded to me of me being a gold digger and wanting to move in on their partnership in the manufacturing company. More than once I'd wanted to let him know that I didn't need Teddy's money, I had money of my own, and that the sum total of my interest in the company was my interest in Teddy's happiness.

Mort said that Teddy had arranged everything: the luxurious flight in the company jet from New York to Mumbai,

India, followed by the two-night ferry cruise from Mumbai down to Colombo, Sri Lanka, with me not completely understanding Mort's explanation why the company jet couldn't fly me directly to Colombo, but not making an issue of it as I didn't want to appear ungrateful. Then an open taxi ride to the Colombo train station and the two-and-a-half-hour train ride to Kandy. A hanging-on-to-the-sides rough ride on an ancient bus from Kandy to Nuwara Eliya brought me into the shadows of Sri Lanka's highest peak, Mount Pidurutagala, on the slopes of which, on very short notice, I had been booked for a two-week stay in a yoga ashram. The jitney ride from the bus station to the Windsor Hotel was probably the most harrowing travel experience of it all, and, once in my hotel room for a one-night stay, I simply showered under a drizzle in the bathroom, not complaining because I was sure I had the most luxurious room in the hotel, and fell, naked, on the bed to sleep the sleep of the innocent dead.

The entire journey I reassessed my relationship with Teddy, who had become quite possessive of me. The argument had been over that and his taking me for granted, and, I'm afraid, it had become quite violent—at least on my end—involving the Bette Davis-style melodrama of raised voices and thrown crystal vases. I'd left the apartment in quite a shambles. I hadn't driven half way to the Catskills in Teddy's Porsche before I realized that I had gone overboard and that most of this was because of the not-so-favorable medical report Teddy had received. But it had been far better than we had expected. We thought that he perhaps had no more than a few months to live, and the doctor had talked to him in terms of years—but years of living more carefully.

Once out on the open road and climbing to a higher, cooler altitude, I was able to see how much of the argument had resulted from both of us being frightened of what "years of living more carefully" meant. Did it mean Teddy couldn't bed me each night as he'd been doing for three years? I had asked, not knowing how that would touch on Teddy's own fears and how well it reflected my selfishness. Teddy had exploded rather than telling me what the doctor had said—but asking me if I was seeking permission to take a lover who would satisfy me daily when and if he couldn't. At that point I had blown up and started screaming the building down around our ears. Mort had arrived just then to speak with Teddy about business but had beaten a quick retreat.

Then Teddy had said just the worst thing, asking me if I wanted to cut and run now, whether, being young and highly sexed, I had no stomach for staying around to care for the man who had taken care of all my needs for three years. That had set me off at even a higher decibel level then, because it wasn't in the least what I was thinking. What I was thinking, no matter how irrational, was that Teddy was deserting me—slowly dying on me. And not that he would leave me with nothing substantial to show for letting him exclusively possess my body for three years of the prime of my youth, but that he was slipping away from me and wouldn't be there for my old age. We had planned so much for his retirement.

We were both frightened by it all, and I fled the scene, needing to get space between me and our problems. When Mort came to the cabin with Teddy's apology two days later and his pledge of trust by offering to let me go on retreat—to prepare myself for the hard year or more ahead—I was recovered and understanding enough to say that the gesture wasn't necessary. It was only Mort insisting that it was what Teddy wanted that won the day—and the fact that Teddy already had it all mapped out, the ashram reservations and all.

It didn't occur to me until I was jetting over the Atlantic that it wasn't like Teddy to be able to put together a travel itinerary like this this quickly. This was more in line with Mort's accountant personality. But if Mort had done this planning for Teddy and given Teddy all the credit, it seems I had been misjudging Mort.

As I stood outside the entrance of the Windsor Hotel and watched the bustle of Sri Lankan activity out on the street, my attention was drawn to a pony-drawn cart flanked by two young men as they approached. The men were notable because they were dressed identically, in loose white cotton trousers and a long-tailed white cotton long-sleeved tunic with a V-cut almost down to their navels, showing that they were both in very good condition. There the similarities ceased, however. The taller and bulkier of the two appeared to be European—probably Mediterranean. Olive skinned, darkly handsome, and hirsute, with curly black hair. The other one, shorter and thinner, appeared to be of northern Indian origin, light-skinned, also handsome but carrying himself with more reserve than the other man.

I was surprised as they came right up to me and the European queried my name. "Are you David Kane?"

"Yes," I answered, only now realizing that this was my welcoming committee from the ashram.

"I am Benito and this is Ravith," the European—evidently Italian, based on his name—said. "We have come to fetch you to the Sanasuma Ashram on the mountainside. Please excuse me, but I can say no more. We cannot speak to the initiates until we have known them."

"Thank you," I answered, looking dubiously at the pony cart and then up at the brooding mountain where I thought I could see the ashram teetering on stilts and projecting out on a steep slope nearly two-thirds up the mountain.

The two seemed nonplused, though, and simply handed me and my suitcase into the pony cart and turned back the way they'd come. I saw that they were both barefoot and the way their tunics and pants hung on them gave a feeling that they otherwise were naked—and that they were both well built. They walked beside the pony cart in silence, although each turned from time to time to give me a shy but also appraising look, as we ascended the mountain. Neither seemed to get out of breath in the climb and both walked with the grace of dancers or gymnasts.

I realized I should not be surprised at this. Yoga was all about developing, maintaining, and controlling your body.

We were met at the door by an older Indian man, perhaps in his forties, in a white dhoti, his well-developed barrel chest and muscled arms bare, his arms crossed and his eyes assessing me as we approached.

He gestured for me to descend from the cart at the gate to the ashram compound and follow him inside. The two young men who had escorted me followed us into the central courtyard but then disappeared. A dark-skinned servant of some sort of indeterminate age, but apparently of Sri Lankan ethnicity, took the reins of the pony and led it and the cart back down the narrow trail we had ascended. The ashram was a double-storied wooden building on a platform projecting on stilts out from the mountainside, set among massive boulders. It pushed into the surface of the mountain itself on the side facing the slope. As we passed into a covered passageway with iron gates on both sides, we emerged into a central courtyard dotted with gnarl-trunked trees, supporting lush, perfectly shaped canopies, set in a regimented pattern in large box planters that bathed nearly the whole atrium in dappled shade. Windows around all four sides overlooked the courtyard, which made me aware that there hadn't been any windows that I could see on the outer walls of the structure.

The older man led me to a door in the wall facing the slope of the mountain, where he paused briefly, to say, "I am Acharya Ahitharan, abbot and instructor at Sanasuma Ashram. 'Acharya' is a title meaning teacher, not my given name. There are stages of your entrance into the ashram. Sanasuma means 'satisfaction,' and total satisfaction is the end state we move toward—in stages. For two days, you will remain in the room I am taking you to, where you will meditate and read and absorb the yoga studies you find in your room—all in silence. Your meals will be brought to you. Do not try to talk to the one bringing your meals. He cannot speak to you inside the ashram until he has known you. After the two days, you will come to me for your first interview, during which I will tell you more of the ashram experience and will inform you of the next stage. There is no more to say now, so a two-day period of silence will now commence. I can only speak to you at designated stages of your initiation until I have known you too."

While I mulled over what the Acharya had said, he took me inside the wooden structure, which looked ancient. The structural supports of the building were obvious, as the beams, made of a polished, darkly stained wood, were left exposed. The walls between the beams were mostly of some sort of ochre plaster, but when I had an opportunity to run my hands over them, I could feel that they were solid and substantial. The room he led me to was on the second floor and had the feeling of a

385

monk's cell, although it was fairly large, probably twelve by twelve feet.

Besides the door from the corridor, the only other doorway opened, without a door, into a primitive small bathroom with a toilet, a sink and a metal pan with a drain in the center and a shower head above. On the wall opposite the entrance, the wall that would face the slope of the mountainside, was located what seemed to be a window enclosure about four feet in width and three feet high. But it was covered by sliding shutters that met in the middle and were locked by a bolt requiring a key that was not, as far as I could tell—or discover later—provided in the room.

The furnishings were limited to a cot with a mattress, a chest of drawers, a straight chair, and a small table, serving as a desk. There was a small stand next to the cot, with a lamp on top of it. Another lamp sat on the desk. Neither was to prove to emit much light, and when they were on, the light wavered in both. It was enough to read by in the evening, if I held the books close. There was sufficient light for reading during the day, though. The corridor outside the cell door ran along the outer wall overlooking the courtyard, included many windows, and was bathed in sunlight. And there were windows high up on the wall of my room on the wall facing the corridor. The daylight from the courtyard filtered into my room through these high-set windows.

And there were books. They were sitting on the desk. Acharya Ahitharan gestured to them, making clear I was to read them over the next two days. He then opened the chest of drawers and took out a pair of cotton trousers and a tunic—just as Ravith and Benito had been wearing—and made clear that they were what I would wear too. Digging deeper, he pulled out a saffron-colored silky robe, which he showed to me, wagging his finger to convey that I should not casually wear that, and replaced it reverently in the drawer. Then he moved to the door to the corridor and departed.

I looked in the drawers and beyond several pairs of trousers and tunics, under the saffron robe, I found a couple of thin-material cotton briefs, which, unaccountably buttoned at the hip with just one button on each side.

I changed into the cotton trousers and tunic, leaving my own briefs on, and set my suitcase beside the desk. I had taken the inference that I wouldn't be wearing my own clothes while I was on retreat in the ashram. Then, with a sigh, and still exhausted from my fast trip out from New York, I tried out the mattress. It was a bit lumpy. That didn't matter. I was out like a light. I woke when Ravith unlocked the door—until that moment I hadn't realized I'd been locked in—and brought a tray of food in, placed it on the desk, turned and gave me a little smile, and then exited the room and relocked the door.

It was simple fare, limited to fruits, vegetables, and nuts. For drink, there was cool water in a jug that contained enough to easily last me into the next day. There also was a strange plastic bottle of something set to the side and a brochure. The brochure explained that the bottle contained a douche, and that I was to clean myself out twice a day, that purifying myself this way was part of the preparation for participating in the ashram. Strange, I thought, but I had no idea what was involved in an ashram retreat, and purifying oneself seemed to make sense.

I intended to start reading the yoga studies that night, but I was still exhausted and went back to sleep after I'd eaten the food. Sometime in the evening I was aware of the tray being cleared away and later than that I had a vivid dream of hearing the sounds of moaning and groaning, as with the sex act, but by many voices—all male voices. I thought I awoke during this, but the sounds continued. Groggily I reasoned that I already was missing Teddy. We had sex every day—I needed almost constant attention—and it had been, what, two or three days, since Teddy had fucked me. I already was missing it. But I had wanted a retreat to an ashram, so this was my own fault, I told myself, and I just covered my head with one of the two thin pillows on the cot and willed myself back to sleep.

The next day, after eating the meal that had been left for me and showering and douching, as instructed, I sat at the desk and read over the yoga studies—somewhat in shock. They covered quite a bit of the standard principles of yoga and of the ashram tradition, but they also were rather explicit on the sexual practices within the Hindu tradition, primarily the positions of the Kamasutra. The illustrations of this included heterosexual couples, but they also included same-sex couples, both female and male. Being in somewhat of a state of want already, my attention naturally gravitated to the illustrations of male couples practicing the positions of the Kamasutra. I felt myself in arousal and realized after several moments that the sounds of my dreams—the male sounds of moans and groans and from multiple sources—had commenced again. And this wasn't a dream as I had thought it to be the previous night. This was a real sound of something happening beyond the shuttered window on my wall facing the mountain slope.

I rose and tried to discover a way to open the window, but could not. Then, fully aroused by the combination of those sounds and of the illustrations in the yoga studies, I collapsed into the chair in a slouched position, pulled my hardened cock out of the waistband of the loose cotton trousers, and masturbated myself to ejaculation.

I barely had time to make it into the bathroom to spill my seed into the toilet when I heard the door to my room open. Ravith carried a tray with my dinner on it to the desk, turned and smiled at me, as I stood over the toilet in his side view, and left the room. I entered the room to hear the rasp of wood on wood and looked at the door, the directional source of the sound. It was only then that I realized there was a window in the door, covered by a sliding panel controlled from the corridor.

Had Ravith been watching me masturbate?

* * * *

"The Sanasuma Ashram is one of providing a men-only tantric journey toward enlightenment and fulfillment," Acharya Ahitharan said to me on the morning of the third day as we sat across from each other, each in the cross-legged lotus position on a platform in a small room with light coming into it from high windows on the courtyard side of the wall.

"Tantric?" I asked. "Isn't that—?"

"Tantric relates to sexual techniques that will channel your erotic energy, unlock your creativity, transform your sexual experiences, and significantly alter all other aspects of your actively homosexual life."

"My homosexual life?"

"Yes, this is a men-only ashram. Homosexual men only. And there are certain, ah, attractiveness requirements. We received instructions about you and your needs before we accepted you as an initiate into the ashram."

"Instructions about me?"

"Yes, we were assured that you needed constant sex. We are in the need of young men who will fulfill the needs of those adherents who retreat with us on a temporary bases. We also received photographs and a record of your statistics, and I must say—"

"I don't understand."

"It's really quite simple. You will be trained in the positions of the Kamasutra through the practice of tantra. Tantra alone is a very energizing experience, but blending the benefits and principles of yoga with tantra sexual practices will transform all aspects of the years you will spend with us?"

"Years?" A chill raced up my spine. What have you done, Teddy? I silently cried out.

"Young men coming to us as you have are initiated into the Tantra and service to our adherents in stages. You have started into the stage of self-denial, which will develop into uncontrollable need, upon which you will be initiated into the training stage by Siddha—the enlightened—Satyanarida himself. 'Siddha' means just that—the enlightened one. And only Satyanarida has reached the level of total tantric sexual enlightenment in this ashram. After the Siddha has marked and accepted you, you will be trained in the Kamasutra by our sub Acharyas, such as the two young men you have already met. Then you will become a sub Acharya yourself and will instruct men who come to us on retreat. Upon reaching the age thirty, if you are still deemed desirable and among us, you will move to the Acharya level until the age forty and—"

"Excuse me. I'm only here for a two-week retreat. I'm only twenty-three. Age thirty? That's—"

"Seven years from now, yes."

I stood, trembling, almost unable to control myself in my anger and confusion. "I . . . will be going . . . now . . . I cannot stay."

"I think not," Acharya Ahitharan said in a calm voice. He clapped his hands, and Ravith and Benito immediate appeared in the doorway. "I have been told of you and I observe it is true. You cannot exist without the sex. Your need and your lack of self-denial have already been in evidence here. But we will train you. You will embrace the journey to tantric sexual satisfaction. That is what we provide here. That is what Sanasuma promises—satisfaction, tantric sexual satisfaction."

He waved to the two men standing on either side of me and holding me tight, and they muscled me, screaming and cursing, back to my cell. They dropped me on the cot, left through the door, and locked it.

I lay there agonizing and seething, throwing my body about and muttering in frustration. He had done it, completely fooled me. Teddy had said he was doing what he knew I needed for me—sending Mort to tell me that it was a peace offering. Not coming himself. I should have known. He was punishing me, not just sending me away, and also having me imprisoned. Getting his revenge for what he thought I was going to do to him—desert him in his time of need.

I was beside myself, my mind racing on where I was and how I was going to get out of here. It was some time before I realized that I could hear the sounds of men moaning and groaning again—and now so much clearer than before. I looked up at the shuttered window. But it wasn't shuttered anymore. I rose from the cot and went to the window. It was barred. The spindles were wood, but where they joined at the top and bottom showed me that inside the wood were iron bars. There would be no escape through this avenue.

But I didn't think of that now because of what I saw beyond the window. The window didn't open to the outside; it opened to a large two-story room, and not just a room, a large cavern. The ashram must have been built into the mountainside at the mouth of a large cave. It was some sort of meeting hall, ornately painted in frescoes—frescoes of waving scenes upon uneven rock walls of naked men fucking in a lush jungle. The positions of the Kamasutra. The positions that I had been studying in the yoga books for two days.

There were men in the hall, in spaced ranks on mats on the uneven stone floor below. As I focused I could see that the men were in pairs. They were all naked, with their white cotton trousers and tunics folded neatly beside them, and they were all fucking. This was the source of the mass male moaning and groaning I'd heard on earlier occasions.

Still snuffling and my heart racing, I raced over to the desk to retrieve the book on the gay Kamasutra positions and went back to the window. Plastering myself there, I studied what was happening below, my eyes darting between the fucking pairs and the illustrations in the book in my hand. They were replicating the Kamasutra positions—in an organized fashion. There was a raised dais at the far end of the room, supporting only one pair of copulating men. Below that, from the back of the room where I was overlooking the hall and toward the dais, the positions seemed to be progressing to the more expert positions.

Nearer to me were examples of the familiar Missionary position, the "catcher" on his back, legs spread, and the "pitcher" lying between his thighs, the two face to face; the Greyhound, known better in the West as the doggy fuck; the Elephant, with the catcher on his belly, his hips raised, and the pitcher kneeling over the catcher's hips, supporting his weight on his arms planted beside the catcher's chest; and the Andromache, known in the West as the Cowboy, with the pitcher flat his back and the catcher saddled on his pelvis and riding his cock.

Further up in the ranks were those practicing the positions of the more confirmed in the art: the Oyster, the catcher on his back, thighs raised and calves hooked on the pitcher's upper arms as the pitcher knelt between thighs; the Anvil, with the catcher rocked up on his upper back and shoulder blades, his thighs pulled up to his chest and his ankles on the pitcher's shoulders as the pitcher stretched out full length on top of him, leveraging on his knees or even just his toes as he rocked his cock back and forth inside the channel; the Spoons, with the two lying on their sides, the catcher's buttocks pulled into the pitcher's crotch and his legs slightly tucked toward his stomach as the pitcher embraced the catcher and penetrated him from behind; the Octopus, with the catcher flat on his back, his thighs running up over those of the pitcher crouched between his legs, the catcher's calves crossed behind the pitcher's back and the pitcher either gripping the catcher's waist or stroking his cock; and the Wolf, the catcher standing on his feet, bent forward, with his hands flat on the mat in front of him, and the pitcher standing behind him, holding and spreading his buttocks, and penetrating him from behind.

Those in the expert positions were just in front of the dais: the Butterfly, with the pitcher on his back, legs straight in front of him, raised on his elbows, and the catcher, sitting on his cock above him, the two face to face and the catcher supporting his weight on all four appendages; the Tree, with the catcher on his back and the pitcher in a standing crouch between his thighs, one of the catcher's legs raised along the ribcage of the pitcher and the other bent, with his foot flat against the pitcher's breast; the Reed, with the catcher on his back, his weight borne on his shoulder blades, his legs bent, heels on the mat, leveraging his own thrusts, with the pitcher on his knees between the catcher's thighs, his arms circling the catcher's waist and raising his channel to the cock; the Swing, with the pitcher on his back, legs spread, and the catcher, facing away from him, crouched over the pitcher's pelvis, legs bent, feet flat on the mat by the pitcher's thighs, and his arms stretched to the mat in front of him; and the Stem, the catcher on his shoulder blades, his torso and legs raised up the trunk of the pitcher, who was on his knees between the catcher's thighs and holding his waist with his hands.

Only the commanding figure on the dais, magnificently muscled, black hair flowing down his back, was using an elite Kamasutra position—on a small-bodied, berry brown, Sri Lankan. The man in control, quite evidently the Siddha himself, was of indeterminate origin. There were aspects of the Indian and also of the larger-boned Westerner, and he likely was some mix of those two. Whatever he was, he obviously was the master of the room.

When I first lifted my eyes to the dais, they were in the Yin and Yang position, the yoga master in the cross-legged lotus position and the smaller man in his lap, facing him, chest to chest, with his legs wrapped around the master's waist and his ankles crossed. It looked like a simple position, but it wasn't, the books on the Kamasutra in my cell explained. It was one in which the cock's penetration was at the maximum, the touch of other body parts was most intimate, and the balance between the two figures was most demanding. I could tell from the way the Sri Lankan was shuddering and how he began to faint even as I watched them, that the penetration was deep. As I watched, the Sri Lankan began to slip backward, the master grabbed his waist but let the young man arch his back to the floor and lay his cheek against the mat. Even from here I could see that the young man was swooning and going glassy eyed.

And then I knew why. The master started to pull the young man's channel off his cock and then pull him back on, in long strokes, impossibly long strokes. The yoga master's cock had to be a foot long.

Trembling, I fell away from the window and, moaning, crouched on the floor below—and masturbated myself to solitary completion.

Later that evening, when Ravith came in for my supper tray, Benito came in with him. They held me down on the bed, and, while I struggled ineffectually, they fitted my cock with a locked, hard-plastic chastity belt that would permit me to pass urine—but not to masturbate.

* * * *

Four days of agony of not being able to resist watching the twice daily tantric ceremony in the hall below but not being able to get any relief from it. A whole week without sex would have had me climbing the walls anyway, but what the demonstrations of the gay Kamasutra were doing to me without me being able even to masturbate were driving me to distraction. On the morning of the fifth day I woke to Acharya Ahitharan standing in the open door to the corridor with Ravith and Benito standing behind him.

"It's time for your interview with the master, Siddha Satyanarida," he said and motioned the two others into the room.

I moaned and protested in a desultory fashion, being totally worn out by the deprivation, while Ravith and Benito unlocked the cock chastity belt and ascertained for themselves by checking the spent douche bottles that I had purified myself.

They stripped me of my white cotton trousers and tunic and buttoned a pair of the briefs with the buttons on the hips on me and then wrapped me in the saffron robe that I had found in the dresser a week previously but not worn, and tied a sash around my waist.

The Siddha was sitting, in a cross-legged yoga position, on silk pillows on a dais in a room richly slathered in gauzy drapes cascading from the center of the ceiling and tied at the corners of the room and oriental carpets under foot. A low teak table was positioned in front of him, supporting a flask and two crystal tumblers.

His chest was bare and he was wearing a saffron-colored dhoti that flared out around his small waist, covering his legs. He was barrel chested, with massive, hard-muscled pecs, shoulders, and biceps. I estimated that he must be well over six feet tall, and perfectly proportioned. There was no beard on his androgynous-featured, beautifully calm face, and long, silky, straight hair hung down his back to his waist. There was an emerald in his navel and a ruby affixed in the center of his forehead.

I would have thought he was sleeping or in deep meditation if he hadn't obviously been aware of my presence. As we entered the room, he lifted one palms-up hand from a knee and gestured to the loose pile of silk pillows beside him. "Please, join me here, David Kane." His voice was rich in tone, smooth, and calming—if I could have been calmed under the circumstances.

As Ravith and Benito guided me to the pillows and made me sit down right next to the Siddha, the yoga master gestured to Acharya Ahitharan. "Drink for our guest, please, Acharya."

Ahitharan poured liquid from the flask into one of the crystal tumblers, and Ravith took it and raised it to my lips. The Acharya leaned down and murmured in my ear, "You best drink this for your own well-being. And position yourself in the lotus position."

Trembling, I drank from the glass and assumed the lotus position. The Siddha waved the other men away. As they left, the Acharya taking the flask and glasses with him, I saw that we were sitting directly across from a full-wall mirror. I could see the serenity that the Siddha was exhibiting contrasted by my own nervousness.

I began to feel a little woozy. But just a little. I had no idea how I was going to prevent what was going to happen, but I certainly wasn't going to let this man know how badly I needed to be fucked. A chill ran up my spine at the memory of how long I had seen his cock was from watching him fuck the young men in the ceremony hall—always smaller men. Never the same one twice, leading me to wonder how well his Kamasutra partners endured the experience.

"I believe Acharya Ahitharan has given you a time line on your initiation period here, David Kane. The time has come for me to formally commence that initiation. What you will receive here, now, is the highest-level tantric experience, elite Kamasutra, so that through all of the coming stages of initiation, you will know what goal you are moving toward, a perpetual tantric sexual high. We will proceed through several positions of the Kamasutra and you will spill your seed copiously. Before we are done, you will become aware of the highest levels of tantric sexual satisfaction."

A moan escaped my lips.

"Do not fear it," he said. "This is the experience you are here for."

"Not really," I murmured, wondering why my voice sounded so distant and quiet. "This is not what I thought I was getting into. I . . . Oh, oh."

He had wrapped an arm around my shoulder and pulled me to him. The other hand had moved into the folds of the saffron-colored robe I was wearing. I felt his long, sensuous fingers deftly unbuttoning the cotton briefs at each hip, and the briefs falling away from my body. I now knew why they were constructed the way they were. He had some sort of rings just below the tip of his thumb and forefinger, with metal balls on the insides of them. His hand slowly glided up my belly and sternum and then he was moving the balls on the flesh of my chest and torso.

I moaned deeply, and he turned my face to his for a possessing kiss—the only time he kissed me.

I . . . must . . . resist, I thought, but it had been too long. I shuddered and groaned as he took a nipple between the balls and rubbed them back and forth. He brushed the robe open, but just slightly, so that, in the mirror opposite us, I could see the metal balls moving on my nipple, puffing it up, making me tremble.

"Please, no, I cannot," I whispered. Too low for him to hear, I feared—not that it mattered, I was sure.

He pulled me half onto his lap, one bare butt cheek on his thigh, and his hand came out of the fold at my chest and moved to below the sash tied around my waist. Without dislodging the sash, he pushed the robe off the thigh I had straddling his lap. He ran the two balls around on the thigh, causing me, involuntarily, to watch the circles—both by looking down and by looking into the mirror—move higher on the thigh, knowing full well where they were going. I trembled and buried the back of my head in the hollow of his shoulder as he moved to the inside of the thigh. And slowly moved up, higher and higher. They were rubbing under my balls and I was hyperventilating and struggling against him—without effect, as he held me tightly in strong arms. But I was moving slowly in my totally inadequate defense, as if I was trying to walk underwater. Something in the drink, obviously, but not something that deadened my senses. Something that dulled my reactions but heightened my senses.

I groaned and begged him for mercy as he moved the balls up and down my already-hardened shaft.

His cock was monstrously hard now too—and in evidence. I could see in the mirror where the cock had erupted out from the seam in his dhoti and was standing up in a long, foot-long curve. I gasped at the size of it—not overly thick, but monstrously long.

"Please, please," I whimpered. "It's too big. It's . . . oh, fuck. Oh shit!" One of the balls on his finger had found my piss slit and he was fucking the opening with it. With a jerk, I came, exploding with cum that had built up inside me with no chance of release over the past four days. Slathered with my cum, the balls moved lower, to the rim of my entrance, where they rubbed as I moaned, and then the index finger penetrated me as the ball on the thumb continued to play the rim. Deeper inside me, searching for, finding my prostate with the metal ball. I writhed inside his strong embrace, panting hard, murmuring the mantra, "Oh god, fuck me, fuck me, fuck me, fuck me," my resolve evaporating before the days of forced abstinence and exposure to the visions of mass sex and his magic touch.

"Fuck me!" I cried out, came again, and collapsed against him, the surrender complete.

"The elite Kamasutra position of the Reverse Bonobo," I heard him murmur. And then I felt him pulling me fully onto his lap, facing away from him. He grasped me under both of my thighs and lifted and spread my legs. He rolled my hips up, and, although still robed, my thighs and cock and balls were revealed to the mirror opposite me and I couldn't have been more naked, and vulnerable, even though I still was fully clothed in the sashed robe. His cock was between my thighs and curved up toward my belly. He raised my hips enough for his bulb to be placed at my ass opening, and he fed the bulb and another inch or two of the cock inside me.

I gasped and cried out and another two inches pressed in, opening the channel as he moved.

He made sure I could see the whole progress of the cock. At eight inches in, leaving a good four inches of the root outside, he started to slowly pump me. I panted and groaned at the deep invasion. But I couldn't help it; I gloried in the fuck. I needed the fuck.

I ejaculated again, fully satisfied, evacuating another white-foamy spurt of the pent-up load from days of abstinence.

But, oh no, the Siddha hadn't come, and he was pushing me over onto my belly on the tea table. I raised my head and stared into the mirror, seeing his chest and head over my back as he raised up over me and, oh, shit, oh, fuck, fed me those last four inches of the foot long pole and began to stroke me in long, long, deep strokes.

"The simple position of the Greyhound," he said in his soft, yet strong, melodic voice. "But I find it quite effective in the full tantric experience. It is one where I can give it all to you."

It might have been the drugs, but I felt like I had a snake, not just a hard shaft, inside me. It rotated and swiveled and screwed and whipped around and bent to where its bulb kissed and sucked and rubbed on my walls—every square inch of my walls. I came for the fourth time, and he, finally, released his cum in a flood deep inside me.

He lowered his chest on my back and hooked his chin on my shoulder. We both were looking in the mirror, cheek to cheek.

"The height of tantric sexual experience," he whispered in my ear. "The perfection of Kamasutra. The position of the Plow." He reached down on either side of me and raised my legs off the floor, resting my weight on my chest on the surface of the tea table. My calves were coaxed to fold on the small of his back, with my ankles crossed. Then his hands moved down my arms and grasped my wrists and I cried out and groaned as I felt him, still hard, a foot inside me, start once more to plow me deep. Moments later, he rose off me, his magnificent chest looming over me in the reflection in the mirror. Grabbing my legs again, he turned me on the cock onto my back and raised my legs to where they stretched up his torso. He grasped my waist in his hands, raising my pelvis with his, and began to pull my channel on his cock in long slides.

"The position of the Stem." I could barely hear him. "Good for the long journey down from the heights of tantric satisfaction."

My ears were ringing with the sound of the ocean. I was completely relaxed, spent. I had lost count of the positions or the care of how many more were to come. Exhausted, I let my arms dangle to the floor beside me and my head arch back over the end of the tea table and watched the tightening and releasing of his massive chest muscles as reflected in the mirror. The tightening came at the end of the foot-long slide into me, the release as he slid back out. This time his ejaculation came in one long, peaceful flow that burbled up the sides of his staff and dripped out of my stretched and throbbing hole.

Beyond Sanasuma now—beyond satisfaction.

I was his featured partner at the ceremony in the hall that evening.

Docile, no longer drugged in any way, but now his complete slave, I was worked through elite Kamasutra positions, with me moving to any position he guided me into, only crying out and gasping when he penetrated deep inside me: the Bamboo, with me lying on my back and spreading my legs, the Siddha bending over me from on top, me lifting one leg and resting it on the Siddha's shoulder while the Siddha moved his own knee forward, penetrating me deep; the Yin and Yang again, in a close lotus embrace with me in his lap facing him, close, our nipples rubbing, until he pushed on my chest and I arched back and he started to stroke inside me, once again, even when I wasn't drugged in any way, making me feel like there was a snake slithering around inside me; and then, to conclude, the Bonobo, me on my shoulder blades, my thighs bent back onto my chest and the Siddha bending over me, his fists buried in the mat on either side of my head, rocking my pelvis with his, kissing every surface inside me with the bulb of his cock, encouraging me to bend enough to take the bulb of my own cock inside my mouth and sucking it—amazing me when I could. I had known I was flexible, but . . .

And pumping and pumping his cum inside me. He had held each position until I had come, but he had the control to hold himself until the end.

On the way back to my room, Ahitharan assured me that I was greatly favored by the Siddha—that he rarely took an initiate to the ceremony as he had taken me. He did not enjoy me enough that he called for me again in the following days of the next stage of my initiation, however. Although I had been thoroughly fucked—and had needed it—I couldn't say I regretted not having a foot of snake working inside me constantly.

Over the next two weeks I was in Kamasutra training with Ravith and Benito. The two of them together took care of my sexual needs much better than Teddy ever had done, even at his most virile. But that wasn't quite enough. I increasingly realized that I loved Teddy himself. I might love the cocking I got from Ravith and Benito—more from the forceful, rougher, less refined in the ways of Kamasutra Benito than from the highly delicate and refined technique of Ravith—but I loved Teddy as a person and a partner. It was during this period that I came to realize that there was so much more involved in a loving relationship than sex.

This didn't make the knowledge that he had delivered me into sexual bondage any more easy to accept, though.

Progressively, I moved out on the ceremony floor with Ravith and Benito and came within a week of moving to the next stage—more advanced Kamasutra with the older, more experienced Acharyas. Acharya Ahitharan was already eyeing me and letting me know by his touches on my body as he guided me to the cavern ceremony room, that the time that he would "know" me too was near. As my training progressed, so did the trust I was given.

On the first morning I found that my cell door hadn't been locked, I quickly changed into my Western clothes, grabbed my suitcase, quietly stole out of the ashram, and nearly rolled down the mountain and into Nuwara Eliya. I knew I couldn't stay at the Windsor Hotel, but I went there first to get my bearings and to decide how best to escape from Sri Lanka and to make my way back to, first, level Teddy for what he had done to me and then to beg for his forgiveness and hold him in my arms until I could get his cock inside me. I knew then that we'd be fine.

I was starving. Of all the indignities I had suffered in the ashram, nothing topped the diet of vegetables, fruit, and nuts. I went into the hotel café and ordered fried eggs and bacon. While I was waiting for it to be served, I opened an English-language paper. My attention was arrested by an article on page 3.

. . . . *Wanted in the murder of New York manufacturer Theodore Drisal, his associate, David Kane, is being sought by New York police. He is thought to have fled the country, and may be in India. He is suspected of having commandeered the company's jet and flown to Mumbai, India. Drisal's business partner, Morten Whitley, who found Drisal's body on April 21st in his apartment, which had been ransacked, reported that Drisal and Kane, who lived in Drisal's apartment, had been fighting of late over Drisal's intention to retire and to turn the company over to Whitley. Drisal is thought to have been diagnosed with . . .*

Tears came to my eyes. My first thought was to the death of Teddy. Only after that did I fully absorb that I was being sought as Teddy's murder. For his murder. Teddy had been murdered. Mort. That was why . . . that was the reason for all of this . . . it wasn't Teddy.

I knew I must—should—go back. But all of the evidence . . . just too much evidence now built against me. I had fled . . . or so everyone thought. Mort would have had plenty of time to solidify the case against me. To cover his own tracks.

I looked up and, through tear-clouded eyes, saw Ravith and Benito standing in the doorway. I looked wildly around the room. There was a door into the kitchen. Maybe I could make it through there and escape them. But did I want to?

Decision time.

The Message

I took one last look in the dingy bathroom mirror of my Strand Hotel room, opening my mouth in a wide, toothy grin to make sure everything was in good order, and then I took a deep breath, muttered an "OK, then, let's do this" to myself, and turned to the door. "Can't keep the general waiting too long."

I would have said something to the hotel management about the condition of the bathroom but from what I gathered of the conversation in the dining room the previous night, I had one of the only functioning bathrooms left in the establishment. As I walked down the corridor to the stairs, not trusting what was offered as an elevator, I did what I could not to look at the smoke-damaged, peeling wallpaper of what had once been the celebrated Rangoon gem of the necklace of colonial grand dame hotels extending from New Delhi, down through the Southeast Asian nations, and up to Hong Kong. I hoped that someday the hotel would again regain its glory, but that was unlikely to happen as long as General Ne Win, now in his twenty-fourth year since he seized power in Burma in 1962, held his stranglehold on power here.

I would be honored to be able to be any part of whatever changed that.

I entered the dining room, where there was just a smattering of diners, just as there was only a smattering of lodgers at the hotel. Most Burmese were not permitted to lodge or dine at the Strand, and most foreigners weren't even able to get into the country. It was a minor miracle that I was able to be here myself, especially considering that my request for a visa was based on an intent to interview the imprisoned emotional symbol of the freedom fighters, Kyine Nyunt, whose father had unsuccessfully led the struggle for a return to civilian rule and had died in the attempt. Kyine Nyunt, who had written elegantly and spoken eloquently in favor of the freedom movement throughout the world, had returned to Burma, only to be imprisoned and held with little contact outside of Mandalay, a long distance north of Rangoon up the Irrawaddy River. Along with the opposition's even more important intellectual leader, Aung Htun, who also had been imprisoned in some unknown place in Burma, Kyine Nyunt, was the heart of the country's freedom movement.

I was here, in the Strand dining room, because the key to my being able to land an interview with Kyine Nyunt for my International Press news agency was sitting at the best table in the room, separated by a considerable distance from any of the foreign diners. General Soe Ye, once (and still) the warlord of a major opium-producing enclave somewhere upcountry in Burma on the Thai border, was dining here this evening. I had known that. There was a whole network of informers willing to put me into contact with the whereabouts of General Soe Ye. The good general was also one of General Ne Win's backers and main supporters. If anyone could get me to where I needed to go, it was General Soe Ye.

My entrée was that I had met the general before. I had been covering an ASEAN mutual cooperation conference in Bangkok that General Soe Ye attended for the Burmese. "Mutual cooperation" was a euphemism for military alliance, but, as ASEAN was not supposed to be a defense organization, all of their talks on cooperation were couched in economic terms. I was covering the conference for the IP. General Soe Ye was royally bored by the economic framework given for the talks, and his eyes wandered. His eyes wandered to me—

repeatedly—which was noted by those with interest in the freedom movement in Burma. As they also knew what General Soe Ye's weakness was, they had come to enlist my cooperation. My own inclinations didn't rail at the assignment, and the general had, in fact, propositioned me before leaving Bangkok and invited me to come to him in Burma, so, with their help from the Thailand end in me getting into Burma, here I was. Making myself available—for a worthy purpose.

Soe Ye saw me, and his face lit up in a big smile. It's not that I wasn't expected; I wouldn't have even gotten this far, to Rangoon, without his intervention. But he nonetheless was happy to see me. As, no doubt, was the waiter, who, when the general's attention was switched to me, managed to slip away from the hand that had been squeezing his buttocks and retreat to the kitchen.

"Mr. Jansen," he said in excellent, if perhaps somewhat overenunciated British English, "welcome to Rangoon. I trust you had no trouble clearing customs."

"Nothing that two bottles of Johnnie Walker Red didn't smooth over," I said. "But thanks for all of your help," I quickly added, having seen the touch of anger my first comment had caused to flit across the general's face. Corruption and bribery were widely practiced here in Burma during these years; it just wasn't anything you would talk about openly, especially not to one of the senior generals of the ruling cabal. "And do call me Gene," I added, giving him a sunny smile, which changed the expression on his face considerably. "I'll call you general, of course, but you certainly needn't be formal with me . . . given the circumstances."

"So, you have considered the little proposition I made you in Bangkok, then, have you . . . Gene? And, please do sit down and have a drink." I sat while he motioned for a waiter. "What is it you'd like to have, Gene?"

"I'll take a vodka screwdriver," I said to the waiter. I wasn't that fond of screwdrivers, but I had winked at the general—playing him—when I'd said "screwdriver," and he'd appreciated the little joke.

The waiter stammered, reluctant to admit the hotel's limitations in front of the all-powerful general. "I'm sorry, sir, we are unable to serve vodka here."

"Oh, that's OK," I said, understanding that to mean they didn't have any vodka to serve. "I'll take whatever beer you have available then."

While he was leaving, Soe Ye leaned over to me and said sotto voce, "I have vodka upstairs in my suite. And a screwdriver too. We can go up there directly to entertain each other with them." His lustful smile was unmistakable.

"That, I'm sure will be very . . . entertaining," I answered him, with a smile of my own. "But first things first. I must serve my masters—I do like to serve masters." I saw the chill of a thrill zing through his body when I said that.

"As you know, I have been sent here with a purpose. My news agency wants an interview with Kyine Nyunt. It would mean so much to my standing there if I could get one. As we discussed in our letters, certainly. The authorities can review the text of the article, of course—before I leave Burma. That's a given, naturally."

Such a game we were playing. I knew the Burmese government didn't want an interview with the emotional symbol of the opposition of any sort floated, and they would have been donkeys to not understand that a censored article run now wouldn't preclude an entirely different version being published once I'd left Burma. But it was all a game within a game, and much of it hung on the lust of General Soe Ye and on what he convinced himself was worth giving up to get what he wanted in the short term.

"Yes, quite all right," Soe Ye said. "And you have a guide to take you up to Mandalay?"

"Yes," I answered. "He's right over there—his name's Saw Win." I waved to the local Burmese guide my friends in Bangkok had hooked me up with, and he smiled back. Soe Ye wasn't smiling. He was looking at Saw Win speculatively. I wondered if Soe Ye had, by instinct, recognized the competition. Saw Win was quite talented and heavy on the muscle and good looks and assessing eye. I had only met him yesterday afternoon, at the airport, at the arrival of my Air Burma plane from

Bangkok. But he'd already spent the night in my hotel bed, fucking me masterfully like we were long-time lovers.

"Shall we go up to my suite now?" Soe Ye asked in a tight voice. I'd pulled his attention away from Saw Win by placing my hand on his thigh, just above his knee, and giving it a little squeeze.

"The letters of access and of passage up the Irrawaddy," I said gently. "I believe we had agreed that I would receive them first."

"Yes . . . I . . . I." The general was struggling for control now. I'd moved my hand to his basket, holding what gave me a lurch of fear and anticipation through the material of his trousers. This was a tricky moment, and I needed to have him in my control and panting for me.

"Here, right here. I have them," he said. And he produced a packet of precious passes worth their weight in gold—certainly worth what I was about to do.

After looking the passes over, I motioned to Saw Win, who approached the table, and I gave them to him and he left the dining room. Soe Ye watched Saw Win intently as he walked away, with seeming mixed feelings. Another obvious rooster leaving the hen house; but leaving with high stakes that Soe Ye had placed on the table in the playing of his hand.

Soe Ye was a forceful, and cruel, and demanding lover. It was all about him; his pleasure. And part of his pleasure was in inflicting pain, receiving full service, having full control. The preliminaries were all about me pleasing him. Me massaging him and sucking him to the heights of desire and the hardness of steel. And the main event was focused on him taking me—by force, at his direction. My struggling against the taking was instrumental in him getting as much passion out of the fuck as possible. I massaged his ample body and gave him suck until he rose up and slapped me hard across the face, sending me to the floor. And then he was upon me, covering me, and thrusting inside me as I struggled, on the tired, almost threadbare carpeting of his room, trying—at his direction—to scrabble out from underneath him and slither to the door. Putting me in a headlock and screwing me to the floor with the force and size and insistence of his cock then, he fucked me in a lengthy

407

campaign for his ejaculative satisfaction, while I whimpered and moaned and groaned at the onslaught.

Then he held me there, me panting, close to exhaustion, while he had barely broken a sweat. He was recharging, but while he did so, I remained his prisoner, pinned to the carpet by his bulk and by the ramrod drilled into me, nailing my pelvis to the floor.

When he was ready again, he pulled me up off the floor, flung me onto the bed, on my belly, the balls of my feet on the floor, my legs spread, and he beat me with a riding crop on my back and thighs and buttocks while he rode me hard to a second completion.

Afterward, he sat, calmly in an arm chair next to the bed, smoking cigarettes and drinking scotch and humming to himself, as I lay, exhausted and covered with welts, still panting hard, on his bed.

"You please me," he said, blowing rings with the smoke of his cigarette. "You will come back to me here after your trip to Mandalay."

It wasn't a request or a question. I could not leave the country without his acquiescence. If all went well, however, I had no intention of meeting him here at the Strand again. And if I was guessing right, he didn't really have any intention of that either.

My guide, Saw Win, was waiting for me in my room when I returned from being debauched by the general. He was all cluckings and soothing words. He gently rubbed salve on my welts—both of us having known what the general would do with me—and then he stretched me out on the bed on my side and covered me close from behind and made languid and deep-delving love to me with his master cock until I drifted off to sleep.

* * * *

Saw Win suggested that, since I had managed to get into Burma and most likely would not find it easy ever getting in again, that we should break our trip up the Irrawaddy on a series of river trader steamers at the ancient temple complex at Pagan,

408

which rivaled Cambodia's Angkor Wat at setting the mouths of archeologists of ancient Asian civilizations drooling. It was here that the expedition turned ugly.

I was exhausted from a full day of moving from one ruined temple to another in a World War II vintage Jeep. Saw Win was an excellent guide. He knew so much about the long history of the building of several hundred temples at Pagan on the banks of the Irrawaddy. And he also was so attentive to me. And loving.

The facilities were primitive, and we showered together in the evening under the drizzle of a water pipe in a half-enclosed shed, soaping each other up and rinsing each other off, running our hands all over the tired curves of muscles and into the inviting crevices of one another. He was magnificent and masterful, and I was panting my want for him while he toweled me off and guided me into the guest lodge and parted the mosquito netting for me to lower myself on my back on the bed and then spread and raise my thighs, so he could maneuver himself between them, slowly glide inside me, and start filling and stretching me with long, languid strokes.

During the lovemaking, we whispered to each other, discussing what lay ahead of us, knowing that if anyone was spying on us, all they would hear were two lovers in high heat, their bodies undulating against each other in primeval passion, whispering what they want to feel or do next.

I had been led to Saw Win by friends of the Burmese opposition forces in Bangkok. So I knew that he knew there was more to my coming than gathering an interview with Kyine Nyunt that would be chopped to pieces before I filed it—if they let me actually talk to her at all, which in itself was highly unlikely. It was time to tell him more. I had been told to tell him more at this point in the journey.

"I am not really here to . . . oh, god, that's good. Again, please. Oh, Shit! . . . to interview her," I whispered. His cock stopped in its probe at that point. He held us there, not moving a muscle other than the throbbing of his centering muscle inside me. I was panting, waiting for the next thrust, wanting the next thrust. But he was waiting to hear the rest of what I had to say. I could feel him beginning to tremble, in anticipation, no doubt having waited for this since that first day in Rangoon.

"Go on," he growled.

"I'm not gathering," I whispered. "I'm giving. I'm carrying a message for her. Something so important that it has to be conveyed this way."

"A message?" he asked. Holding, trying to hold us in suspense. I moved my pelvis against him, trying to get him to push me over the edge, but he placed the palm of a strong hand on the small of my back where it descends into my crevice and held me there, waiting.

"Yes," I murmured. "It's in code. In my interview notebook. A page that looks almost like the shorthand of the rest, but not quite. If . . . if . . . oh, god, YES!" he had started to pump me slowly again. ". . .If anything happens to me, could you? . . . Oh, oh, Ahhhhhh!"

We had been stretched out almost flat, Saw Win's pelvis between my thighs. But now he went up on his knees, rolled my hips up to him, pushed his cock a couple of more inches inside me, and began stroking me hard and fast, as if there was no tomorrow. He was sending me over that edge I had been seeking. I arched my back and thrust my hips into his pelvis in a counterpounding, lost in the fuck, wanting every single inch of him and the tiniest dribble of his spouting deep inside me. Pounding against each other endlessly, both crying out in lust and passion.

When we had both ejaculated and collapsed into a sweaty, spent heap, I started to doze off. I was not yet asleep. Saw Win might have thought I was, though, from my regular, shallow breathing, when he rose from me, parted the mosquito netting, and padded over to the doorway, which had been covered by matting.

The shadows of two monstrously muscle-bound men raced across the ceiling in the light of the small bedside lamp, and I was being manhandled, fucked vigorously by one bulky, cruel attacker after the other, as Saw Win stood off to the side of the room, rifling through my things, looking for my interview notebook.

The truck journey east, away from the Irrawaddy, not north toward Mandalay, but east toward the Thai border area, was a rough one. The track we moved on could hardly be called a road; there was little if any suspension in the bed of the truck, where I was huddled between two burly Burmese hulks, both of whom prodded and pulled at my naked body to their great enjoyment. I wasn't hooded or kept from watching my surroundings in any other way, which I took as an ominous sign that they had no reason to care where I was being taken.

Saw Win wasn't with us. I had seen nothing of him after he had found my interview notebook and left our room in Pagan, while the men who had invaded the room were still fucking me.

Hours later, the truck pulled up into a jungle compound, walled and consisting of several pavilion-style, leaf-roofed buildings set against the side of a steep ravine tumbling down into a rushing stream far below. The canopy of the trees met far overhead, making the compound virtually invisible from the air.

I was hauled out of the truck and set down on my bruised feet and forced to turn around. I was standing right in front of . . . General Soe Ye.

"Welcome to my kingdom, Gene," Soe Ye said. Then he laughed and ordered me to be taken into one of the pavilions and slapped down onto a rough table on my back. My wrists and ankles were bound to the legs at the four corners. And then General Soe Ye, entered, naked now, swishing his riding crop, and smiling an evil smile.

He beat and fucked me almost into unconsciousness, declaring that I couldn't fool him, that he knew I wasn't in Burma just to interview Kyine Nyunt, that he was too clever for me, and that he would hold me here and play with me until I was all used up. No one, he said, would know what happened to me after I'd left Rangoon. I was in his world now and there was no leaving it.

I moaned for him and whimpered and told him that he was the greatest lover and that I didn't need to be bound. That all I wanted to do was please him; that I couldn't get enough of him. That he had the best cock I'd ever had.

Afterward, I was unbound and led to where I could stand under a water pipe and sluice the fucking of so many men off of my bruised and broken body. I was given a native sarong to twist around my waist and led to a small pavilion near the back of the compound. Unlike the other pavilions, its sides were set with iron bars. It was a cage of some sort.

I was pushed through a barred door, into the cage, and the door shut tightly behind me and was locked.

The area inside the small pavilion was dark, but I was able to see the rustling of material back in the corner, and, as my eyes became adjusted to light, I could make out the figure of a small, emaciated man. He turned and I checked the memory of the photographs that had been shown to me back in Bangkok.

"Aung Htun? Is that you? You are Aung Htun, aren't you?"

The figure rose up off the bench and shuffled toward me, reaching for the light.

"Who? What?" he asked through parched lips, in a ragged voice having grown unused to conversation. Aung Htun, erstwhile leader of the National League for Democracy, the coalesced umbrella organization for the Burmese opposition. The intellectual underpinning of the movement.

"Your friends in Bangkok have sent me with a message," I said. And I laughed to myself. A message for Aung Htun, not for Kyine Nyunt in Mandalay. All a game within a game, the opposition in Bangkok knowing that their intellectual leader was being held by General Soe Ye somewhere—although no one knew where. Needing someone to lead them there.

"A message?" Aung Htun asked, in confusion. "But you come almost as you were born. Where is this message? Why have they not taken it from you?"

"I am the message," I said. And then I smiled a broad, full toothed smile for him, reached two fingers into my mouth, and pulled out a molar. "In this false tooth is a transmitter," I said. "When I found you, I was to extract it and disconnect it. That was the signal that where I was, there you would be also. I would suggest that we both stand back toward the back of the

412

cage now, if you don't mind. And perhaps go under that bench. In a few minutes, I think it's going to get very busy around here."

South East Asia

Double Trouble

I knew where this was going.

I was sitting in Kamrod Tikka's lap, both of us naked, me facing him, and with my heels resting on the headrests of the adjacent seats in his business jet high over India en route to Bangkok.

He already had his fat cock up inside me and I felt his hands go under my buttocks from each side, and my buttocks spread and a finger from each hand enter me as well. I was grabbing the headrest on both sides of his head for dear life to stay in place as his hands no longer were encircling my waist.

I moaned as a second finger from each hand penetrated me as well.

"You liked the copilot, didn't you?" he murmured to me. "I can have him back here in a minute. I know he'd like it."

"No, Kam, not now, please. Maybe someday, but . . . oh god, oh god!"

A third finger from each hand had entered me, and he had grasped his shaft with his fingers and was moving it back and forth inside me.

I panted and gasped . . . and came up his hard, dark belly in the rivulet of black, curly hair that descended from his chest into his pubes.

Kamrod wasn't done, though. He was only beginning. He had superb control. The fingers came out of my channel and he was grasping my buttocks and pulling them apart, and with the strength of his strong arm muscles, raising and lowering me on his shaft too, until, finally, as the jet started its descent into Bangkok and I nuzzled my face into the hollow of his neck and gasped and moaned, he gave me his seed in three prodigious jerky bursts.

I lay against him, panting, while he ran his hands up and down my back and went flaccid inside me. I whimpered for him, letting him know he had mastered me. I knew it was what he wanted. India putting America in its place.

I even asked him to do it again in a low whisper of longing, knowing there wasn't time before we landed, but also knowing it excited him to have that control over me and that well into his fifties, he could still have a twenty-two-year old blond beg for it from him. I felt him stiffening again at the thought, but then there was a ding, the red light went on over our bank of chairs, and he muttered with regret that I'd just have to wait—that we were descending into the Thai capital.

I took his face in my hands, kissed him, and wiggled my butt on his shrinking cock, as if I wouldn't listen to reason. And I knew that this excited him as well. I needed to keep him excited.

I knew he wanted to double me. He'd been building up to it for some time. But I had fended that off. I didn't know how much longer I could do that. If I truly didn't want to give in to it, I'd have to find another daddy. And it would be hard to find another man in Mumbai as hard bodied, hard cocked, and rich as the international entrepreneur, Kamrod Tikka. And not having my passport in my possession, Mumbai was pretty much my selection pool.

He had picked me up in a male bordello in Mumbai after I'd been there less than a week, abandoned by the American businessman who had brought me there and suddenly decided he preferred dark-skinned Indian boys to American beach bum blonds.

I had gone with Kamrod willingly, because after a week in the bordello, and discovering that young blond men were in

418

high demand in India, I didn't know if I could survive another week in that place. On the whole, I'd found Indian men small cocked, but they had some peculiar notions of what to do with their cocks. And the Western businessmen who visited the brothel wanted their money's worth and generally wanted rough sex that they didn't think they could get away with in their home environments.

Kamrod had been both the hunkiest and most refined of technique of the Indian men who had bought my time, and he took his time with me. I found the fingers plus cock routine he liked painful at first, but I'd been with him a full month now, and one night I'd even managed most of his hand buried and gripping and rotating his cock inside me. He took it slow and gave me plenty of time to adjust.

He was tall and burly for an Indian. A handsome face and an assured manner. He was dark skinned, telling me that he was from south India, where that was normal. And I liked the black, curly body hair he had on his forearms and thighs and cascading down from his Adam's apple to his cock.

His mouth was sweet and persistent on my cock, and he could play me for nearly an hour at a time, bringing me to the brink and then holding me off. Then suddenly entering my channel with three or four fingers and spreading them and making me cum in a flood as the pad of a thumb thrumbed on my prostate. Sometimes that was the end, but more often, he'd move between my legs then, and I'd feel his thick cock entering me between the fingers and he'd work me for another eternity, showing that he knew how to control himself as well.

And, as I said, he took his time and made love to me with his voice as he fucked me. He had a mesmerizing tone to his voice and he could speak in the rhythm of the fuck.

I was never quite sure how long he would want me. He seemed the type who could keep in thrall a young man of his own choosing from his own business world and who didn't need to go to a brothel.

I actually saw that in the first week I was with him in his home. A young German man, who obviously didn't like Indians and who visibly pulled away from them and showed distaste at their touching manner, came—reluctantly, I'm sure—to

Kamrod's house for a business meeting and no more than two hours later was coming on a toilet stool, his ankles on Kamrod's shoulders, and melting at the love Kamrod was making with his voice in the young man's ear and with his cock in the German's channel.

I asked, apprehensively, why he had brought me from the brothel—and then not just discarded me when he'd done all he wanted to do to me. He told me that he had heard about me from a colleague and that I was just the kind who turned him on. He also smiled and said he hadn't done everything he wanted to do with me yet, causing me to shudder as much from the way he'd said it as from the touch of the backs of his fingers gliding up the inside of my thighs.

He more than hinted that he liked threesomes and double penetrations, but I didn't hop on that suggestion. Increasingly, though, I figured I'd either have to show interest in that or find another way home from India.

I was in India illegally now. I had no papers. Whatever man I was with could pretty much do anything he wanted with me. I felt lucky that Kamrod, hunky, not too old—maybe early fifties—refined, and filthy rich was the man who had me.

When he said he had to go to Bangkok on business and he wanted me to go with him, there wasn't much I could—or wanted to—say other than yes. I started to mention the problem of leaving the country, but he produced my passport, which he somehow had managed to acquire.

He didn't give it to me, though, and I didn't ask him to.

We were booked at the Oriental Hotel, Bangkok's most prestigious hotel.

That night, in a tenth-floor suite, Kamrod was all about my needs rather than his. Although he was a good lover, everything we'd done before was because he wanted to do it. On this night, though, he wanted to know what I wanted. He said we could just sleep too, if that was my wish.

I would have liked the "just sleep" suggestion—Kamrod was quite virile and had fucked me at least once a day since he had, essentially, bought me from the bordello. But knowing his appetites, I didn't want to do anything that lessened his ardor for me.

So, I asked him to take me out onto the balcony overlooking the Chao Phya river, with the Wat Arun temple lit up across the water, and lie back on the chaise lounge out there, while I mounted him and fucked him slowly and gazed out over the exotic river scene, the water still alive with small long-tail boats even in the night.

He seemed pleased with my choice and came twice for me.

The next day, he was in meetings until the evening. I sat by the pool, where I got several propositions—from men and women alike. But it was nice not to have to say yes.

Except for a young, small Thai pool boy, who assured me that he was in his twenties and who I fucked down in a patch of bougainvillea near the river's edge, happy to be the top for once in a very long while, I politely turned aside all other offers.

Near sunset, Kamrod came back to the room and told me we'd be dressing formally for dinner and that we'd be eating with the Belgium businessman he had come to Bangkok to strike a deal with. I didn't ask what sort of businesses Kamrod was in—and he didn't tell me. I surmised there was more than one business, though, and I could tell they were lucrative.

As we were leaving our suite for the hotel's Le Normandie restaurant, Kamrod leaned in to me and said, "I believe I have the deal I wanted, but he has expressed an interest in you. I need for you to be pleasant to him—despite whatever impression he makes."

Of course, I thought. Why wouldn't I be pleasant? But then I met the man. Kamrod introduced him as Hugo Jaguerman. I would have thought that Pig would be a more fitting name.

He was a massive man, even bulkier than Kamrod. But I could tell by the way that he filled out his tux shirt that it was mostly muscle, not fat. His jacket must have been specially tailored for him to accommodate the girth of his upper arms. His head, a pig's head, complete with snout, seemed to lay directly on his shoulders. What little I could see of his neck was as thick as his head.

He was bald, with folds of fat at the base of his neck, and his ears looked like those of a pig too. His eyes were small, buried in puffy cheeks, but as he squinted at me, I could see the same expression of lust that I'd seen in men's eyes most of my life.

He ate like a pig too, his eyes rarely leaving mine, as he chewed noisily on all of the artistically prepared dishes that were wasted on him.

He and Kamrod talked—although Jaguerman looked at me rather than Kamrod. But they spoke in French, which I didn't understand. I was disgusted with how the pig would stuff his mouth and then talk. He left the impression of a coarse man with huge appetites that were almost impossible to satiate. I shuddered at the thought of what I assumed I was there for.

Hearing French coming out of such a hoggish face was a surprise. But he was Belgian, so I suppose it was natural that he'd speak French. It was more of a surprise that Kamrod spoke it—and when he spoke it, it sounded like music. A little chill went up my spine at the thought of him speaking soft French in his mesmerizing voice while he fucked me.

When the coffee was served, Kamrod stood up from the table and walked away without a word to me, although he leaned down and spoke softly in Jaguerman's ear, which was answered by a leer.

And Kamrod didn't come back to the table.

"We go now," Jaguerman said in heavily accented English when he'd finished his coffee.

"Mr. Tikka?" I answered in a surprised voice.

"We will meet him at apartment."

I started to object, but a burly man in a black suit was at the side of our table. He had a chauffeur's hat tucked under his arm and seemed to be well known to Jaguerman. I got that he was Jaguerman's driver and that I indeed was going someplace with Jaguerman. The Belgian alone was muscle enough to manage that even if I didn't want to, but here in the best restaurant in Thailand, his bulky chauffeur made clear that I shouldn't make a scene.

I knew for sure now what Kamrod meant by being pleasant to the Belgian businessman. And I probably knew exactly why I'd been brought along for the jet ride. I would not be surprised to find out that the Belgian had specified what type of young man he wanted Kamrod to bring with him from Mumbai and that this was what prompted Kamrod to take me from the brothel.

The thought struck me that I would not be flying back to India with Kamrod. But this was quickly replaced with the fear that I would not be leaving wherever I was going now alive.

In the back of the Mercedes limousine, where I half assumed I would be thoroughly fucked, I wasn't.

I sat in the middle of the backseat, and Jaguerman, taking up much of the width of the seat, sat across from me and stared at me and picked at his teeth with a toothpick.

"Let me see it," he said in a low growl.

"See it? See what? Oh." He was motioning with his hands what he wanted to see.

I spread my legs and unzipped my trousers and fished my cock out.

I cupped my balls in the palm of my hand, and we sat there for several moments, Jaguerman picking his teeth with a toothpick with one hand, his legs now spread too, and his other hand holding himself through the fabric of his tux trousers.

I assumed this was the start of rough sex. But it wasn't.

"Enough," he said, and I folded my goods back into my trousers and zipped up. He kept his hand on his crotch, though, and it was obvious he was aroused.

We didn't have long to drive after that—to yet another high-rise building on the banks of the Chao Phya.

Jaguerman lived in the penthouse, which, although large, was surrounded on all four sides by terracing that dwarfed the apartment.

I held back a gasp when we entered the apartment and he flipped on the light switch.

The lounge room we entered, with an S-shaped sofa winding its way through the center of the room, lit up in a soft glow—but not from any lights overhead or on floors or tables. Instead, track lighting in the ceiling spotlighted onto paintings on the walls.

My almost gasp was caused by seeing that all of the paintings were male nudes—or, more precisely, male torsos. An impossibly muscled—almost cartoonish in its muscle definition—highly erotic torso and legs, bringing to mind that of a muscle-bound satyr.

"Sit on couch. You want drink?"

"Umm, yes," I answered. "A beer is fine, if you have it."

"Bottle or can?"

"A Bottle's fine, thanks."

He laughed. "You choose wisely. But, then again, maybe not."

On that strange note, he left the room and went into another one overlooking the terrace, which looked like it was a bar.

When he came back, he was swinging four bottles of beer—two in each hand—but I hardly noticed them, as shocked as I was.

He was naked. And what immediately dawned on me was that he obviously was the model for the paintings lit up on the walls. And the paintings no longer looked like exaggeration. His body was horrible and magnificent all in one sweeping impression. All of the muscles were where they should be, but they were almost grotesquely overbuilt. His waist was thick, but with plates of muscle rather than fat—his abs looked like those of a Roman breastplate. His chest muscles overpowered his torso so that his waist looked tiny in contrast. And his arms were as thick as telephone poles, with bulging muscles.

And his cock was as thick as a telephone pole too, with two baseball-sized balls hanging behind it. He was already in full arousal.

I moaned as he set three of the beer bottles down and, sitting down close beside me, took a big swallow from the bottle still in his hand. Then, encasing me in one arm, he pulled me to him and took my mouth in his.

I almost gagged as the beer swished into my mouth, and then I did gag as his tongue followed.

I closed my eyes, not able to look at his piggish face, and let him hold my mouth captive with his as his hands moved across my body, unbuttoning, unzipping, pulling clothes off my arms and legs.

I was trapped in the embrace of one of his arms while the hand of the other encased my cock and he started a slow pump.

My nerves were standing on end. His technique of tease in the car leading directly into this no-preliminary assault had me on edge and confused. It would have been useless to resist him anyway, but I was completely disarmed, yielding to him. The reflex was involuntary, but my hips were going with the motion of his hand on my cock. He loosened the grip, while keeping my cock encased, and I found myself slow-fucking his fist.

He released my mouth and then, thankfully, all I could see of his head was the bald top as his mouth was going down onto my chest.

The hand on my cock was crushing now and was beginning a faster, more demanding cadence.

My eyes went to the paintings on the wall. His body really was a wonder. And none of the paintings showed his face. I could take the body. I looked back down at him and could see—and appreciate—the bulge of the shoulder and muscles on either side of his shiny, billiard-ball-smooth head. He was pulling me over into his lap, and I could feel his hard cock at the small of my back and those thunderous thighs under my naked ones.

I panted hard to the rhythm of his jacking, and I cried out in little huffs of breath in response to what he was doing with his mouth on my nipples.

I shouldn't just be giving it to him. He was a gross pig. I should let him know I didn't want it—or that I'd give it to him but not because I wanted it. Because I didn't have any other choice. Make him demand it and take it by force and then not be able to fully enjoy it, as I couldn't enjoy sex from a beast like this.

If I just didn't have to . . . look . . . at his face.

I brought my hands up to glide over the lines of his fantastically defined muscles.

It was OK, in the almost dark, with the lights just highlighting the paintings. I could let him have it and enjoy it.

I wanted to reach back and grab his cock—to get the measure of it. Both thrilling and moaning to the thought of it inside me. Had I ever taken something that thick and long? Would I have a sense of triumph when I had?

God, I wanted it. I moaned and involuntarily whined, "Please . . . please."

I heard him laugh, a low, rumbling chuckle. I couldn't be doing this. I couldn't want it. Not from a coarse pig. As if in evidence, he bit my nipple and I cried out and stiffened.

Fight him, fight him, I screamed inside to myself. Stay stiff. Make him take it. Don't let him know . . . God, I wanted it. I relaxed, all of my senses going to the rising seed in my cock. My butt twitching. My channel crying out for attention.

Fuck me, fuck me, fuck me. I was surprised that I wasn't saying it—that I was only thinking it. It was the fear of the size of him, though—and the fear of having to look into his piggish face while he plowed me that held back what my aroused body wanted me to cry out to him.

That cock. How much of it could I take? Oh, god, give me that cock. Once more I tried reaching around him for it—but his waist was just too thick.

"Come for me," he said in a low, guttural voice. "Come for me."

I realized that I was on the brink of doing just that. And, shockingly I was overcome with a sense of loss and disappointment. No, fuck me, fuck me, fuck me, my mind was screaming.

And then I came for him.

He laughed and released me. He pushed me over to the side, and I just toppled over on my side on the curving sofa.

He stood over me, in magnificent erection. If my eyes just rose up his body as far as his nipples, I could remain in full arousal myself. I knew I could. Just don't look into the face.

He picked one of the beer bottles up from the coffee table set a couple of feet in front of the sofa and handed it to me.

"Drink," he said. "Drink. Then we fuck. No, I fuck; you scream."

He laughed at his little joke. I shuddered. A few seconds before—before I'd exploded—I'd wanted the cock. Not now.

Now I was scared of it again. I could see his evil, piggish face again.

He had already finished off one of the other bottles. I took the bottle, keeping my eyes at the level of his navel, although they kept moving down to his cock and balls and causing little shivers to go up my spine.

I took several swigs, and so did he.

But then he took the bottle from me and put it back on the coffee table.

He turned and sat on the sofa and ran an arm under me and lifted me up and pulled me over to his lap, facing him. I turned my eyes to one of the paintings on the wall.

Here we go, I said to myself. Remember not to hold your breath. Breathe easily, don't tense your channel, be loose, very loose. Eyes on the paintings. It's the body. You're being taken by that magnificent body. That monstrous cock. Not the face.

But then, rather than setting me down on his cock, he pushed my head toward the carpet in front of the sofa. I felt his thighs go over mine on each side as my shoulders and neck hit the carpet. My thighs were trapped between his and the edge of the sofa. My legs were spread in the air. His feet were on my shoulders at the arm pits, holding my shoulders to the floor.

I shuddered as I saw his face above mine and then, again, when he reached over and took the fourth bottle of beer from the coffee table.

I lurched and gasped and he laughed as I felt the cold beer stream into my channel. And then the neck of the beer bottle.

"Good choice, maybe, the bottle not the can. But when I fuck you will wish you had been prepared by the can."

I whimpered and moaned as he fucked me with the beer bottle, my channel sloshing with beer.

He took my dick in both hands and started to work it again. "You come for me."

I was overcome for several moments, but then I got angry. No, you come for me god dammit. Fuck me. Fuck me.

Again it was an internal cry.

But I managed to reach up with both of my hands and grasp his cock and start driving him as hard as he was driving me.

He let out an animalistic yell, and the first thing I knew, I was dangling from his side with his arm around my waist and we were moving across the room.

Into another room we went, dark, but for only a brief moment. When the lights went on, it was another room with lighting spotting on paintings. Three of them. The same grotesquely gorgeous torso. But fucking a small, dark-skinned youth—a Thai I presumed—in three different positions.

It was a bedroom, with a gigantic king-sized bed in the center of it.

I was dumped on the bed, on my belly. The hand under me, palming my waist, pulled me up onto my knees, while the fist of Jaguerman's other hand grabbed me by the back of my neck and smashed my face into the thick material of the bedspread.

I managed to turn my head and found myself facing a painting of just this fuck position. The cock of the top in the painting was gigantic.

I cried out as Jaguerman's cock head fought for entry in my channel. But only with the bulb of the cock. Pressing in but holding there.

Again the tease, the hint of preliminaries as briefly the bulb moved back and forth just inside my entrance—and then the long plunge, with no further preliminaries.

Yes, fuck me, fuck me. Don't hold your breath, reach back and pull your buttocks apart, relax, relax, relax your channel, relax your . . . oh god, oh GOD. Oh, Holy SHIT! Oh, yesss!

Fuck me, fuck me, fuuccckk me. Moooannn.

Oh, shit, I've got it all. Can feel his pubes on my buttocks. Breathe, breathe. Oh, holy shit. But I've done it. I could do it.

And then, as I felt his balls begin to slap on the tender skin of my inner thighs, the screaming started. It was mine. Giving me no quarter, he was pistoning me to beat the band.

The second painting had me lapped, facing away from him and making love to his cock with my channel. Slower, more sensuous this time. Lovers finding each other's arousal points.

Now he had lost control too. Now he was moaning and groaning.

And it was OK. No, it was great—as long as I wasn't facing him.

But in the third painting position, I *was* facing him. Laying on my back on the bed, with him standing between my legs.

But I was beyond caring what he looked like. Every fiber of my senses was concentrated on the gigantic staff inside me. Deeper, deeper, thicker. Moan. Faster, deeper, deeper. Oh god, oh shit!

He didn't come. I came. He said, "You come for me," and I came. But then he stopped.

I looked up into his face. Just barely being able to do so now. Any man who could fuck me like that deserved to be looked in the face.

With him stopped, inside me, like that, I could get the measure of him as never before. No, I'd never had it like that before. Never as deep, never as thick. And it was pulsating inside me.

I was mewing and sighing and groaning. "Fuck me, fuck me. Don't stop."

It wasn't spoken internally now. I'd said it. I looked him in his piggish face and I was all desire, no disgust.

"Fuck me," I whined. "Finish it. And then fuck me again."

He was smiling. It was an evil, mischievous smile.

He held there, inside me. I half expected a sudden flow, a gut-wrenching drenching to rival that of the beer.

But he was withdrawing from me. And I wanted to cry. I clutched for his buttocks, trying to hold him inside me.

But he laughed and pushed my hands aside.

I was exhausted. I had just realized that. When he was inside me, everything had been focused on that monster shaft and begging it to reach further, to stretch wider. To throb and to flood me.

But now that was gone, I felt the loss of it. I whimpered.

He laughed. And then he reached down for me and lifted me off the bed and slung me over his shoulder.

He padded across the room and out into the hall. Down the hall to another closed door. He opened the door to darkness. He flipped on the light switch.

Again, spotlights on paintings on three walls, the fourth wall a solid sheet of glass overlooking the terrace and the sultry Bangkok night, the noise of a city that never slept spiraling up into the room.

I whimpered again as my eyes focused on the paintings. Three men now. One of them my Belgian satyr. The other another burly Westerner. Again a small Oriental youth between them. Three fuck positions. All doubles. Two cocks, fighting for dominance, within the small youth's channel.

On the bed, waiting for us. Naked and in full erection. Kamrod Tikka. Smiling. Hand encasing erect phallus.

"There," the Belgian boomed out, "I told you Mr. Tikka would meet us at the apartment."

"Oh god, oh god," I murmured. Not able to respond in any other way in my utter exhaustion.

As Kamrod held his rod stiff and licked his lips in anticipation, the Belgian turned me away from Kamrod and lowered my channel on his cock.

Kamrod encircled my waist with his arms and took my cock in one of his fists. He kissed me in the hollow of my neck.

I watched Jaguerman full in the face as he fisted my ankles, spread my legs up and wide and began working his cock inside my channel above Kamrod's already fully encased staff.

"Oh, god, oh, god, Oh shit." But it was barely a whimper.

The Cast Party

I could not have been in any steamier place or time for my sexual awakening. Bangkok, Thailand, in the eighties, was sin city extraordinaire. Anything went there; everything was tolerated. It was a *mai bin rai* ("never mind; whatever, it's OK") place, and everything was not only tolerated, but it also was on offer—and almost always for free or at a very good price. And it was an innocent time. The mellow follow-on years after the hippy era of "if it feels good, do it" and before anyone had ever heard the term AIDS.

The U.S. government was also partly to blame for my development of an interest in the gay life style. I was a young government pilot of the SR71 photo reconnaissance aircraft, and politics had shut us down for several months of my Bangkok tour and had allowed me to turn my interests elsewhere other than soaring higher above the earth than anyone else could at the time.

I had time on my hands, and, thus, when there was a casting call for the Bangkok Community Theatre's production of the new Ira Leven thriller *Deathtrap*, to be performed at the Bhirasri Institute off Sathorn Road, I auditioned and won the part of the young protagonist, Clifford Anderson. I had acted through high school and college, and exotic Bangkok had set my creative juices boiling. Opposite me, in the older man's role of Sidney Bruhl, was an expatriate queen in his late forties who I will call Ron (primarily because that was his name). Ron had taught English for years at the American University Association in Bangkok, banished from the United States by his rich family because he had the gall to be gay at a time when it wasn't fashionable, at least flamboyantly and in public. He had outlived his family, however, and inherited their money and was having the last laugh by living in style in a mansion near Sathorn Road with his choice of young men who were interested in his money (and in each other).

Ron had been attracted to me and he regularly gave me expert, soft-mouthed blow jobs in our shared dressing room throughout the run of the play to release the tension we both felt after an exhilarating performance. I also fucked him doggy style once at his request, but I'll have to admit that I found his blow jobs more satisfying. He asked me to move into the mansion with him and his friends then, but I didn't consider myself for sale—driving a stealth jet paid quite well—and not to mention that I had a wife and children I wasn't going to abandon.

At the time, Ben, a U.S. Army lieutenant assigned to the Joint U.S. Military Advisory Group, was living with Ron, and Ben threw Ron a cast party at the mansion following the closing night of the play.

All of the woman and straight men involved in the play departed the party early, no doubt not all that comfortable with the special friends Ben had invited to Ron's party, but I stayed on. I had realized by this time that this was a special time and place for me, sexually, and I wanted to make the most of it. It wasn't long before my wish was granted.

I was returning from the bathroom, half snookered, down a long, dark hallway, when I was accosted by Ron's live-in, Ben. He just turned my back to the wall in the hallway, planted his palms on either side of my shoulders, and came in for a long, wet kiss. Ben was pretty much a hunk, so I just went with the flow. It was a hot evening, and everyone left was starting to shed clothes. I had my shirt open and Ben had no shirt on at all. He rubbed his chest and basket against mine and made me feel pretty rubbery in the knees.

432

After another kiss on the lips and a couple on my nipples, he told me to turn around, belly to the wall, and I did so. He took my shirt off me and then stripped down my pants and briefs, so that all I was wearing were my loafers. He placed his hands on my hips where they joined my waist, with his thumbs across my butt cheeks, and I remember thinking that this simple gesture seemed to mark his full possession of me, at least for that moment. If I'd ever had the inclination to cut and run, this ended any such thought. He kissed and tongued his way down my back He knelt behind me and must have taken his own pants off then, because I wasn't aware of that happening later, and I felt a hand come between my thighs and signal that I was supposed to open up my stance, which I did. The hand came on through, and he pulled my cock back between my legs and stroked it, while his tongue and lips search for—and found—my asshole in the folds of my butt cheeks. All the while, the music and laughter were wafting down the hall at us from the living areas of the mansion.

I had my hands raised to either side of my shoulders and my palms and cheek hugged the cool plaster interior wall of the old mansion. I wasn't thinking anything except what a new exhilarating experience I was having. All of my senses were focused on the cock and the asshole that this handsome hunk of an Army lieutenant were making love to. I was footloose in Bangkok, my family having gone back to the states early for summer R&R. Everything was allowed as long as it felt good. And this felt great.

Ben was alternating the attention his mouth was giving me between tonguing and rimming my asshole and sucking and twirling his tongue around the tender bulb of my cock. He was moistening up my asshole real good, but my cock was getting too stiff to hold the between-the-legs angle, so Ben told me to turn around, and he sucked me off from the front. His right hand was running over my thighs and my belly up to my chest, and he was using his left hand to either work my balls or gently finger fuck my ass.

Meanwhile, there were men going back and forth down the hallway to use the bathroom. One beautiful blond Scandinavian showed particular interest in what we were doing and came back to observe briefly at various intervals of this fantastic experience I was having. But most took what we were doing for granted—they all were doing similar things all over the house that evening themselves. Ben was one of the best-looking, and certainly one of the best-hung, men at the party, and I was vain enough to be quite assured of my own qualities in both regards as well, so I wasn't at all embarrassed at giving anyone a show who wanted one. What I lacked in experience at that point I made up for in enthusiasm and the willingness to shed all inhibitions.

After I had cum at the back of Ben's throat, he stood back up and kissed me on the lips for a few more moments. Then he sort of stooped down in front of me, braced his arms under my butt, and told me to help lift myself and climb up on his waist. He was very strong and I didn't have to help him raise me up much at all. I hooked my legs above his hips and wrapped my arms around his chest below his arm pits, and I immediately felt his cock head at my asshole.

He entered me a couple of inches and waited for me to adjust to him. He had two strong hands under my thighs. Then he slowly slid a long, slender cock up my ass canal. It felt almost like I was taking in an eel. I figured he must have been a good eight or nine inches long, but he wasn't all that thick. And then, for a good long time he just fucked me against that wall, using his strong leg muscles and those hands under my thighs to move me. He held his cock steady deep inside me and worked my pelvis up and down for the stroking and pumping action. I moved my arms up around his neck and buried my face in the hollow of his neck and savored the fuck, enjoying his hard, strong body, enjoying the feel of his chest and belly heaving and rubbing up and down mine almost as much as I enjoyed the feeling of him slithering around inside me. After he had jacked off in me, he let my feet back down on the floor and gave me another wet and deep kiss on the mouth. He told me how nice I was and that he'd wanted to do that the entire time the play was rehearsing and that he'd planned this party just so he and I could hook up. Then he said he other guests to contend with, so he'd have to leave me, but that he hoped we could be special friends in the future. (As it turned out, we became very special, close friends in various parts of the world thereafter.)

I was told later that the aging queen, Ron, had seen me together with his live-in in that hallway and had retreated to his room in tears. I don't know if that was the case, but he avoided me thereafter for the rest of my tour in Bangkok. I sort of regretted the loss of that very experienced soft mouth of his.

I returned to the party to find that it had become quite raucous. Many of the guests had wound up nude in the pool, and I joined them there. This certainly was a good way to shop what was available in Bangkok and who had the longest and thickest goods and the best build. I was happy to see that in that time of my life I measured up very well to the competition.

I found the blond Scandinavian voyeur from earlier in the evening sitting on the side of the pool, dangling his legs—and very nearly his horse-hung dong as well, I might add—in the water, and I swam up to him and sucked his dick until it was hard and was standing at attention. He enjoyed that so much that he hauled me up out of the pool, and almost literally carried me over to a nearby lounge and side-split fucked me for three-quarters of an hour or more. I'll never forget what wonders he could do with a nipple while he was plowing my ass deep and stretching my canal walls to the limit. I was late in learning that the nipple was an erogenous zone for many a man—and most certainly for me. I have large aureoles around my nipples and get sent over the moon any time a man takes all of that in his mouth and teeth around it and gives it suck. I think that alone can add an extra inch and a half to my hardened cock. All of these "first discoveries" thrilled me.

While I was being plowed by the Scandinavian, I chanced to look over to a nearby pool lounge and saw the man of my dreams, a hulky chocolate brown hunk with the biggest, thickest cock I had ever seen until then—and since then as far as I can remember. He was fascinating to watch as he hunched over a reclining blond and pistoned down into his ass—not the least because his attention-commanding cock was several shades darker than he was. He looked at me and smiled for me, and I knew right there and then that I would be going after him in the weeks to come.

Bangkok in the early eighties was perfect for sexual awakenings. Nothing was taboo. Everything was done for the sheer pleasure of it.

Kasem's Kitchen

If the kitchen of Kasem's family in the upcountry jungle of Thailand hadn't burned to the ground, I possibly never would have found out what the special Bangkok sports massage was all about. Kasem was my masseur at a fancy Bangkok gym, which was open for "men only" a couple of nights a week and which was a major pickup place for prime cuts of male meat. Of course, when I'd started going to the gym, I hadn't known it was "that sort of place," and I'd never experienced a male-male coupling before—although I'd certainly given it some serious thought. With my male model and minor TV and movie "the handsome young stud" role background, I apparently qualified as prime cut, and it wasn't long before I was humping with—and being humped by—the best-endowed of them.

It also wasn't long before I heard about the special Bangkok sports massage that a lot of the guys were getting from their masseurs. But after a couple of months at the gym, with a massage after each workout, my own masseur, Kasem, hadn't shown the least bit of intention of introducing me to any such special massage. I don't want to leave the impression that he didn't give a really good sports massage, though. I never could quite figure out how such a short, thin—almost boyish and shy—Thai man, who I was told was well into his twenties, could have such strong hands and masterful technique. But then, I quickly learned that, with the Thai, looks were deceiving. They could look like they were weak and starving, but they'd show out to be able to manhandle grand pianos up three flights of stairs in a solo effort without losing a key.

Kasem's family house lost its kitchen to a stove fire. Fortunately the kitchen was set away from the main structure of their house, in keeping with Thai good common sense practices. And to get money to rebuild, the family was forced to come to their "rich" city son—which would be the masseur Kasem (who probably was rich by Thai standards from the tips he made from *farang*—foreign—clients). But Kasem was stretched for money himself, so he passed on his family's plight to his clients.

Kasem didn't hit me directly for financial help when he initially told me of his family's dire problem. But he started softening me up while he told me about the tragedy. I was flat on my belly on the massage table, completely naked, as that's how all massages were given at the gym. Kasem was deep massaging the backs of my thighs, when I felt him pull my thighs apart, and he was massaging the inner thighs right up to the groin. This was a little farther than he'd ever gone before, and his touch was sending electric shocks through my body.

Always before his massages had been impersonal enough—and had kept away from the jewels enough—not to arouse me. His massage this time was arousing me. And this time he went right to massaging what he'd never massaged before.

He moved one hand to the small of my back to keep me pressed down on the table and his other, well-oiled hand wrapped itself around my cock, which he had brought back through my legs. And he slowly stroked me to ejaculation—all the time chattering on about how difficult it was to live life in rural Thailand when your kitchen had burned down. He wasn't drawing attention to the almost surreptitious hand job he was giving me, and I—other than the sighing and moaning I was doing—didn't bring any attention to it either. I was afraid that if what he was doing was openly acknowledged, I would be breaking some sort of unspoken rule, and he'd stop short of giving me satisfaction and release.

But he didn't stop, and it was very nice, a whole new, pleasant sensation for me. About as relaxing as a post-gym session massage could get. I left thinking, "So this is what a special Bangkok massage is all about. Very nice; I'm glad I finally found out about that." And I tipped Kasem an extra 50 baht (which was all of about 20 cents U.S. at the time—but which was considered a handsome sum to be tipped on top of the usual 100 baht).

The next week, I was feeling a little deflated when my massage was about over, because Kasem had already done my back and now had me turned over. If he was going to give me what I thought was a Bangkok special, it should have happened by now. I was panicking. Could it be that I hadn't tipped him enough the previous session? That I had somehow insulted him? But then, while he was massaging my chest and belly, he started talking about that kitchen again and lamenting about the exorbitant estimate the family had been given for reconstruction of this very necessary section of their home—it could come to almost as much as 30,000 baht (only some $115, but more than most rural families could make in a year in combined income).

I suddenly realized that only one hand was massaging my chest and belly now; the other hand was rubbing my inner thighs and eventually worked its way to my engorging cock. I drew in my breath with a hiss as I felt the foreskin of my cock being pulled down to the rim of my glans and an oily finger beginning to massage my mushroom cap, mixing oil with the precum that started to bubble up and rubbing it around the cock head. A finger was trying to insert itself into my piss slit. I arched my back in sensual pleasure and tried, quite unsuccessfully, not to groan, as Kasem proceeded to rub oil all over my cock and balls and slowly jerked me off. Once again, we both pretended that nothing was happening beyond the usual sports massage.

I tipped Kasem an extra 100 baht and left thinking, Ah, this must be the Bangkok special massage. Much more than all right!

The third week, while I once more was on my back, was when Kasem broached the possibility that I might be able to lend him the 30,000 baht his family needed to build a kitchen—

and maybe we could think of some way he could work off the debt in installments.

I murmured that something like that might be possible, which proved to be the key to nirvana.

Little doubt was left about what the installments might consist of, because immediately after making the proposal, Kasem swallowed my cock and started deep throating it. I had my hands buried in his thick, wiry black hair and was moaning loud enough to be heard in the next massage cubicle (which was tit for tat, because I had heard enough moaning from the other cubicles during my earlier tame massages). By the time oiled fingers began making little forays into my pulsing asshole, I was ready to give Kasem anything he asked for.

Of course I'd loan him the money to rebuild the family kitchen, I said. I left him with what I had in my wallet, about 5,000 baht, I think, and promised him the balance when I returned to the gym the next week.

He was so delighted the next week, when I handed over a full 30,000 baht and suggested that the family install an extra-special new kitchen that, after he had pounded and prodded and kneaded my body to sheer suppleness, he climbed up on the massage table, straddled my hips between his wiry, strong thighs, and made my throbbing cock disappear up his asshole. He rode my dick for a good thirty minutes, making every pelvis movement imaginable and dispensing love to every square inch of my buried cock. I was letting him know of my pleasure so loudly and graphically that I'm sure that everyone in the surrounding cubicles was envious and made sure he had special massages of his own that evening.

On the fifth week, Kasem wanted to start talking about a repayment schedule. He seemed to think it would take six months or more to pay me off, but I suggested a way of making the schedule much, much shorter. The first installment of my idea of a schedule had Kasem kneeling in a side chair with his belly draped over the chair back and me standing behind him, holding his pert little hips in my hands, and fucking my hot and ready cock up into his hole until the loud groans and moans those in the other cubicles were enjoying were coming out in a throaty, high-pitched Thai rather than English.

I never did learn, in terms of sexual services rendered, where a regular Bangkok special sports massage stopped and fulfillment of a loan repayment plan began. But Kasem must have thought the arrangement was a good one, because when I left Bangkok for a new assignment in Japan, he came to the airport to see my family off and, with tears in his eyes, thanked me for helping his family rebuild their kitchen. My wife was very touched—both that my masseur would make a special trip to bid me farewell and that I was so philanthropic.

Legend of Cowboy

All sorts of expatriate "characters" gravitated to Bangkok, Thailand, in the seventies and eighties, and none were more colorful than the man known simply as Cowboy. Cowboy was a six-and-a-half foot black American stud, who was said, alternately to be an American airman who, once assigned to Thailand, stayed there and, somewhat more romantically, to have been a pro basketball player of some note who had retreated to Bangkok in the face of possible charges for point shaving and racketeering. In Bangkok, Cowboy had built a small empire of girlie (and boy) bars in the Patpong tenderloin district, the most notable one of which was named, appropriately enough, Cowboy's. Later he moved his operations to a short street between Soi 21 and 23 Sukhumvit, which had been named for him and is still there today, providing the same entertainment venues it ever did.

There were a few legends about Cowboy beyond how he got to Thailand. One was that he had the biggest dick in Thailand, which was given some evidence by the women who buzzed around him looking very satisfied. The second was that he would fuck anything that moved, which was at least partially evidenced by the men who buzzed around him as well. And the third was that he never took off his signature ten-gallon hat, chaps, or spurs, even during sex.

Cowboy was one of the most happy-go-lucky, witty, and generous people in the international community, and those who knew him reacted well to him no matter how much effort they had to put into ignoring his past and his reputation.

A few months into my tour as an SR71 photoreconnaissance jet driver living in Bangkok, I decided I'd like to check out the legend of Cowboy. I joined the U.S. embassy's bowling league just because he was on it, and I got as close to his inner circle there as possible. Eventually, he invited me to come up and see him sometime at his flagship Cowboy's bar. As, at the time of the invitation, he had his hand under a table exploring my basket, I didn't have any illusions what his invitation entailed. This suited me just fine, of course, and I wasted no time in scooting over to Cowboy's to see him one afternoon in the next week.

When I walked into Cowboy's, I was told that Cowboy was in his office on the second floor and to go on up. Cowboy's office was a pretty good-sized room, with a desk and other office equipment at one end and a double bed with a red velour bedspread at the other end.

Cowboy was home, as was a dreamy-eyed woman with long, frizzed-up blonde hair and big tits. Cowboy was lying on the bed, feet pointed at me. He was wearing his ten-gallon hat and his boots with spurs, but that was all, so at least the part of the legend of the chaps was false. The blonde was sitting astride his pelvis, with her tits also pointed at me. I therefore couldn't check out the legend of the biggest dong in Thailand, at least for the moment, because the blonde was sitting on it.

She looked vaguely familiar to me, and it slowly dawned on me that she was the wife of one of the U.S. embassy's economic affairs officers. She'd bowled a 280 on the last league night, and, I understand, had gone out on a celebration binge and hadn't been seen for two days. It had taken me a few minutes to recognize her, because the economic affairs officer's wife I'd known had always been wearing clothes, and this woman was naked. Really nice tits, though.

444

When I walked in, Cowboy had his hands on her hips and was helping her to have a bouncy ride on his lap. They both seemed happy to see me, though, and Cowboy boomed out that I should feel free to strip down and come join them. He suggested that the woman might like to suck me off while she was getting her ride, and she seemed agreeable to this. So, I stripped down and went up on the bed with my knees straddling Cowboy's calves and my butt sitting on his boots. His spurs jangled quietly behind me.

Before the woman started to service me, I buried my face between her tits and did some exploration of those with my hands. That seemed to turn her on—or a bit more on than Cowboy had already turned her—and, after a while, she pushed me back on my haunches, and stretched forward and started giving my cock good head with her soft mouth.

Cowboy must have gotten bored with this, because after ten minutes or so of her slurping and me hardening, Cowboy asked me if I wanted to ride too. I said sure, not knowing what he had in mind, but being game for about anything until I was able to fully check out this legend thing. When I had voiced my agreement, his big hands came around from either side of the woman's chest, and he cupped her tits and pulled her back onto his torso, which brought her pelvis up.

Wonders of wonders! Cowboy was in her asshole, not her cunt. Her pouty little cunt was sitting right there, begging for attention from me. So I just slid up Cowboy's thighs and drilled my hard seven inches into her. She was writhing and moaning, having a good time being double stuffed. She took my head in both of her hands and brought our lips together, and I kissed her deeply, thinking that was only polite considering how deeply I was fucking her. All three of us were riding and bucking and rotating, sometimes in synch, sometimes not, but always in ways that gave all three of us pleasure.

While I was kissing the woman, Cowboy let loose of her tits and started to play with mine. I liked the attention fine. He even managed to get my nipples aligned with those of the woman, and he did some rubbing and pinching together that was driving us both crazy.

I came out of my kiss with the woman and dove beside her head and found Cowboy's mouth. We did a battle of the tongues that was more invigorating than what the woman and I had been doing. She was a fine ride, but I knew which side my bread was buttered on.

I felt the woman's pelvis being pushed into mine, so I put my hands under her butt cheeks and pulled her up with me, as I went up on my knees. I heard a long slurping noise as Cowboy came out of her ass and pulled himself up toward the head of the bed from under us. The woman and I went back down on the bed and she held her legs out briefly and then brought her heels to the back of my calves and massaged them while I pumped her. She was making little mewing sounds.

Cowboy was behind me. He was lathering up his cock with KY, and I took a peek. That part of the legend probably was true. He was longer, if not thicker, than anyone else I'd seen in Bangkok. His dick was a darker brown than the rest of his body and had a big pinkish-brown helmet on it. I started my own little mewing sounds at that point.

He took me by the hips and just lifted me up off and out of the woman and I dug my knees into the bed again to prop myself up. Cowboy's mouth went to my asshole and he tongued and kissed me there. The woman slipped out from underneath me and reversed herself and came back under. She took my cock in her mouth and restarted the stimulation there. She played with my balls with her hands, until Cowboy's cock was engaged and nearby, and then she gave his cock root and balls attention. I lowered myself on her and spent my time servicing her g-spot with my tongue, holding her gyrating pelvis within some sort of limits with my hands dug into her butt cheeks. Her tits felt good bobbing against my belly.

Cowboy stopped licking my butt and applied some KY there and then entered me, and entered me, and entered me, and entered me. I didn't think his dong would ever stop sliding up into me. And when he was well in, he started plowing me really good at a depth I didn't remember ever doing any entertaining before. With her soprano, my tenor, and his bass, we had a real good harmony of sighs and moaning going there for a while.

After a good fifteen minutes, Cowboy pulled out of me, sort of pushed me off to the side and turned the woman around to finish his fuck and shoot off his load in her cunt. I didn't mind, because by then, I was drilling his ass to my own climax.

So, other than the chaps, the Cowboy legend pretty much held up to scrutiny.

The Darling

"I'm going to take you to the Darling tonight."

I froze. I'd been chatting with three other guys on the sectional sofa in the conversation pit, not even aware that the major had reentered the house. I was studiously avoiding thinking of where he was. Otherwise I wouldn't have been in this conversation group at all. I normally tried to stay well away from these three. The three pansies we had termed them behind their backs—all three of the limp-wristed type, all affiliated in some way with the music and theater world of the expatriate community in Thailand, even though two of them were Thai. They only went with men as a threesome, joined at the hip. There were men here, though, who enjoyed the novelty of having three at a time. I wasn't one of them. And, thank god, neither was the major. As far as I knew.

I didn't keep track of who the major was fucking. He wasn't the kind who wanted anyone hanging on him like that. As long as he was fucking me, I just let that question be. The major. That's what we all called him then, and now, decades later, I no longer can recall what his real name was, even though Thailand was not the last post where we met up.

"I'm going to take you to the Darling tonight," he said in that rich baritone voice of his, as I looked down to see the strong, chocolate-brown hand he had rested on my forearm. He had leaned down to speak in my ear. I looked up into the eyes of the three pansies. Their litany of whining complaints and snippy gossip had been interrupted and they were all staring beyond my head, over my shoulder, at the heavily muscled barrel chest tapering down to the flat, hard belly and slim waist of the major's. He had come to the party in just low-slung jeans and sandals, knowing that all eyes would follow him around the room. I suspect he'd done that this evening because he'd planned what he was going to say to me—what he was going to do with me—and he wanted me to know that if I didn't go with him, he could have his pick of nearly every other man at the party.

He also, I'm sure, knew how aroused I'd be just to see him walk into the room—and to know that he fucked me.

I saw the eyes of the three pansies slit, almost as if in unison, and their sharp little tongues flicking out to wet their lips in arousal and, could it be, in some remembrance of shared experience. Yes, it could, I guessed. I wanted to think that the major wouldn't have been interested in them, but I claimed no knowledge—or hold—over what the major liked or had done beyond putting his brand on me. I had visions of him fucking all three of them, in quick succession, if only for the variety and exercise that entailed.

"Yes, if that's what you want," I whispered.

"That's what I want," he murmured, running his hands into the deep arm holes of the athletic T I was wearing and cupping my pecs. I leaned my head back onto his sternum and turned my face up to him as he kissed me with those thick, sensuous lips. When I tilted my head back down, I saw that the three pansies were hanging on every movement, their envy barely shielded. I heard a collective sigh as he stood, pulling his hands back from my chest.

"One more drink and we'll leave," he said. And then he was gone.

"If that's what you want," I repeated. But he was already gone, and the three pansies were already leaning into each other, pointedly ignoring me, and resuming their gossiping.

He had won. The major had beaten me. It had been a three-month struggle, but he'd finally gotten me to agree to go to the Darling with him. This was the first time he'd flatly told me I was going to go there with him. It's probable that, if he had said it in declarative earlier, I would have obediently agreed. I doubt I could ever flatly say no to a command from the major. He fucked me like no one had ever done before—nor, as far as I can remember, ever since. He was built like a horse, was a power driver, and was so strong that he manipulated me like I was a rag doll. And I loved muscular, demanding black men.

He'd always phrased it as a question before, and I had begged off, for what I thought were good reasons. But tonight it was a declaration, and, coming on the heels of the news he'd given me earlier out on the terrace by the pool, I couldn't say no.

"I've gotten my orders," he'd said. "It's back Stateside."

I paused for a few moments for that to sink in. He was holding me in his arms, and I'm sure he could feel me trembling. I had his jeans unbuttoned and was giving him a hand job, assuming he'd take me to one of the lounges around the pool and fuck me. We wouldn't be the only ones doing it. He liked to fuck publicly. He liked having an audience gather around him while he was showing his prowess and displaying that thick ten-by-two incher of his. And I didn't mind it when it was him—but only him. With him, I was aroused at the thought of all those men gathered around us, wishing that they were getting what I was getting.

I unbuttoned and unzipped my shorts and pushed them and my briefs down to my ankles. I didn't want to think about what he said. If I didn't react to it, maybe it wouldn't be true. I didn't know what I'd do in Bangkok without him. Well, I'd continue to find big men to fuck me, of course. There was no shortage of offers. But for nearly a year he'd been at the base of those I coupled with. I compared all of the men I went with to him, and all had come up shorter or thinner, or with less drive or inferior technique. I lifted a leg and hooked it on his hip. I used the hand I'd been jacking him off with to move his cock to below my ball sack. I moaned as his cock head rubbed across my perineum.

"Fuck me here, standing," I murmured.

451

"Did you hear me? I have ongoing orders. I'll be leaving Bangkok."

"I always thought I'd be the first to go," I answered. "Agency tours are shorter than those in the military."

"I know," he answered. His hands were palming my buttocks. I thought he was going to do as I asked. Just lift me up and set me on his cock, standing. If he did that, I would arch back toward the terrace, palming the rocky surface with my hands, giving those inside the house, beyond the wide glass doors, the full effect of the fuck—his rippling chest muscles in full view, his straining arm muscles holding my pelvis to him as he fucked down into me. That would please him and those in the house too—and thus, I would be pleased as well. And I could try to dismiss what he'd said from my mind.

He wouldn't go farther toward taking me right there and then, though. He just held me there, motionless, against his chest.

"You know there's something I want you to do with me. I'll be leaving soon. I will be disappointed if I leave without that. It could be your farewell present to me."

"The Darling. You want to bring that up again."

He just gazed at me, expectantly, until I broke down and spoke again.

"We've discussed this before. It's too close . . . and it's one thing with you, but with another—"

"It's what I want."

I broke away from him then, pulled my shorts up, and retreated into the house. Everyone else I walked by was coupling up already, so I had nowhere to go to fold into a conversation—except for the conversation pit. The three pansies had taken up residence there and no one had come by yet to take them all, giggling and wiggling their butts, up the stairs to the bedroom level. I sat on the sofa near them and turned my attention—or pretended to—toward them. They, in turn, pretended that I was part of their conversation. They didn't try too hard, though. They saw me as competition. I wouldn't be taking them upstairs, but the next man who drifted over sniffing for some tail, might choose me instead of them.

452

The minutes ticking by without anything happening—especially since I had no idea at all what I wanted to happen—were excruciating. Even though I couldn't see him, since I had pointedly positioned my back to the door out onto the terrace, my mind was trying to trace where the major was, what he was doing. Had he, out of pique, decided to punish me by pointing to another man and pinning him to a lounge cushion with his cock? If so, most of the men at the party would have gone with him with a smile and a sigh. And, if so, I would deserve it.

I had what I thought were good reasons for my reluctance. The Darling was too close to my apartment—at the head of Soi 12 Sukhumvit. My apartment was farther down the same street. There was only one entrance into Soi 12, and it went right by the forecourt of the Darling. Every time I walked home from the embassy, I had to pass the Darling. And nearly every time I did, there were both men and women out in front of the Darling, soliciting. I would be recognized in the Darling, I had every reason to presume. Beyond that, there was what the major wanted me to do in the Darling. It was one thing to let him fuck me in public—I had become accustomed to that and even, now, was aroused by that. What he wanted in the Darling, though, was something entirely different.

So deep in thoughtful concern was I that I didn't hear him approach.

"I am going to take you to the Darling tonight."

He was leaning over me on the sofa in the conversation pit.

"Yes, if that's what you want."

* * * *

He obviously had thought ahead. A black Mercedes with tinted windows was outside the house when we left. He handed me into the backseat and climbed in beside me. He said nothing to the driver, who apparently already knew where we were going.

As we drove across Bangkok in traffic that still, this late in the evening, was door handle to door handle on the clogged streets, the major put an arm around my back, tilted my head to his with his other hand, and took me into a kiss with those thick

453

lips of his. His hand moved down to the waistband of my shorts. He unbuttoned and unzipped me and pulled my half-hard cock out.

I whimpered for him, moaning a "please," that he knew was not a request for him to stop.

His hand dipped farther down, his fingers moving between my thighs and across my perineum, the tips of his middle finger coming to rest on the rim of my hole. I rolled my hips up to give him better purchase and sighed. One of my hands involuntarily went down and covered the back of his hand, holding him there, wanting him inside me.

He buried the fist of his other hand in my hair and pulled my head back. His face was very close to mine. I knew what he wanted now. He wanted to watch the expression on my face change while he had his way with me.

I heard him grunt, and recognizing that he didn't want me to reach for him in this instance, I just relaxed, took my hand away from his, and let him play my body. He always wanted to be in full control.

As he slowly worked first one and then two and, finally, three fingers into my channel, I ached to put my hand on my engorging cock and stroke it to relief. But I knew he wouldn't want that and would brush the hand away—and in doing so would have to pull his fingers out of me. I didn't want him to do that.

I began to moan and move my pelvis on his hand as his middle finger found and began to play my prostate.

"Please, daddy," I moaned. "Let me ride you."

"Later," he said.

I groaned as he continued to play me.

"Please. My cock. Let me . . ."

That was the signal he was waiting for. He withdrew his fingers from my hole and wrapped his fist tightly around my cock and slow pumped me until I gave a little cry, tightened up, and ejaculated.

He gave a low, throaty laugh and lowered his lips to my cock and cleaned me up.

* * * *

The Mercedes pulled into the forecourt and almost all the way up to the front door, where the light would have been very dim if it weren't for the frenetic glow of the orange neon sign flashing over the entrance announcing that we had arrived at the Darling. The driver opened the rear door and the major hustled me quickly from the backseat of the car into the entry, where we were met by a giant of a man who was bare-chested and bare footed and wearing a striped silk sarong around his waist.

"This is Boonsri. I told you about him," the major told me as the Thai giant turned and ushered us deeper into the bowels of the building.

And indeed the major had told me about Boonsri. Most tend to believe that Thai men are small, willowy figures, and many are. But some are big, heavily muscled men—nearly as stately as the major himself. Boonsri was one of those Thai.

The major had told me several times as he spun out a dream of his that this Boonsri was going to fuck me and the major was going to watch.

We had entered the Darling, the Darling Massage Parlor. In Thailand massage parlors are brothels. If you want minimal massaging leading to sex, you went to a place like the Darling. If you wanted both a good massage and sex, you joined an expensive gym. If you only wanted a good massage, people would wonder why you bothered to come to Thailand at all.

When the major had first told me that he wanted to take me to the Darling and I had begged off, I'd said I would certainly go to a massage parlor with him if that was what he wanted, but it would need to be one other than the Darling. That was too close to home. My wife and children knew as well as I did what happened in the Darling that we all had to pass each time we left our apartment compound or returned to it. But none of us openly discussed what the Darling was all about or wanted to get anywhere close to talking about whether I'd go to such a place—even though it was given as natural that well-heeled Thai men frequented such places even if they were happily married. And I wanted to keep it that way. The first unguarded mention by anyone that they'd seen me at the

Darling, and the whole life and career I had so carefully constructed would have collapsed upon itself.

"It has to be the Darling," he said.

"Why?" I asked.

"Because Boonsri, the man I want to share you with, is at the Darling. He's indentured there. He can't go anywhere else."

"And it has to be him?"

"Oh, yes, it has to be him," the major had answered.

And here we were. When I saw Boonsri I was even more apprehensive than I'd been when the major had described him in the abstract.

The Thai giant turned and moved into the interior of the windowless building. The major took my elbow in a firm grip, and we followed the slapping sandals and the hem of the striped sarong on the polished wood floor. We were moving toward a room with a bright light and the recorded and amplified sound of a whiny Thai songstress singing to a half-toned stringed instrument. When we walked through the door and into this space, it proved to be yet another corridor. but the walls into the rooms adjoining the corridor were glass panels. On one side of the corridor, behind the glass, erotically clad women were sitting and reclining on couches and primping for a few men standing in the corridor who were, with the help of a Darling attendant, making their choices. In the other glass-fronted room on the other side of the corridor were the minimally dressed men and boys. There were more women than men on offer, and most of the attention in the corridor was focused on them, but a few men were turned toward the window looking in on the men and boys too. On both sides of the corridor, the men and women behind the glass were playing up to the men in the corridor, each vying for attention and selection.

Eyes followed us as we moved through the corridor, with most of them, of course, focused on the major. But not a few of the women and men behind the glass were primping for me as well.

I kept my head down, watching the hem of Boonsri's sarong as much as I could as we moved through the corridor. I didn't want anyone to recognize me on the days I walked by the

Darling on my way to and from my apartment. The major was sensitive to me on this, and, indeed, seemed to have conveyed the need for stealth to the Thai giant before we arrived.

We went through another door and were in a stair hall. We followed Boonsri up one flight and then half way down another corridor, past a series of closed doors. The sounds coming from behind these doors left little doubt what was happening there. He turned and opened a door looking much like the rest and stood aside, beckoning the major and me to enter a small, mirror-walled room with a massage table in the center and a couple of straight chairs and a table at the side. I began to tremble as I saw that the table had packets of condoms, bottles of lubricant and massage oil, and various sex toys and restraints neatly arranged on the top of it. An alarm clock was also sitting on the table, but, slightly to my surprise, Boonsri didn't set the timer. This was my first indication that this would not be a rushed assignation.

At Boonsri's direction, both the major and I stripped down and piled our clothes on the same straight chair. When we turned around, Boonsri had loosened the knot on his sarong, let it fall, and was neatly folding it up as well. I gasped at the sight of his equipment. He was erect, leaving little question what service he would be performing for me—or that he would enjoy doing it.

He motioned for me to climb up on the massage table and lay down on my back. The major took a straight chair, reversed it, and straddled its seat. He folded his arms on the top of the chair's back, with his cock hanging down the back of the chair under the lowest rung, and urged Boonsri to start the show.

Boonsri was a legitimate masseur and was very good at his job—at all of his jobs: working my muscles, working my throat, and working my channel. He massaged my extremities in a deep-tissue workout and then my chest and torso muscles, relentlessly working his way to the center, and doing it so sensually that I was sighing for him and mellowing out.

As the major sat there and watched, the Thai took possession of my cock with his hand and slow pumped me until I had come for him. Then he pulled me forward on the table,

457

with my head lolling off the edge. He was working my temples with his fingers, nearly putting me to sleep, when I felt the head of his cock at my lips and I opened my mouth and throat to him.

As was the case when I deep-throated the major in this position, I need do nothing but open as wide as possible for him and try not to choke.

He slowly face fucked me until the major requested a change in positions, and then he had me roll over on my front and gave an equally deep-tissue massage, moving toward a conclusion with his greased fingers invading my channel and massaging my prostate to my second coming. I turned my face to the major to see that he was masturbating himself and fully enjoying the performance. Boonsri finished me, taking a good half hour to do so, by climbing the table, straddling my hips, skewering my ass with a thick cock, arching my torso back in a full Nelson hold that pinned my arms above my head, and rocking back and forth to work my channel with his digging cock.

I was moaning and thoroughly exhausted when Boonsri had come and climbed off the table. With a groan, I turned over and started to sit up. But now it was the major's turn. He rose from his chair, walked over to the table, grabbed my ankles, and split my legs wide, causing me to collapse onto my back. I arched my back and cried out and moaned as he, longer and thicker and more strongly stroking than Boonsri, took me more roughly and completely than the Thai giant had.

The major took his time with me, and as exhausted as I was, I just lay there, tongue lolling, holding my legs as wide as possible to be able to take him, and luxuriated in the fuck of my favorite lover.

I wasn't in any way angry with the major for wanting to share me and to watch another man fuck me. The major had been good to me, and now he was leaving. Nothing would be the same after that. Anything I could do to show him how I had appreciated what he'd done for, with, and to me, I would do.

When the major was done, having folded me in his arms and rocked me like a baby into his explosive orgasm, I climbed down from the massage table and started to move toward the chair holding my clothes. But the major wrapped his arms around me and leaned me over the table surface. He motioned to Boonsri to return and to slide inside me and resume taking me from the rear. And then the major mounted the table, knelt, forced his knees under my chest and guided his cock between my lips.

I heard him murmur, "We have just begun," and I moaned in resignation, knowing that he wasn't lying to me.

* * * *

Six months later, the major still had not shipped out, and I began to suspect that he had made his reassignment orders up just to get me to agree to go to the Darling with him. I never brought the subject up, though. I held my breath and took as much enjoyment as I could from him still being in Bangkok— and with me when he wanted to be.

He never asked me again to go with him to the Darling, however. When he asked me whether I had enjoyed Boonsri's cocking, I had told him the truth.

Singapore Sling

Kyle was an adventuresome, inventive, strong-minded young man. In short, he was a smartass. He'd been raised by maids and chauffeurs, and he was spending his college freshman year abroad with the floating University of the Pacific not because he was brilliant—which, in some ways, he was—but because his parents didn't know what to do with him and better out of sight and mind than under foot and always getting into trouble at home, they thought.

For the most part, Kyle had always pretty much gotten away with his adventuresome and unruly ways because he looked so angelic. His unruly ways were matched by a halo of golden-highlighted auburn curly hair and the facial features and lithe, pleasantly muscled, perfectly formed body of a young Greek god. And his smile was electrifying. He was always forgiven his foibles at least once by anyone on the basis of his beaming, innocent, "who me?" smile alone.

The university ship was docked at Singapore that day, and the students had been taken off in groups to be steeped in the culture of the tiny Southeast Asian nation. The culture that the university faculty thought was important enough for steeping was not necessarily the same that Kyle had in mind for his cultural advancement.

The university officials had made three serious mistakes. They divided their students into groups aligned by no system that made the absence of a specific student easy to identify; they had turned the groups over to tour guides who didn't know the students; and they had undercounted Kyle's group by one and revealed that undercount within the hearing of Kyle.

The university's view of a cultural tour of Singapore was a trudge down to the Merlion statue in the waterside park at the original landing pier of the island nation followed by a motor coach roundabout of the small country dangling below Malaysia and a visit to the national museum to study the country's rich and rocky history. Five hours had been allotted for this experience, which would earn each eager and well-heeled student one college credit. Kyle's goals for Singapore were to get hammered and to get laid at one of the massage parlors he heard made the nations of Southeast Asia memorable.

If the university hadn't made its three mistakes and if the venerable Raffles hotel hadn't been within sight of the Merlion, where the tour of Kyle's group started its outing, he probably wouldn't have had his dreams come true.

But Kyle's mind wandered at the funny-accented English history introduction being droned out in front of the Singapore Merlion statue, and his eyes refocused on the grand porte-cochere entrance to the Raffles hotel across the lawns of the waterside park. The wheels of his mind went into overdrive. He'd read somewhere that the alcoholic drink called a Singapore Sling had been invented at the Long Bar in the Raffles hotel. The university's mistakes and his goals clicked into place in the immediate and overwhelming desire to find out what a Singapore Sling tasted like.

He managed to sneak away from the group without being seen. Sneaking away from a scene of mischief was Kyle's principle talent. It was a piece of cake on this day.

* * * *

Kyle was on his third Singapore Sling and slurring his words and finding it a bit hard to hold his feet on the rungs of the bar stool, when the half-English, half-Singapore Chinese, well-dressed, clean-cut, young lawyer type patron at the other end of the Long Bar quietly moved down the length of the bar and took a position next to Kyle. They struck up a conversation, with the Singaporean showing great interest in who Kyle was and why he was there—and, eventually, what he really was looking for.

Kyle wasn't exactly lost to the world on alcohol, but he was naturally adventuresome and had been raised to assume that everyone else there was present to serve his needs and keep him safe in a way that he never bothered to do himself. And Kyle had always been open and straightforward in enunciating his "needs" and wants.

Kyle's new Singaporean friend wasn't the least bit shocked to hear that Kyle wanted a sex massage and to get laid, and, as a matter of fact, Kyle's new friend knew exactly where that could happen.

"Best massage, best fuck, all clean, a little expensive, so maybe you don't want . . ."

"No problem," Kyle said. "I've got plenty of money."

And indeed he had, as the Singaporean had already noted, because Kyle was indiscriminately flashing his wad of money around.

But it wasn't really Kyle's money that the Singaporean man was interested in. It was something far more valuable.

"But maybe you want something really special; maybe you're used to . . ."

"Naw, just a straight massage and fuck to start with," Kyle said quickly. "Just want to lose my cherry fast. I've only got about four more hours before I have to be back on board."

"Cherry? You mean . . . You mean you've never . . . ?"

Kyle was blushing. "Maybe someone really experienced first . . . someone who'd tell me what to do . . . you know."

How fortuitous, the Singaporean thought. Even more valuable. A meltingly handsome, young Caucasian hunk and a virgin as well. But, "Certainly, no problem. I have just the place in mind," was what he said to Kyle.

* * * *

Less than twenty minutes later, and the taxi driver, who was really one of the Singaporean man's colleagues, had made so many twists and turns in the narrow Singapore roads and alleys that Kyle would have had no idea where he was even if he had been sober. The taxi stopped at a wooden door in a salmon-colored stuccoed wall in a narrow back street deep in Singapore's Alijunied red light district. The door opened even before the taxi's motor stopped, and Kyle's new friend bundled him into a high-walled, lushly landscaped forecourt, down a bricked path cut through the center of the vegetation, and to a stone-block framed moon gate in a solid deep-red-painted brick wall. The space was in the deep shadows from the high walls and tree foliage overhead. There were pin-point lights flickering in the fronds of the palm trees fanned over the vegetation in the forecourt, but the only strong light was pouring out of open moon gate door.

Just inside the moon gate stood a massive Chinese man in a traditional, light-purple Chinese cheongsam. He was smiling broadly and rubbing his hands together in anxious anticipation. His factotum, who floated around the exclusive Raffles hotel trolling for possible well-heeled customers for Wang Jun's House of Perfect Bliss and who had come up with the prize of Kyle, bowed deeply to the Chinese gentleman and proudly presented Kyle for his examination.

Kyle was a little confused—in a way that he attributed to the amount of alcohol he had consumed, however—when his recently acquired Singaporean friend introduced him to Wang Jun, told him that Wang Jun would take care of everything, and then disappeared back through the moon gate they had entered.

Wang Jun was a mountain of a man. Well over six and a half feet and perhaps pushing 300 pounds, most of which was muscle but a good portion of which was fat, earned by gluttonous living. At either side of the moon gate and standing at attention, were two other men, both Chinese, and both as tall as Wang Jun, but composed of much more muscle than Wang Jun was. They were dressed in filmy white harem pants and red silk vests that didn't meet in front over naked barrel chests. Off on either side of the first section of hallway that extended straight back in sections separated by a series of moon gates were two plushly furnished receptions rooms already nearly overflowing with men of various nationalities, all expensively dressed, mostly middle aged. Young women in sarong skirts, their breasts uncovered, nipples rouged, padded among the men with trays of drinks and hors d'oeuvres.

There had been murmuring through the rooms on either side of the wall when Kyle first entered with his friend from the Long Bar, but it increased in decibel rate as Kyle was being introduced to Wang Jun. Kyle felt slightly uncomfortable under the stares of many of the men in the two reception areas.

"Come, young man," Wang Jun said to Kyle after they had stood under lights in the hallway for a few minutes. "Your friend has told me what you are looking for. Come walk with me, and I think we can find something you will want."

He linked his arm in Kyle's and started down the hallway into the interior of the establishment.

Kyle gasped as they entered the first section of central hallway between two moon gates. The hallway was in darkness, but to Kyle's right was a large picture window into a brightly lit room, where a series of young naked women were lying around on lounges on three tiers. As Kyle watched, they all used their hands and bodies to emphasize what they had to offer him and simulated what he could do with them. The appearance of the angelically beautiful young Caucasian man had seemed to galvanize them. Each of them seemed genuinely interested in being chosen.

Kyle could hardly take his eyes off the women. There must have been twenty or more of them. He'd never seen anything like it. His first reaction wasn't arousal. He was scared. His first thought was that he was in over his head. He felt like he could be eaten alive in this place.

"Come, look to the other side of the pathway," Wang Jun said in an unctuous voice. "See, there are three doors. Each door has a window. Feel free to look in. These lovely young women are the picks of the moment from our viewing room."

Kyle tore his eyes away from the viewing room window and looked into the small window in the first door on the other side of the hallway. The room was small, carpeted, but sparsely furnished. A low platform bed occupied the center of the room.

There was a shower stall in the far corner of the room, a small chair, and a clothes tree. The man's clothes were strewn all around the floor, and the man, a heavy, big-boned Caucasian, was hunched over a slight Chinese woman lying on her back on the platform, standing between her spread legs, and fucking her furiously. One of his hands was holding her head down to the surface of the platform at her neck and his other one was squeezing one of her breasts hard. The woman had a somewhat panicked look on her face.

Kyle immediately pulled away, giving way to Wang Jun to look inside so that he could intervene all the more quickly. And Wang Jun did look in the window. But he just went "Tsk, tsk" and then drew Kyle's attention to the second window. Here, a thin, but well-muscled Japanese gentleman with graying hair was using the chair in an inventive position to fuck a red-haired Caucasian woman in also a very inventive position. His clothes were neatly folded on the clothes tree, with his shoes were placed in precise alignment on the floor below. The Caucasian woman's face showed that she was enjoying the fuck.

The couple in the third room were just beginning. The Chinese man was laying on his back on the platform and the young Black woman was still giving him a massage. But it was quite a sensual massage. She was massaging his torso with one hand and massaging his engorged cock with the other hand. The one hand of the man that Kyle could see in play was fingering the woman's cunt, the index finger deeply imbedded inside her.

"I . . . I don't . . . know," Kyle said when he pulled away from the small windows and turned to the larger one. He was both fascinated and overwhelmed by what he saw and finding he was trying to look away, up into the corner of the room where there were no naked women.

"You don't have to choose yet," Wang Jun said with a smile. "In fact, I didn't intend you to. I would like you to see more of what we have to offer."

"But . . . but . . . all those other men ahead of me . . . I don't believe I have the time . . ." Kyle stammered out, trying now to slow this process down or to give it over altogether. No longer as cocky and as sure of himself as he had been when he had started on this adventure.

466

"Don't worry about that," Wang Jun said, giving Kyle a big smile. "You are a special customer. You are being given preferential service. No . . . no. It's only right. Come, perhaps the next section will whet your appetite more."

In the next section, the women were still basically naked, but they were harder edged, wearing bits and pieces of leather, and were more demonstrative in selling their wares. Kyle could hardly do more than glance in the windows of the rooms opposite, where the women were either abusing their clients or being abused with extra toys and equipment. He moved quickly through the moon gate into the other section under his own steam.

This was a smaller section than the other two and had full-length windows looking into just one medium-sized chamber on either side that also had a door to the hall at one end. This was the first section where Kyle and Wang Jun weren't alone. At the one side, men, naked men, were lined up along the window, watching what was going on inside the room, but also queuing up to go into the room through the door themselves. Nearly all of them were masturbating. Wang Jun pushed Kyle between two of the men so that he could see what was inside.

The only piece of equipment in the room was a body sling hanging from the ceiling by chains attached at each corner of the leather sling. The sling was occupied by a young, naked woman, who was slung there on her back, with her wrists and ankles cuffed high on the chains at the four corners. A small, elderly Chinese man was standing on a stool between her legs and fucking her as vigorously as he could manage. The woman was a Caucasian, her head was hanging down from the end of the sling, her long blonde hair cascading nearly to the floor, her face turned away from the window. As Kyle began to watch, the small Chinese man finished whatever he was trying to do, and a big black man went through the door and into the room, kicked the stool aside, lined up a monstrously thick and long engorged cock at her hole, and thrust inside her. Her body began to writhe and twitch and her fists closed hard on the chains. Her head snapped around toward the window, her mouth opened in a big "O." Kyle could hear her howl in the unexpectedly deep and thick taking through the window as he stumbled away and turned to the other side of hallway.

On the other side was a room identical to the one Kyle had just turned from, but it was empty.

"Come," Wang Jun said. "Just two more stations to show you."

The next section was similar to the first except that the figures in the viewing room were young, lithe men, and the massaging and fucking going on in the three chambers across the hallway were men clients fucking young men. Two of the rooms were occupied by massage platforms as in the first section, but the third room had a cube device rather than a platform on which a young black man was cuffed at the four corners near the base, belly down, and a bulky Chinese man was crouched behind him, screwing a long, thick red rubber dildo up the young man's ass channel.

Kyle tried to turn away from this section and retrace his steps down the hall, but Wang Jun grabbed him with a strong grip on Kyle's wrists and forced him back to the window in the third room.

"No, no, my young friend," Wang Jun hissed. "You mustn't leave until you've seen the last section."

He held a whimpering Kyle there, eyes at the window, while the Chinese man finished with his dildo work and started to fuck the young black man in long, deep strokes.

"I'm told you wanted to lose your virginity," Wang Jun whispered in Kyle's ear. "Is it true. Are you virginal?"

"No, please," Kyle whimpered. "I'm not interested any more. I want to leave."

Wang Jun strengthened his hold and Kyle yelped in pain. "Is it true or is it not. Have you had sex with another yet?"

"No, no, I haven't" Kyle answered in an anguished voice.

Wang Jun began to tremble, but he held Kyle there, looking in the window, as the Chinese man pulled out of the young black man, uncuffed him, turned him on his back on the cube, recuffed his wrists, and lifted and spread his legs and renewed his deep fucking. The young black man's face could be seen now. He was trying to keep his expression blank, but he was wincing occasionally, revealing that the Chinese man's digging cock was having an effect on him.

"No, no, no," Kyle was quietly pleading. And he was still pleading that when one of Wang Jun's bouncers arrived and held Kyle in thrall, while Wang Jun pulled a capsule from out of the folds of his light-purple cheongsam, split it open, brought it close under Kyle's nose, and began dragging him toward the last moon gate, this one closed off by a gilded wooden door at the end of the long passage. Kyle weakened almost immediately and was blacked out before they reached the final moon gate.

* * * *

Kyle was jerked awake by the pain of Wang Jun's monstrous member forcing its way into his channel. A naked Kyle was on his back on a vinyl-covered spongy cube identical to the one he'd last seen in use, his wrists cuffed down near the base of the cube on each side. His legs were being held wide on each side by Wang Jun's burly assistants. Wang Jun was standing between Kyle's spread legs. He'd already made the first breaching. He also was naked, and rolls of his fat were flopped down onto Kyle's belly. Kyle's own dick was lost in the folds of Wang Jun's fat, rubbing within the folds of Wang Jun's skin and engorging from the friction. Despite the fat, Wang Jun's torso was heavily muscled and his cock was big, thick, and vigorous.

"Ah, back with us, my little beauty, I see," Wang Jun said in a straining voice. "Good. I have you on your back, because I want to enjoy seeing your expressions at your first taking. You will make me much money tonight. I already have them lined up for first-night privileges. But owner's privilege. Me first. I must protect my customers. I must know you are fresh for them."

And with that and a guttural "Ugh," Wang Jun's plunger was in and exploring virginal territory. Kyle cried out and writhed against the assault. His muscles and the veins in his neck tightened up and his eyes went wild.

"Ah, yes," Wang Jun chortled, obviously very pleased. "I do believe that you have never done this before. Very tight, yes, Very sweet." And he began to pump slowly while Kyle gasped and moaned and groaned and strained at his bonds.

469

"Satisfy . . ." huff, huff, "my customers this well tonight . . .ahhhhh, and I will give you a premium cut."

And then it was over, and Kyle discovered that he had endured it—and that it didn't seem that bad.

He painfully rose off the cube and rubbed his wrists as he hobbled toward the slightly ajar gilded door in the moon gate. But he heard the chilling voice of Wang Jun behind him as he moved. He turned around and there Wang Jun was, rising and falling on the balls of his feet, the great slab of meat between his legs rock hard again. He was gripping a black leather sling of some sort at either end in a fist and he was smiling broadly. It was a plow belt, although Kyle certainly didn't know that, had no idea what a plow belt was for. He quickly found out, though.

"Oh, no my lovely. My prick isn't finished with you yet. Not quite yet."

Kyle turned to run toward the door, but the plow belt was whipped over his head and down to his belly, and he found himself doubled over and lifted off the floor by the tall Chinese monster close behind him. Wang Jun positioned his cock at Kyle's hole and again thrust deep inside, putting the sling into motion with the strength of his grip on the straps. As Wang Jun's assistant ushered prospective clients into the room to fan around the sides and watch, Kyle was swayed back and forth on Wang Jun's deeply lodged cock, as his writhing and cries of indignation and taken pain subsided into surrendered gurglings and whimperings of being beyond salvage.

What followed wasn't really a surprise to Kyle; he had seen it before, although he was only now experiencing it. The empty sling room wasn't empty for long. Kyle was strung up there in identical form to the blonde across the hallway who was still entertaining a procession of men, and then it was Kyle's turn to suffer hard cocks of all colors and sizes for more times than he could count as he swung back and forth in what he was thinking of, in his numbing hysteria, as his Singapore Sling. It wasn't quite the Singapore Sling he had thought he had sought, but he loved adventure, and you couldn't get more venturesome than this.

Throughout the ordeal, Wang Jun's two attendants stayed close to him, making sure the clients didn't get out of hand—and that they paid for services rendered. And one of them occasionally split open one of the magic capsules Wang Jun had first used to silence Kyle's objections and waved it under his nose, giving him periodic relief. The attendants were being so attentive, because Wang Jun had promised them they could have Kyle for the rest of the night after the establishment closed. But this wasn't to be.

Shortly after Kyle's five hours of structured cultural exposure were up, the University of the Pacific's authorities realized that one of their most troublesome—and, unfortunately, one of their best connected—students was missing, and the highly efficient Singaporean authorities started putting recovery operations into motion.

As the telephones at the House of Perfect Bliss began to wring and worried little men padded in to whisper in his ear, Wang Jun knew he could not keep Kyle. And he also knew that Kyle could not lead the authorities back to him on his own, and probably would not do so if he was made complicit. Kyle jumped at the offer of the money for his services, albeit they were not willing services or quite the adventure he had expected. But Kyle was nothing if not resilient. Wang Jun provided him with a great deal of cash his parents didn't know about, and the floating university's next stop was Bangkok, where Kyle had heard there was even more opportunity than in Singapore to get the kind of massage he had dreamed of. And having seen what he had at the House of Perfect Bliss, Kyle now felt more confident in what that was all about. In fact, he wasn't so sure he'd shy away from that viewing room of young men now.

Most of all, Kyle reveled in the story he would have to tell the next time he was home and one of his dad's stuffy friends asked him what they were exposing him to in the University of the Pacific.

Saigon

I was nearly ready, very close to coming. Nguyen had already come. I had felt him stiffen, knowing he was about to come, and had put my hands under him, raising his belly off the sheets with the palm of one hand and encasing his hard cock with the other and stroking him until he had spilled his seed. And then I had taken him by the waist and lowered his midsection on the mattress again and resumed my slow, deep stroking inside him. I covered his brown little body with mine, my arms laced up under his arm pits, my legs covering his with his feet hooked on my lower calves, my lips buried in the hollow of his neck when he wasn't turning his lips to mine.

Mosquitoes buzzed angrily against the protective netting that covered my bed, centered in the room to catch whatever cross breeze could be captured in the hot, humid Vietnamese night. The rain was coming down in sheets outside the bungalow, sounding like the low roar of a train passing by in the distance. Candles flickered in the corner of the room, their light being reflected and scattered by the slowly churning ceiling fan above the foot of the bed. A gecko ran across the top of the headboard, stopping momentarily to watch the fucking and then went on its merry way.

I turned my head and looked up into the roof of the canopied bed, at the mirror I'd had installed when I took Nguyen on as my lover—when he had introduced me to the pleasures of man sex in Southeast Asia—so much more sensuous and guilt free than I had known before—and I became besotted with watching my larger, muscled body, working his lithe, little brown one or his succulent mouth working my cock before I took him. Appearing in the mirror to have full control, to be ravishing a small, powerless man, but knowing all along that Ngyuen was the experienced one, the one who was in full control.

I concentrated hard as I watched myself in the mirror— me holding every part of him still, with only my butt cheeks expanding and contracting, listening for the moan, watching for the moment that Nguyen's hips began to rotate, when his butt cheeks slowly moved in rhythm with mine, nothing else on our bodies moving, knowing that my cock was buried deep inside him. Watching for the moment of my release and the effect it had on his body, the expression on his face, half turned to where I could see it, his cheek rubbing the fine, moist cotton of the pillow casing.

Nguyen gave a little cry as my flow started, and I thought I heard another sound simultaneously—a rustling or a scraping outside the bedroom window of my Saigon bungalow. Maybe both. There shouldn't be anything stirring out there in the downpour. All of the usual night creatures out there knew to just wait a quarter hour and the rain would stop and they could come out onto the fetid earth of their playground once more.

"Shh, little one," I whispered, and I placed my hand over his mouth to stifle further noise. "I think I heard something."

Nguyen's body stiffened, as aware of the possibilities as I was, and he rolled out from underneath me and over the side of the bed to the floor as I reached under my pillow for my pistol, and he reached, at the same time, as he landed gracefully and noiseless on the teak flooring, for the M-16 I kept there under the bed.

I rolled to the floor on the other side of the bed, staying inside the netting, to the great disappointment of the night insects. We lay there, on opposite sides of the bed, breathing heavily for several minutes. But the moment passed; there were no other unexpected night sounds competing with the chirping of the night crickets that started up the instant the rain stopped, abruptly, like the closing of a spigot, and I muttered an all clear—at least I thought it was clear—to Nguyen, and we came back up on the bed and embraced. But that moment was lost now too. Reality had struck, even if it was a false reality—for now—and we had been avoiding the inevitable discussion.

The recent weeks in Saigon had been nerve-racking. We knew now it was just a matter of time. Four weeks if the intelligence Nguyen had passed to me was accurate. The sleuthing he'd done in connection with his news reporting job had concluded that there would be an offensive against the Cam Ranh Bay installations and, if that was successful, soldiers would be streaming down to Saigon for the final coup d'état here. This information had become key to our plans for the defense of the South. Forces had been retained at Cam Ranh Bay that we initially planned to move down to Saigon. Increasingly the embassy staff had been pulled into the compound, not to return to their apartments or bungalows before the danger was past—although few even pretended this was anything other than the prelude to the end—in fear of the night and of what lurked there. I was one of the last still sleeping outside of the compound. And it was now obvious even to me, in my blinders-on optimism, that this would be my last night in this bed too.

I had been putting on an act that fooled only me—not wanting it to be over, so pretending that it wouldn't be, against all indications to the contrary.

That was a sad thought. I had found paradise here in this bed—with Nguyen Van Trinh, South Vietnamese journalist by day and my willing sex slave by night. Although that even was a lie; it was I who was Nguyen's sex slave. I never wanted this to end. But the North Vietnamese Army and the Viet Cong insurgents of the South obviously had very different views on that. And increasingly their views were the only ones that counted.

"You've been a major source of information for me, Nguyen," I whispered. "I've had you on the evacuation list for some time now. Come to the embassy with me in the morning. I think this is it. And when I'm taken out, I want you to go with me. I've arranged for you to be on the list. Come away with me; I will take care of you."

"I must be in Thon Lac Nghiep tomorrow," Nguyen said. "My parents. They call and I must be there."

"We've discussed this before, Nguyen," I said. "I don't think you'll be safe when the Americans are gone. You've cooperated. You perhaps don't fully appreciate all you have told me—or who I work for. You must come out with me. I'll keep you with me. I promise."

"Perhaps, Jim," Nguyen answered, although I got the impression he was only humoring me. "You aren't safe here anymore. On that I agree. It is impossible to hide an American anywhere in Saigon now. You must move to the embassy compound, like the rest. I will come when I can—if I can."

"Promise? I love you. I don't want to lose you. You love me, don't you?"

Nguyen showed his feelings for me by pressing me on my back on the mattress and straddling my hips with his thighs and slowly riding my cock to another, mutual ejaculation, as I watched the languid movements of my lithe, brown lover in the mirror overhead.

In the morning, when I awoke, Nguyen was gone, as was the M-16. I didn't begrudge him that, though. If that got him to the sea and the village of Thon Lac Nghiep to the north of Saigon and then safely back to me again, I wanted him to have it.

I moved into the embassy compound that morning, and the next day we began the destruction of files. This went slowly, because all of us in the Station were called away for periodic Country Team meetings on the military situation. The military attaches kept saying that all indications were that North Vietnamese troops were moving toward Saigon, and, only the Station was holding out that they would divert to the coast, toward Cam Ranh Bay, before coming further south. They did that on the strength of my good source for the information—Nguyen.

Saigon, however, was in a panic. Helicopters were already shuttling back and forth from the embassy roof out to the battleships anchored off the coast with the embassy personnel deemed nonessential—their dependents having evacuated weeks earlier—and a large number of South Vietnamese officials and their families, people who had partnered with the U.S. forces in the futile effort to maintain a South Vietnamese Republic and who now were being evacuated because their loyalty was a death sentence for them, if—no, not if, when—the North Vietnamese took over in the South.

Back at the Station and working the shredders as fast as I could, I took a break when the shredder I was feeding overheated. I went out to the outer corridor to have a cigarette and to wait for the shredder to cool down. I had worked like a zombie all day, worried to death over Nguyen, and for that reason trying to turn my mind off and just sit there and feed sheet after sheet of top secret paperwork into the shredder. Not for the first time I wondered why we'd created such a mountain of paper out of a losing cause. My hands trembled as I lit my cigarette, and my worries flooded my brain—wondering where he was and whether I should go back to my bungalow in case he was there. I was frantic to see him safely with the other Vietnamese we'd brought into the compound for evacuation.

He was so inscrutable; Ngyuen had soldiered along as if the rending apart of his country had little to do with him. I worried that he just didn't understand the danger he was in— particularly if the North Vietnamese ever learned how valuable he had been to us.

The windows in the corridor overlooked the front gates of the compound. A mass of humanity pressed at the gates, begging entrance, trying to claim a spot on the helicopters that were landing on the roof, loading, and then lifting up to bank sharply out toward the sea. Each approach and takeoff was different; there was no pattern—all because of the occasional sound of a rifle shot of a sniper taking a march on the arrival of the North Vietnamese and vying for a medal for shooting down a U.S. helicopter. And at each approach of a helicopter, the arms of those pressing the gate went up in the air, as if they could lift straight up into the copter. And each time an overloaded helicopter rose off the roof of the main embassy building, there was a massive sigh and sob that spread through the whole compound—knowing that one more opportunity for life had passed all still on the ground by.

We had lost a few helicopters, but the pilots by now had become geniuses at avoiding more ambitious fire than this, and the snipers—probably the vanguard of the Viet Cong, composed mostly of young boys—were lousy shots—or were just firing for effect, not begrudging our departure but wanting us to soil our pants in the process.

As I stood at the window, seeing those pressing, five or six deep, on the main gates to the compound, their arms raised in supplication and their voices moaning pleas that I heard at this distance only as a whining cacophony of sound, I forced myself to look at individual faces. I would not see these people as just a mass; I needed to see them as individual people. I felt I owed that to them. They had believed in us, and we had failed them. And when I did this, I saw him. Nguyen. My Nguyen. He was at the outer fringe, too proud to beg and plead, but his eyes were raised to the building, searching, looking worried.

I ran through the building, my eyes already blurry from tears, and down to the beaten-earth outer courtyard inside the main gates. I called out to two of the Marine guards who were guarding the gates, ready, with M-16s raised before them, in case the gates collapsed and rioters had to be prevented from entering the main building. The Marines recognized me—and they knew I worked in the Station.

"One of ours is out there," I cried. "He's on the list. There, there, the young man at the back of the crowd, wearing the tan shorts and plaid shirt. Help me. We must let him in. He's on the list. We've got to let him in."

One of the Marines looked at me, helplessly. "We can't open the gates, Mr. Baxter. That would be disaster."

But the other Marine was whistling, trying to get Nguyen's attention. And he did. And when Nguyen saw the Marine, he also saw me and his eyes lit up and he started pushing his way into the crowd.

He'd gotten close to the gates, with both Marines now yelling for the others to let him through. And the crowd, indeed, was parting as well as it could to let Nguyen near the gate. And they were all pressing in on Nguyen, no doubt thinking that when the gates were opened for him, they'd all rush forward. None of them was thinking any further into the future than just getting through the gates. Once there, surely the Americans would give them sanctuary, would let them on the helicopters.

As Nguyen got to the gates, the Marine who had whistled cupped his hands, lowered them, and pushed them between the bars, yelling for Nguyen to step up into them, that they would somehow hoist him over the iron fencing, that they couldn't open the gates. But they would help boost him over.

Nguyen's eyes were on me, only on me, and he was calling to me. He was ignoring the frantic instructions the Marine was trying to give him. I moved to him at the gates. My face was just inches from him. I too was yelling at him to step up in the Marines cupped hands.

I must still have been crying, because Nguyen put a hand through the bars and gently brushed away my tears, and he said, "This is important Jim. Leave now. You all must leave now. One more day. That's all you have. It's not Cam Ranh Bay. It's here."

And then he was gone, swallowed up by the crowd. I didn't know whether he was on the ground, being trampled, or how he had just disappeared in an instance. Totally.

The Marine stood back from the fence and raised his hands and turned to me. He gave me a sad look and a shrug and, with a heavy heart, I thanked him for trying and trudged back to the main embassy building. I went straight to the COS, though, and told him that the same source who had informed us the assault would first be on the Cam Ranh Bay installations was now saying that the North Vietnamese plans had changed, that the main assault would be launched here, in Saigon. And most of our forces had been kept at Cam Ranh Bay.

The COS was unsure, and it was now impossible to reposition troops, but he could see that, regardless, it would be best to step up the embassy evacuation. We went straight to the ambassador, who pulled together the Country Team for the second time that day, and, after much wrangling, the call went out to the battleships.

Hours later, as we came out of the meeting, various advisers were still arguing over the need to double the helicopter flights, which would quadruple the danger of the flights, putting the helicopters in greater danger of sniper fire and, more significant, of crashing into each other.

But the COS drew our attention to the windows overlooking the front of the compound. Now there wasn't a single person at the front gates. The people of Saigon already knew. They knew it was too late to seek relief through the embassy. They were deserting the city—at least until it had been taken and it was safer to return.

I left on one of the last helicopters. Everyone we'd gathered in the compound had gotten out, but the shredding machines hadn't kept up with the time needed, and my helicopter lifted off in dense smoke and flying ash from the bonfires we'd set in the courtyards to—we hoped and pretended—destroy as much of our mounds of secret paper as was necessary.

I was evacuated to Bangkok and set to work in the Station there, watching and reporting on the dying agony of Saigon from afar—and mourning my lost lover.

I spent too much time at the bar in the JUSMAG compound, the special forces U.S. military mission to Thai forces, where Major Carl Stevens, a seasoned commando, found me and took me back to his billet and fucked me throughout a weekend until I broke down and told him why I was so morose—how my Vietnamese lover, a valuable asset to U.S. intelligence, had simply slipped through my fingers at the gates of the U.S. embassy in Saigon.

Rough and tough on the outside, Stevens was gentle and caring on the inside. We became almost inseparable, and I gladly took comfort in opening my legs to him and found peace and a numbness to the ghost of Nguyen as he made slow, languid love to me.

One morning over breakfast I turned to him and said, "I know I've been a mess, Carl. I'm grateful for all you've done for me. And you are a great lover . . ."

"But," he said.

"Yes, but," I answered. "I can't get Nguyen out of my mind. I'm not really like this. I've been a burden on you. But . . ."

"But there isn't going to be anything but good, casual fucking between us while we're both here in Bangkok," he finished.

"Yes," I answered in a voice full of regret. "I don't want you to—"

"He's alive, and he's back in his village at Thon Lac Nghiep," Carl said.

"Excuse me?" I asked, confused.

"Nguyen. Nguyen Van Trinh. We still have sources in Vietnam. I traced him for you. We can get him out if you want. I have a team going into Vietnam not far from there anyway—on another Op. Thon Lac Nghiep is right there on the coast. If you go with us and talk him into leaving, we can bring him out this time. Off the books, but my CO knows I'm making the offer. If he was a valuable U.S. asset, he shouldn't be left behind any more than we would one of our Marine buddies."

And that was that. That was why several weeks later, wearing camouflage and smeared with black grease, I was hunched outside a window of a native hut at the edge of Thon Lac Nghiep, watching Nguyen's family closing their activities down for the night and going to their own bungalows and leaving Nguyen alone in his.

I watched him strip, lay down on his matting, turn down his lamp, arrange the mosquito net around himself, and close his eyes. And I wanted him then like I'd never wanted him before.

He started to let out a surprised cry when I came down on his body with mine, but I covered his mouth, first with my hand and then my lips, and he wrapped his arms around me, and we moved slowly into our old familiar embrace and rhythms. He reached down and unbuttoned my fly and fished out my cock. I was possessing his mouth, pushing my tongue in as he opened his legs and hooked his heels on the back of my knees and I slid deep into an old familiar sheathing. And then our pelvises were moving in synch and after many glorious moments of becoming one, precision-timed machine, we came almost simultaneously.

We were still panting our release when Nguyen whispered, "You cannot be here. You must go. It's death for both of us."

"I cannot leave you here, Nguyen." I murmured. "I came back for you. They'll learn you worked with the Americans. You'll be executed."

"No, no, you do not understand," Nguyen muttered insistently. "That's not how it is. I have an honored position here."

"Only until they find out. You must come out with me. I have friends . . . and a boat. And there's a ship—"

"I don't want to hear this," Nguyen said, louder, with anger in his voice. "You don't want to tell me this. You don't understand."

I lifted my head from his and, still holding him close, looked down in his face. I had been so stupid.

"You are one of them, aren't you?" I said in a wounded voice. "You are Viet Cong. You were playing me."

"Yes, I am VC. And I was sent to give you misinformation. To have sex with you and make you trust me and listen to me and make as many of the troops guarding Saigon to stay in Cam Ranh Bay as possible. But that's not all."

"What else is there?" I asked dully. My whole world had collapsed. "What else can there be? I have a knife. I could kill you right here. You know that?"

"Yes, I know that," he answered. But I could discern no fear in his voice. I wanted this to make him scared. I wanted to wound him, as his act of betrayal had wounded me. "But I don't think you will," he said.

"Why? Why can you be so sure?"

"For the same reason that I came back to tell you to leave right away. I didn't come back to Saigon to go with you. I came back to send you away in time. And for the same reason that I am going to let you leave here and not report that you have been here. Because, my duty aside, I love you and always will—I'm just from another world, our two worlds now no longer touching. Perhaps someday, but not now."

"And I cannot kill you for the same reason," I said at length. I said it for me, though, not for Nguyen. He was a far wiser man than I was. He already knew. And being wiser than me, he knew I would have to leave him now and not look back.

Our worlds were too far apart—perhaps not forever, but, as he wisely said, certainly for now.

At Sea with Maurice

"So, you fancy him, do you?"

"No, I fancy you Maurice," I answered, trying to make a joke out of it. But I was beginning to get a little irritated with Maurice. We both knew why he'd offered me this trip home, and I was getting tired of him just not getting to it.

"But you do fancy him, don't you?" Maurice persisted. "I mean you have nothing against mixed Orientals, have you? What would you say? A fourth White Russian, half northern Chinese, a fourth Thai, I would say. And I've been around in the region taking on deck hands long enough to be a pretty good judge of that."

"Yes, I suppose that could be right. Hell, I don't anything about that. I'd only been in Singapore two weeks when you and I met."

"I was very selective, Paul. I always am," Maurice continued. If he could tell I was on the edge of irritation, he wasn't admitting it. We were in the dining room of his container ship bound from Singapore to Miami by way of India, South Africa, and up the coast of South America. "Nine days and eight nights to Mumbai, India," Maurice was saying. "Eight deckhands taken on in Singapore and exchanged in Mumbai for the run to

485

Cape Town with a new set. In each port, a new set. Just like always. Carefully picked."

I wasn't half listening to what Maurice was saying. He owned this container ship—and apparently several others—all plying the equator route, picking up here and letting off there, enabling the exchange of goods by countries across the tropics. I guess that made him quite wealthy. He was egalitarian, though. The passenger accommodations on the ship had proven to be surprisingly comfortable and plush. He must have had at least ten well-appointed cabins for passengers beyond the ship's crew, but only he and I occupied any of these cabins on this run. And all, owner, passenger, and crew alike, took their regular meals in the common dining room.

I looked over at the sailor Maurice was prompting me to show interest in. It didn't take much effort to show interest in him. He was a well over six feet and muscle hardened, as a veteran commercial sailor had to be. Maybe thirty-five, maybe older. As Maurice noted, he seemed to have enough of the Oriental in him to be somewhat inscrutable, but to my eyes, he was mainly Slavic. Maurice had mentioned he came from Harbin and claimed to be a descent of tsarist refugees. Certainly enough White Russian in him to have a sturdy, if extremely well-toned, physique and a well-chiseled face. And his hearty laugh and the way the others at his table responded and accepted him— obviously a well-liked man of good humor.

David hadn't been like that. As he'd gotten older—and especially as he came to choose to think that I never aged along with him—and his maladies had set in, he'd gotten more ill-humored and snappish. "When will you grow into looking like a man," he'd mutter at me whenever we had a fight. But what was I supposed to do about that? There were certain attributes that made for a horse jockey type. The grand tour of Asia was supposed to make him happier. Well, that didn't happen.

"So, you fancy him, don't you? Our quarter White Russian."

"Yes, yes, I fancy him," I answered in barely controlled exasperation.

* * * *

486

"So, you fancy him, do you?"

"Excuse me?" I responded. Surprised to hear myself addressed. It was midday in the Raffles Hotel Long Bar, and I hadn't realized that anyone was sitting at my elbow. I was slinging gin and tonics down in some sort of wake, although I had no idea how an official wake should go. I didn't even like gin and tonics. But this is what David drank, so this is what I was drinking. It was, after all, David's wake.

"The bartender. You two have been chatting it up and you both look quite good. I thought you were working up to getting it on."

"No, no, of course not," I said. I might have been a little short with him, but the barkeep and I had been saying enough for him to know what our preferences were.

I turned and focused on the man sitting beside me at the bar who had asked me this strange question. He was maybe pushing fifty, but he didn't drive a desk, I could tell. He had that hands-on worker aspect about him. Salt and pepper hair, and a lot of it. Thick curlings at the V of his open sports shirt and matting on the backs of his thick-fingered hands where they extended from his sports coat. But he also exuded money and power. Germanic would be what I'd guess if I had to make a guess. I wasn't surprised he was chatting me up. I seem to have something that attracts these older men. David had been about his age when he had transitioned from me riding his horses to him riding me and eventually asking me to move my toothbrush into the main house.

"No," I started again. "I just needed someone to talk to, I guess—to share a last salute with. And I thought the bartender was the only one here. I didn't see you at the bar."

"I wasn't at the bar. I was over there in the corner. Waiting for you to come in."

I didn't have time to process this, because he continued.

"Someone to share a last salute with. I don't . . . ."

"My companion . . . Oh, hell, my lover, the man who fed and clothed me . . . died the other day here in the Raffles Hotel. In bed . . . with me. I've just now gotten the paperwork finished and seen his body off for the States. But there wasn't room for me in the box to Boston. So, I'm here, high and dry. I don't know if I'm here to mourn him or to feel sorry for myself."

What was I saying? I blushed in embarrassment. "I'm sorry. I shouldn't have said all of that. I guess I'm still in shock. I hope I didn't say that to the bartender. I just don't remember. Too many gin and tonics, I guess. I'm such a bore."

"No, no, you aren't a bore at all. You're endearing. And, yes, you did mention to the bartender that you had been a racing jockey some years past. That caught me by surprise. You don't look hardly old enough to have had a past—or to be in this bar, for that matter. And you've said enough to the bartender that I thought you might fancy each other."

I could tell a pass when I heard one. I started wondering whether I might string my Singapore stay out for another meal and a night. That was pretty hard as nails of me, I knew. But after tonight my suitcase would be in the hall, and Singapore's welcome mat would be jerked out from underneath me, and I had no more prospect of leaving Singapore than I had of staying here. It was unfair, really, I thought. I'd given up a promising Jockeying career to go with David; you didn't just dip in and out of that, you had to have a progression of recent successful rides to get anywhere. And I'd been nursemaid and lover to him for nearly ten years—all to the horror of his family. There would be no succor in that direction. I'd not get a dime from any of them to get home on, even though I'd been more family to him for nearly a decade than any of them had been.

The man beside me backed right off of what he was getting into saying, though. His whole expression changed. He became jocular, as if he was afraid he'd been too forward. But in my straits, I'm not sure what too forward would look like. I'd given out for my keep for some time now; I hadn't honed any other skills.

"Say, I'm starving," he said—as if he'd been thinking for some time how to move this proposition along and this was the best he could come up with. "You wouldn't like to join me for a bit to eat in the Palm Court, would you? I hate to eat alone."

"Umm, the Palm Court isn't exactly in my budget at . . ." I mumbled.

"Oh bother that," he said. "My treat, of course. My name's Maurice, by the way. And yours is . . ."

"Paul . . . just Paul."

"Well, Just Paul, tell me, *do* you fancy the bartender?"

I must have given him a very peculiar look, because he immediately steamed back into the conversation.

"Ummm, well. Pity that. But come, the Palm Court awaits us."

Over dinner Maurice established that he owned container ships plying around the world in the tropic zones and that he had one he was taking to Miami via the India, Africa, and South America route that was about to set sail.

"I get the impression your David's sudden death has left you here high and dry," he said over coffee. "Would it help to get you to Miami?"

Would it ever. I'd do just about anything for him to get passage to Miami.

"It wouldn't be the fastest route, of course. It would take more than a month actually . . . but if you're interested, I could take you on board tomorrow. No, no problem, no cost to you. It would just be good to have someone to talk with during the journey. I'm not taking on any other passengers this time; you'd be no added cost to me; more than enough provisions are already on board, and what's not consumed will just have to be thrown out."

Manna dropped from heaven. I didn't even try to pretend that I wouldn't jump at the offer.

"Would you like me to come up to your room with you tonight?" I asked as we were rising from the dinner table. I didn't want there to be any misunderstanding how grateful I was and what he had a right to ask of me in return.

"No, no. Not tonight. That's not necessary. Have your bags down by 9:30 tomorrow and we'll leave straight for the docks."

* * * *

We hadn't set down to our evening meal in the container ship's dining room until we had cleared the Singapore Straits and

489

were steaming into the Indian sea. All alone now on the sea; no land and no other ships in sight in any direction. The sun was still bright outside; it wouldn't set for another couple of hours. The ship's mate came into the dining room as deserts were being handed out to report that we also seemed to be steaming into a squall. All hands were called on deck to methodically walk through the stacks of metal containers as big as box cars and ensure that all of the cabling holding them in place was as tight as could be. One container dislodged could roll the whole ship over in a high sea. It was going to be hard work and the sun was still hot, so all of the hands pushed their desert plates aside, stripped down to their waists, and headed for the hatchway.

I sucked in my breath at the look of the White Russian's physique when he was stripped down. Heavily muscled, bulking, a regular Zeus. In fact, all of the deckhands were large-boned, particularly well muscled; and strong looking; it obviously was a career necessity.

Maurice left with them, but he returned in a few minutes, and we finished our deserts and coffee in an otherwise deserted dining room. He was being extremely polite and solicitous— almost fatherly—toward me. Not for the first time did I feel embarrassment at my slight size and young looks. I wondered how I was going to get past him treating me like I might break in two if he touched me. David had never shown me this regard.

Over the day on board, Maurice had grown on me. I was used to going with older men, and, although "of an age," he seemed in better shape than most. And his curly salt and pepper hair intrigued me. I wondered if he was as hairy under that shirt as the back of his hands and the V at his neck implied. And whether he had such a luxuriant bush at his pubes—and how low he was hung. The hair leading me down that path. I was resisting the urge to run my hands under the hem of his shirt and up to his nipples and trying to start the inevitable process of the taking—right here on the dining table. I leaned in a bit toward him and moved my hand to the edge of the table near him.

But then Maurice abruptly rose again from the table and took a step back. "We should turn in early," he said. "If we run into the squall, it will be a rough sailing night."

"Shall I come to your room tonight?" I asked. Maurice had still not openly expressed the price of my passage, and I wanted to make clear that I knew what I owed. I also knew from how he looked at me that he wanted me, even though he was withdrawing from every signal I was sending him.

"No, no. It's not necessary," he answered.

I found this very frustrating. David—at least after my jockey career was shot when I stopped competing and putting horses through their paces so that I could respond to his every whim—had never let me forget that sex was my price for any favor or spending money. I hadn't needed to beg for the responsibility or right to pay my own way with the only coin available to me with David. I couldn't figure Maurice out.

My confusion and funk continued after I had gone back to my cabin, stripped down to my sleeping shorts, and tried, unsuccessfully, to read from one of the paperbacks I'd brought. The ship wasn't churning in the disquieted seas too violently yet, but it was pitching and yawing enough so that my eyes couldn't remain focused on the small print of the paperback. I had left the night lights on as Maurice had cautioned me to do with the comment that you never could tell where the furniture would wind up at night at sea and it would be best to be able to get your bearings if you had to get up in the night. But the lights cast an eerie red glow around the cabin and fought hard with every attempt I made to sleep.

I rose and padded barefooted out to the covered deck at the back of the passenger cabins, overlooking the wide span of the open hold in which the containers were stacked. Those of the deck crew who so recently had been heartily eating and laughing in the communal dining room were still hard at work, checking cables and tightening up anything loose on deck. It had grown dark now, as much from the black clouds scudding in from overhead as from the end of day. The White Russian, still naked to the waist, torso gleaming from sweat and salt water spray in the lights beaming down from the bridge, was there, not more than ten yards from where I was standing at the railing of the covered passenger deck. What came next came to me as if in a dream.

* * * *

He has come to me in the darkness of night in a stormy sea, riding me on the crest of the waves. I have had to raise the side the rails to stay in the berth as the ship struggles through the squall, rolling and churning through the stormy sea. He comes down heavily on my back as I'm stretched out in the berth on my belly. He is heavy with undulating, insistent muscle, invading, consuming.

Unable to sleep in the tossing sea, I had come to the rail and watched the deckhands moving like dancers, tightening the ropes, securing the cargo. I watched him, the burly White Russian, for hours as the ship raced toward the twilight horizon, just ahead of the storm, losing the race by the minute, inevitably being enfolded from behind in consuming embrace.

Stripped to the waist, he worked hard with ropes at the bow of the ship, letting his muscles and hands work as they knew so masterfully to do. Beauty in motion. Sensual. Arousing. No longer watching what he was doing, because he was watching me.

"What was that you said?" I called out over tumult.

"Your cabin number?" he called back. "I can come soon. I want to fuck you."

"Fuck me?" I cried out in shock. Maurice had told him, had told the White Russian I fancied him.

"Your cabin number," He called back. No longer a question.

I wonder if he would have come anyway, even if I had not told him the number.

Heavy, stretched out, covering me. Wet and salty, just come from the sea. Too strong for me, even if I had wanted to struggle. He gives me no choice, however. His strong arms lace under my armpits and back over my shoulders and make a fist with his hands at the nape of my neck.

His knees are forcing my thighs apart. His club of a dick is at my channel, pushing, pushing, pushing. Entering and rising up inside me. And he just holds me there, letting the rolling and lurching of the tossing, storm-cast sea move him deeper, deeper inside me, Rolling this way and that, the hot bulb of his cock kissing and assaulting my sensitive inner walls at all angles in the rhythm of the tossing sea. Ahhhhhhh.

* * * *

He was grunting hard and I was groaning even harder. I felt the bulk of him slip away from me and both heard and felt the slurping of his impaled dick pull out of me, and I thought he'd finished with me, short of my release. Short, I was sure, of his own. I had not invited him in, but I felt a sudden loss of him.

But he wasn't leaving me; his weight momentarily removed, he turned me over on my back, and in one swift movement pushed his knees between my thighs and grabbed me above the hips, his hands so big and my waist so thin that his fingers almost met, and pulled my torso down hard into him as he thrust his dick strongly up in me once again. I cried out and arched my back, writhing and trembling under his new, stronger assault. I reached over my head and grabbed the rungs of the headboard to hold myself in place against the tossing ship and the White Russian's digging cock.

My head lolled to one side, and that's when I saw him. Maurice, sitting in a chair across the cabin. Naked under a robe, which was hanging open at his sides. Sitting there, one leg hooked over the arm of the chair to give him a wide stance, intensely watching the White Russian fuck me, a little smile on his face, his hand pulling slowly, rhythmically on his meat. The reddish glow of the night lights made the curled wisps of his heavily matted silver-colored chest hair stand out prominently. He was breathing heavily, his barrel chest expanding and contracting, bringing movement to the thatch of chest hair that reminded me of a breeze passing over a field of wheat. His engorged cock was big and thick, extending from a luxurious bush, its bulbous head angry red in the glow of the night lights—and glistening with precum. His eyes glued to the spectacle of the slight me being manhandled and fucked by the burly White Russian deckhand.

The rolling of the ship and the thrusting of the White Russian's cock was too much for me. I gave a gasp and my muscles tightened, and then I gave a little scream, collapsed under the relentless pounding, and released my seed up into the muscular, flat belly muscle of the thrusting deckhand. He, in turn, roared in triumph and jerked and ejaculated deep inside me.

Then he was gone but was almost immediately replaced by Maurice, who took up the just-vacated position, his knees pushing under my ass cheeks and thighs, his strong hands digging into my hips, a thicker cock than the deckhand's thrusting inside me. And thrusting and thrusting. Fucking me hard, the rolling of the disquieted sea tossing and turning and churning me on his relentless cock. I ran my hands up through the enticing thick hair on his chest and took his nipples between my fingers and gently squeezed. I smiled into his face, a smile of welcome, of gratitude for the free passage. Wanting him to enjoy the fuck. Enjoying the fuck myself.

But Maurice had worked himself up into a frenzy in his voyeuristic foreplay. My welcoming him wasn't really the image and the fulfilled fantasy he was seeking.

"Fight me," he demanded. "Struggle for your freedom or I'll fuck you unconscious." Then he backhanded me across the face, and I began to writhe under him, trying to escape. But this was probably why he had selected me. I was small and light, and although I was strong, I wasn't strong enough for the White Russian or for Maurice.

I did manage to dislodge his cock and scramble over to the side, but the safety slats on the side of the bed were insurmountable, especially as the ship had taken that moment to lurch to port and roll me back into Maurice.

He laughed and grabbed me around the waist with one hand and scooped up two pillows with the other. He turned me on my face and forced the pillows under my belly, raising my hips to him. The lurching of the ship was tossing us about, but Maurice was used to this. He crouched up over my hips, his thighs encasing mine. I felt his hand positioning his angry red knob at my hole, and then he reared his pelvis back and brutally thrust inside me and started pumping me hard. Going with the lurching of the ship, using the ship's motion to delve deeper into my channel and assault and caress every inch of my channel walls as he drove up inside me. Driving me to distraction.

Sensations I'd never felt before. Completely taken, wholly controlled and invaded.

He was riding me like a jockey in a closely contested race, the image not lost to either one of us. He ran the fingers of one hand into my hair, and grabbed, and lifted my head up toward his face, arching my back painfully. Bringing my ear to his lips, he whispered in a throaty, lust-driven tone, "Did your David ride you like this, my little filly? Was he this big and thick, and did he thrust like this . . . and . . . umph . . . like this . . . and like THIS?" Each brutal thrust made me jerk and spasm. Then he bit me on the earlobe.

I gasped and yelped a reply, but he wasn't listening to me. He wasn't interested in what I had to say. He had been so reserved and mannerly in the light of day. In the light of the reddish night light and on the tossing sea, he was something else altogether. He was a vengeful god; King Neptune. And he was splitting me asunder with his spear. I was completely in thrall to him. Alone out here on the sea. Completely at his mercy.

And his mercy was very thin at the moment. He was riding me like a rodeo bull performer, tossed by the wallowing ship, duplicating the fury of the gale thrusting against the creaking ship. He was slapping my butt cheeks with stinging blows from his hands, and pistoning inside me, and riding . . . riding . . . riding.

* * * *

The next morning, the sea was calm as glass. I remarked on this to the third mate as I was entering the dining room, and he said, "Yes, that's not unusual. But the weather charts say to expect another rough night at sea tonight."

The deckhands—and the ship owner and passenger as well—were quiet and a bit groggy after a hard night at sea— harder for some than others; harder in a different way for one than for the others.

We were all withdrawn into ourselves, needing that first cup of coffee before we could even think of being decent to each other or to struggle for something to say.

Maurice was already there, nursing a steaming mug, when I fairly hobbled in, not all from lack of sea legs.

The eight deckhands were huddled over their own coffee, hoarding their cups from each other like they were treasure chests. They all looked at me as I came in. They had had their heads together, listening to the White Russian whispering, when I entered the room. He stopped whispering as soon as he saw me come in.

I went over and sat next to Maurice, not saying a word. I was trying to think of something to say, when I felt the nudge of a hand against the one I had laid on the table top. I looked up into the eyes of a smiling, blond giant of an Australian. Open smile, a gleam in his eye. A steaming coffee mug in his hand.

"A cup of Joe, mate?" he asked. All smiles, super friendly.

I smiled wanly back at him and took the cup. "Thanks . . . mate," I managed.

He smiled again and backed his way to the table of the deckhands and slowly sank into his seat, his eyes still on me. The eyes of all eight on me. One set satiated; seven sets in lip-licking anticipation.

I turned my eyes to Maurice, who was also giving me "that look."

"So, you fancy *him*, do you?" Maurice said, gesturing toward the Australian, his eyes telling me all I needed to know about the rough nights at sea with Maurice.

Triangulation

"I know you'll leave me. You're just waiting for us to get back to Manila, and you'll leave me."

Stanley was curled up in the fetal position on his berth in the compact cabin of the Bayliner 2855 yacht. He and Lance had been anchored off the Hilton Cebu Resort twin towers in the Philippines for two days, and Stanley had been drinking himself beyond pout and into a blue funk for three.

"Please, baby, please don't be like this. You know I wouldn't leave you; you know I couldn't leave you," Lance murmured.

He sat on the berth beside Stanley and laid his hand on his lover's belly. This had always worked before. It wasn't unusual for Stanley to sink into this mood, if not often this deeply, and the drink always made it worse. Ever since Stanley had passed his fiftieth birthday, he had become convinced that Lance, now half his age, would leave him—that his money wouldn't be enough to hold Lance. Even Lance's suggestion that they take this around-the-world trip, just the two of them, alone, most of the time on Stanley's streamlined yacht, hadn't reassured Stanley.

"I've grown so old," Stanley moaned. "Old and dumpy. I saw the looks you were getting the other night at that club in

Manila. I knew they were thinking 'How can such a well-built hunk like that be with such an old man when he could be with me?'"

"No, you're not too old, Stan," Lance said, the exasperation in his voice clear. "You still have the looks of a model. And here. I grab you here and you are hard as a rock." He had placed his hand over one of Stanley's nipples and squeezed on Stanley's well-worked chest muscles. "And you're still flat as a board here." Lance put his palm on Stanley's belly again. "And you still can get it up here." He grabbed Stanley's cock through his Speedo. "And you still have the sweetest one of these I've never known." Lance was sliding his hand under the rim of the Speedo at the small of his back.

"No, no, no," Stanley cried out. He jackknifed out of the fetal position, pushed off of the bed and away from Lance. "You wanted this sort of vacation because you are embarrassed to be seen with an old man like me. No, I know you'll leave me in Manila. I might as well throw myself off the boat now." Then, grabbing up an oversized beach towel, he flounced out of the cabin and to the bow of the boat, where he laid the towel on the sharply raked windscreen of the cigarette boat and laid down on his back, wanting the sun to bake the liquor out of him while he watched the twin towers of the Cebu Hilton and the activity on its beach.

Only a moment later, Lance popped out of the cabin, a panicked look in his eyes. His eyes wildly scanned the water, looking for a sinking suicidal Stanley, until he saw that Stanley was sunbathing instead on the bow of the boat.

Mad now, having had enough of this, Lance slipped off his Speedo and came around to the bow and stood, legs spread, between the sunbathing Stanley and the vista of the Cebu Hilton's busy beach and two tall hotel towers. He took his long and thick cock in his hand and wagged it at Stanley.

"Suck this!" he demanded. "Can't you see that it's hard for you?"

"What?" Stanley opened his eyes. And then he opened them even farther, focused on the midsection of his naked horse-hung young lover. "Lance," he cried out, "What are you doing? People will see you."

"People will see us, Stanley. Not just me. You said I would be too embarrassed to be seen with you. I'm going to fuck you right here, in full view of everyone in that resort. That's how embarrassed I am to be seen with you. And if you won't suck me, I'll blow you." With that, he knelt between Stanley's legs, stripped off his Speedo and inhaled Stanley's cock.

"Oh, god, Lance, oh god," Stanley cried out. His hands went to the back of Lance's curly head and held him close. "Oh, god. All of it . . . yes . . . yes. Oh, god."

Changing to fisting Stanley's cock, Lance started moving his lips up across Stanley's belly and up onto his nipples and to his lips. He was writhing around on top of Stanley, getting as close into him as he could.

"Lance! Not here. In the cabin. We must go below. Oh . . . ahhhh." Whatever else Stanley was going to say was muffled as Lance brutally attacked his mouth with his own.

After working his mouth until Stanley was almost out of breath, Lance broke away. "No. Here, Right here, Stanley. I'm going to fuck you for anyone to see who wants to see. I want you now, here. I love you. I'm never going to leave you. You couldn't get rid of me if you wanted to."

Lance quickly worked his mouth back down Stanley's torso, and after giving his cock a little more loving, Lance put his hands under Stanley thighs, rolled them up, and was diving into Stanley's hole with his tongue.

As Lance stood back up, his hands still lifting Stanley's thighs up and spreading them wide, Stanley looked down at him. "God, Lance. You're so hard. You're huge. I never know how I can take all of you."

"You always take all of me, Stanley. You've got the sweetest ass. I'm hard for you. You make me hard. Can't you accept that?"

"Yes, yes. I . . . Arghhhh!"

His ass had accepted all that Lance had for him again, and Lance was fucking him hard, power driving up between his spread thighs, pushing his back up and down on the raked windscreen of the yacht.

* * * *

Will Thruston worked hard on the key mechanism of his tenth-floor Hilton Cebu hotel room door. He was in such a state that he was doing more cussing at the unresponsive lock than effective key turning. Once in, he tore off his shirt and threw it on the bed, headed straight for the minibar, grabbed a beer, despite his intent never to take anything from an exorbitantly expensive hotel minibar, flipped off the cap, stumbled out onto the balcony, and stood at the railing, trying to gain control of his anguished trembling. He stared hard out onto the yacht basin, trying to calm down, trying to tell himself these things happened, that it didn't mean anything.

But this was the third time this week. He had to face that maybe he was growing unable to get it up. Maybe he was losing it altogether.

Business hadn't been all that good this week. This afternoon's trick, who he had cultivated for nearly an hour in the hotel bar before landing him, had been ugly and pudgy. And he had to have been at least in his mid-forties. But Will couldn't let that turn him off. Most of the marks at this hotel were ugly and fat and old. The younger guys here didn't have to pay for it. And Will only did it for the money.

Everything had worked OK at the start. The guy was half drunk when Will helped him to his hotel room. And he paid up front—what Will asked for without haggling.

Will had planned to fuck him in the shower and then again after the full body massage he had agreed to as part of the price. Lucky, he hadn't told the trick of these plans, though.

The man had been more than ready for Will. He was half hard before they got into the shower, and Will had gone down on his knees in front of the man while water was cascading over them and gotten him to jack off with a minimum of mouth work on his dick. And the guy had gone hard and come again when Will had turned him belly to the tiles and given him a full-tongue rim job. Then Will had planned to fuck him from the rear, but he hadn't been able to get it up. It hadn't helped that the pudgy guy had already hardened and come twice. Will felt emasculated by that. Twenty years older than him and able to spout out twice in an hour when he himself couldn't even get it up. And the worry about it probably didn't help either. As a substitute, he'd finger fucked the man while covering him close from behind for a while, which seemed to satisfy him.

The full body massage on the hotel bed went OK, too. And the trick hardened and came again while Will was giving him a hand job. Still, Will himself hadn't hardened up. Maybe part of that was that the guy gave Will's cock no attention at all. He seemed happy for Will to be making all of the moves. This was both good and bad. Good because the guy didn't seem to notice that Will wasn't aroused; bad because Will had promised to fuck him.

Will's flexible dildo came to the rescue. The mark was so mellow when Will had jacked him off and then turned him on his belly and rubbed down his back and legs, that when Will at last mounted him, the guy didn't seem to notice—or care—that it was a dildo working inside him rather than Will's cock. The man went to sleep, and, having already been paid, Will quickly dressed and left him there.

And he'd come straight back to his own room. Worried and mad, but mostly scared. Was he finished? Would he ever be able to perform again. This was his "career"; he was a hotel stud for pay. A good-looking hunk hanging around the pool, waiting for an old rich lady or a middle-aged businessman wanting to be taken for a ride and willing to pay big bucks for the fuck. If the hotel got any inkling he was having trouble stepping up to the plate, they'd toss him out on his ear. They didn't keep around any duds to fail to service their rich patrons on demand.

Three more swigs from his beer bottle and Will was able to actually focus on the magnificent vista of the Hilton Cebu seascape laid out before him.

Oh, my god, what was that? Surely not. Will reached for his binoculars and trained it on a gleaming white, sleek cigarette boat yacht anchored off the beach.

What were they doing? God, they were fucking. An older, but very trim guy—much more appealing that any of the marks he'd been stuck with this week—was lying against the sharply raked windscreen of the yacht, and a younger hunk—hunkier than Will himself, he had to admit—was hunched between the older man's spread thighs, pounding away in his ass.

Both naked, fucking, right there, not far off shore, for all on the beach and in the hotel towers to see.

Will couldn't take his eyes off them. He felt the binoculars waiver, and he had to fight to maintain focus on the vigorous fuck the young hunk was giving the older man. The binoculars were heavy in his hand, which was trembling. He'd return the other hand to the binoculars to hold them steadier, but his other hand was busy. Without realizing it, he'd unzipped himself, let his trousers fall to the floor, and he was pulling on his cock. And his cock was big and hard. His breath was getting ragged, and he masturbated vigorously. Gloriously alive again.

Maybe all he needed to do was imagine arousing bodies fucking when he was with a mark. Maybe that would keep him in business for a while. It wasn't because he *couldn't* get it up— because, by god, it certainly was up now! And it wanted lots of attention.

* * * *

Edward Frampton got up from the bed, finding himself unable to sleep in the afternoon despite his exhaustion, and deciding he didn't really need anything more on than his sleeping shorts in the middle of a hot Philippines day, went out onto the balcony of his thirteenth-floor Hilton Cebu hotel tower room.

He collapsed more than sat onto the patio chair. God he was tired. But then he smiled, in remembrance of why he was tired, why he hadn't gotten any sleep last night.

He'd never done anything like this before. He had heard that it was this easy in the Philippines and in some of the other resort hotels throughout Southeast Asia. But he was shocked at himself—and amused and, yes, proud of his audacity and boldness—to have tried it here. And it worked a charm.

The room boy who had brought his luggage up to the room was slight and brown as a berry and achingly beautiful in an androgynous way. Clearly male, but as beautiful and lithe and graceful in his movements as a courtesan. In the elevator, they had chatted a bit, and Edward had been surprised to find that the room boy was in his early twenties. He looked no older than a teenager. It was a trait of the Filipinos, Edward had noticed during his various business trips here from Hong Kong. Perpetual youth. He wished he could latch into that. He was feeling his thirty-six years. Nearly forty and nothing exciting had happened to him yet. He'd fucked around in gay bars in his twenties, but when he'd been sent out to Hong Kong, he'd become respectable—and closely watched. He couldn't get away with much of anything in Hong Kong. And, although he'd traveled to the Philippines twice before, and each time had become aroused by the small, well-formed berry-brown young men of the country, he had been too timid to act on his impulses.

Until this, the third trip. He'd been told that all you had to do in a hotel like this was to ask. So, when they'd gotten to the room and the room boy had asked if there was anything else he could do for Mr. Frampton, Mr. Frampton told him what he could do for him and held out two 1,000 peso banknotes. The room boy's eyes had bugged out and he'd smiled broadly.

The room boy had proved to be very willing, very able, flexible, resilient, and inventive. He also, once naked, proved to be very desirable. The years of an adult, the body of a lithe but well-muscled, perfectly formed youth. And a well-worked hole that not only opened immediately to Edward's thickness but also was trained to make undulating love to Edward's throbbing cock.

Edward fucked him under the cascading water in the shower, the room boy's feet leveraging off the frame of the shower door while his shoulder blades were sliding up and down on the wet tiled walls opposite, propelled by the strength of Edward's driving cock. Edward recharged quickly while the room boy toweled him off and then fucked the room boy from behind as he was bent on his belly over the back of the room's upholstered tub chair.

Exhausted then, Edward bedded the room boy, who, still resilient, massaged Edward's screaming muscles, including eventually, the reawakened muscle between his legs. In the darkness of the early night, Edward drifted off, but the room boy awakened him again within a couple of hours. Edward was stretched on his back and the room boy was riding his loins hard, drawing yet another ejaculation out of him. Yet another fucking only a couple of hours after Edward had drifted off nearly paralyzed him. He was groaning hard and the room boy could get no more than a dribble of semen out of him. Mercifully that marked the end, and when he woke next—to the light—and to entirely too little sleep and too much vigorous exercise, he opened his eyes to the thought that maybe 2,000 pesos was entirely too much to have offered.

It was afternoon before he could struggle out of bed. But he hadn't slept. Besides being exhausted, he was incredibly satisfied and pleased with himself. He would have to make more business trips to the Philippines.

When he felt a bit recovered, he picked up the binoculars from the table beside him and started to check out the sights around the busy hotel complex. He decided to take a sweep of the hotel tower next to his for beginners, moving up from the base. When his view reached the tenth floor of the other tower, he let out a gasp and a "Holy shit!" and had to lift a second hand to the binoculars to steady his trembling hand.

The man, a Caucasian, like him, was stunningly handsome. Edward instantly recognized him as a beefy, suntanned hunk he'd seen at the pool as he was taking a walk around of the facilities before checking in. The man had been a large dose of eye candy, and Edward had remembered thinking "trophy stud" when a beet-red European with a distinct pouch and puffy face had spoken to the young man and they'd walked off toward the hotel together.

Now he was standing at the rail of the balcony of his tenth-floor room in the other tower, shirtless and his trousers down around his ankles. He was holding binoculars in one hand, trained out to sea, and he was stroking the loveliest, hardest cock Edward had ever seen. Edward couldn't take his eyes off him, and he felt his own cock begin to renew its interest in spite of the Herculean workout it had gotten the previous night.

Edward was so engrossed in watching the young man masturbate at the balcony rail that he didn't hear the door to his hotel room click open and the room boy reappear to make up the room.

Suddenly, a hand was taking the binoculars out of Edward's hands. The room boy was pulling his sleeping shorts

504

off him, and he has holding Edward's erect cock in his fist as he moved his thighs around Edward's, positioned his hole on Edward's rosy-red bulb, and started to descend into his lap. Edward threw his head back, took a pert hard brown cock in both hands, driving it like a stick shift on a sports convertible, his eyes closed but still seeing that hunk on the other balcony slowly jacking his gigantic meat off, and he sighed in appreciation of how far 2,000 pesos would stretch.

* * * *

Stanley had already come, in three jerks and heavy spoutings, as he was spread out on the window screen of his Bayliner 2855, the palm of his hands on Lance's tight butt cheeks, enjoying how they contracted with each thrusting of his young lover's rock hard cock up into him. How could he have ever doubted his Lance? It was the liquor. He'd swear off liquor for good if it kept Lance with him, in his bed, churning his cock inside him.

After ejaculating, Stanley lay back against the windscreen, letting Lance pound away inside him, knowing it would be several more minutes before he came.

Stanley loved this, but having reached his own climax, reason flooded in to struggle with emotion, and he started to worry again at the spectacle they were making of themselves. Binoculars were within reach, so he retrieved them and put them to his eyes and started scanning the beach and the Hilton Cebu twin towers, checking on who might be watching.

Lance wouldn't notice. When he was deep in a fuck like this, he became a wild, focused man, all of his attention locked on the working of his cock inside Stanley. Stanley knew this was only further evidence that he was still desirable to Lance. Lance couldn't have even gotten it up, let alone become lost in the fuck, if he didn't still want Stanley. Stanley knew he'd been such a fool to raise doubts.

As he scanned the towers, Stanley's attention focused on the thirteenth floor of one of the towers. Two men fucking. A very well presented young man, maybe early thirties, slumped in a chair, his head thrown back, a look of ecstasy painted all over it. And a small, lithe brown-bodied man crouched over his pelvis and fucking himself on a thick, long cock in long, plunging rhythm.

Stanley began to melt and to quicken all at the same time. His cock gave a lurch and came alive. He reached a hand for it, but Lance slapped the hand away and took charge of the cock himself, stroking it in fast rhythm with his vigorous fucking.

A triangulated cry of simultaneous release shot out over the Hilton Cebu complex, sending a flock of disturbed sea gulls screaming and fluttering up into the air. Five long sighs of satisfaction followed, drifting down in the lapping of the surf onto the resort beach.

The Brigade

They had first met in an insurgent camp outside Yogyakarta in the Indonesian jungle, far from their own country of the Philippines. In the Philippines there was little chance that they would have met, especially while the Americans were still there in force, but even in more recent years when the government had been weak and taken up with internal squabbling. Rahib, long-time leader of the Moro National Liberation Brigade, was seasoned and deliberative and Islamic, and he came from the Moro people in the southernmost island of Mindanao. Hilario, in contrast, was young and vibrant—a regular fire brand—and was nominally Catholic and the result of an excellent mix of native Filipino and Spanish blood and came from the northern island of Luzon.

And beyond this, Rahib and Hilario's father, Humberto, had been political rivals and enemies from the earliest days of efforts by such Third World leaders as Sukarno, Nehru, and Castro to bring all of the undeveloped world together to stand against the Western nations. And in those efforts, these leaders had worked—seemingly unsuccessfully in Rahib's and Humberto's cases—to bring all of the charismatic revolutionary leaders together, and to combine their forces, to stop fighting each other for control over a nation that was in the hands of yet other forces.

Humberto was long dead and his original organization defunct, but out of the ashes of that had arisen another insurgent organization that had become the bane of the Americans and the Manila governments they supported in an urban warfare environment. And the leader of this Philippine Nation Brigade was Humberto's young son, Hilario.

In a never-say-die effort of the old Panchsila doctrine leaders, Rahib and the son of his nemesis were enticed to meet with insurgent leaders from other countries for the first time in a congress of remnant revolutionary groups across Southeast Asia. Hilario was still open to high thinking and had a fire in his belly for change, and he was susceptible to the principles of Panchsila. Rahib who had been around long enough to know that Panchsila stemmed from an effort to keep Islam spreading in Southeast Asia was not.

However, Rahib was sexually attracted to Hilario and could not help but notice that Hilario was attracted to him even more, like a puppy sniffing after a bone. And Hilario was highly sexed and was a pushover for more mature, well-muscled men. The two came together, interestingly enough, for exactly the same selfish reason—disrespect for Hilario's father, Humberto.

As the conference wore on under the heaviness of high-flown speeches that were dusty from decades of useless delivery, Rahib's amusement at the thought of fucking Humberto through the puppy following him around turned into a possibility and then an intention. With Hilario, it started with the attraction to Rahib, the man, solid and mature, well-muscled and silent until discussions were at their deepest quandary and then cutting in with the wisdom of many years on the trail and in the insurgent hunt. And those many hard years were etched in the man's body. The primitiveness of the jungle camp did not accord much privacy, and Hilario saw Rahib in the showers. His body was powerful, his Moro tattooing was intricate and fascinating, his cock was thick, his balls were heavy, and, most intriguing of all, his body was pocked with the medals of combat that can't be properly symbolized by colorful and shiny baubles.

Only after Hilario decided he wanted to be fucked by Rahib did he start thinking of what a delicious revenge that would be on the unloving and abusive father who had never had a favorable thing to say about the Muslim insurgent leader.

Hilario was the aggressor. Rahib had planned the taking, but he was always deliberate and slow in unfolding his campaigns. Hilario was impulsive and direct. He started by wearing nothing but low-slung jeans and always being in Rahib's line of vision. His was a lithe, berry-brown, and perfectly proportioned body that came with the delightful mixing of the genes of dramatically separate races. He moved gracefully, like a dancer, and his beautiful body was always in motion. Rahib was not the only man to watch the youth in motion and want to grab that, and hold it, and penetrate it deeply as it slowly melted down at his feet.

On the day Hilario entered the shower room when only Rahib was there and directly asked Rahib if he'd like to fuck him, Rahib turned the smaller, younger man belly to the concrete wall, crouched below him, and willingly thrust his thick cock up into the soft core of his enemy's son. With each thrust, Rahib declared a death to each person and force that stood between the disparate Philippine revolutionary groups and seizure of the mutually hated, American-influenced government in Manila. Hilario answered, between groans and moans of pleasure, with a pledge of assistance and cooperation. If the Moro leader ever needed him, Hilario said, his insurgent band would be there to help.

And in that strange way of zealots always putting their zealotry at the center of their lives and natural functioning, an exorcism of a mutually hated, long-departed man was consummated, and the seed of future cooperation was sown just as surely as Rahib's seed was implanted deep in Hilario's channel. In addition, the conference attained probably its only success toward meeting its goals—and never even knew it.

For the remainder of the conference, the two very different leaders bedded together, while Hilario endeavored to introduce Rahib to sophisticated and refined sexual positions and Rahib trumped that with lost-to-the-fuck power ravishment. The one technique that Rahib readily absorbed from Hilario's preferences was bondage. Hilario liked to be lightly controlled with strappings and entrapment when he was fucked.

At the end of the conference, ironically enough, while Hilario returned to the Philippines to insert his band of young, energetic insurgents ever deeper into the major Philippine cities and his forces grew, Rahib took his Moro insurgent band to the north island, Luzon. Although in time he was successful in displacing American influence there—especially around the former U.S. service recreation center at Baguio—as the U.S. forces were being pulled out of the region, the toll of combat on his own forces was significant.

As the Americans left, the government in Manila began to take on more of its internal defense responsibilities, and within months of declaring Baguio insurgent held, Rahib's Moro National Liberation Brigade was trapped in the dense forests on the nearby Mount Pulog and the Philippine army was poised to announce that yet another insurgent band had been wiped out.

At that point, Rahib's long-ago rivalry saved his life. A small army of young, inspired hot brands streamed out of the cities and into the highland jungle of central Luzon. The forces of the Philippine Nation Brigade under the leadership of Hilario was reconstituted in the foothills of Mount Pulog and merged with the battered and combat weary remnants of Rahib's Moro band.

The two leaders met, all smiles. They agreed on the spot to merge their forces, without regard to the real differences in doctrine, religion, ethnic origin, and political goals that had made them separate forces. And, not being able to readily agree on a name, they settled on the only shared word in their individual titles, and the combined force now became known only by the bland name "The Brigade."

"We must celebrate tonight," Rahib said with a big grin, knowing full well that the equal nature of the merger was a farce—that to the extent he controlled the impetuous young Hilario's ass canal, he controlled all of the insurgents gathered. He had just rejuvenated his own forces at the mere cost of a title. "We will dine alone, you and I, in my tent."

The look Rahib gave Hilario left little doubt who would be dining on what.

"I should like to bring my lieutenant along with me," Hilario said, reaching back behind him and pulling a tall, solidly built man of greater years than Hilario and most of those in his youthful band forward into the circle of senior combatants. "This is Fernando," Hilario said.

Rahib took one look at the seasoned combatant Hilario had brought forward and at the way Hilario held the man's arm, and Rahib instantly knew that this was competition. He marked himself for a fool for not realizing that the impulsive and randy Hilario would not have a lover, and he decided he needed to establishing the poking order from this new beginning.

"I would love to talk with your lieutenant further and to give him full position in our counsels, Hilario, but I would like this first evening together to be a meeting of the minds of just we two principal leaders. I would be happy to see you at my tent at 7:00 p.m., please." And then he turned and left, not bothering to check the glances exchanged between Hilario and Fernando.

That evening, the wily and experienced Rahib did manage to establish the poking order. He fucked Hilario, with Hilario's wrists tied above his head on the tent's center pole, and Rahib lifting his legs off the ground with hands grabbing Hilario's hips and pounding up inside his channel. Rahib had figured that Fernando had not guessed that, although Hilario said he enjoyed exotic positions and refined fucking, what he melted to was just a controlled deep pounding by a thick cock.

And when Rahib was finished with Hilario, he sent him back to Fernando immediately as a "try to top this" challenge. Fernando's stretched out, sensual, slow-fuck side splitting of Hilario inside their combined sleeping bags did, indeed, pale in Hilario's unconsciousness in comparison with the exciting domination Rahib provided him.

During the following months, Rahib managed to walk a precarious but ever-more-steady line in sublimating the many differences in temperament and beliefs and goals within his expanding insurgent force and keeping Fernando in a distant third place, all through his cocking mastering of Hilario. And as time went on, his position and hold strengthened, and the insurgents slowly regained control of the Baguio region and the government troops began to cordon off the region rather than continuing to try to wipe the insurgents out—and to complain of outside support of the insurgents to their American allies.

At that point a new element entered in the mix.

Rahib, Hilario, and Fernando were standing in the center clearing of the main camp one late afternoon—dancing around an argument over Rahib's minimizing of a one-time goal of the Philippine Nation Brigade and Hilario just standing and slightly frowning as Fernando lost point after point with Rahib—when a commanding, Western-visage, shockingly out of place figure strode into the circle.

All around the periphery rifles were raised and safeties were clicked off, but the figure continued his measured strides right up to where the three insurgent leaders had been conversing. He was a large, hulking figure, cut to demanding military standards, dressed in jungle combat garb with brown camouflage fatigue trousers over combat boots and a brown athletic T stretched over an expansive muscled chest descending into a narrow waist. His biceps were like trunks of trees, and he was easily shouldering a duffel bag over his shoulder, carrying a submachine gun in one hand, and dangling one of the insurgents' perimeter scouts under his other arm. The scout was minus his trousers and briefs and just collapsed and moaned in the dust when the stranger dropped him.

"Not the best of welcomes," the stranger barked, "You'll find another scout out on the trail. Not the worse for use, I hope."

Rahib stayed the progress of the insurgents from the periphery of the circle, who, rifles still raised, were closing in around the stranger.

"Who are you, and who sent you?" Rahib asked, challenge and no fear in his voice.

"They call me Sling," the intruder answered. "And Osama sent me."

"What is this?" Hilario said, turning to Rahib, who obviously had heard the answer to his challenge that he wanted to hear and was motioning the insurgents to lower their rifles.

"He is an expert in commando operations, Hilario," Rahib answered. "We have agreed, you and I—and Fernando— that, as exuberant and motivated as your men are, they lack the training for rural warfare. You have been fighting in the cities. And when we put my men with yours for training, there has been too much friction. Sling here is an expert trainer. He comes to us from comrades in Colombia. He will help make us strong."

"But, he said Osama. That isn't—" Fernando muttered, the concern clear on his face. And there was more than one reason he felt an uncomfortable concern. He had his eyes on Hilario, who was staring intently at the stranger. Fernando knew that look. Hilario was so hard to control. He was a randy brat; he'd open his legs for any mature, muscled man, if Fernando didn't keep him under control. Fernando was already losing ground to Rahib with Hilario. And now here was a brand-new threat. Fernando was listening out of one ear to the conversation between the insurgent who had knelt to help the disarmed scout, and the scout was saying that the hulking Westerner had fucked him after disarming him and he was babbling something about a strap.

"Come, Sling and Hilario," Rahib interjected forcefully into the discussion. "We will go to my tent and discuss plans for the training. It could not have come too soon. We've heard that the government forces are building. They may be planning a dry season offensive."

Rahib did not want to dwell on who actually had sent Sling. He wanted to minimize the Islamic connections. But these connections were key to Rahib's plans for the future. In his mind the insurgency group was fundamentally promoting the interests of the Islamic nation, even if the youths Hilario brought into the mix considered themselves nationalistic Catholics.

Hilario had trouble paying attention to the formulation of plans during the meeting—which Fernando tried to attend but was turned away from at the entrance to the tent by two of Rahib's right-hand men. Hilario's eyes were glued to Sling's pecs and the quarter-sized nipples pushing through the material of his athletic T. Hilario had also heard the scout say that the stranger had fucked him, and Hilario was lost to arousing speculation from that moment.

Sling started his training immediately. It did not go smoothly, although Sling obviously did know his craft well and he was a good enough instructor. What Fernando noticed in watching him at work, though, was that Sling was slyly fomenting unrest between the members of the two disparate bands that had been flung together with little preparation. When he was working with Hilario's men, he slipped in disparaging remarks about Rahib's seasoned combatants. And when he shared rations with Rahib's veterans as they all squatted around the fire, he criticized the abilities and talents for rural combat of the brash and snotty young men from the cities.

When Fernando tried to speak with Hilario about this at night when he was making gentle and slow love to his young leader after Rahib had sent him back to his own tent, Hilario just turned on his side and drifted off to sleep, exhausted at the bound cocking Rahib had already given him.

At the first chance Hilario could get in the next few days, he spied out Sling in the showers, simple woven bamboo-paneled sections set on stone floors with hoses set in frames above them. And the small, young revolutionary gasped at the sight of the man naked. His body was more magnificent than Rahib's even. He was younger than Rahib and his muscles were rock solid and the cock and balls hanging down from his bush were, if anything, meatier than Rahib's. And, like Rahib, his body displayed the honor of combat scars. On him, they just made him seem more dangerous and desirable.

Hilario let out another gasp when he became aware that Sling saw him watching and Sling turned to him and, with soapy hands, began to work his cock, giving it almost impossible length and thickness.

Two evenings later, rather than going to Rahib's tent, Hilario decided that he needed a shower as he watched Sling, only in his combat fatigue trousers, striding toward the showers with soap, a towel, and some sort of black leather thick strapping over his arm.

Hilario entered the shower enclosure naked. Sling turned to him and gave him a half, "I knew it" smile. He was working his cock up with soapy water again.

They stood there, staring each other down, for a long minute. Hilario was unsteady on his feet, and his rising cock was betraying his interest.

"Have you come for this?" Sling asked, moving his hand on his cock.

"Yes," Hilario said in a small voice.

"Come here, kneel, and blow me." Sling growled.

As Hilario knelt and took Sling's cock in his mouth, Sling added, "And work yourself."

After a few minutes, Sling pulled Hilario up, standing, close to his chest.

"Work them both," he directed, and Hilario took the two jutting cocks together in his hands, while Sling palmed the young man's buttocks and then, using soap under the cascading water from the overhead hose, spread the orbs with his palms and began working his fingers into Hilario's channel and opening him up.

Sling reached over to where he'd dropped his towel and came up with the thick black-leather strap Hilario had seen slung over his arm when he was walking to the shower.

"Ever used one of these?" Sling asked. "It's called a plow belt—and that describes what it's used for quite well."

"No," Hilario answered, but the way he said it indicated that he clearly was interested in what it did. It was about four feet long and ten inches deep and padded. It had hand holds at either end.

Sling took one handle in one hand, flipped the sling around Hilario's back and grabbed the other handle in the other hand.

"Climb my cock," Sling directed. And he crouched down, jutting his midsection forward, as Hilario positioned his hole over the head of Sling's cock and, with the help of his hand, moved the cock inside him to the rim of its bulb head.

Sling pulled the plow belt tight under Hilario's buttocks and pulled up in a strong motion as he quickly rose from his crouch, sending Hilario's channel on a deep dive down the length of Sling's long, thick, hard cock.

Hilario cried out at the taking, flung his arms around Sling's neck, climbed Sling's hips with his legs, and held on for dear life and Sling used tightening and releasing of pressure on the strap slung under Hilario's buttocks to stroke Hilario deep with his cock.

Hilario came before Sling did, and then, when Sling came, he just dropped one end of the belt and let Hilario collapse down his legs onto the stone floor of the shower enclosure.

Sling picked up his towel and sling and soap and walked out of the enclosure.

Two nights later, Hilario told Fernando it was time for him to go sleep among the insurgents for a while and work on their morale. This had been Hilario's answer when Fernando tried to tell him again that Sling appeared to be sowing dissension between the two insurgent factions. When Fernando was gone, Hilario asked Sling to move into his tent.

At the same time Hilario stopped visiting the tent of Rahib in the evening.

In short order, tension had mounted and tempers had gotten as short among the leaders of The Brigade as they were among the insurgent underlings.

Two days later, in the midafternoon, with the temperature so hot and the sunlight so intense that the men retired to their tents and to the shade for their midday siesta, Sling was fucking Hilario in Hilario's tent. Sling was standing in the middle of the cleared area inside the tent, in a half crouch. Hilario was bent over the plow belt held at each end by one of Sling's fists and suspending Hilario's belly above the ground, his asshole connected to Sling's midsection by Sling's impaled cock. And Hilario was moaning and groaning in deep passion as Sling raised and lowered the young insurgent leader on his throbbing cock with the black sling under his belly. This was the third such fucking using the sling in this position, and Hilario had begged for it rather than taking a nap.

Sling was standing to where he could see out into the center of the camp from the sheltering shadow of the tent interior. He saw Rahib standing out there, shouting something, and then Fernando lurched into view, facing off with Rahib and waving a pistol. Sling could see the figures of other insurgents, moving about, forming up two opposing lines.

While Hilario was still crying out at his own ejaculation and begging for Sling to finish him, Sling lowered Hilario to the ground, dropped the ends of the plow belt, and reached for

Hilario's throat, his thumbs seeking out the vein that would black the young insurgent leader out.

Hilario wasn't quite out, but definitely was stunned, when the first shot rang out in the camp center. Sling crouched low, grabbed up his fatigue trousers, and pulled the knife out of the sheath attached to the trousers' legs. He was at the back of the tent in a flash, picking up the duffel he's stashed there in one hand and slitting up the wall of the tent with the knife held in his other hand. He turned and, at the sound of automatic weapons fire, Sling saw, past the figure of Hilario, who was groggily fighting to sit up, both the body of Rahib sprawled on the ground and the body of Fernando slowly falling to the ground. Stray bullets were zinging into the tent and pinging against this and that, and although Sling didn't stay around to see anything else clearly, he thought he saw Hilario jerk and grunt and start to topple over in the periphery of his vision.

Silas "the Sling" Collins, a senior member of the Agency's special ops unit that was informally known as the candy store, could still hear the gunfire coming from up the slope of Mount Pulog when he was half way down the mountain. But he also was beginning to tune his ears into the sound of the chopper coming to pick him up, the chopper he'd summoned with the GPS device hidden in his duffel that he'd set off as soon as he felt he was safely away from the fire fight that was imploding the recently created Philippine insurgent Brigade.

It had been a fairly easy and quite effective operation, really. The hardest part was for whoever managed to make Collins believable as a connection between mainstream Islamic terrorism and Rashid's Moro insurgent group.

As he drew close to the whirlwind caused by the blades of the hovering chopper, Silas laughed when he looked down and saw that he was still clutching and dragging his favorite sex toy, the plow belt. He was happy he wouldn't even have to replace that.

Tail in the South Pacific

Joe knew his unit shouldn't have entered the Schwarzwald this close to dusk. The doughboys had been picked off one by one by the Huns, hidden in the trees. But Joe knew someone must get through and warn the big brass. He was the last one alive. He had to press on; he could not fail. This could be the turning point. The Yanks and all of their loved ones across the sea who depended on them to prevail over Old Fritz could be saved if the warning of the impending German troop movements got to the American lines in time.

They saw each other at the same moment as Joe splashed out of a shallow creek; the German soldier was as surprised to see Joe as Joe was to see him. A moment of shock during which it registered with Joe that the German was just a boy, a young and scared boy. Could he possibly be an enemy? He was shaking like a leaf. Could Joe possibly take advantage of that? Was he sent here to hunt young, vulnerable boys? Could that ever be the right thing to do? In the moment of indecision, the boy raised his ancient two-barreled pistol and sent a bullet whizzing through the material of Joe's uniform sleeve.

An overload of sensations: surprise, slight pain from the bullet nicking his arm, the sound of the misfiring click of the second chamber of the

519

youth's pistol, and a new, ominous sound—harsh snuffling and snorting and thrashing about in the underbrush beside the creek. A huge wolf, a magnificent creature, really, broke into the small clearing Joe had been caught in and stood, menacingly between the American doughboy and the young German Hun, his great muzzle turning from one to the other, trying to decide which direction to pounce. With a little cry, the trembling German youth slipped from his precarious perch in the tree and fell to the ground. The wolf was upon him in a flash. Awakened from his paralysis by this new, more worthy, better-defined foe, Joe whipped a long-bladed knife from the sheath at his thigh and fell upon the wolf, slicing and stabbing the beast relentlessly—man against the natural elements, a suddenly clear-cut understanding of the point of the struggle of man.

The battle was furious but short, and once more man was triumphant. With a mighty heave, Joe thrust the carcass of the magnificent wolf aside. The German youth was gashed and his clothes lay on his bruised and trembling body in tatters—but he still breathed and his eyes were filled with panic and fear as they looked up at the panting American doughboy standing over him with raised and bloody knife. Joe . . .

"Jules! Jules! Jules Kincaid, where have you crept off to? Oh there you are. Come in this instant and go to your room. You can see what time it is."

Yeah, right, Jules thought. Time for one of those men to come and start playing hide the sausage with you. With a sigh, Jules left off writing his story, closed his tablet, and slid back into the shabby little Kincaid living room from the Chicago tenement fire escape. The fire escape and his stories were Jules's escape from the sordid world he and his mother had been propelled into by the death of his father the previous summer.

"Jules, hurry up now and go to your room. It's almost eight o'clock." Jessica Kincaid sounded more weary than angry. This wasn't the life she'd planned for either of them. At least Jules had his stories to escape into. All she had was her low-paying receptionist job by day and what she had to do by night to bring in enough to keep the two of them going. All because of Joe. All because of his bravado—and because he'd never learned how to swim.

"Step to, Jules. In your room now. And finish up your homework, or you'll never graduate with your class. Don't be spending all of your time on those adventure stories of yours, do ya' hear?"

Jules heard all right. He heard that hated name, Jules, pounding at him. He certainly heard that. The first thing he was going to do come July and his eighteenth birthday, in the year he'd had his eye on for a decade, 1917, was to get rid of that name, have it legally changed if he could. Reduce it to nothing more than an initial if he couldn't. But as far as hearing, he could do that better than his mother seemed to think. And he had two good eyes too. Who did she think she was fooling?

There wasn't a thing wrong with either his hearing or his eyesight an hour later, when, shortly after hearing the knock on the apartment door, he opened the door to his bedroom a crack and saw them doing it on the couch. His mother was on her butt on the sofa, sideways, with her back arched and her shoulders digging into the sofa arm. And her legs were splayed wide. And some big bruiser of a guy was kneeling between her legs with his knees buried in the sofa cushions and that big fat dick of his buried in Jules's mother.

The guy was grunting and groaning, and Jules heard his mother making all sort of moaning sounds with her mouth. But from where he stood, he could see her eyes. And her eyes were dead and focused on someplace far, far away. This wouldn't have been happening if those Huns hadn't swarmed over his dad—his war hero dad—and gotten the best of him finally after he'd killed hundreds of them. His dad would put a stop to this if he were here. Jules himself was almost eighteen, and he'd learned a thing or two about fighting, but he somehow knew that his mother didn't want him to intercede. She apparently was doing what she wanted to do. But she sure wouldn't be doing it if his father were still alive.

Jules's attention was arrested by the working of the man's dick inside his mother, the rhythm of the movement as it pushed in and pulled out in concert with the man's grunts and his mother's moans. It was almost poetic and was arousing—or would be if it weren't his own mother who was being worked. But then Jules had the most guilty feeling, and he saw now that his mother had seen him watching and that her eyes had become even more dead than before and were brimming over with tears as her mouth formed a silent, wounded scream.

The inevitable confrontation between mother and son the next morning didn't take the direction that either had envisioned.

Jules caused the floodgates to open by trying to deal with the tension between them—and the reason behind it—indirectly by extolling the war hero exploits and high moral character of his dead father—assuming his mother would get the message without forcing them to talk about what he'd seen. But Jessica was having none of that, although she took her reaction to a place she'd carefully never taken it before. And she surely would not have taken it now if her world hadn't been shattered by the undeniable truth of what her son had seen the previously night, a truth that had been there for some time but that she could, until now, pretend wasn't real because it wasn't acknowledged.

"God, will you stop this about your father, Jules. Joe wasn't a war hero. He didn't even make it to France. His ship sank and he drowned. We aren't still fighting because some quirk stopped him from saving the world. He died a useless death— and he left you and me with nothing."

"He loved and protected us and went to France to make the world safe for us," Jules responded stubbornly, refusing to hear the truth. "He—"

"The only one he loved was himself, Jules. He wanted me until he had me and then I was just another one of his possessions. And it was the same with you. He—" She couldn't go on; she recoiled in horror at what she'd said. She'd never spoken of her husband to her son like this. Even though she had spoken the truth. She might have said something before now, knowing that Jules was sinking ever deeper into his misconceptions, but Jules was growing up to be so much like his father. She didn't want to plant any more of Joe's self-possession and disregard for others in Jules's brain than was naturally there.

Both sat there, staring each other down. Jules still worshipped his father. What he was hearing now wasn't the warning that his mother intended; it was more like a blueprint.

At length, Jessica changed tack. "It isn't about last night. I was going to tell you anyway, but now it's just as well that I did it."

"Did what?" Jules asked belligerently.

"Last week I was informed that you won the school system's citywide writing competition. I was going to tell you then, but something else came with the contest win, and I've been struggling with it ever since. I think now, though, that it's the best thing that could happen—for you, certainly."

Jules was interested now. He actually knew he'd won the contest. And he knew what his mother hadn't told him. He had been agonizing for days that she would say no, that he would be trapped in this tenement with her and in this sordid life forever. He'd already decided he would enlist and go off to the building fighting in France and Germany if she didn't agree to the what came with the contest win.

"The novelist, Arthur Brolin, has agreed to take you on as a personal student," Jessica said. "But he's leaving for a year's sabbatical in the South Pacific in late June. If you want to apprentice to him to learn what he can teach you about writing, you'll have to be gone for a year. You'll have to leave Chicago. And I can't come with you."

Jessica had voiced these stipulations like they were negatives. But they were honey to Jules's ears. Each and every stipulation. He was free. He was going far, far away from Chicago and his mother, and he was going to study under the novelist, Arthur Brolin!

* * * *

"It's good, of course," Arthur Brolin said as he handed the typewritten pages back to his pupil, Jules Kincaid. But he wasn't looking at the young man, and he offered no further comment.

Jules followed his teacher's gaze out onto the white-sand beach beyond the palm tree line. Sid—their Sumatran houseboy, Sidharto—wearing a gaily colored sarong pulled up and tucked into his waistband to escape the foam of the waves, was casting his net into the turquoise-blue surf of the perfect beach. For his year of writing sabbatical, accompanied by his young protégé, Brolin had settled on this beach paradise, just up the coast from the coastal town of Bengkulu, yet so isolated that few came this way. Here, Arthur Brolin was like a king in his domain—and few knew or cared how what he did in his domain.

Brolin sighed, still gazing intently on the rippling muscles of the lithe, diminutive, yet perfectly formed houseboy, who was focused on catching their dinner. Jules knew what that sigh was about. He'd heard Brolin fucking the houseboy in the dark of the night in their thatch-covered sprawling hut. Jules had no illusions why Brolin had come this far from the American Midwest for his year's sabbatical of writing. And, now, he also had no illusions about why Brolin had volunteered to bring him along and to mix his own writing with developing the young escapee of the Chicago tenements.

"It's good . . . but?" Jules said, waving the pages of his latest attempt at a short story near enough to Brolin's line of sight to break the man's concentration on the fishing houseboy.

"It's good. It's very good . . . ," Brolin answered again, absentmindedly.

"But what?" Jules persisted. Brolin was usually much more communicative than this. But Jules had been writing story after story for two months now in this Dutch colony paradise, and he still hadn't won anything more than lukewarm comments from Brolin.

"But . . . we've discussed this before, Jules," Brolin said as he gave his handsome, eighteen-year-old student his full, undivided attention now. "It's good in a mechanical sense, but it has no passion."

"No passion?" Jules asked. Brolin had put his hand, that hand with the long sensuous fingers, on Jules's wrist and hadn't taken it away. Jules shuddered at the touch, but not wanting Brolin to feel his trembling and misconstrue it, he let the words tumble out.

"What is this about no passion? I write adventure stories. I write of men struggling against the elements and eventually winning out over nature or the cruelties men force on other men, like war. War stories, like the one we just went through. Situations where people like my father struggle against impossible odds. I pour out everything inside me on these. But you say they have no passion?"

"Your writing is very good . . . no, extremely good, Jules, as I said. And there's nothing wrong in the themes you pursue. But they are missing something nonetheless. And I think what they are missing is passion. I'm sure you put everything inside you into your writing. But clearly the problem seems to be that you don't have nearly enough passion inside you to give to your stories—to make them sing with passion, to put them above what any other young writer is producing. I didn't invite you out here to make a competent writer of you. I brought you out here to make an internationally acclaimed writer of you. And I think you have that in you."

Jules had lowered his head and was trying his best to drink in what Brolin was saying to him. But all he could think of were those searing fingers on his wrist, feeling his pulse, no doubt searching for the passion inside him.

"I do. I do feel very passionate about what I'm writing," Jules stammered out in his defense. "I feel—"

"You only feel within the limits of your experience, Jules," Brolin said softly. "And your experience is limited. You can't really feel passion as a writer until you've experienced passion. That's what the best writers do. They let themselves go and they experience it all. And it comes out in their writing. You are young, so young. You've experienced . . . nothing . . . really, before now. I could—"

"You showed me this picture, this picture of an elk," Jules rushed on, not wanting to hear what Brolin wanted to say to him. "You told me to write a story about it, about a majestic animal, about the relations between all that the elk is and my protagonist, Joe. And I did that. I wrote of Joe and an Indian warrior coming upon each other in the wilds of Wyoming and how they fought each other, meaning to do so to the death. And how the appearance of an elk stag on the mountain ridge above them made them both stop and realize how futile their fighting was and then separate and go their own way. I wrote that with passion. Man against the elements, the majesty of nature, the bonding of men in dire straits."

"That wasn't the bonding of men," Brolin said in a voice both soft and full of steel. "Those men fell away from each other when confronted with the majesty of nature, as represented in the elk, Jules. Don't you see? Nature won. That didn't show the strength of your protagonist; it showed his weakness. What I see inside you, what I think you have to give in your writing is showing the ascendance of your protagonist over nature and over other men. The passion in the protagonist's relationship with nature, as symbolized by that elk stag, is not in accommodating or respecting the elk, but in mastering and possessing it. And the same can be said of the man, the Indian warrior."

Brolin's voice had become insistent; he was flooding Jules's mind with the power of his smooth, honey-toned voice and the strength of his storytelling. Jules felt almost as if he was going into a trance. He could feel the pressure of Brolin's grip on his wrist, and now he could feel the palm of Brolin's other hand on his thigh. Jules felt his chest heaving, and, looking at Brolin, he could see that his mentor was similarly affected. They were both bare-chested and in colorful sarongs, just as Sid was. They had gone completely native. Jules felt what was coming next, but the mesmerizing effect of Brolin's voice and Jules's aching need to produce the writing that Brolin wanted, to become the writer that Brolin said he was capable of becoming, possessed the young man, and he made no move to stop his mentor.

"Bonding is important to a writer, Jules," Brolin was saying. "Experiencing bonding and letting the passion of that build and pour down to your fingertips as your fingers sit on the keys of the typewriter, and imbuing your writing with a full, mature knowledge of passion through experience . . . ." His eyes were fully intent on Jules now, although Jules was still unable to look up at him, and his hand on Jules's thigh had slipped into a fold in the sarong and rested on the warm, smooth skin inside Jules's thigh, high up. He was lightly stroking the inside of Jules's thigh with his index finger and a thumb, sending ripples of electricity through Jules's body.

"You need to acquire a much deeper and richer experience to even begin to know what the passion is, Jules. Bonding. Bonding. I could—"

"Kiai Brolin. Kiai Brolin! Venerable teacher! Look what I've caught." The chestnut brown houseboy, Sid, full of life and laughter and with a smile as broad as his handsome face, was running up the beach toward Jules and Brolin, a big fat fish in his hand. "We eat well tonight, Kiai Brolin. The god's are good to us."

Brolin joined the infectious laughter of his houseboy and also joined in the rejoicing over the catch. When he turned back to Jules, though, his young apprentice was gone and only the scattered sheets of his "only very good" short story and the picture of the majestic elk stag remained where he had been sitting on the pillows beside the low table at the palm-treed verge of the white-sand beach.

Hours later, unable to sleep, burning with the implications of what Brolin had told him, knowing now, instinctively and irrevocably, that Brolin was right—that he would never be able to write with the necessary passion until he had allowed himself to experience passion—Jules crept out of his room in one wing of the thatched hut and quietly moved to the doorway of Brolin's room in the other wing.

They were there. The little Sumatran houseboy was flat on his belly on Brolin's bed, his legs tight together and his hands firmly gripping the brass rods of the headboard above him for dear life as Brolin, nude and crouched above him, encasing the pelvis of the smaller man with his strong thighs, his sensuous fingers wrapped around the Sumatran's wrists, plunged a thick and long cock between the houseboy's pert butt cheeks again and again and again. Sid was whimpering and Brolin was panting hard. Jules stood, transfixed, and moaning slightly to himself as his hand went to his own rising cock and the passion of the moment flooded into him. This, more than anything Brolin had been telling him earlier, demonstrated the majesty and monstrousness of what full, passionate possession meant. Jules's mind started to race and all sorts of sensations and images flooded in. He withdrew from the doorway.

A pen and some paper; he had to find a pen and some paper. He had to write.

Now!

* * * *

Jules wrote far into the night, feverishly. He knew the writing was better than he had ever accomplished before. But he also knew that it wasn't good enough. His mentor had been right. The experience of the passion was what was missing. What he had seen earlier had transmitted to him in some degree, but that wasn't enough. He knew now what he had to do. He had to have the passion; he had to become the writer he wanted to be.

He was focused so intently on his work that he hadn't noticed the sounds until they had become insistent, close by. Drums and shots and screams.

Jules jumped up from his desk and ran to the window and pushed aside the palm frond matting. The sky was aglow over Bengkulu, lighting up the beach and the pounding surf of the Indian Ocean. Bengkulu was burning. It seemed as if the whole sky to the west was ablaze. A shot rang out nearby, and Jules instinctively fell away from the window.

"Quick. No time. The storage shed," Brolin muttered in a guttural whisper as he lurched into the room and pulled Jules up from the floor. He was completely naked, his firm muscle twitching in the shock of the moment, his manhood and ball sack hanging and swinging low.

"What . . .?" Jules muttered, dazed by the sudden eruption of activity on their peaceful, isolated beach.

"No time. There's a hiding place in the storage shed. And it's concrete. We could be quickly burned out here or plugged by a stray bullet."

"Sid . . .?" Jules said idiotically as he permitted Brolin to pull him toward the back door and the pathway away from the beach toward the storage shed. His sarong went to his ankles and constricted his movement so that he hobbled in a shuffling gait as Brolin propelled him along. Brolin reached down and tore the material off Jules, freeing the young man's movement but making him as naked as his mentor was.

"Sid's PNI," gasped through his pants, and then when the sense of that didn't seem to register with Jules, he spoke again. "He's a member of the communist movement. If they come here, it will be because of him. The Dutch are burning out the resistance movement. If they find we're harboring a PNI member, we'll be burned out too. Sid's gone into hiding away from here."

Both of them were panting heavily when they got to the shed. Looking back toward the beach, Jules could see figures of men with lifted torches and rifles, silhouetted against the glow on the horizon from Bengkulu, coming through the palm tree verge and heading toward their hut. Brolin pulled him roughly into the hut, moved some boxes aside at the back of the small room, pushed Jules roughly down on his back in a narrow space been the back of a wooden-back shelving rack that went nearly to the ceiling and a concrete block wall, and then, after pulling the boxes back to cover the entrance to their hiding place, and sprawled down, full-length, on top of Jules. There was no room in the confined space for him to do otherwise, but Jules was fully aware of his mentor's nakedness, and the hairiness of the very fit man's chest, heart pounding and muscles taut, on top of his own naked chest.

Adrenaline was pumping through both of the men. Brolin couldn't help himself, having wanted to be doing what he then did for the entire two months they had been in Sumatra. And Jules, aroused by what he'd seen Brolin and Sid doing earlier and the sudden awakening to passion couldn't help himself either. The danger and the passion of the moment swept them both up into its clutches, and Brolin was cupping Jules's head in his hands and was kissing him deeply in his full and sensuous lips. At the same time his pelvis was grinding against Jules's. Jules reach down and took possession of Brolin's cock and felt it grown long and thick and hard. His own cock was rising too, and Brolin was left with no doubts about Jules's willingness. Brolin took one of his hands away from Jules's cheek and spit on it and moved it down between Jules's thighs and found his young student's virgin hole.

Jules arched his back and rocked his head back, away from Brolin's lips, and opened his mouth wide, preparing to scream out in surprise and pain as Brolin entered him with his moistened finger. Brolin's strong hand went to Jules's mouth, however, and covered both his mouth and his nose, as his finger continued to probe. Jules was trembling and gasping for air beneath the stifling gag and he was beginning to black out. Brolin released his hand over Jules's air passages, but he replace his hand with his possessing mouth. He was kneeling on his knees now between Jules's thighs and pulling Jules's legs up to his shoulders.

Jules felt the large dick head at his hole as Brolin removed his searching and stretching fingers, and Jules arched his back again and silently screamed around Brolin's probing tongue as the head of the teacher's cock obtained purchase just inside Jules's hole.

They both froze at the sound of voices outside the door to the storage shed. The room was full of light now that blazed over the top of the shelving unit that didn't quite meet the ceiling and through cracks in the backside and around the edges of the case.

Voices. Angry voices. Firing off rapid-fire exclamations in Indonesian, clearly not pleased that they hadn't found any communists to exterminate. Jules knew now that their lives depended on him not screaming. This was a moment such as he'd written about. But the reality was so much more intense than his imagination had been when he was writing. He now fully appreciated what his teacher had been trying to tell him about experiencing being necessary to capture the passion of a story that would lift it head and shoulders above the competition—about danger and what a man had to do in the face of danger to survive and to come out as the master.

Brolin took advantage of the moment of Jules's fear of making any noise to start the plowing of his plump, experienced cock up the young virginal ass canal.

Regardless of the danger of the moment, Jules started to whimper and to struggle underneath Brolin, the hard thick possession of the older man being almost more than Jules could take. Brolin covered Jules's mouth and nose with his hand again, and all of the fight went out of Jules as he began to drift out from oxygen starvation and Brolin's dick continued its throbbing invasion up his canal.

And then the light and the voices were gone, and Brolin had removed his hand and was kissing and sucking and nibbling on young Jules's neck and nipples and the pits under his arms as the master's cock bottomed deep inside the tender canal and began to pump and pump and pump deep inside his student. Harder and faster. Jules was gasping and groaning and moaning now.

Brolin had gathered control of himself enough to murmur that he'd try to stop fucking Jules if the pain was unbearable and that's what the young man wanted, but Jules was too far gone in the experience now. He could only manage and breathless, "No-o-o."

"No, what?" Brolin grunted.

"No . . . don't . . . stop," Jules cried out.

And Brolin fucked on. he had Jules's cock in his fist and he relentlessly stroked him off until Jules ejaculated with a gasp and collapsed back to the floor. But Brolin fucked on and on and on. The passion flooded back into Jules and he moaned and groaned and cried out for the fuck, his mind racing, forming words and images and experience-filled themes to pour out onto the typewriter keys.

* * * *

The next day dawned much like any other on Sumatra. Brilliant sunshine filtering through rustling palm fronds at the verge of a bright white sandy beach. The surf relentlessly lapping at the beach and the birds chirping away in the inland pine trees. It was as if nothing had happened the previous night that was in any way out of the ordinary. And the people would continue living their lives as if nothing had happened the previous night, as if the Dutch and their native underlings hadn't conducted yet another of a long series of nights of the long knives. And if the mothers and wives of the young men who had been singled out as PNI members or supporters mourned the permanent absence of their loved ones, they did none of the keening in public. The Dutch were the gods on Sumatra. There might come a day when all of the people of the archipelago were free to think what they wanted to think and do what they wanted to do, but 1918 was not such a time.

Brolin was still abed, having had his fill of both Sid and Jules the previous night, and exhausted from the loss of adrenaline over their near brush with the long knives of those doing the bloody bidding of the Dutch.

Jules, again wearing the sarong from the previous night, was walking the surf line of the beach, grappling in his mind a reworking of the elk story. He didn't want to write a totally new theme. He still wanted to work with the elk image. He wanted to show his teacher that he had been right—that Jules's brilliance as a writer could be touched and could shine out increasingly as he gained passion and experience. He knew now that Sid would not be spending all of his nights in the hut—that Jules's himself would be draining the teacher of far more than words in his search for new and richer experience and for the passion he needed to convey to his readers.

Jules had been walking for long, lost in thought. When he looked up, at the sound of rustling in the jungle beyond the fringe of palm trees, he discovered that he was well beyond their beach area toward the east, in the direction away from Bengkulu. He walked toward the sound.

What he first saw were the bright colors. Lengths of brightly colored sarong material, waving and dipping in the thick covering of ferns under the palm trees. Then he heard the giggling. He moved stealthily to behind a fat palm tree and observed Sid in the process of fucking a comely Sumatran lass. She was on her back with her legs spread wide, and he was crouched between her thighs and leaning over her, his lips working a nipple on her plump breast, his hand caressing her cheek, and his dick thrusting strongly in and out of her cunt. She was thrusting her hips up to meet his downward thrusts and was laughing and moaning for him.

More experience, Jules thought. And he watched the two making love, drinking in the experience of it, trying to merge with them from his position behind the tree. He could feel his cock engorging and he was stroking himself as he watched them fucking with abandon and obvious enjoyment. The passion and enjoyment of the two were obvious. Jules felt that he should rejoice in what they were doing with each other, both fully giving and receiving, no regrets, no shyness, no inhibitions. But there was something missing. What Jules wanted to write about—what Arthur Brolin had defined to him the previous day that he, deep down, wanted to write about—was possession, not mutual satisfaction. No, not the abandon of shared passion, really, but the possession of, the mastery of one over the other. There had to be a winner. Someone had to be in total control.

"You want to fuck her too?" Sid was asking, having seen Jules well before Jules realized that his presence was known. "Come, yayi. Come, younger brother. She is very nice and ripe. She does very nice ju ju. And she likes you. She's always telling me she wants to make ju ju with the serious, strong, young American. And you are beautiful too. She wants you too. Come, yayi, come and share the joy."

What a simple culture, Jules thought. Last night Sid was escaping just ahead of a mob that wanted his blood, and today he was leisurely fucking a comely young lass on the beach. Jules tentatively moved toward the coupling lovers as Sid pulled his cock out of the girl's cunt and made way for Jules. Not being real sure what to do, Jules went down on his knees between the girl's outstretched legs. She looked up at him and smiled a big smile of welcome. Sid leaned down and kissed Jules on the lips to show the complete abandonment of the time and place.

There was no need for Jules to prepare his cock. It was already at full attention and was dripping precum. The young Sumatran girl gave a little giggle and came up on her knees. She took Jules's cock in her hand and straddled his thighs with her own and guided him inside her. She was deep and moist and her passage walls were undulating around Jules's cock. She flung her arms around his waist and began to rock back and forth on his cock with her hips. He joined in that motion and buried his face between the fragrant mounds of her pert, full breasts. The girl gave a little lurch and a gasp and Jules looked up to see that Sid was crouched behind her and obviously had entered her ass with his cock. The three of them rocked on and on and on as Jules's two companions gave small, satisfied exclamations and muttered to each other happily in the sing song tones of the Indonesian language.

Jules and Sid came almost simultaneously and the Sumatran girl cried out her satisfaction of having been doubly ridden and filled. She was the first to move. She extracted herself from the two young men and smiled and chattered to them in low, silky tones as she, rewrapped her colorful sarong around her waist and backed away to a place where she had left a water jug. And then she turned and disappeared into the jungle.

Jules and Sid sat there, on their haunches, facing each other. Jules knew he should feel satisfied. But he wasn't. He wanted possession. He wanted mastery. He wanted to win over the elements and other men. Women were fine, but men were equal adversaries. They were what he needed to master.

Sid gave him a little smile and started to rise and reach for his own sarong. Searing passion flashed through Jules's brain, though. With a cry, he came up onto the balls of his feet and grabbed Sid by his hips and turned him and pushed him down on top of his spread sarong on all fours. Then, crouching behind and above him, Jules thrust his still-engorged dick inside Sid's ass and rode him hard, fucking him like a dog, until Sid collapsed to the ground underneath him, gasping and groaning and moaning. Jules followed him to the ground, grinding his cock deep inside the young Sumatran, while his prey, his majestic elk, writhed under him and whimpered for relief. At last, Jules spouted off deep inside the Sumatran houseboy, who just lay there panting, a big smile on his face, as Jules rose, rewrapped his sarong and turned and walked back up the beach with strong, proud strides.

* * * *

"Excellent, excellent. Ready to be published. Sure to win an award," Arthur Brolin was crowing with pride and full satisfaction after reading Jules's rewrite of a story of the elk stag the following day. Once more they were sitting at the low table at the palm-tree edge of the beach and watching a gingerly treading Sid cast his net in the incoming tide of the Indian Ocean. This time, however, Jules was cuddled into Brolin's lap, his back to Brolin's chest, and Brolin's cock deep inside his student. Brolin was rocking his pelvis gently back and forth in rhythm with the rustling of the wind through the palm fronds overhead, and Jules was doing his best to concentrate. He'd give Brolin is enjoyment for now. But before the year was over, Jules was determined that Brolin would be begging for Jules to fuck him—and Jules would only be doing so when it pleased him.

In Jules's rewrite, his protagonist, now named Pete, had tracked a mighty elk stag up in the snowy and rocky reaches above the timberline of the Wyoming Grand Tetons for days until both he and the elk were near exhaustion. When he finally cornered the elk, he found that an Indian brave had been hunting it as well and had fallen while notching his arrow to launch against the beast, which was upon him, lashing at him with his antlers. Pete had shot the elk, but it hadn't died. And then Pete's rifle had locked up and the wounded elk had pawed the ground and lowered its fourteen-point rack and charged the hunter, forcing him to the ground and piercing him again and again with the sharp points of his antlers. Pete had fought back with his bare hands, helped by a weakened and bloodied Indian brave, and Pete had, in the end, killed the elk. The Indian and the White hunter had briefly stared at each other, taking each other's measure, prepared to take the struggle to its ultimate conclusion. But in the end, the Indian had bowed to Pete's mastery of the elk. The brave had gone off with the hide, but he had insisted on the ascendance of the White hunter, and Pete had its head hanging over his fireplace and the Indian brave's turquoise-beaded breastplate lying on the mantel.

"You are ready to write your novel of man against the elements and of male bonding now," the teacher said, his voice full of approval. "And I know it will strike a note in an America just opening up to its destiny of mastery of the world. Jules Kincaid will soon be a household name."

"Not Jules Kincaid," the student said quietly. "From now on I will be J. Harvey Kincaid."

And J. Harvey Kincaid wrote his novel of the great American west, full of its symbolism of a new, resource and space rich nation coming into its own and possessing and mastering everything in its wake as it reached out to embrace the world. And when his first novel won the Pulitzer Prize, he kept writing the story over and over and over again. And the depth of his theme and the richness of his imagery increased manifold as he lived life on his own terms and sank into being his theme.

And before the year ended, Brolin would be begging to be fucked by Jules, and Jules had met and mastered and possessed many of Sid's Sumatran friends.

Pacific

Hong Kong Canyon Connection

The first thing I learned about the Hong Kong high finance corporations when I was promoted and moved from Singapore to the bustling former British island colony was that in the modern Chinese commercial world, the boss was god. The second thing I learned was that my boss, Henry Lu, fucked the male employees he was attracted to and that I had been promoted to here from the Singapore office because Henry Lu was attracted to me.

For the first month, he bedded me discretely, although even from the beginning there was a touch of the exhibitionist risky about sex with him. He admitted to me early on that public fucking turned him on. He maintained a suite at the Mandarin Oriental, and his car met me at Chek Lap Kok international airport. I was taken directly to the Mandarin Oriental, and with my luggage still in the trunk of the limo—just in case I didn't please—Henry Lu had me suck him erect in a back booth in the hotel bar and then he took me up to his suite and showed me that Chinese men knew a few tricks of swordsmanship that I had not encountered in Singapore.

They take business very seriously, my firm, and after that first "test," it was made quite clear to me that Henry Lu owned me—in several different aspects of my life—and when he called I was to come.

I had been working in the Seng Heng Hong Kong Connaught Road offices for some time when Lu told me one afternoon that that night was one of "those" nights that I was to be prepared to serve his needs, whatever they might be, and that I was to be in his office at precisely 8:15. Such a summons was not that unusual; Hu had been fucking me regularly for a couple of months on the desk top in his office after hours. I didn't mind this, because he was really hot, all taut muscle and flexibility, and he could reach great depths inside me, hold himself in check until I was ready for him, and recharge quickly. He wasn't all that old, and he was being really good to me professionally. But I thought it a little strange that he'd given a precise time I should be there. Unusually he had me stay in my office and he rang me up after his secretaries and assistants had cleared out.

We worked in one of those all-glass downtown high-rises in Hong Kong's Central District, where land was at such a premium that the office buildings faced each other closely across narrow canyons bottomed by busy streets. Hu's office was on the eighteenth floor, and he got off on topping me in front of floor-to-ceiling glass in the early evening hours while it was still light and while the traffic noise from below was still at a high level. But at 8:15 this time of year, it would be darker out than when we usually fucked in his office. Not a problem for me, because I hadn't planned anything that evening, but it meant I had to stay around in the office a little longer than usual.

I showed up to his office early and he kept me up against the wall, just inside the door, for several minutes, while he got us all hot and bothered with his roaming hands and lips. We undressed each other there and then rubbed chests, bellies, and cocks until we were both panting and hard for each other. He went down on me there, my back up against the wall and him kneeling between my thighs. He was really good with his tongue and teeth and the soft inner sides of his cheeks, not to mention his fingers at my balls and back door, and it wasn't long until I'd

540

creamed his tonsils and nearly collapsed on top of him, with my knees buckling at the intensity of the cocksucking.

It was almost precisely 8:30 when Hu stood and led me over to his desk. I couldn't have asked for a more studly guy bossing me around. I took my usual stance on the desk top: on my back; butt at the edge of the desk, legs open wide, held by my hands; my back to those floor-to-ceiling glass windows. I was waiting, all atremble, as usual, for those lips at my ass, followed by the cool feel of the KY, and then by the invigorating drive of that seven-inch, very thick cock that I'd come to love plowing my canal.

But tonight, to my surprise, Hu told me to come down off the desk and turn around, stand on the floor, feet wide apart and lay my chest on the desk top. I did as he asked—he, after all, was the boss. And as he was pressing his face into my crack, successfully finding my puckered hole, and giving that attention with his lips and tongue, I rested my cheek on the desk blotter and sighed and moaned for him, assuring him that I was enjoying his attentions to me. His face came away and his teeth gave my butt cheeks a little nip here and there, causing me to writhe a bit, rubbing my rehardening dick on the leather surface of Hu's executive desk. I gave a little lurch and yelp and instinctively grabbed for the corners of the desk with my hands and jerked my head up as I felt the first of his KY-slathered fingers enter me and begin to probe.

When my head came up, my eyes went to the window, and, instinctively, to the glass office tower immediately across the narrow Connaught Road canyon from our own glass office tower. Few lights were on over there, so it wasn't hard for me to zero in on a brightly lit office in the mirroring building just about opposite from ours and two stories higher. That particular window was arresting, because there was a young, well-cut Chinese man leaning against that window, looking out, seemingly looking directly at me. The most arresting aspect of that young man was that he was stark naked, his hands spread out wide and supporting him against the window, his forehead plastered to the window, his legs out at a wide stance—and another naked, bulky and hirsute, but not exactly fat, Caucasian man kneeling behind him, his face buried in the young man's butt, and his arms around the young man's legs, hands tightly holding the young man's thighs.

I could clearly see the young man's face, and his facial expression at having his ass eaten out was surely, I thought, no less pleasure driven than my own was at what Hu was doing at my back door. Interesting, I thought, An older Caucasian man doing a younger Chinese man over there, and an older Chinese man about to fuck me, a younger Caucasian man, over here.

As I watched, the hairy man across the divide stood. I saw his hand glide back around the young man's hips, and I saw the young man lurch as the hairy man forced fingers into his asshole. I knew that was what he was doing, because at the same time, the second of Hu's fingers forced its way into my ass, and I also lurched. The hairy man brought his body in close behind that of the young man, and his lips went to the hollow of the young man's neck. They both seemed to have their eyes glued on me. I felt Hu lower his chest closely on my shoulder blades, his fingers still in my asshole, and he kissed and nuzzled the hollow of my neck. I licked my lips and moaned, not sure whether I was doing this on my own or suggestively, because the young Chinese man across the glass canyon was doing the same.

Hu came up off my back; the hairy man pulled away from the young man's back. Hu clutched my hips; the hairy many clutched the young Chinese man's hips. In one swift, painful movement, Hu entered me with his seven thick inches and plowed up to the root. I howled to the ceiling in pain and surprise, and grabbed back at him with my hands, trying to pull him off me. His brutality was a surprise. But my eyes were glued to the window, where the hairy man had impaled the young Chinese man in one swift movement and the young man had lifted his head and howled to the ceiling and clutched back at the hands imprisoning his hips with his own hands.

The young man's eyes were linked to mine, beseeching me for help, trying to convey his pain and suffering at having been possessed so fully and brutally. But I couldn't help him; I was trying to seek the same solace from him. Mouths open in a screams that almost made the separating window glass between us reverberate, the young man and I shared our debauching and Hu stroked my ass with his huge tool swiftly and deeply and the hairy man stroked the ass of his prisoner equally swiftly and deeply. All four of us were in a quartet of open mouths, cries of passion, and slitted eyes.

Hu and the hairy man were keeping the same rhythm and tempo, almost as if they were doing so on purpose, and I knew exactly the point at which my pain was overridden by the pleasure of this wild fuck because my emotions were being exactly mirrored in the eyes of that young Chinese man across the glass canyon divide. Everything was all right now. No, more than all right—ecstasy. I was having the hot ride of my life, and it was only being enhanced because I saw that my young Chinese counterpart was also having the hot ride of his life. I writhed and moaned and slammed my hips back to meet each thrust of Hu, just as the young man was doing to his hairy attacker.

And I knew exactly when Hu would release and flood my insides with his rich cream because I could see the point of release in the eyes of the hairy man. And my mouth joined that of the young man in my cry of joy at being filled so fully and so deeply.

Hu collapsed onto my back, and the hairy man collapsed against the young man onto the window across the canyon. The hairy man lifted a hand to the young man's cheek and turned his face fully to the window, making the young Chinese man's eyes latch onto mine for a last time. Hu was doing the same to me, and I could see the hairy man whispering in his young lover's ear just as Hu whispered in mine.

"See that man over there, the hairy one?" Hu whispered. "That's my golf partner, Ned Treadwell. He and I planned this little mirroring encounter for you and his young employee. I hope you liked it."

I'll never be able to fully tell Hu just how hot this glass canyon connection was for me.

Out of the Sun

I was happy that Ti had withered away within the last moon death, because there were now only eight elders in the village of the gatherers. But eight was more than enough. I was already bruised and sore as never before when Ai, the great chief, had taken his staff out of me that first time, having spilled the first of the seedings of the night before I was to die for the village. I did not care. Let the pain and the filling come, I thought. The danger for all of the people was near at hand. An offering to appease the mountain was needed. Once chosen, I did not care what happened to me on the night before the appeasement.

It was an honorable death. And death was ever present here on the more fertile side of the island, in the very lee of the thunder mountain. If scarce harvest did not take us, it was either the body weakening and sufferings, or it was the meat people from the other end of the island—constantly attacking us and taking, taking, taking. They were much larger and more robust than we were; we were like the sand before their crashing waves.

Ai was withdrawing and Ga had moved into his place. Ga looked almost sad. He had favored me for many moon dyings. I had found him enthralling and, as he favored me with extra food he had gathered and the murmurings of his longings and wishes, I had begun to mold to his desires. Now, as he gently turned me on my back and raised my hips with folded palm-leaf matting, he whispered to me of his regret and sorrow. Regret that he had not taken me sooner, because if he had, that would have made me unfit to be selected for the appeasement offering. Sorrow that now this would be our only coupling, because on the morrow, I and the seeding of the strength of the village would go into the burning mouth of the thunder mountain.

Ga came in between my legs, and I arched back and cried out as he entered me. Ga was younger, more virile, and both thicker and longer of staff than the elderly, withering Ai, and for the first time my channel walls were being stretched to the limit and tested for their flexibility. I, also out of regret of what now would never be with Ga, held him inside me and stretched out the taking for as long as possible before his seed joined and mingled with that of Ai deep inside me. It was with a sigh and a groan that he gave up his essence inside me, and it was with a sob of loss that he withdrew his staff and turned from me, not being able to see what my eyes had to tell him.

The mean and vindictive Fre was next. He had wanted me when Ga was showing me favor, but there was nothing about him that I had found endurable. He wanted to own and turn everything to his pleasure, and he was not at all picky about what he would do to own it. Until Ga invited me to gather with him, once I had reached my season, I had to hide from Fre during the gathering. I had heard the stories of young men who did not elude him during the gatherings, most barely into their season, and how he had trapped and ruined them.

Now he was doing all he could to ruin me. I was bent over on my belly on the palm-leaf matting, and he was thrusting into me from the rear. Long, hard, rough thrustings. And he had fisted the hair on my head in one hand and was cruelly arching my torso back to him. And he was slapping me on my sitter cheeks hard as he rode me. The other elders were muttering and telling him to be more gentle, and I was pleading with him to slow and give me more time to take him. But he just laughed and continued on. He spilled his seed, but did not declare it, as ceremony required him to do. He wanted to enjoy me longer, so he kept on thrusting even as his staff was growing smaller inside me.

He could not fool the thunder mountain, though. The mountain knew he had seeded already, and the mountain showed its displeasure at his breach of ceremony. The ground underneath us began to move and groan, and the thunder mountain began to rumble its complaint that ceremony wasn't being followed. There were flashes of daylight outside the open doorway to the hut, as the mountain attempted to move the ceremony straight into the next sun birth—before all of the preparations had been made and all of the requirements met. The wailing in the village at the verge of the beach conveyed the fear of the community of gatherers. They had been sad when I had been chosen, but this was our lot since the dawn of time. We merely served at the pleasure of the gods of the underworld, and we were privileged to live near their entrance at the top of the thunder mountain. It was a melancholy honor to be the sacrifice for my people. I could hardly bear to withstand their fear and wailing at thunder mountains display of its displeasure.

For me, this anger from the mountain meant the elders had to shorten my ordeal, and they clutched at Fre. Knowing of his guilt, knowing that he could not fool the thunder mountain as he fooled his fellow elders, Fre pulled away in fear, and the next of the elders quickly took his place and built up and spilled his seed inside me as fast as he could.

The mountain quieted then, and the elders returned to a more decorous, leisurely fulfilling of their ceremonial duties—filling me with their seed throughout the night so that their authority and strength would go into the maw of the mountain with me and thus placate the gods of the underworld.

An hour before dawn, I was awakened, with an elder still crouched between my legs and mingling seed with seed as an offering to the gods. And I was guided, my knees almost unable to bear me out of the hut and toward the surf, now angry as well, coming hard upon the beach and crashing up in big fountains of spray. The sea felt the rumbling of the ground underneath our feet and joined in the angry demand that we atone—for what, we knew not. Had Fre done something else unspeakable before we became aware that the thunder mountain was demanding an offering to bring balance back into our world? I could only regret that Fre was not eligible to be sacrificed, although I was sure that the mountain would not accept him even if he had been untouched and pure before the ceremony began. I'm sure it would have just spit him back out.

My first duty was to try to calm the sea as I hung there open to it, awaiting the dawn of the sun cycle. If the sea calmed, I would be spared for another sun cycle to discern whether the thunder mountain calmed as well. If it did, I would be free and we would be saved. If the sea didn't calm—and it never had before when a ceremony was required as long as any of the villagers still with memory could recollect—I would be carried to the top of the thunder mountain and thrown into the burning maw of the mouth of the gods with the hope that this would be the gatherers' deliverance.

I hung there in what I knew were to be my last hours, welcoming the rebirth of the sun, hoping for it, as all of the villagers did as well. Sometimes, legend told us, the sun had not been reborn on the sun cycle of the thunder mountain celebration—the sky had remained as black as the sun death cycle. On these occasions, custom required that all of the unseasoned boy children in addition to the newly seasoned offering were to be given to the thunder mountain.

We had lost too many of our boy children this season cycle already—to a wasting away and to a raid from the meat eaters from the dark forest that separated our two peoples on the island.

But as hoped for, at the moment expected, a glint of reddish-yellow light appeared across the horizon out into the sea, and a cheer of relief and joy went up from the gatherers assembled between where I was hung and the village. The sun was being reborn. And gloriously so. The reds and yellows and oranges and purples as the sliver became a line and then a widening band, were heartening to all. Only I would need to be given to the gods. And, as afflicted and sore and bruised as I was, I rejoiced with all of my people.

The sun rose from the water to greet us and to promise life and sustenance, and the people continued their rejoicing.

My rejoicing abated, however, and slowly dawned into a new fear, a new concern of imbalance and danger. I waited as long as I could, willing myself not to see what I was growing to know was a reality.

When I could contain myself no longer, I bellowed out a warning, sending my clarion call above the cheering and rejoicing of the gatherers. "Warrior canoes! The meat eaters! Coming out of the sun in abundance. Run, run for your lives."

It took several moments for the gatherers all to hear me, but no one here was too old not to know what the war canoes of the meat eaters boiling out of the sun in the morning meant.

Shortly I was alone, tied to the crossed palms. A lone offering now to the wrath of the meat eaters, as my people melted into the forest beyond the village.

What had we done so wrong as to bring this upon ourselves, I wondered, as I strained against my bonds, trying to break loose and escape. Thunder mountain was adding its displeasure; it had resumed its rumbling, and the ground was moving in waves again—and the waves were crashing more heavily on the beach, sending curtains of foam into a sky that was darkening. The sun was dimming, perhaps having decided to leave us to our fate.

And then they appeared, as of ghosts, through the curtain of sea spray. Big, bulky men, heavy of muscle, tall of stature, larger and more robust than any of the gatherers. Naked and their staffs thick and long, swaying heavily between their legs as they strode out of the spray. Their eggs bigger than bird's eggs and hanging low. I moaned at the thought of the stories I'd heard of youths who had been captured by them and had escaped back to the gatherers—but not until after they had been sorely used and stretched and split by the meat-eater monsters.

They were all carrying clubs, ready to raid our stores after a good harvest. Striding in front was a particularly large and muscle-bulging warrior, painted for conquest, and obviously the leader of the raiding party.

He strode up close to me, blocking the light from the saving sun, as I writhed on the crossed palms, still trying to free myself. A nearly equally gigantic meat eater moved to stand beside him. The leader waved for the other raiders to continue on into the village, in search of grain and conquest.

The leader of the band laughed at my feeble attempt to escape. He backhanded me once across the mouth, which sent my head snapping to one side. And, as I was trying to bring my vision back into focus, he leaned down, and cut away the bonds at my ankles, grabbed the backs of my thighs in his big, strong hands, and lifted and spread my legs.

I screamed to the gods of the thunder mountain for relief and release as he crouched under my raised hips and thrust his splitting staff up into my already beleaguered channel. All I wanted to do at that moment was to die, and the staff of the leader of the raiders was so long and thick and was being thrust so hard inside me that I thought I was soon to have my deliverance.

But the dark period of taking and the flooding of my insides with the seed fluid of the village elders gave me enough protection to stave off death, although it also denied me the relief of unconsciousness. I found that even when the other meat eater who had stopped before me with the band's leader moved to behind me, grabbed my hips with his big, calloused hands, and set his staff to working inside me in countermotion to his leader, I still could not drift away from this ordeal.

All I could think was that I would not reach the fiery mouth of the gods alive, and even if that were possible, I now was defiled, because the leader of the meat eaters was already jerking and grunting and flowing his accursed seed inside me. As he did so, his hand left my thigh and he grabbed up his club, and I knew my time had come.

But just as he was about to strike and the second man was pumping his seed deep inside me, the rumbling of the thunder mountain turned into true thunder, and the sky blackened. And then it was replaced by brilliant light. And from out of the sun, straight down from out of what was now revealed to be the risen sun, came balls of fire. Hitting the ground and hissing. Hitting the thatched roofs of the village huts and setting them afire. Setting the very palm leaves over our heads afire.

Pandemonium suddenly reigned among the raider band of the meat eaters, and they were running back out of the village, almost entirely empty-handed, and dashing for the canoes through the stormy surf. My assaulters were among the first to reach the canoes and to start paddling them hard back out to sea.

Almost as soon as the mountain's anger had started, it ceased. Totally. Although the balls of fire still hissed in the sand, they were quickly turning from bright red and yellow to a grayish black. The earth no longer was moving; the mountain no longer was rumbling. The sea had calmed. The raiders, however, could not see this. They were far down the island coast and out to sea now, racing back to their own people. Not looking back at what would now be seen as a formidable defense of the gatherers against raids.

It was all becoming quite clear to me now. The thunder mountain wasn't angry with the gatherers. It was angry at the meat eaters for preparing this attack upon our village. The thunder mountain was pleased with us. So pleased that it wanted to protect us from the meat eaters. We were blessed.

As the villagers returned, tentatively, led by the eight elders, I was testifying in loud voice to how the mountain had saved us and prophesying that it would protect us from raids from the meat eaters as long as their warriors could speak of the events of this sun cycle.

Ai approached me, perplexed, and Fre immediately started nay-saying me, claiming that I was only trying to escape the ceremony. But Ga interceded, declaring in commanding, reasoned tones that all that I had said had come to pass had, indeed, come to pass. He challenged Fre to pick up and hold one of the mysterious, still-smoking stones that had appeared in profusion on our beach if he spoke the truth. Or to explain what limited amount they had all seen and heard while they were hiding in the forest. The sky *had* darkened. The sea *had* been angry when they ran away and was calm now. The mountain no longer was speaking to them in its anger; the earth was not trembling its ire beneath our feet.

Fre leaned down to take up a hissing stone, but as he drew near, a grimace set on his face and he snatched his hand up and turned and walked quickly into the now-smoldering village.

If I was lying, Ga went on, pulling the attention of all from the retreating Fre, what explained this calm that had fallen on them without the completion of the ceremony? No, Ga, proclaimed, the gods had accepted me as an offering as I was. I had given the prophesy of long relief from the raiding meat eaters—who everyone here had seen with their own eyes—but who now had disappeared. I therefore was a true prophet of the gods of the underworld, fit to sit with elders.

All were silent, and then Ga became bolder. He took the knife accorded to him by his position in the village and carefully freed me from the tree. All the time he was speaking in commanding tones to all who were gathered about. As the presumed elder who was to replace Ai when his time with the gods came, Ga said, he had much to learn from their new prophet. We would draw rations for three days and withdraw to the sacred ledge half way up to the mouth of the thunder mountain, and he would commune with me.

Ga and I ultimately found the perfect position for communing, with him sitting on a moss-covered stone and me sitting in his lap, facing the great sea below and using the heels of my feet on the ground as leverage to rise and lower my now well-opened channel on his powerful staff as he stroked my staff with one hand and pinched my nipples with the long, elegant fingers of the other.

Perfect Harvest Year

The sun was in half stride to the top of the sky, And Xulatiki stood proudly, his purple cloak billowing around his perfect body in his first year of full manhood. His eyes, and, indeed, the eyes of all those about him, all of the woman of the remote Pacific island who were able to walk or find someone to carry them to this place, were focused at the top of the smoking sacred mountain and the swirl of color that could be seen there. Xulatiki's flawless body, tallowed and glistening in the rays of the god sun, whose full presence had emphasized the perfection of this year's ritual, was taut and trembling slightly with anticipation. Other than the purple cape attached at golden bands around his biceps, wrists, just above his knees, and at his ankles, the young prince was proudly naked.

The full appearance of the sun on this propitious day was only a further favorable sign for this year. Xulatiki was starting his kingship today by right of the ritual; he had been judged to be the most magnificently formed of all the young men in the small Pacific archipelago who had come into full manhood this season. But he also was becoming king by right of position, which would mean there would be no maneuvering for power among the elite this year, maneuvering that could only detract from the purpose of this ritual. Eighteen years before this ritual day, his own father and mother had been the chosen ones, and thus he was doubly chosen, something that not even the oldest croon now staring intently at the stone platform built on the rim of the smoking mountain top above their heads could remember to have happened.

The women spread across the side of the conical, volcano-formed mountain at the center of the main island were the first to notice the change in the activity on the platform above. The cessation of the swirling dancing of the many colors, the raising of arms that brought up a curtain of purple, brown, deep blue, green, aquamarine, yellow, and orange capes surrounding the altar at the center of the platform, and the slinking into a cower to below the lip of the platform of the figures in the black, gray, and red capes. And when the women saw the change, their murmurings and chants changed to loud ululation. They were trilling loudly, clicking their teeth together rhythmically, and raising and swaying their arms in praise and joy.

Xulatiki saw the reclining figure of Queen Norinana, naked but streaked with red, being bundled away from the surface of the altar by white-robed elder woman, and the figures in the brown and deep blue capes rose up above the raised curtain and capes, onto the surface of the altar. They each had a large earthenware jar in their arms, which they tipped over in unison, washing the blood of the queen from the altar. And then, as they receded downward, rising up between them to stand fully erect and majestically, his arms opened wide to those on the hillside, was elevated the most magnificent figure of all, robed in gleaming gold. The highest priest of the sun god, chosen when the previous highest priest lost his virility, chosen by right of having the straightest, most robust body in the empire combined with a phallus of the longest and thickest dimensions.

The highest priest rose tall on top of the altar and raised an object over his head in one hand and a bloody knife in the other, and the woman spread across the hillside cried out in unison but then went immediately silent. The highest priest of the sun god handed the object and the knife to the last of the white-robed ancients, and they scurried down the hillside in the wake of the departing figure of the reclining queen. In response, the crowd of women lathering the mountainside slunk away into the surrounding jungle at the base of the conical peak, which was spewing its puffs of smoke into the air. As the women faded away, they were replaced by a great army of men, naked and tallowed, each with his own color of bicep, wrist, knee, and ankle bands. These were their passports for traveling beyond their villages. The color of the bands designated the village origins of their wearer in the compact but fecund island running around the sacred mountain and to the endless sea, endless in every direction except for that far-off island of the man crunchers barely discernible on the horizon to the west.

The highest priest of the sun god raised his arms and his face toward the sun and let out a bellow that was joined with the deep-voiced yells of joy and anticipation of the men who had replaced the women on the side of the mountain.

This was Xulatiki's cue. the sea of men between him and the top of the smoking mountain parted, and Xulatiki slowly ascended this path, proud and welcoming, his head held high, his bulging breasts rock hard and nipples taut, his comely cock swinging against newly manned thighs, his eyes locked on those of the waiting highest priest of the sun god. He would be king. And kings must suffer for their people.

The colorfully caped men on the platform were moving fluidly about again in their slow-motion swirling dance. They could not be clearly seen because of the smoke coming out of the cauldron the mountain possessed instead of a peak, but as Xulatiki came closer, he could see that they each held a spear in one hand—all except for the three undulating around below the rim of the platform. These three were moving in circles that had a pattern to it. They were moving as if to intercept Xulatiki before he reached the summit. But now the other caped figures—all save the golden-caped one who remained standing astride the altar, legs out wide, cock proudly at full erection—were circling to come between Xulatiki and the other three, and as Xulatiki reached the platform, they had driven the three—the black-caped fury representing pestilence, the gray-caped fury representing the human enemies of the kingdom, and the red-caped one representing devastating fire—back behind the platform and under the lip of the smoking cauldron.

Xulatiki stood at the edge of the platform now. Everyone, priests, furies, and men on the mountainside alike, held their breath for the longest time and looked to the skies to mark the ascension of the sun. It was almost exactly overhead now, and as the sun moved into that position, the minor priests—the yellow-caped one representing the grain, the orange-caped one representing the fruit of the land, the green-caped one representing the game of the forests, and the aquamarine one represented the bounty of the ocean—encircled Xulatiki. As they lifted him straight up in the air, two with strong hands on his arms and above his rib cage and two with hands on his thighs and under his round and firm buttocks, the highest priest of the sun stretched himself out on the surface of the cruciform-shaped altar, his arms spread wide on the cross arms of the altar and his prodigious cock standing straight up in the air. The two high priests, that of the earth, caped in brown, and that of the sky, caped in deep blue, were at the lip of the cauldron, ensuring that the three furies were keeping their distance.

The men on the mountainside started to chant as the minor priests lifted Xulatiki high in the air, suspended over the altar and that monster spike of the highest priest. Benetiki, the purple-caped king, stood at the head of the altar, arms outstretched, his eyes plastered firmly on Xulatiki's eyes, as the ritual of the passing of the kinghead began. Xulatiki was returning the king's gaze, and he was chanting the chant he had been taught to use at this time, a chant that was meant to divert his attention, steel his resolve, and clothe his fears as much as possible to the ritual that had begun.

The sun hit its zenith and the two minor priests who were holding Xulatiki's legs spread them wide and all four of the minor priests brought Xulatiki's virginal passage down onto the erect manhood of the highest priest of the sun. Although both the phallus and the passage were slathered with tallow, the entry was not an easy one. Xulatiki's initial cry of pain was covered by the scream of possession and victory let loose by the reclined highest priest of the sun. This signal of the beginning of the year's seeding cycle released an exaltation of joy across the mountainside, and as the minor priests raised and lowered Xulatiki on the sacred seeding spike and Xulatiki raised his face to the sun to howl the chant he had been taught to use at this time, the women, now as naked as the men, flooded back onto the hillside and mingled with the men. The tension in the air was palpable as the highest priest's flow began to rise for the ritual seeding of the year's crop through the symbolic breeding of the new king.

The highest priest's pelvis lifted off the surface of the altar in rhythm with the downward thrustings of Xulatiki's torso, and at the triumph scream from the highest priest's lips of release and flow of the seed, the multitudes across the hillside fell on each other in an orgy of symbolic—and in many cases actual-seeding—man on woman and man on man and woman on woman, as they pleased. There would be many a new baby to comfort and challenge the men and women of the kingdom in the coming cool season.

The start of the ritual precisely when the sun had reached its zenith was yet another propitious sign of a good harvest year. But even more significant was the dark cloud that blotted out the sun and began to release its life-giving nourishment to the empire at the precise second the highest priest had ritualistic spouted his seed inside the new king, marking the precise moment Xulatiki had become the new king. Miracles of miracles, yet another sign simultaneously came from beneath their feet. The mountain began to laugh, to rumble and move, showing its approval of the new king and giving its blessing on the new growing season.

The old king, Benetiki, not yet a year older than Xulatiki but already a defunct king, was dispatched exactly as the ritual called for. The opening of the sky had brought a deluge of water that hissed loudly when it hit the burning embers inside the mountain's cauldron. In the cloud of smoke that ensued, the three furies, pestilence, human enemies, and fire, crept up out of the cauldron and snatched Benetiki. They stripped him of his purple cape, pulled him below the lip of the cauldron, and, in succession, seeded him deeply and roughly, in succession and two together, in their fury of not having been able to reach the new king. A writhing pile with the old king lurching and twisting in the center as three vengeful cocks found, invaded, and plowed his orifices in repeated thrustings.

It was the time in the ritual now for the high priests of the earth and sky to give their seed blessings to the new king. The highest king of the sun came off the altar and moved to the front of the platform, facing the sexual feast of people of the empire. He stood there, legs spread wide and arms crossed and blessed the seeding of the nation going on before his eyes. The high priest of the earth stood on a ledge running on either side of the altar, the altar between his thighs, and the four minor priests turned the new king so that he hovered over the altar, his back toward its surface. And they brought the new king's pelvis in toward the groin of the high priest of the earth, and he entered the king's passage with his phallus and bred him. The high priest of the sky straddled the altar over the new king's head and entered the new king's mouth with his phallus and bred him there.

When earth and sky had seeded the new king with their blessings, the king was laid flat on the lower arm of the altar table. His wrists were bound to rings on the cross beams of the altar, and one after another, the priests of the grain, the fruits of the land, the game of the forests, and the bounty of the sea straddled the altar below the king and blessed him deeply with their seed. As they did so, the favored maiden Tianana appeared beside King Xulatiki and poured mother's milk on her plump breasts and suckled the new king. This marked the validation of her selection as the new queen.

All of the favorable signs rang true. The crops were bountiful that growing season and the game of the forests and bounty of the sea were plentiful. The winds blew strong across the peninsula, not giving pestilence a chance to place its claw on crop, or animal, or human. The rain was plentiful and no fires of destruction flared. The coastal villages of the kingdom did see a great armada of war ships on the sea, but it floated past the empire's lands. Smoke was seen rising soon thereafter above the island of the man crunchers. And for the first time in many years, no enemy force appeared to try to deprived the kingdom of its crops or bring grieving to the hearths of its people. The year's harvest was the most abundant the empire had ever known.

The sun god having been ascendant for the ritual of the blessing of the crops, the moon goddess was given her due for the ritual of the blessing of the harvest.

On a night of the first full moon following the harvest, King Xulatiki met and coupled with his new queen, Tianana, on the altar of the sacred mountain. The white-clad select virgins of the empire danced around the platform in the moonlight as Xulatiki met with Tianana on the great altar. Xulatiki stretched his bride out on the altar and hovered over her, touching her here and there and running his hands here and there as the moon ascended the sky. And when the moon reached its zenith, he thrust his phallus inside her. She sang to the moon as he thrust and thrust and thrust. The two perfectly formed favored children of the empire merged and coupled and twisted and entangled and sighed and moaned, pleasing the moon goddess greatly in their breedings. The king masterfully seeded his new queen repeatedly through the night, passing on in great flowings of golden seed the blessing of all the gods of earth, sea, and sky that he had received at the beginning of the growing season.

Peace and plenty reigned over the island through its fallow season and there was only joy and nurturing of the human fruits of the growing season ritual orgy throughout the empire.

The new growing season was upon the kingdom once more. The ritual had begun again at the altar on the sacred mountain in keeping with a never-ending rhythm. The high and minor priests were swirling around the altar, the women of the empire were spread across the mountainside below, their ululations wakening the gods in the heaven to the kingdom's supplications. The furies were at the edges of the platform, being held at bay by spears of the priests. King Xulatiki had taken up his position at the head of the altar. He looked briefly down the mountainside at the new king expectant standing nervously, trying his best not to appear nervous, in his purple cape at the base of the mountain. Xulatiki looked back to the altar spreading before him. His beloved queen, Tianana, was stretched out on the surface of the altar. She was groaning and moaning. The highest priest of the sun was straddling the altar and her, standing on the ledge running down each side of the altar. He had a long sharp knife in one hand. He was gently rocking his pelvis back and forth, entering the queen with his phallus and pulling back out and then entering her again.

He was playing the part of the sun god, welcoming the fruit of the queen's womb into the world, the empire's most sacred baby of that year. His phallus was entering the queen and reaching to the new baby, coaxing it to appear precisely at dawn, as would be a perfect sign to cap a perfect year and to bring promise of continued good fortune in the harvest. The queen's attendants, a bevy of old women in white, were moving about her, kneading her belly and doing this and that to either prolong or shorten the childbirth, doing everything they could to have the baby appear exactly at dawn.

At a signal from the attendants, King Xulatiki leaned over his naked wife and started suckling her breasts, causing her milk to flow. And the highest priest of the sun god increased his rhythmic beckoning of the child with his stroking phallus.

There was a gush of blood and fluids and the high priest of the sun god pulled his phallus out of the queen and stepped down from the altar, just in time for dawn to strike and for the head of the new baby, a strong son, to appear. The highest priest of the sun god announced the arrival, exactly at the most propitious moment, of the new prince. As he cut the umbilical cord with his knife, an exultation of joy went up from the throng of women gathered on the hillside.

But then the greatest of miracles. A cloud drifted across the rising sun, and it became night again. But as soon as the cloud had come, it was gone, and there was a second dawn. And there was a second child coming out of the womb of the queen. This one was a girl child, with very healthy lungs. In a trembling voice, the highest priest of the sun god, who in all his years had never thought he'd see the kingdom blessed as it had been in this year's harvest cycle, announced the arrival of a princess, and the women on the hillside went wild.

The queen and the babies were rushed away and the women were flooding away from the hillside and the men were flowing onto the hillside in a ritual pattern that basically never changed no matter how blessed or cursed a particular year was.

Still, King Xulatiki, king for only a few more moments, couldn't help but look down on the young purple-caped man standing nervously at the base of the mountain and to pity him. This had been the perfect harvest year, more propitious than any of the past and probably more so than any of the future. That could not help but be a disappointment to the short rule of the young man standing below. Xulatiki's breast puffed up with pride and self-congratulations.

Yes, the perfect harvest year, the fading King Xulatiki was thinking, not yet aware of the fingers of the furies of pestilence, human enemies, fire that already were seeking purchase on the hem of his purple cape from the rim of the volcano's cauldron.

Cockpitting

After two years in the male-male paradise of Bangkok, a short assignment to Okinawa, Japan, seemed, for most of my tour, like entering a monastery. I was supposed to rotate directly back to the States with my SR71 supersonic photoreconnaissance unit, but the North Koreans were acting up on the DMZ, and the government wanted an intense look-see at whether or not they were building their troop strength up near the border. The flying from Kadena Airbase was fine, but, as far as sexual release, Okinawa seemed pretty much a wasteland compared to Bangkok.

Neither the local women nor men were all that attractive in general and they were wholly unsophisticated and unimaginative in terms of pursuing the options for self-satisfaction. There were some luscious soldiers, airmen, and sailors about, but the U.S. authorities kept them on a pretty short leash, and I wasn't going to be on "the Rock" long enough to develop many liaisons.

If it hadn't been for Keith, another photorecon jet driver on temporary assignment from Bangkok, I definitely would have felt sexually deprived. We had been in the same group of "fuck buddies" back in Bangkok, and we managed to get on the same shift rotation at Kadena. Pilots were put on call for twenty-four-hour shifts, which meant that when we were on duty rotation, we ate and slept in a Quonset hut attached to the hangar housing our two Blackbirds, just waiting for the call to leap into the air and shoot pictures of suspected North Korean troop movements.

A couple of times a week, Keith and I would find ourselves alone in the Quonset bunk room, and, on these occasions, we never needed more than one bunk.

One night Keith had me on my back, sidewise on the bottom bunk, with my feet lodged wide apart in the railings undergirding the upper bunk and my hands hanging on to the tailings of the sheets and covers of the upper bunk, while Keith stood on the floor next to the bunk, hunched down, and with his cock pounding away at my chute. He was a real moaner and must have been enjoying his plowing of my ass immensely that night, because we attracted the attention of an airman doing some late-night maintenance on the SR71s.

The airman was a big muscular blond, and he had a grin that went from ear to ear as he draped himself in the Quonset hut doorway and watched Keith fuck me. He wasn't the type who was satisfied with just watching, though, and in short order he had saddled up behind Keith, and the heightening of the decibel rate of Keith's moans let me know that he was being plowed from behind while he was mining my ass.

The airman must have taken a particular fancy to me, because as Keith was finishing, the airman had pushed his head over Keith's shoulder and was in a lip lock with me.

He hadn't cum when Keith shot off and collapsed beside me on the bed in a panting heap, and he disengaged from Keith at that point and sat down on the other side of me and continued kissing me and pulling at his engorged rod.

"I wanna do you," he was whispering to me.

"So, who's stopping you?" I asked. I liked repeated fuckings by multiple men.

"Not here." he whispered back to me.

"Where then?" was my reply.

"In the bird, man. In the cockpit of the bird."

I was skeptical as to whether we really could do it in the cockpit of the SR71, but we managed. It was a tight fit—in more ways than one. There is very little room for my thighs beside his on the seat as he sat in the driver's seat and I faced him and lowered my ass on his rod. In addition to that, his dick was so thick that this was a tight fit in my ass as well.

I pole danced for a short while, sliding up and down his pole, but then he took control. He lifted my legs up around and behind him onto the cowling of the plane behind the cockpit, with me leaning my back against the instrument panel, and he rode my ass hard in deep upward thrusts that had the jet rocking back and forth on its wheels.

This was every bit as good a fuck as I had been getting in Bangkok.

I learned that my well-hung and horny airman technician's name was Pete. I didn't learn this because he said anything to me that night. He, in fact, left me bent over the cowling behind the cockpit of the SR71 and gasping for air that night, never having identified himself.

But he apparently knew my name, as I was to learn later.

I was fascinated with the medieval castles that could be found in ruins on the small Pacific island. Okinawa had long been real estate that both China and Japan had contended for and, in turn, had forcibly occupied. But the castles of Okinawa were eerily similar to those of medieval Western Europe even though those two cultures apparently never made contact. Before I left the island on my short tour there, I wanted to explore those castles, and the opportunity arose when the Kadena AFB Outing Club posted a tour of one of the best-preserved castles near Bolo Point, on the island's west coast, nearly at the halfway point from north to south.

I didn't think anything of it when the tour leader called me to tell me there needed to be a change in the tour date. I didn't even think twice when he went out of his way to ensure that I could go on the tour on the new date and time.

On the appointed day, I appeared at the recreation building in the Quonset hut near the Koza City Gate Number Two to the air base.

That's when I got my surprise. The tour guide was Pete, the guy who had flown me a couple of weeks earlier in the cockpit of the SR71. He was even hunkier in the daylight than he had been in the airplane hangar late at night.

He introduced himself to me quite politely, acting like he hadn't known me already in the biblical sense, and told me it would be just the two of us riding out to Bolo Point in his jeep—that the rest of the hikers would meet us at the castle.

It was a good thing we took the jeep, because the castle was on top of a craggy outcropping accessible only by a narrow track through a sugarcane field. There weren't any other vehicles on the small cleared apron in front of the castle gate when we arrived; nor were there any other tour takers in evidence—or anyone else for that matter. This was really a remote spot of the island.

When we entered the shadows of the small enclosure between the outer and inner gates, Pete pushed me up against a crumbling, gray stone wall and placed strong hands on the wall on either side of me.

"I have a confession to make," he told me in a low, husky voice.

"Oh?" was all I could manage. I was breathless with anticipation. That night in the jet cockpit had been the best sex I'd had during my Okinawa tour. I was his for the asking.

"The tour wasn't really rescheduled. I saw your name on the roster, and I wanted to give you a private tour," he said, brushing his hand against the side of my face. "Do you mind?"

"No, not at all," I answered in a hoarse voice.

"May I kiss you?" He asked

I assented with a nod and by turning my head to him, and he kissed me deeply and tenderly.

"I haven't thought of anything but you since that night," he said when we'd come up for air. "May I fuck you again?"

My answer was a foregone conclusion. I'd already acknowledged to myself that I was his for the asking, and he'd asked me politely, which hadn't always been the case with my lusty partners. I did, however, make him give me at least a perfunctory tour of the castle first, as my interest in that was genuine, as was the expertise of his tour guiding.

What was most striking in the comparison of Western castles and those of ancient Okinawa was the fundamental difference in their plans. The stonework, towers, and battlements were all quite similar, but whereas a Western castle tended to be fortified from the outer edges in, with the most precious holdings located at the center, the Okinawan castle invariably was built against a precipice, as this one was, with the holy of holies being a sacred grove and ruling family altar at the rear of the castle, hanging on at the top of the cliff.

After a brief tour of the outer works of the castle, Pete guided me back to the sacred grove, which was just that, a grove of pine trees at the very back of the castle walls on a small apron of land suspended over the boiling surf at the foot of the cliff. Here there was a grassy area in the middle of the grove of trees and a stone altar—the center of the ancestor worship for the family that once had ruled the castle and the surrounding fields and had acted as the sentinel for invasion from China to the west or the Japanese islands to the north.

Pete laid out a khaki army blanket on the ground in front of the altar, and after pulling me to him in a standing position and fondling and kissing me into a lustful mood, he undressed me, pushed me down on all fours, prepared my asshole with his tongue and saliva, and covered with his body and fucked me to paradise. As he pumped me, I listened to the roaring surf at the base of the cliff and the wind sighing in the pine trees, and I added my own sighs and moans of ecstasy to the sounds of nature.

When we both had cum, Pete pulled me over on my side within his arms and we both merged with the wild beauty of the setting until our breathing had regularized. We then kissed and worked each other's bodies with our hands until we were in full rut once more.

Pete pulled me up from the ground and took the army blanket and draped it over the stone altar in the middle of the grove. He then pushed me onto my back on top of the altar, spread my legs wide, and we worshipped the exuberance of our youth and vitality and our healthy, lustful bodies at the altar with merging and rhythmic thrusts and counterthrusts and with me crying my passion to the tops of the swaying pine trees.

In Pete I at last found my escape from the somewhat tedious routine of the Okinawa assignment, but I had hardly found him and started to be introduced to a very active male-male underculture on the island, when my government decided that the North Koreans were just rattling rockets they didn't actually have, and I was on my way east across the Pacific Ocean, leaving Pete and the fascinating Okinawan castles behind.

Naval Dilemma

Dutch came first. It was a particularly busy and boisterous night in the Dick Hut, tucked in the back shadows of an alley off the Nuuanu Stream in the heart of Honolulu's red light district. Naval ships were in harbor, more than ninety of them, I was told, and all of Oahu was abuzz at the rumbling of war, with the Japs getting more belligerent with each passing day. All the sailors could talk about was how we were on the brink of something big.

As the night wore on and the drinks flowed and sailor's overflowed our little bar, it was getting a little dicey for me. Hung Lee, the bar's proprietor and my virtual owner as well, kept a string of young Hawaiian men like me in the bar for when the sailors wanted something more exotic, smaller, more lithe and compact—and more undressed—than each other when they poured off their docked vessels, randy, needy, and with a month's pay in the back pockets of their regulation tight whites. Our main responsibility was to keep the men in the bar and paying for drinks. Inevitably, though, we left the bar with one or more of the men and took them to our small apartments in the upper floors of surrounding buildings. This was where the real money was, and Hung Lee let us keep a third of whatever we earned.

I had already left the bar once that night—with a blond, pimply young sailor of no more than nineteen, who was shy and embarrassed and didn't know for sure what to do. All he knew was that he was far from home, he was lonely and a bit scared, and he had had a raging hard on for weeks because he was missing poking some sweetie back in Ohio on the mainland.

I took him to my rooms more because he was being circled by the older, much more experienced and aggressive sailors, and I knew from experience that he was in danger of having something far different happen to him than what he had hesitatingly come into this bar for.

When we got to my small two-room apartment, he didn't seem to know what to do, where to start. So I started for him. I untied and dropped my sarong, the only thing I wore at the bar, and directed him to disrobe, which he did almost furtively in the corner of the room and turned from me. Then I laid him on his belly on my single bed, the most sturdy piece of furniture in the apartment—out of professional necessity—and I rubbed his shoulders and back with fragrant oil, loosening up both his tension and his inhibitions. He was grinding the bed clothes with his pelvis by the time I had finished with his legs and had moved to his well-rounded butt cheeks. He was sighing and moaning like he was in the heights of sex, but then I turned him over and my hands and mouth showed him what real sex felt like. It had been some time since he'd had sex, so he shot off quickly and prodigiously almost as soon as I sank my mouth down on his throbbing cock.

And then he was very embarrassed and was stammering and was quite beside himself with apologies. I felt sorry for him and didn't want him to leave with a bad impression of how he would be with a man, so I shushed him and covered his mouth with kisses until he subsided back on the bed with a sigh. He was young and virile and in need, so he was already hard again. I mounted him and slid my hole down on his cock, straddling his pelvis as he lay back in the bed, and I taught him that all he had heard on shipboard of what a man could give him was true.

I was late in getting back to the bar because I had instilled such confidence in the young sailor that instead of leaving when I thought we were done, he bent me over the back of a straight chair and took control of a vigorous second fuck, covering me closely from behind. I cried out in the taking for him, telling him how good he was and how fully he was using me and how much I wanted him—all to help him get seasoned in this new lifestyle he was trying out.

When he asked me how much I wanted, I asked for far more than my usual fee. And I did so to be kind to him. I didn't want to leave him with a great deal of money to spend. I wanted him to go directly back to his ship from here, not return to the bar with the predators who circled the waters there. I told him that if he just kept his eyes open for the possibilities, that he should be able to find a special friend on the ship who would bottom for him with more opportunities for encounters and less of a risk of falling in with those who would want to use him for their bottoms until he was more seasoned.

When I returned to the Dick Hut, Hung Lee was beside himself with anger for my taking so long, slapped me hard across the face, and pushed me into the thick of the boisterous, rutting crowd of sailors. There were entirely too many ships in Pearl Harbor, too many sailors free in Honolulu. Too much testosterone flying around the red light district. Too much tension in the air. Too much frantic need with an eye on the curfew time.

And there were very few of us bar boys to go around. We were easy to spot in a swirling crowd like this. We wore only gaily colored sarongs knotted at our waists, hanging low on our slim hips. We were barefoot and bare chested and had orchids over our ears. We left the impression that all a sailor had to do was to pull loose that knot and we'd be accessible and ready for action.

The sailors, however, were heavily regulated to remain in their starched white uniforms, with the tight midsections and bell bottoms and the pullover top. The Navy didn't care too much what they did on port leave as long as they remained squared away in their sailor costumes while in public. The only saving grace was that they still had buttoned cod pieces for easy access when they needed to piss. It, of course, provided easy access for other things as well. They didn't have buttoned slits at their assholes, though. Thus encumbered, the sailors, in their urgency, gravitated more to the half-naked, willowy and exotic Hawaiian and Chinese bar boys than to each other.

And there were few even vaguely private places for the sailors to go together. Hung Lee had a back room, but it was quickly filled—at a premium price. As were the surrounding alleys, even if they were free, if you didn't count the danger of being accosted by a roving military police patrol. The sounds of grunts and groans and slurping floated above the whole backstreet and its allies, as white-dressed sailors gravitated to whatever unoccupied shadow to kneel and suck or cover and doggy fuck.

Or, especially close to curfew, they just unbuttoned their flies and, otherwise fully clothed, fucked the bar boys furiously on the table tops. Hung Lee didn't care; he was too busy trying to collect voyeur's fees from the watchers. And he made more money in the last hour before naval curfew than for several hours previous to that.

It was late enough in the evening and there were so many sailors in the bar, that most of the rest of the bar boys were off in the rooms over the bars, servicing the highest bidders.

I was no sooner back in the center of the barroom before the situation got out of control. I was surrounded by a sea of white and of lust-filled faces. A sailor was close behind me, lacing his arms under my pits, immobilizing my arms, and lifting my feet off the ground. A drunken buddy of his had a fist at my knot, pulling at it, and my sarong drifted down to the floor.

He was leering at me and unbuttoning his cod piece fly and pulling out a hardened cock.

Sailors were surrounding us, coming in close, licking their chops, and a rhythmic chant of "Fuck him, fuck him, fuck him" was swelling.

Hung Lee had gone up on the bar top and, red faced, was bellowing at the top of his lungs, yelling that he needed to be paid first—both for all who fucked me and those who watched it—and that this wasn't allowed in the barroom, that the military police would be along at any minute and shut them down. The "isn't allowed" was proforma and in a much softer voice than he used to state the fees for making a bar boy suck cock and take cock or to watch. He even cited a fee for doubling—and an extra voyeur's fee for watching that—which I found the sailors themselves rarely thought about doing until he mentioned it—and almost always considered in that last frantic hour when it was brought to their attention. The fee for that was quite high, though, for each participant, and few sailors had much money left to spend at the end of the night.

I wasn't scared of the sailor's cock or even what he intended to do with it. I got fucked by sailors nearly every night. But I was apprehensive about the ten sailors who might follow him and about the mob conditions in general—that I might be gravely hurt in the process. I knew that Hung Lee wasn't going to do much to save me from a gang bang.

The sailor in front of me was lifting and parting my legs and was crouching his hips under me and between my legs. My feet already were off the ground. Most of these sailors towered over me; all of them were bulked up and at least twice my size.

I winced and flinched as the cock head found my hole and pressed inside and pushed higher and higher into me. The mob was crowding in closer and cheering at the initial invasion and picking up the "Fuck him, fuck him" chanting. Hung Lee was wading through the crowd, demanding and receiving money.

My assailant was sweating and smelled of too much beer. His cock wasn't thick, but it was long enough that he was rising up farther in me with each thrust. He certainly was longer and more insistent than the young, inexperienced sailor I'd just serviced had been. He was palming my butt cheeks and leveraging on them to pull me up and down on his cock. His teeth went to one of my nipples, and I screamed out in pain at that. And the crowd cheered.

The crowd noise swelled and then inexplicably tapered off and my tormentor had pulled his cock out of me and I was being lowered, more gently than I imagined was going to be the case down to the floor. The grip of the man behind me lessened and he was trembling. But he didn't drop me.

I looked up to see a gigantic, broken nose of an angry-faced head pushing its way through the crowd. The mouth was open, showing uneven, broken teeth; it was bellowing at a level that demanded attention. A monster of a man in sailor whites was cutting through the mob that had surrounded me, and the men were shrinking away from him. Those who didn't give way fast enough were being swatted into the men behind them, all struggling hard not to go down like bowling pins. The man mountain was virtually bulging with muscle. His torso was thick, but not fat, and the material of his sailor bell bottoms were straining to hold in his massive thigh and calf muscles, not to mention the privates between the thighs. He was a good foot taller than any other man in the room. And he was ugly as sin.

But he had saved me and had quieted the crowd into docile and skittish sailors instantaneously. The two men who were my principle assailants melted into the crowd, and the mob somehow largely evaporated from the bar.

The man leaned down and lifted my sarong from the floor and held it out for me.

"Are you OK?" he asked.

"Yes, now," I replied, "Thanks to you, of course." He looked away, almost bashfully, while I reknotted my sarong low on my waist. I was trembling, but I fought to regain control. Just another night at work. I looked around in half panic for Hung Lee, but he had collected enough money to satisfy him and returned to behind the bar.

"May I buy you a drink?" he asked, diffidently, almost in a whisper. He still wasn't looking at me.

"Yes, of course. At the bar." This was what I was here for—to push drinks for lonely sailors. I looked over at the bar. Hung Lee was behind it now. Looking at him now, I could tell that he was half in shock at the near riot we'd just had, his whole future having passed before his eyes. I'm sure he figured he came close to having the bar closed down by the naval authorities because a riot had occurred here. And there was no question in my mind that he'd blame me. I'd have to walk very carefully until he forgot this incident.

We bellied up to the bar. I ordered a gin and tonic (which, of course, would come without the gin), and the sailor ordered a Coke. Anybody else in here who ordered a nonalcoholic drink would have been jeered out of the place. But I was pretty sure that no one messed with this monster of a man.

I discovered the source of his almost obscene bulk. He was a boilerman on the battleship the USS *West Virginia*, which was docked at Pearl Harbor. His was perhaps the dirtiest and most muscle taxing—and developing—job on the whole ship. His name was Dutch, which he seemed anxious for me to know. He seemed to want me to know more than that he was just in this bar to get pissed on beer and to find some man to fuck—or be fucked by.

"And your name?" he asked quietly as we worked on our drinks. As required, I quickly downed my first one and was already on my second one, all on the sailor's tab, of course. He had saved me, so I felt badly about doing this, but Hung Lee was right there, watching my every step, and the sailor didn't seem to mind.

"'Ano'i," I answered.

"'Ano'i, 'Ano'i," he repeated, almost in a whisper, treating each syllable like velvet. "What a beautiful name. Is it Hawaiian?"

"Yes," I answered. "I'm Hawaiian. Well, mostly. A little Chinese blood, of course, and I'm told there's a Presbyterian missionary or two from the mainland in there too. Not that they would admit it. We're all a mix of something here."

"And it turned out quite well, too," He said, giving me a smile that was almost pathetic as ugly as he was. I almost felt like laughing. It seemed like he was courting me. Here in a bar, where I got paid to lie on my back and open my legs, no real pleasantries exchanged.

"Thank you," I said. Then "and thank you again what you did over there; I would have been in a lot of trouble if something had happened to get the bar closed down tonight. Now, I guess I should—" I was standing up, ready to mingle with the much smaller crowd in the room in the wake of the excitement.

"No, please. Can't you stay a bit longer?" he asked, his eyes pleading with me. "I have money; I can pay for the drinks. Barkeep, another round over here, please."

I looked at Hung Lee for a sign of what I should do. But he was being inscrutable. I knew he'd want me to jolly up the men around the tables and get them to drink faster to cool down their hard ons as I flirted with them. But it also was obvious that Hung Lee realized that it was only Dutch's presence that was maintaining calm on this unusually crowded night. A night full of tense talk of what was happening, why so many ships were in harbor, what were the Japs up to?

"'Ano'i,'" Dutch said again, almost in loving tones. "A beautiful name. Does it have a meaning?"

"Yes," I answered. "It means desired. And it can be either a boy's or a girl's name. They often use that name when—"

"I know what it means to me," Dutch said in a low, hoarse voice, cutting me off in midsentence.

I didn't respond. I just let that hang there. He was ugly and maybe three times bigger than I was, and it frightened me a bit to think that he was that proportionally big everywhere. And his hulking strength. He could smother me or break me in two in his excitement and lust. An uneducated sailor, a boilerman working in the bowels of a battleship. He might be cruel and rough and incapable of holding himself back at the height of passion. But he had saved me from possible harm, had saved the bar from maybe being closed down when there was so much profit to be made.

"Can we . . . could we . . . would you . . . ? I have money; enough money." he was struggling to get the proposition out. But he wasn't looking at me. He was ugly as sin and frightfully big. He didn't need to be told that. He lived that.

I looked at Hung Lee, who nodded slightly. Not really an acquiescence as much a command.

"Yes, yes. of course," and then an "I would like that." Ever mindful of the role I played the fantasies that were mine to weave for the money. "I have rooms across the street. We can go there. Now, if you'd like."

* * * *

He perched precariously, straddling one of my straight chairs, reversed, his massively muscled arms folded over the back, resting his bulging chest against the slats, as I stood by the bed and unloosened the sarong and let it slide to the floor in swirls around my ankles. He had taken off his tunic, and I nearly gasped at the hard-muscled bulk of chest. I had no idea how much of me he had seen in the gang banging earlier in the bar, but his eyes at first went wide and then slitted when he saw me fully unclothed, and I heard his intake of breath.

He just looked at me for the longest time, and then he stood up from the chair and slowly stripped off his navy trousers. It was my turn to take breath in when he was done. His muscling, from head to toe, was inhumanely bulky, but all in proportion, and his cock, as I had feared, was enough for three men, not too abnormally long as it stood straight out from his thick thatch of reddish pubic hair but as thick as a normal man's wrist. I had never taken anything that thick in a single, and I suddenly was glad that I'd that I'd done doubles. And his balls hung low and were the size of lemons. I hadn't slightest doubt that they could provide semen to pump for hours.

He was holding back, unsure of whether I would want to continue after having seen him. But I lifted my arms in a welcoming, gathering gesture, and, with a sob, he moved to me, picked me up, gently and almost lovingly in his arms, and his mouth went to mine.

I closed my eyes, not least to close out the ugliness of his face. I wasn't resentful, but I wanted him to think my body would respond to him, and I was afraid that the ugliness of him would freeze my desires. But I need not have had any fears about that, because his kiss was soft and tender, and sweet tasting. I couldn't get enough of the taste of him, and sensing that, he tentatively darted his tongue into my mouth, and then when I sighed to that, he probed deeper, yet still tenderly.

When we broke from the kiss, I murmured "Oh god, take me, fuck me. That cock. It's gigantic. I can't wait to see if I can take it. Pound me. Fill me with your cum." It was a line I instinctively used to get sailors to get on with it so I could get back to the bar. But I wasn't at all sure that was what I meant now, in this instance.

"If you think you can't . . . if there's a problem. Maybe just a hand job. That's all I usually—"

"I want to feel your cock inside me." Again it was a line for the second-thought men. But I said it to him, to Dutch, with meaning, because I meant it. If I could take that cock, I could take any man's—at least in thickness. And he was being almost tender with me.

I could feel him shudder at that. He was still holding me in his arms. But I could tell I had broken through the ice. He knew now that I would accept him.

"Yes, yes, in time . . . if we can manage it at all. That's not always possible," he said in a low, hoarse voice, the doubt obvious in his tone. "But first I want to make love to you. Maybe we can manage an inch or too, but I can make you come in other ways too, and you me. You are so lovely."

He laid me gently down on the bed, on my back and sat down on the side of the bed next to my waist. "Do you have . . . ?" he started to ask with hesitation.

"Sheaths? Yes, there, in the nightstand drawer."

"No, not that . . . and I've brought my own. I don't think yours would—"

No, probably not, I thought. And then a chill went up my spine at the realization of what was to come. How monstrously thick he was.

"I meant oil. I would like to give you a massage. I am longing to feel your curves and crevices."

"Oh, that's in the nightstand as well. And . . . well . . . it can be used for—"

"Yes, that's good," he broke in.

He was a divine masseur. He worked all of my muscles so lovingly and deeply and sensually that I was purring and getting close to dozing off when he gently turned me over. And the sensuality of what he was doing was so strong that I was fully engorged when he turned me. He worked my neck and chest and arm muscles and moved down from my chest to my pubic fringe and then up from my legs to under my ball sac.

And while he was working me, I was gliding my hands over any part of him I could reach. When I could reach his cock, he poured oil on my hand and I stroked him. I couldn't get my fist around what he had. And it was hard as a rock and was throbbing. I knew it wouldn't be long now before I was put to the test. He was sighing and groaning. With my eyes closed, I could completely blot out that he was an ogre of a man, in both bulk and visage.

I must have drifted off to a purring sleep, because I came back to full consciousness with a warm, moist, fully encasing sensation in my cock, which was completely sheathed in Dutch's mouth. Then I realized my channel was being filled as well—as fully as most men could with their cocks. Dutch was working on opening me to him with oil and his huge thumb.

His thumb had found and was stroking my prostate, and, with a flinch and a lurch, I exploded into his encasing throat. I murmured my appreciation and the extreme pleasure he had brought me in his sensitive and prolonged preparation.

But we weren't very far along in the preparation at all yet. Now it was time for Dutch's pleasure.

"You opened," he murmured, in amazement. "Wide. Maybe—"

"Of course I have," I said, a laugh. "I'm a whore. And I want it inside me. You weren't expecting a virgin, were you?"

He leaned down and kissed me between my shoulder blades. "For just now we can pretend that you're just that—a virgin. But I think . . . that maybe . . . I can—"

"Then do it. Fuck me. Don't make me wait too long."

He turned me in the bed to where my butt was on the edge. He pulled over the straight chair and sat there now. Placing two pillow under the small of my back, he took my calves in his big fists and pulled my legs apart and folded them up and made me dig my heels in the wooden side piece of the bed.

Then, using large quantities of the oil, he began to open me up, murmuring his pleasure that I could do it. His thumb was replaced with his middle finger. He gently fucked me with this, in and out and around, opening me slowly. This wasn't so bad, and neither was it that difficult when he added his index finger. I began to pant and arch my back, though, when the third finger went it. He fisted my cock with his other hand and stroked me to another ejaculation to take my mind off the opening of my hole to his needs.

Not long before I spouted off, I felt I couldn't wait any longer. "Fuck me!" I cried. "Take me now! Fuck me. And no rubber. I'm clean. I want you to drown my insides! Now!" And it was true. I was doused regularly because some sailors just wouldn't wait. And I'd yet to have a problem. Hung Lee was Chinese. They knew what to do.

"Sorry, Not yet, I can't yet," he croaked, my begging for him affecting him deeply, almost choking him up to where he couldn't speaking. The three fingers inside me were quaking with excitement and anticipation. "I don't want to ruin you, and I'm afraid once I've started I won't be able to stop."

As I shot off, the fourth finger went in, the fingers cupped and gently pressing out, stretching me, if ever so slowly. I writhed under the invasion, moving my pelvis back and forth, trying to help stretch my channel. My fingernails clawing at the bed spread.

"And are you sure about the rubber? I don't want—"

"Yes, I'm sure." I spat out between clinched teeth. "Skin on skin. I want to feel that thick pulsing vein under you cock. Put me directly on your cock. My muscles moving on your cock, making love to your cock, Pulling you into me, being flooded by you. Deep, deep inside. NOW!"

That did it, With a sob, Dutch rose up off the chair and crouched between my legs, and I felt the gigantic bulb of his cock head at my hole, between his cupped fingers inside me. As the fingers withdrew, his cock head tried to push in, slowly and as gently as he could, but I had him worked up to the limit now and his legs were shaking.

I arched up to him and reached down and grabbed at the root of his cock, held it steady, and tried to draw it into me, willing the cock head to breech the sphincter. We were both panting and groaning. With a plopping sound, the cock head was past the entrance, and he was inside me.

I screamed and flopped back onto the bed, arching my back up then, though, and clawing at the bed spread with my hands, taking up great globs of material in my fists. Panting hard and groaning and grunting at the strain.

"I can stop. Tell me to stop," Dutch cried out.

"Don't you dare," I yelled back. "All the way. Fuck me. Stretch me. Ah, I can feel the vein! Oh, Shitttttt!"

And then I was taking all of him. He had prepared me well. He was sliding up inside me and my muscles were making love to his cock, undulating around his huge cylinder, inviting him in, wanting him to force himself all the way in.

We didn't say anything for a half hour or more. We were concentrating on giving and taking as much as each of us could. When he had bottomed out and was sure that I could handle him, Dutch bent down to me and we kissed a prolonged, tonsil-swabbing kiss. He buried his face in the hollow of my neck and kissed me deeply and gently bit me there. His mouth went to my pits, as I raised my arms, one after the other, and he licked and kissed and nipped me there. Then he worked his mouth down my torso as far as he could go, giving loving attention to my nipples.

He was pumping me. Slowly, but deeply. Alternating rhythms so I was never sure whether he was going shallow or deep, whether he was going straight or corkscrewing me. Holding me on the edge; taking me over the edge again and again. Both giving and taking a full measure of pleasure.

He nipped a nipple, and I ejaculated again, up his hard belly.

He picked me up with hands on my waist and turned and sat on the bed. My torso arched back and he crouched up off the bed and fucked down into me. Then he stood, still a bit crouched, with me suspended below him, my hands leveraging off the floor, my legs wrapped around his upper thighs, his hands holding my thighs, as he fucked down into me deeper and I met his thrusts with thrusts of my own, pushing off from the floor with my quaking hands.

With a cry of ecstatic passion, he fountained off down into me and then filled me and filled me and filled me, great flowings of semen burbling up around his cock and out the sides of my hole. Flowing for more than a minute. Emptying those lemon-sized balls inside me.

We lay on the bed panting, time in suspension while I reveled in hearing his ragged breathing of fulfilled passion, my back enfolded into the bulging muscles of his torso. When he entered me this time, I required no extra preparation and we needed no oil. His strokes were long and deep and slow and melting, and the previous flow of his semen was enough to lubricate us. I nestled my butt back into his pelvis, and he lifted my leg for greater access and gently fucked me to an exhausted sleep, his massive calloused fingers gently rubbing my nipples. All the time him whispering in my ear how good I was to him, me knowing that, rather, it was him who was giving me the stretched and sustained loving I hadn't had for several years. The thickness of that cock alone something that few had known and been able to take. Me only taking it because of the patience of his preparation.

I didn't wake until morning. He'd left enough money on the table to shut off any complaining Hung Lee might have done because I didn't come back to the bar the previous evening.

Dutch was a regular customer the next couple of weeks. And I never again needed the preparation to take him that I did that first time. But I always felt stretched to the limit, fully taken.

We had to be careful how we fucked; if Dutch moved to a position on top of me, there was a danger I would be crushed. There was always the fear that he would lose control. Men were afraid of his bulk and the size of his cock, and when he came to me he was full of need and aching with semen. But he never did fully lose control; he always let me determine when we should stop to allow me time to open to him. It was only while he was in those long moments of miraculously long flow of semen at the height of passion that he would stroke hard and deep and fast. And by the moment, he had worked me so expertly that these were the most pleasurable moments for me as well.

He visited me every three days, and the men in the bar grew to know that when he entered the door, they were to move away from me. He couldn't get enough of me; he worshipped me. I invariably started by oiling his awesome muscles, hard and as beautifully cut as marble. I tried to give him suck, but I could hardly get more than the bulb of his engorged cock in my mouth. The rumbling groans of pleasure from him were well worth the effort, though.

Usually we would start with me sitting in his lap, facing him, my wrists locked behind his neck, my lips on his jutting nipples, while stretched me open with oiled fingers. I loved the feel of his pulsating cock pressing against my belly. Then, when I felt I was open enough, I'd rise on my straddling knees and either slowly impale my channel on his tool while facing him and kissing that ugly face of his or turn away from him, arched forward with his big mitts on my pecs, and lower my butt cheeks into his pubic bush. One glorious afternoon, he corkscrewed me, revolving me around and around on his lap as he sank farther and farther into me. In an equally melting, but not so advisable, fuck, he leveraged his back against the wall, crouching down to provide a perch for me on his thighs, and he lap fucked me, moving me up and down on his tool with strong hands at my waist—but the whole building shook when we got lost in passion, so we only did that the once. Invariably we ended stretched on the bed, me folded into his belly, and he side splitting me languidly until we both drifted into sleep. He would be sighing, and I would be thrilled that I had given him satisfaction.

I was awed at the thought of how an ugly sailor like that, only a boilerman on a battleship, could have learned to be such a gentle and expert lover. And a lover he was becoming. All of the rest of the men in my life for the previous three years had been quick-fuck marks—or a young sailor I pitied. But what I had for Dutch was very close to love. It certainly was love for him. And he told me so. And within two weeks of our first lovemaking, he was telling me that he wanted to take me from the Dick Hut and set me up in an apartment in a safer, less seeding neighborhood and have me for his own. That he wanted us to be life partners.

It pulled at my heartstrings. I'd been taught to avoid this. I knew what could and couldn't be. I knew that I would never be destined for that. But now I had received the offer. And within a week, I'd received another. And that was when the naval dilemma set in.

His name was Richard Randolph, and he made a point of never separating those names. They always went together. I gathered that the Randolph was supposed to mean something. Maybe it did, on the mainland, on the East Coast, where he made clear his family was from. He was a lieutenant, serving on the light cruiser, the USS *Raleigh*.

He was all spit and polish, well groomed, extremely well turned out, his body obviously his temple. He marched into Dick Hut one Thursday afternoon, when business was light. He gave the distinct impression that he wouldn't come in such a place at night when the enlisted sailors held sway.

He marched right up to Hung Lee, who was at the bar supervising the Barkeep's cleaning of glasses. I and the other bar boys were milking the few afternoon drunks that we could— mostly civilians, because few of the Navy men were given leave from their ships in the middle of the day.

The lieutenant, standing straight and tall and slim, and pristinely white in his officer's uniform, stroked his thigh with some sort of stick, a swagger stick, maybe, but it looked more like a riding crop, as he spoke to Hung Lee in low tones.

I got both interested and a little apprehensive at the same time when both Hung Lee and the lieutenant started gazing in my direction as they talked. I saw Hung Lee's eyes go wide and his mouth begin to quiver. And then his eyes slitted and he said something to the lieutenant, which caused the lieutenant to take a wallet out of his tight white uniform and slap a big wad of bills down on the counter. And then the lieutenant turned and walked over to the entrance door and stood, as if ready to take a freeing, cleansing step out into the street as soon as he could. He was looking out the door, not at anyone in the bar.

Hung Lee shuffled over to me. "This gentleman has bought you for three days, 'Ano'i," he said. "In your rooms. He says he saw you on the street and wants you and followed you back here. Don't keep him waiting."

As soon as we entered my rooms, the lieutenant kicked the door shut and pushed me over to the table I ate on and pushed my chest down roughly on the wood. he held my cheek painfully to the table top with a firm hold on the back of my neck, while he unknotted my sarong with his other hand. Once my sarong was falling down my legs, he had the palm of his hand on one of my butt cheeks and then worked it over to the crack and was roughly fingering the rim of my asshole.

"Open," he said with mild surprise. "Wide open for one so small." I could tell he was pleased.

Of course it was open. Dutch had been fucking me for weeks now, and I'd been a whore for some time before that.

He had knelt down, and I felt his mouth and tongue at my hole. He was licking and nibbling at me. I started to rise off the table and he slapped me on the rump.

"Stay down," he said. I put my cheek and chest back down on the table, and he went back to eating me out. While he was doing that, he slapped me on both sides of the rump until I felt myself chaffing.

"Where's the lube?" he asked. I noted that he didn't ask for a rubber. I assumed this had been covered with Hung Lee when they were talking. I told him it was in the nightstand by the bed, and he told me not to move until he returned.

While at the nightstand, he stripped off his uniform, neatly folded it, and put it in the center of the bed. That was the clue that we probably wouldn't be using the bed for a while. Before he came back, he glanced around the room, zeroed in on a stool without a back on it, and pushed it over into the center of the room with his foot.

Then he was back at me. Working my hole with lubricated fingers with one hand and arching my back with his fist in my hair with the other.

He pulled me off the table and propelled me over to the center of the room and pushed my belly down on top of the stool. Then he was riding me like a horse and fucking me like a dog and beating on my thighs, arms, and back with his riding crop.

He had a respectable cock, but nothing I couldn't handle. His rough fucking, however, made something other than his cock the center of our sex. Whatever he lacked in cocking, he made up for in invention and maximizing of sensation and risk-edged ecstasy.

He played me alternately like a violin and a set of drums for three days and nights. He was not unlike the sailors I usually served in his intensity and concentration on his own needs and his cruelty in the fuck. But he went way beyond those others; he took me beyond what had become numbing sameness of the act. He would still be fucking when the others would have had their immediate needs met and wanted to get back to the liquor at the bar. And he would take me far out over the edge each time. I would moan for him to slow down or stop and he would quicken his pace and go on forever—and I would find that awakened me. After a while, I would beg for mercy—because it seemed to please him to deny it—but I no longer wanted mercy from this man. I wanted what he was giving me, how he was using me.

He made me hard, something that had been slipping away from me in the routineness of my life at the Dick Hut—except when I was with Dutch—and he kept me hard. And he brought me off—repeatedly in a session. The cruelty and invasiveness was overbalanced by the height of passion he brought me to—beyond, I must admit, even what Dutch transported me to. The sailor had to be very handsome and well built and hung to make me ejaculate these days—and most had no interest in doing so. They were only there for their own temporary needs.

I was only there for the lieutenant's needs too, but his needs included having me writhing and quivering like jelly and begging for mercy while incongruously also begging for the cruel fuck and crying out in passion and release—and not pretending to do so as I normally did with the other sailors. I had come to need the cruelty and explosion over the edge that he was providing. It was sweeping the numbness of my life away.

He'd leave for meals and then return to floor me wherever I was and fuck me and prod me and slap me and beat on me with his riding crop. I'd meet him at the door and he would push me down on the floor and fuck me roughly from behind as I tried to move across the floor, wanting to escape the onslaught, but equally wanting what the lieutenant was giving me. Once as I tried to escape him, he pulled a plump, curved cucumber off the table and fucked me with that, reminding me of Dutch's cock stretching me to the limit.

I'd wake up in the middle of the night flat on my belly with the lieutenant straddling me and working his cock into my ass. Then I'd find he'd bound me to the bed and he'd roll me over and attack my mouth with his hardened tool, slapping my cheeks and tweaking my nipples.

And, amazingly, I found I loved it. The quick, impersonal, missionary- or doggy-style fucks I'd been trapped in for years had deadened me to passion and lust, only relieved by

Dutch's gentle, filling attentions. Now I had another lover, equally melting, but entirely different. For three days and nights, I found that I myself was perpetually hard and ready to ejaculate at the lieutenant's will. I didn't know what turned me on and fulfilled me the most, the giant but sensitive boilerman or the demanding, controlling, and cruel, but inventive officer.

But it seemed I would have to make a choice. At the end of the three days, the lieutenant informed me, while I was lashed by my wrists to a hook in the ceiling and he was crouched under me and fucking up into me and flicking my belly with riding crop, that I had pleased him.

He said nothing then, but the following Thursday night, the young, pimply sailor I had striven to save from the predators in the bar brought the situation with the lieutenant to a head.

The sailor appeared in the bar that night, the first time I had seen him since I had guided his floundering lovemaking. He looked around until he saw me. I saw several of the older sailors assessing him, so I walked quickly over to him.

"I thought I'd convinced you you didn't really need to come in here again," I whispered to him, while I latched on to his arm, as if I was flirting—an attempt to hold both Hung Lee and the sharks in the water off.

"I want to be with you again," he said in a little whining voice. "I brought money."

"Didn't I tell you that you could find someone on the ship to satisfy you? You fuck well. When that's known, you'll have all the bottoms you can handle."

"So far all I've found are guys willing to suck me off," he said. "I know I'll find someone, but my rocks are aching. And they're aching for you."

So, I took him to my rooms and let him fuck me. He took greater control than he had earlier, and I was laying on my back on the bed, my legs spread, his knees under and lifting my butt, and his cock working nicely inside me, when the lieutenant put in an unexpected appearance.

In the space of five minutes, he had the sailor clutching his clothes and escaping the apartment under the flailing of the lieutenant's crop, and the lieutenant had transferred his anger to me in a rough, wild, and totally satisfying fuck.

Immediately after that the lieutenant told me he must own me for his own and that he'd be negotiating with Hung Lee for my contract and wanted to set me up in an apartment away from here where only he could be fucking me.

This set me back on my haunches. I melted to Dutch. I loved what he did to me and the knowledge that I could take a cock that big and that he was so gentle with me, but Richard Randolph drove me wild and made me experience ecstasy to depths that my life of opening my legs for every randy and drunken sailor who sailed by had driven out of me.

Despite what the lieutenant thought, though, he couldn't just buy up my contract from Hung Lee—at least not without my concurrence. My mother had Hung Lee by the balls; he could shove me around like he did at the bar, but he couldn't "sell" me. He didn't own me. No one would own me without my permission. But if I chose to go with Richard Randolph and the condition was that he owned me, than I would let him own me. Certainly when he was fucking me, he owned me. And owning me was part of the thrill of sex with him, the depth of sensation I hadn't felt for years—until he and Dutch entered my life.

Sundays were my off day. When I brought men back to my place on Saturday night, they left on Saturday night. Sunday I slept in and pampered myself. Or at least I did until that first Sunday in December. That Sunday I was awakened before 8:00 in the morning with the most godawful noise I'd ever heard. I tied on my sarong and ran out into the street—only to see the diving of jets over Pearl Harbor and a cacophony of explosions. The Japs were attacking the fleet anchored in Pearl Harbor— more than ninety ships of the line, the largest part of America's fleet.

Like everyone else, I headed up the slopes away from Pearl Harbor, my first thought being for myself.

Later, when all was over other than the salvage of the tonnage bombed to the bottom of Pearl Harbor—not sunk, because the floor of the harbor was only a few feet lower than the ships normally drew, but crippled at the minimum—I remembered my beloved Dutch and the lieutenant who touched me at my very depths and went down as close to the carnage as possible. All I could find out was that my lovers' ships, the USS *West Virginia* and the USS *Raleigh* were among those that had sustained damage and that had lost a large number of crewmen in the Japanese attack.

For three days I agonized. Men were starting to reappear at the Dick Hut, but they were there to bury themselves in drink, not to pursue hookups, and none of them could tell me about either Dutch or the lieutenant. On the second day, the pimply young sailor showed up, shell shocked, and I took him up to my rooms and we made love like he'd never done before. If nothing else, I was able to push the remembrance of that brutal attack out of his mind for a couple of hours.

But he couldn't fill the needs of my life. Only either Dutch or the lieutenant—or both—could do that for me.

On the third day, within three hours of each other, I found out that both Dutch and the lieutenant were alive and recovering from superficial wounds.

That was two days ago. Now I am back to my naval dilemma. Either Dutch or the lieutenant, both of whom are only fleeting pleasures, as they now surely will be transferred away from here quickly. Or neither—the continuing of my life as relief and comfort for needy, now increasingly frightened and endangered sailors, like my young, pimply sailor.

I don't know what to do. My story doesn't end here. All I can say is that both of my lovers survived that terrible attack on Pearl Harbor. And for now, maybe that's enough.

~

ABOUT THE
AUTHOR

Habu is one of the pen names of a former supersonic spy jet pilot, intelligence agent, male model, movie actor, and diplomat. A wild youth in South East Asia was spent enjoying whatever sexual opportunities came his way, and much of his gay male writing is about recalling incidents from those days and inventing ones he'd perhaps have liked to experience. He now leads a very quiet and ordinary happily married family life.

An American, he is a published mainstream novelist and short story writer under another name and in another dimension of his life. He has written or cowritten (with Sabb) over 500 published short stories and nearly 100 published erotica e-books, primarily of gay fiction but also memoir, straight fiction and ménage fiction. His hand and creative writing can be seen in stories and books by habu, sr71plt, Dirk Hessian, Shabbu, and Stephen Kessel—among unrevealed others that might surprise readers. The fictionalized GM memoir *Flying High, Diving Deep* is loosely based on his life experiences. He can be found at the adults only gay male site www.BarbarianSpy.com, which he shares with Sabb and Dirk Hessian.

Our authors always like to receive feedback, and appreciate it when readers post reviews at Amazon, Goodreads, and other distributor and review sites.

BarbarianSpy
FOR LITERARY HEAT

Not all books listed below may currently be on release.

BOOKS BY DIRK HESSIAN

Xtreme Erotica

The King's Men

Shores of Tripoli

Prophecy of Noto

Pretender's Fate

General Erotica/Romance

Fire Down the Valley

Constantinople

The Beautiful Way

Blue and Gray

Colonel's Treasure

Beginning of Time

Labyrinth

BOOKS BY HABU

Gay Erotica

Memoir Faction

Flying High, Diving Deep*

Xtreme Erotica

Second Coming: Emile La Cour Unleashed

Vortex: Sacrificed by Curiosity*

Dark Angel Sounding *(in e-book & included in Sounding:Ultimate Control Paperback)**

Sounding: Ultimate Control *(Print Only)**

Sounding Five *(in e-book & included in Sounding:Ultimate Control Paperback)*

General Erotica

Romance

Four Coins

Lower Than the Heart

Brambleton

Gotta Keep Trying
Finding Amnad
Platres Conclave
Other Novels/Novellas
Prepared in Cape Verdi
Gilded Cage
House on Park
Anything for Ambition
Dance of the Ravishers
Hard Knocks U*
My Neighbor's Spa*
Man's Man: Tales of a High Priced Gay Hooker*
Trip Money
Clint Folsom Mysteries Compendium Volume 1*
Death to Blonds - Stolen Judgment (Clint Folsom Mystery)
Clint Folsom Mysteries Compendium Volume 2*
The Indian Doctor
Sailorboy
Home to Fire Island
Choke Hold
Gay Erotica Anthologies
Doubled*
Doubled Again*
Tails in the Tropics*
Tails in the Med*
Rough Riders*
Grab Bag 1*
Grab Bag 2*
Grab Bag 3*
Grab Bag 4*
Grab Bag 5*
Beyond the Beaded Curtain*
Habu's Christmas Balls
The Sporting Life*
Fetish Galore!*
Literary Gay Erotica
Cairo Surrender*

The Handyman*
Homeward Bound
Journey to Mirage*
Menage Erotica
13 Ways for Halloween
Luther*
The Indian Prince
Literary GLBT Fiction
Summer of Denial

BOOKS BY SHABBU
Finding Jason
Dirty Pool
Operation Black Jade
Cigars!*
Angel in the Barn
Gayly Complicated
Despoiling David
The Tree of Idleness
I Met a Man
The Interview
Rough Road to Happiness
BOOKS BY SABB
Hiring in Hollywood
The Legend of Holleystone Grange
Surprise Encounters
She is He
Wrong Man
Loyal to his King
Barbarian Tales - Book One - Traveler's Tales*
Barbarian Tales - Book Two - Journeys Begin*
Barbarian Tales - Book Three - The Inheritance*
Barbarian Tales - Book Four - Road to Persepolis*
~
* indicates the book is available in paperback and e-

book.

www.ingramcontent.com/pod-product-compliance
Lightning Source LLC
Chambersburg PA
CBHW031020030726
47497CB00004B/938

* 9 7 8 1 9 2 2 1 8 7 5 1 2 *